# DELIVER US

## DELIVER · VANQUISH · DISCLAIM

# PAM GODWIN

*NEW YORK TIMES* BESTSELLING AUTHOR

Visit my website at pamgodwin.com

# DELIVER

# PAM GODWIN

## Book 1

# ONE

Tonight was the night. Nervousness might have been a natural response in her position, but bending to it wouldn't change a damned thing. Liv sucked in hard. A lungful of smoke pushed past her unsteady smile and tumbled into a halfhearted cloud against the glare of stadium lights. Force of will pinned her bowed lips in place.

Another drag. Exhale. She stretched her neck and rotated her shoulders.

Whistles and cheers roared from the stands. Green and gold banners rippled to the stomp of thousands of feet on metal bleachers. Wedged between a trash barrel and a concrete wall, she smashed the cigarette on the *No Smoking* sign bolted to the railing at her hip.

To blend in as a Baylor University Bears fan, she wore a green t-shirt and dark jeans. Her alcove was field level, out of the path of foot traffic, and the best vantage to observe her mark.

The boy.

A goddamned saint.

He likely hadn't known a night similar to the one he was about to have. Her stomach quivered in a war of dread and anticipation.

The scoreboard counted down the final five minutes of the game. *Le Male* aftershave wafted from the nearby huddle of guys. The scent of store-bought pheromones mingled with their sweaty excitement and the nachos clutched in their hands. Smelled like fucking team spirit. Right now she hated *Nirvana* and everything musical expression had once meant to her.

She shouldn't begrudge the college boys their thrills. To be fair, a number of them, with their athletic frames and juvenile energy, could have been her next delivery. But she'd already chosen. A fucking holier-than-thou virgin boy.

The tone of cheers exploded in volume and urgency, drawing her attention to the field. Green jerseys descended upon the turf, cleats kicking up mud, the rush of testosterone led by number fifty-four, the Bears' star linebacker.

He jogged to midfield in long-legged strides, the seams of his sleeves straining to contain his biceps. She leaned over the railing, eyes glued to his gait. Self-assured and powered by trained muscles, he covered the field like he owned it. Given the whoops of his fans, he did.

His helmet, rib protectors, and shoulder pads concealed his pale green eyes and black hair while enhancing all six-foot-two inches and two hundred and twenty pounds of masculinity and sexual innocence that met the *client's* conditions. But she knew everything about the twenty-one year old. She had been watching Joshua Carter for weeks.

Daily surveillance had put her in the woods surrounding his parents' farm at five every morning, stalking the campus halls during his classes and football practices until four, and back in the cotton fields until dusk.

In his four-year college career as a linebacker, he had caught a record twenty-three interceptions. As a trained sex slave, he would catch seven digits in an offshore account.

While his predictable schedule made him an easy capture, his notoriety on the team magnified the risk. But it was the raw beauty in his seductive eyes and honed physique that passed a whisper between her ears, the kind that couldn't be unheard once acknowledged. He was the one.

A stolen password gave her access to his university records. As the only child of poor farmers, he would've needed every bit of financial aid offered had he not received a football scholarship. His scholarship essay supported his pursuit in earning a degree in Religion, stating it would *equip him with the tenet and fortitude to effectively fill a professional ministry role.*

His righteousness chafed her heathen ass, but it avowed his virginity. Not an easy find these days, especially not in one so potently masculine and easy on the eyes. Which was why she'd sought this particular job on Baylor's Christian-centric campus rather than her usual hunting grounds in the slums of Brownsville and Killeen. Besides, he would forget all about his godly endeavors by day two in chains. Just like all the others.

The visiting crowd moaned. Their quarterback lay on his back, the football wobbling beside his grass-stained helmet. Beside him, number fifty-four stretched out a hand to help the guy to his feet.

2

# DELIVER

"A terrific defensive play by number fifty-four, the Bears." The announcer's enthusiasm reverberated above the hoots of Bears fans. "Results in a sack."

Anticipation twitched her shoulders. She came to watch him steal the spotlight. He didn't know it would be the last game in his career, but she would remember the high points for him. She would remind him of his glory right before she peeled it away and rebuilt him into the sum of the buyer's requirements.

Sixteen- and seventeen-year-olds were her forte. Not too young to make her stomach roll with pedophiliac queasiness and not too old to resist her methods. Though, with enough time, she could find the chink no matter the age. The buyer for this job demanded a boy in his twenties, virtuous in his relations with women, and a body disciplined to accept and please a man.

Number fifty-four sprinted to the defensive line, quadriceps flexing against his compression pants. As he bent at the waist, the spandex stretched over jock strap lines and the glorious divide of his ass.

Payday was in sight. She lit another cigarette and curved her lips through the exhale.

"If beautiful smiles could kill," said an unfamiliar voice behind her, "you'd be a spear through the heart."

The lame pick up line sent her molars slamming together. If she looked, she'd find a smirk that needed practice. If she gazed deeper, she'd find an entitled college kid, one who didn't appreciate his family-funded education. No mind-reading required. Seven years and seven captured slaves had taught her how to detect weakness in a voice and smell the waste in its words.

She brushed a length of hair forward, using the thick curls to cover the left half of her face and the four-inch scar there. It was her permanent reminder, not that she needed one. Her insides were gutted.

With deliberate slowness, she turned her head and confronted the annoyance.

Stiffly crooked lips and nervously blinking eyes belied the confidence he was attempting to exude. Hands fidgeting in the pockets of his jeans, feet a shoulder-width apart, the kid was no older than eighteen, at least six years her junior, and in need of a lesson on stranger danger.

She tiptoed her gaze down his puffing chest and paused on the bulge below his longhorn buckle. With a muffled sigh, she reminded herself she was there for a job. That didn't include informing some douche drip that her smile was especially dangerous when wrapped around a cock. She flicked her eyes to his and shed the smile.

"Oh, come on. I'm writing a paper on the life of Moses." He licked his lips. "Let me demonstrate how to part the sea with my staff." His gaze

3

slid to her metaphoric sea.

The fact he wasn't choking on his own douchery was a prick to the nerves. He didn't know she tied people up and fucked them with rubber dicks for a living. With a grab and twist of his nuts, she could humiliate him. But she couldn't draw that kind of attention. She curled her fingers around the railing and shaped her expression into a mask of cruel arrogance.

Whatever he saw in her gaze pinched his face. He shuffled backward with deflated shoulders. Pathetic. If she had thirty minutes and an empty classroom, she'd show him things more painful than a bruised ego.

She turned back to the game and scanned the field.

Number fifty-four sprinted past the five-yard line, leapt to intercept a long pass, and caught the ball mid-turn.

"Interception," the announcer yelled as the crowd jumped up, their cheers as wild as the beat of her heart. One second remained on the clock.

She wanted to clap with the fans, but knowing it was his last victory crushed her celebratory spirit. Truth was, she didn't have a viable reason for being there. She couldn't exactly snatch him out of the crowd. But after weeks of watching him on the field, his games had become something to anticipate.

The ambience of the cheering crowd, the camaraderie of friends enjoying a favorite pastime, and the view of athletic boys showing off in tight pants nourished her longing for the youth that had been stolen from her. Seven years ago, she was the innocent girl who stood before the crowd singing the National Anthem at her high school's football games.

The memory fluttered in her belly and dulled her awareness. She snapped her spine straight. Fuck, she was losing track of time.

Lighting another cigarette, she blew her sentimentality into the night sky and slipped out of her recess. Striding up the stairs toward the parking lot, she twisted to catch a glimpse of number fifty-four running off the field.

Cheerleaders enveloped him on the sideline, hopping and mewling for his attention. He tugged off the helmet and rubbed a hand over his face, his complexion gilded so exquisitely by the Texas sun. He glanced at the scoreboard above her head. If she were watching through her binoculars, she would've been staring into the unusual glow of his innocent sea green eyes. The ones she was about to change forever.

"Excuse me, ma'am?"

*What the unholy fuck now?* She pivoted and met the narrowed glare of a middle-aged man. Dressed head-to-toe in Baylor swag, he was probably some overzealous alumni reliving the *glory days*.

He waved a flabby arm. "This is a smoke-free property."

She raised the cigarette, inhaled, and released a plume of *fuck you* into his scrunching face.

A dramatic cough accompanied another flap of his arm. "The university has strict guidelines—"

"Are you the smoke police?"

A fury of red bloomed from his buttoned collar to his blotted cheeks. "You can't do that here."

Bet his virgin ass clenched as he said that. She shifted to move past him, irritation skittering across her skin.

He stretched an arm out to block her. "What's your name, young lady?"

Before she did something that would get her hauled off in handcuffs, she blew him a smoke-ringed kiss, pushed around his arm, and wove into the exodus of spectators.

Past the cooling charcoal grills and trash-littered tailgates, her ten-minute stroll took her to the edge of the parking lot. In the farthest corner, beneath a broken street lamp, she circled a nondescript sedan. No one loitered. No witnesses to connect her to the car. She tapped on the passenger window.

The locks released and the door swung open.

"How many times did you get hit on?" Van Quiso's timbre bordered on growly.

On a good night, calm reason eclipsed his jealousy. She struggled to remember a good night.

"Wouldn't you love to know?" She winked at him, dropped into the seat, and shut the door.

Despite the consequences, she got off on tormenting him. A desperate and pathetic attempt at revenge.

A toothpick protruded from the opening of his charcoal hoodie where his mouth was, probing the air in restless circles. "You smell like sex."

"I banged three linebackers during halftime." She buckled her seat belt.

"Your sarcasm is juvenile."

"So is your suspicious resentment."

The stench of his possessiveness saturated her skin and bled into her veins. The more he took her, consensual or not, the farther she followed him, down, down, down into his twisted reality.

She rubbed her arms and focused on the empty lot. "The boy is here."

He leaned back and stretched a leg along the floorboard. "The kid's never missed a class or a practice, let alone a game."

"It's flu season, Van. People get sick." At least, that was the argument she'd given him to get one last chance to see the boy play.

The toothpick bobbed and stilled. He fingered the keys where they dangled from the ignition and lowered his hand. "Look at me."

Tension crept through her limbs. She itched to reach over and start the car. The confined space, in the dark, with him, had her crawling out of her skin with reminders of what he'd done to her, what he continued to do to her. His cock stretching her ass, his whip burning across her back, his fist in her face, the tenderness of his lips kissing her wounds.

She pushed her shoulders back, pulled out her phone, and checked the time. "The coach should be finished with his post-game speech. The boy will be showered and headed out soon. We need to go."

"Look. At. Me."

The heat in his command cracked her shell of bravado, tightening the muscles in her face. Only two people in her isolated world had a stronger strike than hers, and Van knew he was one. His breath sawed in and out with enough vehemence to sharpen his teeth as he watched her, poaching her air, waiting.

Avoiding his stare was a means of gaining distance, but ignoring him only delayed the inescapable. She made her face relax and looked at him straight in the eyes.

He stared right back, the toothpick jogging low in her periphery. It could've been the press of shadows in the car, but meeting his gaze was like straining to see into the reaches of the moonless night. Maybe something terrible lurked in there, something malicious enough to end her life in unspeakable ways. Maybe it was her imagination.

The rotating toothpick froze, caught between his molars as he spread his lips into a grin. His hooded sweatshirt hid his high-and-tight cut of brown hair and sharp features and struggled to contain his mountain of muscles. The severe angles of his face added to his dangerous beauty. An unsuspecting glance in his direction promised a double-glance, usually followed by a prayer to God that he didn't catch the admiring look and use it to his advantage.

He seemed to embrace the mold of a convicted criminal, but he had never been convicted. And despite the prayers to ward him off, his sexy smile could coerce a virgin girl's thighs into a spread-eagle sigh.

But that girl no longer existed.

A timeworn ache awoke in her chest. She masked it under a steady breath and let her eyelids half-droop in a display of boredom.

He slid back his hood to his hairline just behind the comma-shaped laceration that connected the outer edge of his eye to the crook of his mouth. Even in the dark, the deep red gash stood out, a threatening brand against the perfect symmetry of his features.

His hand lifted to her cheek, smoothing her hair away. She held herself immobile as he traced the scar that mirrored his. When he stared at it, did he ever regret the events that led to their matching punishments?

"You're sleeping in my bed tonight." The touch of his fingers and the command in his tone jabbed like a knife.

She leaned back, throat dry, and forced her eyes to remain on his. "I have a job to do. If I fail, you'll be digging my body out of the backyard to fuck it."

The skin around his scar strained. "He doesn't bury bodies back there."

"Yet."

He plucked the toothpick from his mouth and pointed it at her. His lips parted to speak and a gust of frustration grooved his face. He knew if she didn't meet their deadlines her threat was a dead-on promise.

Whatever he was going to say was abandoned as he dropped his brow to hers and pressed the seam of his lips to her bottom one. She fought a shiver. This bond wasn't romantic. It was unwanted, sad, and it thrived on her fear of him.

The slide of his tongue along her inner lip hitched her breath. He wouldn't fuck her here and sabotage the mission, but he always made time to fuck *with* her. To speed it along, she remained pliable in her stillness.

With a disappointed sigh, he returned the toothpick to his mouth and started the car. "Let's go get your boy."

# TWO

Liv wanted to be anywhere but in that car, on her way to uproot another life, facing the next ten weeks behind a whip and a mask. She trained them. She delivered them. And after?

They were dead to her. They had to be. Sometimes, it was the lies she told herself that kept her going. Believing anything else made her a danger to the captives she sold.

She pressed her fingertips against the window. If only she could find the strength to end her own life.

The suburban conveniences of Waco, Texas, swept by in the form of drive-throughs, water towers, and churches of every denomination. As Van drove toward the outskirts of town, the scenery transformed. The wide-open freedom of the crop fields, cut by a swath of tarmac and hangars beneath the moonlight, haunted her vision.

Memories took shape, a tapestry of the private airport in Austin where Mom instructed skydiving courses, the adjacent corn field and its maze of childhood adventures, and the acres of paved airstrip where local teens roller-bladed until dusk.

Until one of the kids was taken.

The old sore in her chest opened. Her exhale erupted in a choke, and she feigned a cough.

Van's hand swung into view and collided with her throat, squeezing. Oh God, her mind wasn't on the job, and he had the unnerving ability to mark every fucking move of her body.

She tried to draw air, an empty effort against the vise of his fingers on her windpipe. His *I-control-your-thoughts* conditioning was a technique that once worked on her, and experience taught her the best reaction was no reaction.

Lips pinned in silence, she sought out her defense, a song, any song, and grabbed hold of "Gods and Monsters" by *Lana Del Rey*. Saturating her thoughts with the lamenting chorus, she sang in her head. The rippling effects numbed her heart—and her throat beneath his fingers. Singing was her tonic, the only trace of self she had left.

"Is your head on straight?" He tightened his grip, gave it a shake. "Feels like it is."

Lungs burning, fingers digging into her thighs, she steadied her pulse to the slow beat of lyrics spilling through her mind.

The clamp vanished and his hand returned to the wheel. She let her lungs fill with quiet stoicism and loosened her muscles limb by limb.

"Your mind is wandering." His impatience pulsated between them. "Pull your balls out of your cunt."

She wanted to hate him, but he was all she had. She wanted to love him, but memories tore deep and scarred. "My head is straight. Balls are out. What other body parts are you concerned about?"

Passing headlights illuminated the stone set of his jaw, his eyes piercing the road. "Tell me what you were thinking about."

That command had more power than it should. She summoned a reply with control in her voice. "Your first capture."

"My first…" His hands tightened on the wheel, slackened, and a sick kind of attachment slithered into his tone. "My favorite capture." He squeezed her knee.

Mom used to say no one had truly evaluated their life until they looked at it from 10,000 feet. Liv's arrangement allowed her a certain amount of freedom, so she still skydived between jobs. When she did, her falls always retraced the same path of *should-haves*.

Should have jumped with Mom that day instead of staying behind to roller-blade. Should have skated away from his car when he stopped to ask directions. Should have screamed instead of getting in when he aimed the gun.

A wave of revulsion surged through her. "Your first capture was just a stupid girl."

"A stupid girl who incorporated the client's requirements. Tight seventeen-year-old ass, perky tits, all that innocence bouncing up and down on skates." He hummed. "I have no regrets."

Regret would have gone a long way in their relationship.

He shifted closer and reached for her thigh. She jerked out of the path of his hand and pressed against the door.

Black fields smeared by. If the cold glass against her cheek was the only barrier between her and those fields, she would be sprinting through them as fast as possible away from this car.

He reached again, a full-body lean, veering the car onto the edge of the shoulder. The car righted as his hand made contact, shoved between her legs, and cupped her.

That hand had been her undoing so many times. She was stolen innocence, following the rules of monsters. Somewhere along the way, she'd become one.

The faster he rubbed, the harder he pressed against the denim seam protecting her bundle of nerves, the looser her hips became. It was his words, however, that had the power to own her and destroy her, from the inside out.

"I want to spend the rest of my life looking at you, touching you. Christ, I have to touch you to make sure I'm not imagining you."

She ground against his fingers, hating herself. Her hips shifted up and down, pelvis rolling out, thighs opening, responding in defiance of her own volition.

His voice lowered to a murmur. "Why is fucking you the only way I can reach you, Liv? I want more. More than this."

She released a moan, a sound practiced to seduce. But she couldn't stop her heartfelt yearning from bleeding into the edges of her voice. She covered it by dragging it out into a longer, more robotic groan.

He yanked his hand away. "Save your fucking fakeasms for the new bitch boy."

A shaky breath tingled past her lips. She hadn't been faking, not completely, and that was more revolting than the act itself. "Maybe I won't fake with this boy."

The sudden stiffness of his posture betrayed the calmness in his tone. "The client was very specific about who will be fucking his property."

Of the twelve requirements in the contract, the buyer's first demand took an audacious detour around the usual kinkativity.

*Requirement One. Slave has never experienced sexual intimacy with a woman. Slave is heterosexual but hates women. He desires only his Master.*

There wasn't a buyer who didn't make her shudder, but this one was so openly sexist, he notched a new level of loathing, and she hadn't even met him yet. "His first requirement is so fucked up. I don't like it."

"He's probably some scorned man and wants a slave to sympathize with his misery. He's not any different than the other kinky, fat-wallet pig fuckers you've contracted for."

"Maybe. But this one's a whole new breed of creepiness."

Their previous contracts were straightforward, listing desired physical attributes and demanding the usual kneel-grovel-suck-my-cock training. The cost for that training was ludicrous, and she never saw a penny of it. But everyone had a price. Hers was more valuable than money.

"The job's the same." His voice snapped through the car. "The slave you deliver will be *exactly* as he ordered."

Or she would lose the only two reasons she buckled on a parachute when she jumped.

He wiggled his toothpick. "Though it definitely would've been easier if the contract had allowed us to nab a homo."

Jesus, the world was already a predatory asshole, and here they were discriminating who it should feed on next. The client wanted a twenty-something, straight, virgin male with all the usual attractive, athletic qualities. The fishing pool for such a demand was spectacularly small. Boys who grew up without families didn't retain their virginity.

"I don't like taking this boy from his parents." It fucked up her delicately woven strategy, the only secret she managed to keep from Van.

"So," he said, smirking, "because your previous captures didn't have families who missed them, that makes them less human?"

Absence of loved ones was her own personal requirement when she went through the selection process, but that did *not* make them less *at all*.

His laugh greased the air. "The irony of your ethics is perverse."

The irony of her life was perverse.

He relaxed into a sigh, his head dropping back against the seat. "We make an invincible team, Liv. Just do your thing until the mere presence of your pussy makes him vomit."

With the previous captives, Van held the reins, driving the level and direction of the training. But the first requirement in this contract was sticky. To condition the slave to hate women, they'd agreed that she would be the brute force.

Her stomach wobbled. "Think you can stay out of the way while I handle this one?"

"Yep. Just call me in when your devout jock-bag is ready to suck my cock."

*Requirement Two. Slave will service Master sexually with exceptional skill, and his body will be prepared to make it easy for Master.*

She and Van would play a depraved game designed to turn a straight, virgin boy into the embodiment of the client's twelve requirements. Virgin boys were beyond her expertise. Joshua Carter—with his pious upbringing and family support—was a tangle in their operation, one that could endanger her arrangement. The unmistakable shiver of panic lurched through her.

He eased off the gas. "I think we're here."

Up ahead, a smudge of trees breached the flat horizon of rural Texas.

She checked the signal on her phone. "We're in the dead zone. This is it."

He parked on the shoulder where the trees crept closest to the road and turned on the hazard lights. She stepped onto the gravel, the stir of dust settling around her sneakers. When she raised the hood of their car, he removed a fuse from the engine compartment and tucked it in his pocket. Then they waited.

Wheat fields reached around the woodland and stretched beyond the mantle of night. The lonely cry of a mockingbird pierced the dark hush.

The nearest resident lived two miles down. She knew them through the lens of her binoculars. Daniel and Emily Carter couldn't leave their nightly chores to attend their son's football game. She knew they expected him home soon.

A distant rumble drew her attention down the desolate road. Given the ease at which sound traveled over the vacant fields, she should see his headlights in about two or three minutes.

Van's big body blocked her view, pressing in, violating her comfort zone. She raised her chin and searched the depths of his hood. Shadowed and vacant, his expression mirrored her presence of mind.

The back of his hand made a slow trace of her scar, brushing her hair from its path. When he reached her lips, he coiled several strands around his finger.

She grabbed his wrist, and the tendons in her grip turned to steel, immovable. She closed her eyes and braced.

He yanked, sparking a burn where the follicles gave way.

At the sound of his retreating footsteps, she opened her eyes and watched his broad back move toward the trees. "Someday, we're going to talk about those fetishes of yours."

Without acknowledgment, he continued in a slow, dispassionate stride until the shadows between the trees swallowed his silhouette.

The purr of the approaching vehicle grew louder, followed by the spit of gravel and bobbing headlights. She leaned against the fender and hummed to the tune of her bludgeoning heart.

# THREE

The truck slowed and stopped. Liv held up a hand, greeting the darkened interior and the boy who lingered within.

Her mark.

When the door remained closed, she worried her lip. Were her assumptions about him wrong?

With each unanswered second, her nerves mounted. What if he had a passenger? She'd been so sure about this part of the plan.

Relief came with the creak of his door. It had been just her anxiety making it feel longer.

He hopped out, and the interior light illuminated the empty cab. "Hey there. You need help?"

His voice reverberated through her chest for the first time. It exceeded all her imaginings, a deep underlying elixir, the perfect embodiment of his powerful, masculine frame.

"Hi." She wiped imaginary grease on her jeans and gestured at the engine. "Started clanking on I-35. I pulled off, got turned around." She spread out her arms to indicate the expanse of nothingness around them and quickened her rambling with a display of panic. "I'm lost. Dang car crapped out, and I can't get a signal on my phone."

A chuckle vibrated in his chest, and there was something unnervingly soothing about it. "You definitely got turned around. You're miles from the interstate. Want me to take a look?" He pointed at the engine and cocked his head, his luminescent eyes dancing in the headlights.

Several feet separated them, the closest they'd ever been in proximity. At almost a foot taller and a hundred pounds heavier, he commanded the space he stood in, as well as hers. He could overpower her with sheer strength, which was why she had to lead him to chains by his own accord.

She regarded the ground and tapped the toe of her sneaker on the tire. "It's the alternator. Last time this happened, the mechanic told me I needed a new one. It's expensive, you know?" She peered at him through her lashes. "I'll have to tow it."

"There's cell service about a mile up the road. I can give you a lift."

Soon, he'd give her more than just a lift. Time to zip on the helpless-girl suit.

She inched forward until the beam of light caught the hideous damage on her left cheek.

His Adam's apple jumped, and he seemed to wrestle with dragging his gaze from the scar to her eyes. Sympathy, or perhaps pity, softened his expression. She deserved the latter, especially after she used it against him.

"My dad…he…" She placed a palm over her cheek, cradling it, and trickled out an award-winning whimper.

"Hey." Loose rock scraped beneath his tentative approach. "What's wrong?"

"It's just…Dad was so much harder on my little sister." She stroked the scar and hunched her shoulders. "She's all alone, and she needs me."

There was no Dad, no sister, but a family boy like him needed something he could sympathize with.

"I left Dallas as soon as she called, and now I can't get to her." With a shuddering breath, she gave him her back and wrapped her arms around her midsection. "This can't be happening." A whisper.

"Where's your sister?"

"Temple." She released a sniffle into the darkness.

His silence struggled around her. If she had chosen the right play, he would be working out all the dire possibilities that would justify her driving two hours back to Dallas with a bad alternator. And if she'd chosen the right boy, he would offer a solution that delivered him into her hands.

"Is she in danger?" he asked.

If yes, he would call the cops.

She shook her bowed head and curled further into herself. "She's unstable. I don't think she'd hurt herself, but her mind's in a bad place." A deep breath for effect. "I'm the only person she has."

The scuff of his feet moved in the direction of the truck. "Temple is only thirty minutes from here. I can take you, if you want?"

Touchdown. The victory pulled at her lips.

She relaxed her mouth and pivoted slowly, facing him, her features arranged in a portrait of disbelief. "Really?"

He opened the passenger door and held it in invitation. "If you're okay leaving your car for the tow service. No one will bother it."

No one would bother it because Van would replace the fuse and follow far enough behind to not be seen. She snagged her wallet and phone from the car and shuffled toward him with deliberate caution in her steps.

What would a normal girl in her position say?

"You're not going to kidnap me and rape me, are you?" The twisted callousness in that suggestion tightened her throat. She wanted to retract the words, despising what the end of the night would bring for him.

"No, ma'am." He shifted out of the way as she climbed in. "But there's Mace in the glove box. Help yourself." The corners of his full lips inched up. "Pretty as you are, you can't be too trusting."

A frigid clamp closed over her heart. *Stupid, stupid boy.*

Seated behind the wheel, he turned the truck around and drove toward town and I-35. When the bars appeared on her phone, he held up his. "I need to text my folks and let them know I'll be late. Would you mind?"

As expected, his law-abiding refusal to text and drive put his phone in her hands.

She accepted it and tapped on the call log. Last call was to his mom prior to the game. "Of course. Is it under —"

"Mom. Should be right —" He cut his eyes at her finger on the screen. "Yeah, that's it. Just tell her I'm giving a friend a lift to Temple and I'll be home by eleven-thirty."

It was remarkable how unabashed he was about living with his parents. He didn't know she knew the reasons. That they depended on him to work the struggling farm morning and night. That staying in his childhood bedroom saved them on-campus housing expenses despite some of the offset his scholarship awarded them.

He let her imagine whatever she wanted about a twenty-one-year-old checking in with Mom on a Friday night. His confidence wasn't boy-like at all. It was admirably mature. And problematic. It would require breaking, likely through physical humiliation.

The pang from that thought hit her stomach, and she calmed it with the reminder that to succeed in an important aim, it was acceptable to do something bad. Or lots of somethings bad.

A discreet glance confirmed his eyes were on the road. As she typed out the text, she worked the cover off the back of the phone, let the battery drop between her legs — thank God it wasn't an iPhone — and closed it up. The screen went black, the text unsent.

She placed it face down in the cup holder. "Sent."

"Thanks. Do you need a number for a tow service?"

"I'll call in the morning."

His thumbs drummed on the steering wheel and stopped. "Name's Josh. What's yours?"

She always used her real name. No reason not to. "Liv."

"Liv." He pursed his lips. "L-I-V."

"L-I-V."

Shove it between *DE* and *ERER,* and she had a job title. Mr. E had a jolly cruel laugh about it when he promoted her to a deliverer by way of blackmail.

Josh's face creased in a smile. "Do you believe in meaningful coincidence?"

*Absolutely not.* "Why?"

"I play football and my jersey number is fifty-four. Your name is L-I-V."

What was his deal with the spelling? She cocked her head at him. "And?"

He shrugged. "The Roman Numeral LIV is number fifty-four."

*His jersey number.* Would she know these things if she'd had the freedom to earn her diploma or attend college?

"I take it you believe coincidence is meaningful?" she asked, curious.

"I think it's plausible. There's comfort in believing there are things in the universe that defy the odds, that something beyond common sense can pivot into place and fill an inner need." He angled his head to glance at her, studying her face. He wouldn't find anything meaningful there. He returned his attention to the road. "What do you think?"

The focus of conversation was expected for a boy pursuing a career in ministry. Still, she scrambled for an answer and settled on the truth. "Coincidence is nothing more than cause and effect. You jump. You fall."

He'd unwittingly jumped from his path and fallen onto someone else's. What she had planned for him would challenge his notions of coincidence and every other damned thing in his life.

# FOUR

Josh sensed Liv's huge brown eyes making furtive sweeps in his direction. Addictive eyes, the kind that tunneled through his outer shell and scrambled his mind until he forgot where he was going.

There were moments in his life when he wanted to bypass the road chosen for him. He was staring at one now. The most attractive woman he'd ever seen. In his truck. Watching him.

The scar dividing her cheek flickered beneath a passing streetlight. It didn't distract from her beauty. It was a delicate emblem of her life, of whatever had happened to her. He burned with curiosity to know her story.

"Take 35 south. I'll tell you where to go when we reach Temple." She shifted her gaze to the speedometer. "Watch your speed."

No *please* or *thank you*. Just a quiet authority that stroked his ears and urged him to test her limits. "How 'bout you just sit there, look pretty, and let me drive?"

"The cops are all over, shooting radar. I can't afford more delays tonight."

This girl seemed a lot less vulnerable than the one trembling on the road. Her voice was soft, musical even, but clipped at the edges as if repressing something beneath her scarred exterior, something beyond the hurt. Outside of her fleeting glances, there was a peculiar apathy in her stillness. Like a dormant animal, resting, waiting.

His discomfort swelled, feeding on all the unsaid things about her family. He merged onto the interstate. "Do you want to talk about your sister?"

"No."

He scratched his stubble and grappled with her reserve. "It's a good thing I came along when I did. I'm the only one who passes through there at this hour."

The wind rustled against the windows as the truck gathered speed.

This was when a normal person would pick up the thread of friendly chitchat. Her silence challenged what he knew about girls and their self-involved monologues. He wasn't usually a nervous talker, but seriously, her lack of conversation was growing more awkward and irritating by the second. "I live just down the road a piece from where I found you."

She stared out the windshield, her fingers seemingly dead on her slender thighs. "Mm."

Pity she didn't want to talk. He had thirty minutes with this gorgeous girl. Thirty minutes to speak openly, to be himself in the company of a stranger. "I'm majoring in religion at Baylor."

A sigh whispered past her lips. "Why?"

"Why what?"

"Why the Jesus career?" Her lips rolled as if constraining judgment.

"I promise you, the reason is completely and wholeheartedly…absurd."

She glanced at him. Not just a flick of her scrutinizing eyes. He won a full-on head turn.

A tousle of chestnut curls clung to her face and spilled around her… Sweet Lord, he shouldn't have been gawking, but her chest was very, very mature. He was certainly not immune to feminine attributes, but watching her mouth part, tipping up at the corners and stretching her scar, was hell on his focus. Confusion looked seductively X-rated on her.

A low-burning fire stirred in his groin, a sensation he'd never tried to sate with a girl. He could've blamed his abstinence on Christian principles and a demanding workload. Truth was, he derived pleasure from the exertion that hard work put on his mind and body. The girls hanging around his practices didn't arouse him like the bruise of a tackle, the pains of farm labor, or the mental strain that accompanied religious stringency. He'd accepted his unconventional urges long ago and locked the darkest ones deep inside. If his parents knew the kind of thoughts he entertained, it would destroy them. His chest tightened.

He moved out of the passing lane and merged into an opening between two slower cars. He'd admitted to her the reason for his career choice was absurd. Might as well tell her why.

"My folks tried to get pregnant for years. When they reached their mid-forties and found God, they prayed, made promises, and nine-months later…" He gave her a raised eyebrow.

"You arrived."

"Yep. Here to fulfill their promise. They'd made a deal with God. If He gave them a child, they vowed to raise their miracle to be a servant of His church in Baptist ministry."

She laughed, a sweet sound for such a glaring expression. "Absurd."

"Told you." And telling her seemed to dislodge it just a little from his chest. It wasn't that he didn't believe in God. He just wasn't fanatical like some of his classmates. Like his parents.

"So young to allow all your choices be dictated by a promise to God."

"*My* promise is to Mom and Dad."

"Whatever. It's a promise that controls you. Doesn't that make you angry?"

"It challenges me, makes me a better person. I'm good with that."

A lull settled over her, and her gaze lost focus as she stared at him. She raised her hand, tentative at first, and reached for his face, fingertips resting on his cheekbone. When she traced his jawline, it was a caress so alluring he had to put all his concentration in keeping his eyes open and his hands on the wheel.

"Your life has always been predetermined, huh?" Her words were as perplexing as her touch.

"Mom and Dad gave me life, an honest one. In return, I accept the path they want for me." He leaned ever so slightly against her fingers and murmured, "It's just a job. You never know, it might lead to something extraordinary."

She yanked her hand back, and her attention snapped to the road.

The absence of her touch left a cold shock. He rubbed his jaw on his shoulder. "Did I say something—"

"Take the next exit."

Unease burrowed in him. What the hell happened? He exited, replaying the conversation in his head. Perhaps leaning into her touch had been too forward.

"Five miles up, turn right into the *Two Trails Crossing* subdivision."

He passed Temple's main drag, the emptiness of the streets seeping into the truck. His body knew she was sitting right beside him. Hell, it pulsed to close those few inches. But she seemed so very far away, lost in her thoughts.

Then she began to hum. It started with a tremor, out of the blue and shocking to his ears. Was she singing to avoid conversation or to slice through the quiet?

The fluttering harmonic built into a haunting rhythm. The tune was unfamiliar, yet the notes shifted through him as if breathed from the most secret part of her soul.

"What is that?" he whispered. "What are you humming?"

The enchanting crescendo cut off, and he immediately regretted opening his mouth.

She cleared her throat. Then he heard it. The a cappella melody of a voice so piercing and peaceful it jolted a chill through him, sparking every cell in his body. The shiver faded too quickly but not for long. Her voice pitched, and an electric surge fired down his spine. He held his breath, spellbound.

In unerring key, she sang of wishes and stars and souls that couldn't be saved. Her octave carried a tinkling quality, profound and lonely at the same time. It transported him to the farm, to the isolated pond on a rainy day. Her voice was the pattering of drizzle on the misty surface, infused with nourishment and despair and acceptance.

She closed with a hum and a delicate exhale.

"That was…" His tongue knotted, heavy in his mouth.

"'Lullaby' by *Sia*."

"I was going to say exquisite, bewitching." *Carnal.* "Do you sing for a living?" He slowed at a stoplight and twisted to look at her.

"No." Complex and unflinching, her eyes held his and the key to his secrets.

The light ticked green, and she broke the connection, pointing at the brick archway on the right.

Lopsided letters clung to a wooden sign in tired welcome. *Two Trails Crossing.* He turned in.

Massive elms darkened the rows of lower middle-class homes. Dated wrought-iron gussied up the doors and windows. A couple left and right turns led them to a cul-de-sac, where she nodded at the small single-story at the end. "That's it. I'll go in through the rear."

He followed the skinny driveway alongside the house, around the back, and parked in front of the rear garage. The engine rattled, and he willed it to choke and die. He didn't want to let her go in just yet, and why was that? As the most sought-after bachelor on the football team, he had more female attention than he knew what to do with.

It wasn't that he didn't want a girl. In fact, he was so aware of the way the female body moved with its ample curves and forbidden places that it was often unbearable to hang out with the opposite sex. He was a guy in his prime, for heaven's sake. His restraint had its limits. So he fended off the handsy girls, accepted dates with the proper girls, and late at night, alone in his bed, he gripped his erection and gave into his primitive needs.

Something he would be doing when he got home, because Liv was the summation of all those girls, and more. What was it about her? She sang like a choir of angels and didn't proposition him like the girls at his games, yet her eyes promised experience and indulgences that reached beyond the boundaries of his folks' expectations for him.

She licked her lips, and they glistened in the dim glow of the porch light. "Come in."

Go in with her? Hell, he couldn't think past the pull to kiss her. He realized he was leaning toward her when she spoke again.

"My father isn't here, and I don't expect anything unmanageable with my sister, but just in case?"

The thought of spending more time with her sped his pulse. The uncertainty etching her heart-shaped face decided it. One thing first.

He closed the final inches and tasted her lips. Her exhale caressed his mouth, and her fingers swept through his hair, pulling him closer. He fought the urgency to work his tongue past her lips and kept it chaste. Since kissing was the breadth of his experience, he'd stolen countless lip-locked moments, each one growing bolder but never out of bounds. Though the sensation of her lips whispering over his went beyond that point of contact, spreading south.

He cupped her cheek, holding her to him. Shuddering waves of need heated his insides and gripped his groin. If the kiss continued one more second, his vow to his parents would be put to the test. He broke the kiss.

The seam of her lips separated, the delicate lines of her face magnifying her allure. He grabbed his phone from the cup holder and jumped out. He wasn't a slave to his desires, and she'd asked him to come inside because she needed a friend. That he could do.

She joined him at the garage keypad and punched in the code. By the time they reached the interior door, he'd managed to wrestle down his libido.

A dark hush greeted them in the kitchen. There was a trace of mustiness in the air, the staleness of vacancy, but the red sauce smearing the dishes in the sink appeared fresh.

He trailed her confident pace over the worn brown carpet to the sitting room. A single lamp illuminated dark wood panels, a paisley couch, matching armchair, and a clunky tube-style television.

"This place is familiar." He rubbed his jaw.

Creases formed in her forehead. She scanned the room but didn't really seem to be inspecting it, her gaze more inwardly focused.

"*That '70s Show* was filmed right here in this living room, wasn't it?" He grinned, amusing himself.

Not a hint of a smile on her distracted face. "Poor people have poor ways."

A reminder he didn't know what she did for a living, and he'd probably offended her, dammit. He didn't know anything about her. Except the smooth silkiness of her lips.

"Sis?" She ambled down the hall and poked her head in each of the two bedrooms. "She must be in the attic."

The room chilled, and he shivered. "The attic?"

"She feels safe there." She paused at the enclosed staircase that led up from the mouth of the hallway and held out her hand.

He rubbed the back of his neck. "Sure you don't need a few minutes to talk? I can wait down here if you want privacy."

Her hand remained outstretched, her rich brown eyes watching him with a pleading kind of intensity that told him his presence was important.

He joined her and twined their fingers, her palm cool and damp. What could he do to ease her nervousness? He tightened his grip and followed her up, the unlit stairwell closing in around him. "Where's the light-switch?"

She stopped them on the top stair, the darkness as heavy as her silence. Her clothes rustled. Beeps followed. A small red light blinked on the wall.

Apprehension crawled over him, tickling the hairs on his arms. "Was that a keypad?"

A door opened, and he squinted into the fluorescent glare escaping from inside. Her grip on his hand tugged him over the threshold, and he followed, compelled, curious. *Shocked.*

His attention landed on the center of the room, and he struggled to process what he saw.

A teenage girl knelt before them, completely nude. Her white-blond hair and fair skin looked nothing like Liv. But what sent dread through his veins was how she lowered her brow to the floor, hands behind her back, thighs spread.

The door clicked shut behind him, snapping him out of his stunned paralysis. He averted his eyes to the cot in the corner and the steel rings bolted in the wall above it. Dear God, what was this place?

His pulse roared in his ears, his voice strangled. "That's your sister?"

Liv cocked her head, a smirk pinned on her face.

Holy crap. Did she lie to him? Why?

Realization sank his stomach. She lied to lure him there.

He spun, yanked the door handle. No give. He slammed a fist on the door, a muffled thump. Solid wood. Reinforced with a steel jamb. "Let me out."

"No."

*No?* She was refusing to release him? His blood drained to his legs, leaving a trail of ice in its wake. He pawed at the keypad on the brick wall. His heart rate redoubled. Surely the naked girl was there voluntarily. Maybe they just wanted to have some fun with him, and he'd given the wrong signals.

He turned, pressed his back to the door, and tugged out his phone. "I'm not into this…whatever this is."

The buttons wouldn't respond. Black screen. He jammed his thumb against the power switch. Nothing.

A hard swallow caught in his throat. He raised his eyes, found her watching him with that terrible stillness about her. When she spoke, the voice didn't belong to the girl with the silky lips and enthralling lullaby.

"You will learn, practice, and become the twelve requirements demanded by your Master." She crouched to stroke the girl's head, who hadn't moved or glanced up.

It had to be a sick joke. Just some swinging neighborhood debauchery. He needed to hear her admit it, because imagining the alternative was kicking his heart rate to dangerous levels.

"So you lured me here for some kinky game where I play gimp boy to your…your…she-Master?" He released a laugh, and it was strained and desperate. "Sorry, babe. You've got the wrong guy."

She rose and stalked toward him, her stride commanding, her expression blank. "I am a deliverer. I deliver the strikes that enforce your obedience."

Her voice, sweet Jesus, it was so cold, so wrong.

He slid to the side of the door, choking on panic, and smacked the keypad. "Open the door."

"I deliver the sexual training that justifies your purchase price."

If he screamed for help, would anyone hear? "What's really going on here, Liv? If you're in trouble, I can help you. I know people you can talk to."

She stepped into his space, the wall pressing against his back. "In ten weeks, I will deliver you to be sold."

His breath caught. "You're insane."

What he saw in her eyes wasn't insanity. Deeply-embedded resolve held her pupils immovable.

"Requirement number three," she said. "Slave will keep his eyes down unless Master requests otherwise."

The impulse to fight strengthened his spine. He was a linebacker, trained to run and tackle, so he lunged. Grabbed her shoulders. Slammed her chest into the wall beside the keypad. She didn't fight, didn't squeak under his rough handling.

"Enter the pass-code." He pressed against her back and gripped her neck.

Her body slouched, free of tension beneath the brace of his arms. She wasn't fighting him, and he realized why when the door swung open.

He swiveled, muscles heated to bolt, and met the short barrel of a revolver.

A hulking man strode through, his face shrouded by the hood of his sweatshirt. He kept the pistol aimed between Josh's eyes and closed the door. "Release her."

Josh let go of her neck, his jaw clenching painfully. She'd let him pin her, knowing she held the upper hand.

He took two steps back, hands up, and searched her face in a Hail-Mary hope her rigid mouth would crack into laughter and say, *Ha, ha. You've been punk'd.*

Her hips rocked in tight circles, slowly, seductively, as if an erotic dancer had taken over her body. She sashayed to stand beside the man with the gun and raised her chin.

The chill in her voice stopped his heart. "Eyes. Down."

# FIVE

"Joshua Carter no longer exists." Liv gave him a second to absorb that, though the firestorm thrashing in his eyes told her he might need more than a pregnant pause.

Her heart rate threatened to rob the strength from her knees, and that kind of weakness pissed her the fuck off.

She gathered control over her features, arranging them into the stoniest expression she had. "For the next ten weeks, your name is whatever I want it to be."

"Let me go." Despite the pallor blanching his golden complexion, he glared down at her with the composure of a fearless man.

His maturity was emphasized by the whiskers darkening his square jaw and the carved contour of his rigid muscles.

She needed to think of him as a boy. Boys were malleable, unsteady, and less attractive. "For now, your name is *boy*."

Standing by the locked door as if its proximity could save him, he set his jaw, green eyes sparking with defiance. Van kept his position beside her, the gun level with the boy's head.

"Eyes down, boy." Not that she expected him to obey. That progression had to be paved with his blood and tears. The thought stabbed a terrible pain in her chest.

His unwavering stare continued to press against her skin, and there was so much force in it, she didn't think she could endure it much longer. She would, though. She would do anything for the hope that awaited her at the end of the night. The hope that would feed her famished heart.

In the center of the room, the girl remained folded on her knees.

Since her training neared completion, she could demonstrate some expectations for the boy.

Liv approached her, injecting her command with unfeeling iron. "On the cot, slave. Cuffed."

The girl crawled to the cot and lay on her back, hands reaching above her head to grasp the handcuffs on the wall. She locked in her wrists. The cuffs connected to steel eyehooks and were sturdy enough to restrain the strongest of struggling slaves.

The boy's glare ticked between the girl and the gun, tension rippling over the hard lines of his body.

He closed his eyes, opened them, and met Liv's gaze, nostrils flaring. "I kissed you."

Her insides tightened, and Van's finger twitched on the trigger. Just a twitch. Van's role that night was to keep quiet and ensure her success in confining the boy in the box. The rational part of her was glad Van was there. If she were alone with the boy, she might've anchored her thoughts in the intimacy they'd shared. She might've weakened under the resentment of her betrayal.

Van's presence kept her frigid, focused mask in place. But he was undoubtedly raging with jealousy. *Too damned bad.* He knew the job and what it involved.

She reached up and slid back his hood, caressing his scar. The affection catered to his possessiveness, calming his inward battle, evidenced in the subtle slackening of his finger on the trigger. But unveiling his expression also served as a warning for the boy. Van outmatched him in muscle and cruelty, and under the fluorescents, she knew Van's eyes were blades of silver and cut just as deep.

The boy swallowed. "You said something about—" He gritted his teeth. "You intend to sell me? Like a...a slave? This isn't a game?"

No way did the boy fully grasp what was going on. He was probably still clinging to the hope of release when they were done with him.

"Let him go, Liv." Van scratched his neck. "You got the wrong kid."

While Van was attempting to win the boy's trust, it didn't quite soften his razor eyes. He sucked at being the passive captor, though to his credit, he'd never had to watch from the sidelines before. His sadistic control-freakery was probably tearing him up inside.

"Just stand there and hold the gun like you're supposed to, Van." She met the boy's steadfast expression with her own. "You will be trained. Then you will be sold for sex."

"I can pay." He raised his stubborn chin. "I can come up with the money and cover whatever they're paying you."

Hell, he didn't have a dollar, and certainly not two million of them. His illogical offer meant he was still in the panic stage. She remembered the confusion and how the uncontrollable trembling and desire to escape had made her crazed, hyper-aware, and desperate.

Witnessing him experience the first horrific phases of capture was why she'd avoided conversation in the truck. She hadn't wanted to connect with him as his equal, as a friend. Connections like that birthed concern and sympathy and other touchy-feely detriments to her arrangement.

But she'd returned his kiss. At the time, she'd reasoned it was a luring tactic. Until their lips separated, and she was left with a lingering taste of something she'd never have.

"Follow me." She didn't wait for the boy's obedience. Van's gun would ensure it. She strode to the soundproof wall that divided the attic into two chambers.

At the door, she punched her code into the keypad. She and Van had separate codes to move through the rooms within the house, but only she had a code for this one.

She walked through the long, narrow room. Once her prison, it was now her sanctuary, her bedroom, and the only place she could escape Van. When Mr. E promoted her from slave to deliverer, he allowed her request to hold the only combination to the room. And why not? He could reach through any door with the threat he held over her. But Van could not.

Tossing her phone on the threadbare mattress in the corner, she moved past the open shower, toilet, and sink along the front wall. Reaching the coffin-sized pine box opposite the unenclosed bathroom, she turned and waited for the boy to join her.

There was an illusion that he could walk freely into the room, but it was psychological bullshit. Van wouldn't shoot if the boy slipped-up, but any number of the non-lethal weapons hidden on his person insured compliance.

The brick at her back made the attic feel inescapable, as was intended, but the true barrier was the sound-deadening concrete forms veneering the exterior walls. Its effectiveness was tested by her own lungs during her first year in this room. No one had come to save her.

The boy crossed the threshold with Van's gun at his back. His arms lolled at his sides, his expression growing more wary and alert with each step. What would he do? What was he thinking? Planning?

He scanned her room—the room she would be sharing with him— and his gaze seized on the phone on the mattress, flicked to the horizontal box, and returned to the phone.

"The phone is locked." She kept her posture still and straight, her voice detached.

A storm of frantic ideas churned in his icy eyes. He could try to dial 911, but the modifications Mr. E put on her phone disabled things like the camera and the ability to make emergency calls while it was locked. This allowed her to keep her phone with her, one of his requirements. He used it to track her every call, her every move. At the end of the day, she was just as trapped as the boy.

Van nudged him with the gun, moving him forward.

The boy stopped a foot away from her position beside the box. His breath evened in what seemed to be an attempt at deference. Too many emotions clouded his face to predict what he was planning. But his choices were no longer his.

"Requirement number four. Slave will not wear clothes unless Master requests otherwise." She exhaled slowly through her nose. This would not go over well. "Strip."

His expression emptied. Was it shock? Was he masking his terror? If so, he was doing a damned good job. Maybe he already worked out it would come to this. When she was forced to strip the first time, she'd already played out the worst scenarios in her head. Surrendering her clothes had paled next to her imagination. Hadn't stopped her from pleading for her modesty.

"Why did you skip requirements one and two?" His voice was calm. Too calm.

Had he already reached the compliance stage? That usually took days to weeks of unrelenting pressure. Perhaps he was just being vigilant and probing his hopeless situation from all angles.

She inhaled deeply through her nose. As a cold-hearted deliverer, she couldn't answer his questions. She kicked his knee, hard enough to make him stumble. "Clothes. Now."

He glanced at Van, the gun, back to her. "If I refuse, do I get a matching scar, too?"

The little shit actually grinned. It was shaky as hell, but he had brass balls. Her stomach sank at the thought of breaking them.

Van laughed, playing the part. "Only if you're really lucky. You'd have to fall in love and break the virginity clause to earn one of these." He stroked his scar.

She closed her eyes. The love thing was one-sided, and he'd left out the most important part, the piece that held her there. For that, she was grateful.

When she opened her eyes, the boy was watching her with a demeanor she couldn't interpret.

"Just take off your clothes, man," Van said. "Do what she says, and no one will scar your pretty face."

The boy held her gaze as he yanked his shirt over his head, toed off his work boots, and dropped his jeans and boxers in one shove. He didn't cover himself. Just stepped out of his pants and let her peruse his body.

His thick neck expanded into cut after cut of muscle down his torso. Sinews and tendons stretched the skin in his arms and legs. It was a physique developed through rigorous labor and exercise, wrapped in golden flesh. And his cock… Her breath caught. In its flaccid state, it lay over a loose, full sac and reached a few inches beyond.

"Look at that." Van circled to stand beside her. "And you thought it was the jockstrap straining his pants."

The boy's eyes widened, likely in realization that this wasn't a spontaneous kidnapping. Yeah, she knew all about his jockstraps, but she'd never mentioned his package to Van. Didn't mean she hadn't thought about it. Warmth swirled, uninvited, through her body.

When she was sure she'd mustered strength back into her voice, she tapped the edge of the box. "Get in."

A twitch in his socked foot was the only response.

Van rotated the aim of the gun down, up, left to right, as if deciding what body part to shoot. He settled the sights on the boy's balls. "Liv, you sure Mr. E doesn't bury the bodies in the backyard?"

Fear was the cruelest weapon. It victimized the mind and bred inaction.

She despised the idea of scaring the boy. Fuck, she was scared every damned day of her life, but she maintained the bitchy role she was required to play. "I don't want to know what he does with the bodies."

Truth was, Mr. E no longer needed to dirty his gloved hands since he'd acquired her. His visits were rare, his identity masked.

"You won't shoot me." The boy rolled back his shoulders, flexing his pecs. "How much money will you make off me?"

She leaned up on tip-toes, using the nearness to examine the depth of his bright eyes, the sun-bronzed skin dipping in the hollows of his cheeks, and the velvet pillow of his lips. He was raw, unblemished beauty. Mesmerizing. Distracting.

Relaxing her feet, she dropped back. "Emily Carter has a doctor's appointment tomorrow morning. Your mom goes every Saturday for her weekly allergy shot."

A hitch shuddered around his mouth.

She reached behind Van, slipped her hand under his sweatshirt, and removed the Taurus PT-22 from its wedge between his spine and waistband.

"The clinic's not in a very good part of town." She held up the .22, aimed at the ceiling. The intent wasn't to shoot him. It conveyed a much grimmer purpose. "Would be a shame if she got carjacked."

He stared at the gun, at the pink wood-grain grip. Horror tightened his face as he recognized his mother's pistol. "No." A heartbreaking whisper. "Please, no."

Though he gave her the response she needed, her heart felt like it was shrinking. She relaxed her mouth in a painful smile. "I stole it from her glovebox a few days ago. She's unmolested. For now."

His breath wheezed hard and fast. A moment later, his lungs slowed. He looked at the box, and a long, deep inhale widened his nostrils. He blinked slowly, eyes lowering.

Then he jerked forward, fist reared back and aimed at her. Expecting it, she dropped in a crouch, dodged his punch, and slammed her shoulders into his knees.

The .22 clattered to the floor, a deliberate maneuver to distract him. He wobbled, skirting around her, and scrambled for the gun. She let him. After all, it wasn't loaded.

As he bent to retrieve it, Van pressed a boot on his back and shoved the loaded revolver against his nape.

From a small trunk by the box, she gathered locking metal cuffs and a coil of chain, the clanking drawing his attention. "Van's gun is loaded. Your mother's gun is not. Go ahead. Check."

He did, wrinkles forming on his forehead. After a second check of the magazine, he set it on the floor and slumped under the weight of Van's foot.

"In the box." She kicked the .22 out of reach as he climbed in, his movements wooden.

The cuffs went on first, cinching tight. Next, she wrapped the chain around his wrists until the full length was used. The excess binding was more psychological than practical.

He allowed her to move his limbs where she wanted them, his eyes squeezed shut. What was he feeling? Frustration, denial, hope of rescue, utter terror? Her time in that box had covered the gamut.

With the ends of the chains hooked together, she raised his bound arms above his head and locked the cuffs to one of the many eyehooks lining the wood slats.

The box was a device in repression, used to send a degrading message. She controlled his actions, down to every sensory detail. In twenty-four hours, he would emerge sleep-deprived, hungry, and, with no access to a bathroom, humiliated. Weakened and at the mercy of her commands.

She removed his socks and repeated the shackling with his ankles. He stiffened each time her finger brushed his skin, likely repulsed by the feel of her. She swallowed around the knot in her throat. She didn't blame him.

A yank at his arms and legs confirmed the detainment. She stepped back, followed Van to the door, and entered the code.

As he pushed it open, he swayed toward her, slanting his cheek against hers.

She tensed. With his mouth so close, would he kiss her or bite her?

His nose slid through her hair, inhaling her scent. "I'll let Mr. E know we'll be ready for the videos in five."

The gentleness in his tone and the meaning of his words loosened some of her stiffness. On nights like these, when they watched the footage together and he shared in the assurance it delivered, she could feel the tender caress of affection poking past her deepest bruises and curling around her heart. She nodded.

The door clicked behind him. She hurried back to the boy.

On his back, muscles bared, bound, and stretched the full length of the box, he was an erotic picture. She was a criminal, and as ashamed as she was by that, the disgusting, fucked-up part of her anticipated spending the next ten weeks touching every inch of this man.

*Boy.*

She dragged her gaze from his body to his face, and guilt slammed into her.

He stared up at her with so much pain in his eyes. "Don't hurt my parents."

Her gut twisted. She knew that pain, lived it every day. She leaned in, lips hovering a breath away, and repeated what Mr. E had said to her. "That's up to you."

Resolve hardened his face. She knew that emotion, too. Her time in the box was permanently carved in memory, which had made Van's threats of returning her there an effective form of control in her training.

Tendrils of resentment coiled around her throat. To dwell on her or the boy's predicament would only bring irresponsible hesitation. So she did what she always did to distract her thoughts.

She reached into the cold place inside her, searching for something yearning she could sing with dispassion. The beginning verses of "What It Is" by *Kodaline* fell past her lips and shivered through the room. She sang with an icy pitch as she removed a blindfold from the trunk by the box and tied it over his wide, glaring eyes.

To deprive smell, a swimmer's nose plug went on next. He could breathe through his mouth, and the cracks in the box allowed airflow, but it wouldn't feel that way to him once she shut the lid.

The skin on his face was hot and damp, the muscles beneath jerking against her fingers. She continued to sing as she cuffed headphones over his ears, plugged them into the tablet outside of the box, and activated the timer. Twenty minutes of heart-hammering silence.

The music in her voice strangled, stopped. Twenty minutes alone with his thoughts. Then the misery would begin.

"It's just the way it is," she murmured with an ache in her throat.

His body was motionless, but she didn't miss the goosebumps creeping across his skin or the slight tremor in his jaw. The sudden desire to comfort him drew her closer, bending her at the waist, until her mouth brushed his, softly, unjustly. His lips pulled away in a quiver that she felt throughout her body.

She straightened and rubbed her breastbone, unable to soothe the ache beneath it. "I'm so sorry." A whisper, too low to pass through the earphones.

Then she closed the lid.

# SIX

Opaque fabric pressed against Josh's eyes. The clip on his nose forced his breaths through his mouth. Were there air holes? There must've been, otherwise he'd be gulping lungfuls of nothingness. His throat whistled. His mouth parched. Maybe he *was* suffocating.

Were his captors standing right outside the box? He couldn't hear a damned thing beyond the covers on his ears and the thump of his heart.

The unforgiving wood dug into his shoulders and hips. The thousand-pound chains pinned his hands and feet. The too-close walls caved in around him, firing the nerve endings along his skin in concentrated chaos. It was the kind of tactile assault he imagined could only be experienced within the deafening suffocation of a coffin.

Fear boiled in his stomach and hit his throat with searing acid. Great, he still had the sense of taste, which meant he could savor his puke as he choked on it. He squirmed, tilting his head to the side in case his stomach emptied.

This had to be a depraved prank. They wouldn't leave him chained like this for long. The girl in the next room didn't have visible wounds on her fragile frame. There weren't any instruments of cruelty hanging on the walls. Hell, the gun wasn't even loaded.

He should've grabbed the blonde and threatened to break her neck. Why hadn't he kicked the gun from Van's hand as soon as the man walked in? His chest tightened. He should've left Liv on the road to tow her own effing car.

His pulse elevated, and his body burned and itched. Mom and Dad would be looking for him. How many calls had he missed? His heavy breaths congealed the air around him. She'd done something to his phone.

He bucked against the box, yanking and twisting at the restraints. His stupid freaking impulse to help a stranger had put his parents in danger. He'd left them unprotected and abandoned them with a farm they couldn't manage alone.

He was an idiot. His cheeks burned, and his body fevered with sweat and chills. He tried to punch his legs. The shackles held. So frigging stupid. He kicked again, and pain jolted through his ankles.

Could they hear him struggling? He bit down on his lip, swallowing hard. Had his hostility sent them out to hurt his parents?

A roar clawed from his throat, thundering in his head. How could he have let this happen? Why hadn't he sent his own text to Mom? Why hadn't he noticed these people watching him? He should've investigated the problem with her car himself. He could've prevented this.

His muscles clenched against another bout of trembling. Dad would retrace the route from the stadium to home. He'd find nothing. Likely not even her stalled sedan. She was too well-prepared, luring him with a story, sabotaging his phone while he sat beside her, and coercing him with Mom's routine and her stolen .22. How long had they been watching?

Why him? Oh God, what had he done to earn their attention?

Helplessness ricocheted over his limbs, thrashing against the chains. Mom was probably pacing in the kitchen, wearing down the linoleum, overworking her already fragile heart.

A sob erupted in his chest, taking him by surprise as it escaped with his gasps. *Please, dear God.* He closed his eyes, trapping wells of moisture. *Please take care of Mom and Dad.*

Prayer saturated his thoughts. He stammered through his favorite hymns, filling his heart with the inspirational, joyful words. He desperately needed the power of God to overcome this and to ensure he rose whole and confident and alive.

The walls of the box crept impossibly closer. He thrashed. Useless. He widened his eyes beneath the mask, trying frantically to see, and met a shroud of black. So cramped. Dark. His lungs panted. He needed to focus, to keep his head.

He tried to recall the meditation techniques he'd learned at his retreat. Sucking air through a dry throat, he pictured light filtering through the box's wood planks, spreading a glow over him, chasing away the shadows. The walls around him expanded outward. The coffin doubled in size. Oxygen flowed in. His pulse slowed. He swiped his tongue over cracked lips. Bless the depth of his imagination.

Time stretched. Was it minutes? Or was it hours? They should've released him by now. What were they doing out there? Sharpening knives? Laughing about what a sucker he was? Or were they planning to move the box out back and bury it with him inside?

No, not death. She'd said he would be sold in ten weeks. He would have to be alive for that to happen. He latched onto the hope of survival, even as the implication of his body being auctioned for money brought its own horrors.

A violent shudder ripped through him. Purchased by what kind of person? For what purpose?

He knew. He knew the answers and shoved them away, stretching his jaw to accommodate a panicked rush of breath. *Heavenly Father, please help me.*

Despair gave way to anger and frustration. His prayers weakened in conviction, losing their appeal. He had put himself in this situation. God had nothing to do with it. Doubt trickled in. Doubt in His divine rescue. Doubt in himself.

Too many terrible things could happen to him and his parents. The air thinned, and his lungs struggled against images of Mom and Dad's bodies gutted in their bed and painted in blood.

He curled his hands into fists, picturing Liv slicing off his fingernails with a razor blade. Nausea coiled in his stomach. The glaring possibility was rape. Was he strong enough to prevent Van from taking him from behind?

His heart pounded. His virginity was his to give, dammit, not to be stolen and dehumanized. The thought girded him, even as he knew his restraints enabled them to do whatever they wanted.

He rolled his head back and forth over the wood. What had he learned during his spiral of mistakes? Beyond his stupidity in blind trust? He was in the *Two Trails Crossing* neighborhood in Temple. His captors went by Van and Liv. Calm, physically fit, and armed, they posed a difficult barrier to break through.

Besides the mention of a Mr. E, she seemed to be the one in control. Who was she? Clearly not the girl who cried a sob story on the street. Hindsight punched him hard in the gut.

But she couldn't be a sociopath. Hadn't he glimpsed the real girl in his truck in her moving song? No one could fake the gravity he'd heard in her voice. What was driving her? Money was the obvious reason, but her aim seemed...more profound. Was she motivated by something deeper? Something attached to her?

A deep-rooted sadness had flooded her eyes and creased her mouth when he asked her not to hurt his parents. Then it was complicated by that second kiss, the one she took while he was pinned in the coffin.

Maybe he was only seeing what he wanted to see? Scrambling for the only thread of optimism in his reach? Perhaps the kiss was a design to mess with his head. Except it had conveyed a hesitancy the first kiss did not.

There was nothing hesitant about Van. His composure was fortified by piercing gray eyes, so sharp they didn't blink. Which made the calculation in his chumminess obvious—and confusing. Even as Josh had recognized it for what it was, he couldn't deny he felt a little less tense when Van traded his steely gaze for a full-faced grin.

And the girl, who must've been some kind of slave, had somehow earned a respite from restraints and supervision. A reward for good behavior?

Sweet Jesus, one week in this nightmare and he might be drooling applesauce. He writhed in the chains, his hips banging against the sides. How much longer before they let him out of the freaking box?

He tried again to calm himself, catching his breath, rolling his neck and shoulders through the burgeoning pangs of muscle cramps.

There was a way out of this. Somehow. He just needed to man up and figure it out. Field experience in instructional ministry had taught him how to associate with people, how to listen to them, and guide them through tough situations. He would concentrate his attention on observing what she was hiding and hearing what wasn't being said. He would study her face and learn her expressions. Once he discovered the heart of her, he would offer advice, befriend her, discover her strengths and weaknesses, and predict her next moves.

What if she injured him? Raped him? What were his limits? How much could he endure before he despised her so much he lost himself in hate?

Adrenaline burned through his veins. If he could survive the next few hours or days, he could survive ten weeks. Maintaining composure was paramount.

A sudden ringing sound pierced the silence. It was a consistent lonely tone, like the lingering bong of a brass bell. Was it some kind of tinnitus?

He rolled his head side-to-side, and the frequency seemed to ripple around his ears. It was definitely streaming through the headphones. The volume wasn't elevated enough to hurt. Just one loud, relentless blare.

Minutes passed, and the sound continued. His fingers tingled, as did the skin around his lips. Panic and irritation robbed his ability to catch his breath. He yawned over and over, popping his ears.

No change in frequency. No relief. He buckled down, fought the tremors in his body and the furor of emotions pushing against the backs of his eyes.

"Make it stop!" The scream shredded his vocal chords. "Please, stop."

He counted to one thousand. He couldn't calm his heart.

When would it end? He counted to five thousand.

All that existed was the certainty in one demanding tonality. He couldn't focus.

*Stop, stop, stop.*

"Please...Please turn if off...Stop!"

His throat scraped, his shrieks unraveling his hold on his mind.

# SEVEN

Liv found Van downstairs in the sitting room, reclined in the armchair, a lit cigarette drooping from his lips. She stiffened as he patted his knee in invitation, his eyes twin sparks of silver in the glow of his phone, the room's only light.

The way he looked at her chilled her skin, even as his smoke-curled smile made her heart ache for things he could never give.

Spine steeled against the brutal beauty of his face, she put one sneaker before the other, plucked the cig from his mouth, and perched on his knee. "Ready?"

Moving his arms around her waist, he rested his chin on her shoulder and reached for the device. "Been ready since the day I met you."

Her skin itched where his breath touched her cheek, where his leg pressed against her ass, where his arms brushed her hips. He was both an infectious rash and a soothing touch.

She finished the final drag on the cigarette and squashed it in the ashtray, eyes on the blank screen.

He launched their e-mail account, the inbox empty. Empty for nine weeks. She stared at it, willing it to beep, her exhale trapped in her chest.

A tap on the screen made the phone call. Another tap, and he switched it to speaker mode, his free arm draped over her thigh. The call connected on the first ring.

"Any problems?" Crisp and deep, the voice dragged a shudder from her lungs.

"No, sir," she and Van said in chorus.

The inbox dinged, announcing a new message with an attached file.

"The recording is five minutes old," Mr. E said, "and two minutes long. I'll wait."

Van clicked on the video file and leaned back. She bent toward it, where it perched in his outstretched hand.

On the screen, a woman in her late-forties sat at a table in a kitchen that had become familiar from this camera angle. Wisps of gray curled through her short brown hair, her hands folded around the mug she stared into. If she glanced up, her eyes would be a deep warm brown, set in the determined expression of a woman who had birthed a child on the heels of an abusive relationship. A woman whose passion for skydiving came second to her love for her only child. The woman who said that anyone could fall; the skill was in landing.

When she'd learned her missing daughter's remains had been found in an abandoned house, she'd cried for weeks as Liv watched through video footage from her attic prison. But Mom knew how to land. A few weeks before Liv's one-year incarceration as a slave ended, Mom moved on to a new job and a new home.

The ache to find that kitchen in the video festered inside her. While Liv had the freedom to run errands, scout for new victims, and — not often enough — skydive, her movements were monitored. With anxious discretion, she slipped in and out of public libraries, hunting the web for Jill Reed the skydiving instructor, the pilot, the grieving mother. There were too many skydiving schools, too many Jill Reeds.

She scrutinized Mom's sleeveless shirt. Tepid climate in October? Could've been anywhere along the Gulf. Were the creases in her hair from long hours beneath a skydiving helmet? Or a ponytail holder, pulled back for any job? The print on the newspaper at her elbow was too small to read, and the blinds were closed on the window. No new clues, every recorded clip too meticulously selected before delivery.

The sudden impulse to demand her mother's location from Mr. E cramped her gut and heated her face. Last time she did that, he slapped her with his two-week version of house arrest. So she crushed her reckless notion behind pinned lips and traced a fingernail over the beloved image on the screen.

She earned three video sessions per slave. One on the evening of the capture. One after a successful first meeting between buyer and slave. And one when she made the final delivery and the funds were transferred to Mr. E's account.

Only once had she received a video outside of this schedule. It had arrived after she'd forgotten to take her phone on a grocery errand. Her failure to respond immediately to one of Mr. E's texts while she was out had earned her a video of Mom's demolished car, lying on its side in a ravine. Mom survived with three broken ribs and a shattered femur.

Her chest tightened at the memory and squeezed harder as she watched Mom stand from the table and move out of view of the camera. The video ended, frozen on the empty room.

Each time she watched the videos, she was reminded that she'd sold her soul and the lives of her captives to a man she couldn't trust. Didn't stop her pulse from strumming excitedly as her attention flew to the phone's notification bar. One more email would come, the video meant for her and Van.

"I expect," Mr. E said, "you'll meet your next deadline. Or your future viewings will only include one of the two videos."

A knot lodged in her throat. It was a threat he could only use once. If he killed the only two people she loved, she would no longer have the incentive to work for him…or to go on.

"A camera was installed in the bedroom," Mr. E said. "The recording is three hours old."

The line disconnected.

The lump in her throat loosened. "Did you hear that? Her bedroom, Van." For six years, she'd imagined what it might look like.

"I heard." There was a smile in his voice.

A new message alert popped up. She reached for the screen, colliding with his hand. Chuckling, he offered her the device. Then he wrapped his arms around her waist and leaned them forward on the edge of the seat, hunching over the small screen. She tapped the file, and the video player opened.

Red and brown whimsical birds winged a painted pattern over the bedroom wall. White lacy curtains draped the window, the shroud of night swallowing any clues that could point to location or climate. A red-checkered quilt blanketed the twin bed and the six-year-old girl within.

Liv's breath stuttered, and she felt Van smile against her neck.

The girl grinned, front tooth missing, eyes heavy-lidded with trust and love. Her smile was for the blond woman who sat beside her.

Liv wanted to rejoice at seeing her happy and safe, but bitter jealousy was a noose, strangling her air and failing her heart.

He gripped the back of her free hand, lifting it with his and cupping their twined fingers around the screen. Their fingers an inch from the girl's pixelated face was the closest they'd ever been to touching her. In her mind, she'd named her Mattie.

Warm breath flitted over the curve of her neck, his other arm a brace around her waist. At that moment, his affection was a quietude in shared happiness, their connection suspended in a twinkling of peace.

"She's beautiful," he murmured against her skin.

Dark brown hair curled from Mattie's sweet face and fanned over the pillow. She laughed at something her adoptive mother said and rolled to her side, shut her eyes.

Liv imagined herself a mother, saying silly things to incite that beautiful, toothy smile. She wanted to call her name just to look into her eyes. She wanted to know her *real* name and hug her when she cried. What would it feel like to pick her up when she fell, to help her with homework, to watch her blow out birthday candles? It would have been a complete life.

A burn erupted behind her eyes, her fingers dragging Van's up and down the edge of the screen. She breathed deeply, tried to swallow the choking hopelessness.

The blond woman reached for the bedside lamp.

"No." A whimper escaped Liv's lips. "Not yet."

Van moved their twined hands, hugging her arm to her waist. Her other hand held the device in a death grip.

On screen, Mattie's shoulders rose and fell with restful breaths, her little hand fisted in the blanket.

Then the lamp clicked off, drenching the screen in black. The video stopped.

Liv's heart plummeted. She wanted to restart it, tried to untangle her arm from his, but he held it pinned against her body. She balanced the phone on her leg to punch the play button, and he snatched it away.

"No replays, Liv." He forged his voice in an iron tone. "You know the rules."

Watch it once and delete it. Their phones were monitored and swapped out each time Mr. E visited. No cameras and recordings allowed on the property. No evidence. No replays. No saved or copied files. No distractions from the job.

The job, the job, the job. Focus on the job. Be the job. *Or else.* It was all she was, a mechanical, hollow nothing that did anything needed to prevent the *else.*

A violent shudder snapped through her bones. As long as she lived, Mom and Mattie would be in danger.

Liv's death could set them free. So many times, she came close but couldn't do it. She was a weak, selfish cunt.

She pushed against his chest. "Let me go."

His arm tightened against her waist. "The child will be fine."

*The child.*

"She's *your* child." Spit flew from her lips, her voice rising. "*Our* child."

He dropped the device and spun her off his lap. Her back hit the couch, the weight of him holding her down. Her pathetic struggle ended with her arms above her head, shackled by one of his hands, his other pointing at the phone on the floor.

"She's *not* our child!" His volume hiked, matching hers. "She belongs to that woman."

"A woman who probably works for Mr. E!"

In six years and twenty-one videos, the blonde's face had never been revealed. Mattie's life depended on Liv. A failure during the job or a fracture in the rules promised another accident. Mom had been meant to die in that car. Mattie wouldn't be so lucky. Only Liv could protect her, and the safest way would be to hide her from Mr. E. She could be anywhere in the world. Liv desperately needed her name.

"Wipe that look off your face." He pressed his hips against hers, the steel of his irises resistant and unfeeling. "Even if you could find her, you can't take her from the only mother she's ever known."

"The way you snatched me from my mother?"

His lips thinned into hard lines with clenched teeth in the middle. "Back to this again?"

"You started this when you accepted his proposal. You *chose* to ruin people's lives."

He released her arms, standing tall and imposing, and glared down at her. "Mr. E started it when he freed me from that goddamned slum."

He stabbed a finger at the front door as if indicating the direction of his crackhaggot mother. She slung drugs in El Paso, assuming she still lived. Liv knew he didn't care either way.

Mr. E had freed him from his victimized life, trained him to be a deliverer, and paid him to kidnap a girl of his choice. Lucky for Van, his choice ignorantly roller-bladed up to his car.

Her chest ached, and her body felt cold. "You broke his rules."

Van took her virginity not long after capture. Eight weeks later, he delivered her to the client, claiming she met the requirements of obedience and chastity. The former was accurate. Van had well and truly whipped the insolence out of her and replaced it with the trap of fear. The chastity, however, was disproved when the buyer brought in a doctor while Van waited for the exam results and the money transfer. The positive pregnancy test was a shock to everyone. Except Van.

She sat up, unable to glance away from the scar that perforated his prominent cheekbone, his face otherwise model-perfect from his clear, round eyes and full lips to the high, smooth bridge of his strong nose. His complexion glowed so vibrantly with health, one could almost overlook the four-inch red cut. The laceration Mr. E had given him when the buyer returned her without payment. The mate to the one she'd received minutes after his.

He watched her with a toothpick in his mouth and the harsh lines of intention etched around his eyes. "I saved you."

Did he save her by impregnating her before she was sold? Or when he pleaded for her life as Mr. E held the gun to her head upon her return? What did a human trafficker want with a pregnant slave? In the end, Mr. E gave Van what he'd wanted: Her.

"Yeah, you saved me." She clenched and unclenched her hands. "Instead of a life as a sex slave or a bullet in the brain, I got a disfigured face, my tubes tied, an illegal job, and a promise that I will never hug the only two people who matter to me."

His darkening expression blasted her anger to her stomach. That look had trained her to avert her eyes and drop to her knees. But sometimes, in the dark, the intensity of his stare and the openness of his lust almost felt like love.

A muscle jumped in his cheek. "Someday, I hope to matter to you, because you are the only one who matters to me. You will always be mine, Liv."

The promise propelled her to the night he'd preyed on her fear of him, comforting her while piercing past her virginal barrier. In that moment of frailty, wrapped in his strong arms, that scared, lonely girl had wanted nothing more than his devotion. She should've fought, should've retained some inkling of dignity.

That girl had realized, too late, something wasn't quite right with his adoring smile. After that night, the matching scars, and the loss of Mattie, that girl fell so far the hand of God couldn't pull her back. If manufacturing sex slaves in the house of evil was the only way to protect Mom and Mattie, to hell with God and everyone else.

Van rolled the toothpick between his lips and knelt in the $V$ of her legs. "Shall we head to bed?"

The desire in his eyes knocked her backward.

She pulled her knees up and pivoted, scrambling off the couch. "I have a job to do."

He caught her before she reached the stairs, slamming her back against the wall, his lips a toothpick away from hers. His hand moved over her waist, fingers slipping beneath her waistband.

The way his breath hitched and the heat melting his steely eyes swept an uninvited warmth through her womb. When he spit the pick on the floor and slanted his mouth toward hers, she jerked her face away. *Damn, his fucking lips.* His kisses were potent, and she was too emotionally exhausted to pretend they weren't.

A strong finger on her chin turned her face back to his.

"Don't you dare look away from me." He captured her bottom lip between his, nuzzling, and pulled back.

Her heart raced and her weak fucking knees wobbled.

His gaze roamed over her eyes, hair, and mouth, gorging on every detail. "Christ, Liv, you're so fucking beautiful."

She shivered at the compliment. Or was it the nausea tumbling her stomach? Why wasn't she fighting him? Spitting and punching and running away? Was it his strength holding her against the door? The conditioning instilled in her as a slave? The connection they shared through Mattie? Or was it as shallow as lust in the proximity of those stark gray eyes and talented lips?

He shoved a hand through her hair and licked the corner of her mouth. "I won't touch your defenses. Just give me everything else."

Yet he'd already taken everything, and her walls against him were splintering. Even if she could bring herself to kill him, she was restrained by the contract on Mom and Mattie's lives. A contract that would mobilize a hit man if he or Mr. E died suspiciously.

Her chest hurt, and her heartbeat thrashed in her ears. Sure, she could run. She could disappear somewhere they couldn't find her. But Mr. E had promised that if she vanished, he'd make Mom and Mattie's death so vile, it would reach national attention. Just to ensure it reached *her* attention.

Trapped in paranoia, she was terrified to make a mistake, her every action watched, judged, and used to threaten her family. Her nerves were so raw, she trusted nothing, connected to no one, and her loneliness was exasperated by her complicated fucking relationship with the man peppering kisses over her lips. She wanted to love him even as her fingers twitched to run a blade across his throat.

She spoke against his persistent mouth. "If the boy is suffocating on his own vomit, I won't be around long enough to give you anything."

His face tightened. "Very well. Go check on him."

He stepped back to give her just enough room to slip around him. As she did, a recognizable pang assaulted her scalp. She didn't have to look back to know he held a ripped-out chunk of her hair in his fist.

His creepy hair-thing fueled her race up the stairs, to the safety of her bedroom and to the boy she would destroy to keep her family alive.

# EIGHT

Liv rested her head against the box, absorbed by the rueful tune braiding through her mind, her ass numb from sitting on the subfloor. She should check on the boy, but the sight of his suffering would shred her already crumbling composure. The raw groans echoing from within the box were doing that enough on their own.

The other captives had fought her with vicious desperation. This boy's determination was quieter, more calculating. She heard it in his steady, low-pitched voice, saw it in his alert gaze and tightening fists, and felt it in her increased body temperature and rapid heartbeat.

Dammit, she'd trained herself not to get attached to these boys. She uncrossed her knees and straightened her legs along the floor. She would need extreme mental focus to smother her attraction to this boy and maintain her icy indifference.

The lid was closed, but she could imagine the terror creasing his beautiful face. It set off her own memories, shooting pain into body parts that had been shackled, whipped, and violated by Van's hand.

She pushed that aside. Self-pity would only earn her a stumbling misstep and a black-eye from Van's fist. Her own punishments certainly wouldn't make this experience easier on the boy. He needed a confident hand to guide him through the next few weeks. She climbed to her feet, her muscles tight with reluctance.

She opened the lid, knowing he wouldn't hear the squeaking hinges nor would he sense her leaning over him. The Solfeggio frequency piping through the headphones overpowered his perceptions, his ability to reason, his entire universe. So much so, he probably wouldn't even sense the change of air.

His lips stretched back in misery as he panted through his teeth. Perspiration wet his skin, streaking drips down his ribs with the heave of his chest. A lonely, weak moan reached from his throat and penetrated her chest.

As his body writhed against the walls in the narrow space and a pang of guilt cramped her gut, she forced herself to evaluate his distress. His rush of breath was panicked but not unrestricted. The chains confined his flailing but didn't cut off blood flow. As for his mind, she just needed it intact enough to be trained, to pass the introductory meeting with the buyer, the final delivery, and receipt of the client's payment.

After she delivered him, he would be dead to her. The same way she thought of the others.

Her eyes caught on his sculpted pecs, traveled along the dips and juts of his abs, and lingered on the impressive length of his cock where it lay against his thigh. Her fingers burned to touch him.

She gripped her stomach, disgusted with herself. He was even more attractive than the others, but he wasn't like them. His matured masculinity was prominent in the thickness of his build and the determined set of his jaw. Most importantly, he had a family and community that would miss him. What a godawful choice she'd been forced to make.

The turmoil inside her hardened into resolve. Ten weeks, a disciplined slave, and Mom and Mattie would be safe for another few months. It was how she measured her life, wasn't it? In ten week increments, in the trade of slaves, one body at a time.

She checked the music player. The one-hour recording rolled through its second of twenty-four repeats. He'd only been in the box for an hour, but it would've felt like days to him.

Ironically, the drone of the 528 hertz was used in meditation as harmonic healing. When Van had shoved her in the box and slapped the earphones on her head, he'd said, "That's a load of new age bullshit. After twenty-four hours of the same goddamned electrical wave passing through your skull, you won't be healed. You'll be fucking manic."

He'd been right. She'd emerged wild-eyed, delusional, and willing to do anything he demanded to avoid another minute in that box.

Fuck Van and his thrills. When she'd fled from him downstairs twenty minutes earlier, the desire in his eyes had been vulgar in its blatancy. Why had he let her escape so easily? He didn't give a shit if the boy vomited in the box, and he was too damned calculating to accept that excuse.

Always, he fucked her when he wanted her. Never did she participate with a willing heart. Yet their scrimmages didn't involve physical force. He'd wear her down with a skilled tongue or prey on her guilt through the mistreatment of a slave. Sometimes, he'd simply threaten to alert Mr. E of her disobedience. It wasn't until she'd met him that she'd understood the meaning of coerced consent.

She stared at the door, terrified to open it, terrified not to.

Surely he went to bed in his room downstairs instead of following her to the attic. If he'd followed her, he'd be out there with that poor girl, who had been asleep when Liv had dashed by in the race to her room.

*Fucking hell.* Checking on the girl was the right thing to do, no matter how badly she didn't want to open the door. Mr. E didn't give a shit how Van treated the captives as long as they met the requirements at the end of ten weeks.

Her stomach turned as she agonized leaving the boy alone. Goddammit, she was weakening already, and it was only his first night. Her chin trembled. He had to remain in the box. She couldn't bend the rules and expect to mold him into an acceptable slave. But the girl was already trained and didn't deserve Van's needless tormenting.

She closed the lid and jogged to the keypad. If he was waiting on the other side, she could shut it quickly. If he was messing with the girl, she'd have to distract him. Deep breath. She entered the code and cracked the door.

Across the room, the incarnation of her fears sat on the cot, back slouched against the wall. The girl's head dipped up and down between his spread legs, her face and his dick shrouded by her hair.

Vicious memories ripped in Liv's mind, sharp and desolate. She saw her own brown hair instead of the girl's blond. She felt his cock punching the back of her throat and his fingers digging into her scalp. An echoed sensation of their baby moved inside her, stretching her belly, making her bent position agonizing to endure.

Her blood pooled away from her core, leaving the frigid numbness of her year as a slave—nine of those months pregnant.

She swallowed the apparition of her past before it consumed her. The girl sucking him still retained her virginity, yet she was adept with her lips, mouth, and tongue. As one of the buyer's requirements, Liv had spent the prior eight weeks teaching her the skill on Van. And in two weeks, Liv would deliver her to a man whose hand was as heavy as his wallet.

Van looked up and caught her eyes, flames of greed blazing in his. "Come out here and show her how it's done, Liv."

God, she hated him when he was like this. When he watched her with such hunger as he pumped his dick in whatever hole he could command. This wasn't a training session for the girl. It was about Liv and him, and he was using the girl to tunnel Liv's guilt.

She could tuck her chin, shut the door, and fall asleep in the musty familiarity of her mattress inside the safety of her room.

And let the girl stroke and suck him until he was done with her. She'd blown him a dozen times before during practice. Did one more time really matter?

Van pushed down on the back of her head, and her hands convulsed on the mattress.

Compassion was lethal to Liv's well-being, but she couldn't stop it as it shuddered over her skin and swallowed up her heart. She opened the door, passed the cot, another keypad, another code, and down the stairs, her insides bucking and tumbling. At the end of the hall, she stopped at the only closed door and dropped her forehead against it.

What was more horrifying? The footsteps pounding down the stairs after her or all the creepy shit waiting on the other side of his bedroom door?

His body slammed against her back, his exhales hot on her neck, his erection stabbing her tail bone. He hadn't bothered to put his pants back on.

She mustered a stoic tone. "Let's get this over with."

"Oh, the sweet seduction of your words." He slapped her ass, lighting fire through her jeans, and swung open the door.

# NINE

Liv stumbled into Van's bedroom, unable to look away from the antique gun cabinet on the back wall, with walnut crests carved around the double glass doors. One might've expected a dozen prized shotguns displayed on the racks within. This was Texas, after all.

Instead, the cabinet was crammed with a menagerie of dolls and mannequins piled atop one another. Arms and legs askew, some still attached to molded bodies. Most were not. All of them bald and nude.

She rubbed the chill prickling her arms. "Little girls everywhere want to know, *Where do all the broken dollies go?*"

"Shut up, Liv." He sidled around her, and his foot sent a tiny headless torso careening under the bed, its jointed legs tumbling after.

Why wasn't that one with all the hollow-eyed faces pressed against the glass of the cabinet? Some of the heads were upside down. Others leered to the side or stared out into the room from beneath hinged eyelids. Dust-laced cobwebs drooped between the dirt-smudged body parts. If she shook the case, how many eyes would wiggle and blink back? She shivered.

"You need to"—she cleared her throat, tried to put *oomf* in her voice—"do some housecleaning."

"Nah." He threw himself on the bed, naked from the waist down.

His erection hadn't lost interest. It stood tall and unabashed between the flex of his thighs as he reclined on one elbow and watched her with his unnatural patience.

His interest in his collection, however, didn't appear to be sexual. None of his plastic friends were anatomically correct nor did they look well-loved. Much the opposite, in fact. A hairless mannequin slumped in the corner of the room, grime coating its nippleless coned breasts from years of inattention. One arm lay beside it, unattached. Its face was punched away, exposing the dark cavern of its head.

Above him, another mannequin hung from something like a meat hook jutting out of the wall. Bent at the waist, its arms and head lolled forward as if reaching for the bed, the far-away gaze on its face frighteningly reminiscent of young Pat Benatar.

"Van..." She jerked her chin at the aberration above him.

He'd never answered her years of questions about his fetishes, but he'd agreed to tuck away the ones that chilled her the most. He knew Plasti-Pat Benatar topped the list.

He rose, unhooked it from the wall, and tossed it under the bed to join who knew how many others. Then he turned to her, gripping the base of his cock, and pulled, one long lazy stroke. "Your turn, Liv. Show the pink."

A shudder bunched her shoulders to her ears. God, she couldn't do this. Her panties were bone-dry, and her throat felt like a fucking Texas drought. "I can't do this."

His expression hardened, his thoughts likely sifting through his arsenal of manipulations. Of course, he could punch her or choke her, but he never had to. She wagered he'd either return to the girl or call Mr. E.

She moved to the narrow bed and perched on the edge. "Not like this."

The muscles in his jaw relaxed, and he sat beside her, dragging a blanket over his lap. He didn't touch her. They both knew he would fuck her before she left that room, and his ability to endure her dawdling was something she always used to her advantage. Which was stupid. It never helped her in the end.

He leaned forward, elbows on knees, and stared at the dirt-matted carpet. A wrinkle creased his brow, his tone hesitant. "You want foreplay? Seduction?"

She wanted real. She wanted to feel an essential, basic emotion that wasn't bound to the wounds he'd inflicted on her, the ones that wouldn't heal. "What I want, you can't give."

He swung his head toward her, eyes alight with pain. "I dried your face when you cried. I held you when you screamed. I haven't left your side once in all these years. You have *me*. All of me!"

She masked her flinch with the stillness she'd perfected. The absence of motion made her feel less visible under his constant attention. She didn't want him ogling at her. She didn't want *him*. How could she? His kisses haunted her, the grip of his voice too painfully familiar in the dark. He was the cause of those tears, those screams, her fears.

The cup of his palm on her cheek drew her eyes to his, and the tenderness in his tone snagged her breath. "Sing to me."

His other hand caught her chin, preventing her from looking away. She shook her head in the cage of his fingers.

"If you need your distraction, your defense tonight, then by all means, sing." His timbre dipped, a sultry intrusion in her ears. "Your voice makes me so fucking hard." He shifted his hands to curl around her neck, thumbs caressing her cheeks, her scar. "Sing to me while I'm fucking you."

She hated that he'd figured out her *defense.* There were two mournful truths about their intimacy. One, he understood why she didn't want to fuck him. Two, he was able to convince her to do it anyway. He knew her feelings for him were as complicated as her situation. He also knew that if he led her to that dead place inside herself, she would hide there without struggling while he fucked her. It was a tactic she resented and appreciated.

"Which song?" she asked, defeated.

A happy hum vibrated in his chest, his scar a macabre extension of his smile. "Bring Me To Life."

His requests never strayed from *Evanescence,* the essence of grace in despair.

She let the trembling dread roll off her spine, drew in a long breath, and warbled through the first verse. Slipping into steady, lilting tones, her reluctance to fuck floated away with the notes. She held his eyes and sang the words he wanted to hear as he removed her sneakers, shirt, and jeans. When he traced her c-section scar, she kept her mind on the song, on its expression of the life she couldn't have and the broken shell she'd become.

He touched her hip bones with reverence, kissed the lace that covered her most private parts, and stripped the material with a ragged groan.

"I can't wake up..." she sang, the lyrics infused with a longing he couldn't sate.

In the next heartbeat, she lay bare beneath him, her disloyal body lubricating his entry, programmed to respond. He fisted the sheets, panting and rocking his hips to the rhythm of her faltering vocals. Against her will, his thrusts woke her hunger, massaging sparks of pleasure along her inner walls. She lost her voice and burrowed into the remote pocket of her mind.

He raised up, shed his shirt, and lowered the sweat-damp heat of his chest to hers. Circling his pelvis, he dipped his dick in and out and dragged his teeth over her throat. "Your pussy's so hot, clenching around me." He nuzzled her neck, his arms stretched above them, fingers linked with hers, his biceps contracting beside her head.

"Your voice makes me want to shoot my fucking load. I'm going to come so hard inside you." He sank and withdrew, his girth a piston of stretching, hammering power. His exertion intensified, pounding her raw. "Keep singing."

Beneath a different man, in another life, she might've sang with a passion to match the intimate connection. With Van, she was a cold voice in a warm embrace, her pussy an entity of its own. The needy slit existed objectively, disciplined to accept and serve. She sang from that carnal place of flesh and superficial appetite. The place where emotions didn't dwell.

His grunts deepened, the roll of his body sliding and slapping against hers. "Come now. Come all over my dick."

The command tore the orgasm from her well-conditioned body. She focused inward, singing in her head, safe behind the shield of her mind as the sweep of unwanted sensations overtook the rest of her. She knew it could be truly pleasurable, and it had been many times with him. But she was too jumpy that night. She didn't trust her feelings because every damned nerve in her body irrationally pulsed for the boy in the box one floor above.

Van arched his neck and shouted his release to the ceiling, his pelvis slamming once, twice, and done. Then his mouth covered hers, moved over her jaw, and latched onto the curve of her neck.

"I love you." His whisper laved her shoulder, hot and wet.

It was the part she dreaded most about these unions. Those gentle words bore the strength to shatter her from the inside out. He believed what he said, but she only had to think of him with the girl who, less than an hour earlier, was sucking him toward the same neck-arching finale.

So she responded the way she always did, with thick bitter silence.

He flicked off the bedside lamp, gathered her in his arms, and trapped her hips with a leg. She lay on her back, her face angled away from his, and her cheek pressed against the edge of the mattress.

Her gaze locked on an arm poking from beneath the bed frame.

The night could've gone worse. That could've been a real arm, decaying into the carpet and stinking up the scenery in Van's garden of crazy. Despite all his cruelty and creepiness, he'd never killed anyone. She couldn't say the same for herself.

But obsessing about her felonies was dangerous in this business. Human sex traffickers were systematic and violent. Didn't matter that Mr. E's three-person operation wasn't linked to the realm of nationwide organizations. The punishment was the same. Mr. E could easily be some douche of a car salesman in nowhere Texas, but he was a douche with Mom and Mattie's addresses. The minute she lost her focus, one fucking slip, and they were dead.

Van's breathing steadied into the rhythm of sleep, and the weight of his arm and leg relaxed into pliancy. She eased from beneath him and caught herself before sitting up. Following the curve of the arm beside her pillow, she found his hand entangled in her hair, each finger meticulously coiled through its own strand.

*For the love of all that's psychotic.* She stifled a sigh.

After a long-suffering endeavor to extricate her hair without waking him, she collected her clothes and crept into the hall.

As she walked to her room, her thoughts churned around the newest threat to her arrangement. Over six years, she and Van had captured five boys and two girls. All of them from ghettos along the Mexican border.

Her first slave—a young Hispanic girl—worked side jobs for a cartel, but the girl's business connections hadn't seemed to care when she went missing. None of their captures had been attached to families who would miss them.

None until Joshua Carter.

Not only would his parents devote their lives to finding him, his community would sponsor a massive rally to search for their football star. But the buyer's demand for chastity had given her little choice. Boys without parents lost their innocence at young ages. There were no twenty-one-year-old virgin males among the sediment of broken families.

The virgin boy in the box would be missed.

She reached the top of the stairs, her fingers finding the keypad with ease in the dark as Van's words whispered through her head.

*The job's the same. The slave we deliver will be* exactly *as he ordered.*

The goddamned job. She coded herself into the attic, tiptoed to the closet beside the sleeping girl, and selected tomorrow's costume. Time to put on the mask. One that would hide her face and the fears it might show.

# TEN

*Boy. Eyes down, boy. Strip.* The haunting voice in Josh's head penetrated the never-ending tonality blaring in his ears. The flat line of sound wouldn't shut up. Not for hours. Not a single breach in range or volume. Hours and hours and hours.

*Your name is whatever I want it to be. Boy. Boiyyyyee.* He knew he was imagining the voice, angelic in melody, cutting in its intent.

No matter what they planned to do, no way would he become a sex slave. He would not break.

His thoughts stumbled into stunned silence, battling through the horrifically endless tone. How far would he bend if pushed? Especially without the strength that came with food and sleep. He'd dozed a bit off and on, but his body was flagging. His mind pounded to exhaustion.

He yearned to hear her sing, to invade his isolation and twine her soulful harmony around him. He needed to speak to *that* girl. Surely whatever lay beneath her chilling exterior wouldn't hurt his parents.

*That's up to you.*

Anger lashed through him, curling his fingers around the chain. An achy, unrelenting pain hammered his hips, back, and legs where they pressed against the wood. He wanted to choke her with the unforgiving chain and watch her stillness ripple with useless spasms.

He sucked in a breath, swallowing that hideous thought into the recesses of his gut where it could soften and disintegrate. Why? Because it was God's place to judge her? Or because he'd been raised to look for the best in people? Or was it his need to believe there was a virtuous quality inside of her that he could free and possibly use to escape?

The voice faded. His ears told him the single note stopped, too, but its echo left a lingering shard in his mind. Would the tone begin again at any moment? Had they returned to pull him out of the box? Had they ever left? His ears were playing tricks on him. Or had his sanity finally fled?

Seemed like days had come and gone since the pangs of a full bladder began their unrelenting jabs. He wouldn't be able to hold it much longer, but focusing on not pissing himself had diverted his mind from the weight of the chains, the eternal time in the box, and Mom and Dad's safety.

His throat and tongue withered with each intake of waterless air. Maybe they already buried him in the box out back. Maybe his next exhale would be his last.

No, he would've felt them move the box. And his life was valuable. They couldn't sell him if he was dead.

Something tickled his face. Another delusion. They'd left him alone for so long, his muscles were stiff from inertia, his fingers and toes numb from loss of circulation. Had they forgotten him? But the noise that had embedded itself in his brain was…silent. Nothing. Gone. In its place was the galloping thump of his hopeful heart.

The press on his ears vanished, replaced by the tingle of cool air. Then the blindfold lifted away. Blinding light stabbed his crusty eyes. He blinked, blinked, blinked, gasping, the chains clattering with his spasmodic attempts to free his arms.

Fingers touched his nose, removed the clip. His nostrils responded with greedy pulls of air, widening, clearing the snot, and filling with the scent of sweat and fear.

As his vision adjusted, the figure towering over him took shape. A gas mask encased its head. Three plastic circles darkened where the eyes and nose should be.

Was the air poisoned? Were they gassing him, drugging him? His heart hammered against his ribs, his lungs struggling to keep up.

"What are you—?" He coughed, harsh and painful. "Am I—?"

"Drink."

The voice was a muffled tinkling of ice. He thanked God it was her under the mask but didn't understand why that knowledge had coaxed his joints to relax. *She* had put him in that box.

She palmed his nape, raising his head. Cool water sluiced over his parched lips, his tongue, trickling down his throat, both abrading and refreshing.

The pressure in his bladder twisted tighter. "Bathroom."

"You shouldn't have held it." The mask's filter concealed her mouth.

He couldn't read her and wondered if that was the intent.

"Your bladder is breeding bacteria as we speak." She worked the chains quickly, tugging at his hands and feet.

She'd chained him in a box and was worried about a UTI? The restraints slackened, but his wrists remained locked together. He pulled up his legs, bending at the knees and trembling through the effort. He didn't have the strength to drag his hands to his chest.

Releasing latches at both ends of the box, she let one side fall open and lay flat on the floor. He rolled out in a haphazard tumble, arms bound together, legs free but weak as hell.

A random pattern of eyehooks protruded from the subfloor around him. There were hooks everywhere, the ceiling, the walls. They dangled padlocks, chains, and cuffs of leather and steel.

She left him lying there, heeled boots encasing her calves and clicking on the wood. His view from the floor arrested on the black PVC-like corset dress molding the curves of her waist and hips and stopping just below the creases of her muscular backside.

Wrapped in pleather, she was a promise of suffering and ecstasy.

The sudden stirring in his groin shot a burning stab to his bladder and spurred him to his knees. He slid one foot forward, his muscles screaming, and rose, swaying on his feet.

"How long was I in there?" He swung his cuffed-together hundred-pound arms toward the box.

Her silence magnified his heartbeat thrashing in his ears.

With unmoving eeriness, her blacked-out lenses watched him stagger toward her, his toes catching on the hooks. He could physically feel his body tensing with hatred for this woman, who regarded him without a twitch to assist his clumsy advance.

When his shins hit the porcelain rim, he dropped his shackled fists on the wall behind the tank, and lost the fight with his bladder. He'd meant to sit. Too late for that. Needing his hands on the wall to hold himself up, he melted into the relief pouring from him, the stream of urine spraying unguided. Thanks to his shaking legs, his aim was marginal at best.

Her mask tilted downward. At the mess he was making? At his nudity?

Let her stare. He'd showered and peed in the presence of others every day in the locker room. This was different on so many levels, but he didn't have the strength of mind to care.

He'd never been drunk, but it probably felt like this. His brain struggled to engage, his perceptions clouded by fatigue, his legs and arms wrestling to respond. He was nude and helpless before a woman who meant to sell him as a sex slave, and he grappled to keep his eyes open.

Bladder empty, he dropped the weight of his head on a braced arm and angled his face to glower at her. "My parents?"

Her vinyl-wrapped head cocked. "Last check, Mr. Carter was celebrating his empty nest at the kitchen table, wrinkling the lacy tablecloth and toppling over that godawful ceramic rooster centerpiece as he pounded his cock into Mrs. Carter's ass."

Anger spiked, and he swung his bound arms — *to shut her up? Make her hurt? Knock off the mask?* — and missed. His sideways motion sent him careening into the spot she vacated, tottering past her and into the open shower stall.

The boot slamming into the back of his knee brought him stumbling to the ground in a discombobulation of limbs and defeat. Flopping to his back, he could only glare up at her. Even his frustration required more effort than he could manage.

She squatted over him, a boot on either side of his hips, the gap of her thighs wide enough to expose a swath of black lace. He jerked his eyes away, disgusted with her and himself.

"You can look," she said.

"No, thanks." He tried to buck her off his hips and failed.

"Soon, you won't be able to stop yourself." She grabbed his jaw and shoved her mask in his face. "Requirement number five. Slave will not touch Master or Master's property in a sexual way without permission."

*Master's property?* She didn't mean —

"For the next ten weeks, I am your Master, and this is my property." She released his chin and gripped his penis, sliding downward, stretching brazen fingers to cup his testicles.

Blood rushed to his groin. No one had ever touched him there and definitely not like that. He hated the visible response of his body but couldn't stop it. Nor could he stop his fury.

"You're a rapist." He scuffed his heels on the tile, breaking her grip. His back hit the wall.

Holding her crouched position, she dropped a forearm over one knee. "The first requirement set by the buyer was your virginity. You will never put your cock in me or any woman."

Her definition of virginity was too specific, or perhaps not specific enough. That did *not* sit well. He clenched his butt cheeks, a sheen of sweat icing his spine.

She stood and reached for the yard of chain hanging from a hook beside the shower head. "Raise your arms."

He tucked them to his chest and stared at the drain, fighting his eyes to stay open. Twenty-four hours in the ear-numbing, sleep-deprived box. Leading up to that had been an exhaustive day of hauling cotton bales, classwork, and the big game. He didn't have enough steam left to stop her from hanging him in the shower, but he refused to make it easy.

"If you concentrate every breath on anticipating my orders, your time with me will be much less painful." Her voice reverberated against the tiles, hollow and robotic. "If you swing at me again, I'll suffocate you with much, *much* more discomfort than you experienced in that box." She bent over him, boots shoulder-width apart, hands on her hips. "If that doesn't penetrate your thick skull, I'll collect another keepsake from your mother. Perhaps something attached to her little gray-haired head."

His heart sped up, heated with anger, knotted with dread. When he recovered his strength, he would escape, and he might knock her across the room on the way out.

Straightening to her full height, she slid the chain through her hands. "Swallow your fantasies of escape and rescue. The house is soundproof. There are keypads on every exterior door. I've ordered Van to stay in the garage all day to dismantle your truck. When the parts are dispersed to various dumps and junk yards, they'll be untraceable." She held out her hand, waiting for his. "No one is coming for you, boy."

A guttural, sick hatred for her spread its poison inside him, twisting and taking over. What was next for him after she strung him up in the shower?

"My virginity... You said..." Dear God, he didn't want to say it out loud, but he had to know. "What about sodomy?"

Her hands dropped to her sides, the chain slapping against the tile wall. She strode to the door and raised her finger to the keypad.

Was she bringing in Van? To beat Josh? To bend him over in the shower and pump away in his backside?

"Wait." His attempt to stand on jelly legs collapsed into a bone-crunching sprawl on knees and elbows. "Please. I'll follow orders."

She tapped in the code.

# ELEVEN

"Please, wait." The effort to stand had depleted Josh.

His head swam, and his body screamed for food and sleep. He stood no chance. This had been the aim of the box, he realized. A total mental and physical shutdown. He raised his bound arms and his eyes, reaching toward her goggled mask.

She entered the final digit on the keypad, and the door clicked open. She stared into the outer room, statuesque in her posture. "Requirement number six. Slave will use the title *Master*."

His extended arms shook, the lump in his throat sprouting jagged edges. "Please…" It was just a word. *Too tired to fight. Just a word.* "Master."

She made him wait another agonizing moment before closing the door and returning to his side. In a practiced movement, she locked the end of the waiting chain to one of his wrist shackles with a combination lock and removed the existing chain that squeezed his hands together. One arm dropped to the floor; the other tied to the shower wall.

He probably looked like hell, but he was a strong guy. Even in his weakened state, he could overpower her. Wasn't she afraid he might trap her and squeeze his free arm around her neck? The confident, relaxed pose of her body told him she expected it.

"*Master* is how you'll refer to the man you are training to serve," she said. "With me, you'll use *Mistress*. Say it now."

The bite in those last three words snapped his teeth together. His breath hissed past his lips. "Mistress."

Was she smiling behind the mask? Did she get off on binding and selling men?

Didn't matter. He would *never* serve a man. *Never.* "How many times have you done this?"

She moved to the perpendicular wall of the corner shower. A chain dangled from another hook. "Other arm, boy."

How many had she forced through the horror of this exact moment? Where were they now? Did she even see them as human? What about the kiss he shared with her in the truck? Her actions seemed so genuine at the time.

"How many people have you ripped from their lives, their dreams, their families?" He squinted into the lenses of her mask, his muddy reflection glaring back. "Mistress," he spat.

Her fist slammed into his mouth, spiking fire through his jaw and knocking him off balance. His back smacked the cold tile floor. His arm, chained to the wall, twisted. Pain tore through his shoulder, ripping a shout from his throat.

"Other. Arm."

Well, that was stupid. *And incredibly satisfying.* He'd found a nerve to pick at.

Crawling to his knees, he spat blood on the floor at her feet and offered his arm with a belligerent smile.

She made quick work of tightening the chains to the walls, the pull of the restraints stretching his arms out to the sides like Jesus on the cross. Naked, on his knees, his chin hanging on his chest, he didn't feel the forgiving virtue of Christ filling his heart. It pumped, instead, with the spirit of revenge and loathing.

The cold spray of water pounded ice pellets on his back, and her hands rubbed soap into his skin and hair. He acknowledged that the movement in his muscles wasn't the flex of courage but the trembling of fury. He'd never felt more subjugated in his life.

Worse was the swelling arousal between his legs. She only needed to touch his backside, his hip, or his inner thigh, and his penis stood at half-salute. He stared at the jerking thing, grimacing. At least she pretended not to notice it, though her eyes could've been directed anywhere from within that terrible mask.

The tap shut off, and he wished he'd stolen a few gulps of water. She untied him and led him by the chains to the mattress that sat on the floor. No frame or box springs in this hell hole. He dripped water onto the room's only rug, shivering like a wet poodle, and waited to see what she'd come up with next.

Maybe she'd command him to perform a tumbling act, sing karaoke, or wear a toga and feed her grapes. Hopefully, something low impact. Dehydration, chills, and exhaustion were riddling him with all sorts of irritable problems, from blurry vision to unmanageable mood shifts. He was so recklessly angry and tired his brain was spinning out of control.

"Requirement number seven. Slave will kneel when Master is present."

*Hallelujah.* His legs were wobbling anyway. He lowered, and his knees gave out before he made it to the rug.

She connected the chains to a padlock and eyehook on the floor in the center of the room, spun the combination to secure it, and dragged a cardboard box to his side. "Eat."

With enough slack in the chains, he raised the lid, and the sights and smells of cheese, sausage, yogurt and hard-boiled eggs sliced through his haze. He went for the bottled water first, the metal links connected to his wrists snagging on the cardboard. He suspected the menu was intentional. High protein, high fat, likely meant to give him energy for activities he didn't want to think about.

When he finished the water and reached for a second bottle, she grabbed the cuff on his wrist. "Slow down or it's all going to come back up."

He yanked his arm away and dug into the food, using the spoon provided. His body responded instantly to the yogurt, as if it contained magical little sugar motes that seeped into his system, clearing the fog from his head and soothing the quakes in his bones.

She watched from her perch on the mattress, legs crossed at the knees, breasts threatening to tumble from her corset with each inhale. She looked absolutely uncomfortable. He decided to make it worse.

"Are you supposed to be seducing me with that outfit, Mistress? Because I got to say"—he pointed at his soft penis, cold and shriveled as it was—"epic fail."

*A total lie.* If he hadn't reached his mental and physical limitations, he would've been battling arousal and his outrage over it.

A sound huffed behind the mask. Could've been a gasp. Impossible to guess since he'd heard very few reactions pass her lips.

He swallowed down three hard-boiled eggs, chewing on his original game plan. Making friends with her, unholy creature that she was, gave him the best chance to glimpse beneath the mask and, with time, influence her. To do that, he needed to shed some of the superiority his buddies teased him about and consort on her level.

He bit into a slice of cheddar. "Does th— I mean, *Mistress*, does this job ever fuck with your head?"

"Wow. That's a pretty vulgar word for you, Jesus boy. First time trying it out?"

The cheese stuck in his throat. The muffling of her voice through the mask only made her words more aggravating. She might have known some things about him, but she didn't know enough to judge him. And calling him a Jesus boy wasn't an effective way to get under his skin.

"I couldn't habituate myself to using bad language," he said. "Imagine if it slipped out in the company of a parishioner."

"The horror." Her tone was deadpanned, bored.

His shoulders stiffened. His social circles were comprised of people like his folks, who so willingly devoted their lives to holiness they took their rules to another level. Study the bible daily, never miss worship, and live in perpetual fear of everything: other religions, gays, cursing, bikinis, pop music, alcohol, smoking, premarital sex, and hell. It was as if they believed humans were demons in the flesh.

The laid-back Christians on the opposite end of the spectrum were content to simply have a relationship with God. Without the obsessive focus on rules, they seemed to better appreciate all the good in the world. It would crush his parents if they knew this was the sort of Christian he wanted to be.

He also wanted a career in football, but his decisions had never been up to him. Especially not now. Given Liv's job, he knew discussing his future in ministry would not help her relate to him. "You didn't answer the question, Mistress."

A motionless tension fell over her. She shot to her feet and kicked the box of food across the room. "I do not answer questions."

Her boot swung again, aimed at his head. He caught it, tucked it to his chest, twisting her leg and rolling her. Using her loss of balance and the taut rope of chain to trip her other foot, he dumped her face-down on the floor and threw his weight over her. Strangely, she lay like the dead, arms trapped beneath her body.

Without thought, his hands went to the mask, released the buckles on the back, and chucked it to the side. He'd already seen her face, so the disguise must've been meant to conceal her expressions. *Screw that.* He wanted to force her responses to the surface and bare every twitch and twist of her gorgeous features.

She didn't try to free her arms or raise her face from the rug. Her breath whispered evenly through the mane of brown silk tousled around her head.

He lifted his chest, pinning her legs with his, and flipped her over. "Do you and Van anally rape your prisoners?"

Arms limp at her sides, her expression was a blank canvas. But her detachment seemed to make her eyes look even more dangerous as they drew into slits and locked on his.

The length of chain gave him enough range of motion to strangle her with his hands, but then what? He didn't have the code to the door, and she didn't seem concerned about her safety, which meant she was prepared. Did she have a weapon hidden in her bodice?

"You're a pimp and a rapist," he said. "How many slaves, Liv?"

"It's *Mistress.*" She slammed her brow into the bridge of his nose.

A blaze of fire burned through his nostrils. He wrinkled his nose, fighting the hurt from her hard head, worrying about the costs his parents would pay for his temerity. He needed to make certain the risks he took didn't touch them.

She slid a palm up the back of his thigh and parted his cheeks. No amount of clenching dissuaded her from touching that forbidden place between. If he swatted at her, he wouldn't be able to hold down her shoulders. He could roll off her and lose the upper hand or he could endure her probing finger.

He did his best to control his breathing, and failed.

"What would you call this?" he panted. "Seduction or rape?"

Holding his gaze, she tried to pull her knees to the outside of his legs, but his weight held them in place. So she used the only freedom she had and pressed a stiff finger against his rectum, her eyes hard and fixed on his.

"Try again." She prodded deeper, a dry invasion that crushed his molars together. "With. The. Title."

His blood boiled, and his mouth dried. "Are you going to rape me, *Mistress?*"

"*You* are restraining *me.*"

Her finger, toying shallowly where no finger should go, garbled his brain. He wouldn't give up his position, and as much as the violation made him squirm, it wasn't dampening the heat stirring in his naked groin where it rubbed against the apex of her open thighs.

"You like this." Her lips curled up, perversely smug. "They all do. By the end of the first day, all of my boys beg me to fuck them." Finger in his backside, she ground herself against his traitorous hard-on. "You'll beg, too."

He wanted to roar *Never*, but the way his fatigued body responded to her touch, he knew it would be a lie.

Her finger vanished, and his muscles relaxed but not for long. She slid her hand between their hips, and he jerked his groin out of her way. But she wasn't reaching for him. She cupped herself beneath the lace, massaging and throwing her head back with a moan.

Heat swarmed his face. He'd kissed girls. He'd groped a breast once above the shirt, but he'd never seen a girl naked before him, and this…this open display of masturbation he'd never dared to imagine. Yet he couldn't stop his gaze from clinging the dips and arches of her body and the hand circling between her legs. Was this why the others begged her for sex?

"You rape them." He thickened his voice with accusation, wanted her to hear his objection.

Her hand froze, and her glare slammed into his. The darkest reaches of her eyes seemed to rotate while her pupils remained steadily locked on his.

"You're my first virgin cock, boy, which means you will endure your training without any hope for a charity fuck." A cruel expression bent her face, catching light along her scar. "And you'll address me correctly, you stubborn prick."

She yanked her hand from between them and slapped her fingers over his mouth, trailing a smear of tart moisture on his lips and tongue.

The shock of it arched his back, his restrained hands tightening the chains and halting his backward flinch. She used the distraction to slip from under him and shove a finger into her cleavage. As he scrambled forward to recover his position above her, she whipped out a metal wire, snapped it taut between her hands, and caught him in the throat.

In the next breath, he was on his back, his neck ensnared by the garrote she'd unleashed from her corset. His arms were yanked to the side by the chains clapping against the floor. Just an impulse away from hindering his airflow, he held himself as still as possible.

Her knee dug against his chest. "Requirement number two. Slave will service Master sexually with exceptional skill, and his body will be prepared to make it easy for Master." She tilted her head, a tangle of curls snaking around her chest. "Your cock doesn't belong to me, but if you beg nicely, I'll take your virgin ass before Van gets a hold of it."

It wasn't her words that chilled him so much as the conviction that punctuated them.

She released him, and his hands went to his throat, rubbing the unbroken skin.

On her way to the door, she glanced over her shoulder. "You'll find your restraints don't quite reach the mattress. Sleep on the rug. And if you bend just right..." She pointed at the toilet. "You can balance your tight little asshole on the rim."

The rim that was splattered in his urine. His fingers gouged into his palms.

"If you don't shit before I return, I'll use a rectal bulb syringe to clean you out." With a flick of her finger over the keypad, she left.

Hatred, his new friend, swept through his veins, promising delicious acts of retaliation against every foul fiber in that woman's body. He shook with a violent contraction of muscles, his blood raging. He wanted to shove her against the wall and pummel her.

Sweet Jesus, what was wrong with him? Violence didn't justify violence. He needed to talk with her, dig through the vicious mess of her mind, and show her there was a healthier way to overcome whatever was dragging her into damnation.

He rose on shaky legs and tested the chain's four-foot length. Didn't reach the bed or the door, but if he backed up and doubled-over like she'd said, he could use the toilet. As he stared into the bowl, he knew why she'd want his bowels clean. He also knew he'd follow her orders if it meant forestalling an enema.

As for the heat she'd stirred in him when he'd held her down, that couldn't have been real. She'd concocted those feelings with the curves of her body, the shadowy depth of her gaze, and the musical way she spoke. God help him, her voice was so captivating it could reach over a hundred tortured screams and call a man to kneel beneath her garrote, mesmerized and brainwashed... *Yeah, brainwashed.* His attraction to her was certainly not genuine.

Who was he kidding? Her taste lingered on his lips. His backside still tingled from her invasion, and his erection throbbed merely by conjuring thoughts about her. At what point did he go from exhaustion to full-on erection? Was it a testament to the power she held over him? Maybe it was the yogurt giving him the fuel he needed, because no way in hell was he that easily controlled by her.

Blowing out a breath, he tried to calm himself. She'd awoken things inside him, things he'd kept repressed for the sake of his parents and career.

Assuming it was nighttime, the morning would bring a whole lot more ugly. He could be a pussy about it, or he could shut his eyes and wake energized and ready to break through her vile mask. Without using his fist.

# TWELVE

The door snicked behind Liv, and her lungs released in a noisy whoosh, her heart thundering unguarded. She clawed at the hooks on her corset, the heaving expansion of her ribs hindering the effort. "Girl!"

The girl leapt from the cot and crawled over the floor on hands and knees, her lean naked body swaying sensually through the movement, just as she'd been trained.

"Get me out of this thing." Liv's chest heaved.

Shifting behind her, the girl's fingers worked deftly, loosening the ties that cinched the back of the corset. A moment later, the bodice gaped enough to free the hooks. Liv tossed it to the floor and turned.

Blond hair curtained the kneeling girl's face and shoulders. This captive was so docile and innocent, Liv found her hand moving to stroke the bowed head. She caught herself before she made contact.

Eyes down, the girl rubbed her palms over her bare thighs. Nine weeks earlier, Van lured the eighteen-year-old beauty from a seedy neighborhood in southern Texas, where she had lived with three older brothers. Perhaps they could've been commended for warding off horny boyfriends and protecting her chastity. The sad irony was, her innocence and virginity had set her in Van's sights.

A shiver assaulted Liv down to her bones. Whether it was from dwelling on the girl's future, Liv's damp skin from the boy's shower, or the exchange of words she'd had with him, she needed the warmth of a gentle voice. "You have permission to speak."

The girl lifted intelligent blue eyes. "Are you okay, Mistress?"

The question, although touching, couldn't keep Liv's mind off the boy's allegation.

*You rape them.*

Two girls. He was her sixth boy. She'd shared sexual intimacy with all of them, including the girl blinking up at her. But she'd never allowed sexual intercourse. She'd never considered the other *stuff* rape.

"I'm fine." She smiled, and it felt strained, achy.

What if she was wrong? She'd permitted the boys release countless times, removed from the purpose of *training,* without Van's knowledge. There were no cameras in the house to monitor her actions. They'd pleaded for sex. She'd responded with hand jobs. During those moments, she only meant to offer them comfort. Perhaps that was how Van viewed his unions with her.

Uncertainty twisted her up, and within the turbulence arose an even more unsettling thought. None of her intimate encounters compared to the moment she'd just vacated. Lying beneath that boy, pinned by the burnish of his defiant green eyes and the unwitting seduction of his physique, she'd felt a new kind of stirring. It was accidental in its creation, but the inconvenient truth was she wanted him. Not only that, she wanted him to want her.

Startled by her vulnerable thoughts, she angled her head away so the girl couldn't see the emotions creasing her face.

"You're cold and wet, Mistress. Would you like me to prepare the shower to warm you?"

The bathroom in this chamber was enclosed and, more importantly, out of reach of the boy's studious gaze. Swallowing the bitterness of the job, she made herself answer in the severe tone the girl was conditioned to hearing. "Yes. Don't make me wait."

Twenty minutes later, showered and dressed in an oversize t-shirt, Liv returned to her room.

He lay on his back on the rug, arms above his head to accommodate the chains. His soft snoring thrummed through the room, thanks to the sleeping pills she'd diluted in his water. But even in the grip of sleep, he wore a brooding look that pulled at his eyebrows and sharpened the bones in his chiseled face. A fringe of lashes shadowed his cheeks, and the lines on his forehead drew deep grooves.

Humans adapted quickly, and when they understood the boundaries, they worked within them. His aggressive attempts to overthrow her had been expected. All captives emerged from the box demanding answers and tossing clumsy punches. But there was something subtly different about his temperament. He wasn't desperate enough.

He wasn't scared enough.

She flipped off the light, submersing the room in darkness, and stretched alongside his body on the floor. The whisper of his breath and the clean scent of his skin navigated her toward his face. Lost so deeply in sleep, he didn't stir as she speared her fingers through the thick muss of his textured hair.

The first meeting with the buyer was in two weeks. Two weeks to mold this boy-man into some semblance of a boy-slave, one who would be deemed satisfactory by a misogynist whack-job. Could she beat the contempt and righteousness out of him in that short amount of time?

It was a psychological battle she intended to win, because the boy wouldn't suffer for his disobedience the way Mom and Mattie would.

Resolve guided her hands, lifting the edge of the rug and unfurling a thin latex sheet from beneath it. Half of the sheath was held down by his body. It was also glued to the subfloor. She folded the loose half over him, crawling quietly to his other side.

He coughed as she hefted the closest shoulder and rolled him on his side, the bones in his arm indiscernible through the hard layers of compact muscle. A few careful tugs on the carpet, his breathing stuttering and steadying, and the rug pulled free from his weight. She set it behind her and returned him to his back.

At his feet, she pulled a zipper around the edges of the latex, sliding it toward his head and removing the chains from his wrist cuffs as she went. Through the night, it would be a plastic sleeping bag. With the sides zipped together, she cinched the latex around his shoulders.

That done, she curled up on the mattress, lit a cigarette, and walked through her preparations for the next day. The nature of mornings in captivity was either they woke up remembering where they were and what was expected or they were punished and dropped in hell. The captive's first day was always hell.

# THIRTEEN

The gravity of confinement bore down on Josh's sleep-dazed utopia. It was a relentless press, dragging against his skin and nudging him to wake.

Lying on his back, he reached up to rub the fog from his eyes and couldn't move his hands. He tried to lift his legs. Couldn't move those either. His heart rate exploded, ripping the haze of sleep from his brain.

The oblivion behind his eyelids was replaced with the blank stare of a masked face. It floated above him, a ghastly-white monition against ruffled waves of chestnut hair.

Arms pinned at his sides, he blinked to clear his vision as her brown eyes watched him through the eyeholes of the opaque disguise. A nondescript nose, pointy chin, and cheekbones molded the white, oval-shaped, plastic face. It would've been androgynous, except for the puckered, red-painted mouth, the upper lip arching in two dramatically-peaked points.

He lifted his head, dragged his focus from the mask to where she straddled his ribs and arms, and wasn't sure which had his heart pumping faster. The blood-red bra and panties that bared her body or the latex body bag that sheathed his.

"What is this?" His voice shrilled, and an impending sense of doom sparked the compulsion to fight.

His muscles tightened, heating his skin and constricting against the stretchy rubber. He could give into his rising panic and shout, writhe, and wear himself out. Or he could conquer his impulses, behave with reason, and deny her the satisfaction of his fear. At least his backside was safe at the moment.

He peered into the eyes behind the mask and searched for a

human being. The pupils, lifeless and frozen, might as well have been painted glass.

His jaw tightened. "Damn. I'm still in this nightmare?"

There, a flicker of raw umber in the glass. His heart danced in his chest. Then the flicker disappeared with a sweep of latex as she stretched the covering from his neck to the crown of his head.

He gulped against sudden claustrophobia, catching pockets of air in the see-through plastic wrap. Bucking and kicking and straining his neck, there was no room to maneuver. The transparent rubber clung to every inch of him, his skin sweating and slipping along it uselessly.

His inhales thinned, every other breath sealing the bag against his mouth and nose. He squirmed toward the top opening, but it cinched around the top of his skull. He could lift his head to scan down the expanse of his body through the bag, but he couldn't roll, couldn't sit up. It was as if he was cemented to the floor.

The whine of a motor screeched through the room and vibrated the wood against his back. Oxygen vanished. The latex shrunk, compressing his arms to his sides and sinking his body to the floor. His nerves rampaged with realization. She was sucking the air from the bag with a vacuum, trapping him, suffocating him.

He grunted, tried to scream at her to stop. Breathless. Constricted. Fire lit his lungs, and his heart exploded with terror.

The motor shut off, and the bag loosened. She peeled back the flap, cool air stroking his face and filling his lungs.

She smoothed his hair from his forehead. "If there's a definition for waking up on the wrong side of the bed, this is it."

Was that a joke? Was the vile witch mocking him while she tortured him?

He mustered his most sarcastic tone and smiled. "I'll pray for your soul, Liv."

Her fist slammed into his cheekbone.

*Ow, dammit.* A jolt of pain seared through his skull and burned his eyes.

The bag covered over his face again. The motor roared. He fought for air, his chest burning. The suffocation seemed to double this time. *Trapped. Can't breathe. Too long.* Black spots speckled his vision.

When she turned it off and pulled back the plastic, he couldn't catch his voice. He didn't want to.

One of her cold, heartless fingers traced his jaw. "You failed two of the simplest requirements."

He panted, his lungs on fire. The requirements…the requirements… Strip. Kneel. No sex with her. No touching her. No masturbating. *Eyes down.*

His gaze dropped, taking his heart with it. Chest heaving, instinct screaming to insult her with every curse word he knew, he tried to shed the fear from his face.

"That's one." She placed a hand on his groin, the heat of her palm seeping through the thin barrier.

A moan caught in his throat. He didn't want to feel her hand there, and he definitely didn't want to like it. Dammit, which requirement was he missing? Sifting through the list, he gritted his teeth. "Mistress."

"Good." She stroked his penis through the latex with a skill that infused his body with lust and fury.

Keeping his eyes averted from hers, he flexed his muscles, drew calming breaths, and blanked his mind. Years of practice in controlling his desires should've overpowered the sensations she was weaving through him, but with each twist of her wrist and drag of her fingernail, the traitorous erection swelled.

Her touch disappeared. His pulse tapered then hammered anew as she shifted down his body. Her mask hovered over his crotch, her hands braced on either side of his hips. The long silk of her hair curled around slim, bare shoulders. If his hands were free, he could snap her in half.

She slid the mask to her forehead, her face angled out of view, and the heat of her breath penetrated the thin material, sweeping over his groin. He arched, straining against the compression of the bag. His legs trembled as quivering energy tingled over his thighs and tightened his balls.

This couldn't be happening. He couldn't stop his release from building. He must've looked ravenous, the transparent latex adhering to his genitals, revealing every detail under her close inspection.

It was wrong. She was violating him, molesting him…

Her tongue dragged over his length from root to tip, wrenching a moan from deep within his chest. Despite the layer of latex between them, all he could feel was the concentrated heat, the soft stroke, the atrocious pleasure of it.

With an invasive grip, she adjusted his erection to lie flat between his pubic mound and the latex. "You have permission to speak. Tell me what you want me to do with this monstrous cock."

"Mistress, release me."

She raised up, shifting the mask to cover her face, and straddled his hips. "I'm so wet. If you weren't wearing a full-body condom, you'd slide right in."

She ground against him, and he thought, for a terrifying second, he might come just from the contact.

"My pussy would stretch to accommodate your girth. It would grip you like a vise and cream all over your cock as you rub in and out, sinking deeply, withdrawing reluctantly." She leaned toward his face, her breath whispering behind the mask. "You would finish with hard, hurried fucks, punching every inch of my cunt."

Vulgarity could be a form of torture, along with character assassination. He knew she was taunting him, trying to coax him into abandoning his beliefs and begging her like those before him. Even knowing this, he couldn't stifle the overwhelming desire gripping his body. He'd never wanted to come so badly, but he would *not* beg.

She slid the red satin crotch of her panties to the side and rolled her hips up. The sight of her plump, pink creases of skin, hairless and glistening with moisture, wrestled his wildest, most insane fantasies to the forefront of his thoughts. He curled his toes and tensed against the warmth rushing to his groin. His breathing and heart rate quickened, yet he couldn't look away from her body.

No cheerleader, no pastor's wife compared to her beauty. She moved with the grace of a dancer, lithe and muscular, shifting over his privates as if she were floating. For a thick moment, he was convinced he'd found an angel. Then he remembered she was his captor, a rapist. The devil incarnate.

He squeezed his eyes shut, his fingers digging into his thighs, his penis unbearably hot and uncomfortable.

"Open your eyes, boy." Her voice was commanding, the mask adding another layer of detachment. "Watch me."

Startled by the ease at which he followed her demand, he watched her finger as it traced her slit, up and down, gathering wetness. He couldn't stop his mind from darting to the conclusion of sex, wanting the mystery of her flesh wrapped around him and not caring about his virginity or his parents' promise to God. It was enlightening and reckless.

Lowering her hips, she parted her folds with the latex-protected length of him, rocking, fingers reaching to pinch his nipples through the rubber buffer. The bulges of her chest overflowed the satin, the color of the bra accentuating the red pout painted over her hidden expression.

She was a demon in the form of the most beautiful girl on earth. If he peered into her liquid brown eyes, he might've found the cruelest corners of the world there. But when she ground against him, the lustrous sheen of her hair swishing around her, her fingers curling against his abs, she seemed more human, less wooden. She looked like she desired him the way a girl would a boy.

The thought made him needy in a way he didn't comprehend. He wanted her to slide her heat over him faster, longer, and hear her hypnotic voice cry out in bliss.

No. He blinked, tried to clear his head. He wanted her to stop.

Another bout of quakes tumbled through him, coaxing the climax that was teetering on a razor's edge. What was her true intention? Was any of this real? Could she produce moisture between her legs if she didn't want him?

If he could recognize her authenticity, he might be able to explain the meaning of her actions. "Mistress. Remove the mask."

She threw her head back, the sinews in her slender neck straining against the skin. She moaned, and the sound transformed into a harmony of *Ahh-Ahhhh-Ah*. Her voice was an offering from God and a temptation from hell, a tone so potent it could corrupt a man, or save him.

Blood surged to his penis, raising his testicles, and his inhibitions fled. His heart rate skyrocketed. His lungs labored, and his thighs and butt tightened. She continued to grind on him, hitting the right spot, the right speed. He was doomed.

"Requirement number eight." Hips flexing, she rubbed against him with the mastery to finish him. "Slave will not orgasm without permission."

A series of contractions gripped his cock. He'd reached the point where he couldn't stop, didn't care about anything but the rush of pleasure barreling down on him. It was happening, and oh sweet Jesus, his body shook with the violence of a spasmodic freefall. Sensations flooded him from the waist down, pulsing against the friction of her heat, and he forgot where he was.

Her weight vanished. Latex covered his face, and the vacuum roared to life.

# FOURTEEN

Four more near-suffocations later, Josh knew Liv wouldn't kill him with vacuum-shrunk latex. But every time she sealed it over his face and powered on the motor, he feared it would be the time she miscalculated.

He labored to catch his breath. How did she measure how long he could go without air? What if she waited a heartbeat too long? And what was the purpose of this cruelty? He was supposed to hold off his body's reactions? Wait for permission to come? If she jerked him off enough, maybe he'd run out of juice.

Fatigued lolled his muscles. Sweat drenched his skin, and the stickiness of five ejaculations dribbled into the creases of his balls, itching the crack of his backside. No way did he have the mental or physical capacity to come again.

He'd thought the same thing three orgasms ago. "Mistress, no more."

She leaned over him, her hand working his sore, yet frustratingly swelling penis. "Your cock says otherwise."

A growl erupted in his stomach. He licked parched lips, unsure if she registered his hunger. If she had any reaction at all, it was locked behind the damned mask. Maybe some mysteries, like if her goal was to starve him or masturbate him to death, were better left in the dark.

She stroked and stroked and stroked. He was past cringing from the effect of her touch. The familiar surge of climax tightened his gut. Unable to stop it, his release surged through his body and burst beneath the latex.

The momentary bliss lessened each time with the ache of overuse, but it was still there, owning him. Though, if he was actually ejaculating semen, he couldn't sense it amidst the existing puddle.

When the haze of orgasm faded, he filled his lungs with air and braced for his claustrophobic punishment.

Her legs bent in a squat above him, the crotch of her panties damp and taunting.

"You smell like sweaty balls and spooge, virgin boy." She rose and lifted a bare foot backward to her hip, balancing without falter, stretching her muscles. Then she lowered her foot and repeated with the other leg. "I'm going to release you to use the toilet, scrub the piss from it, and take a shower."

His body melted into the floor, and his lungs collapsed in relief.

"Then you'll wash me," she said.

Maybe she wanted to shock him, but putting his hands on her might be the most pleasant thing he would experience in this room. No matter how much she disgusted him, her body aroused him. It was infuriating.

"Yes, Mistress."

She crouched beside him and rested fingertips on his hardening length, watching him through the eyeholes, allowing him to make eye contact with her.

Her inhuman stillness paired with her apparent disregard for time was hell on his blood pressure. As she squatted there, making him wait, the rest of the world went about their oblivious lives. Except his folks, but he refused to ask about them, fearing the answer.

Finally, she loosened the cinches around his neck and lowered the zipper down the side. "I'll feed you when your tasks are complete...*if* you follow the eight requirements you've been given."

No doubt she had an infinite supply of punishments planned if he lapsed on her perverted rules.

As she worked the zipper on the bag, he walked through the list. No sex with women. Service the Master sexually or some crap. Eyes down. No clothes. Did a latex toga count? No touching her or himself sexually. Use the title. Kneel. No orgasms. Never thought he'd welcomed that last one so eagerly.

When the zipper finished its rotation around the bag, she unfolded the cover and stepped back.

Careful not to meet her eyes, he lifted to shaky knees, debating the wisdom of knocking her off her feet. If he strangled her to death, he probably wouldn't live to see his next meal.

He rubbed his cracked lips. Were there cameras hidden in the ceilings? Was Van watching from another room, waiting for an excuse to kill his parents? And leading his parade of insecurities was a humiliating thought. Was the fluid crusting his pubis an indication he didn't have a chance at adhering to her damned rules?

His body was conditioned to take a beating on the field, his mind strengthened to suppress desires that didn't align with his spirituality. He could endure her punishments as long as he made progress in unraveling the evil knots that bound her soul.

He held out his cuffed wrists, hoping his submission would garner her trust.

"I see through you, boy. Passivity doesn't take root until the first weeks or months, and stems from boredom and lack of contact with the outside world." The mask cocked. "Six orgasms in two hours does not convince me that you're bored and lonely already."

Ugh, she was frustrating. *Deep breath.* Acquiring her friendship would be a harrowing endeavor, but the first step was easy. He wouldn't lie to her. "Mistress, talk to me. I don't want to screw this up. If something happens to my folks... Just help me, and I'll help you."

The dainty bones in her collar and shoulders sharpened against her skin. He didn't dare raise his eyes above her neck.

Finally, the mask spoke. "Follow the requirements, and you'll help us both. No more talking."

Irritation skittered over his spine, but he remained on his knees with arms raised. Helping people was the one aspect of his career he'd looked forward to. Maybe God put him in this situation to test him with the ultimate challenge, to save the darkest of souls. "Mistress, I'd rather you restrain my arms than my voice."

She stepped before him and gripped the cuffs she'd never removed. He expected her to whip some hidden chain from her bra and slap it on his arms. Instead, she molded his hands around the tiny circumference of her waist and squeezed in silent command. *Don't let go? Was this a softening in her armor? Please?*

The velvet of her skin heated his palms. The wet crotch of her panties, in the direct line of his lowered eyes, filled his nose with a tantalizing aroma. Perhaps God was testing him with man's greatest temptation. His confidence in being able to pass that trial fizzled as blood rushed below his waist.

"Requirement number nine. Slave will not speak unless spoken to." Her nails scratched down his forearms. "Your hands will be free to perform your tasks."

He guessed she expected him to *try* to overpower her and was probably prepared to subdue him like last time. He wasn't going to give her the pleasure.

"I'm the only person who knows the code for this room. Stand and follow me." She pushed his hands off her hips and walked to the toilet, though the way she moved couldn't be described as walking. It was more like the uninterrupted flow of a stream, gliding forward with confident disregard.

He trailed her, dodging the floor hooks with much less grace. Though, he strode a little lighter with the knowledge that Van couldn't bust in without her permission. How odd that he didn't have access. Was it because she was in charge? Something didn't seem right about that, and the answer felt vital to understanding her. What was her relationship with that guy?

She stopped before the medicine cabinet above the vanity, swung open the mirrored door, and dropped a threadbare rag in the sink. Her weight shifted to one leg, jutting out her hip, the bottom edge of her panties creeping up the musculature of one round cheek. She was so tiny and sensually-shaped, yet he'd felt her strength in her punch and could see it contracting through the tendons in her back.

As much as he despised her cruelty, his body wanted her to exhaustion and beyond. It pulsed to tackle her, to use its extra mass to dominate her in a battle of physiology.

Heat blazed down his thighs, and he clenched his hands to stop them from massaging his persistent erection. She was raining temptation down upon him in the form of curves and satin and glowing skin. Was his state of arousal normal in this situation? Perhaps another means of intended torment?

He stood over the toilet. Prayer was supposed to strengthen the struggle against lust, so he cycled *The Lord's Prayer* in his head. Holding his partial erection over the rim, he tried to relax it long enough to urinate. *Lead us not into temptation, but deliver us from the evil one.*

Yeah, she was evil, all right. And seductive and exquisite and complex. The repeated verses did nothing to alleviate his wandering thoughts or the weight between his legs.

She turned toward him and leaned a hip against the counter. "There's no video monitoring in this house. What happens in this room stays in this room. If you kill me, you'll be faced with the decision of whether or not to eat my body to stay alive."

*Good God. Seriously?* Where prayer didn't defuse him, her revolting words did.

He softened in his hand and didn't waste the opportunity to aim and empty. "Mistress, are you trying to scare me or offend me? Because I'm already glutted on both."

"Shock has a way of rousing attention." She moved behind him, the satin of her bra caressing his back, her fingers creeping along his abs, circling around the root of his penis, and trailing his hips to cup his backside.

He tried not to purr with the electrifying sensations. *Lead us not into temptation…*

    *Smack.*

    A sting zipped along one butt cheek. His body shuddered. She smacked him again on the other side. He sighed, relaxing with the tingle. Damn. That was arousing and… cute. His lips twitched.

    "No. Talking."

    *That* was his punishment for talking? He freed the grin squirming to escape and flushed the toilet. A slaphappy fog of delusion must have settled in his brain. He didn't *know* her, yet he was dangerously close to letting her see his deepest urges. Surprisingly, he wanted her to dig around inside of him, but the notion raced his pulse. What would she do if she knew he savored physical pain?

    If only she'd remove that mask so he could search for a hint at what she was thinking and feeling.

    Crouching behind him, she rubbed the heat in his gluts. "You have two sexy handprints on your ass cheeks, boy." She rose, clutching his biceps, and whispered over his shoulder, "Wonder what your God thinks about you grinning while I spanked you."

    His smile fell. No way she saw his reaction. He glanced over his shoulder and followed her gaze to the mirrored door she'd left angled open. The reflection of her mask stared back.

    He blew out a breath. He was a rookie in this demented game, and she controlled the line of scrimmage.

    "The next time you speak without permission, we'll find out how easy your ass reddens beneath my cane."

    His backside clenched, relaxed. He wasn't sure what his limits were, but that wasn't one.

    She sashayed to the sink, wet a rag, and flung it toward the floor. He intercepted it and knelt before the toilet to begin his first task.

    To win this, he'd play her game until, eventually, hopefully, they played on the same side.

# FIFTEEN

Toilet cleaned and hair washed, Josh stood under the warm spray of the shower. He attempted to use the few spare minutes to meditate, but the pangs of hunger nudged him from his thoughts. Facing the wall, he soaped away crusty remnants from his ball sac.

A trickling sound cut through the whoosh of the shower head. She was peeing? He leered over his shoulder before his brain told him not to be rude.

Perched on the seat, knees and toes together, she tore off a wad of toilet paper. The mask lay on the tile beside her discarded panties. He turned slowly, not to gape while she did her business but to devour her expression.

Her lowered eyes fanned thick blades of lashes over her cheekbones, softening the elegant lines of her face. Where most complexions washed out under fluorescents, her flawless skin seemed to glow in the glare.

He held his breath, feet frozen to the floor. She appeared so very human and gut-wrenchingly beautiful sitting there doing normal things like peeing and fidgeting. *Fidgeting!*

Did she know he'd turned to watch her? Was this another enactment to mess with his head?

Her teeth sawed along her bottom lip, and she twisted the end of her hair between a finger and thumb. No question the length and shine of her hair was exquisite, but she seemed to be eyeing it with more scrutiny than it deserved. What was she thinking about?

She dropped her hand, and her eyes slid up, finding his unerringly. Her lips bent in a conspiring smirk.

Oh no. What repulsive thing was she dreaming up? He locked his knees, waited.

Without looking away, she dabbed the tissue between her legs. Blotting? Was that how women wiped? Not that he was really watching, but his periphery caught it.

She flicked the flusher and stood. With a forearm over her chest, she reached back, unclasped her bra, and jerked it off without removing the coverage of her arm. What? No seduction or vulgar teasing? What was her game?

The red satin garment dangled from a finger at her side and dropped. On the floor. Where his eyes and knees should've been. *Craaaaap.*

He balled his fists and lowered to his knees. *Crap, crap, crap.*

*I'll feed you…if you follow the eight requirements you've been given.*

Pressing his lips together, he wouldn't make excuses or beg for food. Dammit.

He blinked at the bare feet beneath his bowed head. She could raise a knee and knock out a tooth. Or kick one of her deceptive little toes into his groin. He loosened his shoulders. He could take it.

Fingers touched his chin, lifting his head. "Raise your eyes."

Following the hourglass curves of her waist, the cuts of her narrow torso, his breath caught when he reached the rounded undersides of her breasts. Not too full, they seemed to defy gravity, sloping upward, reaching toward the…cutting slits of her glare.

"Next time I tell you to raise your eyes, I'll be more specific." Her fingers walked from his jaw to his temple and dragged along his scalp. "I'm surprised a big boy like you isn't more focused on the next meal."

Of course he was frigging hungry. As a linebacker, he consumed 5,000 calories a day. But apparently his sexual appetite was running things.

She patted his head. "I'll reevaluate your progress at dinnertime."

What mealtime was it now? Lunch? Dinner? She certainly hadn't fed him breakfast when he woke in the rubber bag. Straining to keep his jaw from locking in a murderous clench, he remained still and stoic.

She held out a bottle of bath wash and stepped under the spray of water. Sitting on his heels, he started with her feet. That was easy enough. Then he lathered soap up her shins. The set of his jaw loosened as he reached her thighs, his palms gliding over taut satiny skin and lean muscle, his erection an eternal aggravation.

Her legs tightened and relaxed beneath his hands, her calves outrageously defined for a girl. Maybe she ran marathons when she wasn't trafficking humans. Or maybe she kicked kittens. Into end zones painted with the blood from dead puppies.

"What are you thinking about? Look at me."

He snapped his eyes up, caught in the rich chocolate of hers. His stomach growled.

"I asked you a question."

Permission to talk? *Thank you, oh hateful one.* "Kittens and puppies, Mistress."

Her gaze froze over. "Do not fuck with me, boy."

*Not a chance, girl.* Holding her eyes, he leaned up, his chest against the flat expanse of her belly, and ran soapy hands up her calves. "Mistress, I was debating whether your leg strength came from running or kicking small animals."

The fierce point of her chin softened. The icy cut of her eyes melted into liquid brown, and pink stained her cheeks. *Absolutely stunning.* But nothing on Earth compared to the mystic beauty of her lips as they curved up, stretching with abandon. Her smile was jewel-like in its discovery, sparkling and precious. And for a fleeting heartbeat, it was his to treasure.

Then it was gone, replaced with a scowl and an invisible wall. "I did not give you permission to stop washing."

Sliding his hands up her backside, firm cheeks filling his palms, the spirit of her smile fluttered inside him. He'd found her. Behind perversion and tyranny was a girl who could enjoy the humor in being teased.

Still on his knees, he lowered his eyes and met her breastbone, paralyzed by a hammering need to press his lips there. He fought the impulse and continued his ministrations up and over her slender hips.

"I run," she said into the silence.

His hands faltered on her waist. He hadn't expected a response but wasn't surprised by the answer.

The angle of the shower head immersed them both in the warm spray. The tile floor dug into his knees, but it was nothing like the aches endured on the farm or during practice. He quickly shoved those thoughts away and collected more soap from the bottle. Angling his face away from the spray, he lathered suds over her ribs. Yeah, his attention skipped the body parts that guaranteed awkwardness and discomfort. Maybe she wouldn't notice.

A sigh drifted down with the torrent of water, swirling around his ears. "I'm giving you back your voice. Use it wisely."

Why would she do that? Because he made her smile? Because she was lonely?

Please God, don't let him mess this up. "What makes you happy, Mistress?"

Her back turned to stone against his splayed hands. "Why?"

Suspicion edged her voice. Not surprising given her line of work. If she kept company with genuine friends, they were probably as cautious with their feelings as she was.

"Mistress, I love your smile. If I could free it once a day, it might make the next ten weeks bearable. Would smiling cause a conflict in your job?"

Her chest rose and fell with steady breaths. Would she punish him with silence or respond with something foul and shut him down? Or would she try out an honest answer and keep the conversation open? The way she stared over his shoulder, her brown eyes turning inward, he suspected those questions warred in her head, too.

She glanced down at him, studying his face. "Freefalling."

*Freefalling?* Like spiraling into hell? Or leaping from a cliff for sport?

"Enjoy the fall, or nothing at all." Her lips remained parted on the *all*, expression vacant. She must have recognized the confusion in his, because she shook her head. "Nothing seduces happiness like throwing yourself from a plane."

*Fascinating.* And positively unhelpful. It had been a safe answer, since he didn't have a plane to *seduce* her happiness. But he didn't think it was a lie, either. Skydiving was sporty and dangerous. It fit her.

His knees slid over the floor as he shifted around her, washing her arms, neck, and hair with an effortless reach. If he were on his feet, the top of her head would stop at his chest, a reminder that he could crush her with his size alone. Perhaps that was why she preferred him on his knees.

"What about singing, Mistress?"

She regarded him, and the molten depths of her eyes rippled, then stilled. "At first glance, you come across as a pretentious wannabe-psychoanalyst."

Uncertainty pelleted his nerves. He nudged her chin, angling her head under the water to rinse. He'd never attempted to befriend someone so misguided, and he'd definitely never washed a woman's hair. A breathtaking woman. A naked woman. With dips and mounds that molded to his hands.

*Stop with the lusting, pervert.*

"You're not asking the usual questions, boy. Like what's going to happen to you? How badly am I going to hurt you? Who am I selling you to?" She stared at his lips, beads of water clinging to her thick brown lashes. "I think you know those answers won't help you. When you're able to think beyond your hard dick, you're focused on your Jesus-saves-all mission. Which I admit is more appealing than fatalistic whimpering. But Jesus isn't going to save you from washing the two areas you've been avoiding."

He bit back a groan. Apparently, ignoring her privates wasn't going to make them go away.

"Eyes down. Mouth shut. Hands busy."

Her commands hovered between them, protecting her like a raised gun. This girl required a lot of patience. And prayers. A megachurch full of prayers. He soaped up his hands. Knees quivering on the tile floor, insides tightening, he looked at her chest, really let himself behold her for the first time.

Symmetrical, round, heavy on the bottoms, and tipped with pale-pink nipples, they outclassed every pair he'd seen on screen or in magazines. They weren't airbrushed or oversized or marred with tan lines. And because of his much taller height and kneeling as he was, her breasts were right at eye-level, waiting to be washed.

He started with circular patterns, both hands painting lather around and around the outsides. They were firm yet soft. Springy when he rounded the sides too fast. Heavy when he slid along the creases underneath. His heart rate kicked up, pushing his breaths faster.

He avoided the hard peaks because... Did nipples really need to be cleaned? How dirty could they get? He pressed a little harder against the supple curves, tightened the circles, brushed the taut beads. Once, twice... Ugh. Where the hell was his will power?

"Are you washing them or checking for lumps?"

Wow, was he that awful at this? It wasn't like he was trying to pleasure her. He clutched her waist and shifted her chest under the water.

"How often did you beat off?" Her voice sliced like a scalpel, dissecting.

"Once a day, Mistress." At night, alone and dreaming of girls half as pretty as she was.

"I bet you think about touching titties when you stroke yourself. When you're worked up enough, you fantasize about banging a pussy with your finger. Then you replace it with your cock. Probably missionary position. Hard, fast humping. You take her without guilt, because it's only a dream, a fleeting thought that vanishes when you come."

She only had it partially right. He didn't want to *take* a girl. He wanted to give himself to her. He wanted to watch his touch soften her eyes, hear it in her breathy exhales, and feel it shudder over her body as she arched against him. The fantasy of a sated smile on a pretty face was what sent him spinning over the edge every time.

An inferno raged in his body, and his hands clenched on her waist. It was Liv's face he'd imagined just now. It was her smile that made him tremble and harden. So very, very hard. Were his fantasies forever changed? The need to look into her eyes, to put a sated smile on her face, had his molars sawing together and his muscles straining to hold her.

He pushed his chin to his chest and focused on his breathing. *Our Father who art in heaven...*

"You used up all the hot water." Her voice was soft, distant.

Then she seemed to snap out of it and rubbed a soapy hand between her legs. That done, she pivoted to rinse and twisted the lever. The shower stopped, and she breezed past him.

The sheen of water on his skin chilled. With his body flushed and battling arousal, he hadn't noticed the change in water temperature.

She returned to his side with a rope of chain. "Well, you're horny enough." She snapped the ends on his wrist cuffs. "On your feet. Van is waiting."

# SIXTEEN

Liv led the boy into the outer chamber and inhaled the intangible fume of rage seeping from Van's fists-on-hips stance by the door. She steered the boy around him, her defensive hackles shooting her shoulders to her ears.

Anything could've set him off. She'd sneaked from his bed the previous night. She'd made him wait too long for her to emerge from her room, and she'd come out without clothes on. Or it could've simply been one of his cruel-for-the-hell-of-it days.

She could handle Van's venom when it was directed at her, but the way he glared at the boy made her stomach knot. Granted, he was as uncertain as she was on how to convert a straight boy into a woman-hating sex slave, but she still expected him to be better than this. She needed to defuse him before they began the planned training session.

Across the room, the girl knelt on the cot naked, chin tucked to her chest and hands secured to the wall behind her. She seemed invisible to Van at the moment, and in two weeks, she would be out of his reach completely. Thinking of the man waiting to buy her wrung an entirely different wrack of tension in Liv's shoulders.

She was a fool to dwell on it. After the delivery, the girl would be dead to her. Just like the others.

Angling her back to Van, she shackled the boy's wrists to the chains hanging from the apex of the room. He must've sensed Van's volatility, because his muscles contracted against his skin, and his eyes bore a fiery path over her shoulder. Dammit, there was only one place his eyes should've been.

The simplest commands seemed to be the hardest for him to remember. Van would expect her to whip the boy for it, and of course, the sadistic buyer anticipated a battered body. But there would be enough of that after lunch.

A dull pound ignited in her skull. Her logic didn't even make sense in her own head. If she were honest, she was putting off whipping him. She dreaded it down to the marrow of her icy core. This boy was fucking with her detachment.

Using her body as a barrier between him and Van, she tapped the boy's steel jaw and whispered, "Eyes and knees down."

With slack in the chain, he descended to the floor, his exhales a hot caress on her chest. She knew he was in self-preservation mode, but the way he leaned toward her, as if trying to enfold her in the limited cage of his restraints, breathed an irrational warmth through the hole inside her.

All of the slaves had become protective of her at some point during their captivity. The captor-captive bond was just one of the many ways the mind dealt with trauma. But this boy hadn't been under duress long enough to develop that kind of psychological response.

His calm focus and rugged linebacker build was so unlike the mold of previous slaves. He looked at her like he thought he could save her. Maybe he could.

Except he was supposed to despise her. The hammering in her head increased. What a hopeful, romantic idiot she was.

When she shifted to meet the eyes burning into her back, Van flung a sleeveless sheath dress at her face, the most demure outfit from her costume closet. She kept her casual wear in a trunk in her room, but her frayed jeans and printed t-shirts endowed her with human qualities and expressions she couldn't possess in that house.

She stepped into the black nylon sheath and rolled it over her hips and ribs, tucking her breasts in the top. It wrapped her from nipples to upper-thighs and clung to every dip and bend of her body, revealing more than it covered.

Van crossed his arms over his chest, his lips in a flat line. His unusual reticence meant he was holding in something particularly unsavory. The sharpness of his eyes matched his razored tone. "Let's get started."

The knot in her belly intensified with the pressure in her head. To soothe it, she hummed the woeful melody of "Pretender" by *Sarah Jeffe,* the lyrics reinforcing the roles they were playing. Van was supposed to be a passive bystander, but his foul mood tainted the already unbreathable air.

So she left the boy on his knees with his wrists padlocked to the chains in the ceiling and paced to the outer door. "I'm hungry."

Van's footfalls chased her down the stairs. She did her best to outrun them, which was stupid. She'd left the room to confront him, but she wasn't ready. Was she ever ready for him?

He caught her in the kitchen, an arm around her waist, a hand around her throat, and lips pressed against her ear. "Why are you running?"

The beat of her heart drummed against the collar of his hand. He wasn't choking her, but the promise was there. Thankfully, years of practice had taught her how to manage him, and keeping her cool was a vital response.

She relaxed her stance and leaned her back against the granite surface of his chest. "Why are you chasing me?"

"Because you're mine."

His hand cinched tighter with that heated oath. She coaxed her pulse to match a gentle tune in her head and waited. Finally, he released her and strode to the kitchen sink.

The turbulence rolling off him clotted the small room as he stared out the window. She rushed through sandwich preparations and blamed the lump in her throat on Van's pending tantrum, not on the fact that she'd returned the fourth plate to the cabinet because the boy wouldn't be eating with them.

Unable to meet Van's eyes, she kept her back to him under the guise of arranging potato chips on three plates. "Talk to me."

"I don't like him."

Her hand flexed, crinkling the foil bag in her grip. Apparently, his jealousy had reached a new degree of crazy. He never liked the male slaves, but this was the first time he'd vocalized it.

"I want him gone." His sharp tone punched her in the back.

Objections amassed in her throat. They wouldn't find a replacement slave in time. And they couldn't just send the boy back. He knew where they lived, had seen their faces. Van's *gone* meant one thing, an unthinkable alternative he'd never suggested before.

Somehow, she mustered an exasperated sigh and a bored tone. "Why?"

"His parents are all over the fucking news." His voice grew louder, more guttural. "Their whole goddamned town is searching for him."

This wasn't about jealousy? She shivered as he paced behind her, the air frosting with each pass, sending ice through her lungs.

"He's not like the others, Van. We knew he'd be missed."

She didn't have to turn on the news to know what love and desperation looked like. Haunting images stabbed the backs of her eyes. She squeezed them shut to trap the remembered videos of Mom grieving alone and the godawful need to reach through the screen and hug her.

His fingers bit into her bicep, spinning her so violently her hip slammed into the counter's edge.

"Why did you choose him?" He shook her shoulder, his grip punishing. "Answer me," he shouted, his fury a hot mist in her face.

She blinked rapidly, grasping at the most logical answer. "He fit what the buyer wanted." She dragged her gaze to his and flinched at the feral expression twisting his features.

"Bullshit." He captured her jaw in a steel grip, lifting her chin until she stretched on tiptoes. "A hundred other fuckers would've met the requirements. This one fit what *you* wanted."

The truth of his words paralyzed her, shriveling all of her justifications for choosing Joshua Carter. The real reason made her throat tighten. He represented purity, beauty, family, all of the things that had been taken from her. He was a glimmer of goodness in her dark fucking world, a warm spark she could hold, if only for a fleeting span of time.

Her fingernails stabbed her palms. She was such a selfish, vile bitch.

Van shoved her away, turned her over the counter, and pressed her face against the laminate. "And the way he was looking at you really pisses me the fuck off."

When his hand tunneled between her thighs, her heart sputtered.

"No." She jerked beneath the prison of his immovable body. "No, Van. I have a job to do. I need to be in the right frame of mind."

The intrusion of his fingers speared between her labia, pinching dry flesh.

"What frame of mind is that?" His tone, as cold and penetrating as his touch, froze her to her bones.

"I am a Mistress, not your sex slave." She tried to match his iciness, but it came out desperate and high-pitched.

He yanked her from the counter and slammed his knuckles into her face. She managed to stay on her feet as jolts of pain fired through her skull. A warm trickle wet her lashes and smudged her vision. The ache in her heart was worse, but she would not give him the perception he'd hurt her beyond the cut of his fist. She kept her hands to her sides and met his biting silver gaze head-on.

Angry red splotches stained his neck and cheek, and she imagined his blood simmering beneath the skin. He clutched the counter's edge on either side of her hips, his face level with hers.

"When I dispose of your body, no one will ever find it." His voice dropped to a chilling rasp. "You know why?"

Her heart sped up, increasing the throb above her eye. She held her muscles as motionless as her glare.

"Because no one will care enough to search for it." He angled over the plates and hocked a foaming bubble of spit on one of the sandwiches. "Clean up your face." His smirk flared the bruise around her heart. "You look more like a slave than your little cunt boy." He grabbed an unsoiled sandwich, sat at the table, and dug into the roast beef.

What they were, what they'd become together, wasn't sane or healthy. It was in his blood to spew nasty things in a fit of rage, including threats on her life, and she'd conditioned herself over the years to bury it. His temper would eventually ebb, and the hurt from his words would, too. Because she didn't love him. He didn't have the power to leave a permanent scar on her heart. But that reminder didn't help the rawness of the moment as she moved to the sink and turned the tap to warm.

Ducking her head, the spray showered her face, renewing the pain around her eye. The water ran red, but no amount of cleaning would remove the evidence that she was just as much a prisoner as the ones in chains. And somehow, she would have to stand before the boy with a black eye as his Mistress.

Van finished his meal and reclined in the chair, studying her. No hint of civility, but the tension in his jaw loosened. "If you spent your allowance on makeup instead of your skydiving bullshit, you'd be able to cover that before you went upstairs."

She dried her face, blotting the hurt over her eye. Her fingers recoiled from the bubbled scar on her cheek, the cut that makeup could never cover. Not that she would waste a dime on meaningless luxuries. Their monthly funds from Mr. E paid for basic expenses, groceries, gas, and tools for training. She and Van split whatever was leftover, and she used her allotment on freefalling. Her only freedom.

As she replaced the ruined sandwich top with a new slice of bread, Van tossed a bag of frozen peas on the counter beside her. It wasn't an apology, but an offer to move on.

She held the icy bag to her eye. Too bad it couldn't numb the emotions swelling her throat.

# SEVENTEEN

Josh chewed the hell out of his cheek. Fifteen minutes alone with the naked girl and she wouldn't answer any of his questions. She was probably thinking, *Fifteen minutes with the naked man, and he wouldn't shut up.* Too bad. The need to hear about her experience coiled him into a restless chatterbox. He didn't just want to make sure she was okay. He needed to hear everything she knew.

He tried to draw her in with highlights from his family farm, his coursework, and football achievements while shifting his weight from one knee to the other to transfer his discomfort on the hard floor. When she said nothing, he switched back to questioning. "Do you know what they have planned next or why Van was ticked off?"

She remained statuesque in her folded pose on the cot.

He pressed his lips together and tried to rein in his frustration. "Does anyone ever visit?"

Her hands and arms were limp, her silence ominous, indicative of psychological trauma.

He drew in a deep breath and released it slowly. "Have you ever left this room?"

She stared at her lap.

"Who is Mr. E?" His stomach growled. What he wouldn't do for Mom's biscuits and gravy right now. He winced, thinking about her safety. "Have you ever met him?"

A big empty nothing.

He sighed but refused to admit defeat. "You seem like a nice girl. Pretty, too, though I've yet to see beyond the top of your head." Okay, that last part wasn't entirely true. "I'm not looking at the rest of you, I promise."

Funny how quickly he'd become unconcerned with his own nudity. He yanked his wrists, clattering the chains, and her head didn't move from its downward position.

"We're in this together, right? I just need your help understanding what *this* is."

Was she even breathing? The threat that compelled her to ignore him could walk through the door any moment, which only fueled his impatience.

"Look at me," he shouted.

Her head snapped up. *Finally!* The deep set blue of her eyes widened, flitted to the door, and back to him.

"Hi." He kept his smile soft and unassuming. "I'm Josh."

"Your name is *boy*." A whisper. "Please, stop talking." From the thready plea, the tensing of her body, and the heave of her chest, she seemed to be crawling in her skin with fear.

Pressure swelled behind his ribs. "Hey, it's okay." He stretched his arms to reach for her. Impossible. He let them drop, his elbows bent on either side of his head. "We're just chatting. What's your name?"

"Girl."

He had to strain his hearing to make out her heartbreaking whisper. Commands were clearly more effective than questions.

He hardened his voice. "Give me your birth name."

She glanced at the door, and the nervous twitches in her cheeks tightened his chest. At least she wasn't peeking around the room at hidden cameras. Perhaps Liv had been honest about no recording devices. Or maybe the girl was as in the dark as he was.

Her attention dropped to the floor between them. "Kate."

*Kate.* The excited race of his heart redoubled as he considered what to ask, or demand, next. How much time did he have? Something had been tightly stretched between their captors when they left. Perhaps they were just eating lunch. Or planning the next training session. Maybe they were having sex.

He slammed his teeth together. *Good grief.* Where the hell did that thought come from? "Tell me about the relationship between Van and Liv."

With another peek at the door, she shook her head. Did the huddle of her shoulders mean this subject terrified her?

"Does he force you or Liv to have sex with him?" he asked.

Her chin lowered, her body returning to its earlier frozen state.

Dammit, now he was glancing at the door, the hairs on his nape standing on end. What bothered him wasn't the hostility vibrating from Van so much as the song humming from Liv's throat when she ran out.

She'd sung in his truck as she'd led him into this nightmare. She'd sung when he was in the box, right before she closed the lid. Singing seemed to be a mechanism she employed when something bad was about to happen. So what was going to happen? What made her bolt from the room?

All of his questions liquefied to one conclusion. "Van's in charge, not Liv. She puts on a good show, but the fact is he's a rapist—"

"Master is not a rapist." Her eyes flashed to his, lit with fire, her words heated and rushed. "He doesn't touch me like that, because he loves Mistress, and she loves him."

What? No way in unholy hell did Liv love that man. His insides twisted and turned at the idea, and it pained him to see Kate's perception so emotionally distorted by what she'd been through. And what did she mean, he didn't touch her like that? Forcibly or not all?

"You've been here a month?" He leaned toward her. "Two months?"

She shrugged, and it was wooden and completely absent of hope. "I don't know."

Was he staring at the harbinger of his own future mental state? How would his judgment fare after ten weeks of captivity? His head ached, and his impatience with her and the chains that held him set his skin on fire.

He rolled his arms in a useless attempt to escape the shackles. "I want to help you, Kate. Please, talk—"

The door clicked open.

Rage cinched his throat and accelerated his pulse. He lowered his head with a frustrated jerk and glared at the floor.

# EIGHTEEN

Josh's breathing grew heavier, louder. His body temperature boiled from his blood to his skin.

Liv's bare feet skimmed over the floor and passed by his knees. Van's sneakers trailed close behind. They stopped at the cot, and the mattress creaked under Van's weight, a plate of food balancing on his lap. Josh's stomach gave a miserable groan.

"Tell me what I missed, girl." The cool clip of Liv's voice sliced the air, but there was a strained edge to it. "I want to hear every word that was uttered."

Surely her other slaves talked and even befriended each other when they were alone. Did she punish them for it?

Locking his eyes on her feet was pure torture. He wanted to read her face, observe what wasn't being vocalized. In the outer edge of his vision, Van raised a sandwich toward Kate's mouth.

"He said his parents are cotton farmers. He plays football at Baylor." Between meager bites and swallows, she repeated the conversation verbatim with much better recollection than his own. When every morsel was consumed, and all of his words betrayed, she finished with, "I told him Master wasn't a…rapist, that you love each other."

The heels of Liv's feet twitched outward so slightly the movement would've gone unnoticed if he'd been staring a couple inches higher. Her knees bent even more subtly as if she were pressing her feet to the floor to mute the reaction. A sign of objection.

He was so distracted by the dichotomy between her genuine responses and her facade that he hadn't considered the consequences of Kate's tattling until Van stood.

"Roll to your stomach, girl." He moved out of Josh's field of vision, his voice pitching through the room. "Face pressed against the mattress. Ass and pussy in the air and spread for your Mistress's punishment."

*Punishment?* The biting claw of dread shivered down Josh's spine. No, it hadn't been nice of Kate to tattle on him, but she didn't deserve a punishment for answering his questions.

Van returned with a thin rod that resembled the riding crop Josh had used in his horse riding lessons as a boy. His brain twisted into knots trying to piece together what was happening and what he could do to stop it.

With his eyes on the floor, his field of vision was limited to below their waists.

When Van pressed the handle into Liv's hand, she didn't close her fingers around it. The exchange was swift, but Josh was certain Van bent her pinkie at an awkward angle to persuade her to take the crop.

She traced Kate's raised backside with the leather-tipped end. "Boy, you violated requirement number nine."

Requirement nine? He didn't know them by number. Hell, he wasn't sure he could recite them all. But nine was the last requirement she'd taught him, right? The one about not talking—

*Whack.*

The crack of the crop left a red mark on Kate's upper thigh. Her legs trembled, and her cry muffled against the mattress.

Josh drew a lungful of air and swallowed the protests springing forward. Kate would suffer even more for his outbursts.

Van crouched beside Josh, his scar pulling at his lips, intensifying the threat of his proximity. "Hey, buddy. The Mistress is a real stickler about rules, but don't worry. The girl will accept your punishment."

A roar pummeled through Josh's throat, and he slammed his jaw shut, trapping it. This horsecrap wasn't directed by Liv, and Van knew that punishing Kate would hurt Josh the most.

Van stood, sidled up to Liv, and circled a finger on the back of her thigh, just below the hem of the minidress. "Twenty strokes. Right, Mistress?"

A battle of emotions coursed through Josh, heating his blood and rushing his breaths. He clutched the chains with white-knuckled fists and braced for the most messed up moment of his life.

And so it went. A garbled scream followed every whack, each one corkscrewing through his heart, stripping away pieces that would never be recovered. Liv kept unimaginable control of her swings, bringing down her arm in a rhythmic tempo as if moving to a cadence no one but her could hear.

He shuddered with the smack of leather on flesh, the pierce of Kate's wails in his ears and the twitch of her small body receiving his punishment under his gaze. Guilt fisted his stomach and shoved the turmoil to his throat.

Each strike fell hard and steady, but the more Liv swung, the more noticeable the trembling became in her free hand. Her fingers pressed against her thigh and her body seemed to lose its upright, stiff posture. It was a subtle change, but something was definitely pulling at her resolve.

Finally, she lowered the crop. A pattern of red welts striped Kate's backside and thighs but did not break the skin.

Liv circled around him to stand at his back. He hadn't seen her face since she'd returned, didn't know what mask she was wearing, if one at all. What was she feeling beneath her stony exterior? What held her here, bending her to do things he knew she didn't want to do?

Maybe he was just imagining her reluctance. Lord knew he prayed for it. There were so many unyielding barriers between them. Her masks. His chains. Van.

When Van released Kate from her restraints, she lowered her eyes and her knees to the floor, crawling toward Liv, legs trembling. "Thank you for the discipline, Mistress."

Her words plunged Josh deeper into the cold clutch of his new reality. It was a terrifying feeling to be enchained by people who could break a girl so unequivocally she thanked them for it. And while Liv delivered the strikes, he was convinced she was nothing more than an instrument operated by another.

Across the room, Van leaned against the wall, arms crossed, expression slack but watchful.

No doubt there would be a profusion of defining moments in the weeks to come, but Josh suspended this one in his mind, branding it to memory, and made a vow to himself. He would adapt to this environment, but he would not become an instrument, an empty shell, or a grateful slave. His parents would surrender their lives before they'd want him to become something less than he was. His heart ached at the thought of anything happening to them, but he sat lighter in his resolve, his shoulders loosened and his jaw unlocked.

"This training session will focus on requirement two." Liv's detached voice tiptoed over his shoulder. "Given your inability to remember the requirements, repeat after me. Slave will service Master sexually with exceptional skill, and his body will be prepared to make it easy for Master."

Ugh. He never wanted to hear that rule again. He climbed to his feet. "Slave will break through Mistress's mask with exceptional skill—"

*Crack.*

Fire erupted on his backside, a concentrated burn in the crease of his butt and thigh. Dear God, she had an arm on her. He breathed through it and hung on the support of the chains. He glanced over his shoulder, not giving a crap about the rules. His throat dried at what he found there.

Red bled over the white of her left eye, surrounded by pink, swollen skin. His heart roared in his ears, and his fingers curled into his palms. With the ragged half-inch cut on her brow bone and the scar marring the length of her cheek, she looked like a battered mess. Worse was the pleading fragility softening the edges of her gaze. She was begging him for something. To obey her? To ignore the beating Van had obviously given her?

Van held his relaxed pose against the wall, but there were signs of edginess. His arms were crossed too tightly, his fingers pressed against his biceps, and the skin around the indentations of his grip blanched.

With Kate in her kneeling position beside Josh and Liv at his back, a division was drawn in his mind. There was a significant intersection in the room. Josh stood with the girls and faced the true threat.

A toothpick rolled slowly between Van's lips as he studied Josh. Perhaps Van was measuring him the way he weighed Van. Josh's limited counseling experience taught him that an abuser's violence was rooted in arrogance, in a belief that no one was as good as he was. Liv was someone Van could control and possess, someone to serve him. That sense of ownership bred jealousy not love.

Van was a problem that couldn't be resolved with a few anger-management sessions, not that the man would be willing to talk through his issues. Because even if he could be rehabilitated, one harrowing fact remained. Josh was on the wrong side of the bars—or chains.

If Van moved close enough, could Josh hold himself by the chains, swing his legs up, and wrap them around the man's throat? What then? He'd seen them both remove weapons hidden in their clothes. Even if his arms were free, he would still be outmatched by muscle and whatever Van was armed with. Despite the challenge charging his nerves, there was nothing he could say or do to stop this training session.

To top it off, Liv's pleading eyes held a desperate grip around his heart. He didn't want to make this harder on her, and with that certainty, he turned toward her with his head lowered. Kneeling at her feet, the chains crisscrossing above him, he tried to repeat the requirement from memory, with a few adjustments. "Slave will service Mistress with exceptional skill, and his body will be prepared to make it easy for her."

Her toes flexed. She seemed to be digesting his wording changes. "Slaves, stand and face me."

He rose with Kate, surprised by her wide eyes when they locked on Liv's swollen face. Kate's shock flashed for only a second before she averted her gaze. Van, who appeared bored by the whole exchange, picked his teeth with the toothpick. Was his abuse a rare thing? Or did Liv usually hide the evidence behind her masks?

She pinched Kate's chin, capturing her focus. "We're going to teach the boy the proper way to kiss."

"Yes, Mistress." Kate wet her lips, pressed her bare breasts against Liv's larger ones, and tilted her head.

At a similar height, their mouths brushed with ease and familiarity. Slowly, enthrallingly, it bloomed into a jaw-stretching, tongue-touching, hands-wandering-curves pleasure to watch. The intimate slide of bodies and lips was sweet, gentle, and hell on his libido. Throughout the kiss, Kate held her mouth open and accepting, her tongue tracing her own lips as if inviting Liv to lead. The fluidity of their shared breaths drew him in, heating and hardening his groin. He gripped the chains to steady his balance.

"Very good." Liv pulled back, her smile quivering. No doubt the muscle movement aggravated her injury. "A slave's kiss anticipates her Master. It's intuitive, an articulation in submission, total perception-by-feel. Return to the cot, girl."

Beneath the delivery of her words lurked a strained emotion. It didn't sound like a scripted speech. More like a remembered feeling leaking from a deep well within her. Something akin to the inviting kiss she'd let him steer in his truck. What did that mean? How did it fit with her motivations? Those answers held the key to unlocking her.

"Boy." Liv stared up at him. "As with all your requirements, number two is commanded by your future Master, for his purpose, which means you will learn how to kiss a man the way a man desires."

# NINETEEN

Josh's pulse sputtered and his stomach bucked. He should've expected this. Van's role was suddenly and devastatingly clear.

As if he'd conjured the devil, a hot, sweaty palm gripped the curve of his shoulder and throat. Fingers added a warning pressure to his nape, punctuated by a thumb on his trachea.

Van leaned in. His mouth was too damned close, reeking of roast beef and ill-intent. The toothpick protruded from one upturned corner.

Restrained by the hand and the blasted chains, his thrashing only pressed him closer to Van's body. "No. No way in hell. I won't do this."

The swing of the crop whistled behind him, and the sharp burn of leather struck the rise of his backside. *Ow, Jesus, that hurt.* He clenched his jaw.

"Open your mouth and accept his kiss."

His muscles tightened. "No."

Another strike, harder. He sucked in a breath. "I won't kiss him." He ground his teeth and prayed for his parents' safety. "Not happening."

The lashes that followed came quicker, spreading out over his buttocks, thighs, and lower back. He held onto his resolution as his body swayed on his feet and his head swam through a haze of pain. At some point, she switched to a whip. Still, he refused the kiss.

She and Van gave him a wide berth as he fell to his knees, his torso held up by his arms in the chains, the tip of the whip cutting so sharply he felt it scorch through his blood.

The strikes turned into hours, the hours into days, and so his training lunged into full swing. As those days passed, they didn't seem like days at all. With the absence of windows and the constant pull of fatigue, it was always night. But he gaged the stretch of time by the healing of Liv's face. When he slept, it was on the rug beside her mattress. When awake, he was chained to the ceiling, the floor, the walls, or her bed.

While her tactics varied in creativity, her drive was steady, unyielding, and rife with trickery. Hours of silence would spur him to speak. Twenty lashes. A tender caress on his cheek would draw his eyes to hers. Twenty lashes. Her gripping strokes along his penis guaranteed an orgasm. And twenty lashes.

Some sessions were better than others. Sometimes the pain carried him to a strange space of unawareness where time and chains didn't exist. Where he mindlessly accepted the punishment. He anticipated that feeling of bliss. In fact, when he was in the moment, he didn't want her to stop.

On the third evening, she restrained his naked and kneeling body to the floor and opened the door. Van's swift gait sounded through the room followed by the click of her heels.

His blood pressure doubled as Van circled him. He lifted his shoulders, protecting his neck, and held his elbows close to his sides. After countless beatings, he'd learned to protect the most vulnerable parts of his body.

Luckily, he hadn't seen Van in three days. It didn't take long to find out why she'd finally invited him in.

She slammed her spiked heel into Josh's back, knocking him forward. "Accept his kiss, boy."

Violently shaking on his hands and knees, he glared at the floor and bit down his cheek. His anger boiled so hot his skin flushed with fever.

Van squatted before him, hands laced together beneath Josh's bowed head.

Screw them. He'd rather stab the bastard with a three-foot toothpick than kiss him. He would *not* become a broken grateful slave.

"No." He pinned his lips and braced for twenty new welts.

The silence in the room drew tightly around him, overtaxing his nerves as he stared at Van's unmoving hands. Finally, she spoke, using the empty voice he'd become accustomed to hearing.

"Raise your eyes and sit back on your feet." She walked around him, the pointed toes of her black heels stopping beside Van.

He lifted his upper body, his bruised muscles screaming in protest, and lugged his gaze to meet the frigid sharpness of hers.

Van rose and tucked his hands into his jeans pockets. "It's okay, Liv. He doesn't have to kiss me." His tone was casual, but his gaze was molten silver and aimed on her. "You'll give me what I need."

A flash of fear lit her eyes, and Josh's blood ran cold. The scar on her cheek seemed to draw the corner of her eyelid downward into a miserable reflection of his own thoughts. He didn't want her to give that man a damned thing.

She snapped her chin up and looked down her nose at Josh. Then her expression blanked, and she stared through him like he wasn't there. With a roll of her hips, she stepped into Van's body and cupped his groin, squeezing him through the denim. Josh slammed his teeth together.

The slide of Van's hands up the back of her thighs pushed her skirt to her waist and revealed her panty-less backside. The profile of their hips pressed together and Van's grinding and groping sent Josh's pulse careening, his heartbeat pounding, and every muscle in his body tensing. He tried to shake off the anger. It was just a game, a psychological torment meant to break him.

Van freed the button at his waistband, shoved his jeans to his bare feet, and kicked the material away. Naked from the waist down, he grabbed her hand and curled her fingers around his erection.

The chains held Josh to the floor, but it was the heaviness in his chest that pulled him down and squeezed his lungs. Would Van rape her? Was it rape if she wasn't struggling?

She captured Josh's eyes and pierced him with a look so cruel it struck harder and deeper than any implement she'd used on him.

He dropped his head, eyes burning and arms hanging numbly at his sides. What was the purpose of this?

"Watch us." The snap of her voice splintered through his spinning world.

His neck ached with tension as he raised his head.

The manifestation of her sudden smile seemed forced, blanching along the seam despite the glaring curls at the corners. She angled her chin away, and Van caught her mouth.

He attacked her lips, licking and sucking. With a hand in her hair, the other wrapped around her fingers, stroking his fully aroused length.

Josh's throat thickened, and a guttural roar burst from his throat. "I'll do it. I'll kiss you. Just..." He trembled with the violent need to bash Van's face in. "Just get away from her."

Why did he care? She'd whipped him for days. He should hate her. Yet the pain of watching her with another man eviscerated his insides and destroyed his ability to see a future beyond that room.

Van released her lips, his arm pinning her against him, and cocked his head. "Maybe next time."

He returned to her mouth, his tongue whipping aggressively, dominating the movement of her jaw. He lifted her, hooked her legs around his waist, and backed her into the wall a couple feet away.

When Van's hand shoved between their hips, Josh barreled forward, the strain of his body caught by the web of chains.

"Mistress?" He jerked and yanked, the cuffs on his wrists scraping along his skin. "Mistress, don't let him do this."

Her glassy eyes peered at him over Van's shoulder. She lay her palms flat on his back, her shoes dangling from her toes where they hung behind Van's flexing thighs.

A vicious force of nausea spun through his gut. Why was this affecting him so furiously? There was no love between him and that woman. He sucked in a breath, his mouth thick with saliva. Wasn't this possessiveness he felt for her a method of control? Maybe he was supposed to feel sorry for her. Sympathy was more effective than hating her. The proof was in the painful collapse of his chest as Van thrust his hips, sinking inside her and grunting his pleasure.

His ears burned with the sound of his heart ripping, bleeding with loss and crushing into the shape of betrayal. Why the hell did he feel betrayed? Because she didn't fight? But the skin around her mouth blanched and strained. When he snagged her eyes, she looked away.

The hammering of Van's hips accelerated. The color drained from her face, and she pressed her grimace against Van's shoulder. Josh aged ten years as he watched beneath the weight of his chains, his perceptions grinding into a jaded palate of anguish, helplessness, and jealousy.

The fact that she wasn't struggling snarled and thrashed through his head. If he thought about it, really pushed past the shock and fury of his emotions, the truth was painfully obvious. She couldn't control him with punches and whips, but this...this would leave a permanent mark. She was doing her job by any means possible. His lungs constricted, his mind a mess of twisted conflict.

As Van pummeled into her limp body and pawed at her breasts through the bodice, a wet sheen glazed her eyes. When a lonely tear escaped, she looked at Josh, startled. She quickly brushed it away on her shoulder and averted her gaze.

His chest hitched. She didn't want this. His belief in that didn't mute the pain as Van buried himself deep inside her and released with a revolting groan. But it renewed his faith in his ability to expose her goodness and gave him the strength to keep fighting. For her.

Two days later, he lay on his stomach, stretched over her mattress, his nose burrowed in her sheets. Her familiar womanly scent warmed his inhales as the strikes of her cane pommeled his backside.

The passing of time had warped into an ugly mass of emotions, the intensity and direction of his thoughts changing as frequently as her masks. He flailed between hating her, wanting her, fighting her, and praying for her. And through it all was the incessant urge to screw her. The latter formed a knot of guilt in his stomach. After witnessing Van's treatment of her, his arousing thoughts were selfish.

The air whistled. *Crack.*

Burning pain stole through his thigh and cut his breath. He held tighter to the chains connected to the wall.

*Crack.*

His tender skin flinched, shuddering away from the hurt. But the warmth that remained spread tendrils of heat to his groin. When her footsteps clicked over the floor, he loosened his muscles, anticipating her next hit.

*Crack.*

The impact stabbed his backside, flexing and quivering his gluts. His lungs labored. He relaxed into the lingering twinge, and his arousal mounted.

*Crack.*

He ground his pelvis against the mattress, seeking relief. He tried to muster the shame in it and failed. He'd reached that place in his head where the pain transformed into a lofty phenomenon, his body floating through an immersion of sensations, every nerve ending devouring her attention. He rocked his hips.

Her knee pressed between his spread legs, and her hand wedged beneath his groin. She gripped his erection and stabbed her fingernails into the throbbing, sensitive skin.

"Slave will not rub Master's property against the mattress in a sexual way." Her tone was as cold as the absence of her hand as she stepped away.

*Crack.*

Fire seeped into his bones and smoldered in his joints. He thrust his arousal against the bed, wanting more. It was strange how badly he longed for her full focus on him, only him, whether or not that attention came with pain.

Her fingers grabbed the hair on the back of his head and yanked, exposing his neck. Her lips caressed his ear, and his penis throbbed.

"Stop. Grinding. Your dick." She released him with a shove. "Kinky fucker."

*Crack.*

*Ahhh.* He melted into the heat of her strike. He couldn't remember what the infraction was that led to the current punishment. Couldn't recall what day it was. Didn't care. It was during these highs that he trusted her implicitly. And ignorantly. The flow of his thoughts whispered in jumbled bursts of nonsense, his give-a-crap drifting beyond reach.

The mattress dipped as she knelt on the edge.

Time passed. He might've dozed. Somewhere along the edges of his drowsiness, her phone beeped. When he opened his eyes, her knees hadn't moved.

He licked dry lips. It would've been delusional to expect leniency from her after every punishment, but sometimes, while the pain ebbed, she gave him a small window of sympathy. Sometimes, during these moments, he tested her.

"Come here," he breathed.

She sighed, and it was sexy soft. His lips floated into a smile. At least he thought they did. Her gentle response surprised him as much as it had the first time he'd given her the same order. In those rare moments when she came to him tenderly, it didn't last long before the detached Mistress appeared again. Still, he wanted her, craved her body against his, and this time she obliged.

Black pleather encased her from chin to ankle, and she wrapped all that material around the length of his side, stroking a hand over his sore muscles, soothing him as he fell out of the sky.

It was the only time she held him, and he didn't try to understand her intent. He simply savored her tender attention, turning his head to peer into her eyes.

In place of a mask was an expression he hadn't seen since Van had sex with her in front of him. Beneath the yellowing bruise around her eye was pure, unrestrained fear. It paled her complexion, hardened her jaw, and flattened her lips.

"Liv?" He raised his head, his stomach hardening. "What's wrong?"

She recoiled, clutching a cell phone to her chest. In the next breath, her face blanked, her tone equally vacant. "I'm failing. I've tried everything I can think of." She released a shuddering exhale. "You're the worst slave ever."

He wanted to laugh at that, but something was wrong. She hadn't let up her grip on the phone.

"What's going on?" His scalp tingled. "What are you doing with the phone?"

She lowered it, staring at it like it was about to detonate. Then her eyes flashed to the door. "Mr. E is on his way upstairs."

# TWENTY

Josh was treated to the soft strains of Liv's a cappella as they stood side by side before the door in her room. She stared at her phone, perhaps waiting for a text. He stared at her profile, trying to capture the quiet words woven in her melody. Something about hounds and chains and teams. The tune was familiar, but he couldn't place it.

Her dark chestnut hair was smoothed into a ponytail that swung over the toned lines of her arm. Black vinyl painted her limbs and torso, giving her a sleek, wet look. The catsuit was so compressed, he could've spanned the cinch of her waist with two hands. He knew her costumes were intended to intimidate and hypnotize, but her musical voice held that power all on its own.

Her lips froze mid-verse, her attention locked on the phone's blank screen in her hand.

"Where are your eyes, boy?" The stiffness in her neck matched the aggravation in her voice.

She wasn't pleased with his wandering eyes, but his last punishment had ended with her body curled against his. It gave him enough temerity to break more rules.

"What does this visit from Mr. E mean exactly?" He watched her beautiful, expressionless face.

She turned, facing him with her back to the door and her stony eyes packed with grim promises. He considered it an accomplishment to stand before her, as he did every day, with his wrists wrapped in chains, every inch of his flesh bared and unprotected, and his backbone proudly intact.

Her scrutiny leveled on his raised chin, and her brown eyes melted for a millisecond before hardening again.

"I saw that." He was being reckless. Despite the bumps and bruises riddling his body, the threat of her whip had lost its edge.

But she could still threaten his parents. Or have sex with Van. His jaw locked, smacking his teeth together.

"You saw nothing, boy." Her stillness suggested a disciplinary strike would follow, but her expression was hesitant, as if distracted by some inward conflict.

He stepped closer, raising his hands between them, the coil of chain around his wrists a reminder that he wasn't the enemy. "If your boss is right outside this door, why are we in here?"

Her throat twitched as if she'd stifled a swallow a second too late. "Eyes down."

Of course, she wouldn't answer him.

He'd have to make a guess and read her reaction. "He's out there with Kate. Van's probably catching him up on her training. When that's done, he'll text you to open the door, so he can inspect his new property. Do I have the gist of it?"

The flash of her eyes told him he'd guessed right. "On your knees. Now."

*Arrgh.* He stayed on his feet. "You always do that. You deflect with those damned rules."

Still, she seemed off-kilter, and he might not get another opportunity to poke around for a soft spot.

"I'm just trying to understand." He searched her face.

She kept it guarded. So he rested his fists against the door above her head, no physical contact, but the bond was there.

"Step. Back." Her jaw set.

Maybe *bond* was too strong of a word, but she could've ducked out from beneath his arms. Instead, she stared up at him with an unfathomable mien on her face. Something was hidden there, an expression, a truth, etched in the delicate creases around her mouth. Her lips parted and pressed together, bending the scar that mapped the struggles in her life, the ones he suspected she fought alone.

Then it clicked. "I know that song you were singing. Isn't it about loyalty and friendship and—?"

"Team." Her eyes were wide, watchful, and maybe a little skittish.

"That's right. 'Team' by *Lorde.*"

He wanted to ask what the song meant to her, but she wouldn't have answered. Didn't matter. He could guess its significance, knew it had to do with why she slept where her prisoner slept, confining herself with him for five days, only leaving to fetch food.

"Better to be enchained with someone on your side," he said, "than to be alone with a false sense of freedom."

The expression on her face transformed from that of captor to equal. Her posture loosened, her features gentled, the phone forgotten in her hand. She stared into his eyes, blinking, nodding slowly, subtly. It was a poignant moment of connection, the opening he'd been searching for.

He touched his forehead to hers, his chains rattling above her head, and waited for the punishment that never came. "We may not be trapped for the same reason, but we're looking in the same direction, reaching beyond these walls *together*. Tell me what we're up against."

A low-pitched noise groaned in her throat, and her head relaxed against his. He kept his shackled arms balanced on the door, afraid the smallest movement might spook her.

Was she considering his words or formulating a safe response? Maybe she was worried about Van hitting her again. Or raping her. His throat hurt as he replayed Van's groaning thrusts and the pain in her eyes. The two times he'd asked her to talk about it, she'd whipped him for speaking without permission.

Too soon, she straightened, breaking the point of contact. She took her time meeting his eyes, and when she did, a smile tugged at the corners of her mouth, her chin slowly moving left to right. "I give you an inch—"

"And I'd be six-foot-three." He lowered his arms, nudging her chin with his bound hands. "I love your smile."

Her lips trembled and stilled. The smile remained, but her eyes dulled. "You've got balls, distracting me despite the consequences."

He blew out a breath and retracted his arms to his waist. "So you're tallying my infractions?" He dreaded what those consequences might be and tried for a light tone. "When do I get my spanking?"

Her fingers touched his navel, sending a quiver through him. She traced the dusky trail to his groin and coiled a finger tightly through the thatch of hair.

"Spankings aren't effective." She tugged, sparking a twinge of discomfort over the sensitive skin there. "You're a pain slut."

A half-laugh, half-groan escaped with his exhale. "I am not a pain slut, whatever that is."

"Oh, please. Five welts and you fall into a hypnotic trance."

Okay, maybe he felt some out-of-body weirdness. Wasn't that normal in adrenaline-charged situations?

She glanced at her phone, and a sharp line rutted between her eyebrows. Her anxiousness was bleeding onto him.

"What is it?" he asked.

She angled the phone long enough for him to glimpse the text. *Unknown number: Open the door.*

An unnerving metamorphosis washed over her, stripping the

emotion from her eyes, smoothing out her breathing, and hardening her body into an armored shell.

"You want to be on the same team?" Her voice was cold and terse. "You want to save me?"

He nodded, hoping it wasn't a trick. Her sudden change in demeanor tightened the muscles in his jaw.

She dropped a hand to her side, snapped her fingers, and pointed at the floor beside her feet, an unmistakable order to kneel. "Then don't fuck this up."

Whatever was about to happen, it was evident that her bearing, as well as his, needed to broadcast that she had the upper hand. He knelt at her side, holding her gaze as he lowered. Sure, she appeared dispassionate at a glance, but the hand at her side trembled.

As she entered the code in the keypad—too quickly for him to catch the pattern—he gripped the fingers digging into her thigh. The door clicked open, and she pulled her hand away but not before giving him a tentative squeeze in return.

He kept his eyes on the floor, taking in the scuffed black boots that entered first, followed by Van's sneakers. The door shut, imprisoning the room with silence.

He'd expected trousers, paired with an expensive suit, a wardrobe that signified wealth and power. Instead, black cotton work pants gathered over the dusty boots. The mystery surrounding Mr. E compounded, surging dread through his veins.

"Raise your head, boy." Her voice was so detached, even its iciness was absent.

His breath caught as he lifted his eyes and met the drab material of a cotton jumpsuit. The kind one would zip over regular clothes to change a tire or carry out an activity that might be messy. He stopped breathing altogether when his gaze reached the man's head.

It was wrapped in a potato sack hood, cinched at the neck, with two crudely cut eyeholes and vertical stitching where the mouth should be. Rough-hewed seams rounded the skull, pulling the material taut to maintain the curvature. Then it spoke.

"Stand, slave." The mouth, stitched as it was, didn't move. The voice was soft and masculine and cruelly calm.

Van leaned against the closed door in a display of arrogant composure. Liv stared at her feet, frozen and pale, as if the masked man had chased her into some unseen recess of her mind.

*Don't fuck this up.*

Josh climbed to his feet and let his bound wrists loll over his groin. At his full height, he stood four or more inches taller than Mr. E.

"You'll address me as *Sir*." Mr. E glanced at Liv and back to Josh.

"Did you give her the black eye?"

His shoulders tensed. "No—"

"That was me, sir." Van's smirk oiled the tension in the air.

"Ah." A chuckle rustled through the canvas mask. Mr. E reached a gloved hand to Van's jaw and patted it. "I suppose you can't fuck up her face worse than it already is."

"Nope." Van popped the *P* with a smarmy exhale and slid a toothpick between his curved lips.

A storm of rage boiled Josh's blood, twisting and shaking his insides. She should've been defending herself. And what compelled Van to be at such ease with a man who hid behind a potato sack? The man who, Josh suspected, had given them their matching scars.

The whites of Mr. E's eyes shifted inside the depths of the eyeholes and settled on Liv. Under the decomposing scrutiny, her shoulders curled forward, her gaze fixed downward.

It was in that moment that his assumptions about her place in the hierarchy were confirmed. Just because she wasn't a slave didn't mean she wasn't viewed as property and used as such. They seemed to think of her as scarred and ruined, and she certainly wasn't sexually innocent. Her usefulness to them was limited to her proficiency in training slaves. A replaceable skill. Was Van's apparent ownership of her the only thing that held her there?

There was so much obscurity surrounding the operation, and seeing her like this shook the hell out of Josh's hope. He bit down on his cheek, checking the turbulence of his emotions, and put on his own phlegmatic expression.

"Have you fucked him yet?" The potato sack cocked toward Van, and Josh balled his fists.

The silver cut of Van's eyes sliced through Josh, but it was Liv who answered. "He's not ready."

Mr. E's stillness was deafening, cranking the room's temperature to scorching. Then those elusive eyeholes shifted to him. "Let's see how well he kisses." He curled a gloved finger. "Van."

Josh fought the heart-pounding urge to swing his bound arms into that stupid mask and stared directly into the soulless eyes. "I will not kiss that man."

Liv's finger twitched against her thigh, but she was otherwise unresponsive.

"I see." Mr. E clasped his hands behind him and spent an eternal moment moving through the room, testing the strength of a dangling chain, nudging the mattress with his boot, and building a terrible anticipation. Then he returned to Van's side. "She still sleeps in here."

A muscle jumped in Van's jaw. "Yes, sir."

"You haven't won her over yet."

"She's mine."

"I'm not arguing that."

Josh felt like he'd fallen into a state of surrealism, where crap that should never ever make sense was sickeningly transparent. They talked about her like she wasn't standing right there while ignoring the fact that Josh refused to kiss Van. It was a game, a tactic to mess with his head, and maybe hers, too.

Mr. E snapped his gloved fingers under Liv's bowed head. "Get his clothes."

Her stillness unfurled into a steady, flowing stride to the trunk by her mattress. She placed her phone on the bed and returned with the jeans, t-shirt, and boots he'd arrived in. They were just things, inconsequential possessions, yet the sight of them made his heart race.

"I'm a huge Baylor Bears fan." Mr. E scratched his chin through the mask. "The news reporters are saying you're the best linebacker in college football."

Josh's shoulders curled in. How much was the news covering his disappearance? Would they be camped out on the farm, shoving cameras in his parents' faces, and magnifying their grief?

"Get dressed." Mr. E pointed at the clothes.

The taunt of freedom thrilled in his chest as she removed the padlock on his wrists and unbuckled the cuffs. He massaged the skin that had been rubbed raw by metal for a week. Were they letting him go? "What is this?"

"Too many people are searching for you." Mr. E angled his mask toward Liv. "She picked the wrong boy and has made no progress in your training. You're a liability." He placed a hand on Josh's shoulder and squeezed. "Besides, the Bears are getting crushed. They need you."

What? No. This was crazy.

Mr. E laughed. "I was kidding about the last part. The Bears are doing just fine. Seriously though, you're a risk I can't afford." The hand on Josh's shoulder shifted to his throat, gripping his jaw to tilt back his head. "I'll drop you in the middle of nowhere. By the time you find your way to a phone, we'll be gone from this house."

Letting him go home was a risk. Even if they fled, he could identify Liv and Van. There were no suspicious bulges on the men, but Liv had proven how easily a weapon could be concealed. He imagined a gun trained on his head as they pushed him from their car. Boom! Body dumped, never to be traced backed to their operation.

His chest hitched. "You'll kill me before you'll let me go."

The grip on his throat released as Mr. E said, "Been doing this a long time, boy. Never killed no one. And this is the first time I've offered freedom."

He could taste the promise of it, felt it awakening every cell in his body. Liv pressed his clothes to his chest. He stared into her eyes, searched for the truth, and found an expression as lifeless as Mr. E's mask. Even Van was gazing at his feet.

"What about Liv and Kate?" Josh asked.

"Not your concern." Mr. E waved a dismissive hand. "Take the offer, boy."

It would be so much easier to help the girls if he were free. Even if the operation vanished, detectives could track it.

Why was he even debating this? Would he seriously choose the woman who'd been beating him over his parents' happiness?

But he couldn't protect Liv if he left. She was as much a victim as he was. His head swam. He couldn't protect her in chains, either.

He dressed, and with each piece of clothing covering his skin, he felt more hopeful, more anxious. He watched her expression as he tied his boots, wishing she'd look at him and give him some sign she understood. He wasn't abandoning her. He was going to get help. He was going to save her.

Clothed and trembling, he waited at her side while she punched in the code. Was this really happening? He was wearing his clothes. They were letting him go home. Mom and Dad's joyous faces filled his vision and spread warmth through his chest. He was going home.

The door opened. Mr. E and Van exited first. When Liv stepped through to follow, Mr. E pivoted, grabbed her throat with two hands, and shoved her back against the door jamb. Her mouth gaped, gulping without sound, hands clawing at the ones on her neck.

Josh leapt forward, pulse racing, a roar bellowing from his chest. "You're choking her." He tried to break the grip, yanking on unmovable wrists.

The barrel of a gun moved into his vision. Van jerked it at his face. "Move back. All the way into the room."

Liv stretched her jaw, her eyes squeezed shut, tears leaking down her red face.

"Let her go." Josh's heart thundered, his voice thick with spit. "You're going to kill her."

"Step. Back." Van's tone was steady, but his eyes shifted rapidly between Mr. E and Liv, as if warring with whose side he was on.

Oh God, she couldn't breathe. He was going to choke her to death. Josh shuffled back, hands in the air.

With a violent heave, Mr. E slammed her head into the jamb and tossed her limp body onto the floor at Josh's feet.

Josh dropped to his knees and put his ear over her chest, then her mouth. Unconscious, she lay listless, her breaths labored. He didn't know CPR, had no medical training. What was he supposed to do?

Van lowered the gun, his muscles flexing, his teeth bared, but he made no move to help.

"You're not going home, boy." Mr. E clutched the door handle. "You were never going home."

Deep down, Josh knew it. Didn't stop the pain from splintering his chest. He turned her head and followed the river of blood to the cut on her scalp. Head wounds bled a lot, right? Did she need stitches?

"She needs a doctor." Josh cradled her head in his hands.

"She needs to do her job. You meet your future Master in two days. If you want her to live, you'll kiss him with ardor and skill. You'll grab your ankles if he wants to test drive your ass. You'll be fucking willing and obedient."

Van stepped out of the room, and Mr. E followed. The door slammed shut, shaking loose the last forgiving piece of Josh's heart and replacing it with a sharp-edged thirst for blood. Mr. E and Van seemed to be using her in the most vicious way. Maybe she could outsmart them, but she wouldn't need to do it alone.

As he carried her to the vanity to search for a medical kit, he glared at the door. God was neither hot tempered nor did He rush to judgment. Josh could be patient, but when the time came and God delivered those bastards before him, he would defeat them.

He would utterly destroy them.

# TWENTY-ONE

Something warm and hard and decidedly alive lay beneath Liv's body, coaxing her awake. Her throat throbbed, and a pounding ache fired through her skull. She was face down with her cheek on a brick chest of muscle, which could only belong to the boy. She tried moving her arms, dragging them along with her thoughts from the comfort of oblivion.

Mr. E's hands on her throat.

The impending meeting with the buyer.

Her phone.

She snapped her eyes open and met the fathomless green of the boy's gaze.

His hands skimmed heat along her back beneath the blanket, his thumb tracing the length of her spine.

"Good morning." His voice was raspy, relaxed. "Or afternoon. Or whenever it is."

Her stomach told her it was afternoon. She pushed against the cotton covering his shoulders. He was dressed, and by the scratchy feel of her skin against his jeans, she wasn't wearing a damned thing.

He watched her closely, his hypnotic eyes and sensual mouth producing a tremor through her aching body. She struggled to drag her attention away from the masculine lines of his chiseled face, the thick mess of black hair, the defined cheekbones. The sudden and intense longing to be cared for by him filled her with dangerous hope. She would address that—all of that—as soon as she gathered her strength.

She pushed again to sit, but the hands on her back held her in place with gentle determination.

"Easy," he whispered against her hair. "How are you feeling?"

Her whole fucking body hammered like the aftermath of one of Van's beatings.

She reached up, flinching as her fingers met the lump beneath her hair.

"Let me go." Her command came out hoarse and thready, blazing more pain through her throat.

"Nope." Holding her with an unyielding arm, he reached to the floor and lifted a glass of water to her mouth.

He let her arch up enough to tilt her head back. The first gulp over-flexed the bruised muscles in her throat, reigniting the burn.

She continued to drink, scanning the room. "Where's my phone?"

He studied her, eyebrows shifting downward. "Why?"

*Mom and Mattie.* If Mr. E wanted to further punish her for the previous night, he'd give her the news in a text.

A sinking feeling pulled on her insides. "My phone. Please."

His gaze narrowed.

Yeah, her tone was desperate. She was begging. "Please?"

He set the glass on the floor, and his hand returned with the phone. He held it out of reach, watching her with those compelling pale-green eyes. "If I give this to you, will you talk with me? Let me help you?"

If he intended to take advantage of her vulnerable state and force her to talk, he would likely succeed. But there was no manipulation in the wrinkles that worried his chiseled face. His drawn eyebrows and the supportive way his arm rested against her back wasn't rooted in coercion. He seemed content with simply comforting her.

Her heart contracted, massaging an unfamiliar sensation through her chest. For the first time in seven years, someone held her in a nonsexual way. She didn't know what to do with that, so she nodded, unbalanced.

The phone dropped into her outstretched hand. He could pluck it away as soon as she unlocked it. And why wouldn't he?

He let his head rest on the pillow, studying her, and touched a tentative finger to her scarred cheek. His concerned gaze as he stroked the raised line of flesh told her escape wasn't at the forefront of his thoughts. Another thing she'd need to examine. Later.

She angled the screen away and tapped in the passcode.

Seventy-eight texts from Van. Nothing from Mr. E. She released a lungful of air.

He grabbed her wrist and jerked the screen toward his face. Her breath caught as she pressed the power button, locking the phone.

"What the fuck?" She let the phone drop from her hand, her molars grinding. "Don't I feel stupid for trusting you."

He released her hand and narrowed his eyes. "Now you know

how I felt when I learned that the stranded girl I helped was a sex trafficker."

*Ouch.* She deserved that. Remembering her own capture magnified her shame, stirred an old ache inside her, and shoved her self-loathing to the surface. "I already know that feeling."

Though her words were whispered, he flinched as if she'd shouted. Their eyes locked, and a long look suspended between them.

His expression hardened. "What does that mean, exactly?"

Not for the first time, she wanted to confide in him. For five days, she longed to expose her arrangement, with the hope that he'd understand her position, and trust he wouldn't use it against her. She'd never burdened a captive with the truth of her situation. At least, not while they were bound in her chains.

Her composure was wrecked, and his perceptive eyes seemed to capture every crumble and twist of her face. She needed to toughen up, put on her best mask. The scary part was she didn't want to wear one with him.

His features softened. Even when frowning, his lips formed a serene curve. "Okay, Liv. I'm going to let that sit for a minute." He blew out a breath. "First, I wasn't trying to steal your phone. You're not exactly forthcoming, and I need to know what you're not telling me. Second, why did that bastard text you seventy-eight times?"

"He's probably worried." *Or horny.*

"Really? He let the friggin' door shut while you were bleeding and unconscious on the floor." His nostrils flared at her flinch. He scrubbed a hand over his stubble. "Look, I don't know what your relationship is with him—"

"There's no relationship." She let her heavy head fall to his chest.

The protection of his body was a persuasion she couldn't resist with her mind as fuzzy and achy as it was. He felt like the safest place on Earth.

"Have you told him that?" His voice vibrated through her, powerful, dependable.

She should've been punishing his disobedient ass, whipping him into the shape of a dutiful, cock-sucking slave. Even if the thought wasn't so ludicrous, she had neither the energy nor the will to hurt him. "Let me just lie here a minute."

"Thank you, God," he murmured as his fingers combed through her hair, not coiling and yanking, just soothing the strands and stimulating the roots along her scalp. "How much pain are you in?"

"I'll manage." Every inch of her bare skin relished the support of his warm musculature. She brushed a hand down his ribs, hooked a finger around the belt loop of his jeans, and yanked it hard enough to pinch his balls with the pull of denim. "Why am I naked?"

A deep noise strangled in his throat. "Your sprayed-on leotard was constricting your breathing." He bent his knees, and she settled snuggly in the cage of his hard thighs, chest to chest. "Don't think it's passed my notice that I'm supposed to be the slave, yet you're the one lying here battered and troubled."

The beat of her blood accelerated.

"I'm just going to talk through this and hope that you'll fill in the gaps." He stroked her hair. "I've tried to figure out why I need to consent to do *things* with Van." His caressing paused and began again. "Van doesn't hit me, hasn't raped me, but he wants to. What's his deal?"

She tightened her hand on his waistband. "The buyer wants the appearance of a willing slave. One who desires a man despite his innate heterosexuality. If Van raped you, that outcome wouldn't be achieved."

He laughed, coarsely. "Thank God for that. So, that's a requirement?"

"Requirement one. Slave has never experienced sexual intimacy with a woman. Slave is heterosexual but hates women. He desires only his Master."

A soft chuckle rumbled through his chest. "I could never hate women." He wrapped his arms around her. "Nor can I hate you."

His tender embrace made her heart thump against her ribs. The backs of her eyes burned with the kind of ache she hadn't felt in a long time. Swear to God, if she cried over a hug, she'd never regain her position with him.

His lips touched the crown of her head and retreated. "If you fail to deliver a slave as prescribed..." His silence stretched for so long she raised her head and found him staring down at her. "Mr. E will kill you?"

A swallow hung in her raw throat. "Worse."

His face twisted. "What's worse than death?"

Mom always said if she could confront the wind at 10,000 feet, she could confront anything. But falling out of the sky felt a fuck of a lot safer than exposing her awful, selfish truth. "Ask yourself that question."

He stared at her with such intensity she closed her eyes against it. He was the only person who had ever tried to peek beneath her masks, and damn her, she wanted him to find what he was searching for. After a long moment, he rolled her off his chest with gentle arms and settled her on her side. Then he sprang from the bed.

She shifted to sit with her back against the wall, pulling the blanket around her chest. As he paced through the room, the contraction of his tense body captivated her.

Powerful legs stretched the denim of his low-waist jeans. His biceps flexed as he ran his fingers through cropped strands of his black hair.

"Who is he threatening? Your parents? A husband?" He stopped at the mattress, fists on his hips. With the agitation straining the tight fabric of his t-shirt, the hard line of his lips, and his eyes sharply focused, there was no way he could pass as a boy. In fact, he looked like a man prepared to take on the world. Especially when he shouted, "Who, Liv?"

Why did she feel so compelled to open up to him? She pressed her fist to her lips, stifling the song that suddenly and violently ripped through her mind. He wouldn't hurt her, wouldn't use her fears against her.

Drawing a deep breath, she swallowed her panic and whispered, "My mom."

In the next breath, he was kneeling beside her, holding her hands in his. "Your mom?"

She pressed her back to the wall, her hands sweating and shoulders stiff. "And my daughter."

She kept her eyes on his, but her voice was so small she was sure he didn't hear her nor did she want him to. She would've done the world a favor if she'd died giving birth. But her body had recovered, just like it always did. A fucking curse she couldn't bring herself to end.

His face paled, and his hands convulsed around hers. He lowered his head and tilted his ear toward her. "Say that again."

An onslaught of dizziness spread through her head. Her cheeks numbed and her throat tightened. "My daughter."

He leaned back, searching her face as a whirlwind of emotions crashed over his.

# TWENTY-TWO

Liv held her breath, waiting for her revelation to sink in. She circled her thumbs over his hands. What would he do with this information? How would his reaction impact Mom and Mattie?

"Say something," she whispered.

His jaw hung. He closed it, blinked. "Who's her father? Where is he?"

When her eyes flicked to the door, he sucked in a breath, his face contorting in disbelief.

"*Him?*" His voice was guttural, strained. "You have a child with Van?"

A wave of nausea rolled through her, trembling her body. Disgusted with herself and his reaction to her, her eyes averted from his. She forced them back, met his steady gaze. "There's a story."

"Then you'll talk while you're eating." He cupped her chin. "But you sure as hell aren't going out there." He stabbed a finger toward the door. "Not until we have a plan."

Her back stiffened, and she jerked out of his hold. "A plan? Don't you think I've thought through every possible solution?"

He climbed off the bed and scanned the room. "Do you have anything to eat in here?"

She pointed at the trunk. Why wasn't he badgering her with questions?

As he strode around the mattress, his eyes held hers, heavy with intent. "We'll walk through our options after you eat."

Clearly, she was no longer steering this...whatever this was. Not that she'd ever really gained control of him. The thought both petrified and thrilled her, a testament to how wildly her world was tilting on end. She knew she should order him to strip and kneel and kiss her feet. She also knew if she peeled away the layers of bullshit around her heart, she'd find a hopeful girl who wanted him stubborn and fierce and whole, exactly as he was.

He returned with an armful of energy bars, apple chips, bottled water, and surprisingly, one of her long nightshirts. "I thought this might make you more comfortable."

Her heart tripped. The shirt was a kindness she wasn't accustomed to receiving and certainly didn't deserve, considering his week-long nudity. She slipped it on, her insides quivering with the realization that he could destroy her at a fundamental level. She'd hidden her vulnerability by pretending not to care, but in the span of a week, he'd sliced a deep cut in her mask.

He unwrapped an energy bar, folded her fingers around it, and pulled her legs over his lap. Then he regarded her, one hand curled around her calf. Not eating, he seemed content with watching and waiting.

After a few deliberating moments and two energy bars, she told him about her kidnapping. Her slave training. The loss of her virginity. The day she was sold. The pregnancy and the scar.

He listened without interrupting, his hand soothing the shivers along her leg, his eyes unwavering. She maintained a steady monologue until she reached the part about Mattie's adoption and the conditions of her arrangement as a deliverer. Her voice thickened, and her heart ached with memories and longing. "The videos are the only assurance he gives me."

"Which is why you wanted your phone. No text is good news?"

She nodded, crumbling under the reminder that she still had a job to do and a slave she couldn't train. His attention honed on her change in breathing and the wobble in her chin.

He gathered her in his lap and scooted to lean against the wall. He touched her brow, her cheek, and the line of her neck, the tenderness melting her against his solid body. "You know exactly how I felt when you locked me in the box, huh?"

Guilt squeezed her gut. "Which makes what I did a hundred times worse." She stared at him, miserable and conflicted about what to do next. "I'm so sorry."

His hands gripped her waist, lifting her and adjusting her legs to straddle his hips.

"What are you—?"

His thumbs pressed against her lips, his palms cupping her jaw. Bound by the strength of his gaze, her body went completely still as his thumbs parted, sliding over her cheeks to join his fingers. There was no hint of harshness in his demeanor. His eyes shifted between hers and dropped to her mouth. His lips parted.

Oh God, was he going to kiss her? A sudden rush of hope blasted through her, and she rode that gust, the filthy perimeter of her existence sweeping away. He lowered his head, and she could only squeeze her eyes shut and anticipate the connection, his acceptance, and maybe his forgiveness.

His lips touched hers, achingly sweet, soft, cautious. A chill replaced the sensation as he leaned back. His breath released, taking hers with it. She shuddered and opened her eyes.

They stared at one another, faces just a kiss apart, and it was the most intimate moment she ever experienced. As he looked at her, the pale glow of his eyes softening, asking without words, *Is this okay?*

She nodded, her body liquefying in the cradle of his lap, molding against his tense abs and thighs.

His fingers flexed on her back, and he swept forward, taking her mouth, opening her lips with the warm flesh of his. Beneath the spice of toothpaste, she tasted his natural purity, his breath flavored with sweetness and hope.

With his hands spread over the rise of her ass, he pulled her closer, kissing her deeply, his tongue chasing and tangling with hers. She devoured the heat of his mouth, the strength of his embrace, the precision of his movements. Neither submissive nor forceful, he clutched her hips and controlled the rock of her pelvis. His strong jaw guided the speed and motion of her mouth, his lips burning a trail of sparks as his whiskers scratched a pleasurable twinge across her skin.

His chest heaved, and a moan rumbled in his throat. She savored the response, wanted to hear more, feel him closer. She wanted to crawl inside of him. She slid her hands down his chest and slipped under the hem. Gliding back up the warm taut brawn of his abs and the velvet skin wrapping his pecs, she paused over the beat of his heart against her palm.

He gripped her nape, angled her head, and intensified the kiss. She didn't know if it was her emotional exhaustion or if he was more experienced than she'd thought, but his mastery over her was assured and exquisite. Every lick and nibble tingled through her body, curling her toes against his thighs, racing her heart, and fuzzing her brain.

Too soon, they came up for air. After a few noisy breaths, she gave him a smile, which he returned with warmth and affection.

"Wow." She shook her muddled head. "You've done that a lot, haven't you?"

He captured her lips again, his mouth just as maddening and curling as before, leaving her body shivering when he finished. "Kissing is the only thing I *can* do."

Her heart pinched. Unfortunately, her bladder, too, but she refused to leave the embrace of his arms. Emotions swept through her as she snuggled against his chest, swirling her thoughts into a jumbled knot. She wasn't ready to voice her worries and ruin the moment, but he did it for her.

"Does Van know Mr. E's identity?"

Their eyes met and she nodded.

"Do you?"

She traced his strong jaw, the whiskers rasping against her finger. He held still as she followed the smooth skin stretching over his cheekbones, between his enchanting eyes and disappearing beneath the soft inky hue of his hairline. His beauty had the power to enthrall and distract.

She dropped her hand. "If I knew Mr. E's identity, we wouldn't be sitting here." She would've tracked him down. Perhaps he had a family she could've threatened. "Van claims he's only seen beneath the mask once, when Mr. E lured him from his mother's meth house. I have my doubts." Her bladder prodded again.

Something shifted through his eyes, and his jaw twitched. "Mr. E basically pushed you into my arms last night." His embrace tightened around her, punctuating his point. "Why would he do that? And I see the way Van watches you. Why would Van let him do that?"

The answers weren't simple, most of which were based on her own theories. "I need to go to the bathroom."

He carried her to the toilet. She might've refused out of pride if she weren't so reluctant to leave his arms. He lowered her to the rim and squatted before her.

Her head spun from the sudden loss of his supportive strength, but she still mustered a glare when he propped his chin on a fist and settled in.

"You look like you're about to fall over." His tone was gentle.

Too tired to argue, she closed her eyes and released her bladder. "Van may not agree with everything Mr. E does, but he's never challenged him. He loves the cocksucker like a father." She glanced up and found him observing her steadily.

The set of his jaw matched the hardness of his eyes. "Van thinks he loves you."

That truth didn't need acknowledgment. She flushed the toilet and moved to the shower. "Mr. E's actions aren't always transparent. Last night was the first time he'd ever raised a hand against me. Other than..." She touched the scar on her cheek and turned the tap to warm.

He sat against the wall outside the open shower as she undressed and washed. Her movements were robotic, but her thoughts were an utter mess. Now that he knew her situation, what was he willing to do?

She needed to know where his head was. "Maybe Mr. E pushed us together to wrangle your sympathy for me, a ploy to persuade you to do what needs to be done, using me as leverage."

Though his eyes followed the motion of her hands, they were unfocused, turned inward.

"He's never attempted anything like this." It seemed too complicated to be worth the effort. As she washed her belly and thighs, she lay a soapy hand over the horizontal c-section scar below her bikini line. It was one scar she wished hadn't faded. "Honestly, I don't know why he's kept me alive all these years."

"Do you have sex with Van privately? Or do you just screw him in front of your slaves?" Quiet words at odds with his finger digging restlessly at a frayed hole in his jeans.

Her throat convulsed, her stomach caving with humiliation. Was he regretting the kiss they'd just shared? He wasn't glaring at her with judgment or pumping his muscles with jealousy. But he'd also been raised to approach problems with civility and grace.

She shut off the water and faced him, wet and naked, with a quiver in her voice. "It's complicated."

The hand on his leg curled into a fist, and his chest heaved. He straightened his fingers, cleared his throat, and imprisoned her eyes. "Complicated how? Is it consensual?"

Was it? She nodded. Unsure, she shook her head then nodded again.

He stood, slowly, his expression tight, and wrapped a towel around her. "I really need you to explain that answer, Liv." He rifled through her trunk while she talked through Van's tricks, his mind games, and his threats to involve Mr. E.

"He doesn't physically force me." She felt sick, weak, frozen in the shower stall. "Having sex in front of you..." She shivered with self-hatred. "I was cornered. He'd told that morning he was going to fuck you. I convinced him jealousy was more effective."

He glared at his hands, gripping the edge of the trunk, his eyes full of pain and face red. When he returned, he handed her a t-shirt, jeans, and a pair of panties that matched the mint green of his irises.

He touched her face, his fingers lingering on her mouth. "Do you come for him?"

Shit, she didn't want to answer that, but he looked at her as if he were consumed by the need to know.

"Yes." She gripped the towel around her chest.

Tension vibrated from his body as he stormed through the room. He seemed to be trying to drive it away with his swift strides back to the trunk and whatever was distracting him there. She didn't own anything personal. Only meaningless things she'd collected while living in that room. She dressed and sat on the mattress.

While he rummaged, she told him what the news had been reporting about his disappearance, highlighting the resiliency his parents exuded during their interviews. Then she talked about her own experience with Mom's grieving and her eventually moving on. "When enough time has passed, your *fake* decomposed remains will turn up somewhere and put an end to all the searching. I don't know how Mr. E arranges such a thing, but he pulled it off when I disappeared." Her throat dried, scratching her voice. "Van says Mr. E intends to do the same with you."

During her one-sided conversation, he'd found a tennis ball in the trunk, a gift she'd *earned* as a slave. He tossed it against the far wall, caught it, tossed it again, over and over. He didn't seem to be listening.

"Am I boring you?" she asked.

He snatched the ball out of the air and jerked his head toward her, his eyes clouded under the *V* of his dark eyebrows. "Mr. E has a pretty twisted hold on me by threatening your life. How does this affect the threat against my parents?"

"That threat was my creation." She felt sick. "An empty one."

Harming his parents had never been an option. She wanted to go back to the day she took him and erase the worry she'd planted in his head. She also wanted to bury her pen knife in Mr. E's jugular and watch his stupid mask soak up the blood. Damn him for manipulating Josh into feeling sorry for her.

He watched her with eyes too perceptive for his age. "Is Van a threat to my parents?"

She pressed a cool hand against her burning cheek. "Your parents are entangled with media and detectives. He wouldn't dare go near them."

Even without the risk, she didn't believe Van would murder an innocent person.

Josh's fist flexed around the ball, his other hand scraping roughly over his face.

"What's bothering you? Besides the obvious." She gestured around the room, indicating his prison cell.

He glanced at her, the tightness of his chest visible in the muscles straining his shirt. "I work my parents' farm at dawn and dusk." He flung the ball, caught the bounce back. "At practice, I sprint, tackle, and sweat through endurance exercises for hours every day." His voice lowered. "Now I'm locked in an attic with the most gorgeous woman I've ever laid eyes on." The ball sailed through the air, returned to his hand. "Whom I just shared a very. Arousing. Kiss. With." A toss and catch punctuated each word.

A warm tendril of pleasure shivered through her. She wanted to close the distance and wrap her arms around him, but he seemed to be trying to control his arousal and pent-up energy. She had no interest in taunting him.

Lowering his head, he pressed the ball to his brow. "And there is a tyrant waiting outside that door to have sex with you. Again." He resumed pummeling the wall. Bounce. Bounce. Bounce. "I'm trying really hard to keep myself in check, Liv."

His words tied her up with heartache and compelled her to silence. She clung to the sounds of the thumps against the wall and the way he controlled his body despite his turmoil.

He caught the ball, clasping it in his hands behind his neck, and looked heavenward. "If I escape, I might be able to track Mr. E down. But he will kill you before I do. If I take you with me, he'll kill your mom and daughter."

Her breath stumbled with the acceleration of her pulse.

"If we follow all the rules, your arrangement is safe." He dropped the ball and sat beside her on the mattress. "Given my background, I think he knew you would trust me with your predicament, and he's counting on me not to put you or your family in harm's way. We're both being played, Liv."

Hearing him voice her fears churned her gut, boiling bile through her chest. "I want to kill him."

"Murder's not the answer."

Maybe he'd meant to find some preacher comfort in his response, but the sinews in his neck were taut against his skin.

She pinched the bridge of her nose. "I can't kill him anyway. He has a contract out on Mattie and Mom. It's part of our arrangement. If anything happens to him or Van, the contract will be activated."

Blood drained from his face. "A hit man?"

She lifted a shoulder, swallowed. "Something like that. He's in the business of trafficking humans. I don't doubt he has connections with an assortment of criminals. But I'm inclined to test his threat."

He leaned forward and laced his fingers through hers. His perceptive eyes projected an intrusive quality, one that could unearth her weaknesses or nurture her strengths. "You're going to teach me all the rules. Train me as your slave."

Regret pinched her chest. Mr. E succeeded where she failed. The boy would be cooperative. *What an elegant fucking play.* "I can't—"

"You will." He squeezed her hand. "And since there's no way I'll let you go out there alone—"

"*Let* me?" She pulled her hand from his. "You're pushing it, boy."

He barked an unsmiling laugh. "I've stomached the *boy* crap long enough." He stood on the mattress, feet planted on either side of her knees, and stretched out his arms. "Do I look like a boy to you?"

Dark stubble shadowed his masculine jaw. His biceps were damned near the size of her thighs. The brick wall of his torso narrowed into low-hung jeans that cupped his groin. She knew too well the shape and girth of the cock that formed that bulge, and it could only belong to a man.

"Cocky bastard." She hid a smile.

He dropped to his knees and straddled her thighs. With a dip of his head, he stole a kiss. "You're going to text Van and tell him to bring us food."

"He won't—"

He kissed her again. "Shut up and listen. You'll tell him I'm becoming the perfect little slave— Don't look at me like that. I can act out the damned requirements." Determination sharpened his eyes.

"Van will test you before the buyer's meeting tomorrow."

His face slacked. "Does the buyer expect to have sex with me at this meeting?"

The other boys she'd enslaved weren't virgins, and the buyers *did* fuck them during the introductions. But this deal was different in so many ways.

"I'll do everything in my power to prevent it." She filled her eyes with the truth of her words. "I promise."

"Then we'll get through the next few days and figure out the rest." His tone sobered. "But Liv?" He held her eyes, drew in a long breath. "Requirement number two is my limit. The only way I'd have sex with those men would be by force. Do you understand?"

She could hold her promise about the buyer's meeting. And she could calm down Van by sending him a text. Once he knew she was okay, he'd leave her alone to do her training.

It was the rest that made her want to throw up.

She nodded, her heart lodged somewhere in her stomach.

# TWENTY-THREE

Josh knelt in the center of the room, naked, and fixated on the nimble movements of Liv's fingers. His insides quivered from holding still for so long.

Crouched before him in her jeans and t-shirt, she tied a long coil of rope into loose bows, sliding his arms through the loops and cinching the knots along his sternum.

Flashes of dizziness reminded him he'd only eaten a couple energy bars. He nodded toward her phone. "Send Van the text, Liv."

She'd texted him an hour earlier to check in but had yet to request food. She slid another knot in place, her eyes narrowed in concentration on the laced web that began with a noose around his neck and intertwined a dragonfly pattern down his chest.

Her tongue touched her upper lip. "We're not ready for him yet."

The urge to suckle that taunting tongue sensitized his skin where it rubbed against the nylon bindings. The knotted bows formed taut sleeves over his arms, holding his elbows in an X over his stomach.

"You made a straight jacket from rope." He waited for the panic to set in, but all he felt was wonderment.

"I've learned how to do a lot of awful things." Painful memories pulled at the corners of her eyes. Then they were gone, and her calmness returned, flowing through the fluidity of her fingers as they moved down his abs.

The torturous caress of her full attention both soothed him and made him antsy. Van was probably prowling on the other side of the door. Or beating on it. She'd said it was soundproofed.

"Why are you the only one with a code to this room?" he asked.

Her rich dark eyes, lashes fanning thickly through slow blinks, were as arresting as her hands on the rope near his groin. She pulled his hips closer to her. "When I was returned by the man who bought me, Mr. E put me in Van's possession." She kept her eyes on her hands, plaiting and twisting the rope. "I requested to have the only code to the door, and I think Mr. E agreed because he knew if he didn't limit Van's access to me..." Her voice wobbled, strengthened. "I wouldn't have survived all these years if I had to live every minute under Van's thumb, sleeping in his bed with nowhere to escape."

Her courage knew no bounds. Maybe it was God working through her, but she radiated an inner strength he was certain she'd never acknowledged. "You've done a hellacious job surviving. You don't have it in you to give up."

"I would have." She glanced up, eyes hard, and returned to her rope work. "But this living arrangement, this room, has kept those thoughts at bay."

For how long? Mr. E could take it away any moment.

"Van's okay with it?" He peered into her eyes. "How long before he swings a chainsaw at that door?"

"He's accepted that this is the only way I'll be a part of his life." She yanked on a knot with more strength than was needed. "As long as I'm around, Van has an outlet for his desires. The virgin slaves remain virgin. Mr. E knows this and lets me keep the code."

His heart ached for her. She deserved a life beyond masks and locked doors and black eyes. Something about her, captor or not, brought out a fierce drive in him to take care of her, to serve her. Not that he could do anything with his hands tied, but she'd asked his permission before restraining him with rope. It was the *asking* that compelled his cooperation.

She wound the ends around his upper thighs, tightened the final knot, and sat back on her heels. Rather than studying her intricate work, she peered into his eyes, her posture motionless and her face framed by ribbons of chestnut hair.

When her silence stretched, he tilted his head. "What is it?"

A deep groove appeared between her eyes. "You're not broken or defeated." The side of her mouth tipped up into a trembling curve, making his chest swell against the restraints. "But you let me do this." A whisper.

When her gaze lowered, he bent his head to remain in her line of sight. "I have faith in you, Liv. You know how to handle Van. What's wrong?"

The furrow in her brow deepened. "This kind of bondage is about trust, not control." She traced a finger over the rope harness and adjusted a knot to line up with the others. "I would've never attempted it on one of the captives." She glanced at him through her dark lashes. "I practiced a lot on a borrowed mannequin."

Given the labyrinth of knots, it was a binding that couldn't be easily forced, a position he certainly wouldn't have volunteered before Mr. E's visit. He pressed his lips to her forehead. Maybe his trust was too soon, but somehow it had braided a bridge between them that was as complex and sturdy as the rope that bound him.

"You trust me." She wasn't asking, but disbelief creased her face.

He captured her parted lips, stroked his tongue over hers, tasting her sincerity, and straightened to behold her. "I trust your intentions."

Soft brown eyes stared back, her hand settling on his inner thigh. He felt that single point of contact through his whole body, warming and stirring. She stretched a finger and stroked down his semi-erect shaft. "You shouldn't."

His breath strangled. "Liv." He groaned, his penis jerking against her touch. "What are you doing?"

"Before I text Van, you need to memorize the requirements. A *perfect little slave* could recite them verbatim." She curled her fingers around the pulse between his legs, massaging him to hardness. "And you need to do it while I distract you."

She grabbed his nipple and twisted it to unholy hell, sparking pain through his chest. The rope between his arms and thighs halted the bow of his back.

"Arruugh!" He moaned for long seconds after she released him.

"What is requirement number one?"

He ground his teeth, reeling from the lingering bite of her fingers. "Slave can only have sex with felonious men—"

She yanked on his other nipple with a brutal pinch and let go. The sting thrummed through his body, and his groin heated, stiffening to the point of pain.

Her hand clenched around his erection. "Slave has never experienced sexual intimacy with a woman. Slave is heterosexual but hates women. He desires only his Master." She arched a slim eyebrow.

He repeated the requirement. "How would anyone know if I've slept with a woman?"

Those gorgeous eyes roamed his face. She trailed her other hand along his hairline, around his ear, and down his neck, watching the path of her caress. "Experience. Skill. Confidence. These things surface in a man's eyes when he regards a woman." Her gaze flicked to his, the hand on his penis sliding up and down. "Don't gape at me like that."

"Seriously?" He released a ragged breath. "You're stroking me."

"When we're in the presence of others, don't look at me at all. You need to practice that now."

If he was going to be tied up and naked around Van or the buyer, he wouldn't be looking at her with anything but panic.

"Tell me requirement number two." She added a second hand between his legs, fondling his balls while she twisted her wrist along his length, her heavy-lidded gaze clinging to his.

"Slave must—" A shudder rippled over him, his biceps flexing against the rope. "Service the Master. Slave's body is prepared and—" His release coiled, tightening, threatening. "You have to stop."

She leaned in and bit his lip. Hard. Consuming. The pang snapped his control, the build up tumbling over in a powerful wave of heat and sighing relief. His head dropped back on his shoulders, his body shaking in the constriction of rope.

As the bliss of his orgasm drifted from his muscles, he realized he'd closed his eyes. When he opened them, she stood above him, her cute little nose wrinkled in annoyance. He wanted to kiss it.

His lips twitched. "Um. I guess I need to work on requirement seven."

"No. Number seven is kneeling, one of the only fucking rules you haven't broken." She rubbed her eyes and glared at him. "Number three. Eyes down. Four. No clothes."

"I've got number four covered." He tried to check his smile, but his cheeks were persistent.

"Good job." Her monotone response matched her disapproving stare.

Hard to believe he'd considered her vicious. With the set of her stubborn jaw and her lips in a plump flat line, she looked decisively non-threatening. "You're adorable."

She spun, striding to the locked cabinet where she kept her crops, whips, and paddles. "You're patronizing me, you little prick."

Oh, he'd really ticked her off. Her aggravation vibrated with the slap of her feet on the floor. He peeked at his lap, and the sight of his come tightened his chest with guilt. Dammit, he needed to try harder.

She unlocked the cabinet and returned with something he knew existed but had never seen in person. Shaped like a cone and made of black rubber or plastic, the phallic shape sent a shiver of dread down his spine.

"No." He shook his head. "No way. Go get the flogger."

"I could beat you until you're bruised and bleeding, but it's ineffective." She squatted before him, her pretty features etched in thought. "You know why?"

The ropes suddenly felt tighter, scratchier. "Because I'm a terrible slave."

"The worst." Her free hand drifted to his ball sac, reawakening his bottomless well of arousal. "How often did you get a woody after a hard hit at football practice or during an excruciating exercise?"

He shifted his weight on his knees, her question poking at experiences he never spoke about. Feelings he'd wanted to express but never had a tolerant ear to whisper them to. Until now.

"On the farm…" He coughed, unable to loosen the discomfort tightening his throat. "Some of the grueling chores worked my body pretty good." His muscles would burn with exertion, his penis would rub against his jeans. He met her eyes.

"It made you hard."

As the room filled with weighted silence, he examined the expression softening the peaks of her lips and rounding the depths of her eyes. He knew her features wouldn't harden and twist with judgment. "Yeah."

She dipped her head, her breath tickling over his cheek, lifting her hand from his balls to toy with the hair behind his ear. "You get hard every time I punish you." She kissed his jaw and nibbled on his ear lobe, whispered, "Kinky pain whore."

Her teasing tone and the playful bite of her teeth on his neck exposed the girl she kept tucked away. His already excited heart hammered against his ribs.

"The problem is…" She turned her head to glower at him. "The whip lost its thrilling danger after the first time I used it. It takes you to an out-of-body place, and all that's left is the thrill." She held up the plug. "But this—"

"Is *not* going inside me." His pulse accelerated, and his rectum contracted.

"It is." She smiled, soft at the edges, but no less determined. "It's up to you if I'll lube it, if I'll be gentle, if I'll prepare you." She licked the tip of the plug, wetting it. "Requirement number ten."

His heart rate redoubled. Sweet mother, he didn't know that one. Sweat beaded on his nape, and his pecs twitched, ready to fight.

"Shh." She brushed a kiss on his chest between the crisscross of rope. "This is a new one. Slave will show gratitude for punishment and discipline."

His lungs sighed in relief. "Thank you, Mistress."

And just like that, their roles reverted. He understood why she rose and stripped down to her panties, why she tied a black kerchief around her nose and mouth, and why she gathered her composure into the unnatural stillness of dominance. It was her masked persona, the Deliverer who performed without mercy or emotion. To enforce the training. To deliver the punishments. To protect those she cared about.

But who protected *her*? Now he was one of the people she would come to defend. This certainty was a visceral grip of faith, and it filled him with a new sense of purpose. Her hidden expressions, costumes and nudity, and penchant for restraints were meant to disarm a slave. It was her cross to bear, and he would help her carry it.

As she repeated the rules over and over, he kept his eyes down with respect, his mouth shut in obedience, and his mind focused on memorizing her words.

Liv sent the text to Van, and thirty minutes later, she walked to the door and put her hand on the keypad. Josh was ready. As long as he didn't look at the yet-to-be-used butt plug she'd left on the mattress.

She glanced back, her shadowy gaze peering over the kerchief. "You can guess why I'm only in panties."

He raised his eyes, swallowed. The test with Van would be sexual in nature. Since she wasn't asking a question, he kept his guess to himself and drew a deep breath.

"I don't know what Van has planned, but he *will* test your limits." With her chin tilted up, she faced the keypad.

As she punched in the code, he knew she would do what was necessary for her family. He returned his attention to the floor and girded his spine.

# TWENTY-FOUR

The aroma of greasy food followed Van into the room. Josh's mouth watered. He couldn't stop the growl escaping his stomach, but he kept his lips clamped, his eyes down, and his knees on the floor.

A takeout bag dropped within grabbing distance, not like he could steal a French fry. The rope-entwined straight jacket held his arms firmly around his torso.

Van's ratty sneakers paused in the space between Josh and Liv, and the toes turned toward hers.

Without moving his head, Josh strained his upward line of sight, marking the tension in Van's legs as they flexed against the denim.

The man's broad shoulders curled forward, his hand lifting her chin gently.

"Liv." His whisper was strained, presumably from the sight of the bruises Mr. E left on her neck.

The distraught reaction set Josh's blood afire, considering the yellow-purple marks around her eye still lingered.

"Don't." She stepped back and turned away. *Good girl.*

Van stood motionless for a moment. Then he reached for her hand. She pulled it away before he made contact.

"What can I do to fix this?" Van gestured between her and himself.

She was impossible to read with her body turned away and her voice so damned wooden. "You could've warned me what he was planning *before* you left me unconscious, bleeding, half-strangled."

Van kept his back to Josh, his fingers flexing at his side. Seconds passed, indicating some kind of deliberation. "You're right, Liv. I fucked you over, and I hated every fucking minute of it."

As much as Josh didn't want to believe him, the man's voice cracked with soft-spoken guilt.

Eyes on the floor, Josh held his spine straight as Van shifted and sat before him.

He pulled a paper-wrapped burger from the bag and addressed Josh. "Sorry about the gun thing last night. That was a dick move on my part. We cool?"

Was this guy for real? If he glanced up, he'd probably get nicked by the sharp silver gaze of crafted bullshit.

"She's starving you, isn't she?" Van held the burger beneath his nose, taunting him with the heady fragrance of grilled meat and ketchup. "Go ahead. It's yours."

Not gonna lie. It was going to chafe like hell to eat from that hand, but he needed energy more than his pride. He opened his mouth.

"That pleasure belongs to his Mistress." Liv's bare feet moved into his periphery.

God love her. He would thank her later. With his mouth. On her satiny skin. Something to anticipate. His penis jerked.

Van lingered, the burger hovering before Josh. The hesitation produced a burgeoning hum that dragged beneath the skin. Unable to see their expressions, Josh was excluded from whatever unspoken communication passed above his head. Not peeking was torture.

At last, Van relinquished the food and traded places with her.

The soft curves of her bare breasts filled Josh's view. The impulse to reach out and run a fingertip over one of those pink nipples was consuming. Good thing his arms were restrained.

She took two bites for every one she gave him. From the unhurried offerings she placed on his tongue to the possessive hand curled on the juncture between his shoulder and neck, she radiated an aura that compelled lowered eyes, humbled gratitude, and an unquestioning desire to please her. No wonder the girl, Kate, had fallen so spectacularly into her subservient role.

But he was not a terrified slave, crawling in compliance to escape the bite of her whip. Initially, he was supposed to be emasculated, hopeless, empty. Mr. E changed the game when he threatened Liv. Now he was supposed to be the slave so consumed with fear that he would risk his life to make sure nothing happened to his Mistress. Instead, his heart drummed with faith in the power of God, in her courage, and in his ability to save her.

As she fed him, Van perched behind her on the mattress, hands clasped between his bent knees. "How did you get him to hold still for rope bondage?"

She brushed a thumb over the corner of Josh's mouth. "You may speak. Tell him how I did it."

They had discussed how the questioning might go. Since their plan didn't extend beyond surviving the buyer's meeting, they'd agreed honesty was the best approach.

He swallowed the fry she'd placed in his mouth, savoring the fried, salty taste. "I trust her." Oh, how he wanted to meet Van's eyes when he said that.

"Really?" Van's voice punched in disbelief.

"And I don't want to see her harmed again." His words, though rehearsed, came from an empowered place inside him. She'd already been hurt so much, but she was not beyond saving.

"You and me both, buddy."

His veins heated with rage. Did the hypocrisy burn Van's mouth as it huffed out?

The conversation fell quiet as she kept the food coming, brushing his lips under the guise of catching crumbs. With the hard floor grinding into his knees, he wanted to remove the distance between them, wanted to strip the kerchief that covered her nose and mouth, and plunge into her eyes. He wanted to be alone with her. Hell, he yearned to speed forward into the future. A future free of shackles. A future with her in it. He dared God to challenge his desires.

Two burgers, a cola, and a bag of fries later, his stomach settled.

Van lifted a foot and nudged her back. "Let's see what he's learned, Liv."

She stuffed the trash into the bag and set it aside. "Say the requirements in order with an eagerness and accuracy that will please your Mistress."

While Van made a decidedly sucky *buddy* in this ridiculous game, he seemed to have his temper under wraps. In fact, he was shockingly passive. Why?

Josh's shoulders stiffened with realization. If he messed up the buyer's meeting, if Liv was killed, Van would suffer the loss. The volatile bastard had just as much at stake.

He exhaled, "Yes, Mistress," and recited rules one through ten slowly and carefully, imagining himself performing each one for her, trusting her not to use his obedience against him.

Her finger caressed a warm path over his knee, her body blocking her affection from Van's predatory eyes. She removed her hand.

"Impressive." Van rose. "Show me how he will service his Master."

A flinch jerked Josh's insides, but he remained outwardly still on his knees. He knew this moment would come and told himself if she could endure Van's touch, he could, too. He waited for her command.

She reached back toward the mattress, but he couldn't see what she grabbed. She touched his jaw. "Look at me."

*With pleasure.* Connecting with her, by any means possible, would make this more bearable. As he raised his head, he leaned forward, subtly, into her personal space, inhaling the peppermint and lavender scent of her shampoo. Peering over the black kerchief, her magnetic eyes pulled him in further. Her pupils widened with an indiscernible emotion.

She held up the butt plug. "Requirement number eleven. Slave will wear and accept toys Master chooses to adorn him with." She paused, seemed to wrestle with her words. "You can open your mouth to Van's kiss or spread your ass for the plug. Both prepare you for your Master tomorrow, but which would please your Mistress now?"

The movement of her mouth paused beneath the cloth as if she were considering the answer, but he suspected her diabolical mind had already choreographed the proceedings from beginning to end.

Van crouched behind her, his eyes alight with interest, his toothpick seemingly forgotten as it lolled in the crook of his lips.

Josh's breaths quickened, his eyes searching hers. One flawless eye, one bruised, the surrounding skin furrowing as her eyebrows drew together. In the complexity of her gaze, he saw concern, a sense of responsibility, and maybe even possessiveness. If he read her correctly, she didn't want Van near him. Or maybe he was just projecting his own desire.

The kiss would be the least intrusive, and if it were with any other man, it might've been his preference. She'd warned him the plug would be used *eventually*, and he'd resolved to accept it *eventually*.

"The plug for now." Her tone was bored, bordering cruel, but the gentle look she shared with him helped smooth the tumble in his gut. Meanwhile, his nerves were shrieking in horror.

With a strong voice and an open expression, he embodied his consent. "Yes, Mistress."

She and Van rose, and she angled her mouth toward Van's ear. Whatever she whispered sent him bolting to her cabinet of tools.

Minutes later, Josh lay face down on the mattress, knees on the subfloor, arms roped around his torso, backside in the air. Shifting into his line of sight, she squirted gel from a tube over her fingers, making sure he saw her apply it to the plug.

He wished he had the tennis ball to slam against the wall and distract his impulse to scream and fight. Instead, he focused on something more soothing. Like the tender touch of her hand as it eased between his crack. The measured caress around the entrance she'd only ventured in the one time. And the fact that it was *her* pressing against the barrier and not the man climbing onto the mattress and reclining beside him.

Face-to-face, Van stroked the back of Josh's head. "Relax your rectum and push against the plug. I know it's scary, but you're in good hands."

He flinched inwardly, burning to crack the guy's skull. The cold hard tip of rubber pressed against the ring of muscle. He tensed instantly then forced his butt and legs to loosen. It must've been the work of God that kept his heart from tearing out of his chest.

The plug inched in, stretching, burning, building a terrifying pressure. He slammed his teeth together, his breath hissing, loud and fast.

Van released a long exhale. His eyes glazed over, and the torment etching his face was startling. "I bled a lot my first time. I was young. He was…huge." His hand cupped Josh's nape, twitched, his gaze refocusing on Josh. "My mom didn't keep good company. She was too blitzed to notice her companions' interest in me." His voice was soft, horrifyingly serious.

A sudden burn sparked in Josh's anus, followed by a dull fullness. She rubbed his gluts as his body adjusted to the intrusion. Breath by breath, his muscles relaxed.

Her footsteps retreated, and the bathroom faucet sputtered on. His legs trembled. With relief that it wasn't as bad as he'd expected. With Van's revelation.

Josh met his eyes and willed himself to listen if the man wanted to talk about it.

"You probably want to counsel me, yeah?" Van leaned up on his elbows and watched Liv's approach. "She's dragged all the messy details from me over the years. No counseling needed."

*That* was debatable. She'd said there was no relationship, but they shared a history, an intimate one. Hell, they had a child together. The thought turned his stomach. He resented their bond, whether or not it was fused in tragedy. Remembering them having sex made him sick with jealousy.

The direction of his thoughts was ludicrous in his trussed up position, face in the mattress, his rear plugged and clenching. Didn't he have enough to worry about?

Van moved to sit on the edge of the mattress. "I think my girl's going to put on a show for us."

*My girl.* Jealousy burned anew, hot and painful. But she didn't want Van. She hid in her room to escape him. The reminder cooled his blood but didn't extinguish the nauseating pang.

She snapped her fingers and pointed to the rug by the mattress. He'd told her he trusted her intentions. Still did. He scooted backward on his knees, the plug both discomforting and oddly stimulating.

Standing before him and removing her panties, she rested her hands on his shoulders. "Your eyes stay on my pussy."

# TWENTY-FIVE

Josh had seen her bared sex countless times, but he'd never stared long enough to take in the details. Out of awkwardness. Out of respect. But the mastery in her command and the potency of his arousal raised his eyes from the floor.

Wrong or not, it was a picture that would be forever branded in memory. Hairless, plump, taut flesh. The slit parted just enough to give him a glimpse of the dark, alluring depth within. When he'd washed her, he'd never ventured inside the crease. Would the delicate lips grip his finger? She was so small he couldn't imagine what it would feel like to slide his penis in there. Dear God, he wouldn't last more than a few thrusts.

"He's already hard." Van's voice held way too much awe as he crouched behind one of her spread legs and curled a hand around her thigh. His other hand held a purple silicone dildo, presumably what she'd sent him to fetch from the cabinet.

Would Van use it on her while Josh watched? Would the bastard have sex with her again? His heart raced, and his blood heated. Beneath the dread of Van's participation was a selfish hope that she would masturbate right there, so close to his face.

She took the dildo from Van and held it to Josh's lips. "Wet it."

His inhibitions fled as her free hand slid between her legs, fingers separating the folds and disappearing inside. He licked the silicone with a dry mouth, tried to gather spit, and spread it over the tip. The glide of her fingers between her slit and the hitch in her breath melted his body into a thrumming pulse of need.

At the edge of Josh's periphery, Van shifted stiffly, angled toward her, his breaths quickening.

She turned, kneeling on the mattress, and thrust her beautiful heart-shaped rear so close to Josh's face, he could see the freckle in the crease between her cheek and thigh. But the freckle faded next to the sinful view of her sex splitting her from anus to clitoris.

The smooth arches of her cheeks curved into the divide and led to folds of skin so pink and velvety and enthralling. A rush of wet air whistled past his teeth. The pulse in his erection intensified, quivering sensations through his body. He jerked his arms in the restraints and tried to distract his lust with rules. *No talking. No masturbating. No coming.* He groaned.

How was this training? Perhaps over time, he'd learn to hate it or resent her for putting him through it. Was that even possible?

She lowered her forehead to the mattress and reached the dildo between her spread thighs. The tip separated her folds, the soft-looking skin clinging to the silicone as it slid in, inch by inch. Sweat slicked his palms. The rope dug into his heaving chest.

She withdrew the toy, slid it back in. Out. In. The dildo glistened with her moisture, filling the room with a sucking sound as her channel swallowed it greedily. It was torture. It was beautiful. He wanted to put his mouth on her, his cock in her. He burned to know how deep he could go, how fast he could thrust, how long he could hold on while staring into her eyes and tasting her lips.

The pull of a zipper sounded beside him. Josh kept his eyes on Liv but could make out the movements of Van pushing down his jeans and taking himself in hand.

No. No, not Van. Not with her. Rage boiled to the surface, straining his muscles, searing his skin. He ground his teeth, seething to chase Van from the room. He couldn't do this, dammit. Not again. His arms twisted in the rope. He had to get free, to protect her, to fight for her.

A grunt muffled beside him, followed by a shouted exhale. Van jerked, shoulders twitching, and groaned out a sigh.

Josh was, at once, relieved and revolted by Van's orgasm. But how quickly would he be ready to go again?

Her dark eyes flickered over her shoulder, skimming over Van's groin, and collided with Josh's gaze. There was a softening in her expression, in the skin exposed above the kerchief, as she accelerated the strokes of the dildo. The shared eye contact made him want to hold her tight and glide his length deep, their bodies so close, so intimate, he would learn everything about her. Every bump and turn inside. Every dream, every secret, hidden away in every nook and crevice of her heart. He craved that knowledge more than he'd ever craved anything in his life. He craved *her*.

His hips rocked, his erection stabbing the air, the plug sharpening the sensations. She flexed her pelvis, riding the dildo in sync with his movements. Their eyes held, her desire feeding his. Veins pulsed in his cock, his arousal coiling, straining, unable to reach the relief he so desperately needed. He couldn't come without stimulation. He couldn't come without permission.

She blinked at Van, back to him. Josh's body shuddered. His penis ablaze, it swelled further, stretching painfully.

"Hey," Van said gently, touching his leg, shooting electric sparks over his oversensitive skin. "Let me help you."

Josh glanced down at his shockingly red and swollen erection jutting from beneath the ropes, his balls so tight they'd disappeared into his body. His brain muddled, and his body overheated. Was this the plan? Work him up to the point that he'd accept Van's touch?

He raised his head, meant to search her eyes, but couldn't see past the drugging beauty of her flesh wrapped around the thrusting dildo.

God forgive him, he jerked his chin up and down, breathless, lost to lust, crazed in his urgency to climax.

"Open your mouth." Van's words breathed in his ear. "Accept my kiss."

Anything to keep that man away from her. He stretched his jaw, instantly, wantonly, his butt flexing around the plug. Lips captured his, tongues whipping and battling for control. Exhales pummeling in the hot trap of their sealed mouths. Van's breath was sour and terrifyingly sweet. They kissed like they would fight. Rough, merciless, impassioned. And seething with rage.

A large hand gripped his erection, and he surged up on his knees, slamming his cock into the clench of fingers. With Van's head angled to the side, Josh kept his eyes glued on her clasp of skin as it stretched around the toy. Was she imagining the dildo was him?

He thrust his hips, having sex with her in his mind, panting noisily, his peak coiling tighter and tighter. Almost there—

"You will not come." Her voice rasped at the edge of his awareness.

Frustration slammed into his gut. The hand on his cock was an extension of his own hand, stroking him at a hard and consistent pace. The tongue in this mouth shoved and licked.

He hung on the precipice, balancing, trembling to rush forward. Her command was unbearable. *No coming without permission. No coming without—*

Ughhh, her pink folds looked so wet, her toned thighs flexing, her fingered grip on the dildo blanching her knuckles. He wasn't going to make it. He tensed against it. Focused on the heat of Van's mouth, the coarse stubble scratching over his jaw.

"Come, boy." She panted. "Come for your Mistress."

Her command tore the orgasm from every frenzied nerve inside him, surging forth in powerful, shivering waves. He rocked into the fist around his cock, his fingers digging into the rope on his torso, pressing into the man's mouth on his, and moaned a hoarse, strained exhale.

His body tingled, trembled, sighed. He collapsed, shoulders deflating, the plug pressing against his heels, throbbing to the beat of his blood.

She set the dildo aside, squatted before him, and removed the cloth from her face. Van raised his arm, his wrist striped with come, and licked it clean in one swipe.

Josh shuddered. Seriously, that was jacked up.

Van held out his tongue, lathered in semen, and leaned toward Liv.

What the unholy hell? She wouldn't. *No way.*

Her moment of hesitation passed quickly. She caught his jaw between her hands and drew his tongue into her mouth, her eyes squeezed shut.

Every muscle in Josh's body stiffened, the urge to interfere overwhelming. He trusted her intentions. She was playing a game. He bit down on his cheek and waited.

When Van's hand shoved between her thighs, his fingers slipping inside her, Josh jerked forward.

She broke the kiss, caught Van's wrist, and pushed his hand away.

"Thanks for the burgers, Van." She rose, gathered up the trash, and entered the code at the door.

A red flush stormed over Van's expression. He stood, yanking his jeans into place, and strode toward her, his voice low. "You're sleeping with me. Get him out of the ropes. I'll wait."

# TWENTY-SIX

Fear, anger, and jealousy stormed through Josh, pulling at his insides and squeezing his ribs tight. He strained his eyes to keep his chin down while glaring over his shoulder.

Liv's arms lolled at her sides, her head tilted up, her face a blank canvas. "Another time, Van. I'm working." She smiled, but it was tight at the corners. "You owe me an orgasm. Don't think I won't collect."

Van raised his hand, caught a few strands of her loose hair in his fist, and yanked. His eyes flicked to Josh.

*Crap.* Josh dropped his gaze, praying he didn't rouse suspicion about his obedience.

"Okay, Liv." Van sighed, his voice tired. "Get through the meeting tomorrow. Then come to me."

The unmistakable smack of lips followed, colliding with wet sucking sounds. The door clicked shut.

The gravity of what Josh had just participated in settled like lead in his gut. The burger and fries gurgled to come up. He jumped to his feet. "He needs a damned padded room."

She slumped against the door, her stoic mask falling away, exposing the heartbreaking expression of a trapped woman. Her eyes fluttered shut.

He moved to her, the rope web pulling on his thighs, the plug rubbing sore tissues. He leaned into her space, frustrated he couldn't hold her, and pressed his forehead against hers. "It worked, at least."

"For now. We still have to get through tomorrow."

And the next nine weeks. He inhaled the scent of her skin at her temple and let her closeness soothe his nerves.

"Do you resent what I did tonight?" Her voice was small, unsteady.

His sins were mounting. Of course, he hadn't been given a choice, but he *orgasmed in another man's fist*. Did it really matter in the scope of their situation?

"No, Liv. You got me past some pretty big barriers. If I hadn't been so horny for you" — he dropped his head on her shoulder, laughed, groaned — "that would've gone much worse." He straightened and looked into her eyes. "What was the semen-licking thing about?"

A ragged sigh pushed past her lips. "It's his thing. He does it during training sessions. In the past, it wasn't a battle I'd chosen to fight. Changing that tonight would've stirred up questions about us."

*Us.* The sound of that stirred up all kinds of questions. But that was for another time.

Her hand traveled over his butt and gripped the plastic base of the plug. She leaned up and bit his lip as she pulled it out with one tug.

He blew out a breath, the muscles in his backside clenching away the tension. But his relief was accompanied by a flush that spread through his body. She'd awoken something in him, and he wanted…more. He followed her to the sink.

She washed the plug and tackled his ropes. As the knots loosened so did his knees. He perched against the edge of the vanity and relaxed into the satiny feel of her hands trailing over his chest.

Her breasts swayed beneath the movements of her toned arms as she freed each length of rope. He wanted to lean in and lick her parted lips. He wanted to lick her everywhere, and his penis responded immediately to that thought. Her gaze lowered to his glaring arousal, and a slow smile built on her gorgeous face. She flicked her eyes to his and shook her head, grinning.

"I wasn't like this before I met you." He laughed. It was kind of true.

"Bullshit. You just wore a jockstrap to keep your endless boners tucked away."

"Actually…" He puffed his chest defensively. "I tucked it into the waistband of my briefs."

A laugh bubbled from her, and she tossed the last of the ropes on the floor. "Let's take a shower, you dirty boy."

Showering with her was a thrilling mix of gratification and torture. He knelt at her feet, caressing soap along the contours of her slender body. Every curve he stroked reminded him how desperately he wanted her. His breaths quickened, and his hands lingered on her inner thighs, his erection oh-so painfully aware of her naked proximity.

His fingers ached with the need to touch her breasts. So he did with a lather of bubbles and a devoted hand. He was in love with her body, the perfect size of her chest, the dramatic dip of her waist, the pink flesh between her legs. Simply watching her stirred a shiver of pleasure through his groin and a fluttering feeling near his heart.

There was nowhere in the world he'd rather be than on his knees, worshiping her body. It felt *right*. The thought should've made his blood run cold. Instead, it flooded his chest with a fulfilling warmth.

When they finished the shower, they turned off the lights and collapsed on the mattress.

He pulled her back to his chest and hooked an arm around her waist, her clean minty scent clearing his head. He'd become accustomed to her nudity, but with both of them bare in this position, it felt new, intense. Her belly warm beneath his hand, her feet sliding over his shins, he couldn't quiet the endless stirring he felt in her presence.

"You're hard." There was a smile in her voice.

"You're naked. And I'm going to burn in hell."

Her musical laugh lifted through the darkness. "For snuggling with the devil?"

"The devil with the voice and heart of an angel." He buried his nose in the soft damp strands of her hair. "I want you so damned much, Liv."

The curve of her body along the length of his lay motionless, unresponsive.

How many times had a captive made the same declaration to her? Damn his big mouth. "That doesn't mean I'm going to—"

"You don't want me." Her whisper cracked. "You want...someone who deserves you."

An ache tightened his chest. He heard her. Not her words but *her*. For a fraction of a moment, he heard the girl he'd been searching for. The girl who yearned to be loved. "Will you do something for me?"

She tensed against him.

He caressed his hand from her belly to her breastbone and settled it over the galloping beat of her heart. "When it's just you and me, lose all those guarded layers. Let me see you." He raised up on his elbow and strained his eyes through the dark to make out the outline of her face. "Don't hide this from me." He tapped the spot over her heart.

A noise hitched in her throat. "It's ugly in there, decayed by lies and shame, endlessly bleeding for all the lives I've ruined. You're the eighth reason I don't deserve affection."

Eight slaves worth of guilt. He wanted to ask where they were, if she could trace their buyers. But those questions would derail the conversation and dredge up the one thing they hadn't discussed. His future. "That's not who you are, Liv."

142

"Don't do this."

The anguish in her whisper gutted him. He pushed through it. "Don't do what?"

"Don't make me feel things for you." Her voice rattled. "It will end badly."

So much fear and hurt. He wanted to take it from her, longed to heal her. But she needed to open herself up and let him in.

"You think having feelings for someone puts them in danger?" He was in danger whether she cared for him or not.

Her breaths quickened.

"Did you have a relationship with any of the others?" he asked.

Had she fallen for a captive and sold him into slavery? No amount of praying could have prepared him for the answer.

"I've never been in love." A weighted exhale. "And I've only had sex with one person in my life."

His pulse spiked. She'd told him her original buyer hadn't touched her before he tested and rejected her, but the rest? No sex with slaves? No dating between captives? Maybe he should've been relieved, but all he could feel was outrage. The only intimacy she'd known was with a person who coerced her, raped her, and beat her. "Do *not* let him dictate your self-worth, Liv."

Her entire body went rigid. "Do *not* preach your self-righteous bullshit. This is not a therapy session."

Though her reaction made his hands curl into fists, he knew he'd plucked a nerve. It was progress. With regard to her irritation, he could fix that.

He rolled her to her back and took her mouth, tasting the mint of her toothpaste, relishing the instant stretch of her jaw. She welcomed him with a heated gasp and a teasing tongue, swirling and whipping and stealing his breaths. He ran his hands down her arms, up her ribs, lifting and kneading the fullness of her breasts.

She licked and sucked his lips, shooting tingles across his skin. Her fingertips grazed the arch of his butt and brushed a trail of warmth along his spine. Each of her caresses, every breath of her attention, flowed through him and settled between his legs, aching, hardening, needing. Too soon, she tried to lean back and break the kiss.

He surged forward, deepening the reach of his tongue, clinging to the connection, wanting more, wanting all of her. "Let me inside of you." He rocked his erection against her thigh, groaning, wanting in her so badly. "Please, Liv."

"No." Her tone was a sharp prick. The rejection cut.

He dropped his face against her neck, moaned. There were dozens of reasons why she would refuse him. He needed to know *her* reason. "Tell me why."

She pushed on his chest until he conceded a few inches of space. "I've been where you are. I gave the wrong person my virginity and have resented him every second since." Her hand cupped his jaw and fell away.

He had a long way to go on salvaging her self-worth if she put herself in the same category as Van.

"Fine, Liv." He blew out a breath. "We'll work on righting your perceptions."

"We're not—"

He pressed two fingers over her lips. "Let me touch you. I've been here eight days and haven't seen you orgasm once." He released her mouth to trace the line of her neck.

"Just hold me?" Her request was tender in its delivery, but potent in its significance.

"Gladly." He curled around her back and tucked a knee between her legs. His hand on her breast, his heart paced in tune with hers.

Holding her, melding with her, his virginity felt so inconsequential. This connection extended far beyond a physical union. He'd give her anything. He wanted to give her everything.

"Liv?"

"Mm."

"You said there were twelve requirements. You've only given me eleven."

She laced her fingers through his and held their hands to her chest. "Requirement number twelve. Slave will not sleep in Master's bed."

His laugh coaxed hers, and they tumbled into comfortable silence.

The ceiling's A/C vent breathed a steady whoosh. He tried to sleep, but his mind wouldn't shut off as he traced through the events of the night. "You awake?"

"Yeah."

"Why did Van pull out your hair?"

A sigh. "It's his thing."

It was a common occurrence? "He has a lot of *things*."

"You have no idea." She wiggled her back closer against his chest. "Go to sleep. We've got a four hour drive tomorrow."

*The meeting with the buyer.*

He would leave the attic, taunted with freedom, enchained by the threat on her life.

# TWENTY-SEVEN

*Crack.*

Liv raised the four-foot stock whip, the rigid handle sweaty in her palm, her stomach twisting. They had to leave for the meeting in one hour.

She swung again. *Crack.*

He flattened his hands on the wall, feet spread on the subfloor, and accepted each strike with a twitch in his sculpted back. No chains, no clothes, no words. When she'd told him she had to mark him, he'd stripped wordlessly and gripped the nearest wall. The knot in her gut doubled.

Mr. E had taught Van the art of whip cracking, and they used her body as Van's cutting target. Van eventually passed the skill to her. But it didn't matter if she was on the end of the handle or the fall, she had never experienced the kind of trust evidenced in the relaxed muscles before her.

That he would find credibility in her despite the cruelty she'd inflicted upon him twisted her insides.

She snapped back the single tail, popped it forward, and let the fall lash his upper thigh. *Crack.*

His legs trembled and his back rippled, but he refused to move, bound by trust alone.

Her heart squeezed, but she kept the whip moving over her shoulder, elbow in. A hairpin wave uncurled like an extension of her arm. *Crack.*

Another welt joined the others striping his back, ass, and thighs. His head dipped between his braced arms, the hair at his nape damp with sweat.

She swung her arm back. Held it.

Every strike left a new scar inside her. No more. She dropped the whip, her blood beating cold. "I'm done."

Turning, he closed the distance, cupped her jaw, and rested a hand on her hip. "I'm kind of starting to like those feverish little love taps."

A glimpse of his erection confirmed it.

"Kind of starting?" She sighed. "You've been getting stiffies under my whip since day one."

If he weren't locked in her room, facing an unknown future, maybe she wouldn't feel so sick about her part in it. Maybe she would wrap her legs around his waist and fuck him like she'd wanted to the moment she first saw him.

But he deserved a good, clean girl. She drew in a slow breath and raised her eyes.

His smile creased his clean-shaven complexion, lighting up the pale glow of his green eyes and chasing away some of her overflowing guilt. It also wobbled her footing as his Mistress.

She glared at him, her insides melting under the warmth of his affection. "Remove your hand from my face, boy."

"What's your last name?" His hand dropped, but only as far as the bust of her corset, fingertips caressing the pillow of her breasts above the binding. He bit his lip, watching her with a lopsided grin.

Fuck her, he was so damned charming. She emptied her expression. "I'll break your fingers."

He arched a challenging eyebrow.

She arched one in return.

He ducked his head and took her mouth, lips brushing, tongue teasing, flicking, kindling a slow-burning fire. His hands traveled around her ribs and clutched her back, tugging her close. He ate at her mouth, and she met him lick for lick.

She loved his kisses, his confidence, his stubbornness. She loved every goddamned thing about him. He only had to glance in her direction, and the floor dropped away. She was freefalling, riding the wind of his breaths, hoping he'd catch her.

She rolled her hips forward, the hard heat of his desire jabbing her hip.

"Reed," she breathed. "Liv Reed."

His lips floated along her cheek, his smile tickling her jaw, one hand returning to her breast, curling fingers beneath the binding on her corset. "Are you worried, Liv Reed?"

By using her name, he was prodding her to say his. But she needed the designations to resume her role. Just needed to get through the meeting.

She stepped back, chilled by the distance she'd put between them.

"My worry is none of your concern, boy. Stand straight. Shoulders back. Eyes down."

He bent his knees to meet her eyes. His grip on her hips was hard and soft all at once. "Then whose concern is it?"

Her heart fractured. *Think about Mom and Mattie.* "If the buyer is satisfied and doesn't back out after tonight, Mr. E will send new videos." She left out the part about watching them with Van. She would deal with that detail later.

His jaw slackened, and his arms fell to his sides. "All right." He straightened, squared his shoulders, and lowered his eyes. "Will you explain why you just whipped me?"

She clicked through the room in her thigh-high boots, the stiff leather mini-skirt pinching her legs and shortening her strides. "The buyers aren't just purchasing slaves. They're paying for the training of their *property*." The cold words shivered through her.

"And the marks on my body show you've been beating me properly?" He leaned a shoulder against the wall, arms crossed, unabashedly nude.

A swallow dragged down her throat, her skin tight with a strange, intense emotion. With the others she'd delivered, she experienced remorse, regret, self-hatred. With him, she burned with a sense of possessiveness.

She grabbed his jeans from the trunk and tossed them to him. "The slave's obedience during the introduction proves the validity of the training." She moved to the cabinet. "Since the sale is not final until delivery, Mr. E claims fresh welts are a marketing tactic. *Seals the deal.*" Mr. E's words. She unlocked the door and removed what she needed, avoiding his eyes. "Sadists get excited seeing a body marked up."

Her breath strangled. She couldn't tell him how cruel these buyers were at these meetings. She didn't want to give him any more reasons to run.

Clothing rustled, sounding his approach. "Look at me."

She raised her chin, fell into his eyes.

"We'll get through this."

His affirmation gave her strength. She rubbed arnica into his welts and gave him Tylenol, something she'd done for every slave after every beating. Then she held up the long rope of chain in her hand. "Ready?"

He answered her in a heady, tongue-swirling, toe-curling kiss.

Ten minutes later, he followed her into the outer chamber. The girl lay on the cot, her eyes closed. Liv suspected she feigned sleep to avoid attention. The thought didn't help the knot in her belly.

Josh walked beside her, wearing only his jeans and boots. Chains wrapped his torso from neck to waist and locked his forearms together. Metal cuffs secured his wrists to the links on his chest.

The restraints she hated most forced his hands into fists against his sternum, encasing them in a tangle of strong wire. The strands of metal twined in and around his knuckles and thumbs, preventing him from straightening his fingers. He couldn't clasp a door handle or squeeze the trigger on a gun. The gun she would carry and hoped she didn't have to use.

Van was waiting in the kitchen with lunch. She ate her burrito in silence, feeding her prisoner between bites. Van watched with panic straining the edges of his eyes. He feared these meetings as much as she.

Van wasn't allowed to join them. The first time they met a client together in her role as a deliverer ended with Van's fist in the buyer's face. He hadn't liked the way the man was gaping at her. Fortunately for Mom and Mattie, the transaction went through despite the *misunderstanding*. Since that night, she was the only face of the operation.

But without Van's overbearing protection, she was on her own. And given this buyer's expressed hatred for women, the clench in her stomach was threatening to double her over.

She forced resolution into her knees and stood. "Time to go."

With her phone, a hood, and a long scarf in hand, she snapped her fingers and walked to the garage and the waiting van.

The van's only two windows and windshield were tinted to conceal the interior but not enough to risk getting pulled over. She and Van restrained Josh on the floorboard in the cargo area. He lay on his back, eyes on his boots, retractable tie-down straps holding him in place.

She wedged a ball gag in his mouth and covered his body and face with a sheet, smothering her unproductive emotions with long, deep breaths. Then she climbed behind the wheel and rolled down the window.

Van opened the garage and approached her door. "I put the cooler in the back."

"Thank you." She meant it. She hadn't remembered to pack dinner, wasn't thinking past the meeting.

He handed her a small LC9 handgun and a disposable phone through the window. "He'll call at seven o'clock."

The clock on the dash read *3:58 PM*.

"Take 35 south until he calls. He'll tell you where to go from there."

She nodded, gut churning.

He placed a hand on her jaw and a kiss on her opposite cheek, over her scar. She held miserably still as he kissed the corner of her mouth then fully on her lips. The skin around his mouth was colder, harder than Josh's smooth complexion. The movements of his lips forced, pried, and dug in. The scent of his breath wasn't unpleasant, but it was *wrong*.

His hand fell away. "Come back in one piece."

"I always do." Key in the ignition, she started the van and backed out.

He stood in the driveway, hands in his pockets, his expression tight, worry rimming his eyes. If she never returned, that would be the last look she saw on his face. Her chest hurt, a complicated pain.

Ten minutes outside of Temple, she pulled into a vacant parking lot, tucked the gun in her thigh-high boot, and climbed into the back. A whisper in her head begged her to not to deter from the routine. Slaves always rode in the back.

Would he cause her to wreck in an attempt to escape? What if she was pulled over by a cop?

She didn't listen to logic as she yanked back the sheet and removed the gag.

"I can't...I don't want you back here...like this." She pinched the bridge of her nose.

What the hell was she doing?

She raised her eyes, clung to the calm strength in his. "Will you try to run?"

# TWENTY-EIGHT

"Not going anywhere without you, Liv." The intensity in Josh's eyes slammed into her chest, knocking her shoulders loose and freeing her lungs.

She hadn't trusted another person since Mom, and experiencing that feeling again was thrilling. *And stupid.*

Releasing the straps, she waited, frozen beneath the gravity of her decision.

He rose, sidling past her, the chains straining across his back and arms, his jeans molding distractedly to his ass. He dropped into the front passenger seat.

With a glance at his wired hands, he faced the windshield and let his head fall on the head rest. "Will you buckle my seat belt?"

Her heart hit the floorboard. More restraints. More trust she didn't deserve. Maybe some day they could drive to an unknown destination without shackles and stomach-curdling anxiety. They could sing along to music on the radio and talk about the future. They could dine together in a restaurant, and maybe he would hold her hand.

Her hopes died in her chest. She'd surrendered her chance at love the day she roller-bladed to Van's car. There would be no carefree car rides or dreams about the future. There was only her videos and his chains and the man who awaited their arrival.

As she drove, he sat sideways in his seat, arms locked to his chest, watching her with a maelstrom of thoughts turning behind his eyes.

She chewed on the inside of her cheek. "What are you thinking about?"

"Why does Mr. E require ten weeks of training?"

This would be difficult to explain to a guy who didn't fit the hostage mold.

"He allows the stages of captivity to run its course. Panic and denial consume the initial seconds to hours. Hostility and escape attempts happen in the first few weeks." She swallowed. Never had she considered allowing captives to ride up front on their way to an intro meeting. Two weeks into their confinement, and their eyes burned with a desperate need to escape.

The pale green eyes studying her were patient, thoughtful, and nothing she was accustomed to dealing with.

He rolled his lips. "And after the first few weeks?"

She stretched her neck, eyes on the cars zipping along beside them. "True acceptance is gradual and doesn't fully materialize until the first couple months. Acceptance is necessary for the kind of slave Mr. E is selling. One who can follow his Master around without noticeable restraints." Complete and total submission. Broken and hopeless.

"Eight slaves in seven years, if you count me." His steady gaze warmed her face. "Nine, if you include yourself. That's little over a captive a year. What do you do the rest of the time?"

"We hunt. Our selection process is based on the buyer's requirements, family and social situations, but most importantly, the captive's ability to conform. The latter takes months of surveillance to determine the ideal candidate."

He shook his head. "You watched me for weeks and —"

"I knew." Her stomach clenched, conflicted and lost. "I knew you weren't the right choice for this." She met his eyes and found her way. "You were the right choice for *me*. When I saw you, I couldn't walk away."

A smile tipped the side of his mouth. "There's my girl, honest and open. Was that so hard?"

Her chest lightened, her pulse pumping in an untroubled rhythm. "You're easy to talk to." *And easy to love.*

As she drove, she explained what she knew of Mr. E's network, how he never had contact with the clients, and how he'd created a referral system for new buyers. "Each buyer must pass along a reference at the intro meeting. It's Mr. E's requirement in the contract. Since I'm the only one who meets face-to-face, Mr. E preserves his and the clients' anonymity. Once the delivery is made and the transaction is sent, we never hear from them again." *There's so much more to that last part.*

His silence pulled at her skin, scratching with unasked questions. No doubt he was thinking about how impossible it would be to find her previous captives. If he asked where they were, she would lie to him the way she lied to herself. They had to be dead to her, because the truth was too risky, for him and everyone involved.

When he finally spoke, his question surprised her. "Are there female buyers?"

She imagined him growing hard beneath another woman's whip, and a double knot of jealousy tightened her tone.

"You think a female buyer would've made this easier for you?" It was unfair to accuse, and she immediately wanted to take it back.

He sucked his teeth at her, his voice low and aggravated. "I'm struggling to understand how I'm supposed to be a straight guy who hates women."

She flicked the blinker and changed lanes. "There was one female buyer. She wanted a male slave." A corporate, power-charged bitch with a chip on her shoulder. "I don't know what prompted the unusual demand of misogyny with this one, but it's imperative you give the impression that you despise me and any other woman who might be present."

A miserable silence followed as they watched the open pastures blur by. How would someone *make* a person hate women? It was an impossible requirement, but she'd known that going in.

She grabbed a pack of cigarettes from the console, cracked the window, and lit one. "Recite the requirements. The better you know them, the easier it will be for you to embody them."

He narrowed his eyes on her cigarette. Oh, he wanted to scold her, and if they were on their way to somewhere normal, he probably would have pulled out his preachology. Instead, he smirked and dictated the rules. Listening to him practice the loathsome words, knowing he was doing it for her, made her want him with a ferocity that burned the backs of her eyes and swallowed her destination.

He repeated the twelve requirements with fewer and fewer errors, until he relayed them perfectly. His body molded to the words, his chin dropping, thighs opening, no hint of resistance in his voice. She knew he wasn't losing himself. He was acclimating. For her.

Her body heated and tightened. He was the strength and heart of the most dangerous jump. He was the soul of bravery wrapped in chains. He would never fall, no matter how much metal weighted him down. He was a man who loved selflessly and honestly, and she was taking him to a monster who would slice him open and fuck the incision.

She gripped the wheel with two fists, unable to steer off course, unable to save him from herself.

An hour into the drive, flat fields tumbled into the scattered tower blocks of Austin.

"I grew up here." Her voice sounded distant to her ears. Memories could tear her apart, but they were there, gathering in the clouds that hovered over the metropolis. "Just a few miles that way."

He turned to face her. "What was your childhood like?"

"Spent a lot of time up there." She pointed at the blue sky that spanned beyond the reinforced concrete and steel. "When I wasn't at school, I was jumping with Mom." She smiled past the burn in her throat. "I used to sing to the first-time jumpers. Mom said it calmed them, but it's so noisy on the plane—"

"Sing to me." His gentle tone competed with the hard set of his jaw.

She wanted to, desperately needing the distraction. She began with "Pretty Face" by *Sóley*, letting the misty notes rise to her lips and carry them out of her hometown.

When she hummed the song to a close, he regarded her as a lover might, affection softening his eyes and lips, his shoulders curling forward as if reaching toward her.

"Gives me chills, Liv. Every damned time. Your beauty isn't just an experience for the eyes. It breathes through the ears and evokes a reaction so consummating it claims the soul."

Her boot slipped off the gas pedal. She regained her footing but not her voice. It was flattened somewhere beneath her galloping heart.

"I can feel you." He leaned back, inhaled deeply. "Inside me. Everywhere. You own me. You will always own me, and I will walk through hell to keep it that way."

Eyes on the road, her breath shivered from her lungs, cracking her voice. "You own me, too."

"I know." He pinned her with those mesmerizing pale eyes. "Sing another one."

She shuffled through her favorite atmospheric tunes, serenading him, drawing out every minute they were side by side, beyond the prison walls, speeding in the same direction.

An hour south of San Antonio, her phone buzzed in her lap. They both jumped and stared at one another until it buzzed again. She lifted it to her ear.

"Take 85 west toward Asherton." The buyer's voice was suave, smooth, and thick with a Latino accent. "There's an abandoned railway station." He gave the address and disconnected.

She entered it into the GPS. "One hour away." And minutes from the Mexican border.

How easy it would be to disappear. She could toss the phone Mr. E tracked her on. Maybe he wouldn't try to find her. But she couldn't escape the news coverage. His promise to punish her with national headlines of Mattie's death made her hands shake. Her fingers turned to ice on the steering wheel.

Josh's gaze was tangible, pressing into her skin. "You okay?"

"It's just a meet and greet." She angled her head to see his sharp expression. "I won't let anything happen to you."

Muscles contracted in his arms as he tried to pull his hands from his chest. "I can't repeat those words to you, Liv. Not when I can't use my arms."

"You don't need your arms. Focus on the requirements and remember to hate me."

He reclined in the seat and stared at the roof. "Right."

An hour later, she stopped a mile outside the GPS destination on a vacant gravel road. "Bathroom break."

She released her nervous bladder into the dust-covered weeds. Then she pushed down his jeans and held his cock so he could do the same. No words were uttered when he returned to his seat in the van, when she unlaced and removed his boots, or when she stripped his jeans and left him bare.

With a tremble in her hands and an ache in her chest, she covered his trusting eyes with a black hood. "This is for both of us." An accidental glance between them could be fatal if the buyer was perceptive.

As she stepped back to close the door, she hesitated for one heart-clenching second. She didn't deserve him, but goddammit, Joshua Carter was hers.

The black shroud of night held still and patient, coaxing her to risk a stolen moment. She climbed onto his naked thighs and lifted the hood just enough to expose his lips.

The first kiss was for him. A brushing of lips, a promise of protection. The second kiss was for her. A deep-reaching dance of her selfish tongue, a curl of love with a man who deserved so much more.

She lowered the hood, slid off his lap, and left him panting.

"Liv?"

"The requirements begin now. Who am I? Say it."

"Mistress."

She shut the door on the hiss of his breath through his teeth, wrapped her hair, nose, and mouth in a long scarf, and drove to the red dot on the GPS.

A single story building squatted, tired and alone, beside overgrown railroad tracks. Surrounded by shadowed fields and woods, no one would stumble by this end-of-the-road depot. A black sedan parked in the empty lot. No license plates. It looked outrageously sleek and out of place beneath the sagging gloom of the unkempt property.

She checked the handgun's concealment in her boot, tucked her phone in the other boot, and guided Josh to the door.

Her strides glided over the crumbling sidewalk with precision, shoulders cut back, lungs regulated, her thoughts beating to the seditious hymns of "Ghostflowers" by *OTEP*.

# DELIVER

She was a deliverer, a killer, a soulless captor.
She shoved through the door.

# TWENTY-NINE

Over the years, the intro meetings had instilled certain expectations in Liv's mind. The buyers were paranoid, often armed and protected by bodyguards, and always masked. As Liv led Josh inside behind her, gripping the chain at his waist, her sphere of preconceptions evaporated, along with the air from her lungs.

The door creaked closed, and she tried and failed to shield his too-large frame with her smaller one. He bumped into her back, his head hooded and his body tight with tension.

A man reclined in a dusty chair at the center of the room, seemingly unconcerned with the grime rubbing onto his expensive suit. He wore no mask, and there were no obvious bulges marking concealed weapons. Even more unnerving, there were no bodyguards. He was either stupid, confident, or planning to kill her. Maybe all three.

Fifty extra pounds lolled over his belt and tested the button threads on his shirt. Late-forties, round nose, bald head, his oily gaze greased through the air, slicked past her, and clung to Josh's nude body.

But what made the hairs on her neck bristle was the naked woman restrained to the ceiling. She stood off to the side, in the shadowed edge of the room, staring out of twitchy, unfocused eyes. Her arms stretched over her head, tethered to the rafters, her feet weighted to the floor with chunks of broken sidewalk.

Thank fuck for the hood over Josh's head. He was temporarily oblivious to the depravity she'd led him into.

A ring gag held the woman's jaw open, secured in place with straps around her tangled black hair. Her tongue rolled in her mouth, pushing saliva through the ring and down her chin. A reflective orange collar cinched her throat. Belts fitted around her waist and upper thighs, connecting a wide strap that covered her vaginal and anal entry points. To fuck her, he would have to remove the three padlocks dangling between her legs.

If he hated women, why did he have a female slave? Most likely, misogyny was the reason he kept the woman confined in a chastity belt. So why did he want Josh?

Her stomach tightened painfully, but she forced her most dominant voice through the scarf on her mouth. "This is an introduction only. You will view what I've brought. If you approve, your down payment is required in the form of a phone number. As you know, we operate on referrals only. Call me Deliverer. What do I call you?"

"Traquero." His accent slithered with his gaze, his neck arching so he could steal a better look at Josh.

A yellow bulb drenched the wood floors and plaster walls in a dirty glow. At the perimeter of the light, the bound woman began to writhe. A moment later, she shrieked, muscles convulsing, drool stringing from her gaping mouth.

Behind Liv, Josh's breath hitched. She tightened her grip on his chain, a silent command to remember his role.

The woman's chin fell upon on her chest, and she drooped in her restraints. Traquero held up a remote, pushed a button, and the woman screamed again.

As Liv made the connection to the shock collar, images assaulted her—Josh collared under the hands of this man, his beautiful face shattering in agony, his faith in humanity shredding with each press of the button. *No fucking way.* Not while she still sucked air.

She jutted out her hip, creased her eyes with a calloused smile, and laughed. "Who the fuck is she?"

"My wife." Traquero flared his nostrils. "She used to be my life. Until I found out she was just a fucking whore." He stood, yanking the tie loose at his neck, his accent clotting with long *i*'s. "Fucking all my colleagues. Making me a goddamned laughingstock, the filthy fucking bitch."

He strode toward his wife, rolling up his sleeves, and backhanded her face.

A normal person would've regretted asking the question. Hell, a kind person would've ran for help. But Liv was neither. She needed Traquero's commitment to the deal to ensure her family's safety, and she *couldn't* leave without it.

Marketing 101. Know the customer's needs and use the information to influence him.

She met his eyes. "You want a lover who won't" — *can't* —

"undermine the dominion you've worked so hard to establish?" *Fucking lowlife.*

"Yes." He folded his hands behind his back and swaggered toward her. "Move. Let me see him."

She didn't want that motherfucker anywhere near Josh. The thought alone spindled around her lungs, tightening its oxygen-depriving tendrils. But she couldn't shove her gun down his throat and pull the trigger. She could not. She could not. She breathed through it, focusing on the reason she'd stripped Josh of his clothes. He was there to be viewed. Seal the deal.

She stepped aside and exposed Josh to the man's sickening gaze.

"At last, I see you, *mi belleza*," he said, referring to Josh's cock. Traquero's attention was fixated and slack-jawed. "Out of the way, whore." He shooed her with a hand, his voice thick with spit.

"It's Deliverer, you sexist cunt." Her lashing tone was a pitiful attempt at maintaining her position.

Didn't matter who she was. She had a vagina. He considered her no more important than the woman he strung up and electrocuted, and he glared at Liv now like he might hit her.

She backed up, hands at her sides, fingers resting on the edges of her thigh-high boots.

He circled Josh, his gaze scouring the flexing muscle encased in chains, and paused with a hand over the raised welts.

"Magnífico." He reached up and yanked off the hood. "Face me."

Never had she expected to become so overwhelmingly possessive of a man, and it terrified her. The fear of losing him was as painful as her loss of Mom and Mattie.

Josh kept his eyes down, but she knew he could see the woman hanging in his line of sight. Other than the twitch in his shoulders, he kept his reaction to the horror behind an empty expression. When he turned and Traquero cupped his lowered jaw, her heart pounded wildly to smack the touch away. She locked her knees, forced herself to wait it out.

"Has your dick been corrupted by pussy?" Traquero breathed. "Speak. Give me your eyes."

Josh was several inches taller and regarded the sweaty, suit-clad man with a calm expression, his tone admirably smooth. "I'm a virgin, Master."

"Good. Good. *Muy bueno.*" He caressed Josh's bicep and followed the chains over his chest. An unmistakable erection bulged below the girth of his gut. "The slut I married will watch me fuck you. She will see honor and respect as you accept my dick, my rules, my power. *Then* she will know what her cunt has lost."

*So fucked up.* His requiting desires should've made his twelve requirements more plausible. Instead, the perversity of his oath and the lust smoldering in his eyes magnified his madness.

When he palmed Josh's cock, she grappled for an excuse to stop him. She hadn't told Josh that fondling was acceptable at these meetings. Stopping it would raise suspicion.

Josh held still with a heavy-lidded expression and intense patience, but that didn't mean he wasn't cracking beneath his stoic exterior. Her helplessness was an agonizing knot in her throat.

"Your limp pecker pleases me." He cupped Josh's balls, weighing them in his hand. "Not interested in men, no? Since I only employ men, you won't fuck my colleagues? My servants? Answer."

She shook her head, inwardly. Traquero liked the idea that Josh wouldn't be tempted to fuck his colleagues, but what the megalomaniac wasn't considering was that also meant Josh wouldn't willingly fuck him, either.

"No, Master." Josh's voice was soft, but a vein pulsed in his forehead.

"No, you won't." Sick satisfaction congealed in the crook of Traquero's grin, his eyes locked on his groping hand. "I want him."

The three words she needed to hear and had dreaded with every fiber of her existence. Time to get the fuck out. "Delivery will be in eight weeks. Do you have the down payment?"

His referral would be her next client. One with a new list of requirements for a new captive. An endless cycle she couldn't break.

"I said, I want him." Traquero hardened his jaw.

The force of his declaration punched through her, stealing the strength from her legs. Did he mean—?

"Right now." He continued to molest Josh's cock, his audacity slicing through her rising fear.

She brightened her eyes with the vicious smile he couldn't see beneath the scarf. "He hasn't been prepared for you, and he'll fight like hell." She hoped she hadn't misunderstood his desire for a willing victim. With her hands on her hips, she rolled her head on her shoulders and stretched her mouth in a yawn. "He needs more conditioning." She yawned again. "Hence, the eight weeks." *Now get your fucking hands off him.*

"He's not leaving until he gives me something. No deal without this." He squeezed Josh's cock, stretched it from his body. "I want you to come for your Master."

Her heart skipped a beat. How would she stop this? Mr. E didn't care what happened during these meetings as long as she secured the deal and the contact info for the next client.

He grabbed the chair, scratching the legs across the floor, and slammed it down in front of his wife. He pointed at the seat and frowned at Josh. "Sit."

Josh's muscles strained against the chains as he paced to the chair, head down. His wire-wrapped knuckles were bloodless, his jaw a hard line of anger. She stayed on his heels, the weight of her promise to protect him a splintering pang in her chest.

When he sat, she stood in front him. His heavy exhales rushed against her back. He was pissed, probably scared, but he hadn't done anything to foul up the meeting.

She needed to wrap this up by any means possible. Strike that. By any means but one. "You will not fuck him tonight." *Or ever.*

Traquero removed his suit jacket. "Then I'll fuck you."

The room was fetid, reeking of desperation, the air thickening every second she hesitated. Vibrating through the stench was the silent wall of rage behind her. Josh's knees tapped against the backs of hers, bouncing violently, begging her attention. It was a terrible reminder of the horror she'd subjected him to. At the same time, she found comfort in his jostling presence. He didn't want this for her, and his concern was a fiery spark in her chest, a pulsing light that energized her with so much warmth.

She glared into the eyes of a monster who didn't respond kindly to disappointment and dragged her response, bucking and sour, from the pit in her gut. "You want to fuck my filthy cunt? I'm just a whore."

Traquero stepped into her, toe to toe, his exhale scorching her face. "That's why I'm fucking your ass. I'll come in your bowels while my property comes in your face. Turn around."

The floor tipped. Her ankle gave out, and she righted herself. She was teetering in unchartered territory. Josh was her first virgin boy. The other boys had not only been promiscuous but also experienced in anal sex. And by the time they'd attended their intro meeting, they'd been conditioned enough to accept the kind of demand Traquero was making.

If she denied Traquero, would he pull out a hidden weapon? Would he back out of the deal? Even if he let them leave unmolested, her rejection would wound his sense of superiority. An unhappy client meant a death warrant for the two people she'd sacrificed everything to protect.

A shiver chilled her blood. *Shit. Fucking shit.* She swallowed, held her spine straight. Van had taken her anally countless times. She was already ruined and would do anything to spare Josh that fate.

As she turned, a moan bellowed from the woman hanging beside them. Her mewls transformed into an ear-piercing shriek. Good God, he was shocking her again. Her body thrashed and fell quiet. Liv choked back the bile burning her throat.

"Bend over." Traquero's hands gripped the hem of her skirt, shoved it to her waist, and fisted her panties, ripping them off. "Eyes on me, slave."

*Fuck, fuck, fuck.* No way could Josh look at him without a face full of emotion. If he lost his shit, they might not leave there alive. If he showed any concern for her, the raping twat-hater would see through their facade. She hoped to hell Josh was working this out in his head.

As she bent over his lap, their gazes collided. The connection lasted a fraction of a second, but it was all she needed. He wanted to fight for her. It was there in the pink rims of his eyes, in the blotch of red staining his cheeks. His lowered chin was fiercely set, his mouth a pale line of anguish.

He raised his head, blinked up at Traquero, the emotion gone. He'd swallowed his struggle deep inside where it would fester and eat him alive. He did that for her. For Mom and Mattie. Her eyes filled with tears. Not for the pain she was about to endure, but for the man who would suffer it with her.

When a zipper sounded, reality slammed into her in violent waves of tremors. Her teeth chattered behind the scarf, and her stomach heaved bile through her chest. *Think of Josh. Protect Mom and Mattie.*

She bolstered her voice with steel. "Condom."

Traquero's pants rustled, and a foil wrapper fluttered to the floor. Sweat trickled beneath her corset. She grabbed hold of the seat back and planted her elbows on Josh's thighs. His body was a stone pillar to which she clung, every hard inch of him bracing her.

Fingers singed her hips. The cold, hard tip of Traquero's dick pressed against her rectum. Her muscles tensed on the verge of springing. He shoved.

The burn ripped through her and cut her breath. Pinpricks seared the backs of her eyes. He didn't give her time to adjust, pounding her in a relentless beating. Oh God, this wasn't how Van fucked her. Not even close.

Dots blurred her vision. Her fingers cramped around the chair back.

"Slow down, goddammit." Her command was thick with saliva and cracked with tears.

The vicious gouging in her ass sped up. *Cruel, motherfucking prick.* She shook with so much hate, her thoughts swarmed toward rash decisions, all of them involving Traquero's insides splattered over the room. As his dick punched a fist of fire inside her over and over, she tucked all those images into the harsh, broken chambers of her soul and soothed herself with a promise. The son of a bitch would die. Her throat burned, her eyes smearing. Maybe not tonight but very fucking soon.

His punishing stabs punctured and branded. Fire and ice. Stretch and rip. Fuck, it hurt so much. She was sure her skin was tearing. She wanted to die.

Eventually, her mind recoiled, pulling her into that lonely corner inside herself where it was just her and her songs and numb paralysis.

She searched for the right tune, a calming verse, fumbling, arms outstretched. But instead of her voice, she found Josh's waist, hugged it, pressed her forehead against the chains on his abs, the velvet skin on his back warming her fingertips.

The hurt in her rectum was a dull burn, rising through her. She cleaved to Josh with her hands and her heart. He was all around her, his breaths singing for her, his shackled arms floating above her, his tensile muscles absorbing her pain.

Traquero's grunts punctuated each forceful jab. "Come with me, slave."

Josh's cock remained unresponsive beneath her chin. He wouldn't be able to come, not like this.

A hand fisted the scarf on her head, tangled with her hair. Traquero used it to angle her to the side, exposing Josh's flaccid state. "Damn you." He panted, slowing his thrusts. "Make him come. Use your mouth, whore." He released her head with a shove.

A shiver swept through her. He was either mindless in his methods or he was testing her. Did this violate the first requirement prohibiting sexual intimacy with women? No, she'd jerked him off countless times in training. Blow jobs were allowed, and Mr. E expected her to do *anything* to seal the deal.

"Do it," he bellowed and slammed into her so hard the chair screeched backward.

She balled her hand until the trembling subsided then tugged the scarf from her nose to her neck.

Josh would hate her for doing this. In this place. While her ass was getting fucked. Guilt gnarled in her chest as she gripped the base of his soft cock. The merest lift of his hips nudged her hand.

She glanced up at his face, hoping to find acceptance there. But his eyes were on Traquero, his features heartbreakingly blank. He flexed again, the clench of his ass and thigh muscles urging her.

It wasn't consent, but it was enough to lower her head. She kissed the tip of his cock, closed her eyes, and drew him into her mouth.

# THIRTY

*Oh, sweet God in heaven.* Josh's boiling anger shuddered off his body the moment Liv's lips wrapped around him. Every molecule of thought descended into the wet clasp of her mouth. He swelled against her tongue in a violent surge of blood, his balls alive with electric shocks.

Nothing compared to the unfathomable suction of her lips, and he would've been lost in the pleasure if Traquero weren't brutalizing her backside. It required a double-backboned power of will to stare into Traquero's eyes of soulless black and regather his brain cells.

Maybe if he hadn't lived such a sheltered life, he could've predicted this, would've been able to stop it. Now all he could do was trust that she'd made the best decision for her loved ones without destroying herself in the process. No matter what happened, he intended to be there to help her heal.

He squeezed his fists so tight the wires broke skin, grounding him in a way his prayers hadn't. Why didn't she just let Traquero force *him* instead? Didn't she know watching her suffer was a torture worse than experiencing it firsthand? Perhaps the same rang true for her. She'd promised to protect him, and he hadn't realized what it would cost her.

What could he do? He didn't have his arms, but if he stood, kicked high and hard in that vile face, he might... Might what? Buy them time to run? That wouldn't save her family.

Her trembling fingers clutched at his waist, and he was thankful for the cage of chains and the command that held his eyes hostage. One downward look at the savage motion of hips, or worse, if he found a haunted expression on her face while she sucked him, his obedient slave routine would shatter.

"Come now." Traquero's voice was an abrasive rasp, bred by a hundred stolen thrusts.

She responded by accelerating the speed and intensity of her sucking, pumping her fist in sync with her mouth, urging him to comply. And he would. He would end this for her.

He kept his eyes on Traquero but didn't see him, his mind chasing every beautiful and painful thing he loved about this girl. Her guarded brown eyes, her rare smile, the purity of her voice, the cut of her whip, her lips sliding over his length. The grip she held on his heart and her control over his body made him ache, sped his pulse, tightened his groin, gathering, reaching.

Traquero grunted. "Come."

Only for her. He held it, let it coil, until she pinched his backside in a silent command. His climax barreled through him, strangled his breath. He gave it to her, all of him, raw and willing, his release in her mouth so intimate the room melted away. He was on her tongue, dripping down her throat, fusing with her body. Just the two of them. He was hers.

The horrors around him snapped back with Traquero's gasp. "Unnngh."

The bastard's body doubled over her arched spine, trapping her chest against Josh's thigh. The wife wailed a pitiful moan, and he laughed. Then he stood, stuffed the used condom in his pocket, and tucked himself into his slacks.

"Get up." He jerked his bald head at Liv.

She replaced the scarf over her nose and mouth. Josh ached for her, and that ache erupted into a burning rage. He wanted her to remind Traquero she wasn't a slave, even as he knew she wouldn't be able to reason with a man whose evil bled from his skin to his bones.

She adjusted her skirt and rose with shoulders stiff, hands fisted, and eyes smoldering like embers of a dying fire. "Boy, go stand by the door."

*Dammit, Liv.* He knew she was sending him out of harm's way, but what about her safety? If he disobeyed, the deal would fall through and her family would suffer.

He fixed his gaze on the floor and crossed the room, sweat dripping down his back in his effort to obey. Every step away from her killed him.

"Give me the referral, and we have a deal." She wielded her voice like a blade slashing the air, but there was a slight hitch in the inhale that followed. Pain from the brutality she'd endured? Fear of what might happen next?

Traquero paced a circuit around the room, gathering his suit jacket and straightening his tie. "I don't like what I see."

Her laugh was a cold shiver. "What, his cock's too big for you? His face is too pretty? What the fuck do you not like?"

"He comes for you, not me."

The man just did unspeakable things to her and had the balls to sound petulant. Josh was a hairsbreadth from body slamming him. He locked his legs. To stand there and do absolutely nothing flung his nervous system into a havoc of messed-up signals. His muscles pumped to use physical force while his brain bellowed the consequences.

Despite what just happened, she'd dealt with predators like Traquero before. She was their best shot at getting out of this. So he kept his eyes down, his periphery rising no further than their waists.

"You wanted a straight boy. Of course, he's going to come for me." She leaned a shoulder against the wife's suspended body as if she were a lamp post. Her fingers rested on her thigh, just inside the top of her boot.

Traquero's pacing stopped behind a narrow counter. "Get away from her."

Liv straightened but didn't step away. "After ten weeks of training, he will crawl to you on his belly, lick the cheese from your nut sac, and plead for your cock in his ass, all while quivering with anticipation to come on your command."

The godawful image boiled bile into Josh's throat. He stood by the door, his distance from her a heavy frustration, his chains equally so. At least, the width of the room separated her from Traquero.

"There's something else going on." Traquero buttoned his jacket. "You're protecting him."

"I protect my assets, you delusional fuck. Until you pay, he's mine to keep undamaged and unused. If you're not man enough to want him, another Master will be. Do we have a deal or not?"

Her voice was ice, but beneath her taunting, Josh could hear a crack. If Traquero were listening past her words, he would've heard it, too.

"No," Traquero said. "No deal."

Silence, so stagnant it clotted Josh's inhales and clung to his skin. His muscles contracted, preparing. What was she thinking? What would she do? Her temerity scared the ever-loving crap out of him.

"Go to the car, boy," she growled.

She was out of her mind. He rooted his feet to the floor.

"You go." Traquero shifted against the counter. "He stays."

Josh snapped his head up as Traquero pulled a snubnosed revolver from beneath the counter and trained it on Liv. Blood thundered in his ears. He jerked forward and crashed to a halt when he saw the gun in her hand.

She shoved the barrel through the ring that held the wife's mouth open. "Are you a good shot, Traquero? Maybe you'll hit me at that distance. Maybe you won't." Her dark eyes blazed with ruthlessness, but flickering in the depths was a hint of desperation. "We both know *I* won't miss."

Josh's heart died in his throat. Liv was gambling on Traquero's caliber of bullet, his accuracy from thirty feet, and his level of duress. If he didn't hit her with the first shot, chances were he'd kill her with the second.

The room stood still, waiting for Traquero's response.

# THIRTY-ONE

Josh's breathing shallowed. His heart knocked against his ribs. Every frenzied thought concentrated on the aim of Traquero's gun.

The glow from the filmy bulb gilded Traquero's distorted face in a putrid yellow. "Don't shoot her." He tipped the revolver's nose down, just an inch. "Please."

There was nothing shocking about a man begging for his wife's life. Unless that man was Traquero. But Liv didn't seem shocked. Somehow, she'd figured him out.

"Empty the gun. Toss it."

She spoke as a Deliverer, a Mistress, a cold criminal. But that wasn't who she was. No matter the mask, Josh had never wanted anything more than the courageous, reckless woman trapped beneath it.

Falling bullets plinked on the floor. Traquero chucked the revolver, and it clambered somewhere beyond the reach of light.

Holding her gun in the woman's mouth, she removed her phone from her boot. Probably the same place she'd concealed her gun. "The referral."

As he rattled off a phone number, she typed with her thumb and, given her subtle exhale, sent off the text.

"Don't fucking move." She stared at the screen, her gun hand unwavering. A moment later, she said, "Confirmed."

Thus, securing the lives of her family. Her drive to protect was fierce. Josh wanted that same kind of protection for her. He wanted to be that for her.

She returned her phone to her boot and kept the gun aimed on the woman as she backed toward the door, her feet gliding smoothly and confidently. "I need a phone number for the delivery."

Traquero stared at his wife like he wanted to run to her. "Maybe I want a different boy. One who doesn't look at you like that."

She stumbled and resumed her backward walk. "They all look at me like that. You'll change your mind when the training is done."

"We'll see," he said, absently.

There was no indecision in her need to get out of there. She held the door for Josh and quickly followed him out and to the car.

For five minutes, she drove, silent, eyes darting to the side mirror. Josh wanted her to fall apart the moment she hit the gas. He needed to see *her*, not the damned Deliverer. The stink of fear and sweat oscillated through the dark interior, but somehow she held it together.

His nerves stretched, and his pulse refused to slow down. He tried not think about the battered wife, the botched deal, or Traquero raping her from behind, but his thoughts surpassed turbulent. His hands ached in the wires. He wanted out of his chains. He needed to hold her. He felt so damned useless. "Liv? Talk to me."

She turned off the road and followed a long dirt path through a thick cluster of trees. Deep within the grove, she stopped and turned off the engine, her eyes hidden by the moonless night.

Wrestling with the scarf, she untangled it from her hair and tossed it to the side. The screen on the phone in her hand awoke, casting a soft light over the dash as she knelt in the space between their seats.

A flash of pain sparked in her eyes. "I have to call Van."

He clamped his teeth together. He knew she'd need to check in. The nightmare was never-ending.

She connected the call, her gaze watery and heartbreaking. She squinted at the screen, at Josh, then switched it to speaker and set it on the dash.

"Already talked with the referral." Van's voice prickled across his skin. "He wants a girl. The usual requirements."

Kate was still at the house, waiting for her delivery day. So another girl would be ripped from her life. Dread clamped Josh's stomach.

"I'll leave in the morning," Van said, blandly.

Leaving? A rush of possibilities jump-started Josh's brain.

She touched his fists with trembling fingers and untwisted the wires. "I didn't secure the deal."

"What do you mean?" The question dripped from the phone, a slow ominous reverberation.

Her face paled in the screen's dim light, her expression tight. "He wants a heterosexual boy to come for him on demand. It didn't happen the way he wanted."

"What the fuck *did* happen, Liv?"

She sucked in a sharp inhale. The wires loosened between their hands. Circulation rushed to Josh's fingers in biting stings, but the sensation dulled with the rush of her next words.

"He fucked my ass, Van. Then he fucked me again by rejecting the deal." She pulled the wire free and flung it at the back of the van, her teeth grinding so violently Josh could hear the enamel scraping.

The line went quiet for a heartbeat, two... The sound of shattered glass crashed through the speaker. "Goddammit, Liv. God fucking dammit." Heavy exhales. "Get home. Now."

She winced then recovered with squared shoulders. She unscrewed the quick links connecting Josh's chains and paused on the last one. "The videos."

"There won't be any fucking videos." The line went dead.

She ducked her chin, hiding her face. A surge of anger rocked Josh backward. He knew Van didn't have any control over the videos or what would happen to their daughter, but the man sure as hell wasn't putting his ass on the line to fight for her. Josh suspected he was more afraid of losing Liv and this fragile arrangement than anything else.

The chains fell off his chest and arms and pooled around his waist. His freedom swept through him in ragged breaths.

She gazed at him with stiff lines of determination on her face, an expression he'd seen a hundred times, the unwavering glare that tortured him, aroused him, conjured his nightmares, and filled his dreams.

He memorized each twitch of her lashes, the delicate point of her raised chin, every faltered breath. He was consumed with having her and terrified to lose her.

"Tell me what you're thinking." He reached up to brush his fingers through her thick dark hair.

She recoiled before his hand made contact. A blank mask fell over her face, a wall of ice slamming between them. She moved to the driver seat and faced forward.

His momentary calm burst into a roaring fire. Hands fisting, heart pounding, he didn't know what do with the fury burning through his veins. He tagged his jeans and boots from the floorboard and jumped out.

He dressed as he walked, jerking on his boots, kicking branches out of his path. His muscles heated, and sweat slicked his bare chest, chilling in the night air. He wasn't angry at her. He was angry *for* her. The abuse done to her body. The helplessness of her situation. His inability to free her.

He slammed a fist into the nearest tree trunk. Again. Again. Pain ricocheted through his hand, down his arm, and fed his breaking heart.

Out of the corner of his eye, he caught her silhouette standing a few yards away. A slender shadow, shrouded by darkness. And in her raised arms, she held a gun, trained on him.

He threw another fist. Absorbed the burn. Expelled the rancor. He knew she was holding a gun on him to prevent him from running and putting her family at further risk. Regardless, she wouldn't shoot him. Not because she needed a slave, but because she loved what was hers with a self-destructing passion.

He faced her and held out his arms. "I'm yours."

The girl and the gun didn't move.

"Lose the damned mask and stop hiding from me." He raked his throbbing hands through his hair. "Scream, cry, hit something. Hit *me*. But for God's sake, let it out."

The shadowy lines of her body wavered. The gun lowered, returned to her boot.

He stretched out his arms, savoring the cool breeze brushing over his unrestrained skin. "I stand here without rope or chains, Liv, tethered to you by my own will." His blood beat with the ferocity of his words. "I won't be free until you are."

Her head jerked back, her body rigid. Then she walked straight to him and unleashed her fists on his chest. She clobbered him over and over, her gasps accelerating with each fall of her hand.

The lashing didn't hurt. Not like the whimpers rising from her chest. She was hurting, lashing out for the wrongs that had been done to her. A sharp pain swelled in his throat. The only thing he could do was take it in, try to bear some of it for her.

He held his arms out and his body open. When her hits ebbed into weak slaps, she stumbled back, hugging herself and clutching her elbows.

His heartbeat slogged through the ache in his chest. He kept his arms outstretched and whispered, "I'm here."

Disbelief widened the whites of her eyes, and her breath caught. He waited.

In two running steps, she launched at him, climbed up his chest, and curled her hands in his hair. He lifted her, pinning the curves of her thighs around his hips, and took her mouth. His knuckles burned with fever, but the heat from her lips was overriding. She whispered kisses over his jaw, around his mouth, caressing, assuring.

He angled his head, deepening the reach of his tongue and drinking her in lick by lick. Her hands in his hair, the sweetness of her breath filling his mouth, there will never be another kiss like hers. She knew how to suck his lips and trap his tongue in a way that stroked every nerve ending in his body. More than that, she knew how to reach inside him. She found him, her ferocity defying the odds and pivoting them into place, perfectly interlocked.

Her thighs squeezed around his waist, her breasts soft against his chest. He palmed her backside with a cautious gentleness, and chased her tongue, spiraling, stretching deeper, falling heart-first into an existence where only she mattered.

When their mouths separated, gasping for air, she cupped his cheeks and pressed their foreheads together. "I'm so sorry."

He knew she was referring to the atrocities of the meeting, and she had nothing to be sorry about. "You should be sorry. Getting a blow job from you was a real hardship."

She rested her lips on the corner of his mouth and sighed. "We need to go."

"I'm driving." He shifted her, hooking an arm beneath her knees, and carried her to the driver's side door.

The way she curled against his chest and hugged his neck produced an obscene amount of pleasure for his emasculated ego. She was finally turning to him for comfort. Though, the fact that she didn't protest him driving was a testament to her physical and mental state. She trusted him not to cause a wreck or drive to a police station. He kissed her head, let his lips linger there, branding her peppermint scent in memory.

He scooted behind the wheel, sliding back the seat to accommodate his longer legs, and found the keys in the ignition. She snuggled into his chest, settling in, exactly where he wanted her. Her knees folded under his arm and allowed him plenty of room to see and steer. Holding her like this, her soft body half the size of his, she didn't seem so tough and intimidating. In fact, the quiet tremor shaking her breaths made his muscles heat with the need to avenge her.

He veered onto the main road, the tires kicking gravel into vacant fields. No cars. No buildings. Only a black dome of sky and a thousand questions beating against his skull. He stretched his hands on the steering wheel, igniting a burn through the gashes. "What happens now?"

Her lips moved against his neck. "The intro meetings are always strained with tension, but I've never walked away from one without securing the delivery." Her voice wavered. She cleared her throat. "Mr. E will try to sell you to another. Though, the next buyer wants a girl."

"And Van captures the girls?"

She nodded, fingers curling against his chest. "He'll be gone a few days. Maybe a week. Scouting only. Watching. We hunt as far from home as possible. You were an exception."

She'd already explained her reason for choosing him, one he'd accepted with ease. Better him than someone else. He hated to ask, but they needed to talk about the ramifications of the meeting. "Does Traquero's referral safeguard your family?"

"I don't know." Her voice was desolate, tearing the lining around his heart.

"We *need* to know." He tried to choose his next words carefully, but there was no way to soften what she needed to hear. "If they're dead, you will be, too." Mr. E would no longer have a means to control her. "We can't go back there."

She stiffened. "I have to go back for Kate."

*Kate.* She'd never used her name, and doing so now was monumental. And terrifying. Was she giving up? Or giving in? "Then we'll go back, wait for Van to leave, and make our escape."

"Her delivery to the buyer is in two days. If Mom and Mattie are still alive, I *have* to deliver her."

He slammed a hand on the steering wheel, and she didn't even flinch. For the love of God, this was so jacked up. "How is delivering her better than not returning for her?"

The passing fields illuminated with the flickering lights of the emerging town. She slid out of his lap, dragged the cooler to the front, and perched in the passenger seat.

"When I deliver her, I'll kill the buyer." She held a forkful of salad to his mouth and looked at him as if she were talking about football stats.

He accepted a few bites and tried to consider her suggestion with an open mind, but he couldn't be moved from the conviction ingrained in him. Murder must always be a last resort. "You're not killing anyone. Murder is a *big* sin, Liv."

She stuffed another bite in his mouth with more force than necessary. "So if it had come down to leaving you with Traquero or pulling the trigger, you would've preferred the former."

"Yes." He would've found another way out, God willing.

"You're an idiot." Her tone was scolding, at odds with the weariness sagging her eyes.

"Repay no one evil for evil. We *will* overcome evil with good."

"Ugh. Shut up." She threw the salad container into the cooler. "I *am* evil. Destined for hell. What the fuck am I saying? I'm already there."

"I'm not even going to respond to that." He glared at the road.

Her self-perception punched him in the chest, but he wasn't helping her, either. She needed a solution, not a bible study session.

"Contact Traquero and request another meeting," he said.

"We only get one-time-use numbers. A number for initial contact. And a number to make the delivery. Outside of that, the buyers call Van. Mr. E's rules. He prides himself on buyer confidentiality." She leaned back in the seat and stared out the windshield. "Traquero will have a change of heart and call Van again."

She seemed confident, and he wasn't sure how to feel about that. His self-preservation objected to the notion of Traquero making that phone call, but his trust in her was unremitting. If it had come down to leaving him with Traquero, she would've pulled the trigger, damning herself to hell.

They passed through San Antonio and Austin, and the conversation circled around ideas that wouldn't form into a plan. She put holes in every suggestion until there was only one option left. One he couldn't accept. Premeditated murder was not a solution. Nor would it save her family and return him to his.

As he drove, he evaluated his feelings about resuming his old life. Returning home meant exchanging twelve requirements for a hundred more. Did he really want to go back to their rules? Mom and Dad's restrictions were morally acceptable but no less confining.

When he exited the interstate at Temple, edginess stretched between them. Her mask fell in place, and her posture gathered into that unnerving stillness.

He pulled off into the same vacant lot she'd used ten hours earlier and climbed into the back. They were no closer to a solution, but they were together, bound by a connection that was deeper and stronger than keypads and shackles.

He lowered to the floorboard, and the chains went back on.

# THIRTY-TWO

The next twenty-four hours tested Josh's faith in God's presence in Temple. As Liv sank slowly and deeply inside herself, he questioned if maybe this was hell. Perhaps she was right. God had abandoned him on a threadbare mattress, locked in an attic, with his heart hemorrhaging in his hands.

He fed her the meals she retrieved from downstairs, showered with her, and tended his swollen knuckles and the small rip on her rectum. But his single-minded outpouring of questions, affection, and worry were failed attempts in breaking through her steel-plated chest, which grew colder and more rigid with each passing minute.

She curled in a ball on the mattress and clutched her phone. Waiting for the videos that never came. Watching the blank screen as if, at any moment, it would stare back with lifeless eyes.

If Mr. E intended to kill her Mom and daughter, he would do it *after* she delivered Kate. Van had left Temple before they'd returned early that morning. Mr. E needed her and wouldn't risk her dissent. Josh knew she knew that.

He dropped the tennis ball he'd been throwing for the past hour and stood over her, hands on the waistband of his jeans. "What time is it?"

Her thumb tapped on the phone's screen. "11:48 PM."

Only fifteen minutes had passed since the last time he'd asked. He was out of excuses to coax her out of the attic. Kate was free to roam the outer room, and Liv had brought up enough food to hold the three of them over until the delivery tomorrow.

He knew Liv intended to kill Kate's buyer. Every time he counseled her against this decision, he was met with a litany of colorful words. Liv seemed completely unconcerned about her own safety.

Numerous times, he'd considered calling his parents to let them know he was okay. He would've had to trick her into unlocking her phone, but that wasn't what quashed the idea. He didn't know the outcome of their situation until she delivered Kate. Giving his parents false hope would be cruel.

"No more waiting." He perched on the edge of the mattress. "We need to leave. Escape with Kate."

"No." Her answer was cold, final. She turned away and stared at her phone.

It hadn't passed his notice that she was the only one going downstairs for food. With Van gone, there was no need for pretense. Beneath that icy mask, she still believed he would leave her.

He drew in a breath and matched her chilly tone. "If you haven't heard from Mr. E before the delivery, then what?"

She'd said Van would send her the address for the delivery when he received it.

"Are you still going to deliver Kate?" he asked.

Her body turned to stone, her voice grinding. "I'm going to do what I have to do."

He rubbed his temples. He couldn't ask her to choose whose lives to protect. It was an impossible decision. One that would make the strongest person lose her bearing.

Laying on her side with her back to him, she folded in on herself, arms and bedding wrapped around her belly. She needed someone to hold her on the shore of decision, to cradle her fears, to contemplate what was best for *her*.

He leaned in and touched her bare shoulder with his fingertips, with his lips. "If you need a place to go, Liv, I'm right here."

A shiver twitched down her arm. Her hair swept over the pillow in ripples of mahogany. The naked curve of her spine disappeared beneath the sheet that bunched at her waist. He was conscious of her lack of clothing under there, and while her nudity was no longer a mystery, it was no less alluring. Even in her misery, he wanted her, in every way possible.

He trailed a knuckle along the dip of her waist, over the rise of her hip, taking the bedding with it. He expected her to jerk away as she'd done all day, so he decided to surprise her. He yanked the sheets to the floor, exposing her slim lines and milky skin, stripping her bare.

She rolled to her back, her lips parting in disbelief, her phone seemingly forgotten at the edge of the mattress. What a gorgeous opportunity. He pinned her chest with his and captured her mouth before she could close it, swiping his tongue, finding hers on the second pass, warm, wet, and so damned promising.

She arched into him, the heated satin of her flesh molding to his hands as he caressed her backside. He was instantly hard, his balls tightening with an achy need. He palmed her breasts, his thumbs rolling over her nipples, his tongue licking and stroking the sensual reaches of her mouth.

The most private part of her body ground against his, her calves hooked around the back of his thighs, her fingers clutching his biceps. As their mouths moved together in synchronized surrender, he wished he'd had the foresight to remove his jeans. He wanted to feel her against his skin. He wanted *in* her.

Her hands twisted through his hair and tugged, breaking the kiss. Her lashes lifted, carrying her gaze from his mouth to his eyes, and held him, heart and breath, in eternal suspension.

She licked her bottom lip, and he felt it pulse through his erection. She blinked and something shifted over her expression. Angling her chin to the side, the hands in his hair pulled his face to her chest, and her thighs tightened around his waist. "Please don't give yourself to me."

He broke the crush of her embrace and gripped her face with two hands, forcing her to look at him. "I already have. This"—he rocked his groin against hers—"is part of the deal."

Her eyelids shuttered closed, and a breath spasmed through her chest, her lips in a flat line of rejection.

His hands fisted in the pillow. He couldn't, wouldn't, force her, beg her, or otherwise guilt her into it. He lowered his forehead to her shoulder, inhaling the clean scent of her skin, savoring the intimacy of her body against his.

A haunting melody strummed from her lips. He recognized it immediately. "Possession" by *Sarah McLachlan* was a sad but fitting choice, its tune reflecting the tragedies in Liv's life. He shivered against the sweet breeze of her vocals, holding her tight as she expressed herself the one way she knew how.

She sang about trapped memories and solitude, but when the lyrics shifted to aching bodies, her huge brown eyes moistened, welling in the corners, staring up at him, piercing. Her conscience emerged through the words, her voice cracking, yearning. He realized she wasn't rejecting him. She was beseeching him. Asking him to love her.

He sat back on his heels, curled her legs around him, and beheld the beauty of his world. Uncertainty misted her eyes. He drank in her fading hymns, her feminine allure. The parted seam of her mouth, gentle swells of breasts, flat expanse of belly, vulnerable spread of thighs. Her fearless heart.

His chest swelled, overcome and pounding frantically, as her love gathered before his eyes, twining her fingers around his, rolling tears down her cheeks, whispering a word he'd ached to hear in her angelic voice. "Josh."

Not *boy*. She called him *Josh*.

"Liv… I want this. I want *you*." He bent forward and collected a tear on his fingertip.

His pulse beat in his throat as he lowered his finger and traced the slit between her legs with the teardrop, sliding deeper and deeper with each pass. His lungs panted. His finger breached her opening, and warm, slick flesh sucked him in.

Just thinking about putting his penis there sent a shock wave to his groin. He sank to the knuckle, her channel flexing and gripping. A moan tumbled out with his exhale, and he fell forward, catching his weight with his free arm beside her, laughing at himself, overwhelmed with desire.

He pressed in and out, and added a second finger. Her eyelids dipped to half-mast. Her lips freed a smile, her body glowing with life. He cherished every breathy gasp, marveled at how wet and hot she was, and couldn't let go. He wanted in, and given how violently his muscles shook, it would happen quickly and with a great amount of energy.

The naked light bared her arousal in all its curves and glistening flesh. His hand braced his larger frame over hers, his other exploring her sex with fumbling urgency. "Wish I had ten hands. I want to touch you everywhere while I'm doing this."

"Just keep doing exactly what you're doing." She reached down, found the button on his jeans, released it, and lowered the zipper. "You'll have me coming in no time."

Oh, those words stroked him, made him harder. He concentrated on the depth of his touch, the velvet heat of her folds drenching his palm, and the sound of her exhales. When she pulled him from his pants and glided a fist up and down his length, he quickened the thrust of his fingers, wheezed on his laboring breaths, and felt his release barreling down.

He bucked out of her grip, pulling his fingers from her, squeezing the base of his erection and halting the orgasm.

"I…uh…" A ragged laugh shook from him. "Wow. I'd like to get at least one thrust in before I embarrass myself."

Stretching her arms above her head, legs spread in offering, she grinned. "I'll keep my hands here." She sucked on her bottom lip, her gaze sobering. "I'm all yours, Josh."

Ahhh, his name on her lips. The arousal straining her face and the sultry caress of her voice accelerated the gallop of his heart and the throb between his legs. He lowered his face to her mound, slid his hands under her butt, and kissed a path down the line of her sex.

The sweet scent of her moisture infused his inhales. His mouth watered as he spread his lips over her, licking, sucking, imbibing the salty, sugary essence of her. He kissed her like he would her mouth. Deep, hungry pulls with his lips, burying his face, his tongue circling and lapping. The more he explored, the hotter her flesh grew, her entrance swelling, widening, wanting. He was doing that, tweaking her body, giving her pleasure.

Her legs flexed around his shoulders, her inner muscles pulsing against his tongue. Fingernails scraped the wall above her head. "Ohhh, fuck, fuck. Don't stop."

*No way.* He ground his hips against the mattress, working his jeans off with one hand and kicking them away. His heart raced toward implosion, his hard-on so hot and painful, he was consumed with the primal need to fill her, to make her his. He curled his fingers around her thighs, spreading her further, deepening his kiss.

Her curvaceous backside went tight in his hands and loosened with her full body sigh. "Ah, ahhh, I'm coming. Oh fuck, Josh, I'm coming."

He devoured her through the twitches and pulses, the muscles inside of her beating against his tongue. Soon, she melted into the mattress, her breaths falling like lingering tears. She gazed down the length of her torso, eyes heavy-lidded and clinging to his.

One more tongue-delving kiss, and he crawled up her body, taking his time, dragging his mouth over her quivering belly, capturing every bead of sweat, following the dips of her ribs. He got sidetracked when he reached her nipples, flicking and biting until she pulled his hair and covered his mouth with swollen lips.

She drew in his tongue, humming, hands sweeping down his back. Her fingers burrowed into his butt crack and pressed against his rectum. Fire sparked in her eyes. "Take me."

He shivered, his voice strangled. "Yes, ma'am." He rolled his hips forward, cock in hand, and lined it up to her opening. They'd tied her tubes, but... "Condom?"

A smile shook the corner of her mouth. "Van doesn't sleep around and has blood tests to prove it. I trust him on that." Her eyes asked, *Do you trust me?*

He nodded, his heart hammered. This was it. He found her eyes, smoothed the hair from her face. She touched his lips then his chest, over his heart.

He thrust, a hard breathless slide, and they bled into one. Hot and wet. Soft and tight. Freedom. It was everything he'd wanted and nothing he expected. Her body stretched around him, gripping him, spinning stars through her brain. Buried to the root, he inhaled her breaths, sweating profusely, afraid to move.

She stared up at him with a yearning look, her dark eyes framed by wet lashes, the corner of her mouth trembling.

Connected inside her in a way he could've never imagined, he tasted her lips, a caress of soft, swollen bliss. "You okay?"

Her fingers speared his hair from his temples to his nape.

"I never thought…" She drew in a deep breath, tightening her hold on the back of his head. "This tenderness…you and me…" She blinked rapidly, her inhale hitching. "This is an intimacy I never thought I'd experience."

A deep level of satisfaction washed over him. He was able to give her something she'd never received from another man. Hope fluttered in his stomach. Maybe his love for her was big enough to heal her emotionally.

Her warm sex clenched, spurring him into motion. He withdrew, dragging his length along her walls, igniting a million sensations, and slammed back in. His hands scrambled for purchase on the mattress. Oh, God. His vision blacked, and his release tore from deep inside him, pummeling through his cock, shredding his throat.

"Ah, ahhh, ughhh." He shouted incoherent sounds over and over, his muscles jerking in spasmodic bliss, his heart tripping in his chest.

His head hit the pillow, the remnants of his climax thrumming through him, tingling his skin. When he regained his voice, he shifted his weight to his arms, bracketed her face, and searched her eyes.

"I intended to last longer than two thrusts." A smile pulled at his lips, and he let it loose with a laughing sigh. He circled his hips, still seated deep inside her, with no plans to pull out. Ever.

She shook her head, biting down on her own smile. "Just like a teenage boy." She kissed him, gliding her tongue and heating his mouth. Then she pushed her hands through his hair and leaned back. "But you fuck with your heart."

"Then my heart is aching to move." He rocked his hips, relishing the connection. Grinding harder, he circled his pelvis, feeling her everywhere, and worked into a furious tempo.

She cupped his jaw and arched a brow. "Again?"

"As long as you'll have me."

Her legs and arms hooked around him, and she rolled them. With his back against the mattress, she straddled him, folding her arms behind her head. "My turn."

What a glorious vision. With her body bared before him and a gleam in her eyes, she rotated her hips, breasts swaying, waves of dark brown hair cascading around her. "You gave me a gift, Joshua Carter. I'm keeping it. Always."

He gripped the curves of her butt, holding her to him, lifting his hips, and sliding deeper. "Good. Because I'm yours. Always."

When she came, she took him with her, milking him, crying his name. He would never forget that moment. The merging of their passion, peaking together. Two parts of a whole, lost together.

They curled up in silence, her back to his chest. She laced their fingers and brought them to her mouth, kissing the cuts on his knuckles.

A few moments later, her musical laugh tiptoed through the room. "You're hard?"

He bit her shoulder, stroked his erection along the crease of her butt. "I'll never get enough of you, Liv."

She angled her hips, reached between her legs, and guided him inside. He was home.

Hours passed. Outside, the sun would've been climbing the sky, but he didn't care. He had so much light in his arms, it was easy to pretend nothing else mattered. Just for a little longer. They made love incessantly and intensely, slow and fast, hard and soft. He was lost in her body. Lost in *her*.

Eventually, exhaustion pulled him under with her curves against his, limbs entwined.

When he woke, it was with a head full of sexy dreams and blood swelling him to a full hard-on. Never enough. He grinned and reached a hand over the mattress, searching for her. Not finding her.

He lurched to his knees. The mattress was bare. The room empty of life. His heart went wild, his thoughts crazed. Maybe she was checking on Kate. Or making breakfast. He climbed to his feet, and something crinkled beneath his toes. A white piece of paper with scrawled handwriting. Beside it, a car key.

He dropped to his knees and a picked up the letter with shaking fingers.

*Joshua,*
*Van called with the buyer's pickup location. Meet me at the Sleepy Inn on 35. If I don't make it there by tomorrow morning, go home. Go home to your family.*
*The code is 0054. The key belongs to the black Honda parked out front.*
*Liv*

The letter wadded in his clenching fists, a fog of red clouding his vision. All business. Nothing from the woman he'd spent the day in bed with. She might as well have signed it *Deliverer*.

He spun to the trunk and found his clothes inside. Hers were gone. She wasn't coming back. He shoved his hands through his hair.

*The code is 0054.* Number fifty-four. She was freeing him. What would happen to her Mom and daughter?

# DELIVER

His heart collapsed, spilling panic through his blood. What the hell was she planning?

# THIRTY-THREE

Liv drove the van out of Temple, with Kate strapped to the floor in the back as she headed west on 190 to make her seventh and final delivery. Darkness descended over the horizon. Street lights flickered on. Her pulse beat a frenzied vibration in her ears.

Josh would be driving to the motel by now. A motel that would never be one of her destinations. *If* he obeyed her instructions, and hopefully, without revealing his identity to the motel clerk. God, she needed him to just wait somewhere safe and hidden until morning. By then, everything would be done. Surely, he wouldn't go to the authorities before going to the motel?

Fuck, it was a risk, made more excruciating after spending the previous seventeen hours in his arms. She'd tried to keep him at a cold distance when they'd first returned from the meeting. She'd been fighting through her uncertainty about Mom and Mattie's future and trying to come to terms with what she had to do. She needed to protect him from her, refused to endanger him with the details. But most of all, her plan would've devastated him.

When they became entangled, they brought with them all their convictions, pursuits, and pains. Whether it was scriptures from religious study, record-breaking interceptions, or delivery deadlines with sex traffickers, he'd taught her that one's purpose in life had no sway on who the heart latched onto. And while she'd managed to keep her plan hidden, he exposed the rest of her with a fierce loyalty behind his gorgeous green eyes and a blaze of determination burning in his touch.

She yanked the seat belt pinching her chest, strangled and trapped by the tragedy of her miserable fucking life. She loved him, goddammit, but she had to let him go. Covering her mouth, she smothered a sob between trembling fingers. Fuck, it hurt so damned much.

*Focus. Breathe. Don't fuck this up.* Gripping the wheel with two hands, she glanced at the passenger seat. A mask, change of clothes, the LC9 pistol Van left for her, the pen knife he didn't know about, the phone Mr. E would be tracking her with, and her letter to Van. What was she missing?

*Josh.* His absence was a bleeding fucking hole inside her, the stitches around her heart unraveling and ripping. She inhaled deeply. Gasped noisily. *Fuck. Keep it together.*

A glance over her shoulder revealed Kate's heaving chest beneath the restraints on the floorboard. Liv's throat burned, stinging pinpricks of pain through her head. She wiped at her nose and eyes, hands shaking.

A few miles later, a gas station emerged, the lot half-full with customers. The first stop.

She pulled off and parked at a pump beside a minivan. Bright lights fringed the canopy over the pump islands, flickering with winged insects and bleaching the starless sky. A woman leaned inside the minivan's sliding door and hollered at the wailing kids within.

Liv approached her with her thumbs hooked in the front pockets of her jeans. "Excuse me, miss?"

The woman turned her head and blew a wayward hair away from her face.

Liv shaped her mouth into a friendly smile. "Sorry to bother you. Is there any way I can borrow your phone for a minute? Mine's out of juice, and I really need to check on my dad."

The woman shifted to face her, and her eyes widened, fixed on Liv's scar. She looked away quickly. "Uh, yeah. Let me grab it."

Funny, Liv never really thought about her fucked-up face until she ventured into public. Her internal damage had always been much more distracting to her.

"Here you go." The woman offered the phone, the pity in her eyes negating her smile.

"Thanks. I'll just be a minute." She stepped away from both vehicles until she was out of hearing distance and dialed the number she knew from memory. It was the sixth time she'd called it, and it'd been eight months since the last call.

"Who is this?" Camila's sultry voice, though always straight to the point, had a way of warming Liv every damned time.

"It's me."

"Where?"

The reason for her calls was always the same. "Brady Reservoir." She gave Camila the GPS coordinates Van had sent. "10:00 PM."

"Shit. We're three hours away." A muffled noise scratched down the line. Then Camila's voice came back. "We'll make it. How many?"

"At least one extra man. Maybe two."

"Stall them. We'll be there." The line disconnected.

*Stall them?* Buyers and their bodyguards did not stall, and it was eight fucking o'clock. Camila would have to make up a full hour. Liv sighed, rubbed her eyes. It wouldn't be the first time Camila overextended.

Fear crept in, like it did before every delivery. Deep breath. This was the last one. She pinched the bridge of her nose, drew in another calming breath, and returned the phone to the woman.

For the next two hours, she smoked one cigarette after another. The stimulant intensified her edginess, so she sang while she smoked. When the tears sneaked in, she changed up the song. The towns grew smaller with each passing mile, stretching farther apart, separated by rocky scrub land. Fifteen minutes outside of Brady Reservoir, she stopped on the side of the road and changed into her costume.

The Deliverer wore a silver under-bust corset over a bra and boy shorts, both made of black latex. The gun went into her thigh-high boot. The knife's scalpel blade folded in, and the pen-like design fit down the center of the bodice, snug in the corset casing that had originally held a steel bone.

With a few minutes to spare, she knelt beside Kate and brushed the girl's hair from her sweaty forehead. "I delivered another girl once. Six years ago." Her chest tightened, testing the seams of the bodice. "She was very brave." She leaned down, pressed a kiss on trembling lips. "You remind me of her."

Thanks to the pitch-black interior, she couldn't see the fear in Kate's eyes. She didn't need to. It breathed through the van in a ghastly shudder, desolate and needful.

She returned to the driver's seat, a sheen of dread dampening her skin and chilling her spine, and faced the next phase of the plan. As she maneuvered the winding roads, dipping and curving around hillocks and banks, she couldn't escape the grip of doubt.

The emotionally detached letter she'd left Josh weighed on her the most, but she couldn't leave him with the damaged whispers of her heart. He might've clung to her words, searched for her, tried to save her. There were too many people involved in her deliveries, too many identities to safeguard. The less he knew in his freedom the better for everyone.

Stunted bushes crowded the landscape, forming smudges against the inky backdrop of barrenness. The last building was ten miles back. The occasional headlight bobbed in her side mirror and vanished behind the bends in the road. The desolation preyed on her nerves.

The navigation system directed her onto a narrow path that faded into a gnarled expanse of wilderness. As the clutch of trees closed in, she put on her mask, tying the strings to hold the round white face in place.

Up ahead, an arced glow rose through the dark, striping through the skeletal branches. Her boot shook against the gas pedal, and her palms slicked the wheel.

"Glory and Gore" by *Lorde* invigorated her lungs and heart as she scanned the trees, searching for a sign of her secret saviors.

Ricky, Tomas, Luke, Martin, Tate, and her very first captive, Camila.

She knew them by the names she'd once refused to use, by the bruises on their skin, and by the strength of their forgiveness. Her six deliveries in seven years were dead to her. Until she called. Her freedom fighters always came when she called. And they came for blood.

A car blocked the road, its headlights aimed at her and cut by the silhouettes of two men. She shielded her eyes with a forearm, turned off the engine, and grabbed the phone. In the back, she unstrapped Kate, straightened the girl's knee-length cotton dress, and led her out.

"Stay beside me," Liv whispered. "Shoulders back. Eyes down."

"Yes, Mistress." No chains or cuffs. The girl was broken in her despair.

With the confidence of the Deliverer, she swayed her hips and flexed her bare thighs with each stride toward the waiting predators.

# THIRTY-FOUR

Liv closed the final few feet with her chin held high and her strides wide and easy. Her insides, however, shook with a violence that strangled her breaths.

The shorter of the two men wore a Guy Fawkes mask, painted with a mustache, goatee, and a cynical smirk. The bodyguard didn't share his employer's creativity, his face distorted in a transparent sleeve of nylon.

"Good evening." Guy Fawkes cocked his head.

"We'll see." Her cool voice tangled in the autumn air.

The bodyguard approached her, and she remembered the drill from the intro meeting. She stretched out her arms, her phone in one hand. Beside her, Kate stared at the ground.

He prodded around Liv's mask and hair and patted down her bra, corset, and skin-tight shorts. When he reached her boots, he lifted the gun as she'd expected. Pocketing it, he moved to Kate and repeated the search. That done, he stepped back.

The Guy Fawkes mask turned toward Kate. "Come to your Master."

Liv clasped her wrist and walked a step ahead of her, holding her to the side. Was Camila there yet? Could Liv cut the fucker before his bodyguard shot her? Stall, stall, stall.

She released Kate's arm. "Kneel."

As the girl descended to the ground, Liv arched into Guy Fawkes' suit-clad body, inhaling the stench of musk and greed. She cupped his groin.

He swelled in her grip and held a palm out, halting his guard's advance. "How much for both of you?"

Same question he'd asked last time. If he saw her scarred face, he'd probably choke on his persistence to buy her.

"Pay me for one slave." She tightened her fist around him. "Then we'll discuss the prospect for two."

He pulled out his phone, his fingers tapping on the screen over her shoulder. She stroked his erection, bile burning through her chest and challenging her steady breaths.

"Sent." He pocketed the device and slammed a hand down on her ass. A heavy fucking hand.

The sting rippled down her leg and burned through her muscles. He reared back and hit her backside again. Her fingers fell away from his dick to clutch his hip. She was sure he broke blood vessels, the sadistic prick.

Her phone vibrated in her hand. She held it between their chests, unlocked it, and glanced at the text.

*Van: Funds received*

Her heart soared. It took a great amount of discipline to hold in the relief blubbering to escape. She breathed to the beat of "Glory and Gore" and lowered the phone to her bodice. As she worked it beneath the binding, she slipped the pen knife free, her body pressed to his in a wretched embrace.

The bodyguard stood a few paces away, his nylon-smashed expression skimming the surrounding woodland.

She flicked the blade open, her hand hidden beneath the rise of her chest, her pulse thrumming wildly. Trusting that the Guy Fawkes mask limited his field of vision, she swung the scalpel upward, and sliced his carotid artery. He shuffled back, cupping the spray of blood beneath his mask.

The bodyguard straightened, drew a pistol from his hip. She stopped breathing.

One shot fired from the trees. Two. Three.

He jerked back, stumbled. *Oh, thank God.*

The beam of headlights illuminated a crimson stain at the center of his white shirt. He snapped his gun up, aimed at her, and fired.

The bullet whistled past her. She leapt on him. Took him to the ground. Landed on his chest, the knife slick in her grip, her heart beating at a dangerous velocity.

The buyer hit the ground beside them, one hand squeezing the flow of red at his throat, the other clawing through the dirt to grab her leg. His fingers caught her calf in a blood-slicked grip.

She jerked her leg free and stabbed downward, hitting the bodyguard's chest. The blade sank an inch and stopped. The sternum? A rib? Shit, shit, she couldn't push it in. He shoved her away, raised his gun.

A gunshot cracked from the brush.

The beige of his nylon hood turned red, seeping blood. His gun dropped, and his body slumped.

A ragged breath tore from her throat. She unlocked her limbs, shaking violently, and checked the pulse in his throat. Nothing. She scrambled toward the buyer.

He lay on his back, arms lolled to the side. She tore off his mask and stared into the lifeless eyes of a weathered face.

She sat back on her heels, removed her own mask, and choked on the copper-tainted fumes of death and defeat. Nausea gripped her insides. The torture of her first seven captives had fattened Mr. E's off-shore account, but they were free and their buyers dead. And her eighth captive...

A sharp pain ripped in her chest. She inhaled deeply. Josh was safe.

Kate knelt a few feet away, curled over her thighs, shoulders trembling. Liv needed to go to her, but her legs wouldn't move, the gravity of what came next weighing her down.

One more kill. In Van's bed. Where he would find her dead and rotting and clutching her letter.

The stampede of foot falls crashed through the trees. A moment later, arms wrapped around her, Camila's familiar spicy scent a temporary comfort.

"I'm sorry, Liv. We tried to get here in time."

Shoes scuffed the rocky terrain around her, sounding the movements of young men gathering the dead and cleaning up the evidence. Young men she'd abducted, humiliated, whipped, and jacked off.

Killing herself would free them for good. It would also free Mom and Mattie. Mr. E would have no reason to harm them if she weren't around to experience the horror of it.

She should've ended her life years ago, but Josh had been the push she needed. Releasing him back to his parents was the right thing to do. Perhaps it was his integrity that had given her the strength to be honorable.

She hugged Camila's slim shoulders and dropped her face in the black silk of hair. "Don't be sorry. You still managed to fire a kill shot. Thank you."

Camila pulled back, shaking her beautiful round face, her eyebrows drawn in confusion. "We didn't shoot anyone. We just got here."

Her blood ran cold. "What do you mean?"

"Liv?" The deep accented voice behind her belonged to her second captive.

She pulled to her feet and came face to face with Ricky, who aimed a gun at a pair of pale green eyes. Eyes she never thought she'd see again.

*Josh.*

In his hand, dangled a Taurus PT-22 with a pink wood-grain grip.

# THIRTY-FIVE

Six guns aimed at Josh's head. Five men, one woman, all of them young, irrationally attractive, and glaring at him with fight in their eyes. He should've been scared shitless, but the cold blood settling around his heart suspended him in a state of shock.

He'd just killed a man. Even as he feared God and shunned evil, he knew without a doubt he'd do it again. For her.

Liv watched him, her eyebrows in a stark *V*, her complexion pale and splattered with blood. "Lower your guns."

The weapons lowered, disappearing in waistbands and pockets. Her friends, whoever they were, shifted closer, forming a bulwark at her back.

The Latina woman opened her mouth, and Liv held up a finger, silencing her and glaring at him. "How did you find me?"

"You might call it a lucky break. I call it divine intervention." He flicked the safety on the gun and held it up. "Why'd you leave this in the Honda?"

"So you could return it to your mom." Her eyes flashed. "I did *not* expect you to use it in a reckless gunslinging rescue." She spoke low, repeating her question. "How did you find me?"

He tucked the gun into his waistband at the base of his spine. "I left as soon as I woke. Got to the front of the neighborhood, and there you were, in the van, only a few blocks ahead of me." God hadn't abandoned him after all. "I followed you."

Her lips pinched in a line. "I freed you."

The woman at her side covered her mouth, eyes wide. "Oh my God. He's that missing football player from Baylor." Her head snapped to

Liv. "He's one of us?"

They were three hours from Baylor in the middle of nowhere. It was surreal that news of his disappearance had traveled that far. And what did she mean, *one of us*? His vision prodded through the nighttime shadows, searching the faces of her gun-toting, backup team. "Who are you?"

Liv pulled out her phone and squinted at the screen. "I have about twenty minutes before Mr. E wonders why my phone isn't moving." She blinked up. "Josh, this is Camila."

Camila gave him a chin lift. "I was her first delivery."

The hand of darkness seemed to lift from the trees, the stars singing together and the world crashing into place in a duh-faced moment. He took in their handsome features, their muscular builds, and their youth. Some were of Spanish descent, and they all fit the same desirable mold, including Kate. All seven of her captives. Here. *Free.*

All the signs had been there. She had never shown remorse over the fate of her captives, refused to talk about rescuing them, never veered from her plan to deliver Kate. And Van's inability to attend the transactions made it all possible.

Camila gave Liv's hand a squeeze. "Liv gutted my buyer the minute he sent the transaction. I screamed like a maniac, covered head to toe in his blood." She half-laughed, half-groaned. "When she calmed me down, she told me her story. Her history with Van. Her Mom. Her daughter." A sad smile touched her lips. "I refused to abandon her, so she let me dispose of the body and gave me an anonymous e-mail address. I sent a phone number there, one that couldn't be traced to me. A year later, she called. That's when I met Ricky."

The man closest to him held out a hand. "Ricky. Slave number two."

Josh accepted the handshake, awe-struck, his tongue not functioning.

Another guy flicked up three fingers. "Tomas. Number three. Her favorite."

Someone coughed, "Bullshit." Then each of the remaining men stepped forward, their names threading around him, pulling him into their huddle. Luke, the only redhead, number four. Martin, who had to drag his eyes from Liv, number five. Tate, huge smile, number six.

A familiar blond head emerged through the wall of men, her hands twisting in the front of her dress. She peered up at the strangers with a shell-shocked expression. "I'm…my name is Kate." She stared at Liv, her lips parted and eyes wide. "Does this make me number seven?"

"Yeah." Liv moved to her and cupped her face, bending to meet her eyes. "You okay?"

With a jerky swallow, Kate raised her chin and nodded. "I'm still trying to catch up. I…I had no idea. I thought I was going with that man." Another swallow. "I didn't expect you to kill him. Have you ever lost a slave?"

A deep inhale billowed Liv's breasts above the cups of her bra, and a quiver skipped over her arm. "No, Kate. We're all here."

*We.* They were all free, yet Liv was still a prisoner.

Liv smoothed Kate's hair from her face and spoke to her in a low, rushed tone about her mom and daughter, the significance of the other slaves being there to help her, and why she does what she does. The whispered conversation went back and forth for a moment longer, and Liv turned Kate toward Camila. "I trust them with my life, Kate. They'll protect you with theirs."

Camila embraced Kate in a hug. "Finally, a girl. And blond?" She glanced at Liv. "Still hunting in the border towns?"

"Until Josh." Liv moved to the hood of the sedan and picked through the cash, weapons, and phones that had been gathered from the dead men's pockets. "Kate's buyer wanted blond and innocent. Took Van a year to find her in the southern slums." She turned toward Kate. "Your brothers were protective of you, but they're drug dealers, and they're involved with some really bad people."

Kate's face pinched. "I know."

"It'll be fine." Camila grinned and waved a hand at the men. "You can help me air out the testosterone in our house."

Josh startled. "You live together?" Were they still considered missing?

Ricky strode around the buyer's sedan and shoved the lolling arm of a body into the trunk. "We come from broken families and ghettos who wrote us off as runaways." He slammed the lid shut. "If we return to our hellholes, it might initiate investigations that led to Liv." He walked back toward the group, eyes on Kate. "You can't go home."

She stepped away from Camila's embrace and rubbed her head. "I…I know."

Martin pointed a finger at Tate. "You know, that guy threw a fit when we told him he was stuck with us. Look at him now. He's been trying to fuck me since he moved in."

Hands laced behind his head, Tate glared at him. "I come into your room at night, because the entire house can hear you shouting Liv's name while you're jerking off. You need to get over her, man."

Martin flipped him off. "Fuck you." His eyes lit with laughter then shifted back to Liv with unmistakable longing.

Liv's shoulders squared under Martin's gaze as she blinked up at Tate. "You look well." She smiled. "Happier."

"I *am* happy, Mis—" He coughed in his fist. "Liv."

Tate was number six, so he would've been her last delivery, which she'd said was eight months earlier. Thick black hair and one of those boxy jaws women love, he smiled like he was posing for a camera, but it was warm and sincere when he regarded Liv. Josh believed she'd never had sex with him, but she knew him intimately. She knew all of their bodies intimately. With her hands. And her mouth.

Jealousy surged through his lungs and tightened his muscles. It was ill-timed and immature, but it couldn't be helped. His fists clenched, itching to drag her away and pretend that none of this existed.

Ricky nodded at him. "Liv, your boy's about to pop a vein in his forehead."

She closed the distance, her shadowy gaze caressing his face, her nearness replenishing the oxygen in the air. She clasped his fists and uncurled his fingers, her hands sticky with blood.

"Why'd you free him without a transaction?" Martin crossed his arms over his chest.

Her eyes didn't waver from Josh. "He's stubborn, disobedient, and untrainable."

He saw so much behind those words. Her spine straightened defensively, her lips flattened with fear, and her eyes hooded with affection.

"He failed the buyer introduction." She raised their laced hands to her chest. "You would've failed the next one, too. It was only a matter of time before Mr. E and Van saw this…" Her lashes lowered, her gaze on their hands, and fluttered back up. "They would've killed you."

A mass of regret clotted his throat. He didn't mourn loving her, never that. But he wished he was smarter. There had to be a safe way to end this with her family protected, but he couldn't see it.

The guys continued their road cleanup, but their attentions lingered on Liv. Without hesitation, his possessive heart led his lips straight to hers. With a hand on her neck, his other clasping hers against her chest, he kissed her deeply, nipping, licking, stealing her breaths, swallowing the hum in her throat. She was his, and he owned her mouth with a kiss that would leave no misunderstanding.

When he released her lips, her eyes clung to him, dark and hungry. Exactly how he wanted her. *After* all his questions were answered. "You freed me. Freed Kate. How does this save your mom and daughter?"

Camila paused in her effort to kick gravel over a patch of blood-stained dirt. "That's what I've been trying to figure out."

The crimson gore slicking Liv's cleavage gleamed in the headlights as her chest heaved. She unwound their hands and walked toward the van. "We need to wrap this up."

He shoved his fingers through his hair, watching the uncharacteristic wobble in her retreating strides. "Camila, why didn't she tell me about you? About this?" He gestured at Ricky and Luke, who were pouring jugs of acrid-smelling vinegar over the crime scene.

"She freed you," she said, softly. "When you return, you'll be swept into the investigation of your disappearance. Lots of interrogations." She jerked her chin at the group. "How are you going to keep this a secret? We're killing people, Josh. And Liv is crazy protective of our identities. In fact, she's terrified her expressions or reactions around Mr. E and Van will give us away. So she lies to herself when she's in that house. She thinks of us as dead." She turned toward Kate, whose eyes were glazed and distant, and stroked her hair. "Until she needs us."

Across the road, Liv leaned against the passenger door of the van, stripping her boots and wiping the blood from her chest with a t-shirt, her expression downcast and inwardly focused. He never once suspected this endgame, and he liked to think he knew her better than anyone else did.

He watched her with a renewed appreciation for her mystery. She was a complicated puzzle, one he planned to enjoy for the rest of his life.

A new life. What did that look like? He wouldn't return to his old life without her. Yet, she'd sent him on his way as if she expected him to do just that.

His spine tingled. "She wouldn't have freed me unless she had a solution to save her family."

Kate's shoulders bunched as she watched Liv wrestle with the front clasps of the bodice. "She's going to kill herself."

His nostrils flared, his pulse spiking in objection. "Did she tell you that?"

Her head shook as she hugged herself. "I was just thinking about her behavior since we left the house. She cried a lot on the way here. Then her voice grew cold and weird. She started singing "Last Resort", you know, that suicide song by *Papa Roach*. Definitely not her usual genre of music."

Muscle-clenching fear shot through his legs. He sprinted toward Liv, watching her movements, his entire body aware of her fingers on her corset and her feet pacing in a tight circle. Did she have a weapon on her? Would she attempt it right there? In front of him?

He skidded before her and slapped her hands from her belly. "Do you have a blade under your clothes?" He wiggled the remaining hooks free, dropped the corset, and tackled her bra, searching the seams. "Answer me."

"Fuck you." She gripped his arms, tried to stop his hands from unclasping the back hooks.

The bra dropped, her breasts bare and streaked with red. No

weapon. He dropped to her latex shorts, shoved them past her hips.

"What the hell are you doing?" She glowered down at him, kicking off her shorts like she was going to kick *him*.

Well, screw her. He was a breath away from tying her up. He opened the passenger door and shifted her until the door gawk-blocked her nudity from the nosy onlookers.

With her arm twisting in his grasp, he pulled her chest against him and pinned her back against the inside of the door, his voice low and vibrating. "Did you consider me in your suicide plans?"

A gasp shuddered through her. *Good.* Let her feel some of his wretched horror.

Her shoulders rose, and her eyes sparked. "Yes, I thought of you. So much so I made a covenant with my heart to stop cutting you with its jagged, damaged pieces." She spat the words, her voice growing louder, her eyes watering. "Don't you see how wrong I am? I'm a kidnapper. A murderer. A fucking monster."

"I see all of you." He wrapped his arms around her and pressed his lips to her temple. "I claim every jagged piece of you."

She shoved at his chest, tears escaping, screaming, "I freed you. For you."

His feet dug in, his arms caging her against the door. He put his face in hers and stared directly into her eyes. "And I will free you. From you."

Her eyes fluttered closed for a moment. She seemed to be struggling to hold her composure in place. Then a heartbreaking sound keened in her throat. She grabbed him, clinging, her arms twining around his neck, her thighs climbing his body.

He hoisted her backside and wrapped her legs around his waist. His heart fractured and bled out, but as he held tightly to her trembling body, his fortitude strengthened and beat anew.

With her face against his neck, her rushed breaths stroked his skin. "Staying alive is the most selfish thing I've done. Every day I live risks them." She gestured behind her. "And you. Mom. Mattie."

"Yet you rise out of the storm, faultless and upright." He gripped her chin, angled it until he won her eyes. "With every delivery, you release another captive. Then you return to your cell to begin the cycle again. The buyers exist with or without you. You lure them out and stop them from preying elsewhere."

She peered up at him, lips parted, her body going soft in his arms.

He kissed her lips, treasured the salty tears there, and rested his forehead against hers. "Let the one who has never sinned throw the first stone. You were the first slave. The one who has never been freed." He cupped her beautiful, tear-stained face, and traced the scar with his thumb.

"Don't give up. On me. On us."

The hammer of her heart against his chest slowed with her breaths. She hugged him tighter, nodded. "Thank you for coming. For shooting that man." She trailed a finger over his lips, watching the movement. "You saved me." She glanced up. "You can mark that off your to-do list."

She still needed saving, as did her family.

Camila strode toward them and held out Liv's handgun. He snatched it before Liv could and set it inside the glove box, along with Mom's PT-22.

Camila's face creased with concern. "You won't come home with us, will you?"

The others talked amongst themselves in the background.

"She sure as hell ain't going to kill herself."

"Fuck no. But she can't go back to that house."

"He's right. We need her. Our lives, this whole operation, is fucking pointless if she's dead."

Liv untangled her body from his, wiped her cheeks, and shook her head. "I have to go back."

Using the wet rag Camila held out for him, he wiped Liv's face, neck, and arms, removing the remnants of blood. The others hovered around the sedan, grumbling, dismantling the cell phones, and pocketing the cash and other valuables that had belonged to the dead men.

Questions piled up in his aching head about the dangers of this operation. "What do you do with bodies and evidence?" He tossed the rag back to Camila.

"I'll explain on the way back." Liv grabbed a t-shirt from the passenger seat and pulled it on. "We need to go."

"What do we do with the Honda?" He handed her a pair of jeans.

"Where is it?"

"About a quarter-mile back." He pointed down the road. "Keys are in the ignition."

"It's yours," Liv said to Camila as she dressed. "I was supposed to get rid of it anyway."

With the bodies stuffed in the sedan and the road cleared of blood, they said their good-byes. The guys hugged Liv a bit longer than he thought was needed, but there was no talk of future contact. Everyone knew the stakes, and no one had a solution.

Kate lifted a hand to him and gave a small smile. Her demeanor seemed to already be transforming, her chin lifting higher, her shoulders relaxing. She would be fine. Probably better than fine with that fierce pack of protectors.

"I'm driving." Liv climbed in the van, her gaze lingering on her friends.

Some of them slid into the buyer's sedan. The others faded into the woods. Her expression was wistful as she watched them leave, her fingers curling around the wheel.

"You'll see them again." He would make sure of it. "Under better circumstances." He hoped.

As he moved her extra clothes from the passenger seat to the floor, his hand brushed a folded piece of paper. He held onto it.

The van crunched along the gravel road, the same path he'd taken by foot in his race to catch up with her. At the time, he'd had Mom's pistol out and ready with no intention of using it. But when he saw that gun aim at Liv, it was a terrible ache, a flashing of his own life, a loss of breath. There was no falter in pulling his trigger. No guilt. She was alive.

He put on his seat belt and unfolded the paper in his hand.

"Don't read that." She stared straight ahead, navigating the winding road, her expression lost in the darkness.

When he flicked on the ceiling lamp, she tried to grab the paper from his hand. He caught her wrist, pinned it to her thigh, and held up a letter that was addressed to Van.

# THIRTY-SIX

Van,

> The reasons that chained me here were my reasons to go.
> I've never asked you for anything. I'm asking now.
> Keep them safe.
> Liv

Every mournful word stabbed Josh in the gut. As he read to himself, Liv stared straight ahead, her jaw locked in unapologetic stubbornness. He folded up the note, turned off the light, and spoke as calmly as he could. "You were going to do this at the house?"

"Where he'd find me." Liv's whisper was cautious.

He let that sink in. Would he have done the same to save his parents, damning himself to hell?

Maybe. He didn't know, couldn't wrap his mind around it.

His throat burned as he freed the heartache piling up there.

"I would've missed your smile, how it lifts your eyes and rounds your cheeks. And your voice. God, Liv, your voice is so mystical and arousing. I've never experienced anything like it." He pinched the note between his fingers, loathing its purpose, feeling its strength. "I would've missed your kiss, that incomparable connection when your lips brush mine. But most of all, I would've missed our future together, the one you would've taken from us." He turned in the seat to face her. "You said you freed me, but freedom isn't defined by chains or walls. You, alive, with me. That's my freedom."

Her profile nodded in jerky movements, and her hand reached out for his.

DELIVER

He caught it and entwined their fingers. "I need a promise, Liv. A promise to survive."

She glanced at him, swiped at her cheek, and steered onto the main road. "Wish I could say that if I went back to the day I first saw you, that I would've looked the other way." Her hand tightened in his. "I can't. I found my redeemer, and I know where you'll still be in the end. I won't give up. I promise."

Damn, those words felt good. He traced her knuckles with his thumb and settled into a comfortable silence until a hundred and ten questions penetrated his solace. "How did it start with Camila?"

"She has associations with a cartel. Not family relations. It's some kind of business connection. I don't know the details. She was doing side jobs for them before Van took her. When I killed her buyer, she drove away with his body, saying she knew people." She let go of his hand and raked her hair from her face. "I was so damned scared, unsure if I could trust her. She went back to work for her connections, and now they help her dispose of the bodies, cars, weapons. I don't know. I only talk to her on delivery days, and our interactions are as brief as you saw tonight."

His heart raced, his mind spinning. "Has she looked for your mom and daughter?"

With her connections, Camila should've been able to trace Liv's mom at the very least.

"She's tried. I don't know my daughter's real name and there are no Jill Reeds that match Mom's description."

He drummed his fingers on his knee, gathering his thoughts. "Did you plan to kill Camila's buyer?"

She nodded. "Camila didn't know. I think she thought I was going to kill her, too."

No doubt. Liv was the fiercest woman he'd ever met. "How does Mr. E not know about this? With every buyer disappearing after his purchase, someone would notice."

She stretched her legs and reclined behind the wheel, eyes flicking to the side mirror. "The buyers are supposed to disappear. They crawl out of whatever hole they come from, make the transaction, and return to their holes. Which happen to be in shady places south of the border. They're all from Mexico."

That part made sense. Traquero had the accent.

Josh shuddered, knowing the fat freak was walking the streets then going home to torture his wife. "What about the referral system? They're all connected."

"Wrong. Camila is the connection. When she drove away with the body of her buyer, she also had his phone. And the contact number for his referral. She used it to create a network, initially on her own and now with the help of the guys. They sell referrals to potential buyers." She took a breath, bit her lip, and glanced at him.

Yeah, he was listening, shocked speechless, his head pounding.

"They lure would-be slave owners," she said, "often acting as previous buyers, collect the contact number, and sell it to the next client in line. The buyers aren't connected to each other. They're connected to Camila." She barked out a laugh, rubbed her eyes, and sighed. "Camila actually charges each fucker for the referral number of the next fucker. Then he sits back and waits for Van's call. A year later, she's emptying his pockets and disposing his body."

*Jesus.* He scrubbed a hand over his mouth. Fields of black whipped by the window, passing him by, leaving him reeling in another dimension. "What is Mr. E's role in this?"

Her gaze ping-ponged between the side mirror and the road. "He started this horrific operation. I think he owned slaves before he brought in Van and me. I mean, he taught Van how to train slaves. Why would he know that?" She tugged at her ear, her expression pensive in the passing headlights. "Now he just sits on his greedy ass and collects money while Van and I scramble beneath his blackmailing thumb."

Nausea rolled through his gut. What would've happened if he'd been the obedient slave she'd intended him to be? His own delivery would've played out. Traquero would've been gutted. Then what?

"I'm not like the others." His chest tightened. "My parents are searching for me. I would've wanted to go back."

She flinched. "I know. I chose you anyway, without a clue on how to deal with the aftermath."

The whole operation was risky. So damned risky. One misstep, one slipped word from the buyer to Mr. E, and the whole thing would fall apart with Liv at the center. Yet they'd pulled it off six times.

"Where does Mr. E think these referrals come from?" he asked.

"Why would he care as long as he has his next paycheck lined up? Van makes the initial call, gathers the buyer's requirements, and establishes Mr. E's rules on anonymity. Mr. E never deals with any of them."

"It takes months to hunt and capture a new slave? Ten weeks to train him? And you're doing this, knowing the slave will never see the inside of a buyer's prison?"

"Hoping." Her voice wavered. "Never knowing. Van was banned to tag along after Camila's intro meeting. That ban could've been lifted. Or I could've been overpowered during a delivery. Or my freedom fighters could've been delayed...like tonight." She peeked at him from the corner of her eye.

"Freedom fighters." His lips twitched. "I like that."

"I've been thinking." She glanced at him and back to the road. "Van knows who Mr. E is. What if he also knows where my family is? Maybe we could tie him up and torture him until he tells us everything he knows? We'd keep him alive so the contract isn't triggered."

Wow, that was the thinnest idea he'd ever heard. "You're serious?"

She shrugged. "I've got muscle now." She gave his arm a pointed once-over. "What would Jesus do if he was built like you?"

"Cast the first stone?" Honestly, he didn't know. "What if Van doesn't know anything?"

"Then we're fucked either way."

For the next two hours, she answered his questions about Camila's operation, and he still wasn't sure he understood all the intricacies of the process. When she turned into the *Two Trails Crossing* subdivision, she stopped the van a block from the house. "Meet me on the front porch. He's not due back for a few days, but we're running out of luck. If he's there, I'll find a way to sneak you in." She left him on the curb with a heart-pounding kiss and trust in her eyes.

The walk was quick, but the wait on the porch dragged ten minutes too long. Drapes blacked out the windows. There was no light peeking through the creases. No sounds coming from within. What if Van was in there? Hurting her? His nerves stretched by the second until he finally snapped.

Down the driveway, past the garage, he stopped at the back door, found the keypad, and punched in 0054. She'd said all the doors but hers opened with multiple codes. Van and Mr. E had their own.

The door opened into the kitchen, lit by the lamp over the sink. Soft sobs crept from behind the bar and tore through his chest.

He sprinted around the counter and found her curled up on the floor, clutching a photo and a newspaper clipping. "Liv? Liv, what happened?" His pulse roared in his ears. "Are we alone?"

She nodded, expression pallid, voice empty. "Mr. E was here." When he jerked back, she grabbed his t-shirt, her face twisted in horror. "Oh God, Josh. It's...it's..." Her gaze was lost to the papers shaking violently in her hand.

Stomach plummeting, he pulled her into his lap and wrenched the pages free. The photo showed a small smiling girl, her dark brown hair the color and length of Liv's. Same milky complexion. Same delicate chin. The date and time printed on the bottom indicated it was six hours old. On the back, neat cursive scrawled, *Do not fail again.*

Liv coiled her arms around his ribs, her body trembling. "Mom got married." Her voice was hoarse, desolate. "That's why I couldn't find her."

He kissed her head, his lips numb with dread, and dragged his eyes to the news article printed by the *Key West Examiner,* dated today.

*Local woman killed in plane crash*

*The pilot killed in a plane crash near Key West is being described as a skydiving adventurer and a generous volunteer in the community.*

*"It's devastating," said Wyatt Keleen, husband and co-owner of her skydiving school. "Jill was a warm-hearted woman and well-known in the Keys for her charitable efforts with families of homicide victims and missing persons."*

*Keleen said Jill's only child was kidnapped and murdered seven years earlier.*

*Jill's body was discovered off the coast of Lois Key in a swampy area. The wide cavity surrounding the wreckage indicates her life came to an end after a high-speed impact.*

*The Transportation Safety Board is investigating the crash. Officials have yet to confirm the cause. Memorial services were held today at 2:00 PM at Summerland Key Cove Airport.*

# THIRTY-SEVEN

Liv lay on her side on the mattress, showered, fed, and *depleted*. Josh had kept her talking through the night, prompting her to share memories of Mom and preventing her from crawling inside herself. Eyes itchy and sore, she'd cried more than she had in seven years. If she didn't stop, she would find herself ass-up in the prison of her own self-pity.

Mom had survived Liv's death. She could survive Mom's. And she would. With Josh's hand in hers.

He'd run their dirty soup bowls downstairs two minutes earlier. Her fingers were clenched so tightly in the sheets, one would've thought he'd been gone for hours. Her lungs didn't seem to suck enough air, her focus blurring on the door, awaiting his return. When had she become so fucking needy?

The angel in the photo she'd tacked to the wall smiled down at her with eyes and hair as dark as hers. So much better than a video. She had a snapshot of her daughter's face, forever looking back at her. Perhaps Mr. E gave it to her to cushion the murder of Mom. Or to lessen his own regret. But she knew that was bullshit.

She'd failed to nail the deal with Traquero, which earned her Mom's death. But he'd still given the referral, which earned her Mattie's photo. His motivation for not sending a video had to do with the fact he didn't trust her with access to e-mail without Van present.

That thought awoke an unwelcome feeling about Van's departure. It wasn't odd for him to hunt immediately upon receipt of a buyer's specifications. But given his enraged reaction to the meeting with Traquero, why hadn't he waited for her return and the opportunity to punish her?

What if Van had left to kill Mom himself? Was he cruel enough to not only let it happen but *make* it happen? Despite his violent nature, she struggled to believe he was the hand that brought down Mom's plane, but how well did she really know him?

She and Josh had discussed going to the FBI to request an investigation into the plane crash. Hell, they wanted to divulge everything. How closely was Mr. E monitoring them? How easy was his access to Mattie? Could the authorities hunt down a masked man before that man hurt her daughter? It was too much risk.

The door clicked open, and Josh's broad frame brimmed her horizon. Relief whooshed from her lungs. He tilted his head to the side, and his alert eyes narrowed on her fists. She uncurled her fingers.

A muscle jumped in his bare chest. "You still think I'm going to leave you?"

She shook her head swiftly. No, the stubborn bastard wasn't going anywhere.

"I think I'm just feeling a little raw." And exposed. Definitely not a feeling she was used to.

The sharp lines in his face softened. He closed the door and strode toward her, the towel around his waist hung low beneath crowded bricks of abdominal muscles.

He bent over her and planted his fists beside her hip, the mattress depressing beneath the weight of his vascular arms and upper body. Jesus, his proximity was distracting to a fault. It wasn't just the cuts of his body, crystalline green eyes, and strong lips that demanded attention. His pursuit to please her was a perceptible aura that charged the space around him.

Looking up into the face of a man who would damn himself to protect her, she knew she'd found her sanctuary, her deliverance, her future.

He swooped in to kiss her, and she got a lungful of his nourishing scent. Clean, pure Josh. She kissed him back, licking his mouth, tasting the familiar intimacy, and clinging to his love.

His tongue trailed fire around hers, leaving no part of her mouth untouched. It was impossible to be afraid when he was so close, so intense, that the barriers between them burned away. He moaned against her lips and kissed her with a pressing necessity, stoking a flame in her belly and coaxing a curl of something she hadn't felt in years. *Joy.*

Guilt breathed through her, a foul-smelling intruder, whispering her failings. Seven years of slavery, chained by a threat, and she still lost Mom.

Her lips stretched back. Their teeth tapped. She turned her chin away, but he caught it. Then he caught her eyes.

Fingers pinching her jaw, his expression swam in contemplation. He stared at her, panting from the kiss. "What would your mom say to you right now?"

A quiver interrupted the rigid set of her chin, her lungs pumping to hold in a thousand clogged tears. She closed her eyes and saw Mom laughing, jumping into the wind, her hair whipping around her smiling face. "She'd say, use a condom."

He huffed. "I think your mom was much more profound than that. Try again."

She opened her eyes, diving straight into his. "She used to say, what defines us is not how we fall but how we land."

He leaned in and stroked his nose along her scar. "You've survived the hardest landings. You'll survive this one."

Was that what she'd been doing all these years? Landing? "Feels more like plummeting out of control."

Every harrowing moment was chained to the next one. What if the cycle was finally broken? If she could find Mattie, then what? She'd never considered a future outside of the attic walls.

Until Josh.

He stood and adjusted the towel at his hip, watching her. "You're hurting, Liv. I want you to give it to me. All of your hurt."

Her eyebrows snapped together, her chest pinching. "What?"

He studied her, rubbing his jaw, gears spinning behind his eyes. Then he turned and paced to the cabinet. The round brawn of his ass flexed beneath the towel. The muscles in his back compressed and expanded as he worked the combo lock. Clearly, he'd figured out all her lock codes were the same. He opened the door. What the hell was he doing?

With a length of chain and a flogger in hand, he returned to the mattress. "You feel like you're plummeting? Like you don't have any control? Then control me." He grabbed her wrist and put the implements in her hand. "Do this on our terms. Not Traquero's or Mr. E's or anyone else's."

She glanced at the flogger and chain then searched his hopeful eyes for a long moment. He wasn't just new to sexual submission. He was new to sex. He might not have consciously known what he was asking, but it was a request voiced from a sequestered part of his identity, one she'd seen rise to the surface with the first cut of her cane. Of course, he wanted her to fuck him. But he also wanted her to hurt him. His hard powerful body seemed to crave the rough handling, being pushed to its limits.

Letting the chain spill into her lap, she slapped the leather tips of the flogger against her palm.

He didn't flinch, his eyes hooded and penetrating as he crouched before her. The towel separated at his thigh, the downward angle of his legs hiding what was between.

"You want to explore your naughty side, Josh?"

His chin tilting slightly, his cheeks sucking in with a steady inhale, he traced a knuckle over her nipple where it tightened against her t-shirt. His eyes didn't waver from hers, a luminescent glow beneath the determined mantle of his dark eyebrows. "I want to explore everything with you."

The idea sent a tremor through her, fanning a needy blaze between her legs.

It was around three in the morning, but they were both too restless to sleep. They had nothing but time on their hands until Van returned. She could either spend the days wallowing in misery or…

She let her gaze take a leisurely stroll over the messy spikes of black hair raking away from his forehead, the stubble roughing his jaw, the vein pulsing in his thick neck, and the taut skin stretching over bulges of shoulders and biceps. His cock jerked beneath the towel as he watched her devour every gorgeous detail.

Fuck, he was a lot of man. Chiseled, powerful, perceptive, and his attention remained resolutely fixed on her. She gathered the chain and rose to stand beside him. He'd said she needed control, but he'd initiated this, and he held the power to end it. The moment he said *no* she would stop.

There were a few things she could regulate, however, and she would use her mastery of dominance to help him find his boundaries. Her ratty, thigh-length t-shirt didn't exactly exude an authoritative air, but she didn't need a costume or mask. Not with him.

"You want me to have control? I'm taking it. Now." A stillness swept over her, measuring her breaths, loosening her shoulders. "I decide the how, the intensity, the purpose, all for my pleasure."

The depressions outlining his shoulder blades twitched. His hands flattened on the mattress. "Yes, Mistress."

The appellation was shockingly arousing, fluttering through her belly with nipping tingles. The title had never stirred a response in her. But now, it was given willingly, on his terms. For her and no one else.

At the center of the room, she connected the chain to the latch in the ceiling. "Stand here with your back to me."

She didn't wait for him to obey. She returned the flogger to the cabinet and gathered a pair of cuffs and three things he would've never chosen.

He stood where she'd directed, arms crossed above his head. The vertical indentation down the length of his back led erotically to the rise of his firm ass peeking above the towel. His torso, wide on top, narrowed to a slim waist, its appeal punctuated with two dimples where his back met his hips. The sight alone rolled the heat between her legs into a pulsating clench.

She wanted to just stand there, relish the burgeoning rise of desire, and stare at him. So she did, taking in the carved angles of his body. The backs of his ears twitched, probably from a flexing jaw. Oh, she knew he was squirming with impatience, but he remained where she'd told him with his back to her. Still and silent, awaiting her next order.

After another long, taunting moment, she crossed the distance and stood behind him. Not touching but close enough to let him feel the heat of her body. "Are you hard?"

"Yes, Mistress." A rasp.

Her heart thumped. It didn't matter how rare his innocence was, how fast he ran a football, or how respectable he behaved among his parishioners. It was the sexy, honest pain slut under it all that enthralled her now.

She placed the toys on the floor and strapped the cuffs on his wrists. Once his arms were restrained to the dangling chains, she grabbed the blindfold from the pile. "I'm going to open your eyes."

She tied it around his head and smiled, certain his imagination was running rampant. What kind of dirty thoughts were spinning through his mind?

A tremble skated down his back. She chased it with a fingertip, sliding through beads of sweat, memorizing each dip and peak of muscle. "You won't come without permission."

He tensed, relaxed. "Yes, Mistress."

Feeling his skin creep beneath her touch and controlling him with just her voice and the pad of her finger was intoxicating. She ran her hands down his sides, caught the towel, and dropped it to the floor. Circling him, she trailed her fingers over his warm flesh, touching him everywhere. Everywhere except the very swollen erection jutting from between his legs. She caressed his thighs, the indentions in his hips and abs, savoring his shallow gasps.

She returned to the items on the floor and raised the rattan cane, the most advanced tool in her cabinet. It took her years to learn how to use it without splitting the skin and leaving a scar.

It whistled through the air as she swung it back.

*Thwack.*

The single strike of the cane's rigid width formed two side-by-side welts on his ass with a narrow depression of skin in between. The nerve endings in that depression would be stinging like a son-of-a-bitch.

He drew gulps of air, his fingers curling around the chain above him. He was likely feeling a fire of pain spreading outward from the impact site, blazing through his legs and back.

She whacked him again, an inch above the first marks. He breathed, clutched the chain tighter. Three more thwacks. Ten red lines striped his ass. His head dropped forward, his body shivering.

Shit, did he not know he could end this at anytime? What was the protocol for consensual beatings?

"Tell me *no,* and we're done." She rubbed her eyes, nauseous with guilt. She should've talked this out with him before they started.

He stood taller, raised his chin. "Don't stop." His voice was thick with arousal.

She walked around him to see his face. The blindfold hid his eyes, but his lips were parted, his jaw slack. Between his legs was the hardest, longest cock she'd ever seen. She squeezed her thighs together and returned to his backside.

Pacing back and forth, she varied the cane strokes between hard and soft so that he wouldn't know what to expect. "What does a future with you look like, Joshua Carter?"

*Thwack.*

"A lot of prayers." His ass flexed.

*Thwack.*

"Bible study three times a day."

*Thwack.*

He lifted up on his toes, his voice hoarse. "No smoking and cussing."

Very funny. *Thwack.*

"Missionary position only."

A laugh burst from her throat, and she stumbled, her swing missing him completely.

"No sex until we're married," he said.

Oh my God. Did he really just mimic her practiced deadpanned tone?

She moved to stand in front of him, so she could watch his mouth. "You're going to hell."

His lips twitched then erupted into a full-faced smile. "Oh, good. I was worried you'd be there without me."

Her heart swelled, tightening her chest. Fuck her, but she loved this man.

Dropping to her knees, she set the cane on the floor and lowered her lips to the tip of his erection. A gentle kiss pulled a moan from his lungs and a bead of pre-cum from his cock.

She grinned. "No coming without permission."

His head fell back on his shoulders, his thighs quivering. "You're going to kill me."

"Over and over again."

Gripping the root of his cock, she drew him into her mouth, the velvety skin burning against her tongue. She sucked him greedily, drinking in the flavor of salt and man. She ran a hand over his contracting muscles, squeezing the back of his thigh, careful to avoid the welts. The throb in her pussy intensified, releasing moisture along her inner thighs.

When his hips started rocking, she didn't scold him. His movements were confident, needy, stubborn in his desire to please her. Exactly how she wanted him. She ran her teeth along his cock and twisted her fist in time with the long consistent pulls of her mouth.

His breathing strangled, and his thrusts ceased. He was holding back his release. She was mesmerized. And trembling with desire.

She tormented him with a few more dragging suckles along his length and breathed around him, "Come."

Taking him over with a one word command was the ultimate high, exceeded only by his willingness to give her this. He groaned as he came, filling her throat, the steel of his cock jerking against her tongue, his body shaking violently. She licked him clean, humming, smiling, so damned pleased.

She rose and stepped behind him as he slumped in his restraints, catching his breath. She didn't give him time to catch it for long. Shedding the t-shirt, she grabbed the last item on the floor, stepped into it, and cinched the straps around her waist and thighs. Next came the lube, on her fingers and the attached dildo.

She'd never enjoyed the strap-on with the boys she'd trained, which was why she'd chosen to do it now. This was Josh, and it was on their terms.

Her body thrummed as she pressed against his back and prodded his crack with the dildo.

"What are you doing?" There was no hint of alarm in his voice, only curiosity. Evidently, the butt plug had chased away his fears.

"I'm going to fuck your ass." She kissed his shoulder, her pussy slick and pulsing. "Tell me *no*."

He pushed against the strap-on. "I'm yours, Liv. Inside and out."

She didn't have to see his eyes to know what was behind them. He was once a captive in her attic. Now she was the one held captive, enraptured by his unwavering trust.

She took great care stretching his tight ring with her lubricated fingers, stroking and circling the opening. She nipped at his back, and finger by finger, he loosened around her intrusion. His feet stepped farther apart, his body settling into complete submission.

Pressing the tip of the dildo against his rectum, she reached around his hips and gripped the stone-hard girth of his cock. She smiled against his back. "You're an incredible man."

"I'm a lucky man." He panted and rocked against her, helping her work in the first inch. His voice choked. "When you're done having your way with me, I get to return the pleasure." He bucked backward. "Now quit talking and work those hips."

She half-gasped, half-laughed, and smacked his thigh. With a few strokes up and down his erection, she teased him into a trembling frenzy. Then she thrust and held still, her pelvis flat against his ass, allowing him to adjust to the pressure.

His sigh filled the room. That was her cue. She did work her hips, driving into him, her fist jerking his cock, her other hand roaming his chest, his abs, his balls. The leather strap behind the dildo ground against her clit, building her into a panting mess.

Maybe she hadn't reached his limit, but after a few minutes, she'd reached hers. She pulled out, untied his blindfold, and released the chain on his wrist cuffs. As she washed her hands in the sink and stepped out of the strap-on belt, she felt his eyes scaring every inch of her skin. But he remained where she'd left him, waiting, watching.

"Where did this obedience come from?" She dried her hands and turned to face him.

He tapped his fingers on his chest, directly over his heart, a fire flickering in his eyes.

She nodded, her throat swelling. "I relinquish control." Not that she'd ever fully had it.

In four swift strides, he was on her, lifting her, and slamming her back against the nearest wall. His hand pushed between their hips, gripping his cock, and aligning their bodies.

He drove hard and true in one long stroke. They groaned in unison. She hooked her legs around his waist, her arms around his neck, and let him pound her against the wall. He moved in urgent thrusts, his lips finding hers. She felt the joining in every part of her body.

The wet slapping sounds of their lovemaking echoed around them, their bodies moving together as one. Guttural breaths. Heated moans. His muscles bunched around her, supporting her, his hips hammering to the tune of her heart.

The hands on her ass clenched, fingertips digging in. Their tongues swiped and slashed and curled together. Her release was climbing hard and fast. Her toes flexed. Her arms around his shoulders wobbled. Her desire knotted, double knotted, and tightened.

"Josh," she gasped into his mouth.

He released her lips, worked his hips, and cupped her jaw, staring into her eyes with an intensity that pushed her over.

The sensations lifted her up, up, up, and burst outward. The ecstasy of stimulation softened her bones, melted her body, and robbed her breathes. He continued to thrust, her pussy convulsing around him, her skin tingling.

Grinding his pelvis against her, his hands squeezed her ass and his smoldering gaze collided with hers. "That was so damned beautiful."

Then he took her mouth again, gently, letting her feel his words. She kissed him with the same tender tempo, rotating her hips against him, ratcheting his already labored exhales.

A moment later, he dropped his head on the wall beside hers and thrust once, twice. A long groan vibrated his body. His arms coiled around her waist, tightening. His muscles quivered, and his cock jerked deep inside her.

The hum of contentment whispered through them. At last, she was exhausted enough to sleep, and it would be a restful sleep with him wrapped around her in a blanket of protection and love.

They showered, she treated his welts, and they lay between the sheets, chest to chest, sharing breaths. Their legs entwined, and his toes caressed her ankle. She felt him with her entire body, every nerve ending reaching for him.

Through the absence of light, she found his eyes. "You freed me."

His fingers stroked down her back and rested in the crack of her butt. "Then we'll tackle the next few days knowing we're already free."

The strong beat of his heart against her breast filled her with hope, something she'd never depended on until that moment. "We need to find Mattie."

"We will."

She drifted to sleep with a heart full of trust in those two words.

# THIRTY-EIGHT

Liv woke however many hours later, sweating, panting, her mind fluttering with erotic images of Josh. Face down on the mattress, her breaths steamed against the pillow. Her pussy was a furnace of wet heat, throbbing with its own demanding heartbeat. And sliding along its slit was a strong and skillful tongue.

The bathroom light cast a subdued luster through the room. She glanced over her shoulder and met Josh's sparkling eyes peering above her ass cheeks.

With his hands under her hips and his body stretched out between her legs, his gaze burned into hers. He lifted her pelvis, rocking her against his mouth and kissing her pussy with a single-minded ferociousness. He glided his lips through her folds, sucking, curling his tongue, his hips grinding on the mattress.

His groan hummed through her core as he pushed her thighs farther apart and deepened the kiss. His intensity was contagious, shuddering over her spine and coiling her body inside and out.

Her climax exploded, wrenching a moan from her lungs and rolling her eyes into the back of her head. He licked her through the sweep of sensations, thrusting a finger inside her, his breathy noises magnifying the ecstasy.

Then he bit her ass. She shrieked, and he laughed, dragging his lips over her back, nipping and pecking as he crawled toward her head. She buried her face in the pillow. Apparently, his libido was making up for lost time.

She sighed, smiling, her voice muffled in cotton. "You're such a horny slut."

Chuckling, his mouth reached her nape, sucking the skin below her ear. He covered her body with his hot leaden weight, his thighs bracketing hers. His palms slid beneath her chest, massaging and cupping her breasts. Oh God, the sensation of his touch combined with his body pressing down on her was indescribable.

His cock prodded, wedging into the tight space between her thighs. He reached between them, guiding the connection, and thrust. She clutched at the pillow, arching her back and pushing against him to deepen the drugging stimulation.

The position and angle of her legs pressed together limited his thrusts to short, shallow fucks. She couldn't get close enough and bowed her body into his. She wanted him to fuck harder, though he was hammering his hips, his cock filling her with each forceful drive.

He was inside her, his body enveloping her and shaking violently with need, yet she wanted more. Couldn't get enough of him. Her heart pounded against the mattress, and her ribs felt bruised inside. Needy and crazed, she twisted her neck, seeking his mouth. He met her tongue and responded with the same urgency, feeding her his desire, swallowing her exhales.

His toes curled against hers, his powerful body rubbing along the length of her smaller one. One hand shifted beneath her hip, his trembling fingers fumbling around her clit. He found it, circled through her wetness, and flicked it with precision. *Right there. Oh fuck, right there.*

"Come," she breathed against his lips. "Come with me."

He rotated his hips, rubbed her clit, and ate at her mouth until they stiffened, gasped, and fell together.

When they caught their breaths, he leaned in and nibbled on her earlobe. "Morning."

"Morning."

An hour later, they realized it was, in fact, afternoon. They stood at the keypad, showered, dressed, and stared at the digital *3:18 PM* on her phone. Despite their shared smiles, unease buzzed between them. Their bodies needed to be fed, so they were forced to leave the room.

She stuffed her phone in the back pocket of her jeans and clutched the door handle. "Let me go down first. I'll make sure he's not back and return to get you."

He reached around her and punched in the code. "We went through this last night. You're not going down there, or anywhere, without me."

The door clicked open. She flashed him her most threatening glare. "Then stay behind me and out of sight."

Through the vacant outer chamber, another keypad, and down the dark stairway they went. Silence greeted her at the bottom. Daylight leaked in through the kitchen window, spreading a sparse glow into the hallway.

She reached back, placed a hand on his chest, and gave him a silent command with her eyes. *Stay.*

In the kitchen, dirty soup bowls filled the sink. The refrigerator hummed. Outside the window, the trees rustled beneath the afternoon sun. With a stuttering heart beat, she opened the door to the garage. The van sat alone. She held her breath as she checked the driveway and the front curb through the windows. Van's sedan wasn't there, and he had no reason to hide his car from her. Her edginess loosened, but remnants of uncertainty remained.

Returning to the stairway, she found Josh gripping the door frame, his impatient eyes blazing from within the shadows.

She touched his abs and met a wall of rock-hard tension. "He's not here. Follow me."

Leading him down the hallway, a familiar dread gripped her gut. She needed to check Van's room of horrors, if only to ease some of her lingering anxiety about Van being there. But she didn't want to go in that room alone.

Hand on the knob, she inhaled deeply. "This is his room. As you know, he is…" How did one sum up morally, mentally, aesthetically, and theoretically damaged? "Fucked up."

Impatience vibrated from Josh. "Open the door, Liv."

She did. And gasped. Stumbling through the room, she spun in a circle, hand over her mouth. An empty mattress. An empty gun cabinet. The drawers hung from the dresser. Empty. The closet door stood open. Empty. No mannequins. No clothes. There was nothing but worn carpet and the musty reek of vacancy.

"He's gone." Huge fucking alarm bells blared in her head. Her heart raced and senses heightened.

Why would he leave? Was it fear? Was all hell about to break loose?

Josh clasped her fingers, his forehead furrowed in thought. "Tell me what you're thinking."

She rubbed her head. "Van's a sadistic dick, but he wouldn't have left me if my life was in danger. Something prompted him to leave in a hurry, though."

Shards of glass littered the carpet in front of the gun cabinet. The door was a toothy frame hanging on its hinge.

Her stomach turned. "That's what he hit when I told him about Traquero." Had he been angry *for* her? Or *at* her? It shouldn't have mattered, but when it came to Van, her feelings gnarled and bled in complication. She thought back to the last conversation she had with him.

"He said he was leaving in the morning to begin his scouting."

"Only, he left before we got back." Josh strode out of the room and into the spare bedroom.

A square of ratty green carpet buckled between the walls. The metal blinds on the single window hung lopsided and yellowed by age.

"This one has always been empty," she said. A room reserved for her, one she'd refused to move into.

He turned and walked down the hall, his gait quickening as he approached the kitchen. "He was pissed about what happened with Traquero. He must've packed immediately and blew out of town."

She ran to keep up with his longer strides. "Why? To kill my mom?" She flinched and clenched her fists against the stabbing reminder. "Or to protect himself from Mr. E?" *But why would he need to do that?* "Van's a lot of things, but he's not a coward."

Josh veered into the kitchen and opened the fridge door, scanning its contents. Of course, the linebacker was focused on his stomach. Her thoughts were on a crash site, somewhere off the coast of the Keys, and the man who might've caused it.

Josh tossed deli meat and cheese on the counter. Then they sat through a nerve-stretching meal. She picked at her sandwich, her stomach souring with each bite. He barked at her to eat when she sat still too long, his anxiety feeding on hers. They finished in silence, staring at the door to the garage as if it would open any moment and let in all the answers.

Thirty minutes later, they tackled the filing cabinet in the hall closet, the only place in the house that could've held a clue to Mr. E's identity. She'd dug through it countless times, but maybe she'd missed something amongst the bills, receipts for generic items purchased for the house, tax filings, and news articles.

"Who is Liv Smith?" Josh held up two hands full of paperwork.

"The fake identity Mr. E gave me."

"Everything is in that name. The rental agreement for the house. Liv Smith." He thumbed to the next one. "The titles to the vehicles. Liv Smith." His face twisted beneath clenched eyebrows, his voice rising. "The friggin' repair bill for the A/C unit. Liv Smith."

She looked up from her drawer. "I see that."

"You see that?" His cheeks burned red, and his eyes widened in a state of disbelief. He wiped his forehead with the back of his paper-filled hand. "Not a single document shows Van Quiso paying taxes, consuming groceries, or living here at all. Ever."

Her hackles rose in defense. "He told me to sign stuff. It was legitimate stuff related to the house. I signed it with a fake name." But she didn't realize the name was on *everything*.

"What about the neighbors? Do they know him?"

"No. He comes and goes from the garage. Tinted windows. Just like Mr. E." She picked the edge of the paper in her hand and said, dejectedly, "I cut the grass."

He blew out a long exhale. "It's like he doesn't even exist." He returned the papers to their hanging folders, none too gently. "What does it mean, Liv?"

It meant Van was smarter than her. "He can disappear." And she couldn't. Not if she wanted to keep Mattie safe.

"Why would he do that?" He slammed the drawer.

She lifted her chin and collided with the sharp green of his eyes. "Mr. E could be planning to shut this down and kill us. Or Van could've decided on a career change after my fuck up and bolted." Without saying goodbye. Her heart squeezed. *Stupid asshole heart.*

Josh crouched beside her, shifted her hand from the thick file hanging in the drawer, and pulled it out. Her swallow clogged in her throat, along with her breath. How would he react to the news clippings about his disappearance?

Kneeling, he leafed through each one, his face paling, his brow furrowing. She'd skimmed through all of them. Seemed Van had added more in his paranoia about Josh's notoriety. The file was filled with reports about the dead-end investigation, Baylor University's on-going support, search parties, and walk-a-thon's to raise money and awareness. Her heart twisted as she imagined all the pain and resentment barreling through Josh.

Scooting closer, she straddled one of his knees and wrapped her arms around his neck. He welcomed her with an embrace around her waist, holding her tight as he read.

When he finished the pile, he returned it to the drawer. "Where's yours?" His voice was quiet and strained.

She reached in the back of the drawer and handed him the thin dossier. "My disappearance didn't get the publicity yours did." She offered a smile, but it quivered at the corners.

With a kiss on the crook of her mouth, he opened the file. They read the first article in silence.

*Body of missing Texas girl found in Del Valle*
*Officials in Texas say that remains found in an abandoned house this weekend are those of a 17-year-old girl who has been missing fourteen months.*
*Austin police confirmed Monday that the remains were burned beyond recognition. Police said that autopsy results indicated they belonged to Liv Reed. A 9mm shell casing and two unfired .38 caliber bullets were discovered at the crime scene.*
*Reed's mother, Jill, told KRPC-TV that roller blades were found in the*

*house. Liv was wearing them when she disappeared from Fentress Airpark. Her class ring from Eastside Memorial High School was also recovered.*

*Austin Police Chief, Eli Eary, said it's believed that Reed was shot and killed in the abandoned Del Valle house, and her body was burned to destroy any evidence.*

Her eyes blurred, unable to read further. An old ache clawed through her throat. Regret for Mom having suffered through her death and the terrible frustration for not being able to prove she still lived. And searing the edges of that ache was a harrowing sadness for the nameless victim who died in her place.

Josh stuffed the documents in the drawer, closed it, and shifted her legs to wrap around his waist. His lips stroked across her brow, his hands rubbing over her back. He held her as if he'd never let go. She held him the same way, arms tightening, fingers curling into flesh and muscle.

"There are no articles on the other captives." His tone was distant, somber.

A ragged inhale hitched through her. "There was no fanfare with their disappearances. Those who did miss them wouldn't have involved the police. Kate's brothers are criminals. Camila was a gopher for the cartel. The others came from crack houses or no homes at all." She kissed his neck, inhaling his scent to chase away the toxicity of the conversation, and leaned back. "What now?"

He rose, lifting her with him and standing her on her feet. His jaw was hard, his eyes equally so. "Now, we wait for Mr. E to come looking for Van. Or for us. And when he does, we'll be ready."

Her pulse kicked up in approval. She wanted him to color his words and fill her mind with images. *His* images. "Ready to do what?"

"To trap him and beat the ever-loving crap out of him until he exposes Mattie's location. Then we'll slice his throat from ear to ear."

Hope spun around her, curling her lips. It continued to lift her through the night as he led her upstairs, fucked her, cuddled her, fed her, and fucked her again.

They remained in the safety of the attic for two days, waiting for Mr. E's text, closing the door only when they were sleeping, planning and exploring each other. The latter was a new experience with whips and ropes and creative sexual positions. She only egressed for food, and her sentinel was always an arm-length behind her. They never emerged unarmed. He carried his mom's .22 in his hand. She carried the LC9 in the waistband of her jeans.

On the third afternoon, she crept down the stairs and stopped. Her toes touched the bottom step, illuminated by a glow of light. Josh bumped into her back.

Her scalp tingled. The hairs on her arms stood on end. The kitchen light didn't reach the staircase.

*Fuck, fuck, fuck.* She stretched her neck to peer into the sitting room. The lamp drenched the dated decor in a sickening yellow wash. She never turned that damned lamp on.

Her heart thundered in her ears. Mr. E hadn't sent her a text. He always sent a text.

She spun and pressed a finger against his lips, shaking her head. His eyes narrowed, his body vibrated, and his stomach hardened to stone against her hand. She drew the 9mm from her waistband, flicked off the safety, and turned back. Choking on the thickening dread in her throat, she stepped into the hallway.

With a final glare at the silhouette of aggression vibrating in the staircase, she pointed a finger at him and strode toward the kitchen with the gun at her side.

She tripped in the doorway, her heart stumbling with her breath. A mannequin sat at the table, a naked woman with a head of hair, holding a doll. All the blood in her face dumped to her stomach.

She scanned the corners of the room for Van, unsure what to do with the gun. Raise it? Conceal it? Should she go for business as usual? She held it at her side. Where the fuck was he?

Her eardrums throbbed, straining for the sound of footsteps. She positioned herself so that she could see behind the bar, the entrance to the sitting room, and the mannequin at the table.

"Van?" She shouted loud enough to dissuade Josh from charging after her.

But what if it wasn't Van? What if this was one of Mr. E's games?

A few feet away, the brown marbled eyes of the plastic woman stared back at her. A painted red line connected one glass eye to the pink hand-drawn mouth. Propped on the mannequin's lap, the doll was the size of a small child, clothed in a red checkered dress.

Liv's scar tingled in her cheek, her muscles stiffening to the point of pain. Staring at the morbid reproductions of her and Mattie, she tried to keep the contents of her stomach from painting the floor.

Gut-twisting curiosity shuffled her feet forward. With the gun rattling in her hand, she slid her other hand through the sparse hair on the heads. Each strand was different from the other but also…the same. They varied in hues of brown, intricately combed together and sewn into some kind of mesh cap glued to the scalps. The fibers between her fingers weren't glossy like synthetic hair. They felt thinner, some damaged, realistic. *Familiar.*

She jerked her hand back, her stomach bubbling toward her throat. *Oh God.* Her hair. Why? Jesus, fuck, what did it mean? She pressed a fist against her belly, backed up, and slammed into a hard body.

A hint of cologne touched her nose. The width of torso was too big. She turned, but Van's arm around her chest caught her, pinning her back to his chest. His hand squeezed her breast, and she sucked in a breath. If she shot him, the contract on Mattie's life would be activated.

She pressed the side of the gun against her thigh to thwart the shaking in her hand.

His lips touched her shoulder, her neck, the scar, creeping goosebumps over her skin. "I know you don't approve of them, Liv. But I needed something to remember you by."

# THIRTY-NINE

"What are you doing with the gun, Liv?"

Van's voice was a low, strumming pulse in her ears. But there was an unraveling edge to it that scared the shit out of her. She drew in a breath and hoped to hell Josh stayed out of sight.

She trailed her fingertips over the back of his hand where he cupped her breast, to soothe him, to reestablish their fucked-up connection. "I thought you'd taken a permanent vacation."

He sank his teeth into the side of her throat, not enough to break skin, but the sharp pinch stole her breath and raised her on tip-toes. One shift of his hand and he could break her neck.

She leaned into the bite. "Did you come back to kill me?"

His arm and teeth released her with a jerk. She fell forward, righted herself, and spun with the gun raised in both hands.

Three days of stubble darkened his jaw. His steely eyes were void of their usual glint, sagging beneath his hood. His smirk seemed forced as he slid a toothpick in his mouth. "You're the one pointing a gun."

She aimed at his chest. His jacket concealed the strength of his body, but she knew every muscle, every twitch, every scar. He'd taken her virginity, trained her as a sex slave, whipped her, fucked her, and loved her. She wasn't any different from him. With one exception. She responded to the word *no*.

The light in the doorway behind him rippled. She didn't shift her eyes, fearing it would give away Josh's presence.

To distract Van, she backed to the wall, until the length of the room separated them, and jerked her chin at the dolls. "Do they mean you won't be pulling my hair anymore?"

"I won't have a choice." He searched her face longingly, desperately, as if collecting every detail into a special pocket of memory made just for her.

*I needed something to remember you by.*

She shivered and steadied the gun. "Why did you come back?"

The heat in his eyes said, *To fuck you.* His suspicious non-answers said, *To kill you.*

"Just say it, Van."

If she shot him, Mattie was dead. If he killed her, Josh would kill him. Mattie was dead either way.

"I'm sorry about your mom." Sincerity wrinkled the skin around his eyes, but his voice was a monotone hum.

His lips clenched on the toothpick, flattening into a line. His gaze hardened.

He was planning something cruel.

Her molars sawed together, her nerves stretching. She bit down so hard on her cheek the taste of copper filled her mouth. "You murdered Mom."

His face clouded, his timbre scratchy. "I'm sorry. I…" His expression blanked. He reached behind his back.

Jesus, he was going to kill her. Her heart stopped, and her finger slid over the trigger.

Time throttled into a series of choices, measured by the slam of her heart and the cascading motions that followed. Van tugged at something in the back of his jeans.

She squeezed the trigger, and Josh yelled, "No!"

The recoil reverberated down her arms, and Van stumbled sideways.

He slumped against the bar. A dark circle of blood spread on the shoulder of his black t-shirt. He frowned at the crumpled paper in his hand, and the toothpick fell from his slack mouth.

"Oh, God." Her voice was an echo in her fuzzy head.

She lowered the gun, blinked. He hadn't been reaching for a weapon.

He laughed, coughed. "I deserved that." His legs slid out from beneath him, and he toppled to the floor.

Josh skidded through the room, tucking his gun in his jeans, his panic jolting her to move. Numb with shock, she handed the gun to him and knelt beside Van.

A river of blood soaked his shirt, coursed down his arm, and pooled beneath him. He lay on his back and peered up at her with the most heart-breaking expression on his contorted, beautiful face. No hint of anger or blame. It was as if he knew he was dying, and he was okay with it.

    She pushed his hood off his forehead and cupped his damp cheeks. "You killed my mom. I thought you were going to kill me."

    He shook his head in the frame of her hands. "Tried to save her." His chest heaved. "Drove…wasn't fast enough." He gripped her wrist and held her eyes, his nostrils flaring. "I was too late." His eyebrows clenched together, and his breaths rushed out as he squeezed his shoulders against the floor. "I'm sorry."

    A low, agonizing hum vibrated her chest. He wouldn't lie about that, and the realization tore through her in a barrage of buckshot.

    "Oh no, Van." Her chest convulsed, and a sob climbed her throat. She stroked his cheek, staring at the blood soaking his shirt. "Oh, God. What have I done?"

    His eyes fluttered closed for a moment and snapped open, glassy with pain. "It's okay. There's no—" His spine arched, and he moaned. "No contract."

    She gulped at the thinning air and pressed her hands to the bullet hole. "No contract? No hit man to collect on your death? Or Mr. E's?"

    She glanced at Josh, his eyes wide and locked on Van.

    "A bluff." The corner of Van's mouth wavered as if attempting a smile. Sweat trickled down his temples. His gaze landed on Josh, and his lips bowed downward.

    A *bluff*. She knew Van's coercions intimately, and this wasn't one of them. He would never fuck around with Mattie's life. Tears rose up and burned trails down her cheeks. "If he doesn't hire hit men then who killed Mom?"

    "He arranged it." His voice quaked. "His job—" His chest caved in, and his teeth snapped together in agony.

    Warm streams of red pumped over her fingers. The steel in his eyes dulled, his complexion a pallor of white. He was losing too much blood. Josh disappeared behind the bar, banging things around in the cabinet.

    The paper crinkled in Van's fist. "You love him?" His chest stilled as if he weren't breathing at all.

    She didn't glance away as she nodded, slowly, confidently. If anyone understood the connection between captor and captive, he did.

    He closed his eyes and released a slow, easy breath.

    Josh returned with an armful of dish towels, pressed them against the wound, and lifted Van's shoulder to see beneath his body. Van hissed, his lips pulling away from clamped teeth, his eyes rounding in shocked pain.

    "There's no exit wound." Josh lowered him to the floor and held the towels in place.

She caught Josh's eyes, and they shared a harrowing look. The bullet was still in there. She reached in her back pocket and handed him the phone. "The code to unlock it is 0054. Call 911."

"No cops," Van murmured. He raised the wadded paper in his hand. "He'll know."

She flattened the edges of the news clipping, watching at Van's shallowing breaths, and read the first sentence of the article.

*Austin Police Chief, Eli Eary, stood at the podium during a recent celebration to honor his career...*

"Mr. E." Van's voice jolted through her.

Her veins seized with shock, her body shivering. "Eli Eary? The police chief who handled my disappearance? *He's* Mr. E?"

Van nodded, his hand gripping her knee. "My dad."

She choked, her throat thick with tears, panic sprinting through her blood. She gave the paper to Josh and wrapped her hand around Van's cold, sweaty one. Her thoughts wheeled violently around the axis that was her arrangement. "That's why he gave me to you, why he's so lenient with you."

It also explained why Mr. E hadn't punished him for his stunt at the intro meeting with Camila. He'd simply banned him from future meetings and deliveries.

Van's eyes flashed, his voice straining. "He turned me into...this." His lips curled into a weak snarl. "He killed your mother. I never —" He coughed and slapped a hand over Josh's, adding pressure to the towels. "My mom was one of his."

"One of his..." She searched his red-rimmed gaze and found a haunting, deeply rooted pain. "She was a slave?" She looked at Josh, seeking his reaction and perhaps his comfort.

Josh pressed one hand on the towels, the other settling on her back. His gaze formed a grim mirror of her own, creasing at the corners.

Was that why his mother fell into a life of drugs? Because she'd been a slave? Resentment engulfed Liv, shaking her limbs. Mr. E had ruined so many lives.

"I came back to kill him." Van panted. "Needed your help."

Across the room, the dolls waited at the table, his morbid things to remember her by.

Her lungs shuddered. "Then you were going to disappear. You were going to let me go." Guilt ravaged her insides, twisting and fraying.

"Have to kill him." His eyes glassed over, his gasps weakening. "He'll avenge me." He choked. "He'll kill Livana."

"Livana?" The unfamiliar name hit her where she breathed. A

223

name formed from… *Liv. Van.* "Mattie's real name is Livana?"

He closed his eyes, his nod so devastatingly subtle beneath his short, bucking exhales. She was losing him.

"Van? Where's Livana?"

"She's…" His eyes flickered open, unfocused, and confused. He reached for her face.

She leaned in to meet his hand, eyes blurry, heart collapsing. "Van." Her voice rasped, clogged. "What's Livana's last name?"

His clammy fingers fumbled over her scar, across her lips, and lingered on her chin. He opened his mouth and strangled on an incoherent noise that died in the air. His eyes drifted closed, and his hand dropped.

*He's gone.*

"Nooo." She scrambled atop him, fingers trembling over his bloodless face. "No, Van. No, don't go," she screamed.

Anguish took hold in a series of wails, raging in her throat, shaking her limbs. He'd tried to save Mom. He was a fucking victim of his own father's greed. Why had she thought he'd kill her? He never would've done that. He loved her.

Oh Jesus. Fuck. Fuck. Look what she did to him. "Oh, Van. I'm so sorry."

She couldn't take it back. The bullet. The blood. She clung to his limp body, weeping, nose running, her heart shredding.

Arms came around her chest and pulled her to her feet. She elbowed Josh, dropped to her knees, and hugged Van's waist.

Josh gave her a few more minutes to release a torrent of sobs. Then his arms were back, wrapping around her and dragging her up.

He half-walked, half-lifted her to the sink, dragging her blood-soaked hands with his under the water. "I know you're not thinking clearly, Liv, but we need to make a decision and act quickly."

She wept in breathless starts and stops, staring at the pink-tinted water spiraling down the drain.

With his body wrapped around her back, his hands slipped over hers, rubbing her arms and rinsing away the evidence. "We have two choices. One, we go to the cops. Mr. E is brought in for questioning. His corruption may be embedded amongst his peers or he may be working on his own."

"And Mat— Livana? If he were incarcerated, he could still kill her." Goddammit, she hurt. Her head. Her heart. This shit with Van shouldn't hurt this badly.

Josh tore off some paper towels and dried their hands and arms. "Two, we look up his address and stop him ourselves. By whatever means possible. Right now. Before he tries to call Van. It's the safest option for Livana."

Turning to face him, she gathered strength from his eyes and curled her hands around his neck. "Then it's the only option."

"Agreed." The resolution in his taut expression matched his voice. "Mr. E tracks both of your phones?" He pulled her phone from his pocket.

"Yeah. Leave it on the counter." She scrutinized their clothes for blood. Both in dark t-shirts, the smudges were inconspicuous. With a final glance at the blood-soaked body on the floor, she pressed a fist to her chest and blinked away the watery ache in her eyes.

"There's a handwritten Austin address on the back of the news article." He held it up. "Mr. E?"

She closed her eyes. "God love you, Van." And goddamn him. He wasn't making it easy to walk away on sturdy legs. She grabbed his car keys from the counter and headed toward the garage. "Van's phone stays here. Mr. E is in contact with him hourly."

Josh remained a breath behind her. "If his phone is here, Mr. E will know he's here. You're hoping he doesn't call?"

She punched the code in the keypad and grabbed two long scarves from the hook beside the door. "Yeah. It'll buy us some time to make the drive to Austin. Or if he does try to reach us, maybe he'll think we're asleep."

Van was asleep. *Forever.* Fuck, she should've been relieved, but the ache behind her breastbone burrowed in with brass knuckles.

Fifteen minutes later, she parked Van's sedan in the *Daddy's Grill* parking lot outside of town. The sun clung to the horizon as the gray cast of night crept in.

She left the engine running. "I'll be a minute. Try not to let anyone see your face."

He glanced through the tinted windows at the three cars in the lot and said, sarcastically, "I'll do my best."

Inside, the waft of cigarettes and bar-b-que thickened her inhales. She stood before the only pay phone in the area, pumped it with coins, and lifted the receiver.

"Who is this?" The smooth, feline voice answered on the first ring.

"It's me."

Silence.

"This isn't—" Liv cleared the rasp sticking in her throat. "This isn't my usual call."

"No, I don't expect it is." Camila's tone was casual, but worry lurked beneath the surface.

"I need the house cleaned." The tears broke through. She wiped them away. "There's a mess on the kitchen floor."

A gasp pushed through the line. "Your boy?"

"No. This one was never mine."

"Oh." A pause. "I feel like I should be happy." Camila sniffed. "I feel…"

"Same here. I'm on my way to finish this. You have about an hour before the house gets crowded. Two hours tops. Code is 0054."

In a perfect scenario, Liv would kill Mr. E and sneak off with Josh into the night. If she were busted during an assassination of the police chief, she would use the slave house as evidence in her defense. But she didn't want to explain two bodies. If she failed in her attempt, she didn't want Van discovered by Mr. E.

"Is the time-frame doable?" she asked Camila.

"It will be."

Liv thought the line disconnected, but Camila's voice came back. "Be careful."

"Thank you." *For everything.*

The phone went dead.

Liv drove in silence for ten minutes before Josh breached the conversation she'd been expecting. "I'm trying to understand what you're feeling right now and what you felt for him exactly."

"I'm not sure *I* will ever understand it."

Van protected her from Mr. E in the best times, and her body bore his bruises on the worst days. Above all, he gave her a daughter.

"I loved him and hated him with damaged devotion," she said. "He was embedded in my life for seven years. You don't rip that away and feel nothing."

He nodded, unbuckled his seatbelt, and gave her exactly what she needed. Twisting in the seat to face her, he slid a hand over her belly and clenched her hip. His other hand combed her hair from her nape, gripping the strands at the back of her head. With his body curled around her side, he dropped his head on her shoulder, the warm tendrils of his breath twining around her neck. He didn't move for the length of the drive, and it was in that loving clench that she found the strength to forgive herself for killing Van.

Forty-five minutes later, they sat in the car, glaring across the street at a two-story home. Middle-income neighborhood, manicured lawn, well-lit walkway, and hanging flower baskets, it resembled every other house for ten blocks.

Dusk had settled. Cars lined the curb on both sides of the sparsely lit street. Van's sedan blended in, but if Mr. E glanced at the car from his front window, he would spot them. The sedan was a generic car, but he knew what Van drove. He could make the connection if he were suspicious enough.

Josh caressed a warm palm over her thigh. "Mr. E hasn't spent a dime of his illegal money, huh?"

She wrinkled her nose at the simple lines of his lackluster home. "He's a police chief. How would he explain million-dollar luxuries?"

Josh's strong profile watched the street. "He could've cut ties, retired to the French Rivera, and lived off of his fortune. Why is he doing this?"

She blew her cheeks out. "Maybe he likes trafficking humans. The power. The corruption. Maybe he's just greedy and wants more money before he retires." She grabbed the two black scarves from the backseat and coiled one loosely around Josh's neck. "Better than chains, right?"

He leaned in and stole a kiss. "I love your chains, Liv."

A flutter lifted in her chest. She looped the second scarf behind her neck. They would sneak in with their faces concealed, shoot the greedy motherfucker, and leave before anyone noticed. Easy as gutting all the other millionaire slave-owners.

Across the street, the front door opened. Josh gripped her hand as an older man strode along the walkway, shoulders squared, eyes on his phone. The outdoor lighting accentuated the streaks of silver in his black hair. She recognized the police chief in the news articles.

The road was free of traffic noise. If she rolled down the window, they'd be able to hear his footfalls. Could she shoot him at this distance? A shiver licked down her spine.

"What if he's texting Van? Or me?" Her blood pressure skyrocketed. "What if he's on his way to the house? Fuck, what do we do?"

"Deep breaths, Liv." Josh squeezed her hand tighter. "We'll follow him."

When Mr. E reached the SUV parked in the driveway, the front door opened again.

A little girl ran out in blue-jeans and light-up sneakers with long brown hair winding around her shoulders. Her tiny chin pointed up, her eyes alight with laughter.

Fear and joy collided in a rush of nausea. "Josh. Her smile…Oh God, her smile." Liv slapped at the button that rolled down the window just in time to hear, "Daddy! Daddy, wait up!"

A disgustingly familiar chuckle bounced down the driveway. "Come on, Livana. We're in a hurry."

# FORTY

"No, no, no, no."

Liv's whisper seeped into Josh's pores and chilled his bloodstream. Hooking his arms around her chest, he pulled her away from the window.

"Are you sure that's her?" He hoped to God she was wrong.

"Yes." Her voice was a tearful hiss, whipping through the dark interior of the car.

He pressed his lips to her cheek in an attempt to soothe her, holding tight to her heaving body. "If he's going to Temple, I don't think he'll bring your daughter with him."

Liv's daughter. The daughter Mr. E raised. His son's daughter. His granddaughter. It made the decision to kill him a cluster of confusion.

Josh dragged his nose through her hair, his head swimming. Fifteen days ago, he'd sat in his Christian Ethics class, rooted in the belief that murder was a grave moral evil. A capital crime punished with eternal damnation. That was before he'd met Mr. E and the buyers' network of soulless greed. Before his convictions had been tested.

He stroked his thumbs along her rigid arms. He certainly hadn't felt unclean after shooting the bodyguard. Killing that man had been a last resort, one that saved her life. As for Mr. E...the bastard strangled Liv. Bashed her head against the wall. Scarred her face. Stole her child. Enslaved Van's mother. Trained his son to kidnap and torture people. He was beyond saving.

Hell, there were countless examples in the bible that justified homicide to protect one's self and the lives of others. A heady sense of responsibility heated Josh's blood and tightened his muscles. Liv was his to protect.

Across the street, Livana interlaced her tiny fingers with those of a man who trafficked sex slaves. A man who followed through on his threats, evidenced by Liv's dead mother. A reminder that, once again, there were no nonviolent options left. As long as Mr. E lived, that little girl's life was in danger.

As Mr. E looked down at the child, it was difficult to interpret his expression in the dim light. If there was love there, tenderness even. What would killing the only father she'd ever known do to her?

A soft mewling noise rattled in Liv's throat, her round panicked eyes locked on Livana's affection toward Mr. E.

"Oh God, Josh, why did he raise her as his daughter?" She pressed a hand to her abdomen, rubbing, her body shaking.

His arms locked around her waist, hugging her close. He wanted to believe Mr. E raised Livana because she was his granddaughter, but he suspected the reason was more perverse. What better way to keep his arrangement with Liv tightly fastened than to keep her daughter as close as possible?

"What if he figures out Van is gone? He has my daughter, and I killed his son."

"He'll investigate why neither of you are answering your phones before he eliminates the only hold he has on you."

Maybe Mr. E considered Livana his daughter, but it wasn't a mercy Josh would count on. The man had abandoned his own son to a woman who was too stoned to prevent her child from being raped. What kind of life was Mr. E giving Livana?

He buried his rising panic and kissed Liv's head. Leaning her backward against his chest, he lowered their bodies below the windows.

The front door opened a third time. A blond woman stepped out, slender frame, hair in a pony tail. She was maybe a decade younger than Mr. E given her swift strides, the muscle tone in her arms, and her trendy jeans and blouse.

With her purse in hand, she strode toward Mr. E. "I'm starving."

Mr. E stared at his phone. "Change of plans. I need to be somewhere." His gaze shifted to Livana who yanked on his hand in a futile attempt to move him forward. He untangled their hands and patted her head. "I'm going to drop you and Livana off at the station. We'll pick up dinner on the way, and you can eat there."

For a heart-stopping moment, Mr. E glanced at the street, his eyes probing the lines of parked cars. Then he climbed in the driver's seat.

Josh's muscles ached with tension. "Why would he take them to the station?"

"He's paranoid." She stroked his fingers absently. "For the first time in seven years, we're not answering our phones. My mom's murder gives me a damned good reason to revolt, and he knows the first thing I'd do is search for Livana."

The woman clasped Livana's arm, holding her in place. "We'll just stay here."

"Get in the car," Mr. E barked from within the SUV.

The woman jumped and hustled Livana into the backseat. As she slid into the front seat, the engine started, and the brake lights illuminated the driveway.

"Shit. He's backing up." Liv slumped lower on his lap, dragging him down by his shirt. "Josh, he's going to Temple. We need to be there."

His pulse raced. "Shh. It's okay." He hugged her against him. "As soon as they leave, we'll head back. We'll beat him there."

She pressed her face against his chest, nodding, her body trembling. "She'll be safe at the police station. We'll kill him at the house and…Jesus, what if he doesn't come? It's a huge risk."

He stroked her hair as the rumble of the SUV grew closer. "This is a blessing, Liv. We're captives. We'll end this where he imprisoned us. It'll be self-defense. We won't have to run or try to cover it up."

Josh would see his parents again. Liv could live a normal life. His muscles clenched, his heart thundering. He wanted that for her so badly.

The rumble came to a stop beside them. Was the darkness and the tinted windows enough to conceal them? He popped open the glove box where the guns were stored and held his breath, his pulse drumming in his ears. Her fingers dug into his ribs, her body heaving against his.

The engine growled and the soft whir of tires on asphalt sounded the SUV's retreat down the street. He blew out a shuddering exhale.

She melted against him, rubbed a hand up his chest, and curled her fingers around his neck. Raising her head, she blinked at him with watery eyes.

"I"—she kissed the spot over his heart, leaned up, and kissed his lips, softly, breathlessly—"you."

His heartbeat catapulted, strumming every cell in his body. "You, too, girl." His mouth moved against hers, and during that brief, stolen connection, he felt her lips curve up.

For the next hour, they detailed their plan as they drove. The setup. The strike. The aftermath. When they pulled into the driveway in Temple, they had the story they would give to police ironed out and rehearsed.

She used the remote to open the garage door, and the emptiness within tingled down his spine. "Where's the van?"

Her forehead furrowed as she parked the car and climbed out. "Camila probably took the van to transport…" She rolled her lips, chin quivering, and rubbed her nose. "To transport the body."

The tingle on his spine receded, replaced with a fortitude to do anything needed to ensure they survived the night. He handed her the LC9 from the glove box, grabbed the PT-22, and followed her to the kitchen door. His muscles burned through his strides, amped up and ready.

Her pass code released the door, and he slipped in before her, gun raised in two hands. He had three bullets left. He'd only need one, unless someone was waiting for their return. Did Mr. E have a larger network? Would he have called someone to meet him here?

The silence in the kitchen stood as still as the dark. She moved behind him, her footfalls trailing to the sink where she flicked the switch. Light flooded the room.

The yellow linoleum floor showed no evidence of blood. The matching yellow sink was also scrubbed. The chairs were pushed in at the table. No body, no bloody rags, and no dolls.

"I'm glad they took the mannequins," she whispered.

*No joke.* In the end, Van had surprised the hell out of him. Perhaps Liv's influence in Van's life had altered his journey to one of redemption. Nevertheless, the memory of that man would be an eternal prickle creeping over the back of Josh's skull.

She lingered above the spot where Van had bled out, eyes on the floor, her arms wrapped around her torso. Her pallid expression produced a sympathetic ache in his chest.

Trusting that her friends had been thorough, he gave her the two phones from the counter and pulled her by a hand up the stairs, his gun out as he scanned the sitting room and hallway. The absolute stillness of the house was both reassuring and nerve-wracking.

She checked her phone as they climbed the stairs. "Mr. E sent one text, a little over an hour ago. All it says is, *Where is Van?*"

"He would've sent that around the time he came out of his house." At the top of the stairs, he entered the code with his gun hand. "You're not texting back, right?"

"Of course not."

*Good.* No communication would force him to show up. "What about Van's phone?"

"I've tried every code I can think of to unlock it." She walked through the outer chamber and snagged a black costume from the cabinet. "It's a no-go."

Fifteen minutes later, he knelt in the middle of her room, facing the closed door, his naked body prickling with goosebumps. With his wrists crossed behind his back, he was her slave.

She stood by the keypad, phone in one hand, the LC9 concealed in her thigh-high boot, the sheath of her minidress clinging to her curves. Holding her body motionless, she was his Deliverer.

Chains spread out around him and locked to the hooks in the floor. They led to the cuffs on his arms, but it was all a ruse. They didn't attach to the cuff rings. Instead, they wedged beneath the leather straps. One jerk of his arms, and they would fall away. With his hands hidden behind his back, he held the PT-22.

The minutes stretched, his heart beating to the unfamiliar melody floating from her lips. Her lyrics were indiscernible, but the beauty of her haunting voice massaged its way into his muscles and invigorated his blood.

Their foremost priority was to lure Mr. E far enough into the room to close the door. Once locked inside, he wouldn't be able to escape if something went wrong. And while she'd been adamant about being the shooter, he'd denied her pleas to relinquish his mom's gun. No way would he allow her to defend them on her own.

Finally, her phone buzzed. She glanced at it and tossed it on the bed. "It says, *Open the door.*"

# FORTY-ONE

Sweat formed on Josh's skin. His heartbeat thundered against his ribs. He dropped his chin to his chest and rested his finger beside the trigger guard, the gun held tight against his back.

Liv opened the door and stepped back.

Black boots stopped in the threshold. The door opened all the way, and a bath towel landed on the floor. Mr. E kicked the terrycloth until it was wedged beneath the crack, propping the door open. "Van's phone is somewhere in this house. Where is he?"

Josh's blood pressure spiked. There went their plan to lock him in.

Her heeled boots shifted a step backward, her silence constricting his chest. If Van had planned to kill his father, he certainly wouldn't have told the bastard where he was going or what he was doing. Why wasn't she answering him with some kind of lie?

Josh raised his chin as subtly as possible, and his breath caught in his throat.

Mr. E wore his cotton jumpsuit and that godawful canvas mask. His body angled toward Liv. She stood a few feet away, staring down the barrel of his semi-auto pistol.

Josh locked his jaw in a painful clench, his entire world a trigger-squeeze away from death. His fight response pummeled at him to attack, hardening his muscles and heating his veins. Timing would be everything.

A tic bounced in her cheek as her fingers stretched along her thigh, dipping into her boot and grasping her gun. "I'm not Van's babysitter."

The pistol swung, colliding with the side of her head. She fell to one knee, and her gun clattered on the floor.

Josh jerked so hard one of the chains fell loose from his wrist cuff.

It clanked behind him, drawing the mask's eyeholes in his direction.

She lurched for her gun and collided with Mr. E's boot as he kicked it toward the shower stall.

"You gonna shoot me, you fucking whore?" He shoved the barrel beneath her chin, forcing her to lift on her knees. "Where the *fuck* is Van? You've got one second to answer. One—"

"Dead." Her eyes burned, wide and fierce.

The compulsion to protect her wracked Josh with indecision. His pulse raced. No way could he level his gun before Mr. E fired.

Mr. E crouched and shoved his canvas mask into her face. "I don't believe you. Last chance." His gloved finger began a slow squeeze of the trigger.

A tremor gripped Josh's spine as her throat bobbed against the press of the barrel.

Her fingers curled against her thighs. "Your son cleared out his room before I killed him. Go see for yourself."

*Oh, God, Liv.* Josh tightened his grip on the gun.

"You're dead," whispered from within the hood.

In that everlasting second, as Mr. E's finger pulled the trigger and the hammer released, Josh plummeted, gutted. Lifting his arms, he met his breaking point with a single-minded focus to join her in death and take the son of a bitch with him.

His heart roared with fear for her as he snapped his arms forward, clattering the chains and aiming the gun.

Mr. E's semi-auto clicked, a jarringly quiet sound.

Josh stopped breathing. It clicked? The pistol jammed? *It misfired! OhGodOhGod, thank you, God.*

Liv swung her arm, knocking the barrel from her neck, and Josh trained the .22's sights on the mask. He squeezed the trigger as Mr. E jerked his hand to readjust his aim. Both guns fired.

The double *boom* pierced Josh's ears. He choked on his terror as Liv's eyes widened, her hand cupped around her neck. *No, no, no.* She couldn't be hit. He bit his tongue, tasted blood, and forced his attention on the threat.

Mr. E's pistol dropped. Red spouted from a hole in his canvas-wrapped neck, and he collapsed beside her. Josh had aimed true.

He scrambled toward them, his pulse thrumming in his throat.

"Liv? Are you hurt?" He kicked Mr. E's pistol, skidding it across the room, and pulled her hand from her neck.

Milky, unblemished skin stretched against the delicate lines of her throat. She glanced at the ceiling, and he followed her gaze. The bullet hole marring the sheetrock sank a surge of relief deep into his lungs. His eyes ached with the aftermath of jumbling emotion, and he wanted nothing more than to hold her.

The masked head twitched on the floor. Josh clenched his fist, vibrating with the need to take away the last of the man's power. He found the ties on the back of the canvas hood and yanked it off.

Silver striped through thinning black hair. Bags of wrinkles hung from pain-filled eyes. The older version of the man in the news articles worked his jaw, unable to drag in a breath.

She leaned over the police chief, her nostrils flaring. "Van flew to the Keys and tried to save my mom."

His eyes flashed, and his head rocked side-to-side.

"That's right, cocksucker. And he came back to kill you." Her voice strained with tears.

Kneeling beside her, Josh uncurled her fingers from Mr. E's jumpsuit.

The man's jaw opened and closed soundlessly, red trickling from the corner of his mouth. From the neck down, his body lay limp. Maybe the bullet damaged his spinal cord. He was definitely choking on his own blood.

"I went to your house and found Livana." She grabbed his bobbing chin. "When your pretty blond wife returns from the station, I'm going to show her all the things you taught me to do. Then I'm going to kill her."

Josh probably should've been bothered by her taunting a dying man, but his righteousness was buried beneath the huge freaking desire to crush the bastard's skull with his fist.

A gurgle of blood bubbled from Mr. E's mouth, followed by a strangled sigh. His face slackened, and his head fell to the side.

She checked the pulse in his neck. Josh pulled back the edge of a black glove and felt for a pulse on the wrist.

With her face only a few inches from his, he could feel her tension releasing with the slowing of her movements. He waited for her to glance up. When their eyes collided, a surreal moment hovered between them, fueled by their unified breaths. It was over. He leaned in, touched his lips to her trembling ones.

Her face crumpled. "I wanted him to die in a horrible way. This..." Her voice scratched. "This was too merciful."

His heart fractured for all the torment Mr. E caused her. He spoke against her quivering chin. "He'll be judged and spend eternity suffering for his sins."

She shifted, staring at the body, her eyes welling, blinking. A quiver rippled across her lips. She turned toward him and coiled her arms around his neck, her lungs hauling tearful gulps of air.

"It's done, Josh." She cried, quietly, her cheek against his. "I'm so sorry you had to be the one to kill—"

"Don't, Liv." He cupped her face. "I'm not sorry, and you won't be either."

"Okay," she whispered, nodded. "Livana..." She pressed her face in his neck, her fingers clenched in his hair. "She's free."

And so was Liv. Free of fear. Free to live. Free with him.

As he held her, wiping away the streaks of tears on her face, he let fifteen days of tension twist free of his body, muscle by muscle, exhale after exhale. He waited for the guilt, for the darkness, for some indication to show him the wrongfulness of his path, but all he felt was liberation breathing through this passionate woman and the salvation that kept her heart beating.

God's will led him to that house, but it was love that bound him within its walls. He was born with choices and would die with his decisions. Looking down into her huge brown eyes, her emotions so raw and beautifully exposed, he knew she was the most important decision he'd ever made.

He scooted to the mattress with her curled in his lap, snagged her phone, and dialed. Pressing a kiss to her salty lips, he lifted the phone to his ear.

"Bell County 911. What is your emergency?"

"This is Joshua Carter. I just killed the man who abducted me."

# FORTY-TWO

Ten hours later, Liv shuffled out of the interrogation room in the Temple police station, her boots scuffing along the stained carpet squares, the arches of her feet igniting pain with each step. *Damned heels.*

The highlights of the detectives' examination swished through her weary brain. *We believe Eli Eary acted alone in his crimes. Killing him in self-defense is permitted by the law. Your actions are not legally punishable. No actus* reus. *You and Mr. Carter are free to go.*

The investigation was far from over, but for now, they were free. She and Josh had been separated the moment the driveway flooded in blue and red flashing lights. They were transported to the station in handcuffs, separately. They were questioned for hours, separately.

She stepped into the corridor, searching the unfamiliar faces for pale green eyes and came up empty.

No one followed her as she walked, but detectives and uniformed men stopped mid-conversation to watch her pass. *Fuck them.* She tugged down the short hem of her dress, feeling awkward and really fucking exposed.

She hugged her mid-section, dropped her arms, crossed her arms again. This feeling…this insecurity was so foreign. The last time she lived in a free world, she was just a kid. But in her twenty-four years, she'd never been unsupervised, never went anywhere without checking in with someone…Mom, Mr. E, Van.

As she passed offices and holding rooms, looking for Josh, she felt lost. She needed his hand on her hip, his fingers laced through hers, his eyes studying her with his bold affection. She missed him with every dry, achy breath.

Turning the corner, she entered a long hallway, anxious to see how he was doing after all the questioning. Their carefully crafted story to the police painted Eli Eary as a sadistic slave owner, not a slave trafficker. They claimed he acted alone when he abducted and imprisoned them. The detectives were overwhelmed with the discovery of the allegedly-murdered Austin girl from seven years ago and the nationally-mourned linebacker from Baylor.

She and Josh had agreed to omit the existence of other slaves, the dead buyers, and Van. Too much murder, way too many complications. In their story, Eli Eary used her and Josh—his only two slaves—for his sexual, sadistic pleasures. No one knew she abducted Josh. And no one mentioned Mr. E having a son.

Her longer captivity was more complicated. To expose her connection to Livana, she accused an unknown man of raping and impregnating her a few weeks after her abduction. She'd told them Eli Eary threatened the child's life as a way to control her. She was allowed limited errands outside of the house but lived in constant fear for her child. When she'd revealed that truth to the room of detectives, her painful tears fomented the story. The seven-year-old scar on her face might've garnered some sympathetic votes as well.

When they told her she was free to go, she asked for a visitation with Livana. They promised to do what they could with a cautious message. "Mrs. Eary is struggling with her husband's death and his crimes. Give her time."

They'd said the wife and daughter were safe in Austin. Mrs. Eary had been oblivious to her husband's corruption, which meant she'd raised Livana as a legitimate mother. It was good news, right? Livana was loved and taken care of. Yet a deep ache flared in Liv's chest. Her limbs felt heavier, her body colder.

It wasn't as if she had aspirations to take over the role of Livana's mother. God, she'd been so focused on just keeping her baby alive. But if she were to examine her dreams of the future, they did include her daughter. Losing Livana had left a hole inside her, and perhaps that hole would always be there, but she needed to see her child. Needed to understand Livana's relationship with her adoptive mother.

At the end of the hall, she paused at the doorway of the waiting room, halted by the hiccuping sobs tumbling from within. Across the room, Josh sat on a couch between his parents with their backs to the door. Their heads bowed together, their private huddle enveloped by a chorus of whispered prayers.

It was four in the morning. Her stomach hurt at the thought of them waiting for her. They should've gone home. Of course, Josh would never leave without her. But would they be together the next day? Or next month? Would he go back to school, live with his parents, work the farm, and become a minister?

What was her place in his life? She was a master at rope bondage. She could crack a whip without splitting skin. She knew how to suck a cock. As for the Bible, well, that was just an anthology of well-written fairytales. She wasn't a minister's wife.

He clasped his mother's frail shoulder, his broad back twice the size of hers. At least, they let him put clothes on before hauling him to the station. They hadn't given her the option.

Emily Carter's graying brown hair had unraveled from her bun. Her flowery collared smock dress fell loosely around her skeletal frame. The woman Liv used to watch through binoculars had lost a lot of weight.

Guilt landed like a bullet in Liv's stomach. She'd caused his poor mother so much grief.

Daniel Carter grasped his son's neck. The humped curve of his spine and the weathered skin on his nape reminded that most of his sixty-six years had been spent beneath the unforgiving Texan sun. Silver peppered his full head of black hair, and she knew if he turned around she'd see Josh's pale green eyes in the older man's face.

The sight of the three of them together, praying, and crying happy tears produced a sharp pain in the back of her throat. For a flickering moment, she entertained an unrealistic desire to receive some of the love they shared between them, but she didn't deserve it. Taking him from his parents was the most selfish thing she'd ever done, but she would *never* regret choosing him.

She lingered in the doorway, unsure where to go or what to do. Should she interrupt their private reunion? Her fingers shook as she adjusted the clingy top over her nipples. The bottom hem reached just below her ass. One of the detectives had offered her his suit jacket. Now she regretted declining it. She resembled a homeless skank.

The truth in that thought clawed through her chest and burned her eyes. She *was* homeless. Also penniless, jobless, and without a family. Hell, she didn't even have a change of clothes. Aching for Mom, miserable on her lonely side of the room, she backed out of the doorway.

What the fuck was wrong with her? She was free. Livana was safe. Josh's parents had their son back.

*Pull your balls out of your cunt.*

Van's words steeled her strides down the hallway. She'd wait on the bench at the end of the hall until Josh was ready. Her toes pinched in her boots, and her stupid eyes burned with stupid tears. She slapped at her cheeks and pretended she couldn't hear the desolate echo of her heart in her ears.

Halfway to her destination, an arm hooked around her waist. She gasped and inhaled Josh's clean familiar scent. Tension shuddered from her body. She let her head fall back on his shoulder and compulsively reached for his hand at her hip. Christ, she hadn't realized how badly she needed him to hold her.

"What are you doing?" His breath caressed her ear, and his other arm crossed her chest.

She turned in his embrace, wrapped an arm around his muscled back, and pressed her palm to his whiskered jaw, savoring his heat seeping into her skin.

"I don't know where I'm going." Her nose thickened with tears. Fucking hell, she was sniveling.

"Hey, it's okay." He was heartbreakingly beautiful, even more so when he regarded her as if he were searching, not her eyes but what lay behind them. "I'm not going anywhere without you." He touched a knuckle under her chin and raised it. "The worst is behind us. It's just you and me. Everything else is trivial. Got it?"

Her insecurities dimmed in the intensity of his gaze. She traced the curve of his bottom lip. "How do you do that?"

With his arm braced around her, he dipped two fingers inside the front of her dress and pinched her nipple. Leaning in, he kissed the corner of her parted lips. "I'm a horny slut, remember?" He adjusted her top, twined their fingers, and led her back to the waiting room. "Time to meet my parents." He peeked back at her, grinning.

She shook her head and followed that gorgeous, confident smile. She'd follow him anywhere, even if it was to meet his parents with her tits creeping out of the minidress.

"Mom, Dad, this is Liv."

The air shifted with the horrified widening of their eyes. Judgmental energy prickled over her cleavage and down her legs. They didn't openly gawk at her body. It was a flash, a gasp, a quick glance away.

Holding their chins stiffly upward, their eyes locked on Josh as if another accidental glimpse in her direction would damn them to hell. What had he told them about her? Not the truth, certainly. But had he told them he loved her? His fingers were laced with hers, but that could imply friendship. She rubbed her sweaty palm over her belly, stared at the exit longingly, and met their narrowed eyes.

Emily clutched a wad of tissues to her chest, her face etched in wrinkles. Her gray gaze flicked to Liv's scar and returned to Josh.

"Oh dear." Her voice was cold, forced. "You poor thing."

Liv cringed. "Nice to meet you, Mr. and Mrs. Carter." She held out her hand.

Daniel clasped it, his fingers gnarled from manual labor, and let go. The hue of his eyes were indeed the same as Josh's but duller and surrounded by dark circles. Worse, those eyes studied her as if they were putting her in a box labeled, *Things To Keep Away From Josh.* "You're welcome to stay with us until you get on your feet. We don't have a lot of room, but we'll make it work."

"She's staying with us." Josh gripped her hip, pulled her chest against his hard body, and rested his lips on her forehead.

She hooked her thumbs in his belt loops and kissed the hollow of his throat.

Daniel's harsh squint was slightly more subtle than the ugly twist of Emily's mouth. They knew their son had been imprisoned and used as a sex slave. She doubted Josh had gone into details with them, but imaginations were limitless, even for church-goers. They would've been told that she was a victim like their son, but she was still part of the evil that defiled their virginal boy.

"Excuse me, Mr. Carter?" A uniformed officer poked his head in the doorway. "If you're ready to leave, we can escort your family to your car. There's a lot of activity out front."

Minutes later, she stepped into the cool evening air with Josh's arm hugging her shoulders. A small assembly of news reporters lined the walkway to the parking lot, flashing bulbs and shouting questions. But their voices were smothered by the cheers of college kids, waving *Welcome Home* posters and Baylor Bears memorabilia.

"Somebody's pop-u-lar." Liv squeezed his waist, and his chuckle vibrated through her.

They walked behind his parents and two officers, weaving through the crowd that spilled into the parking lot. The college kids stared openly with wide eyes, likely imagining all the horrors of their star linebacker's captivity. Some shouted friendly greetings. Others held candlelit prayer circles.

Suddenly, Josh's muscles stiffened around her. He stopped their forward movement and turned them toward a huddle of pretty twenty-something girls.

*Seriously?* "Josh, what are you — ?"

A flash of long black hair caught her attention.

Camila shimmied between two girls and held out a plastic grocery bag filled with clothes. Her huge dark eyes were cautious, flicking over the crowd.

Josh grabbed the bag, and Camila vanished behind the crowding bodies.

"Keep moving." He held her tight to his side, his height allowing him to see above the bystanders. His eyes were focused straight ahead. He must've spotted the car.

A knot formed in her stomach. Camila wouldn't have risked exposing her connection with them just to bring a change of clothes. The thought niggled as she followed Josh into an old station wagon and shut the door. His parents climbed in the front, and she sat directly behind Mrs. Carter. Josh reclined in the middle, his big body crowding the bench seat.

He set the bag of clothes on the floorboard and whispered in her ear, "We'll talk when we get home."

She nodded, agreeing that a conversation about Camila in front of his parents would raise questions.

Headlights from passing cars flashed across his face as Mr. Carter pulled out of the lot. Something was working behind Josh's eyes, and it had her sitting on the edge of the seat. He buckled their seat belts and tucked her close to his side.

The drive to Waco was filled with his parents' gossip about church, accolades for the community's support after his disappearance, and updates on the farm's crop losses. Josh assured them everything would resume to normal soon, and Liv's doubts about where she fit in sat heavy in her chest.

As Mr. Carter brought Josh up to speed on the business side of the farm, Josh caressed the skin above her thigh-high boots. Sliding toward the hem of her skirt, his fingers slipped between her legs and traced the edge of her panties. She held her breath and stared at his profile. Why was he doing this?

His attention seemed fully absorbed in the conversation with his dad as he eased beneath the crotch of her panties, found her wet, and pressed his index finger in to the knuckle.

She released a soundless breath and gripped his wrist, her body flooding with warmth. Still, he didn't look at her.

"You fired the contractor, right?" he asked his dad, curling his finger inside her.

Her head dropped against the seat back, her thighs parting. Nerve endings tingled along her inner thighs. She realized he was telling her without words that nothing would change between them. The church talk, his parents, his previous life wouldn't sever their connection.

She relaxed around his grinding hand, her lap shrouded in darkness. Her breaths quickened. Her mouth moistened.

He stroked her until she couldn't contain her panting. His hand pulled away, and he drew his finger into his mouth, watching her with a smile playing at the corners. "Liv will be sleeping in my room."

"That's fine, honey," Emily said. "I'll make up the couch for you."

He leaned back and closed his eyes, his arm resting over her lap. "No, Mom. She'll be sleeping in my room *with me*."

That was not how she'd envisioned him exposing their

relationship. She slipped down in the seat, wishing she could disappear.

Tense silence pulsed through the car. He squeezed her thigh, and his eyes remained closed.

"Son." His dad shifted, his gaze on the rear view mirror. "I don't know what you've been through, and we'll work through that. But the rules haven't changed. You ain't gonna be hitched and not churched. Not under my roof."

Josh sat forward, slowly, his eyes narrowed on the mirror. "Your rules haven't changed, but mine — "

"I'll sleep on the couch." Fuck, she didn't want to cause this family anymore pain. She turned toward him and cupped his face, shifting his attention to her. "Please, Josh? I want to sleep on the couch."

He'd hear the lie, but she trusted he'd understand her intention.

He reclined against her, shoulder to shoulder, and traced the skin between her fingers. For a stubborn pain in the ass, he let the subject drop too easily. Which meant he was probably going to do whatever the hell he wanted.

Emily shifted the conversation back to church stuff, promising that the ministers held all the answers to helping him heal. Forty minutes later, they shuffled into the Carter's small, single-story home. The front half was split between a sparsely decorated sitting room and a galley kitchen. A short hall led to two bedrooms and a bathroom in the back.

Josh stopped Liv at the bathroom door. "Take a shower if you want. My room's right there."

He pointed at the door across the hall. Following her in, he set the bag of clothes on the counter and dug through the jeans, cotton dresses, and t-shirts.

A comfortable warmth tingled through her chest. She owed Camila for so damned much.

"Can you sleep in this?" He pulled out a camisole and sleep shorts.

She nodded. "What happened back there with Camila?"

"She said something to me. The crowd was loud. I don't know. I read her lips." He scraped a hand through his hair. "I swear she said, *Watch your back.*"

What? Her spine tingled. "Why would she say that?" *Their enemies are dead.*

He unfolded the camisole, and a piece of paper drifted to the floor. Handwritten scribble bled through the thin folded stationary. Her shoulders tightened as they stared at it.

He picked it up, his eyebrows pulling together, and handed it to her.

Her heart raced as she unfolded the note. "Camila has no way to contact me."

Why would she need to? Liv gripped his arm and held up the note so they could read it together.

> *We're so happy for you! When you're ready, our home is your home.*
> *A couple lingering concerns...*
> *The kitchen was clean when we arrived. The job was gone. No cars in the garage. Were you able to take care of this on your own?*
> *Traquero and his wife are dead. Found two days ago. We're not sure who did it, but the how was passionate. Definitely personal.*

# FORTY-THREE

Van's death replayed through Liv's head in slow motion. The gunfire. The river of blood on the floor. His final words. *He killed your mother…Needed your help…He'll avenge me.* Leading her surge of emotions was the overwhelming relief that Traquero's depravity had met a bloody end.

Josh closed the bathroom door, his complexion a sheet of white. "You shot him in the shoulder." He rubbed the back of his neck, studying her. "Is it possible he survived that?"

She opened the toilet lid, flushed the note, and tried to keep her argumentative voice to a whisper. "He bled out."

"Or passed out." He shoved his hands through his hair and dropped his head back, staring at the ceiling. "So stupid." He shut his eyes. "We didn't check his pulse."

Her mouth went dry. She closed the toilet lid and collapsed on top of it. Her chest felt hard and cold inside. "We left him there to die."

"Except he didn't die." Stunned realization cracked his voice as he crouched before her and tucked her hair behind her ear. "When he returned to the house last night, he already killed Traquero."

She blinked, the movement irritating her gritty, tired eyes. "He must've *flown* to the Keys to help Mom." She nodded to herself, swallowing past a tight throat. "He could've killed Traquero on his way back. But how did he know how to find him?" A horrible thought clenched her stomach. "What if he knows about Camila and the others?"

His hand wrapped around her neck, his thumb stroking the skin below her ear. "Think about *why* he killed Traquero."

The only things predictable about Van were his jealousy and his hypocrisy. "Traquero hurt me."

Van had no qualms raising a hand to her, but Traquero had overstepped, recklessly. Van probably killed the wife in front of him just to make him suffer.

Her breath stuttered. "I think he packed up and left with the intention of protecting Mom and disappearing. When he failed, maybe he came back to avenge Mom's death."

Would he do that? For her? The ache in her chest said, *Yes*.

"I despise Van." He tilted his head. "But his behavior in the kitchen when you shot him…" A line formed between his dark eyebrows. "I got the sense that he was done. With Mr. E. With the whole operation."

She sifted through her memories of the prior night when Van was bleeding all over the floor. She couldn't pick out a single word, expression, or action that suggested ill-intent.

"If he knew about Camila and the others, he'd have no reason to harm them." Her shoulders loosened. "He's not a threat."

Josh pulled her to the edge of the toilet seat, wrapped his arms around her waist, and rested his forehead on her belly. "You're not leaving my sight."

Her hands went to his hair, raking through the messy black strands. "I can work with that." She lowered her lips to his head and filled her nose with his warm, comforting scent.

A fist knocked on the door.

"Joshua?" Emily called. "Are you in there?"

His moan rumbled through her. He raised his head and kissed her lips. "I'll be right outside that door."

# FORTY-FOUR

Twenty minutes later, Liv was showered, dressed in the pajama set Camila gave her, and wrapped in blankets on the couch. The kitchen light trickled into the sitting room, accompanied by low murmurs. Josh and his parents were still awake, gathered at the kitchen table around the corner.

She declined the biscuits Emily made, too exhausted to eat. Stretching out on the sofa, she closed her eyes. It must've been around seven in the morning before sleep finally took her.

Not long after, she woke, cradled in his arms, her body pressed against his chest as he carried her through the brightening house. Stubborn man was breaking his parents' rules.

"Aren't your parents due to get up?" she whispered.

"We've already done all the morning chores. They just passed out."

She hooked her arms around his neck and found his mouth.

His tongue met hers eagerly, his lips wet and inviting. In his unlit bedroom, he closed the door with a quiet click and dropped her on a mattress. The shades blacked out the daylight, drenching the room in darkness. She hadn't been in there yet, and when she scooted back to make space for him, she quickly learned how damned small his bed was.

Her head thumped against the wall, and she cringed, hoping she hadn't awakened his parents. "How the hell do you fit in this?"

Clothes rustled, his breaths deepening, growing closer. "You're about to see how both of us fit."

The mattress dipped and hands grabbed her top, stripping it over her head. Her sleep shorts went next. Then he was on her, spreading her thighs, his naked body sliding over hers, his cock prodding between her legs, coaxing a delicious spark of fire.

His teeth caught her nipple, tugging and stretching. Her hands fisted in the sheets. His fingers swept along her sides, his weight wonderfully heavy, his hips grinding against hers.

Her back arched, and she bit her lips to trap a moan.

"Josh," she whispered.

The box springs creaked as he lifted his body and flipped her to her belly. Kneeling between her legs, his fingers skimmed up her inner thighs, dipped through her wetness, and entered her.

Pleasure shivered through her. He thrust his hand, his fingers dragging along her inner walls, his panting so incredibly erotic. Her hands ached to touch him. Her body burned to be stroked harder. When his fingers slid out, she held her breath, expecting his cock. Instead, a soaked fingertip pressed against the pucker of her ass. She looked over her shoulder but couldn't see him through the dark.

"Van has taken you here?" His whisper was hoarse.

"Yeah." She closed her eyes, knowing his jealousy would be rising to the surface and stirring his instinct to claim her.

"Are you healed?"

"Yes."

It had been a week since Traquero had hurt her. A couple times, during moments like this one, she'd watched Josh spread her cheeks and stare at her anus while fucking her. She knew what he wanted. She'd never willingly given her ass to anyone, but he wasn't just anyone.

"It's yours," she whispered.

His breath stammered, and his finger pushed past the ring of muscle, intensifying the throb in her pussy.

"Holy hell, Liv. You're so tight. And hot." He moved his finger in and out, and his thigh trembled against hers. "I want this. Badly."

"Take it, Josh. Do you have lube?"

"No." He groaned, circling his finger. His other hand held her waist in a death grip.

The sensations from his invasion vibrated across her skin, electrifying every cell in her body.

"Use spit," she panted.

The hand on her waist vanished. She heard him spit and pictured him stroking himself, lubricating his cock as he fingered her ass. Fuck, she was going to come quick. She dropped her head to the pillow.

His finger slipped away, and something much larger nudged her opening. Lifting on hands and knees, she pushed back against him. He swept a warm palm up and down her spine. His fingers lingered on her tail bone, pressing down, and he worked his cock in slowly, cautiously, despite his quickening exhales.

They gasped in unison as his hips bumped her ass, his length buried fully inside her. He bent over her back and cupped her breasts. "Not gonna last long."

"Me neither." She rotated her hips. "Now move."

He moved. Oh God, did he move. She gripped the edge of the mattress and smothered her yelps in the pillow. He pistoned his hips, filling her over and over with an overwhelming tempo of speed and power. The bed squeaked. She didn't care. Her body was on fire, her desire for him tunneling through her and awakening all her pleasure points.

His tongue dragged up her spine, and his fingers slipped into her pussy. She exploded in a spasm of quivering limbs and stammering breaths, her inner walls convulsing around his fingers. His strokes slowed, his mouth open and panting against her shoulder. He came with his face buried in her neck and his arms locked around her, clutching her back to his chest.

She sighed, smiling, as he rolled them to their sides. "You just fucked my ass with your parents on the other side of the wall."

"At least, they didn't come in." He pulled out, rubbed something soft and cottony between her legs and cleaned himself. "There's no lock on the door."

Her gaze flew to the vicinity of the door. Was he *trying* to get busted?

"Did you just clean your dick with your t-shirt?" she asked.

"Yep." He tossed it through the dark room, and it landed with a thud in the corner. "I'll make sure it gets in the hamper."

"Let me guess. Your mom does your laundry?"

He curled against her back, enfolding her in his arms. "She's been washing my cum filled t-shirts for years. Go to sleep."

She lay awake with her cheeks stretched in a silly grin and a flutter in her chest. Sleepless minutes passed, and her thoughts drifted to Van. He'd been a bastard to her for seven years. If he hadn't abducted her, Mom might've still been alive. But there would've been no Livana. She would've never met Josh.

For the first time since Van entered her life, she thought of him with a tiredness that was fulfilling rather than draining.

When Josh's breaths evened out, she carefully untangled his arms and kissed his temple, inhaling the scent of his skin. Then she crept back to the couch.

The next three days rolled into a repetitive cycle. She used the Carter's phone every morning to inquire about a visitation with Livana. She helped Josh haul bales and clean farm equipment. In the evenings, they ran together, just the two of them, the dirt road beneath their sneakers, and acres of freedom.

After his parents retired each night, he carried her to his bedroom and showed her how much he loved her. When he fell asleep, she crept back to the couch. But his irritation with the sleeping arrangements was mounting, if his narrow-eyed glower at his parents every morning was anything to go by.

When she approached him about his attitude toward his parents, he said, "They're more concerned about what happened to the farm while I was gone than what happened to *me* during that time. You'd think they'd be more invested in what I need and less concerned about church gossip and farm chores."

While his parents pretended his time in captivity never happened, the news stations begged for details. They called from all over the country, buzzing the phone so often the Carters turned off the ringer. A number of times, Josh had to run off reporters who were rude enough to show up at the house. He wanted to avoid the press for as long as possible, which meant he was also avoiding school, football, and church. All his attention was on the farm and catching up on the tasks his parents had fallen behind on.

On the third morning, her call to the Austin police department was answered with a message from Carolyn Eary. Mr. E's wife finally agreed to meet with her.

The next day, Josh drove her to Austin in the family's station wagon.

She sat beside him in a spartan holding room at the police station. Her palms sweat, and her mouth dried as Carolyn stared at her with pink-rimmed eyes.

Liv swallowed, tongue-tangled, and searched for the appropriate thing to say to the woman raising her child. "Thank you for seeing me."

Carolyn raised a trembling hand to her face, brushing away an invisible hair. "I'm trying to come to terms with this." The woman gestured at Liv and Josh. "But my primary concern is for my daughter. She's lost her father and—" She choked on a sob. "She's all I have."

A maternity test would prove Liv's parentage. A court order might give her custody. But what was best for Livana?

Liv leaned forward, the long table separating them. "I'm not here to uproot Livana's life. I just want to meet her and, with time, get to know her." She closed her eyes, opened them. "I have so many questions."

"You can ask me anything." Carolyn smiled, though it faded quickly.

"How and when did she come to you?"

Carolyn rubbed her forearms, her blond eyebrows gathering over her blue eyes. "We adopted her. She was only a few days old."

Had Van kept her during those first few days? Or had she gone to the hospital for care? She pressed a hand to her abdomen. She couldn't ask those questions and reveal Van's part in this.

Carolyn's lips pinched in a line. "My husband claimed he had an estranged son who contacted him and asked him to raise his child. Said the mother didn't want her." She averted her eyes and took her time dragging them back to Liv. "My husband and I couldn't have children, so of course I was ecstatic. He dealt with the paperwork." Her cheeks flushed. "It all seems so very obvious now. I should've questioned more. He never mentioned having a son before Livana came to us, and now I know it's because he never really had one."

Josh grabbed Liv's hand under the table, and she laced their fingers, squeezing. Did that mean Van had never met Livana or Carolyn? Was that Mr. E's doing? Isolating his son from the only family he had? Remorse sat heavy in her stomach.

Carolyn leaned back in the chair, her eyes cold, flat. "It was all one big lie."

*Not exactly.* Liv believed Van and his confession to being Mr. E's son, but she wasn't going to correct Carolyn.

"My husband never paid attention to Livana." Carolyn's firm eye contact held Liv immobile. "Please believe me when I say I have loved her enough for the both of us. And she has *never* been mistreated."

Warmth circulated through Liv's body. Fuck, she'd needed to hear that. "Who named her?"

Carolyn tucked her hands behind her elbows. "He told me his son chose the name." She shrugged stiffly. "I guess my husband named her after you." She blinked away.

Van named her. Liv was sure of it. A bloom of warmth curled through her chest, and her lungs filled with a deep, content breath. "Can I see her? Is she here?" Hope bottled up inside of her, quickening her pulse.

"Yes, of course." Carolyn rose and left the room.

Liv clutched her chest. "Oh my God, Josh. OhmyGodOhmyGod. Pinch me."

She swallowed rapidly, light-headed and giddy, gulping deep breaths. Her hands shook over the front of her cotton dress, straightening it. She combed fingers through her hair. Should she brush the strands over her scar?

He hooked an arm around her, touched his lips to her cheek, and chuckled softly. "Stop fidgeting. You're breathtaking. Livana will adore you."

She leaned her forehead against his. "Thank you. I'm so glad you're here."

The door opened, and she stopped breathing.

# FORTY-FIVE

Liv's heartbeat boomed through her body. She leaned forward in the chair, her *Hello* strangled.

Huge brown eyes scanned the room and collided with hers. Livana blinked, tilted her head. A dimple appeared in her pink cheek and a beautiful, shy smile stretched across her face.

Liv had waited six years for that moment, imagined it every day, and never expected one smile to connect her to life so completely. It was a floating sensation, as if all her past and future failures were lifted. Her soul had everything it needed right there in that room. She tightened her fingers around Josh's hand.

Livana entered before Carolyn, her dark hair swishing around her shoulders in long waves. Ladybugs embroidered her t-shirt, and her tiny hand clutched a tablet, which connected to the ear buds poking from her ears.

"Livana?" Carolyn closed the door and regarded Liv. "I'm sorry. She has this thing with music. Always singing."

Josh's thumb brushed over Liv's fingers, and a sense of unity drifted through her, balancing her pulse into a slow, happy beat.

Livana approached, her mouth moving silently, her knees bouncing to some unknown melody. She paused a hug away, and her delicate chin raised. Her lips parted as she stared into Liv's eyes.

Carolyn tugged an ear bud from Livana's ear and sat two chairs away. "Livana, this is Liv and Josh."

A tentative hand reached toward Liv's face with starts and stops until tiny fingers brushed her scar. Too soon, the gentle touch fell away.

She couldn't breathe, her throat too thick. She gathered her voice.

"Have you seen a mark like this before?"

She tapped her scar. Carolyn wouldn't know why she was asking. Livana shook her head. "Nah uh."

It was a sad confirmation. Livana had never met her father.

Liv hunched down to peer at her daughter's dainty features. "What are you listening to?"

Those brown eyes widened, fringed with Van's thick lashes. "Katy Perry. She's really pretty. Like you."

Oh God, that sweet voice. A tingle burned her nose. "May I?" She gestured at the dangling ear bud.

Livana nodded enthusiastically and shifted to sit in her lap. Carolyn watched with tense shoulders, but a small smile touched her lips.

Liv's pulse thrummed in her throat as she released Josh's hand. She lifted the beautiful girl, hugging her close and adjusting the ear buds. One in her ear, the other in Livana's. A tiny finger swiped through Katy Perry songs on the tablet and selected "Unconditionally."

The tune clapped through the ear buds. When Livana's vocals launched, strong and perfectly pitched, a shiver crept over Liv's skin, raising the hairs on her nape. She sought Josh's eyes and found him studying them, his arm propped on the table, a knuckle resting against his lips. Behind his hand, the corners of his mouth curved, his gaze warm with affection.

The chorus kicked in, and she joined Livana's voice in a higher octave, their tones harmonizing as if they'd sung together for years. They watched each other, smiling, laughing when Liv stumbled over the words.

When the song finished, Livana flashed a toothy grin. "You sing good. Let's do another one." She swiped the screen on her tablet.

Carolyn pressed her fingers to her lips, her eyes watery. "Well." She smoothed her skirt and gave a shaky smile. "That explains Livana's beautiful voice."

Liv felt taller, stronger. She'd passed on something of herself, something that was considered beautiful. And she'd done it without meeting or touching her daughter. Her heart froze then pounded with overwhelming wonderment.

A dozen Katy Perry songs later, Livana said goodbye with her arms wrapped around Liv's neck.

"Would you like to see Liv and Josh again?" Carolyn asked.

Liv's heartbeat thrummed heavily, sluggishly. Ripping Livana from the only mother she'd ever known would be so damned selfish. As badly as Liv wanted to demand custody, no one would benefit but herself.

A tingling sensation fluttered in her belly. She wasn't a self-serving monster. Not anymore.

Livana grinned, looking up at Carolyn with love and trust. "I'll bring the music."

Carolyn clasped her hand. "I bet they'll come see you whenever you want."

"Thank you," Liv mouthed to Carolyn.

Two hours later—and after a stop behind a deserted building where she thanked Josh passionately for coming with her—they walked into his parents' house. Actually, she danced. She wiggled her hips, bumping into his as he walked. Her heartbeat drummed in her chest. A light-hearted feeling dispersed through her body, loosening her muscles. She was high on laughter, and his beautiful smile and playful shoves spurred her elation as she spun around him, rejuvenated by the best day of her life.

As they flitted around one another through the sitting room, his hands tackled her ribs, wrenching a laughing scream from her lungs. She pivoted away from him and collided with the hard, narrowed stare of Mr. Carter.

He stood in the kitchen doorway, his distaste evident in the pressed line of his lips. "This was in the mailbox."

With a stiff arm, he handed her a confidential envelope, addressed to Liv Reed in typed font. No postage stamp. No return address. Her stomach tumbled.

Josh led her to his room and closed the door. His hard jawline sawed side-to-side. "I don't think I can handle any more surprises."

He paced the small room, pivoting between the spartan furnishings. A twin bed with a handmade quilt. A dresser with a bottle of aftershave. Shelves lined the walls displaying years of football trophies. He stopped in front of her, crossed his arms, and waited.

Adrenaline flared through her veins, firing her brain to act. She sat on the bed, tore the seal, and slid out a single letter.

The name, address, and phone number of an international bank in the Cayman Islands printed across the top. The body of the letter included three lines.

*Liv Reed*
*Account number 00145481720*
*Balance $6,000,000*

# FORTY-SIX

A flush of dizziness swam through Liv's head.

The mattress shifted. Josh sat beside her, his hand curling around her wrist, angling the paper. "Am I reading this right?"

"Hand me the phone." Her voice trembled.

She called the toll-free number, confirmed the account and the balance, and disconnected.

He rose from the bed and resumed pacing. "Why would Mr. E put his money in your name? Your *real* name."

She stared at the letter, the words blurry. He'd put the house and everything else in her fake name. He and Van had been ghosts in the slave business. She was the face and the name connected to the entire operation.

"So I could take the fall?" Her chest pinched. "But someone personally delivered this to your parents' mailbox."

His mouth slackened, voicing her assumption. "Van."

*Van.* He'd spent seven years trying to break her, and it had only taken him a few minutes of near-death honesty to make amends. She'd already forgiven him. She didn't need the money to mend things between them.

"There were seven transactions, at least a million each. He probably kept a portion." She sucked in a breath. "Regardless, I can't accept it."

Josh stared down at her, his fists on his hips. "Why the hell not?"

"Eight lives, including yours" — she ground her teeth, her voice rising — "were torn apart for this money."

He crouched between her legs, tugged the letter from her fist, and set it on the bed. "Nine people, Liv. You're one of us. And you *know* our lives are better for it." He placed his palm beneath her ear, his thumb caressing her cheek. "*My* life is so much more damned meaningful. Because of you."

Her head ached and her chest squeezed. She rubbed the middle of her forehead. What were her options? She couldn't send the money back. She could donate it to charity. Or... "I can divide it among the eight of you."

He searched her eyes, his hand lowering to tap his fingers on her thigh. "You'll divide it between the nine of us, and I'll give my portion to my parents."

She smoothed a wayward lock of hair from his forehead, mesmerized by the iridescent glow of his eyes. He wouldn't need his own money if she kept a portion of the account. Neither of them knew what the future held for them, but one thing was certain. They would be together.

She wrinkled her nose to thwart the sudden burn of emotion. She had a future to look forward to. With him.

"Joshua?" Emily's voice muffled through the walls. The door opened, and her gray eyes darted between them. "Son, I'm not comfortable with the door shut when there's a girl in your room."

Liv bit her lip. Good God, they treated him like a child.

He flattened his hands on her thighs and drew a deep breath. "Sorry to hear that, Mom. And the *girl* has a name."

Emily raised her chin. "Yes, of course. I didn't mean to be rude."

"Anything else?" He squinted at her over his shoulder.

Her chest hitched. "Can I see you in the kitchen?"

"No. If you have something to say —"

The door hit the wall behind it with the force of her shove. She turned on her heels, her strides fading down the hall.

He bowed his head in her lap. "God grant me the serenity to accept the things I cannot change."

Liv combed her fingers through his hair, massaging his scalp. "There's going to be churchventions all over McLennan County praying for your soul tonight, Joshua Carter." She touched his rock-hard jaw and raised his head. "Go talk to her." She gave him her coldest Mistress glare.

A laugh barked from the back of his throat. He held up his hands. "All right." He rose, smiling. "What's a churchvention?"

She shrugged and batted her eyes. "Interventions for churchy people?"

Shaking his head, he scratched his jaw and lingered in the doorway. "You're splitting that money between the nine of us."

She picked up the letter, hugged it to her chest, and fell back on the mattress, biting back her smile. "Fine."

Early the next morning, he caught her waist with a determined arm as she tried to sneak from his bed. "Not this time."

Twilight bled a faint glow beneath the window shade. She swatted at the hand creeping between her legs. "Your parents will be up soon."

He rolled to his back, shifting her over him, chest-to-chest, and gripped the sides of her head.

"Then muffle your moans." He pulled her mouth to his and used his tongue to awaken her from the inside out.

Ten minutes later, she faced his feet, straddling his thighs and riding his cock. His body trembled beneath her. Each rock of her hips made his toes curl. She wanted to bite them.

His hands skimmed her back, spreading tingles of sensations over her skin. His pelvis lifted to meet the grinding slide of her ass, the motion bouncing her breasts and tightening her nipples. The fullness of his girth dragged along her inner muscles, her body flooding with warmth.

She stroked his balls between their spread legs, and the sight of him gliding in and out coiled her release to a teetering edge.

"Josh, I'm close," she whispered.

His fingers dug into her hips as he slowed his thrusts. In the next heartbeat, they came together, their sighs floating through the room.

A fist knocked on the door.

"Joshua," Emily hollered. "That girl didn't sleep on the couch last night. I think she's gone missing."

Liv's hands flew between their legs where they were joined as he shouted, "Be out in a —"

The door opened, and a laundry basket tumbled to the floor.

Emily covered her horrified gasp with a trembling hand and slammed the door, her screams penetrating through the wall. "Daniel! Oh dear Lord, Daniel!"

Liv slumped over his legs, her heart hammering in her throat. "I miss my keypad."

His body jerked beneath her, vibrating through his hitched breaths. Oh God, was he crying? She rose off his cock and twisted around.

His forearms crossed over his face, his chest heaving. She crawled toward him, yanked his arms down, and found his mouth curved and his eyebrows crawling up his forehead. He was laughing?

She smacked his chest. He laughed harder. She smacked him again. "Shame on you. Your poor mother is probably out there rallying an exorcism."

He regarded her with a dimple in his cheek and light in his eyes. Why was he so nonchalant? Then it dawned on her. "You wanted her to walk in on that?"

A sigh rippled from his gorgeous lips. "I want them to see *me*, not who they want me to be." He tucked her hair behind her ear. "A really pretty girl told me once that shock has a way of rousing attention."

She caressed his jaw, her fingers lingering on his mouth. "She's a stupid girl."

His eyes hardened. "Bull." He scooted to the edge of the bed and perused her body over his shoulder. "As much as I love you without clothes on, you should probably get dressed for the family meeting."

In the kitchen, Emily sat stiffly at the table, holding a tissue to her nose. "You just haven't been right since the kidnapping. You need to talk to a minister." She nodded. "You need the influence of *good* people."

Liv hovered in the corner. Fuck, she didn't want to be there, but when she had emerged from the bathroom in her jeans and t-shirt, he dragged her along behind him, saying, "This needs to be done."

He leaned against the fridge, arms crossed over his bare chest, his legs clad in low-hung jeans. Despite his casual pose, there was a fire burning in his eyes. "Liv is good people."

She and Josh had discussed their options the night before. With their financial issues resolved, they could go anywhere, and they would. He wanted to ease his parents into his impending departure.

Her insides quivered with anxiety. This was ripping off the band-aid before they'd healed from his last departure.

Daniel sat beside his wife, his green eyes narrowed on Liv. "We have rules in this house, and we expect you to follow them."

Josh's nostrils flared. "Don't you dare blame her."

"She's as loose as ashes in the wind," Emily whispered, as if only Josh could hear her.

Liv caught her sigh before it billowed out and dropped her head on the wall behind her. His parents were hurting. They'd lost their son, and he'd returned with his own view on life, one that had veered from their belief system.

"Be careful, Mom." He straightened and stormed toward the table, the muscles in his back flexing and hardening. He raised an arm and, for a fearful moment, Liv thought he might sweep all the dishes to the floor. He snagged the gaudy ceramic rooster centerpiece. "Apologize to her or the rooster's gonna get it."

Liv bit back her smile and tried to imagine how her mom would've reacted to catching her in bed with him. She honestly didn't know and that realization tugged at her chest. She was a seventeen-year-old virgin when Van took her. Her relationship with Mom had never reached this kind of trial, and it never would.

Emily fanned her fingers over her breastbone and flicked her eyes to Liv. "I'm sorry. It's just...my boy's going to be a minister. He has schooling and farm work. He doesn't have time for—"

"That was an embarrassing apology, Mom." He set the rooster on the table and strode toward Liv with wide steps, his eyes roaming her face. Placing his hands on the wall on either side of her head, he leaned down and kissed her forehead. "I love you."

Her heart wobbled. "Love you, too."

"Let me remind you that you're *not* married." Daniel rested his forearms on the table. "Tell me this was the only time you...shared a bed."

Liv sagged against the wall. Their son was kidnapped and trained as a sex slave. Jesus, they were in serious fucking denial about his captivity.

Josh turned and hooked a thumb in his belt loop. "I love her, Dad." He pointed at her. "And I'm *sharing a bed* with her every which way to Sunday. Because I. Love. Her."

Daniel paled, and Emily gasped, her face crumpling. "You need to go to church. And you need to finish your religious studies."

He let out a booming laugh. "No amount of church is going to keep me from sleeping with her."

Liv pressed a fist to her lips, her chest swelling. She wanted to kiss him for standing up to his parents, but her stomach sank as she considered what it might do to his relationship with them.

"You've changed." Emily straightened her spine and pursed her lips. "That man who took you put something bad in you. You need help, Joshua."

He raked a hand through his hair and groaned. "I need *her*." He sat in the chair beside Emily, turning it to face her. "I'll finish school. *When I'm ready*. I'll worship God. *On my own terms*. As for the farm, I'll help you financially." He twisted and met Liv's eyes over his shoulder. One dark eyebrow lifted.

Oh God, he wanted her to step in here? They already hated her. She rubbed her forearm, wrinkling her forehead. He wanted her support, and she had a sure way to give it to him.

Two confident strides put her behind his chair. She rested her hands on his shoulders. "I inherited some money when my mom died." She rubbed her thumbs over the skin on his back. "We'll leave you with more than enough to retire."

Daniel stiffened, his eyes on Josh. "What is she saying? You're not leaving."

"I am." His shoulders rolled back.

"You will not disobey me." Daniel jumped up, his face red. "You're not leaving. That's final."

Josh stood with his hands in his pockets, chin lowered, and his body angled toward his parents, but his eyes cut to the side and met hers. A small smile played around his lips. "No more requirements."

She swallowed around a lump of guilt and moved to stand beside him.

He reached for her hand and looked at his dad. "I'm not leaving *you*. I'm leaving your rules."

He was telling his dad, man-to-man, how he was going to live his life. She was certain he'd never done that before. She wished his parents could see what she saw. Joshua Carter would never be enchained by someone else's rules. He was a man of strong convictions. His *own* convictions.

Emily sagged against the chair back. "You don't even have a car."

"I'm taking the bike."

# FORTY-SEVEN

Josh moved through his bedroom with a high-energy buzz and an overwhelming lightness in his chest. Before Liv, his path was narrow and predetermined. Now it was a wide open field that reached the horizon and beyond. He wanted to fling his arms up, break out into a run, and whoop like an idiot.

Liv lingered by the door with a gleam in her eyes and a smile struggling to punch through her stern expression.

"What bike?" She closed the door and crossed her arms. "I stalked you for weeks. I would remember a bike."

He transferred her clothes from the grocery bag to his backpack. "I've got an engine strapped to two wheels."

"That sounds safe."

*Said the girl who threw herself out of airplanes.*

"I started putting it together out in the shed when I was fourteen." He grinned. "Old school pipes. Uber fat tires. It has enough torque to make my parents stutter through their prayers."

"They wouldn't let you ride it?" She joined him at the bed and helped him fit her clothes in the bag.

"Nope." Not even slow in the driveway. "But it still runs. I fired it up yesterday when you were in the shower."

She stuffed the last shirt in and put her hands on her hips, staring at the sum of every possession she owned. "Where are we going?"

He opened a drawer and tossed a few shirts, briefs, and jeans on the bed. "We need to go to a bank, open an account, and transfer your funds. We need phones so my parents can call us. Oh, and helmets for the bike." He sidled in front of her, prompting her to look up and meet his eyes. "We can go to Austin and live near Livana. Or we could call Camila. You think they have room for two more in their house?"

"Nine adults in one house?" She threw her head back and laughed, her gorgeous brown eyes alight with amusement.

Probably not the best idea, especially given the way the guys longingly tracked her every move.

"Tonight…" He wrapped his arms around her lower back and squeezed her addictive backside. "We're staying in a hotel with no keypads and no parents and…" He scanned his room, his attention snagging on the hook behind his door. That would work. He released her, grabbed a leather belt from the hook, and held it out to her. "And this."

She could strap him to the bed or shackle his wrists or whip his backside. A pulse of warmth curled through his groin. He needed to buy more belts.

She took the one from his hand, folded it, and whacked her palm. Her upturned face glowed, her soft cheekbones curving with her smile. "You want me to beat your ass, you dirty slut?"

Her cool voice sent a shiver down his spine and stiffened his penis to a throbbing hard-on. "Yes, Mistress."

She twisted her fingers through the hair at his nape, her long lashes blinking slowly. Then she pulled him down for a kiss that tunneled his vision and rocked his hips.

"Finish packing." She released him and stepped back.

He adjusted himself and returned to his dresser for one more thing. Digging beneath the clothes he would leave behind, he pulled out his favorite childhood toy. He clutched her wrist and set it on her palm. "I want you to have this."

Her slim eyebrows pulled together, her face arranged in an adorable expression. "A Rubik's Cube?"

The square stickers peeled at the edges, each of the six sides grouped by color.

"I solved it when I was eight." He laughed, shaking his head at the memory. "Took me a year. I refused to undo it after I figured it out."

"Wow." She stared at it, confusion lingering on her face.

"It wasn't the satisfaction of solving it that was meaningful. It was the experience in pursuing an endeavor of my choosing. I never found another puzzle I connected to the way I did with this one." He touched her chin, held her eyes. "Until you."

She clutched the cube to her chest and pulled his forehead to hers. "Thank you."

He kissed her nose. "My jersey number was based on that cube. There's fifty-four squares."

A huge smile spread beneath her glistening eyes. "My name."

Roman numeral LIV. His favorite number, his fate, his freedom.

An hour later, he hugged his dad in the driveway. The bike rumbled a few feet away. Liv stood beside him with everything they owned on her back.

"Love you, Dad."

Dad squeezed him until his ribs complained.

Mom's embrace was gentle but no less caring. "You call us as soon as you have a phone."

"Yep." He climbed on the bike under the remorseful gazes of his parents.

Their lips pressed tight, their expressions stony, but they were there to see him off. They loved him, and time and patience would sand away their disappointment.

Liv straddled behind him and curled her arms around his waist, her thighs clenching his hips. He licked his lips and pointed his feet forward. A breeze ruffled his hair. The sun warmed his skin. His heart beat a steady, peaceful tempo.

He twisted his neck and collided with her eyes over his shoulder. "Where to?"

She didn't look at the road. Didn't gaze at the sweeping hillside. She raised her eyes to the sky and smiled.

# FORTY-EIGHT

Three months later, Liv gulped the cool air rushing through the open door and gripped the bench seat beneath her. The aluminum walls of the narrow cabin vibrated with the roar of the wind. Her palms collected sweat in the thick gloves. Her goggles steamed with humidity. And her smile was so big her cheeks hurt.

Josh sat on the bench across from her, his complexion a kaleidoscope of grays and greens. He looked like he was going to throw up all over his red jumpsuit.

Mom had always said to reach for the sky, so Liv decided to do just that and followed Mom's jump boots. Liv's instructor position at the skydiving school outside of Austin enabled her to take Josh on his first jump without the nervous chatter of other newbie skydivers. It was just her and him and the sun-bleached sky.

She leaned forward and shouted over the shrill of the engine. "Changed your mind yet?"

He snapped his arms out and bellowed some kind of indiscernible battle cry. Then he flashed her a panty-soaking smile.

The man had balls, and fuck her but she loved those balls. She'd had them bound in a ball stretcher the previous night while she paddled his ass to a gorgeous shade of red. The memory kindled a damp heat between her legs. She wiggled, grinding her pussy against the seat.

His boot nudged hers. "You thinking about me?" he yelled.

She caught her lip between her teeth and shook her head, the whir of the turbo-props piercing her ears.

He'd transferred his classes to Austin University to pursue a teaching degree. He wanted to coach high school football. With only two semesters of schooling left, playing college ball wasn't feasible. He shrugged it off, saying that wasn't part of his *Freedom Plan*.

Mr. and Mrs. Carter called daily. They were warming to her but had yet to visit their rental house of bed-sharing sin. The freedom fighters, on the other hand, popped in frequently. Overwhelmed with their sudden wealth, they spoke of the future with glimmering, wide eyes. A future that included her and Josh.

She visited Livana several times a week. It was surreal, sitting in Mr. E's house, in the rooms she'd memorized from the angle of his camera. Her time with Livana filled that empty hole inside her. Some of that happiness included thoughts of Van. Despite the painful memories, she focused on his goodness with a tingling warmth in her face. Sometimes, while running errands or working in the yard at the rental, she'd feel a prickle on her spine and would catch herself squinting over her shoulder, scanning the street for a charcoal hoodie. He was out there somewhere, and she deeply hoped he found something worth living for.

Her gloved hand reached for Josh, and he caught it, squeezing her fingers, his smile cartwheeling through the wind.

The pilot shouted over his shoulder, "We're one minute to drop zone."

"Ready?" she mouthed.

"Yep." He shook his head, still holding onto that sexy grin.

They shuffled toward the open door, weighted down by gear. She checked his emergency parachute one more time, spending unneeded seconds adjusting, tightening, and readjusting the harness between his legs. He laughed and ground his cock against her hand, the horny slut.

Satisfied with the buckles and position of the vest, she shifted his back to the open door with his heels touching the threshold. She grabbed his face, pressed her cheek against his, and shouted into the wind, "Trust me?"

He answered her with his tongue in her mouth, slashing and whipping, his lips strong and determined. His hands clutched the door frame with nothing but empty space behind him.

She pulled back with a kiss on his bottom lip, cocked her head, and shoved his chest.

With an *Oomph*, he was gone.

The wind slapped at her body, thrashing her hair around her face. She sucked in a breath and leapt into the sea of blue, surrendering to the turbulence as it shot her through the air. She watched the plane fly away, her pulse thundering and her lips pulling away from her teeth. The shock to the heart was such a fucking thrill.

She flipped to face downward and spotted her entire world coasting above the curvature of the Earth. He arched his pelvis, limbs out and steady, adapting to his environment so easily, just like he always did. Christ, she loved him, and she would never let him get away.

She arrowed her body, her arms balancing her legs. Using velocity and angling to manipulate the aerodynamics around her, she gained on him.

With the wind deep in her ears and flapping her clothes, she reached out her arms and caught him. The gusts smothered his laugh, but his smile tangled around her, his eyes flickering through the goggles.

He entwined their legs, locked his hands around her back, and covered her mouth with his. Spinning them to descend heads down and feet up, she matched the elated movements of his tongue, answering his affection with the slide of her smiling lips.

Nothing compared to the freedom of floating in his arms.

He would say the hand of God was holding them up, delivering them.

She called it love. Her heart didn't fall. It flew.

# PLAYLIST

"Gods and Monsters" by *Lana Del Rey*
"Lullaby" by *Sia*
"What It Is" by *Kodaline*
"Bring Me To Life" by *Evanescence*
"Pretender" by *Sarah Jaffe*
"Team" by *Lorde*
"Pretty Face" by *Sóley*
"Ghostflowers" by *OTEP*
"Possession" by *Sarah McLachlan*
"Glory and Gore" by *Lorde*
"Last Resort" by *Papa Roach*
"Unconditionally" by *Katy Perry*

# VANQUISH

## PAM GODWIN

Book 2

# PROLOGUE

Pain. Dense, maddening bursts of pain splintered through Van Quiso's shoulder and reduced him to a pathetic mouth-breather on the kitchen floor. Heaviness settled over him, pooling down his arm and collapsing his chest. Each slogging beat of his heart drained more blood from his body, chilling his veins, soaking his t-shirt.

He should've known Liv Reed would be the death of him. If he could focus past the throbbing wound, maybe he'd hear a haunting serenade beneath her breath, beckoning him toward the cliff of oblivion with seduction dripping from her lips. He could only hope his descent into hell would be so enthralling.

He dragged his eyes heavenward and met the bleak despair wetting hers. Their gazes clung, motionless, as shock deadened the air between them. She'd shot him. Too damned late to take it back. He wanted to slam his fist into her beautiful face. Even more, he ached to kiss the path of tears streaking her scarred cheek.

The cold linoleum pressed against his back. He'd fucked her on this floor countless times, bent their joined bodies over the wobbly kitchen table, and slammed her against the fridge until her moans drowned out the whine of the old motor.

But their best moments had happened in the attic chamber, where her ass reddened under the fall of his whip as her lithe body hung from the ceiling, the sound-deadening walls absorbing her screams. For seven years, she'd been his to discipline, fuck, mentor, and keep.

Pulsating shadows framed his vision, closing in and threatening to take him from her permanently. Final judgment awaited him in death, but his punishment had already been inflicted. She no longer feared him. She was no longer his. The burn in his shoulder ignited. If he died, what would become of her?

His lungs clenched, not from injury, but from something more debilitating. He suffocated with the need to tangle a fist in her hair and never let go. She knew better than anyone the justice of his death, yet her full lips quivered. Lips that tasted like butter-soft caramel.

She knelt over him, shocks of brown hair tangling around her arms, the curve of her body taunting him. What he wouldn't give to feel her tight, reluctant cunt gripping his cock one more time. But she loved another man.

His ribs squeezed against the swell of rejection. She'd actually pulled the trigger. How could she think he was going to kill her? Didn't she know he'd die without her?

Dots blotted his vision. From the blood loss? Or was it the tremor of ice-cold fear passing through him? Hard to deny that he'd earned her distrust, kidnapping her when she was seventeen, taking her virginity without asking, and blackmailing her into delivering slaves for Mr. E.

Despite all that, every second at her side had nurtured Van's stupid-as-shit hope that she'd grow to love him. A hope that slipped through his grasp the night she abducted Joshua Carter against her will. She'd fallen in love with her newest slave, and that betrayal hurt worse than the lead buried in his shoulder.

But the blow that turned him against Mr. E's operation came six days ago. Van had sent her to meet with a slave buyer. There was a disagreement, and the buyer brutally raped her.

Renewed rage boiled in his gut. If he'd gone with her, he could've protected her. Sweat beaded on his lip. What was he thinking? He couldn't even protect her from himself.

He stared into the gorgeous, watery eyes of his first captive as her fingers caressed his jaw. He'd beaten and fucked her into submission and failed to stop Mr. E from killing her mother. Still she cried for him. His breath hitched. He loved her suffering in a way he couldn't rationally understand.

When he'd gone after her rapist, it hadn't been some chivalrous act of heroism. He'd fucking reveled in the dismemberment of limbs, the flaying of skin, and the gurgled screams of a man as atrocious as he himself. With the stain of his first kill dripping from his hands, he'd put his exit plan in motion. One that would free them from Mr. E's operation and bind them together. A family.

But her pretty boy was a menacing blockade to his plan. Joshua hovered behind her, his ridiculous linebacker brawn flexing to finish the job if the bullet failed. Despite the boy's apparent willingness to sacrifice his life for her, he couldn't protect her from their boss.

Was she still trying to wrap her mind around everything she'd just learned? Her face had blanched a chilling shade of white when he'd told her Mr. E was not only his father but also the police chief of Austin. And he hadn't disclosed the worst of it.

His pulse weakened, and his breathing thrashed. He needed to get the bullet out. If he survived, it would take days to recover. Days he and Liv didn't have.

"Have to kill him." He blinked through fading flashes of light. "He'll avenge me." Now that she knew Mr. E's identity, he was certain she'd hunt down their boss and finish the job, but she needed motivation to do it quickly. "He'll kill Livana." If Mr. E hadn't killed her already. His throat tightened, choking his breaths.

"Livana?"

The angelic quality of her voice and the shape of her lips forming their daughter's name for the first time produced a wet burn in the corners of his eyes. There was so much he needed to tell her.

The flat line of her mouth wobbled. "Mattie's real name is Livana?"

He lifted his chin, attempting a nod. Beyond the infrequent video footage of their daughter, they'd never been allowed to see her. Liv didn't know where she lived, didn't even know her real name. For six years, she'd heartbreakingly referred to her as Mattie.

A helpless, foreign feeling stabbed his chest from the inside, over and over, pulling him further into darkness. Killing Mr. E meant he could finally meet their daughter. He was so damned close. He *would not* die.

Shivers wracked his body, and Liv's features vanished behind a veil of black.

"Van? Where's Livana?"

"She's..." He forced his eyes open. The outline of her face seemed so far away, yet he could make out her slim brown eyebrows as they formed a sharp *V*. He reached for her cheek, his fingers tingling, numb.

She leaned in to meet his hand, her eyes swimming in tears. "Van." Her voice rasped, and the tears fell over, splattering his chin. "What's Livana's last name?"

She needed a name to find their daughter, but she wouldn't have to look far. His fingers fumbled over her scar. From her eye to her lips, the seven-year-old laceration mirrored his own. Even now, he didn't regret the actions that had led to their matching punishments. Her pregnancy had given him immeasurable relief, a means to ensure she wouldn't be sold as a slave. She belonged to him, his greatest accomplishment.

The pain in his shoulder jolted deep into his bones as he traced her lips and lingered on her jaw, dreading the answer he'd kept from her for so long. He'd had no say in who raised Livana, but he'd controlled Liv by withholding Livana's name and whereabouts. He didn't carry Mr. E's last name, but his daughter did. Liv might very well shoot him again when she learned Mr. E had been raising Livana since birth.

He opened his mouth and strangled on the words. Pinpricks assaulted his body. His vision blurred. He clung to the edge of consciousness as the muscles in his arm shook and gave up. His hand hit the floor.

"Nooo." She scrambled atop him, fingers trembling over his face. "No, Van. No, don't go," she screamed.

Wails bellowed from her throat. Such an outpour of emotion from a woman who always remained guarded behind a stone-cold mask. Her anguish filled him with warmth, pumping his heart. She cared. He tried to open his eyes and failed. His body grew heavy, struggling against the leaden weight of gravity. But that was okay. She thought he was dead and fucking cared.

"Oh, Van. I'm so sorry." She hugged his waist, weeping, nose sniffling.

He melted against the floor, blacking in and out. Time seemed to stop and start, his mind full of cotton, spinning around...something. He'd lost so much blood, but there were things to do. He needed to get up.

The warmth of her body vanished, and a scuffle of rubber soles squeaked on the linoleum. Joshua must've dragged her away. Was she fighting him? *Come back.*

He couldn't lift his arms. Couldn't open his eyes. Her hiccuping sobs teetered off. Or did he teeter off? He strained his ears through the hum of white noise. Somewhere, water dripped. *Plop. Plop.* Too soon, his world faded to nothingness.

He woke to the silence of an empty room and blinked rapidly, catching the low rays of the sun where it had dipped below the kitchen window. Christ, he'd passed out. For twenty, thirty minutes? Long enough for Liv to determine him dead and leave, but it wasn't dusk yet.

Now that the shock of watching her pull the trigger had passed, he needed to find his balls and get the fuck out of there. He wiggled his fingers and toes and tested his strength in his wrists and ankles. Breathing noisily but still coherent, he slowly bent his elbows and knees. With a surge of impatience, he rolled his shoulder and jerked against the sudden stab of pain. "Fuuuuck."

If she failed in her attempt to kill Mr. E, the cops would come. If she succeeded, she might alert the cops anyway. He needed to get his ass up, make a call, and disappear.

Getting shot wasn't part of his plan, and dealing with a lodged bullet magnified his aggravation. A hospital would report the gunshot wound. He could wedge it out with a steak knife. And inflict nerve damage. And gouge a damned artery. Or he could drive to Mexico and pay a seedy doctor to take care of it.

Fucking Mexico. *Ahi vamos.*

He tugged a disposable phone from his pocket and dialed.

"Yeah?" rasped the CTS Decon technician.

"Change of plans." Van had approached the professional cleaner a day earlier and offered a quarter of a million to discreetly and quickly mop up a crime scene. The blood was supposed to have been Mr. E's, the prearrangement to remove Van's DNA from the scene, therefore, eliminating him as a murder suspect. Liv's bullet changed that. Now, she would have to deal with Mr. E on her own while the technician dealt with Van's blood.

He rattled off the address of his location. "Need this done by the end of the hour."

"On my way." The technician disconnected.

Now for the grueling part. He gnashed his teeth and dragged his body up the side of the counter, stars invading his vision. After a few long, ragged breaths, he finished the climb and stumbled to the medical kit beneath the sink.

As he collected bandages, he tried not to think about what Liv was doing, if she had killed his father or if he'd killed her. He pulled his shirt over his head, and the damnable pain staggered him sideways.

He gripped the counter-top and panted through the blades of heat ripping up and down his arm. The pain was real, pushing his pulse and inflaming his skin. He was breathing, hurting. Alive.

With Liv and Livana's uncertain future, he had a helluva incentive to live. And to avoid arrest. He draped his upper body over the sink, splashed water over the dime-sized wound, and taped up his shoulder. He needed a bottle of Tequila Herradura and a long nap in the worst fucking way.

Blood smeared the counter, the cabinets, and the linoleum. He had no choice but to trust the expertise and discretion of the technician to erase all evidence of his existence. Hopefully, it would be enough to deceive detectives if they went hunting for DNA.

He dragged his feet to the kitchen table, each step heavier than the last. Two mannequins sat in the chair where he'd left them. When he reached them, he slid his fingers through their silken mahogany hair. Liv's hair. He'd collected it for years, meticulously weaving it through the mesh caps made for the dolls, one large, one small. His perfected replicas of Liv and Livana. No one could fucking take them away.

Liv didn't understand his need for the dolls. Only someone who'd experienced a lifetime of loneliness could comprehend what they meant to him and why he couldn't let them go.

With his arm hanging limp at his side, he gathered them under the other, careful not to overextend their joints, and carried them to the van in the garage.

Liv thought he was dead. And he was certain she would succeed in killing Mr. E, which meant she would be free for the first time in seven years. Would she leave town and try to disappear or would she stay in Austin, near their daughter? Either way, he'd find her. He'd always find her.

# ONE

*One year later…*

Simple, mutually-satisfying sex was an acceptable way to alleviate loneliness, even if it was just twenty minutes in the dark with the delivery guy. At least, that's what Amber Rosenfeld told herself as she flicked off the table lamp in her bedroom, perched on the bed, and waited.

It was silly the way she collected those twenty minutes, treasuring them like souvenirs. Her mementos of normalcy. Proof that fear didn't own *every* minute of her life.

The overhead light flipped on, and her breath caught. She blinked through the unexpected glare, narrowing on Zach's finger where it poised over the wall switch. Oh no. Something was wrong.

She straightened her spine as he regarded her with a heavy slant in his eyebrows. She fidgeted with her hair, arranging the curls to lay in a sensual fall down her chest. Maybe he didn't like blondes. She brushed it behind her shoulders, out of view. Did he desire a prettier girl? If he turned the lights off, he wouldn't have to look at her.

"The lights, Zach." Her tone held steady despite the pleading drum of her heart.

He fingered the collar of his *Saddler's Tool Company* work shirt and freed the buttons down the front, revealing a thin, hairless torso. Brown hair hung in strands around his whiskered jawline, his blue eyes watching her with too much scrutiny. "Let's mix it up today."

A swallow stuck in her throat. The only thing he was mixing up was the neat edge of carpet beneath his boots. He rocked on the molding between the hardwoods and the bedroom, the rubber-soled toes smashing the fibers with each lift of his heels.

Why did he insist on disturbing the carpet? Couldn't he see the uniformity of the vacuum lines, how the threads lifted in one-foot rows of symmetry? Her walk to the bed had followed the outskirt of the small room. She'd hopped the lines easy enough, leaving four tiptoed indentations she would comb after he left.

Fuck, she was doing it again. She pinched the bridge of her nose. The carpet didn't need to be perfect. *She* wasn't perfect.

He shrugged off the shirt and tossed it on the floor, flattening two rows.

Her stomach clenched, but she forced herself to look at the disorder, to accept it. "It's better without lights."

"No, it isn't." He bent to remove his boots, trampling more fibers. "What if I trip in the dark and put an eye out?"

What a joke. The floor had been spotless before he arrived. Besides, "You don't need eyes for this." She shaped her mouth into a smile, lifting a shoulder. Did he notice the hollowness in her movements? What if he gave her an ultimatum about the lights or said something hateful? Did he have a cruel side?

*Fat, worthless cunt.*

*When are you going to do something about your udders and schedule a boob job?*

*You're a fucking head case. Just like your mother.*

She bent her fingers and cracked each knuckle in order. Index, middle, ring, pinkie. Zach wasn't *him.*

As he watched her knuckle-cracking ritual, lines formed in his brow. He should've been used to it by now, but something was off. He had never put this much focus on her quirks.

Finally, he blinked away, pushed his jeans and briefs to his ankles, and stepped from the unfolded mess. Pale skin smoothed over a narrow thirty-something physique. He scratched his flat stomach, eyes on hers, his partial erection hanging long and lean like the rest of him. He was attractive in a nonthreatening, easy-to-please manner. And he seemed to like her in a way that hardened his cock. A tingling awoke between her legs and fanned heat through her body.

But the light remained on. He touched the switch, staring at it as if he were asking it useless questions.

Her palms grew sticky and hot. For six months, he'd delivered her supplies, brought in her mail, taken her to bed, and left with her shipments. If she had trash, he would kindly drop it at the curb. He didn't make demands, express opinions, or try to complicate the routine. However, their unspoken arrangement had already extended twice as long as the previous delivery guys.

She knew what came next, and her gut twisted. "Just say it, Zach."

His attention shifted to the hem of her dress where it covered her thighs, roamed over her chest, and rested on her eyes. "I want to see you. Just once with the lights on and your clothes off."

A cringe jerked her shoulders, and her tongue thickened with all the wrong things to say. He waited for a response, one she knew she'd fuck up. She raised her chin. "I like it dark." For twenty minutes, every Tuesday and Friday.

His jaw stiffened, and he averted his eyes.

An empty feeling gutted the pit of her stomach. *Please, don't leave.* He was her only tether to the outside world, but she needed to nip this desperation for his company. Distancing herself kept her safe in her self-made asylum.

She attacked the middle joints of her fingers, synchronizing her exhales with each flex and pop. It took twenty-four minutes for the gas to redissolve into the joint fluid. If she continued cracking at this rate, she'd run out of knuckles. She really needed a better distraction.

His gaze flitted around the room, never settling on one thing for long...until something behind her gave him pause. What was he looking at? She followed his line of sight to the blacked-out window.

Oh God, no. Stinging heat crawled over her cheeks. If he opened the shade, the absolute terror and despair waiting on the other side would find her. It would liquefy her bones and seal up her throat until she had no control, no power to stop it.

His sigh penetrated the clamor in her head. "All right." He flicked the switch and smothered her storm with blackness.

A gust of relief freed her lungs and loosened her fists. Jesus, she needed to stop spazzing about what-ifs. She didn't want to be this scared little mouse trapped in her cage. What if Dr. Michaels was right? If she let the panic in, would it really show her a way out?

A shiver lifted the hairs on her arms. Yeah, right. Screw the free world.

She clung to the sound of Zach's footfalls and rationalized his tracks on the carpet as a form of therapy. She was supposed to challenge the anxiety, vary the landscape. He helped with that, even if he didn't know it.

The fifth footprint landed an inch away, and her teeth clamped together. Why did he have to take that last step? Four was even. There were four sides to a square. Four seasons to a year. Four fingers on a hand. Four was complete. Exact. Calming.

His palm touched her bicep, distracting and warm. She gripped his fingers and pulled him onto the bed, reclining on her back. Chest-to-chest, the weight of his body strengthened her in a way solitude couldn't. Her nerve-endings pulsed against every point of contact, her only connection with another human being. The tops of his feet around her ankles. His fingertips on her face. His thighs and groin exquisitely aligned over hers.

Soft lips brushed a stimulating path over her jaw, her cheek, her mouth. Slowly, her doubts and fixations gave way to anticipation of his kiss and his cock and the comfort they would bring. Fuck her unhealthy mind. Her carnal nature, her flesh hummed with vitality.

Lifting his body, he slid the dress up her thighs and tugged down the lace panties she wore for his visits. Fingers found her opening, gently circling, spreading her wetness, and coaxing a tremor of excitement. "I bet your pussy looks as beautiful as it feels." He pushed in two fingers, shooting shock waves down her legs. "Will you let me taste you this time?"

*Don't ask me to put my mouth down there. Smells like a dead cow.*

She cringed at *his* voice in her head. "Not today." Never again, no matter how badly she wanted it.

"Okay." He reached for the condom on the side table. The wrapper crinkled as he knelt above her. "How do you want me?"

"Rough, unrestrained, and perfect." Everything she wasn't.

Chuckling, he fell over her and thrust his hips, entering her in one liberating stroke. His ass flexed beneath her hands as he glided his length. In and out, he rubbed her inner walls into a blaze of sensations. Through the darkness, he found her mouth, his tongue rolling with hers and his fingers tingling over her ribs. Every caress and attentive lick left a trail of vibrations.

Until his palm cupped her breast. She jerked back against the mattress. Even through the dress and bra, he would feel the hard, oversized implants. What must he think of her? Maybe she should explain how much she hated them, how the surgery had dulled the sensations there. No, that would be worse. Only a weak woman would get a boob job she didn't want.

He let her pull his hand away and move it to her throat. His grip tightened as he pounded into her. Ahhh, right there. He didn't squeeze hard enough, but she was in the zone, rocking against him and holding onto the moment with both arms.

The thrust of her hips didn't come from a place in her mind. Fucking was a primal impulse, an urgent action that dulled the noise in her head. The musk of his sweat wrapped her in a cocoon. The hum of her pulse swished through her veins. Almost perfect.

Repeatedly, his cock hit the spot, the right tempo but never enough pressure. Did she feel good to him? Was her pussy tight enough? She clenched her inner muscles with each invasion of his length and moaned. *Come on, Zach. Let out a groan.*

He remained unnervingly quiet as he rotated his pelvis. The scent of sex filled the air, sweet and tangy. What if he didn't like the way she smelled? Was he holding his breath?

His exhales brushed warmly across her mouth, his exertion heating and slicking their bodies. Was it difficult for him to get off with her? Was he imagining fucking a different woman?

She shook off her hateful thoughts and savored the moment, biting at his lips and angling her pelvis. If only he would thrust harder. That brief stretch of solace was in reach. It tingled the flesh that spread around his cock and tiptoed up her spine. She trembled, anticipating the moment when everything inside her would still.

Then it came, the gallop of climax beating along her scalp and booming behind her ears. She moaned as the ripples washed over her, numbing her legs and carrying her to a place where voices and shame didn't dwell.

He followed with an erratic buck of his hips and a breathy groan. She buried her face in his neck, twitching with the aftershocks of tranquility.

Too soon, disappointment invaded her peace. First, came the dissipation of orgasm. Always too weak, too fleeting, it never sustained. Then, the absence of his body as he disposed of the condom. And finally, his tracks across the carpet and the click of the light switch. Her stomach sank.

She shoved the dress over her thighs, despising the chill of loneliness creeping into her skin.

"Your mail and supplies are in the kitchen." He pulled on his clothes, shooting sidelong glances in her direction.

She swiped her thumbs beneath her eyes to clear away mascara and combed fingers through her hair. "A bag of trash and my shipments are ready by the door." She hated her dependency on him as much as she dreaded the post-sex awkwardness. Nevertheless, her merchandise had to be mailed or her bills wouldn't be paid.

She'd tried the door-to-door mail service once, but when her packages were stolen right off her porch, she'd lost a month's income. She couldn't risk that again. Zach was the dependable solution.

A knot tightened beneath her breastbone. How the hell did she become so lonely and helpless? Perhaps those traits had always existed, hidden beneath beauty pageant crowns and fake smiles.

Separation from people hadn't cured her need to please. She longed to lift the hem of isolation, look into eyes full of acceptance, and see in them the reflection of a woman who didn't give a rat's ass.

Neither of them spoke as he laced his boots, each second straining longer than the last. Should she say something? Maybe compliment his performance?

He straightened and lingered in the doorway, deep lines etching his forehead. *Stay* trembled on her lips, but he didn't owe her anything. They didn't have dinner dates or interact beyond their routine. He always arrived at the scheduled time. She always left the front door unlocked and waited in the bedroom. No conversation. No deviation. No questions.

What did she have to offer him besides a scheduled orgasm? If he stayed, he might suggest they go out and do normal things. If he found out she hadn't ventured beyond her front door in two years, he'd never come back.

She cracked her knuckles. She needed to stop the unproductive waffling. Either she continued with him as a detached fuck buddy or she pursued the relationship with a deeper connection. She couldn't have both. The former worked. The latter would end swiftly and painfully.

Squaring her shoulders, she met his eyes. "See you Friday."

A subtle inhale flared his nostrils. He studied her for a long moment, nodded his head, and left.

She curled her fists in the bedding, her muscles straining to run after him.

The slam of the front door knocked the wind from her lungs. *Way to go, Amber.* Might as well add a few dozen cats to the paranoid, anti-social routine and call it what it was.

She hung the dress in the closet, where it would stay until Friday, and put on yoga pants and a t-shirt. She vacuumed, ran four miles on the treadmill, and showered. A few hours later, she finished the filigree carving on a leathercraft order, ate a pancake, and showered again.

As the nightly news ended, she stood before the bathroom mirror and pinched the flab hugging her hips.

*If you exercised more, maybe I wouldn't be thinking about your sister all the time.*

She shouldn't have eaten that pancake. If she weren't ten years older than Tawny, maybe she would've held *his* attention. Her stomach clenched painfully, and she bent at the waist, gripping her knees.

Was he in bed with Tawny now? Kissing her sister the way he'd once kissed her? Of course, he was. They were married now.

She turned away from the mirror, squatted before the toilet, and gagged with the reflex of a practiced vomiter. Her eyes watered, and her throat contracted and burned. The partially-digested pancake splattered the bowl.

She didn't look in the mirror as she brushed her teeth. Didn't glance at her midsection as she dressed and sat on the couch. She had zero resistance to self-deprecating thoughts, and the white envelope on the coffee table didn't help.

The notice of default was proof of her worthlessness. She had ninety days to reinstate the mortgage or she'd lose the house, her safe place.

Her head hurt, and her chest felt hollow.

She would have to increase the sales on her leather goods, but it wouldn't be enough. She'd already cut all her expenses. All but one.

She popped her knuckles and dialed Dr. Michaels.

# TWO

"Good evening, Amber." Dr. Emery Michaels' warm greeting was always unassuming, despite the fact that her calls were sporadic and often panic-stricken. "How are you doing?"

Which problem should she tackle first? She blew out a breath. "He wanted the lights on."

A pause. "The young man who delivers your supplies?"

Zach wasn't that young. Probably older than her thirty-four years. "Yeah."

"Is this the man you want the lights on with?"

His tone wasn't judgmental, but her hackles flared. "He's the man I want to fuck, Dr. Michaels. Lights or no lights, you said my libido was a good thing."

"Yes, as long as sex doesn't become an addiction."

"I can live without it." The thump in her chest disagreed.

"Has your relationship expanded beyond sex? Have you talked with him about your healing path?"

Secrecy and shame were interwoven with her condition, and she excelled at being a psychiatric textbook. "No and no."

"Have you given more thought to attending a self-help group?"

Sweat trickled down her spine, and the muscles in her neck went taut. "I can't—"

"*Agoraphobics Outbound* meets bi-monthly at Austin State Hospital. It's a ten minute cab ride from your house."

She chewed the inside of her cheek and imagined all those people staring at her, examining, criticizing. How would she escape? What if she got lost, stuck in a crowded place, or fainted?

Not only that, her mother was a patient in that hospital. Her breathing quickened. She couldn't bear to be in the same building with a woman who wanted nothing to do with her.

"Amber, you need the solidarity of a support group."

Something she would never receive from her family. She gripped her knuckles. *Crack. Crack. Crack. Crack.* Strangers would be worse. They wouldn't know her, yet they'd weigh her worth as she lost her shit.

"Amber." His soothing timbre steadied her pulse. "Tell me what you're thinking."

"They'll see how undesirable I am."

A sigh whispered over the line. "You are a lovely woman, but you will never hear that until you believe it yourself."

"*He* didn't think so." She winced, hating herself for mentioning him.

"Yet he didn't want to give you up."

She'd once viewed marriage as a sacred covenant, arrogant in her belief that only three A's justified divorce. Adultery. Addiction. Abuse. *He* had committed none of them—never acted on his desire for her sister while they were married, never hit her, never so much as got drunk—yet she'd divorced him. She'd given up, taken the easy way out. "I failed him."

"Eliminating the toxicity in your life is not a failure. It's curative and courageous and never, ever easy."

She blinked against the achy burn in her eyes. Brent hadn't always been toxic. Sixteen years ago, he looked at her like she was so much more than a sparkling accessory on his arm. She deeply missed the man she'd fallen in love with. "Leaving him was the hardest thing I've ever done."

"That's right. So the *Outbound* meeting would be a piece of cake in comparison."

She straightened the envelope on the table, leaving a four-inch, right-angle gap from the table's corner. "I won't be calling you anymore."

"These sessions are necessary in your recovery."

"I know what I need to do to get better." Face her fears. Remember to belly breathe. Ask for help.

"What have you eaten today?"

The purged pancake floating in the toilet. Had she remembered to flush it? Gripping the phone, she ran to the bathroom and relaxed when she saw the clean bowl. "I can't afford to pay you."

"I see." Wariness breathed through his voice, but he didn't offer to counsel her for free.

She wasn't worth his charity. Not that she would've accepted it anyway.

His movements rustled through the phone. "The self-help group is free. That's your next goal. I'll forward links to online support groups and see if I can find a therapist who might be more affordable."

She'd already looked, but maybe he'd have better luck. "Thank you." Jesus, she was going to miss him. "I'll look for your bill in the mail." And hopefully, she'd have the funds to cover it.

"Be patient with yourself, Amber. Sometimes you have to step back to open the door."

Three days later, she glared at the front door, her legs paralyzed with fear. Clutching the cell phone to her ear, she said into the receiver, "I call bullshit."

"Amber, ring my boss if you don't believe me." Zach sniffled through the speaker, his voice leaden with congestion. "He sent me home. I feel like I'm going to die."

"You can't die from a cold." But a heart attack was fatal. She could feel one coiling around her chest, squeezing the life from her body. "What about my mail?" She covered the phone to muffle her panicked gasps.

"Why can't you get it?" He sneezed, followed by a nasty, wet inhale. "Are you on house arrest or something?"

Unbelievable. They'd had this arrangement for six months. He was just now asking why? She released a thready breath. "I just can't. Will you ask someone else at the store to bring my mail to the door? Or maybe you know someone who wouldn't mind swinging by?"

"No. No one lives near you, and I can't just ask people to do that." He coughed. "Listen, I need to go."

The palpitations in her heart wobbled her legs. "I need my mail *today*." She needed it two days ago. The leather dye she'd ordered sat twenty-six steps from the door. She couldn't finish the knife sheaths without it. If she didn't mail out the completed sales by tomorrow, the water would be shut off.

He hacked through the phone. "I'm sorry, Amber."

Guilt formed a hard, jagged lump in her stomach. "Please don't apologize. This isn't your fault." She rubbed her forehead with cold, shaking fingers. Her stomach gurgled with dread. "Get some rest. Hope you feel better."

"Yeah, okay. See you Tuesday."

The phone disconnected, and she slumped to the floor, sucking harshly for air. She hugged her stomach against an onslaught of queasiness and glared at the front door. It stood between her and her paycheck. The damned thing wasn't a terminal disease. It wasn't swinging a chainsaw. It was just a door. A bolted, four-sided shield against certain suffering.

*Sometimes you have to step back to open the door.*

One step back and twenty-six steps to the mailbox. She could do it in twenty-four, a semi-perfect number. Twenty-four hours in a day. Twenty-four carats in pure gold. Four and twenty blackbirds baked in a pie.

Good God, she was drowning in her own crazy. *Just get it over with.* She swiped a palm over her face, smearing her makeup with sweat. Shit. She darted to the bedroom and changed into a white halter dress and matching heeled sandals. A check in the bathroom confirmed her hair held its curl. Her makeup was still flawless. She returned to the door.

Deep breath in. Out. Twenty-four paces there and back. She used to make that trek before Zach and Kevin and Chet and...oh, fuck it. She could take her phone. If she panicked, she could call Dr. Michaels.

No, she couldn't. She swayed and gripped the doorframe. Okay, not a deal breaker. She wouldn't need him. She had this.

Her heart rate doubled. What if she broke down so spectacularly she couldn't walk? What if she couldn't get back to the house?

She flattened a hand over her sternum, hating this, hating herself. What happened to the brave girl who stood on stage time after time, shaping her mouth into a practiced *O* of surprise as tiaras were placed on her head? Oh yeah. That girl tried too hard to please people, and look where it got her.

She smoothed down the dress and stared at the knob. *Reach out and turn it.* Twenty-four steps. She could walk them to the tune of *kick the fear habit, embrace the new, don't beat yourself up* and all the other psychosmart mantras that sounded invigorating until they were put into action.

How about the shit that kept her up at night? Overdue utilities, no showers, no flushing, no clean dishes?

She flipped the deadbolt four times and yanked open the door.

The sun hit her face in blinding white. She raised an arm to shade her eyes, the blanket of humidity seeping into her pores. A winged insect buzzed past her ear. The smell of fresh-cut grass tickled her nose. The hum of air conditioning units had her spinning in every direction. Were the neighbors home, watching from the shadows of their windows?

A truck motored by, and she jumped, stumbling into her first step.

*Don't look at the street.* Her gaze caught on the bushes lining her porch. Jesus, they'd doubled in size, blocking the bench she hadn't used in two years. The wood seat was weathered, neglected, forgotten.

Dammit, she couldn't dwell on that, on any of it. A terrible pressure already pushed against her ribs. She bent into the next step, dizzy, fighting for breath.

*Ignore it.* She ground her molars. Two steps, eight percent of the way there.

Tremors assaulted her body. The landscape spun around her. The mailbox. A passing car. Open windows on houses. A woman walking her dog. Everyone showed up to watch the freak show.

God, she was so fucked up. This should've been a thousand times easier than being crowned Miss Texas. She was wearing her heels. Her curls shimmered around her arms. She could take the third step. Just like on stage.

She raised her leg with the grace that came from years of discipline. Suddenly, as if her foot had landed in the spotlight, she turned on her pageant best. Fingers relaxed and together, shoulders back, chin up, bright eyes, and big smile, she held the pose. The persona strengthened her stance. She was the best. Knowing it meant winning it. She was doing it.

The honk of a slowing car scattered her delusion. She flinched, blinked. Bright green lawns, twittering birds, and the scent of hot asphalt knocked her back to reality.

She glanced down and took in her ridiculous pose. Decked out in heels with one leg bent and a hand on her hip? Her smile slipped, and her ankles teetered.

*Stop it.* She held her arms at her sides. Tingling numbed her fingers, her sense of control slipping.

Why couldn't she stop these reactions? She wanted this step, needed it. *Move, dammit.*

Spots blackened her vision. The pressure in her chest... It was stifling. She couldn't breathe. Oh God, her body was giving up on her, overheating, growing heavy. The ground tilted.

She squatted to avoid collapsing and fell back on her ass, shaking uncontrollably. "Noooo." She cried out in anguish and curled into a ball. *Make it stop hurting. So scared.*

The open crack of the door wavered through her tears, an arm's length away. She crawled on elbows, stiffened by chest pain and gasping for air. She dragged her body over the threshold and kicked the door. It shut with a thunk, silencing the cars, the windows, the witnesses. She folded herself into the corner of her cage and wept.

Eventually, she peeled her tear-soaked face off the oak floor and leaned against the door. The sun no longer glowed through the cracks, and she was no closer to the mailbox.

She'd have to try again.

As if. She was still strung out and trembling like a mouse. She'd only fail.

Yeah, but she always felt that way.

She could call Zach. He might feel well enough to drive over.

Maybe he would. Or maybe she could do it herself and feel better for it. Nighttime might conceal her from onlookers.

But the predators came out at night.

Fucking ridiculous. Everyone went out after dark. Except her.

Forget it. She'd tried once already and failed.

But she'd stepped outside. Three huge steps. *Not four.* That was the opposite of giving up.

Damn right. The corners of her mouth relaxed. They might've even curved up a little. She rose on quivering legs and walked to the bedroom. She needed to change clothes and fix her makeup. Maybe it would take her all night to walk twenty-four steps, but she'd do it. The alternative was unimaginably worse.

# THREE

For a while, Van pretended he didn't miss her. Not her fierce looks or her hot, wet pussy or her beautiful agony. The ache she'd left behind should eventually seal up and scab over like the wound in his shoulder.

But it didn't. It inflamed and festered until he had woken weeks later, twisting in sweat-soaked sheets and fucking his fist, unable to think about anything but Liv Reed.

That was a year ago, and still, she possessed his thoughts every second of every day. He imagined the satisfaction she must've felt when Mr. E died. The quiver in her arms as she hugged their daughter. Her thighs spreading for that cumgargling bible-basher, the fuck who had stolen his place in her life. That shit really fucked with him.

Stagnant air coated his skin in a wet sheen as he locked up his 1965 Mustang GT Fastback. To think the humidity in Austin was relatively mild this time of year. In a couple months, the heat of summer would suffocate his nightly walks.

The hood of his sweatshirt sloped over his forehead, his chin tucked discreetly to his chest. The street's only source of light flickered overhead, months overdue for repair. Somewhere in the distance, the trill of a frog warbled through the silence, calling in the darkest hour of night.

If he were a man with uncontrollable urges, he would've grabbed Liv the night she'd killed his father. When he'd followed her from the police station to Joshua's farm, the bullet wound painful but patched up, he could've snatched her from the cocksucker's bed and taken her to Mexico with him. If he were a psychopath, he wouldn't have been able to stop himself.

Instead, he gave her six of the seven million they'd earned in slave trafficking, the gift alerting her he was still alive. When he'd healed from the bullet, he'd looked for her in the one city he knew she'd be.

Surrounded by one-story bungalows, he strode across the suburban Austin street, dangling a grocery bag from one finger. He cut between two houses as if it were a Sunday stroll. As if it weren't past eleven on a Friday night.

His strides fell in harmony with his pulse, steady and confident. He'd cased the neighborhood long before he'd claimed this route. He knew the names, habits, and lack of awareness of every resident for two blocks. Knew the elderly occupants on either side of his shortcut had been tucked in bed for hours.

Past the overgrown side yard, ducking beneath the low-hanging hickory behind the houses, he followed the path he'd taken hundreds of times. If he weren't trying to pass unnoticed, he might've whistled one of Liv's favorite tunes.

She loved their child so selflessly, he knew she'd never take Livana from Mr. E's wife, the only mother Livana had ever known. Though he'd known his daughter's location since the day she was born, he'd only ever seen her through the lens of a camera—Mr. E's video footage her first six years and his own camera the last year.

Christ, he wanted to meet her, to touch her angelic face, to hold her tiny hand, and look into her brown eyes and see them smiling back. But she lived with Mr. E's widow, who hadn't been part of his father's slave ring but was wrapped up in the aftermath of the police chief's death. Authorities didn't know Van existed, and his freedom depended on maintaining that anonymity.

It'd only taken him a couple weeks to find Liv in a modest rental house minutes from where Livana lived. No surprise she hadn't spent the money he'd given her. Perhaps she'd never touch it because of where it came from and the memories that clung to it.

Which was why he'd kept one million. It served as a parachute should his daughter need it. Livana had come into the world same as him—born of a slave and a slave owner. He would do whatever was needed to ensure she didn't end up like him.

But he didn't mistake his intentions as selfless generosity. He didn't want the fucking money. He wanted Liv. He wanted his daughter. Whether he deserved them or not, he would have his goddamned family.

Loose, curling bark snagged his hoodie, and the ground covering was redolent of sweet peppermint as it stirred beneath his sneakers. He broke from the trees, sheltered by the black sky, and crossed the backyard of his destination.

The single-story house faced the street one block over from where he'd parked. Though no one lived there, he approached the back porch with tightening muscles, ready to slip away at the first sign of life.

Three windows and a glass door broke up the monotony of weathered brick. Heavy-duty shades blocked light from escaping. The shades hadn't moved, not once, in the six months he'd been coming to Liv's neighborhood. A lawn service maintained the small lot of grass, but there were no flowerbeds, no lawn furniture, no inhabitants.

His black hoodie and dark jeans blended with the backdrop of the unlit house as he checked the locks on the rear windows and door, looking for a disruption in the pattern, any indication that someone had moved in.

All clear, he approached the south side that would take him to the front porch and the bench that awaited him. As he rounded the corner, he dug his heels into the wet grass, flattening his body against the vacant house.

One of two windows on the house next door cast a warm glow between the foundations. His pulse sped up, and an excited warmth of energy swirled through his stomach. Liv lived next door to the abandoned house.

He crept toward her illuminated window. His crouched position below prevented a good look at the inside, but he knew it was her kitchen.

The dark window beside it drew his attention. Her bedroom. Was she in there now? Removing her clothes? Humming a seductive melody? He closed his eyes briefly as his dick pulsed against the tight confines of his jeans.

When he regained his focus, he edged around the band of light on the grass and removed two wireless microphones from the bag, following his nightly ritual. The high sensitivity mics penetrated glass and transmitted to his phone. A whole lot safer than bugging the inside of her house.

He powered them on and left them on Liv's brick windowsills. Camouflaged by shadows, he ducked across the yard between the houses, retreating from Liv's and slipping onto the front porch of the vacant house. He strode past the bench and reached a finger inside the porch lantern. The bulb he'd removed months ago hadn't been replaced. Good. With a suspended breath, he checked the lock on the door. The knob wobbled but didn't turn, as expected.

On his way back to the bench, he stopped at the wide picture window and leaned his cheek against it. At that angle, he could see a sliver of light along the bottom of the blackout shade. Always closed with the same millimeter glow.

Though the mail was addressed to Amber Rosenfeld, the only person who came and went was Zachary Kaufman. The *Saddler's Tool Company* employee arrived at noon on Tuesdays and Fridays—a simple inquiry at the tool store confirmed the man's identity and his schedule.

After watching him for months, Van was certain the moron was using the house to grow marijuana. Given his stupid smiles and flushed cheeks when he exited the house, he was toking the merchandise during his visits.

Who cared? As long as Zachary Kaufman didn't get busted, Van had an ideal place to squat.

Hidden from the street by overgrown shrubs, he reclined on the shadowed bench of a house where no one lived and looked to the right. The elevation of the porch put him at the perfect height to peer through the two windows on the side of the house next door. The opening in the foliage gave him a sliver of sight into Liv's life.

He connected ear buds to his phone and pressed one into his ear. A few minutes later, he cracked open a beer, lit a cigarette, and watched Liv's windows like the dirty voyeur he was.

The mic picked up indiscernible voices from deep within the house, and his heart skipped. He squashed the cigarette and concentrated on the sounds in the earpiece. Footsteps?

Liv's front door opened and a tall man with dark, shoulder-length hair strode down the driveway. Van leaned his head back, slouching deeper within the hood. It wasn't necessary. Ricky wouldn't have been able to see him through the foliage.

Good ol' Ricky. The second of seven slaves she'd delivered. Seven million dollars had been paid by seven buyers. Yet seven *sold* slaves flitted in and out of her house, carting side dishes for bar-b-que parties, drinking beer, and braiding her friggin' hair as if she hadn't spent ten weeks beating the ever-loving shit out of them.

Van had discovered the depth of her deceit the night she'd shot him and left him. He'd driven to the police station, his shoulder throbbing like a motherfucker, and watched her walk out of the station and make contact with her first slave. Fuck, he'd never in a million fucking years guessed she'd been freeing the slaves after delivering them.

During the months of monitoring her house, he'd gleaned the details from their conversations, how she'd delivered them, secured the financial transaction then killed the buyer by bullet, knife, garrote, or any means possible. The fact she hadn't been caught was beyond impressive. Perhaps, she'd made it look like they were killed by rival gangs or cartel.

She'd outsmarted him, his father, and a network of buyers. Her treachery only made him want her more. She wore his scar on her face. She was the mother of his child. She'd saved him the unsavory task of killing his father. She belonged to him.

The sac of misery in his chest contracted and heaved. As Ricky climbed in the truck and drove away, he wanted to run after him, drag him to the pavement, and pummel his face. Not because the boy was free, but because he was free to see *her*. To make eye contact. To touch.

Lighting another smoke, he stared at her windows, willing her to appear. As he inhaled the last drag, the hum of a heavenly voice trickled through the ear bud. He sagged against the bench as every molecule in his body absorbed the decadent notes.

Through the window, he saw her hourglass figure fill the doorway of the kitchen. Her full lips moved, and her voice rose in a deathless composition of memories, evoking emotions in him that patched his heart and shredded it all over again.

She glanced to the side, a smile stretching her mouth. Her hum tumbled into a laugh as Joshua appeared from the room beyond and enfolded her in his arms.

"You look gorgeous tonight." The bastard's voice was grating. Besides, she was always gorgeous.

She turned in his arms and whispered something, but he didn't miss the last three words. "I love you."

The beefed-up Boy Scout palmed her ass. "Love you, too."

Van's chest clenched. He'd said those words to her often, but it hadn't changed a damned thing. Hadn't prompted her to say them back. Hadn't prevented another man's hands from groping her now.

As those hands caressed her, he remembered her velvety skin, the minty fragrance of her hair, and the biting flavor of her pussy. His dick grew warm and hard, throbbing for her touch.

He unzipped his jeans as Joshua removed his. He stroked his length, anticipating and dreading the scene he'd witnessed so many times. They would fuck on the table, their go-to in the kitchen. As she slid off her panties, he jerked his fist, hating the man she loved and hoping one of these kitchen romps would roll him onto the fatal end of a butcher knife.

She angled Joshua's bulky body against the table edge, pushing him onto his back and pinning his arms above his head. Her skirt hiked up, and the view of her heart-shaped ass rushed more blood to Van's cock. He stroked harder, his breath quickening with the sound of hers.

After a few wriggles of her hips, she seated herself on Joshua Carter and fucked him the way she did every night. Hard and wild, her face slackened with passion. All the ways she'd never fucked Van.

He knew he should stop. He should stop coming here and fucking his hand. Stop fucking up his head with something he'd never have.

But he could have her if he took her.

His fist tightened, and his balls pulled up. He was close. So was she. Her head fell back, and her features morphed in pure bliss as her body bucked. On another man.

He lost the rush to climax, which happened more often than not. The lonely, wretched feeling that took its place made him want to knock on her door and remind her he existed. Then what? Wait for her to invite him in for a beer? What if she turned him away and started closing her blinds? What if she shot him again?

He relaxed his fist, his insides squeezing in a miserable grip despite the needy throb in his engorged dick. She was happy, and her happiness meant more dark porches and unreachable orgasms in his future. He needed to let her go.

Same damned thing he told himself every night.

Had anything changed since that night six months ago when he decided to put mics on her window? The intel he'd gained through spying hadn't brought him any closer to his daughter. As for Liv, he'd tried for seven years to make her want him. It was an impossible pursuit then, and even more so now.

Watching her night after night with Joshua might've killed some of his desperation for her. But for some perverse reason, he couldn't stop. Witnessing her get off gave him more satisfaction than the faceless men and women he fucked when he left her window.

A click sounded from the door behind him, lifting the hairs on his neck. The deadbolt twisted three more times. What the fuck? He turned, yanking the ear bud from his ear, and his blood ran cold.

Five feet away, the front door opened, and a high-heeled foot tapped slowly, inch by inch, over the threshold. The interior light highlighted long, toned legs and a narrow body wrapped in a short skirt and business jacket.

She lingered in the doorway, half-in, half-out, fingers gripping the frame. She stared at the street as if unsure whether she was coming or going. In fact, she clung to the house as if it were supplying her air. A house that no one lived in.

He didn't move, didn't blink. He could slip off the side of the porch, but he was glued to the bench, captivated by shock and curiosity.

Her breaths grew louder and more shallow, and her profile shifted from the concealment of the doorway. A mass of blond curls framed her face, her delicate features twisted in indisputable pain and horror. It wasn't him she feared. Her focus hadn't moved from the end of the driveway, her wide eyes cutting a circle around the mailbox.

The empty street was dimly lit. Not a car or a snake or a bogeyman in sight.

She stumbled forward, releasing her clutch on the doorframe, and choked on a sob. Another step. Her heels wobbled, and her hands flew to her busty chest as she gasped.

Fuck, she was a beautiful sight. Dainty fingers, tiny nose, pink cheeks streaked with tears. His cock twitched in his hand. He was sick and selfish and insanely turned on by her body and the lost look in her wide eyes, the whole damned package. He stroked his arousal, praying she wouldn't turn his way, hoping she would.

She threw herself forward, her heels landing with a clop. She bent over, hands on knees, and whispered, "Four."

The light from inside outlined the cuts of muscle in her calves, thighs, and ass. Muscles that quivered so violently he was surprised she could stand. But the girl was built. Not an ounce of fat. Perhaps too thin, like body-builder dehydrated, but Christ, she worked it with those huge tits and tiny waist.

And she still hadn't noticed the pervert rubbing his dick behind her. She cracked her knuckles and shook out her arms, seemingly lost in her head. Then her shoulders jerked back and her chest heaved. He leaned forward. What was she up to?

She took off. Amazingly fast in heels, she sprinted down the driveway, her ass flexing with her strides. She slammed to a stop in front of the mailbox and yanked out the envelopes. Her free hand covered her mouth, and the muffled sound of her sobs reached the porch.

What was wrong with this girl? The intensity of her fear resonated deep within the depraved part of his being. It was as intoxicating as her beauty, but where did it come from? What was she afraid of? How the hell did she live in this house? That would mean she never left. Watching her stagger up the driveway, it made sense. Kind of.

She was heading back to the door, and however breathlessly and hunched over, she would surely see him. He tucked his semi-hard dick in his pants and shoved his things in the bag. The side windows on Liv's house glowed from within, the rooms empty. He needed to get the fuck out of there.

Wobbling, she squeezed the mail to her chest, eyes fixed on her feet as if willing them to keep moving. Her shoulders curled forward and seemed to be dragging her toward the ground with each step. She didn't look like she'd make it to the porch.

A few steps away, her attention jerked up, fixed on the cracked door. As she inched toward it, her gaze cut right, then left and collided with his. The anticipation in his stomach coiled into a knot, and he stared right back, daring her to look away. Would she scream? Run? Or confront him? Fuck if he couldn't wait to find out.

Color bled from her face, the whites of her eyes rounding with terror. Her muscles spasmed, shaking her arms and loosening packages from her grip. Several dropped around her feet. Was she having a seizure?

She reached back, squatting, as if she knew she was going to fall. Fuck it. He jumped off the porch and closed the distance in three strides.

# FOUR

Sweet God, why was there a man on her porch? Oh fuck, a murky, fast-moving wall of man. He charged toward Amber in a blur of dark clothes and unimaginable purpose. Why was he running toward *her*? She didn't need help. She just wanted to be left alone to return to her house.

The door was so close. Eight feet at most. But convulsions shook her hands so uncontrollably she lost her grip on the remaining envelopes.

Silver eyes stabbed from the depths of his hood, seizing every cell in her body. She couldn't look away, couldn't breathe. Not when her stomach bucked and her chest simmered with bile. And not when his hands shot out and locked around her elbows, preventing her fall.

Saliva rushed over her tongue, and vomit hit the back of her throat, hot and humiliating. What if he was trying to help her? She couldn't puke on him. Please, no. She swallowed past the burn and breathed through her mouth as bursts of black dotted her vision.

The man's fingers clamped her arms, his chest too close to hers. She needed air, tried to jerk back. Her knees buckled. No, she wouldn't let her panic beat her. Not when she was so close. But she couldn't stop it as the assault bore down in crippling dizziness, the path to the door whirling around her feet.

Another surge of nausea ripped chills through her bones and liquefied her joints. She twisted to face away, stumbled, and fell into the darkness.

The steel brace of his arm caught her mid-section, and she hung there, mucus and anxiety spewing from her mouth and stringing over the mail at her feet. Thank God there was nothing in her stomach to eject. The saliva on her lips was embarrassing enough.

He bent over her, his body surrounding her back, hard thighs supporting her butt, his arm hooked beneath her folded waist. "There you go." His low, steady whisper sounded like a shout in the wind, snuffing out her surroundings. "Better?"

Her vision tunneled. Ringing blared in her head. She couldn't focus. "I'm fine. You can let go."

"Do you have meds? Do you need a doctor?"

A paralyzing freeze spread through her veins, sucking heat from her face in tingling waves. No doctor. No medication. None of that fixed a damned thing. She clutched the muscled forearm at her belly, pushing at it, dry heaving.

Who was this man? No way was he just passing by in the middle of the night. Was he going to hurt her? Rape her? Or do something that would disfigure or permanently damage her body? Did he have a gun?

She choked. Why her? The rapid wallop of her heart accelerated. She yanked at the arm, an unmoving restraint, and forced bravado in her voice. "What do you want?"

He leaned in, his chest heavy against her back and his breath feathering her hair. "You live here?"

His gentle tone conflicted with the pressure of his fingers. She rammed her head backward. He dodged her strike, and the cage of his body curled around her, straightening her with his arms around her chest.

Blood thundered in her ears, and her heart hammered to escape, to give up, to shrink and die. She stretched her jaw and wheezed a pathetic shout. "Help." Need air. The door. She angled toward it, throwing her fists behind her and colliding with nothing.

"Easy." The coil of his arms held her upright, his body a brick wall at her back. "If there's no heart condition, no epilepsy, then what's wrong with you?"

She might've laughed if she weren't failing to breathe. This man didn't give a shit about her condition. No one did. With his arms wrapped around her and his exhales on her neck, she'd never felt more helpless. She wanted to drop to the ground and retreat into herself, but she was better than that, dammit. "Let go."

He didn't. She might not be able to overpower him, but she still had her voice. If all he wanted was an answer, she could give him a revolting one. "You want to know what's wrong with me? My genital herpes has flared up. You know, blistering sores, cracked open and itching? My Valtrex prescription is in one of these packages." She scanned the ground, gasping, humiliation screeching through her voice. "To make matters worse, I started my period. I can feel it dripping down my leg." There. That would send any guy running.

He laughed. The motherfucker *laughed*. Either he knew she was lying or he was a sick fuck.

Somehow, her struggling only shifted her closer. A waft of cut hickory and citrus flooded her nose as his lips brushed her cheek. "You are a captivating surprise, Amber Rosenfeld."

Oh my God, he knew her name? Her muscles heated, more desperate than ever to get away from him. She threw an elbow, and it bounced off his rigid stomach. "If you don't let me go, I...I'm—" She sucked in a breath, her voice gravelly and broken. "I'm going to bleed all over you."

He chuckled. "I don't mind a little blood." He tightened his grip. "Besides, you can't even stand on your own."

Ragged sobs swallowed her breaths. She lurched forward, hands slashing at the air, reaching for the door, going nowhere. "How do you know my name?"

He kicked at the scattered envelopes. Her name and address labeled overdue bills, fliers, and catalogs in block print, glowing in the stripe of light that escaped the crack in the door.

Okay, so he knew her name. She just needed to grab the package with the dye and hustle her ass inside. She twisted in his arms and swept a foot, toeing for an envelope with bulk. Her lungs burned with exertion. Fucking shit, where was it?

A renewed bout of panic hiked her pulse and sealed her airway. What the hell was she thinking? Fuck the package. She had to break free. Lock the door. Call the cops. She could reach the door in one or two running leaps.

Her heart raced, nearly exploding, as she thrashed against him. His arms pinned her biceps, so she swung her fists, aiming for his groin and missing. He wrestled her hands to her sides, everything moving too quickly to process. She simply reacted, slamming her head back again and collided with his chest.

The grunt of pain that followed resuscitated her flight response. She thrust all her weight against his arms, her heels scraping the concrete. "Let me go, you psycho."

His exhales grew heavy, curling over her shoulder and pitching her into a breathless frenzy. The more she shoved against him, the tighter his arms constricted, lifting her until her feet kicked air. "What are you fighting? Fear?" His mouth touched her ear, his timbre a silken noose around her neck. "Fear is an imposture, little girl. It doesn't bruise or thrust or bite." His grip tightened. "*Fear* is not your Master."

Oh, holy mother. What was he saying? The terrible dread that occupied her belly bristled with thorns, impaling her with nightmares of public places, crowds, nowhere to hide, loss of motor control. And now her superficial fears embodied a very real, in-the-flesh threat.

He was going to take her, discover all her imperfections, and reject her. Abandon her somewhere away from home. Or kill her.

A furor of tears shot through her eyes and soaked her lashes. She clawed at his arms and stabbed her heels at his shins. If she could refill her lungs, she might be able to muster a scream big enough to wake the neighbors.

But she'd never seen a single person who lived on her street. How judgmental were they? If they came out, would they just stand there and gape? Oh God. "I have nothing you want." She panted, choked. "I'm nothing. Let me...go."

"As you wish." His arms vanished.

The concrete stoop crashed against her knees, and pain ricocheted through her legs. Oh God, maybe he'd only been trying to help her stand? She'd overreacted, made a freak of herself.

She gagged on a sobbing exhale, and her fingers scraped the ground, searching for the package and coming up empty. Another torrent of nausea gripped her body, singeing her insides and spinning the ground beneath her.

She pushed through the disorientation and crawled toward the door as fast as she could. The metal threshold sliced her knees, but she was too numb and dizzy, seconds from fainting. She could feel him behind her, a thick cloud of judgment with eyes scorching her skin, witnessing her shame.

*You think they don't know how fucked up you are? Everyone knows. You're a fucking embarrassment.*

Oh, if Brent could see her now, dragging her body, snot dripping from her nose. What a fool she was. Maybe the prowler would shoot her and put her out of her misery.

She gripped the doorjamb. Fuck Brent. Fuck all of them. She pulled her legs inside and glanced at the blockhouse of muscle behind her as she swung the door. And froze.

The interior light caught the face within the hood. Her heart constricted, and her hand stopped the door, just a crack.

He hadn't moved from where he'd released her. Hands in his pockets, he regarded her with a lift of one dark eyebrow. His full lips pursed around a toothpick, hollowing his cheeks. A strong jaw and hard gray eyes roughened his model-like prettiness. But the thick scar bisecting his cheek was what stayed her hand, pinning her to the floor and summoning the deepest, most troubled part of her.

The gash curved from the outer crease of his eye to the crook of his mouth. It should've impaired his confident gaze and brutalized the symmetry of his deep-set eyes and chiseled nose. It should've made her look away.

Instead, it demanded tolerance, homage even, and fortified the savagery of his beauty. He was a perfect imperfection.

Her ogling had only lasted a heartbeat. Perhaps, another second drinking in his good looks wouldn't hurt, but as she leaned in, the door swung closed and erased him from view.

The air returned to her lungs. She locked the dead bolt four times and collapsed onto her back.

Who was he? How did he get the scar? What did he want? She replayed the potency of his voice, the strength of his arms, and the flaw in his flawless face. He was fascinating. Though to be fair, she hadn't been outside in two years. A stray dog might've been just as enchanting. Actually, what was more fascinating was that she was thinking about him and not her lost mail.

She sat up, her pulse redoubling. Her mail. Her fucking package. Goddammit, she couldn't go back out there. It was a guaranteed panic attack, one she might not survive. She gripped the middle row of knuckles and exhaled with each crack. If she didn't go back out there, she wouldn't have the dye to finish the leathercraft orders. She wouldn't get paid. Wouldn't be able to stop the water from being shut off.

She released a heavy sigh. She'd made it to the mailbox, albeit ungracefully and shamefully. She could make a few more steps to gather the packages. She rose, exhaustion weighing down her limbs.

God, her silly fears had such incredible power over her. Just a quick sprint right outside, and she'd have what she needed to finish her orders.

With a spike of courage kick-boxing her heart, she placed a trembling hand on the knob—

A fist pounded on the door.

She jumped, rattling her teeth.

"Amber?"

His voice shivered through her, and her breaths burst in and out. Why was he still here? Should she call the cops? Would they force her outside or to the station to make a statement? She faced the door and shouted, "Go away."

More pounding. "Amber, if you want your mail, you're gonna have to open the door."

# FIVE

Van narrowed his eyes at Amber's door as a restless vibration itched behind his ribs. What the hell was this girl's problem? And why was he so hypnotized? Was it her slap-it-hard, fuck-it-harder physique? The breathless waver in her voice? Or the challenge of not knowing what made her freak the fuck out?

Beneath her trembling, however, lay an assload of backbone. And a very, very fine ass. What if every torrid trigger that had ever set him on fire waited behind that door?

He dropped his brow on the weather-beaten frame and tilted his face toward the dark windows next door, his real reason for being there. Liv and the dick monk had moved to the other side of the house and out of hearing range. He should move along, too, return to his cold, empty cabin, and forget all about the fear widening Amber's gorgeous eyes.

And yet, despite the risk of being seen, he gathered the last of her mail and knocked on her door a second time. Christ, he was riding a vicious need to discover her secrets, a craving to break her apart and play with the pieces.

He knocked again and infused his tone with authority. "Amber."

"You should run," she shouted. "I've got a gun aimed at the door."

Sure she did. "What kind of gun?"

"The kind that shoots ball-seeking super-bullets at unwanted visitors."

Cute. Even if she owned a gun, she wouldn't be able to still her fingers long enough to pull the trigger. He released a slow breath, an attempt to expel the impulse to pop the deadbolt. He should leave the poor girl to deal with her demons, but instinct demanded he take control of this...of her.

He was the worst combination of his parents, his very blood blackened with human slavery. Hell, his moral code was fucking fried the moment he was conceived by a ruthless slave owner and a weak, used-up slave. Besides, it was easier to blame his DNA than to examine the decisions he'd made or, rather, the choices that continued to choose him.

A nice guy — like Saint NinnyBalls next door — would stop, but he ripped the edge of one envelope, slid out the document, and activated the light on his phone. "You should see this, Amber. Looks like your electricity is going to be shut off" —he skimmed the red print— "in five days."

A thump jiggled the door. Her fist? "Opening peoples' mail is a federal offense, you sick pig."

He smirked. Couldn't argue with the truth. "Don't insult pigs. It's dirty, and the pig likes it."

"Until they're slaughtered," she yelled, "and served with eggs and coffee."

A smile tickled his cheeks. "You inviting me to stay for breakfast?"

Funny how brave she sounded behind the barrier of a door. A cheap door, in fact, given the hollow rattle and the sorry-ass lock. Didn't she realize one kick would bend it from the casing? He tapped the tarnished kick plate with his sneaker and made it clatter, just to taunt her.

"I'm calling the cops." Her threat pierced through the door, but the waver in her shriek lacked conviction.

She wouldn't be calling anyone. Was it a general fear of people? Or something far more complicated? He leaned a shoulder against the jamb and thumbed through her bills and leathercraft catalogs. "What would keep a beautiful woman locked up in her house?"

His stomach hardened in anticipation of her voice as soundless seconds crawled down his spine. Her silence deterred him more than the door. What was she doing in there? Texting a friend? The friendly neighborhood delivery guy, perhaps? Or was she pressed against the frame, same as him? Was her hand on the knob? He didn't dare twist it. Didn't want her to flee deep within the house where he couldn't talk to her. Instead, he opened the largest package, ripping through the bubble wrap. Four bottles of...leather dye? "I'm waiting, Amber. What's the reason?"

More silence. He rolled the toothpick between his lips. If she didn't respond in three seconds, he'd simply move the mics to her windows. Three, two —

"Why does there have to be a reason?" Her voice reverberated through the wood, soft, close.

He shifted, his mouth hovering over the seal in the door, and matched her tone. "What's the leather dye for?" He turned the bottles in the envelope, revealing directions on how to dye shoes and furniture. "Fixing up a pair of cowgirl boots?" Fuck, those toned legs would radiate sex in a miniskirt and boots.

She growled, loud and guttural, and the door thumped again. "After I flay the skin from your body, I'm going to dye it and sew it into a handbag. Special order from your momma."

A laugh erupted from his throat, and he darted a glance at Liv's windows. "Hate to disappoint you, gorgeous. My dead mother has no use for handbags."

The door held as still as the quiet behind it. If she felt bad about his mother, she shouldn't bother. Isadora Quiso chose the slow death of crack over feeding and protecting her son. She could burn in hell.

"C'mon. Just open the door." He dropped his forehead on the frame. What would he do if she let him in?

Fantasies spilled from the oily, malignant lesion that was his mind. He would take her was what he'd do. Strap down those toned limbs until they strained in agony and bury himself in her so deep she'd never be able to purge the stench of him. He was his father's son, after all.

Except Mr. E had not only enslaved and ruined his mother, he'd left her to rot in an El Paso *colonia* with her unwanted infant.

Van bit down on the toothpick, snapping it in half. He pocketed the pieces, his bitterness cursing at him to embrace his nature. The rancid bits of his life in that ghetto were inside of him. He wanted to pocket those, too.

Yet here he was, growing hard at the thought of ruining another life.

She'd grown too quiet on her side of the door. Had she decided to end the conversation and retreat to another room? He tightened his hands into fists. "Amber?"

The door jostled with her movements.

He sighed in relief. "Just give me one reason why you're holed up." Give him something vulnerable he could break off and sharpen into teeth.

"I'll give you several." Her tone was clipped, angry. "I'm allergic to pollen. I'm hiding a dead body. And I don't like you."

There it was. She *did* like him. He hadn't missed her gape of appreciation when she'd shut the door. What she seemed to be oblivious to, however, was her enjoyment in their verbal scrimmage. But where was the terrified girl who could barely utter a sentence outside? She really put a lot of faith in that door. He grinned. "Maybe I'm the reason."

"Mighty full of yourself." Her volume rose. "Let me clear it up for you. Fuck. Off."

He'd rather fuck *her*. And he would. The brick walls of her bungalow might've suspended her earlier panic, but it was a deception he could shatter with little effort. He could wait till she fell asleep and pry open the rear sliding door. A precaution he should've taken six months ago rather than assuming the house was vacant. He'd been careless, and now his favorite bench — and its view — was compromised.

Though, since the moment Amber had stumbled out, something had happened to his focus. "Are we done talking through the door?"

"What are you doing on my porch in the middle of the night?" She sounded tired, defeated.

"I was looking for some old friends and got the wrong house. You're not exactly rolling out the welcome mat, but I kind of like here. It beats going back to an empty home." It was more truth than he'd planned to share.

"You don't have—"

He pressed his ear against the wood, desperate to hear the rest of it. *Let it out, Amber.*

"You don't have anyone...at home?"

His pulse hopped through his veins. His honesty had opened a precious doorway into hers. "No one, Amber. There's not a soul that cares if I live or would miss me if I died." Maybe he'd laid it on too thick, but the truth was always denser and darker than shit.

The flooring creaked beneath her footsteps. Was she pacing? Considering another swine-related retort?

Finally, the creaking stilled, and her voice drifted over him, sealing her fate. "I'd like to make you an offer."

# SIX

Whatever sanity Amber had left evaporated in her desperate state of do-or-die. The decision roiled through her stomach. She needed the dye to complete the projects, and even more troublesome was how she would transport the finished orders from the door to the mailbox before the Saturday mail carrier motored by.

Was enlisting the help from this man the smart thing to do? It felt right, like a nuzzling, belly warming, union-of-lonely-souls kind of right. She knew, too well, how forceful loneliness was, how it could make a person desperate enough to grasp at strangers.

She rubbed her temples and released a frustrated breath. She was making an emotional decision, as Dr. Michaels liked to say, anchored in empathy and illogic. And Brent had always said she was too stupid to think for herself.

Her hands dropped to her sides. There had been a time in her life when she'd ignored Brent's commentary, when her self-image was as true and sturdy as her pageant pose. Perhaps too sturdy. The more she'd let his disgust roll off her shoulders, the crueler the words had become. For years, he'd tried to penetrate her pride, to elicit a reaction. One she'd refused to give. Until, eventually, he'd cut too deep.

Maybe she'd hardened herself so much she'd become an undesirable person, a detached wife he could no longer love. For that, she only had herself to blame.

*You're excusing his behavior.*

Dr. Michaels was right. Besides, she was anything but hardened now, and Brent wasn't around to savor it. She squeezed her over-popped fingers, and the silent bend of joints pushed her pulse to her throat.

"What's the offer, sweetheart?"

Interest wove through his timbre, and the endearment had no business shivering over her skin. Nothing was more comforting, or more narcissistic, than feeling desired.

She leaned toward the door and placed her palm on the cool surface. Even if he did desire her, it had no weight in her decision. His intention did, and she didn't know what that was. She didn't know him.

But she hadn't known any of her previous lovers. Hell, her *I'd like to make you an offer* was the first thing she'd uttered to Zach through the door.

*Zach.* The recent change in their interactions was the beginning of the end. Perhaps, she'd made such a fool of herself he didn't plan to come back at all. Sometimes, they didn't.

Lack of options was all she had left. "What's your name?"

His pause was brief but unnerving. "Van."

"Van." Her voice rasped past a sandpaper throat. "I'll invite you in for four hours while I dye a project and wait for it to dry. In exchange, you will take my finished packages to the mailbox." She held her breath.

"Does the dyeing and drying involve my skin?"

Her lips twitched, and it felt...safe. "If you misbehave."

"Are you going to give me herpes?"

She laughed at his teasing tone and covered her mouth, startled by the sound. She lowered her hands, but the smile persisted. "If you ask nicely." Her face inflamed. Jesus, she was flirting. Oh, fuckever. Wasn't that what she was offering? The same thing she'd offered the last six delivery guys? Sex in exchange for her deliveries?

But Van's name wasn't stitched on his shirt. He wasn't on his lunch break, for twenty minutes on Tuesday or Friday. He'd opened her mail, for Godssake. He asked questions. *He* pursued *her*.

"It's a deal." His voice was firm, final.

Ohshitohshitohshit. It was one thing to flirt and joke through the safety of the door, but letting him inside after she'd run off her mouth and made an ass of herself? What was she thinking?

Her pulse jumped from zero to a hundred and forty, her legs weakened, and the chest pain barreled in. No, please, not an attack. Not going to happen.

She breathed deeply, flexing and holding her abs on each inhale, four times. She would slap on a fresh face and pull herself together, dammit. The four clocks lined on the far wall read 12:40 AM. "I need twenty-four minutes."

Without waiting for a response, she ran to the bedroom and continued her belly breathing while she changed from her sweat-soaked suit to a clean black minidress. That done, she finger-combed the carpet lines and freshened her makeup in the bathroom.

Blond curls falling perfectly around her heaving chest, she stood by the front door and waited for six minutes.

At 1:04 AM, she spoke. "Still there, Van?"

"Even more impatient than I was twenty-four minutes ago."

His voice matched his words, but she didn't let it stop her from unlocking the deadbolt four times. What if he tracked in dirt or poked around in her things? Would his personal questions continue? Should she maintain a far distance? What if her *Aw, he has a lonely soul* warped into *Sweet God, he has a knife*?

She opened the door, enough to leave a sliver without feeling the malevolent force of the open air. Then she sprinted down the hall, fighting for oxygen and towing a thousand-pound string of reservations behind her.

# SEVEN

The deadbolt slid free, not once but four times in rapid succession. Huh. Was this some kind of neurotic indecisiveness? Or was the crazy woman taunting him? Amber was probably the kind of girl who would leave bite marks all over his dick.

Van grinned.

When the knob twisted and a soft glow illuminated the slivered opening, his pulse electrified. There it was, her free will dangling in the open door. He could take it, violently and recklessly, the moment he walked in. He flexed his fingers, anticipating fistfuls of her hair.

His cock pulsed as the thrill of possibilities heated his blood. It would be so damned exhilarating to throw her against the wall, mar her pretty skin, and fuck her before the stunned effect of terror released its first breath.

He stood taller, lighter, no longer bound by slave-buyer virginity requirements or his father's bullshit tyranny. He could be greedy, merciless, unrestrained. He could beat her just for letting him in. He could fuck her any way he wanted. Then he could take her home, chain her in *his* room, and keep her until *he* was done.

He hadn't taken anyone against their will since Joshua Carter, limiting his sexual encounters to quick fucks with men and women to take the edge off. Had it really been a year since he'd felt this rush? Why the hell was he giving into it now?

Because this fearful, sassy, crazy woman had awoken something inside him.

He slid on his leather gloves, unconcerned with how she might react to them. When he nudged open the door, the sound of her heels speed-clicked around the corner and faded into another room. He hadn't expected a red carpet welcome, but seriously? She didn't know his intentions, yet she'd opened the door and run? That was fucked up from the tits up.

As he crossed the threshold, the aroma of bleach and springtime fumigated his nose, a peculiar concoction of citrus, girly gardenias, and enough disinfectant to saturate a morgue. Maybe she *was* hiding a body. He locked the deadbolt and followed the aseptic wisp through the small sitting room.

Up ahead, a doorway opened into the kitchen. The hallway branched off to the left, leading to three rooms. Shadows gathered around the entrances of two. A soft band of light gleamed from the third, presumably where she'd run off to. She could wait. If she was stupid enough to let him roam alone, that was her problem.

Dated but well-kept furniture formed perfect right-angles, enclosed by gray walls, wood floors, black fabrics, and the sheer absence of color. What halted his steps, however, were the four round wall clocks, hanging side-by-side, identical in style, and synced down to the motherfucking second hand.

The oddity propelled him to examine the room closer as he listened for her footsteps. Four candles lined the glossy coffee table, four black pillows sat at rigid attention on the gray couch, and four bookshelves filled one wall. No TV. No knick-knacks. No picture frames. And definitely no trace of the pungency that would come with harvesting marijuana. Not that he still entertained that assumption.

Which raised new questions about her twice-a-week visitor. Zachary Kaufman was an unknown who would need to be dealt with.

With the envelopes tucked under one arm, he brushed a gloved finger over the dust-free surfaces, turning in a circle and searching for a deviation in the patterned decor. Everything was in symmetrical groups of four. The row of leather coasters, the books on the shelves, and the five-light chandelier...yep, missing the fifth bulb. Even the damned orchid on the sofa table had four white blooms with four petals each, as if she'd plucked the poor thing to fit an obscene idea of perfect proportion.

While the impersonal space offered little insight into who she was, one thing was certain. She was a straight-up freak of orderly foursomes.

"Come here, Van." Her voice skipped down the hall, strong and confident.

He stiffened, and his head tilted. *She* was beckoning *him*? Oh, how he wanted to answer with a cruel laugh just to expose her misunderstanding. Little did she know, he'd moved the mics during the twenty-four minute wait and had listened to her frantic footsteps running in and out of the back rooms. And why had she made him wait exactly twenty-four minutes? Was it an even-numbered thing or something more practical, like setting up a plan to trap him? If it were the latter, the pistol tucked in his ass crack would let her know she'd surrendered the instant she invited him inside.

He slid his tongue over his lips, seeking the toothpick he'd forgotten to replace. The worst part about being a sick bastard was the internal view of his perversions. He'd watch, like a helpless witness, as his body instilled fear in the eyes of his captives, his memories molding them into a weaker version of himself. In those moments, when his hands became manacles and his strikes connected with flesh, he beat the living shit out of the pathetic boy he once was. Nothing was more therapeutic. Or fucked up.

A jolt of heat pulsated his groin. Christ, he couldn't wait to introduce her to the realm of his imagination.

He leaned over the coffee table and stacked three coasters in a lopsided pile. As he passed the couch, he rotated one square pillow to sit on its cornered edge. His grin stretched so big his mouth hurt. Sometimes, it was the little things that teased sadistic pleasures.

Circling back to the front door, he toed off his sneakers and left them there. His silent gait carried him to the kitchen where he unlocked the sliding door. Would she check the locks? He dropped the thick drape back in place to cover the glass, adjusting the pleats to their former order so she wouldn't notice he'd touched them.

A couple of minutes had passed since she'd let him in. Was she clutching a butter knife, waiting to pounce? Counting to four over and over? He smiled at the thought of keeping her waiting.

With easy breaths and slow strides, he entered the short hallway, embracing the pursuit, stalking the innocent, preying exclusively on trust.

She'd willingly opened her door for the last time. Her naiveté would be the first thing vanquished by the hard, heavy weight between his legs.

Filling his lungs, he swallowed his enthusiasm and paused at the first of the three doors in the hall, an empty bathroom. As much as he craved an impulsive fuck-fight, he would take her the way he'd captured all the others, with planning and patience.

He dug a toothpick from his pocket and gripped it between his teeth, buying a few seconds to relax his dick. To speed things along, he shifted his thoughts to the one pure thing in his life. His daughter's vibrant smile, her lively mannerisms, and the crescendo of her precious voice spiraled breathless warmth through his chest and eased the strain against his zipper.

God, he wanted a place in her life, but she lived with Mr. E's widow. Revealing his identity to Livana was a long-term plan-in-progress.

It'd been easy for Liv to slip into Livana's life. The authorities knew she was Livana's biological mother. Legally, she was entitled to claim custody. She had a steady job, plus the six million he'd given her. But he didn't think she'd ever take their daughter from her stable home. Liv was a recovering slave after all, with her own aftermath of healing and maturing to work through.

Unfortunately, his ability to claim custody was nonexistent because *he* didn't exist. Not to the authorities and not to Mr. E's widow. Exposing his identity would link him to Mr. E's trafficking operation and land him life in prison. So his safest avenue to Livana was through Liv.

He gnashed his teeth. Before he could approach Liv, he needed to understand how she'd freed eight slaves and made the buyers *disappear*. Cartel? Hired hit man? Last thing he wanted was to become one of her disposed bodies.

With a swift adjustment of his finally-flaccid cock, he strode toward the only illuminated doorway in the hall and stopped at the entrance, his thumb on his hip, fingers near the concealed gun at his back.

She perched on a stool at the center of a bed-less bedroom, facing him, her back rigidly straight and her gaze on his gloved hand.

Four leather knife sheaths lay on the workbench behind her. His eyebrows crept up his forehead. Definitely a far cry from cowgirl boots. Would she ever cease to surprise him?

Rubber utility mats lined the floor. One wall held a treadmill, a Smith machine, and a metal rack stacked with free weights, arranged by size. No wonder her ass was a wicked bounce of muscle. He imagined her bent over and the inviting space her firm cheeks would create between her thighs.

Heat pierced through his body, contracting his muscles and leaving little room for patience. Fuck, the wait felt like a hundred searing needles, but he relished it, wanting her beneath his skin.

His bulk filled the doorway, legs spread wide, arms loose at his sides, confident he could draw the gun before she could wedge a hidden weapon from that tight dress. While he waited for her to look up, he drank in her features. The regal curves of her face. The tiny slope of her nose. The way her lips naturally tipped upward despite the tension around her mouth. But why the hell had she changed her clothes?

The overhead light reflected off the blond curtain of her hair. The color seemed...wrong, too pale for her honey-light skin. It fell over her face as she stared at the floor, a paradox of insecure beauty.

He tilted his head. Of course, he knew very little about her, but he was missing something crucial, a fragile facet beneath the pristine makeup and trained physique.

He rolled the toothpick with his tongue. "Why do you bleach your hair?"

Golden-brown eyes connected with his, blinking furiously, so deliciously nervous. "It's..." She huffed. "None of your business."

Slowly, cautiously, he slid back the hood of his sleeveless sweatshirt. Her breathing quickened as her gaze skimmed his exposed biceps, his face, and lingered on the scar that divided his cheek. She looked away, her shoulders curling around her ears.

He knew the effect he had on women. Whether it was their fascination with big, scary men with scars or their complete dismissal of danger, he only needed to flash a smile to lure them in. Amber was no different, despite the self-berating that was likely occurring in her flustered mind.

Short breaths rattled her lips. Her knees squeezed together, and her fingers entwined beneath her perky tits, pressing against the knuckles of the opposite hand.

Watching her battle her distress felt a little like foreplay. For every tremble across her skin, his mouth moistened, his pulse purred, and the nerve-endings in his fingers stirred and tingled. His body fed from the energy clashing between them, rushing blood below his waist and hardening him for a fight between her uptight thighs.

She glanced down, and her breath caught.

He followed her gaze, past the discomfort straining his jeans, to his socked feet. He flexed his toes. "What?"

"Where are your shoes?"

Her disregard for his arousal was a shocker. No matter. He'd prepared for this line of questioning. "By the front door."

Her nose scrunched in a naively erotic way. "Why are you wearing gloves?"

"Same reason my shoes are by the door." He lifted a shoulder, deliberately vague, letting her squirm.

Her lips pressed together, and her chest heaved. "I don't understand."

"Your house is obscenely clean." Which had fuck-all to do with covering his fingerprints and softening his footsteps. He caught her eyes and winked. "So I put on my driving gloves and left my shoes."

"Driving gloves haven't been fashionable since the sixties."

"My '65 Mustang might be dated, too, but it's bad-ass.

He savored the little nuances of her floundering expression. The skin tightening over arches of her cheekbones. The vertical lines between her eyebrows. The bounce in her gaze, ping-ponging everywhere but in his direction. And finally, her wavering sigh.

Got her. Earlier, when his arms were locked around her, she might've sensed his cruelty. But now that she'd let him in, she would be fighting that intuition, convincing herself he wouldn't bother with conversation if he intended to harm her. Lucky for him, she didn't know how he operated.

He held up his gloved fingers, wiggling them. "You should thank me. You don't know where my hands have been."

Her nose twitched again, her eyes fixed on the packages beneath his arm. "Um...thanks?" She squared her shoulders and dragged her gaze to his, the display of courage ten times more forced than her voice. "My mail?"

As he crossed the room, she rose like an animated mannequin, a vision of posed glamour, an artist's illusion. He stopped a few feet away, mesmerized by the unnatural yet graceful way she held herself, until she raised a stiff arm and gestured for the packages.

He handed them over and nodded at the sheaths behind her. "Should I worry about where the knives are?"

"Probably." She turned toward the bench and removed the bottles of dye, arranging them in a neat little line with the labels facing her.

"Your vagueness isn't very friendly."

She sighed. "I don't forge blades. I make things from leather and sell them online."

Her only source of income? That would explain her financial problems and her urgency to ship this project.

She unscrewed the first bottle, and the plasticky smell of chemicals singed the air. "You can sit on the stool while I finish and tell me the real reason you were on my porch."

Perceptive little thing. Bossy, too. He let it go and sat, facing her backside as she worked. "When was the last time you left the house?"

Her shoulders bunched. "Thirty minutes ago."

"Before that."

"None—"

"Of my business?" He stretched his legs out in front of him and angled his head to watch the glorious flex of her ass. "Do you know your neighbors?"

Her hands paused; then she blotted a rag with brown stain. "No, so I won't be able to answer questions about your *old friends*."

The six months he'd spent watching her house, he hadn't seen a twitch in the shades. "Gonna go out on a limb here and say you've never even seen your neighbors."

Her hip cocked out as if she'd lost her balance, but her hands continued to work the dye into the carved designs.

The flourish of knotted swirls in the leather appeared impressively intricate, even if the details weren't clear from where he sat. "You always work in a dress and heels?"

"You always chatter like a fourth grade girl?"

He snapped his molars together. Fuck, she was frustrating. "If you'd answer my questions—"

"You didn't answer mine." She bent over to inspect her work, and sweet Jesus, the short dress rose a good two inches up her thighs. Much more of that and those hard cheeks would be gripping his dick.

He swiped a gloved hand over his face. What was her question? Oh. "Why was I on your porch?" He smirked at her back. "Your bench has a great view of your kinky neighbors. Did you know they fuck on their kitchen table?"

She spun, her wide bright eyes colliding with his.

His smile stretched, giving her a good show of teeth.

She studied him, nibbling the corner of her lip, and her face relaxed. "You're fucking with me."

He hadn't even begun. "If that's what you think."

Her eyebrows pulled together as she returned to her dye. "I'm almost done," she mumbled. "Then it'll need a few hours to dry."

And he needed to poke around, unsupervised. "Got anything to drink?"

"Juice and beer in the fridge. Tequila under the sink."

He moved toward the door. "Want anything?"

She glanced over her shoulder, eyes on his gloved hands. "No, thanks."

Smart girl, but not smart enough.

In the kitchen, he opened every cabinet and drawer and found the same diabolical order as the rest of the house. Condiments and plastic containers grouped in fours, organized by size, labels facing out. Same thing in the fridge.

He poured two fingers of gold tequila. Cheap stuff, but even a watered-down mixto pretending to be tequila was better than domestic beer.

Drink in hand, he slipped into the sitting room and made a beeline to the books. When he'd sought out his victims as a human trafficker, he'd been bound by the contract of the slave buyers. Gender, hair color, body type, temperament, everything had a requirement. Now, he was free to choose whom he wanted for *his* pleasure, and tracking, watching, and studying a quarry was the most exhilarating part of a capture.

He had no reason to enslave another person again, but he couldn't fight his nature forever. Would Amber be an adaptable slave? Would she be missed? Did she have any nasty secrets he wouldn't be able to work with? Who *was* Amber Rosenfeld?

His investigation began with the top shelves of her bookcases, which held hundreds of hardbacks. Stacked in a repeating pattern of vertical and horizontal groups of four, the covers featured moonlit mansions, bloody handprints, shadowed doorways, and demonic eyes. While the horror collection was unexpected, the alphabetized order wasn't. His fingers twitched, and his smile built.

It took him less than a minute to fuck up her program, swapping out books and rotating some upside down. As he switched the final books, one of the flaps opened, revealing a signature and a personalized message. *For Paul, with best wishes.*

Something pinched in his chest. Who the fuck was Paul?

He opened another. *To Teresa.* He released a breath. The next five he checked were also autographed and personalized to random somebodies.

He gnawed on the toothpick, his mind racing. Did she steal from people's autographed collections? Why would she do that?

Crouching, he inspected the spines on the lower shelf, which was hidden behind a leather ottoman. He shoved it aside, and the font on the spines told him these texts didn't contain stories of ax murderers and ghosts. He leaned in closer to read the titles, and oh baby, there she was, all laid out in a dozen manuals.

*Break Out Guide for Shut-ins. Face Your Phobia. Imperfect OCD. Living With Agoraphobia.*

OCD was a term he knew, and one that had been scraping at the back of his mind since he'd walked in. But what the fuck was agoraphobia? He cracked open the text *Out Without Fear* and flipped to the first page.

*Agoraphobia is an anxiety disorder in which a person has a fear of being in open places where it is hard to escape. The individual might feel embarrassed, helpless, or trapped, and the intense fear can manifest into a panic attack. Agoraphobics avoid attacks by restricting or completely eliminating activities outside the home.*

No shit? That solved the mystery behind her meltdown outside, and maybe why she'd run from the door when she unlocked it. He skimmed a few chapters as a weird mix of emotions clumped in his stomach. Part of him felt bad for the girl, a quaint feeling to be sure. If he were a fucking pansy, maybe he'd explore that. Instead, he focused on the sharper, more familiar sentiment that clung to his gut.

He wanted her vulnerability. To use her body. To bleed off the pent-up shit inside of him. To fill the emptiness. To get his fucking mind off Liv Reed.

Amber was the one he'd been waiting for, and considering the irony that she lived right next door to Liv, maybe Amber had been waiting for him.

# EIGHT

Van knew the risks in kidnapping all too well, but taking an agoraphobic outside her door? Christ, that was a new one. Were there medical considerations? Would Amber keel the fuck over and die from an aneurysm?

Wait, why did he care if she had seizures and shit? *Because he didn't want to kill her.* If he managed to successfully move her, she probably wouldn't even try to escape. His muscles swelled with heat just thinking about her locked in his house. *Locks optional?*

The swoosh of the bathroom faucet interrupted his romantic thoughts, followed by the approaching click of her heels.

"What are you doing?" Her horrified whisper sent a quiver of pleasure down his spine.

Just to rile her a bit more, he didn't stand, didn't turn to acknowledge her. Instead, he pocketed the toothpick, lifted the glass of mixto tequila from the shelf, and drained half. He took his time, drawing out the tension that wafted from her, savoring it. Unlike the piss burning his throat. Lighter fluid would've gone down smoother.

Eventually, he returned the book, out of order, and rose with his back to her. "How long have you been shut in, Amber?"

"You need to leave." Her voice was so strangled it sounded like she'd lost the ability to breathe.

He shifted to face her, his expression relaxed, his tone more so. "Are you medicated?" An inventory of her medicine cabinet was on his list of to-dos. He needed a better understanding of the disorders.

"Leave right this minute, and I won't call the cops." She clutched her knuckles and raised her chin, the sinews in her neck pressing against delicate skin.

Was she telling him to leave because he'd discovered her phobia? A smile crooked one corner of his mouth. "Go ahead. Call in the pigs." He waved a hand at the door. "If you don't mind them tracking the outside world all over your nice floors." The self-help text had said, *The individual might feel embarrassed.* "Maybe they won't jump to conclusions about someone with a mental disorder going ape-shit on her house-guest."

A noise squeaked in her throat, and her eyes darted from him, to the front door, and back again. Then they lowered, as did her chin. "What do you want from me?"

Ah, fuck, he was screwed. The only thing missing from her response was *Master.* He drew a deep breath through his nose and tried to calm the *fuck-her-take-her-break-her* rap against his ribs.

"I'm going to finish my drink" —he raised the glass, his voice soft and casual— "while we wait for your projects to dry. Then I'll drop them in the mailbox when I leave. Isn't that why you invited me in?"

She shifted her weight from one foot to the other, her hands twitching at her sides. So damned beautiful, all dolled up with nowhere to go. "Yes." She swallowed. "Of course."

He leaned against the bookshelf and hooked a thumb in his pocket. "A shallow bastard might've bolted after discovering your disorder, blabbering some excuse as he ran far, far away." He watched her sharp inhale and suppressed the satisfaction tugging at his lips. "So you have issues. Don't we all?" Fucking understatement.

"I don't want to talk about this." Even as she said it, her eyes fell on the coffee table, and a tremor overtook her body. She charged toward the source of her horror, sucking air as she realigned the coasters with trembling fingers.

He hid his grin behind the lip of his raised glass.

A gasp followed, and she tackled the pillow on the couch, straightening and fluffing with asthmatic breaths. Then she stood, brushed down the hem of her dress, and leveled a hard stare in his direction. "Stop fucking with my things."

He stared right back, but what he really wanted to do was yank up that dress and sink his teeth into her twisted panties. With the casual swipe of a hand, he shifted the swollen head of his cock.

She didn't seem to notice, her eyes too busy shooting fire at his face. "And no more personal questions."

For a little thing, she sure had a big voice when she was angry. It was really quite cute, and he suddenly wanted to know if she was ticklish. What a fucked up thought, and probably not the time to explore it. She appeared to be seconds from self-destructing.

Her heels echoed through the room as she paced, seething through her teeth and wiping fingers beneath her dry eyes. Then she stopped and glanced at the clocks, at the door, back to the clocks. Was she weighing her options? *Go to the mailbox herself? Or let him stay to do it for her?*

When her eyes landed on him, they had cooled by several degrees. "No more snooping. Don't touch my stuff. Don't even look at it."

*Terrible choice, little girl.* He tipped her a crooked smile, made of sugar and shit. "Right on."

She nodded, her bottom lip caught between polished white teeth. "Then the offer to stay four hours stands. Follow me." With that, she turned and clickety-clacked down the hall.

He watched her ass until it disappeared within her unlit bedroom. For all his smugness in manipulating her, he knew better than to pursue this. She had some serious dysfunction—perhaps worse than his—and he'd only scratched the surface. He glanced at the front door. He should be the shallow bastard and leave, but the challenge invigorated him. God help him, but he wanted to lose his mind with this crazy woman.

He threw back the remainder of the mixto and set it on the coffee table. Flicking a coaster to the floor, he strolled down the hall, a hand in his pocket and dark dreams in his head.

At the doorway of her bedroom, he took in her most personal space. A dim lamp now glowing on the nightstand, a single blacked-out window, a small TV that should've been thrown out two decades ago. And a stunning woman sitting on the edge of the bed.

She watched him from beneath her lashes, her slender legs dangling off the side, the toes of her shoes flexed above the carpet. Not a single footprint indented the threads between her and the door. Had she hurdled the ten-foot distance? Impossible. How did she erase her tracks so fast?

Her silence pushed against him, scattering into the hallway and pulsing with the faint rasp of her inhales. She sat motionless, eyes lowering, as if held by an innate need to please. As if waiting for her Master to speak.

A warm current ran the length of his body, prickling his skin. Subservient Amber did *not* help his obsessive thoughts. His cock ached, but the greedy bastard didn't run things. He wouldn't take her impulsively. Not without planning. Maybe not ever.

He pushed off the doorframe and crossed the room, subtly scuffing his heels to smudge the vacuumed stripes in his path.

She glared at his tracks, and her jaw clenched. Yeah, her OCD harbored some affection for clean lines.

He paused before her, brushing his knees against hers and coaxing an exhale from her sweet lips. A discreet scan of the room revealed the same rigid order as the rest of the house. But what the fuck was the bizarre

319

display in the corner?

A glass aquarium sat on a stand, brimming with twisted bits of filigree metalwork, broken bronze statues, and beveled gems—some attached to strips of metal, others loose and chipped.

He narrowed his eyes at her. "Are those—?"

"*Those* are nothing," she snapped, meeting his gaze.

Either she designed metal art, or she'd unleashed a pissed-off hammer on a trophy collection. Her locked jaw suggested the latter. Strange she hadn't covered it the way she'd concealed the self-help books, but he let it go for now.

"Why are we here?" He nodded at the bed.

"Why not?"

Because phobic girls didn't invite strangers where they slept. He gave her a human smile. "It wasn't a personal question." But he hoped it would incite a personal answer.

"Right." She looked at the bed and smoothed the white quilt beside her hip. "This is part of the offer."

His head jerked back. What the—

"Sex in exchange for dropping off my shipments." Her tone was unshakably and incautiously determined. She'd done this before.

The cold splash of realization doused his brain. And his libido. Christ, why hadn't he seen this coming? Of course, her mental condition would force her to depend on people. People with hard dicks weeping to accept her non-cash payments. People like Zachary Fucking Kaufman.

Goddammit, her offer stung. He wasn't some delivery bitch boy, earning pussy for a walk to the mailbox. He was there for his own purpose, not hers, and he'd damned well fuck her on his terms. "No."

Her face fell. "Oh. I thought—"

"I was so hard-up I had to run errands to get my dick wet?" His tone was harsh, though his anger had nothing to do with being hard-up.

Hell, eight years ago, *he* had been the whore, exchanging blowjobs for crack. No doubt, he would've been bent under some rutting drug-dealer at that very moment if Mr. E hadn't returned for him. Twenty-five years late, and still, he'd been overjoyed to meet long lost Dad.

A vein pulsed, hot and angry, on his forehead. Well, didn't that memory darken his mood? He should thank the good people of Austin for promoting Mr. E to police chief. The new position had come with too much scrutiny for a figurehead who trafficked slaves on the side. Mr. E had needed a front man to run the operation and remembered he had a twenty-five-year-old bastard son. A son, as it turned out, who had no qualms about profiting from sexual services.

Unless those services involved Amber and dipshit deliverymen. A beautiful woman should never sell herself so cheaply. She deserved better than Zachary Kaufman, and she definitely deserved better than what *he* had planned for her.

Fuck it. This irrational jealousy, or whatever it was, pissed him the hell off. He wanted to wash his hands of her. More than that, he wanted to brand her with a hundred possessive welts.

She fussed with her hair, hands shaking, and eyelids heavy with shame. "Can we just forget I said...that?"

Seriously? He squeezed his fingers into a fist, fighting the impulse to swing and knock her on her ass. He didn't want to scare her too badly. Not yet. Nor did he want to let this Zachary shit go. "Do you fuck all your house-guests?"

"That's a personal question." Her stubborn chin and hard eyes only fueled his need to punch her.

He leaned over her, hands on the bed beside her hips, and pushed his face into hers. "Your offer to fuck bowled straight through personal and landed smack between your legs. Might as well spread 'em and air it all out."

"Oh my God." Her chest rose, brushing his, but she didn't lean away, didn't look away. "Can you please step back?"

His lips were so close to hers he could taste the toothpaste on her breath. "Answer the question."

"No. I mean, yes." Her voice was angry and rushed, her dilated pupils resolutely locked on his. "I like sex, okay? I thought the attraction was mutual."

A burst of lust ignited through his cock. He grabbed her hand and pressed it against his erection, grinding his hips. Nothing said *I'm attracted to you* like a thrusting boner.

But the tentative squeeze of her fingers sent his head spinning. With her mouth so close and wet from her breaths, he took her lips. It wasn't a gentle touch-and-tease kiss, either. He went for it, dominating her mouth, spreading it open with his jaw, and angling her head with a fist in her hair. His tongue chased hers, lashing and taking.

She didn't fight back, so he unsheathed his teeth, catching and slicing her lips. His pulse raced, and his lungs pumped. Jesus, he couldn't reach any deeper, and she met him stroke for stroke, bite for bloody bite.

Her taste was insufferably sweet, much like the fingers stroking his cock. Which reminded him of his position on her offer.

He released her, and the room stumbled to a dizzying standstill. They shared a suspended look, panting in unison. He stepped back and wiped his mouth with the back of his hand. "The answer is still 'No'."

She slapped a palm over her mouth, eyes closed and forehead pinched. Then she shot from the bed and ran out of the room, leaving a trail of messy footprints in her wake.

He scratched his jaw. Huh. Apparently, OCD-ness came second to Oh-God-he-rejected-me-ness.

Perhaps he should've assured her of her attractiveness with words.

Maybe he should wear a tutu and over-pluck his eyebrows while he was at it.

He crossed the room to the aquarium and dug out a cracked statue of a bronze woman missing her head. The marred scratches across the base were vicious, but the engraving was still legible.

*Fitness Model World Championship*

*1st Place*

*Amber Rosenfeld*

His mouth fell open, though he shouldn't have been surprised. Her body rocked some killer biceps, thighs, and calves, and God knew what lay beneath that dress. It was a rare thing to find a woman with a ten body paired with a ten face, but this fitness model was a hundred from head to toe. So when he pulled out a wad of sashes printed with *Miss Tri County, Miss Heart of the USA, and Miss Texas*, it wasn't shock that caught his breath. It was a very strong feeling of wonder, reverence, and something akin to fear.

There must've been fifty demolished tiaras and trophies in that tank. Why would she destroy something she'd worked so hard to earn? Or had someone else hurt them? Hurt her? The notion sent blood roaring through his ears, leaving him shaken, edgy, and, worst of all, heartsick.

The sudden urge to flee shuffled him back a step. He needed to shed these feelings, this room, *her*. The last time he involved his emotions, he got a blade across his face and a bullet in his shoulder. Hard to forget those lessons.

He dropped the sashes in the aquarium and strode toward the hall, not stopping until he heard muffled sniffles through the bathroom door. He braced an arm on the wall beside it.

Could he be the kind of guy who apologized? How about the guy who walked her mail down the driveway?

He pulled a toothpick from its holder in his pocket and stared at the white cotton of his socked feet. The heavy thump of his heart felt way too foreboding.

Thump noted and rejected. He slid the pick between his lips. Her sniveling didn't affect him. Nope. He backed away from the bathroom door, pretending he didn't feel the thump growing harder and faster with each step.

He wasn't her guy, and he sure as fuck didn't need more scars.

At the front door, he slipped on his sneakers and shifted the hood over his head.

He most definitely wasn't Zachary Kaufman, and the fuckwad

would be back in three days to honor his Tuesday/Friday tradition.

Could her shipments wait until then? Would she attempt to walk them out that night? What if she had a seizure on the way?

He pressed his gloved fingers against his eyes. Not his goddamned problem. He opened the door and gripped it, fighting not to close it and return to her. Instead, he stepped beneath the somberness of a sleepy sky and slammed the door behind him with enough rattle to reach the bathroom.

# NINE

The slam of the front door lurched Amber's stomach into a fit of cramps. Van was gone. *Gone.*

She dropped before the toilet and hung her head. Her mouth swelled with a burst of saliva, and she dry-heaved until her throat was raw. But the pain was nothing compared to the hot stabs of self-loathing perforating her insides.

What did she expect? She'd strutted her crazy all over the house and thought he'd hang around and maybe have sex with her? No shit, she'd overestimated her worth. Though, to be fair, he'd been the first man to reject her offer.

This was her fault. She hadn't even tried to seduce him. She should've said something sexy, maybe flashed a nipple. A man like Van could have any woman he wanted. He wouldn't have just shoved her on the bed and fucked her because she wore a skimpy dress.

A strand of hair fell in her face, and she shoved it away. She used to turn heads once without even trying, but that was *then*. She'd lost her edge. Beauty faded, and certainly being shut in and crazy for two years had sped that along.

And now she faced an impossible trip to the mailbox. *Thumbs up, Amber. Job well done.*

Her chin quivered. *Pathetic crybaby.* She locked her jaw, pushed away from the toilet, and sat on her heels. Beside her, the shower plinked a steady drip, a reminder that it would be several more months before she could afford to repair it.

It took four attempts to stand, and when she finished brushing her teeth, her heart rate rallied, ready to panic all over again.

Fuck that. She breathed deeply, engaging her abs, and forced her feet to move to the front door. Her head swam with dizziness, and by the time she locked the deadbolt four times, the heave of her lungs had elevated into hyperventilation.

*Stop it.* She could peek out the window and make sure he wasn't on the porch.

She sucked in, sharply. No, she couldn't. Looking outside was a surefire way to make this night worse. Besides, there was no way he stuck around.

She stomped to the kitchen, slamming her heels four times on the wood floor to drown out her gasping breaths. That man had been intrusive, rude, dangerous...sexy as fuck. His departure was a blessing. She grabbed a beer from the fridge. The first sip burned the cuts his teeth had left on her lips.

Oh God, that kiss. Her taste buds tingled, not from the hops but from the remembered pleasure of his skillful tongue, the bite of tequila on his breath, and the spicy flavor that seemed to be inherently him. A taste she would never experience again.

Good riddance. She tipped back the bitter ale, hellbent on creating a new night through alcoholic osmosis. In a few days, she would be contemplating her life while sitting in the dark without water or electricity. Because she wouldn't be going to the mailbox. Not tonight. Not ever again.

Might as well drink the beer while it was still cold. She dropped the empty bottle in the trash and grabbed another. "Fucking sucks." She sucked. Shallow bastards with silver eyes sucked. She slumped onto the kitchen stool, hung her head over the counter, and cursed her sucky self and the sucky bastard who had just ran far, far away.

A six-pack later, she'd vacuumed out the footprints in the bedroom carpet, packaged up the sheaths, printed the postage labels, and barfed as much of the caloric beer as her stomach was willing to release. Then she spent the next hour engaged in a standoff with the front door.

"This is all your fault." She struck the wood panel, and her palm landed like a sloppy slap. "If you weren't in my way, I'd be out there right now shipping my shit."

It was a lie, but the door didn't know that. It just stood there like an unfeeling asshole.

"Ever heard of a sledgehammer?" she yelled then burped and laughed hysterically. "That's right, motherfucker. All I have to do is smash your hinges, and you won't even be able to stand." Momentarily distracted by the jumping sensation of her hiccup, she touched her chest and swayed not-so beauty-pageant–*hic*– ably in her heels.

Now what was she doing? Oh right. She lunged for the door, determined to open it, just drunk enough to not give a damn. She wobbled as her hand touched the knob and jumped back, dizzy and confused.

"You're nothing. You hear me?" She thrust out a finger at the deadbolt to punctuate her point.

What was her point again? Jesus, her brain felt heavy as she watched the slow, mesmerizing movements of her arms. She tossed them in the air and stumbled. Whoa, the floor was rocking. Earthquake in Texas? Nah, it was just a blowout of pent-up funk along her psychotic fault lines and stuff. She laughed, bent-over, snorting, though she couldn't recall what was so damned funny.

Probably a good time to call it a night. With a middle finger aimed at the door, she grabbed the bottle of tequila from the kitchen and climbed into bed. Tequila made the tongue taste delicious, especially when it belonged to sinful lips and sharp teeth. She unscrewed the lid and drank. And drank. Until she couldn't remember why she didn't do this every night.

The next morning, she woke with a second heartbeat pulsating behind her eyes and the hot burn of tequila-laced vapors in her throat. At some point during the night, her mouth had forgotten how to produce saliva, and her tongue had withered into a suffocating gag of sandpaper.

Then she remembered the prick who had the nerve to be offended by her proposal. And the fact that she deserved it. Death sounded like a great plan for the day. His. Hers. Definitely his.

She tried to raise her head, and a starburst of pain stole her vision. Not happening. She rolled to her side and her cheek landed in a puddle of drool on the pillow. Not just slobber but the vomit-scented variety that sent her stomach contracting to the tune of *curl up and die.*

What a miserable thing she'd become. A victim of her own destruction. But self-indulgent pity did little more than exaggerate excuses. True comfort came from order and routine. She glanced at the clock.

Oh, no, no, no. She was late. The pounding in her head exploded, and her hands started shaking. Hangover be damned, she needed to get her ass up.

She pushed with weak arms to a sitting position and waited for the queasiness to pass. The bedside lamp was still on, its light intensifying the headache. She swung her legs over the side of the mattress and stopped breathing. Footprints indented the carpet from the bed to the door. Man-sized tracks. But she'd vacuumed sometime between the sixth beer and the tequila chaser. Or were the fumes in her head making up memories?

A terrifying thought hurdled her stomach to her throat. She stumbled from the bed and ran to the front door, clutching her churning belly.

She wiggled the door handle, and the deadbolt held as it should have. She knew she'd locked it before she'd destroyed all her brain cells.

Glancing around, nothing seemed out of order, until her attention narrowed on the books.

Oh God, the titles were rotated and no longer alphabetized by author. The lines weren't there, the spines zig-zagging along the shelves. Her hands clenched and unclenched, and her skin swelled so hot, she was surprised it didn't catch fire. The meddling dick!

She scrambled to the shelves, breathing from her diaphragm. Terrible, unimaginable chaos invaded her head when the lines weren't straight and things weren't grouped as they should be. Sweet mother, she'd slept all night while the spines lay in a shuffled, incongruent mess.

Her hands flew through the books, fixing and straightening. Why had she let him anywhere in the house alone? She hadn't even looked at the shelves when he'd left. How could she have been so sidetracked?

Halfway through reordering the novels, her mind wandered back to the footprints in the carpet. When did those happen? Surely, he hadn't messed with any of the other locks while he'd been there and come back after she'd passed out? Her fingers turned cold, and an ache ballooned in the back of her throat.

Heart racing, she sprinted through the house and checked the windows and the rear sliding door. With a trembling hand behind each and every drape, she confirmed they were all locked. She buckled over the kitchen counter, her skin clammy. Jesus, that little freak-out had not helped her nausea.

She gulped down a large glass of water. Then she returned to the shelves, sagged onto her knees, and straightened the self-help books. He knew she was fucked up. Of course, he wouldn't return to mess up her carpet. She wasn't worth the trouble. She must've left the footprints in a drunken sleepwalk.

Never again. No more drinking. No more muscled men with alluring scars and invasive questions. And no more acts of desperation.

The clocks on the wall read 9:54 AM. Her daily routine was one hour and fifty minutes behind schedule. She'd just have to start in ten minutes and skip the two hours of baseboard scrubbing and furniture polishing to reset the clock. Her pulse elevated at the notion, but she would survive this. She had to. Soon, she would be back on schedule and realigning her world.

*10:04 AM:* She vacuumed, mopped the floors, and washed the bedding.

*12:04 PM:* She ran four miles on the treadmill, sweating tequila and hops from her pores.

*1:04 PM:* She ate lunch—a baloney sandwich and four pickle slices. Just like every Sunday. Twenty minutes later, her stomach felt grossly distended. She purged the sandwich.

*1:34 PM:* She lifted weights — back and biceps on Sunday and Wednesday.

*2:04 PM:* She worked on her remaining leathercraft orders.

Eight hours later, she finished the carvings on two belts, three wallets, and tied off the last stitch on a sweet throw pillow made from the recycled leather of men's worn loafers.

At 10:04 PM, she slumped onto the couch with her laptop, fresh from a shower and dressed in a tank top and boy shorts. The straight lines and symmetrical flawlessness of the sitting room soothed her heart rate, even as she probed every detail for an imperfect tilt or wrinkle. She exhaled a heavy sigh and relaxed against the cushions. Her world felt pretty damned realigned.

She hadn't thought of him or her overdue bills once in twelve hours. So she didn't feel too obsessive when she logged into an online agoraphobics group and searched the discussions on *I told him to leave when he found out about my disorder.* Zero results returned.

Not surprised, she tried, *He won't sleep with me.* Zero results returned.

Her face heated. "Bullshit." She bit her lip and typed, *He thinks I'm nuts.* Thirty-three pages of results, but none of the discussions applied to her situation.

Had she overreacted when she found him reading her self-help books? She sniffed and rolled her shoulders. Didn't matter. He left anyway. She closed the laptop and leaned back. It was for the best.

Except she couldn't distract her mind from the prior night, reliving the strength of his arms around her, the spicy scent of his breath, the pressure of his mouth against her lips, and the way he owned her with a flick of his tongue.

She tried not to listen to the silent slither of loneliness as it snaked its way around her. Tried not to analyze why she felt colder and more hollow tonight than any other night. Tried not think about how much she missed the intoxicating warmth of a man sleeping beside her, skin on skin, even if that memory had been created and destroyed by Brent.

None of that solved her financial problems. If she could ship her completed sales by Tuesday, maybe she'd only be without water and electricity for a few days.

She grabbed her cell phone and opened a text to contact Zach. They never communicated this way, and she waffled with how to start the conversation. She went with courtesy. *Are you feeling better?*

Thirty seconds later, he replied, *yes will b there tues.*

Her heart soared then plummeted. Would he still want sex or had she scared him away from that? She imagined his lips on hers, and the remembered sensation suddenly seemed...uncertain. Maybe, he'd kissed her weakly because he didn't want to kiss her at all. A swallow lodged in her throat. She was flawed, after all.

After Van's repulsion to her offer for sex, she felt used and unclean. She cracked her knuckles not really feeling them. Her insides twisted in knots. Sleeping with Zach had lost its appeal, but she had nothing else to offer him.

She wouldn't be so dependent if she'd gone to the mailbox while soaring on liquid courage. But no amount of tequila would help her conquer the fear. She didn't want to conquer it, because she needed it, the adrenaline rush and the lung-squeezing pain. Like an addiction, the fear fed her, made her feel alive, and gave her something to focus on. She was so messed up.

The phone dinged with a new text. *will u keep the lights on this time?*

An onslaught of trembling tightened her muscles. If she said *Yes*, it would be a new low in her desperation. If she said *No*, she would lose the one person she had to depend on.

*Is this the man you want the lights on with?*

Unbidden, Dr. Michael's words filled her mind with another man, one with a seductive smile and a perfect scar.

# TEN

With visions of a sleeping Amber teasing the surface of his mind, Van pushed the key into the deadbolt on her front door. The key he'd swiped from her kitchen drawer the prior night *after* he'd sneaked back in.

He'd tried to stay away, but it was a compulsion. Coming to this neighborhood. Watching Liv. And now, he had an even more compelling motive to *stop by*.

Strange how Amber hadn't moved the drape on the door and checked the lock before her alcohol-induced haze. He knew this because he'd used that unlocked door to slip back in after she'd passed out. Apparently, the agoraphobia thing had a stronger hold on her than the OCD. If not the agoraphobia, then it had to have been *him* knocking the little compulsive-order-checker off her game.

Whatever the reason, it worked in his favor. He'd crept back in after she'd passed out, locked it behind him, and quickly located a house key.

His pulse thrummed a calming tempo as he closed the front door soundlessly behind him. Just like the night before, he'd listened through her windows with the mics and ear buds, tracking her movements and waiting for her breathing to fall into an even rhythm of sleep.

A grin stretched his lips as he recalled her slurred monologues. She'd been wildly entertaining. Even more satisfying was knowing *he* had driven her to drink. Because let's be honest, she was entirely too uptight to drink for no good reason. So when he'd found her snoring with a bottle of mixto tucked beneath her arm, he'd left tracks in the carpet just to mess with her little hungover mind.

Tonight, she'd fallen asleep sober. Tonight, he would be more cautious. Besides, he was only there to run reconnaissance and return the key—now that he had his own copy.

He wore his quiet-soled sneakers, which dampened his footfalls as he crept through the house. In the kitchen, he placed the key in the kitchen drawer, rotating it to lie exactly how he'd found it.

He entered the hall, his path illuminated by the lamp in her bedroom. There was a chance she might've woken in the short time that had passed since he left her window, but it was worth the risk. He needed to see her, to attach her tangible body to the fantasies he'd been envisioning all day.

A sudden realization halted him midway down the hall. He'd taken the same backyard stroll that night he'd taken every night for the past six months, yet he hadn't even considered setting up the mics on Liv's windows. He pushed a gloved hand through his hair and stared at the light from her bedroom, watching for a flicker of movement.

Amber was a conundrum of distraction. In one night, she'd managed to divert his obsession from Liv. For the first time in eight years, he'd woken without the burning need to beat and fuck his former slave. But Liv was a crucial component in obtaining his daughter. Monitoring her conversations with the slaves she'd released would eventually reveal if Liv had any cartel or FBI connections and if she could use them to stop him in his pursuit of his daughter.

Heavy pressure pushed against his chest. He fumbled through the pocket of his hoodie and pulled out a toothpick, certain he should walk away from Amber and utterly perplexed by the fact he wouldn't.

He'd spent the past ten hours investigating the fascinating beauty queen on the Internet. He was already in too deep, his focus unwaveringly set on the outcome. Especially when he reached her bedroom and took in the view.

Long, blond hair spread out in waves around her head. She lay on her side, facing the door, her tiny hands curled beneath her chin. A thin sheet draped the curves of her thigh and hip, stopping just below her bare shoulder. Christ almighty, was that firm ass accessibly bare beneath the sheet? Would her cunt feel as tight as the rest of her?

His mouth dried, and he licked his lips around the toothpick. There were more important things to investigate before he could even think about taking her, namely Zachary Kaufman.

He couldn't, he shouldn't, but he approached her anyway. Despite the blood rushing to his dick, he lengthened his gait, patiently and carefully, as to not disturb too many carpet fibers.

Three long strides brought him to her side. His arm moved before his brain could argue, his finger hooking the edge of the sheet between her tits and moving it down, down, slowly, until her pinkish-brown nipples appeared.

He snapped his gaping jaw shut and inhaled quietly through his nose. Fucking breathtaking. She certainly hadn't struck him as the kind of woman to sleep naked. Amber was a little hidden world of seductive surprises.

Her eyes shifted behind her lids but remained closed, her dark lashes fanning over her delicate cheekbones. Jesus, she was a heavy sleeper. He glanced at the bedside table and spotted a bottle of sleeping pills.

He squatted, chin level with the mattress, and lowered the sheet to the flat expanse of her belly. Little dips and cut edges defined her feminine abs, framed by the soft curves of her hip, waist, and tits. He leaned in, his knees loose and growing weak. Just a few more seconds of looking, then he'd finish what he came to do.

Her breasts were huge, round, and definitely not real. The faded scars beneath her nipples confirmed his suspicion. Maybe implants had given her an edge in her modeling career, but she wouldn't have needed them. Her natural attributes were enough to make him come in his pants, her raw beauty superior to every woman he'd ever laid eyes on.

Schooling his breaths, he slipped the sheet past her shaved mound and clamped his teeth on the toothpick. His heart swooshed in his ears, and his body heated.

Her thighs were pressed together, giving him a tiny peek of her cleft. He angled his head, his face and fingers hovering over her shadowed pussy. The sweet scent of oranges and flowers bathed his nose. Fuck, he wanted to shove his fingers inside as much as he wanted to roll her over and bury his cock in her soul.

With a great amount of willpower, he returned the sheet and stood. *Soon, Amber Rosenfeld.*

Stepping back on the tracks he'd left on the way in, he balanced awkwardly and brushed up the smashed carpet with curled fingers as he crept backward toward the door.

Two more days. Until Zachary Kaufman's scheduled visit. Until she was all his.

On his way to the kitchen, he stopped in the bathroom and checked the medicine cabinet, the drawers, and under the sink. The sight of the condoms made his blood boil.

The toiletries were grouped in fours, labels aligned. Not a pill bottle in sight.

His research on agoraphobia had come up with a plethora of anti-depressants to numb the disorder, but the recommendation for treatment was consistent. She needed exposure.

He breathed deeply, letting loose a smile. Yeah, he'd expose her, all right.

The prior night, he'd verified she didn't have a landline phone. Now, he found her cell on the charger in the kitchen, and worked the stylus from the case with a gloved finger. A couple taps showed there had been no calls or texts since he'd checked the night before. In fact, the log's six-month history only showed two contacts. One was a Dr. Emery Michaels, whom she hadn't spoken with in five days.

The other was Zachary. His last text — *will u keep the lights on this time?* — induced the same bloodthirsty, muscle-tightening reaction he'd had the first time he saw it. His vision blurred and the phone case groaned in his clenched fist. He set it down and strode to the front door with determined steps.

By this time tomorrow, he would be quite intimate with the fuck digger.

# ELEVEN

The next night, Van drummed his fingers on the steering wheel in the *Saddler's Tool Company* parking lot, listening to "Stay Wide Awake" by *Eminem* and waiting for Zachary McToolLess to leave work.

His jaw ached from clenching, and his muscles were stiff from his shoulders to his ass. Where the fuck was his target? The store had closed a fucking hour ago.

He squinted through the dark empty lot and reached for the camera on the seat beside him. Flipping through the photos, he paused on the shots he'd snapped at the schoolyard that morning. Long brown hair, angelic face, and a glowing smile, Livana looked so much like Liv it made his chest hurt. But as he studied a close-up of her features, he recognized his own thick eyelashes fringing her brown eyes and the exact shape of his lips outlining her grin. He closed his eyes and tipped his head back.

Now seven-years-old, she was safe and cared for by Mr. E's widow, the woman who had raised her. But nothing compared to a father's love and protection. He'd never had that, and he'd be damned if his daughter grew up without it. She needed him as much as he needed her, but she was ferociously guarded by Liv and her circle of freed slaves. He knew Liv would never allow him even a brief encounter. Unless he could convince her.

Ten minutes later, a pickup appeared from behind the building and took off in the opposite direction. It was the same truck he'd seen parked in Amber's driveway while scoping Liv's house.

His heart rate elevated. He threw the Mustang in drive and followed at an unassuming distance. Fifteen miles brought them into the heart of Austin's entertainment district, surrounded by historic buildings, old-fashioned neon signs, and live music.

Was her fucktoy headed for a bar? If so, he'd soon have a new drinking buddy.

Monday night traffic was predictably sparse. Zachary parked beside a little bar off Sixth Street called *Cyanide* and went inside with a prissy little hop in his step.

Okay, maybe he'd imagined the hop, but fuck if he couldn't see how Amber let that skinny rodent put his dick in her. He pressed a fist against the burning sensation in his chest and parked in a nearby lot. When his blood pressure cooled to normal, he locked up and strolled to the bar.

The sky was dark, but the interior of *Cyanide* was darker. Soft electronic beats and a thin crowd set a casual ambiance. He wove around the high-tops and winked at a gaggle of college girls who openly stared at him with *we're-dumb-and-in-heat* googley eyes.

Van's white button-down shirt opened at the collar, and his crisp, dark jeans rode low on his hips. Not his usual attire, but he was dressed to kill.

He found his target straddling a stool at the bar and chugging a domestic beer—*alone*. He approached, thumped the counter, and nodded at the silver-haired bartender. "Three shots of tequila. Neat, not chilled."

When the old geezer reached for *Jose Cuervo*, he growled. "No, man. I said *tequila*." Fucking Americans. "If it doesn't say one-hundred percent agave, it's not tequila." He scanned the top shelf and pointed at the bottle of *Real Gusto*. "That one."

As the bartender poured the shots, Van grabbed a stool two down from Zachary without acknowledging him. A few minutes later, he splashed the first shot down his gullet, relishing the smooth, complex flavor. Then he leaned back and waited.

It didn't take five minutes before the first bitch approached Van.

"Hey, there." She cocked a round hip against his knee. "The girls and I voted." She flicked her claws at a table of giddy women in the corner. "You are by and far the sexiest man in three counties." Her gaze landed on the scar on his cheek and skittered away.

When her eyes returned—they always did—he made a show of checking her out, from the fake-baked tits to the sparkled heels, and moved his leg away from her hip. "Not interested, honey."

She huffed. "You're no fun."

He held his mouth in a flat line of no-fun and didn't blink.

She picked at a plastic fingernail, lingering two seconds too long, and strode away.

Five women and five rejections later, the cock stuffer beside him finally spoke. "You...uh...gay or something?"

Van threw back the second shot to smother the raging words burning up his throat. Fucking twat. Yeah, he fucked men. For his one-night delights, all he required was a submissive body and a clean hole. So what? He also made dolls with the same hands he fingered assholes with. If any of that made him gay, then he'd take it up the ass all the way to hell.

No, that wasn't true. He hadn't endured it that way since he left the ghetto. Now that he was free of his mother's drug-dealing bottom-feeders, he was the one who did the fucking.

Tilting his head, he looked directly at Zachary for the first time. Those twinkling, beady blue eyes made him want to gouge them out and pop them between his curled fingers. "Just want the right girl, man." The girl Zachary Kaufman would never fuck again.

The beady eyes blinked. "Damn, dude. All those women you turned down seemed pretty fucking *right* to me."

He lifted a shoulder. "I want a gorgeous girl with spirit, know what I mean? Quick wit, blond hair, brown eyes, big tits, and lots of personality." He rubbed a finger on the counter, delivering the spiel with a monotone, down-on-his-luck kind of vibe. "You know, someone...unusual. Special. With crazy little quirks and stuff."

A laugh choked in Zachary's throat, and he shook his head. "Boy, do I have a *special* girl with quirks."

Bastard didn't have shit. He covered his scowl with the third shot, slammed it down, and tempered his tone. "Oh yeah?"

"Yeah. She's got my damned head reeling nonstop. It's messed up, but I keep going back for more."

Motherfuck, he didn't want to hear this, but he needed to know the depth of Zachary's attachment. Killing him would be gratifying. And messy. But that wasn't his style. Manipulating him was the smart play.

Van bounced his eyebrows, and his insides twisted with nausea. "She hot?"

A smile took hold of Zachary's face, toothy and weasel-like. "Tits out to here." He cupped the air in front of him as if juggling watermelons like a goddamned retard. "Pretty face. Tight little pussy."

Van's vision clouded in red, the blood in his veins boiling to burst. Zachary was a dead man. He slapped a hand on the counter. "Another shot, and hurry the fuck up, old man."

The tool on the stool must have mistaken his rage for excitement. He let out an ear-splitting cackle. "Thing is, dude, she's got serious issues. Talk about quirks. I don't think she leaves the house much. She won't let me fuck her with the lights on. Been doing her for six months. Always at her place. I still haven't seen her naked."

Six months and the ass didn't know she was agoraphobic. The shot slid in front of Van, and he tossed it back, swallowing down images of

Zachary *doing* her. His stomach hardened, and his breaths pushed out so fast and coarse. No way would he be able to speak without roaring.

Goddammit, he could handle this conversation. This was his fucking forte. Control and coercion without physical force. Hell, he'd spent weeks drinking with the drug-dealing slime who'd lived with Kate, the last girl he'd taken for Mr. E. Her brothers might've protected her virginity, but their drunken, wagging tongues had lost her in the end. He liked to think he'd saved that girl, seeing how he'd freed her from her brothers' crack-house and Liv had freed her from Mr. E's trafficking.

Zachary nursed his beer, all quiet and thoughtful, as he pushed his hair away from his puckered eyebrows. When he opened his mouth, he seemed to be talking to himself. "I have to go to her house at a set time on the same days. Thirty seconds early or late, and she freaks the fuck out." He swiped at his hair. "But there I am, syncing my clocks to hers and showing up *right on time.*"

This wasn't like the other captures. Amber wasn't going to a slave buyer. She was...unique and fascinatingly crazy. And she was *his.* Hell, he'd take her even if the sole purpose was to make sure she wasn't Zachary's—which it wasn't. But the moron didn't deserve her. Of course, neither did he.

He set the empty shot glass down and plucked a toothpick from a container on the bar. He'd only killed two people in his life. Shooting the wife of Liv's rapist had just been a means to torture the monster before killing him, too.

Zachary wasn't a rapist. He was just a ball-less queef in the fucking way.

He shifted to face the queef. "She the only pussy you're banging?
"Yeah, why?"

He thrust his chin at a flock of ladies who had just walked in. "Want to stick your dick in a real woman? With the lights on?"

Zachary's dark eyebrows rose beneath the falling strands of his hair. "Seriously?"

What a cunt. "Follow my lead." He pivoted on the stool toward the women and let his thighs fall subtly apart, knowing the stretch in his jeans cupped his junk just right. He leaned his elbows on the bar top behind him and gnawed on the toothpick.

Four pairs of eyes looked his way. He blanked his expression in a portrait of indifference, his eyes roaming the group as a whole with little commitment.

Like a pack of hungry Chihuahuas, they scampered as one in his direction. A stagger of *Hi's* came next, followed by flushed cheeks, cleared throats, and smoldering stares.

Time to put them out of their misery. "I'm gay."

A chorus of whiny *Oooooh's* blubbered out.

He chuckled. "I know the feeling. This guy here" —he squeezed Zachary's neck, probably with more force than was necessary— "turned me down. I saw his cock in the men's room. Un-fucking-real, ladies. Have fun with it." He dropped a wad of cash on the counter, patted Zachary on the back, and gamboled to the door.

He moved the Mustang a few parking spots down from Zachary's truck and set up his camera. Forty-five minutes later, the two-timing prick strolled out of the bar with one of the girls under his arm and his tongue down her throat. Took the fucker long enough to snag a girl.

Camera raised, Van clicked away from his shadowed position in the Mustang. Zachary pressed her against the passenger door of the truck, one hand fumbling for his keys, the other shoved up her skirt.

*Click. Click. Click.*

Van's lungs expanded to their fullest with each deep, satisfied breath. Damn straight, he was smug. Not only did he restrain himself from gutting the guy, but also he did Amber a favor. She might not have cared who Zachary was fucking—especially given her willingness to fuck *him* a couple days ago—but he'd read agoraphobics didn't just cling to their homes. They attached themselves to people, too. At the moment, there was only one person she could've been attached to.

Zachary pushed the girl onto her back across the truck's seat. Without bothering to close the door, he proceeded to eat her face then her cunt beneath the glow of the streetlight.

After a few more clicks, Van set the camera down and lit a cigarette. Tomorrow, Amber wouldn't have a choice when she cut ties with Zachary Kaufman. But he needed her to be convincing when she did it.

# TWELVE

Ordering groceries online was a Tuesday morning task, an item to check off a list. But as Amber squinted at her online bank account balance, she knew her routine was about to change. A tic twitched in her eyelid. Everything her sanity depended on required electricity or water. The vacuum, treadmill, shower, laundry, online groups...

She tucked her hands beneath her armpits and hugged herself, burrowing into the couch as the weight of her situation pushed air from her chest.

This fear was different from what she was used to. When she'd stepped outside, the paralysis, suffocation, and loss of body control was a physical, heart-rate-in-the-red-zone kind of fear. But the horror of losing her connectedness — to her house, her schedule, her courier and lover — made her feel breathless, empty, and lost, like a non-person.

Who would she be without order and routine? If not a beauty contestant or a neat freak, then what? A hollow husk in a padded room like her mother?

But the most tangible threat was losing her house. Foreclosure meant she would have to leave. She'd have to go *outside*. She'd rather die.

She closed the laptop. She didn't need groceries anyway. There would be no cooking and no refrigeration when the electricity shut off. The city had already turned off her water service that morning.

The clocks on the wall told her she had fifteen minutes before Zach's arrival. He would ship all her packages and, in a few days, she'd receive her payments and get the utilities back on. Until next month.

She stared at nothing for a long moment, searching inside herself for an answer, a reaction, something, but all she found was the absence of value and meaning.

    She set her phone and laptop on the coffee table, lining them up in right-angles, and trudged toward the hall to prepare for Zach. As she reached the bedroom doorway, the hairs on her nape lifted. She paused. Something felt...off.

    A click echoed from the front room, followed by a creak in the floor. A shriek crawled up her throat, and she snapped her mouth shut, listening without breathing, heart thundering. Was someone in the house? How was that possible?

    A few silent seconds passed as she trembled in a gridlock of clenched muscles and stifled breaths. She should've heard a crash if someone had broken in. She gripped the doorframe to her room, her legs shaking to run, her brain telling her not to make a sound.

    The stillness of the house gathered around her, squeezing her chest and slowly, maddeningly, dispersing with her exhale. Was she paranoid now? Fabricating new horrors in her head?

    Then she heard it. The soft rasp of socked feet on hardwood, approaching, gaining speed. Time seemed to slam to a halt as her body moved to escape and her eyes swung over her shoulder.

    A man stood in the mouth of the hall, with broad shoulders, a baseball cap, a scar on his cheek, and a gun in his hand.

    Why was Van in her house, pointing a gun? The shock of it rendered her speechless.

    "You won't run." His voice was soft and casual, exactly the way she remembered it. But his outstretched arm aimed the gun at her head, a gloved finger beside the trigger. A tablet dangled in his other gloved hand, and her phone was wedged beneath the buckle of his jeans.

    She stood half-in, half-out of the bedroom, her blood pressure rising with every second that passed. Ten feet separated them. How good was his aim? If she ducked into the room, she could escape through the window. *Outside.* OhGodohGodohGod. She couldn't swallow, couldn't breathe.

    "I'll shoot through your door before you make it to the window." His lips slid into a terrifying smile. "And we both know you'll have a panic attack the moment you lift the shade."

    Hard to argue, but the fact that he knew what crippled her surged anger through her veins, heating her skin and garbling her words. "What do you want?"

    "We'll get to that. Stand in the center of the hall with your arms at your sides."

    The audacious command made her skin crawl. Worse, she hadn't finished dressing because she didn't want to wrinkle her dress for Zach. The only clothing she wore were white lacy panties and a midriff cami.

"Let me grab a robe." And something sharp to stab him with.

"I won't repeat myself." The eerie calm in his voice crept through the narrow space, stealing the strength from her knees. Not a hint of humor surfaced in the rigid lines of his face. He wasn't fucking around.

Maybe he wouldn't shoot her, but he knew about the agoraphobia. If she angered him, would he force her outside?

She shifted into the hall, fighting to keep her hands at her sides as the intensity of his gaze raked her legs, her panties, and lingered on her nipples pressing against the cotton.

He met her eyes. "You have three seconds to tell me how you greet Zachary Kaufman at the door."

The blood drained from her cheeks, and a shiver raced over her spine. "What are you—?"

"Two seconds."

"I don't—"

"One second."

"I unlock the door and wait in the bedroom," she said in a rushed breath. "Please, don't hurt him." Even if she wasn't emotionally attached to Zach, she didn't want to see him harmed.

He prowled toward her with the gun leveled at her chest. Her pulse hammered in her ears, and her neck strained with tension, but she kept her chin up and eyes full of *fuck you*.

A foot away, he stopped and pressed the barrel of the gun against her breastbone, his eyes fixed on her breasts. The cold metal slid down the center of her chest, taking the thin cotton with it, until the neckline reached her nipples. He leaned in, his timbre low and authoritative. "Walk into your room and sit on the bed."

Her body quivered against that voice, itching to obey. But the glow of his silver eyes rooted her to the floor, chilling her with the ferocity that hardened their depths.

She looked away, clenching her hands at her sides and popping the finger joints with her thumbs.

"Now!" he shouted.

She jumped, gasping for air and stumbling toward the room. He followed her in, and when she sat on the bed, he shoved the tablet under her nose.

She didn't look at it, couldn't drag her eyes from the man who towered over her. Thick, dark energy hummed around him, and he oozed malicious, predatory power from his pores. Not wild or manic, not throwing fists or flinging spit. It was calculating, in control, warning her.

With her arms wrapped around her chest and hips, she glared into his eyes, shivering against their sharp animalistic beauty. Maybe if she said his name, it would remind him he was human. "Van, are you going to make me go outside?"

The only thing that moved was his lips. "Look at the screen and swipe through the photos."

Maybe he'd lied about his name. She glanced down, and her brow furrowed as she took in the image. It showed Zach in a parking lot with his hand beneath a brunette's skirt. She blinked rapidly, startled, confused, and shook her head. "How did you—"

"Flip to the next one."

Her mind raced as she swiped the screen with a numb finger. The girl was on her back in the truck with Zach's shaggy head between her spread thighs.

Nausea twisted her stomach as she swiped again. Same scene, same girl, Zach's hips now wedged between her legs, his pants stretched beneath his bare ass. Amber's body temperature skyrocketed, and her chest tightened. What did this mean to Van? Why would he show her this? "How do you know him?"

"I met this guy in a bar on Sixth Street last night. He told me he was fucking a whack job named Amber on Tuesdays and Fridays, and he wanted to stick his dick in a real woman."

Her hands locked into fists. He could've been making that up.

He tucked the tablet beneath his arm. "With the lights on."

Her stomach dropped, and an ache swelled, angry and painful, around her heart. "So you thought you'd...what? Enlighten me? While waving a fucking gun?" It was too much, too many surprises coming at her too damned fast. "Well, guess what? I *am* a whack job, and he can fuck whom he wants. Why do *you* care?"

His pupils flared, swallowing the silver rims of his eyes. "He's due at noon? Yes or no."

Son of a bitch. "No. Twelve-o-*four*."

He glanced at the side table, and she followed his gaze. 11:58 glowed on the clock.

No way did he just happen upon Zach at a bar after he *just happened* upon her porch. She gritted her teeth. "How long have you been watching my house?" And how the hell did he get in? "Oh my God. You stole my key? You arrogant, thieving dickhead!"

"Be careful, Amber." His icy glare raised bumps over her skin. "Cover yourself up." He waved a hand at the closet. "You have thirty seconds."

Of all the women in Austin, why her? If he knew her schedule, maybe he'd figured out Zach was the only person who would notice if she disappeared. Hell, he had her phone. If he'd looked at the log, he'd know she talked to no one, had no one.

She strode to the closet, trying like hell to keep her shaking arms over her thinly-covered boobs. "What are you going to do to him?"

"If you ask another question, I'll kill him, slow and messy, all over your carpet."

Her mind played out that scenario in Technicolor, and her thoughts degraded to a sick, selfish place where her disorder bred and thrived. The damage to her carpet would be permanent, a constant reminder, and she couldn't afford to replace it.

"If you convincingly chase him away, I'll let him live." He glared at her, his lips pressed in a line. "And I do mean convincingly. The fucker better walk out of here without a doubt in his mind he'll never see you again. I just gave you the ammo to do it. Use it. Fifteen seconds."

She dressed in a hurried daze, fumbling on jeans and tugging a t-shirt over the cami. This wasn't happening. If she chased Zach away, how long would it be before someone found her body? Or worse, found her house empty?

Would he try to kidnap her? Her skin grew clammy, and a tremor shook her legs. "I can't go outside. You'll have to shoot me first." Either way, she wouldn't survive.

"I'll be right in here." He stalked to the closet and gripped the door, with the gun trained on her. "If you fuck this up, if Zachary shows a hint of suspicion, I'll shoot him. Sit on the bed."

How had she not seen this coming when she met him? She'd let this man into her house, for fucksake. Such a stupid, stupid girl. She deserved this. She wiped at the copious sweat clinging to her face and arms, her ramping heart rate thrashing pinpricks through her head.

Breathing deeply, over and over, she sat on the bed and prepared to drive away the only person she had in her life.

Van faded within the shadow of the closet, leaving the door open a sliver, with a line of sight directly on her.

Six huge breaths later, the rumble of Zach's truck sounded in the driveway. Her heart hammered so painfully, she wanted to double over from the agony of it. She could do this. Her odds of surviving sucked, but she could save Zach.

The front door opened and rattled shut. Van must've left it unlocked, already knowing her routine. Knowing too much. She didn't dare look at the closet door for fear she'd unravel into a worthless blob of panic.

Footsteps pounded down the hall, and Zach's tall, thin frame appeared in the doorway. Images of him with that girl girded her spine, even as a lump clogged her throat. It wasn't jealousy. It was the strangling reminder that she hadn't been good enough.

He smiled. "Jeans today? Didn't know you owned a pair."

This was going to hurt. She swallowed. *Just do it quick.* "We're done, Zach. No more deliveries. No more sex." Her voice wobbled, dammit.

He narrowed his eyes and pushed a hand through his chin-length hair, gripping it at the back of his head. "What...what do you mean?"

She drew a deep breath and sat taller. "I saw you last night."

He flinched, and his arm flopped to his side. Then he squared his shoulders and started toward her.

"No. Stay where you are." *Get him out of there. Get him safe.* She hardened her eyes and her voice. "I said we're done."

"How —" His eyes widened. "You left the house?"

Dammit, of course not. But he wasn't as perceptive as the prick in the closet. "I saw you with a girl at a bar on Sixth Street. I want you gone. Don't call. Don't come by. I'm taking my business elsewhere."

"Hey, no. Just wait a second." His eyes pleaded, and he swiped a hand over his face. "I can explain."

When he started forward again, she held up a palm. "Don't come any closer." Sweet God, the tension in the room made it impossible to breathe. "If you try to contact me, I'll file a restraining order." *I'm saving your life.* "Now, leave."

"Jesus, a restraining order? On what grounds?" His voice was thready, and his shoulders slumped. "Amber, she meant nothing. It was a mistake."

"I'll tell them you raped me." She cringed inwardly, her insides threatening to heave. "I still have your semen on my sheets. They'll believe me." If Zach knew her at all, he'd call her out on her cleanliness. But he'd never paid attention to her neurosis, which was what she'd liked most about him. She rose and thrust a finger in the vicinity of the front door. "Get. The fuck. Out."

His jaw clenched, and his blue eyes turned to glass, losing focus. He nodded a few times, staring at the floor. Then he smacked a hand against the door, knocking it into the wall. "Crazy bitch." He turned and stomped down the hall. A moment later, the front door slammed.

The truck rumbled through the walls then faded into the distance. Gone. She was officially on her own. And her packages weren't mailed. She released a ragged breath, her eyes burning with tears she refused to shed. She sniffed and looked at the closet door. God help her. It would open any second now.

When he emerged, she met his eyes and spat out her words. "Convincing enough for you?"

"Watch your fucking tone." He strode past her to the doorway and glared down the hall. "I should've killed him for calling you a bitch."

Sudden warmth hit at the core of her. The sentiment touched a needy, vulnerable piece of her psyche she refused to examine. He confused her, and maybe that was part of his game. "So you can break into houses and threaten people's lives, but name calling is a crime?"

"Yes." His pale gray eyes, so contemplative and unnervingly focused on her, made her feel more exposed than a dozen pageant walks before a hundred judges. He de-cocked the gun and tucked it in the waistband at his back. "You can run, but there's nowhere to go but *outside*. If you don't follow my orders, I'll restrain you...*outside*."

She shook her head in denial and clutched her throat. What he suggested was the worst possible outcome, unless... "Are you going to cut me up in little pieces?"

A cold smile tipped his lips as he chuckled. Then his expression sobered. "Walk to the kitchen."

Fucking psychopath. He stood right in the doorway, taking up the whole damned hall. At over six feet tall with a muscled body cut from stone, he could squash her without breaking a sweat. She didn't want to go near him. He was terrifying. But being forced outside was worse. She straightened her back and headed toward him.

As she slid by, his arm caught her waist and yanked her back against his chest. She slapped at his hand, bucking against him, and his arm clenched tighter. His erection jabbed against her backside, his breath hot at her ear. "Fighting and squirming only turns me on. Don't stop."

She immediately stilled. God, he wasn't lying. His dick was undeniably more pronounced against her back. Feeling him like that, so close, so huge and hard, rushed heat between her legs and prickles over her skin. Why, oh why was she responding this way? She hated and wanted it, and mother of all fucks, she couldn't have been more completely and totally out of her mind.

She drew a ragged breath. *Think, think, think.* But his intention blatantly rubbed against her, scattering her thoughts. "You're going to rape me, aren't you?"

His torso moved up and down with his breath. "I thought you wanted to be fuck buddies. Don't make it weird."

"What? Oh no. Nononononono. I'm not offering now!" Her voice shrilled, and her elbows rammed into his ribs. "This is me saying 'No'."

Restraining her with an arm around her chest, he pulled off a glove with his teeth and shoved his hand down the front of her jeans, beneath her panties. She gasped and tried to reach for the gun at his back. The glove dropped to the floor as he kept his back twisted away and the brace of his massive arm effectively immobilizing her movements.

The fingers in her jeans descended with strength and determination. They slid over her mound, between her lips, reaching, curling, and oh God, fucking her. He pressed his palm over her pussy, his fingers hooking inside her. The grip yanked her back, grinding her ass against his erection.

Her inner muscles pulsated around the invasion, clenching and shameless. She wanted to cry, knowing how wet she was, humiliated that he was swirling through the depraved evidence of her frail mind and touching her in a place she never wanted anyone to see.

"Please." She squeezed her thighs together, tried to angle her hips away from his fingers. "Please, I don't want this."

He thrust harder and twisted his fingers inside her. "Your cunt disagrees." Without warning, he yanked his hand from her pants and shoved his fingers in her mouth, pressing down on her tongue and jaw. The tang of her arousal mixed with her saliva as he angled her jaw with his hand, forcing her cheek against his chest and shoving his face into hers.

Every human being had a cruel side, but as she looked into the blackness behind his eyes, she didn't see a facet of varying traits. She saw the entire man. He *was* cruelty incarnate.

He released her, and she stumbled. He reached out to catch her arm, but she jerked away, refusing to be dragged. He grabbed his glove from the floor, slid it on, and gestured toward the kitchen. "After you."

His soft gait followed closely behind her. She tried to focus on a plan, a useful weapon, anything but the way her wanton body was reacting to the feel of him behind her, around her, dominating her space.

He stopped beside the kitchen sink and set the tablet on the counter. "Get me a glass of water."

Apparently, breaking-and-entering, fucking with women, and being an all-round asshole made him thirsty. "The water is shut off." She couldn't stop the flush of humiliation that crept up her neck.

The look of detachment on his face irritated her as much as it frightened her. "I bet you prepared for that. Open the fridge."

Her molars crashed together as she stormed to the fridge and yanked out one of the four pitchers of water. When she finished pouring a glass, he tugged a baggie from his pocket and dumped the powdered contents into the water, stirring it with a gloved finger. "Drink."

"No way." She backed away from him with rasping breaths. "What is it?"

In the next heartbeat, he was on her, chest-to-chest, arms around her back, hauling her to the sliding door. He yanked the shades aside, and the blinding light of the backyard set her skin on fire and her heart into overdrive.

Her legs gave out, and she swung her head away from the horror of the open, inescapable space. If she went out there, it would be her ruination. She wouldn't be coherent, wouldn't be able to talk or scream without breath.

She clawed at his hands, to break his hold, to escape the door.

Black bursts spotted her vision, and her heart slammed against her ribs. She panted for air and couldn't fill her lungs. Her eyes smeared with hot tears, blinding her. She fought harder, but his arms were everywhere, too tight, constricting and suffocating. Consciousness teased at the back of her mind as a blanket of warmth and aftershave swept in.

The slide of the drapes sounded, and the sunlight receded. Too late, she realized she was on the floor, curled in his lap, with her face buried in the crook of his arm.

She pushed against the hand cupping the back of her head as the rim of the glass touched her lips.

"We can do this all day." He rolled the glass over her chin, sloshing cool water against her mouth. "Or you can drink and fall asleep gently."

So he wanted to knock her out? Well, he could eat a dick. She sealed her lips together and turned her head. "Then what?"

"Then…we go for a ride."

# THIRTEEN

Van knelt on the bed beside Amber and drew a deep, calming breath. After three more stubborn confrontations with the sliding glass door, she'd worked herself into a sniveling, spasmodic conniption. And promptly fainted.

Shaking his head at the irony, he tied her limp arms to the headboard with the belts from her closet. Then he grabbed the drugged water from the side table.

Fainting wouldn't keep her under long enough for the thirty-minute drive, but the Roofy in the water would. Wrestling with her in front of the open door had been a gamble, but he knew the neighbors on either side were at work and the trees out back blocked the view from the other houses.

Still, it had been a risk that could've been avoided by simply pinning her down and forcing her to drink. But watching her struggle with the choice, seeing how far she'd take it, had revealed a lot about how her mind worked.

She'd convinced herself the biggest threat was out there, beyond her doors and windows, and the least amount of pain was in her house, with him. He was certain she would welcome a bullet before drinking the water, knowing the tranquilizer would result in her removal from the house. It was absolutely fascinating.

In his online research of Amber Rosenfeld, he'd validated she'd won countless first place prizes in prestigious contests in fitness modeling and beauty pageantry. Then, after a fourteen-year career, nothing. For two years, no news articles, nothing in the search results except a profile on an online crafts store selling leathercrafts. Why?

Only a year older than his thirty-three years, her firm figure and youthful face would've provided her a comfortable income from modeling. Yet, here she was, carving leather and drowning in debt. What the fuck had happened to her?

She had no social media profiles, and no friends or family mentioned in the public search results. She'd simply vanished from the spotlight with a disqualification from what might've been her fourth win in an international beauty pageant. The significance of the number four hadn't been lost on him.

He straddled her hips, anxious to dig into her complex mind and savoring the feel of her tight little body against his balls. Christ, all her struggling had wreaked havoc on his control. But he wanted to fuck her in his house, on his bed, where the surrounding acreage's dense timber would swallow her screams.

He stabbed the water with the drinking straw he'd found in the kitchen, sealed it with a finger, and trickled it down her throat.

She coughed, swallowing, and gasped awake. He had another strawfull waiting before she opened her eyes. She blinked, lips parting, and he emptied it in her mouth.

Her throat convulsed, her arms yanked uselessly at the restraints, and she angled her neck to look at her hands. Her eyes rounded, her fists clenched, and she roared, "You dirty, conniving" — she bucked her hips — "heavy-ass dick, let me go!"

He slapped a hand over her mouth and nose and howled with laughter. "I'm going to show you how dirty, conniving, and heavy my dick is. First, you need to take a long nap."

Christ, she was cute, but it really wasn't funny. If the neighbors were outside, they might've heard her. He cocked his head and watched her struggle for air beneath the clamp of his hand. Time to get ugly.

Releasing her face, he reared back and slammed a fist into her stomach. Not enough to damage organs, but plenty of *oomph* to knock the wind out of her and get her attention.

She gulped silently, her body straining beneath him. Her lower lip rolled inward, trembling, as she bit down on it. Her eyelids fluttered, brimming but not quite shedding tears. When the pain faded from her eyes, she narrowed them at him.

He held out the glass and raised his brow.

Her lips formed a white stubborn line.

Slowly, he trailed a finger over the cotton covering her stomach, circling the hurt and taunting her until her pupils dilated with fear. She shivered, and sweat beaded along her honey skin. Earlier, it hadn't just been fear that prickled and dampened her flesh. She'd been aroused, too, by his fingers in her pussy, or maybe just from the feel of his erection at her back, from having a man attracted to her. But she'd fought it, fought him, and that had turned him on far more than the juices slicking her cunt.

His finger followed the line of her sternum, traced her collarbone, and roamed over her chin and cheek.

"What are you going to do to me?" The quiver in her voice teased the darkest pleasure centers inside him.

He leaned forward, and his touch caressed a path over her full lips, the bridge of her nose, and her slim eyebrows, drawing out her anxiety. When he reached her nose, he pinched tightly, blocking the airway. Her gaze flew to his, white-eyed and red-rimmed.

Holding her face immobile, he angled the glass beside her chin, using the mattress to balance it. As her lips opened to inhale, he poked the end of the straw between her teeth.

With his fingers clamping her nose, he used the heel of his hand to hold her head down and her jaw shut around the straw. "I'll let you breathe after you drink through the straw. If you pass out, I'll wake you up, and we'll do it again."

Those huge brown eyes glared at him until the pressure of her lungs overpowered her stubbornness. Her throat began to work, swallowing the drug. Gorgeous, watery pools of desperation engulfed her lashes and trickled down her temples.

"Shhh." He bent over her, without releasing her jaw and nose, and kissed the paths of her tears.

When air coughed through the straw, he set the glass on the table and lowered his face to hers. She drew heavy, greedy inhales, tucking her chin to escape him. He chased her lips, catching them with his own and sucking, teasing, enjoying the heave of her chest and her useless struggles to get away. Then he sat back.

She pulled on the restraints and gave up quickly, evidently exhausted. Her eyes slid over the room as if memorizing every detail and locked on the aquarium of mutilated awards. "I can't go outside. I can't." Her voice crept over him, somber and resigned.

"Why did you quit?" He nodded at the aquarium.

She looked at him, her gaze wet and glazed, not really *looking*. "You'll see."

He narrowed his eyes, wanting to press, but he only had twenty minutes before the Roofy took effect. So he offered the same obtuseness. "I'm going to fix you; then *you'll* see."

Tuning out her objection, he strode to the closet. He yanked three duffel bags from the top shelf and stuffed them with the bulk of her wardrobe.

When she figured out what he was doing, she wailed more nonsense about not going outside until he gagged her with a balled up sock from the dresser.

He added her toiletries from the bathroom to the last duffel, followed by the empty water glass with the Roofy evidence, her powered-off phone, laptop, and his tablet.

Twenty minutes later, he found her sleeping heavily, made sure the airway in her nose was clear, and left the gag in place. Then he slid on sunglasses and entered the garage.

Empty. Not even a car. Guess that made sense since she didn't go anywhere. Snatching the garage opener from a bare shelf, he closed the doors behind him. Because it was daylight, he strolled down the street and around the block.

He returned five minutes later in a minivan, parked it in the garage, and shut the door. The van was a purchase he'd made the prior day. A dated model with tinted windows. He'd even gone as far as swiping someone's *County Maids* advertisement, the huge magnet now clinging to the passenger sliding door.

A hired house cleaner wasn't the best explanation for the sudden activity at a seemingly vacant home. Liv certainly wouldn't have bought it, but she was at the airport, instructing skydiving lessons, and Joshua was tied up in his coaching shit at the high school. While a nighttime capture was preferred, taking Amber during the day avoided the most suspicious neighbors.

He shouldn't have been taking her at all, but after he'd researched the disorders, an idea had formed in the back of his mind. Amber might have many uses, one being an unknowing tool in solidifying a relationship with his daughter. First, he had to redirect her attachments until all she needed was him.

As he strode down the hall and into her bedroom, his insides vibrated with excitement. When he freed her arms, removed the gag, and lifted her listless, vulnerable body against his chest, something strange shifted through him and settled around his heart. It felt warm and gentle and...uncontaminated.

Impossible. Besides, his daughter was the only person he would allow himself to nurture a soft spot for. Anyone else would jump on his weakness and twist it into something they could use against him.

He shook off the unnerving feeling and quickened his pace to the garage. He was a cold-hearted fuck with an appetite for blood, come, and tears. And he had the perfect girl to feed it.

# FOURTEEN

A dreamlike blur of sensations sloshed over Amber. Thick darkness. The sluggish thump of her heart. A draft on her skin. The familiar scent of aftershave.

She blinked, tried to clear the haze, and her eyes met a veil of black. Why was her lamp off? She slept with it on. The mattress felt too firm against her back and head. And no pillow? That wasn't right.

Cool air whispered over her body. Her very naked body. Blood rushed past her ears as she tried to sit up, going nowhere.

Nude, dark, cold, she had to be stuck in a dream, tangled in the sheets. She always slept without clothes when no one was looking. No one would be there. Not in her room at night, in her safe place of flawless lines. If only she could see the order to ground herself in her symmetrical world. *Wake up.*

She lifted her head and tried to get her bearings. Fabric rubbed her forehead, cheeks, and the bridge of her nose. Pinpricks bit at her hands. She couldn't move them, so she scrunched her face, wiggling the obstruction, and her eyelashes dragged against whatever held tightly over her eyes. *A blindfold.*

She jerked, and nausea surged through her gut. Her arms and legs wouldn't bend. She yanked and kicked, caught in a web of restraints that dug into her wrists and ankles, pinning her in a spread-eagle position on her back.

A tremor awoke in her chest and exploded outward, shaking every muscle in her body until her limbs numbed and her jaw ached from clenching. Her mind spun through fuzz. She couldn't remember falling asleep, couldn't remember the last thing she did. The nausea, the disorientation, the pounding headache... Had she drank too much again?

Memories swirled in a mist of dizzy fragments. The fading rumble of Zach's truck. A water glass. The drape wrenched from the back door. A fist slamming into her stomach.

*Van.*

Her heart rate spiked, and pain pounded behind her eyes. Oh shit, oh shit, oh shit. She let out an ear-piercing shriek that echoed around her, and she immediately regretted the outburst. She did *not* want to draw attention, couldn't bear for anyone to see her naked.

Her pulse redoubled. Where was Van? Was he watching her with sick amusement? She stifled her breath and listened. No reassuring hum of the A/C unit outside her window. No dripping from the leaking shower down the hall. Oh wait, her water had been shut off. But the mattress... It was too hard, too bare.

She wasn't in her bed. Her heart stuttered and stopped. OhmyGodOhmyGod. She wasn't in her house!

"No, no, no." She jerked her head side to side, writhed against the restraints, and choked through panting breaths. "Where am I?"

The mattress shifted between her legs, and a tickle of wiry hair brushed her inner thighs. Then the press of hard muscle. Someone's legs. "You're home."

She froze. His voice, oh God, it came from above her. He was kneeling between her thighs, where he could look at her stretched, godawful shame. She tried to close her legs and failed. The mattress was indented on either side of her shoulders, and she knew his hands were propped there. How long had he been bent over her, watching her, waiting? Or doing whatever he wanted to her while she was unconscious?

Her lungs slammed together, starving for air. Were the lights on? Jesus, fuck, they couldn't be on. He wouldn't want to look between her legs.

Something hard and slick nudged her opening, and his heavy body flattened her against the bed. Her mouth dried. No, this couldn't be happening. She thrashed, pinned by his weight, unable to escape as objections gathered in her constricted throat.

In the next heartbeat, he shoved himself inside her, his girth stretching her hideous flesh with the brutality of the dry thrust. She bit down her tongue, tasting blood, as the invasion tore her open, plowing ruthlessly and igniting a scorching friction along her inner walls.

Her eyes watered behind the blindfold, the agony and humiliation of what he was doing seizing her heart. Her screech escaped without sound, and her body locked in paralyzing shock. Numb, breathless, her fear was stunned into silence, cringing in the corner of her mind.

"Scream," he breathed, his thick exhale searing her ear.

A wail built in her throat, but he slammed into her, giving her no time to free it. No pause to catch her breath. No gentle coaxing to prepare her for his size. He fucked her harder, forcing her body to accommodate him, taking her beyond the point of pain and hurtling her into muscle-locking terror.

The straps chewed into her skin, grinding her bones. His fingers pinched and pulled her nipples, and the spread of her hips extended painfully beneath the unrelenting strength of his driving thrusts.

This was happening. He'd taken her from her house. Bared her before his eyes. He was raping her.

Her heart panted, a helpless terrified thing trapped in her chest. She wanted to ignore it, to be stronger, but as his powerful jabs shredded and battered her insides, death seemed to be a better option.

His teeth scraped across her shoulder, his grunts lashed her skin with wet exhales, and his arms squeezed around her ribs. Could he see all her flaws in the light? Who else had laid eyes on her, judged her? If she wasn't home... Oh no, oh God, he'd taken her *outside*.

Her pulse went wild, tearing through her body. She bucked in his embrace, but there was no escape. He was too heavy, too strong, plunging in and out of her abused flesh.

The horrifying image of her body spread out beneath him collided with the shackles chafing her raw skin and the cramping pain of her cervix or whatever it was inside her he hammered against so mercilessly.

She closed her eyes behind the blindfold and tried to calm her heart by counting the slam of his hips. One...two...three...four. One...two...three...four. Over and over, she counted until her mind tumbled so far away her body grew numb and limp.

His hand gripped her throat and squeezed. "What are you doing?"

Bright hot reality burned through her, sensitizing every cell in her body. She'd always wanted it harder, rougher, with a firmer hand around her neck, strangling her thoughts. But not like this, with no choice, no safe word. And not with the lights on. "Are the lights...?" Her voice quivered, tiny and reedlike. She swallowed around the clamp of his fingers. "Are they on?"

He tsked and slowed his thrusts. "You don't really know someone until you see them in the dark." His timbre rumbled through her as he rolled his hips and tightened his hand around her throat. "I'll show you the dark, my beautiful slave."

*Slave.* The blackness burst in a constellation of stars as his fingers bit into her tender throat. He flexed his hips, surging forward, pumping faster than the heaving of her chest. Her lungs caught fire, unable to draw air, as her life burned away beneath the vise of his hand.

A prick of light flickered in the dark void, beckoning. She floated toward it, couldn't stop it from taking her. The moment she gave in, the second she stopped fighting, her body felt lighter, her mind quieter. The pain of his thrusts and the clench of his fist receded as wave after wave of serenity sifted in. It nibbled away at her fear and splintered her thoughts until nothing was left but a hundred vibrating tongues licking along her inner walls, swelling wet heat through her pussy, and soaking his entry.

"Aw, God." He loosened his grip, grunting a sound full of lust and satisfaction, and sped up his pace. "There's my girl, dripping all over me."

Her bruised throat sealed up as his words spilled fiery shame through her veins. She'd fantasized about being punished, to be fucked raw and savagely, and maybe she was depraved. But now? Oh God, she didn't want it. Something was missing, something crucial. He took without permission. Every nerve in her body thrummed for more, but he'd stolen her power to stop it.

His balls slapped against her ass, his cock growing thicker inside her. "You love to be dominated." He ground his pelvis against her clit and bit her earlobe. "Even as your conscience tells you to hate it. I dare you to fight it."

Somewhere in the recesses of her fucked-up head, a rational voice screamed in horror, lamenting his truths, hating him. But her pussy swelled with desire, throbbing and gripping him harder. The gluttonous flesh grew slicker with every thrust, welcoming him, urging him on.

After two years of fucking in the dark, she was spread open under the lights. It would've been a huge step for her, but she hadn't chosen it. As she lay there, absorbing the brute force of his cock pounding inside her, she discarded whatever self-worth she had left and replaced it with something she could endure. She let the pleasure in.

His fingers scraped through her hair, ripping the strands and tingling her scalp as he yanked her head back and licked her mouth. "I want your release." His mouth imprisoned hers, sucking the air from her lungs as he drove his tongue in maddening swirls. "Give it to me. Now."

The orgasm exploded from an unbound place inside her, thundering through her body, every muscle rippling with electric tingles. His hips jerked against hers, and he kissed her with a ferocity that buckled her spine. She didn't have the faculties to bite off his tongue, her release so powerful all she could do was ride it as he dragged a piercing cry from her throat. She dug her feet into the mattress, and the ecstasy carried her into oblivion where she drifted in utter peace.

Without warning, he yanked off the blindfold. The quietude evaporated, replaced with the horrifying intrusion of natural light. An A-frame ceiling soared above the bed, its exposed rafters reaching beyond the railing that lined the long, narrow loft where she was held.

She didn't want to look at him, but he was as much a threat as the windows towering above him. She lifted her eyes, and his terribly beautiful face filled her vision. Still deep and hard inside her, he leaned back, his gaze smoldering with blatant lust. Sweat beaded over his forehead, gathering in the furrows and threatening to drip. Oh God, why couldn't he just wipe that away? She couldn't bear for it to fall on her and averted her eyes.

In the corner, a staircase spiraled into a two-story room. The only way to escape was down. Was the room below walled with glass, exposed to the outdoors? She didn't know. All she could see was the source of the light, the glow of twilight bleeding through the triangular windows that crested the two-story wall beyond the railing. The pinkish clouds against the purple sky might've been picturesque if the view of outside wasn't shuddering through her, chattering her teeth and shortening her breaths.

*Jesus, stop.* The windows were too high to see in. It was just the sky looking back. None of this could hurt her. Breathing deeply, she could feel the heat of his eyes watching her from his kneeling position between her legs, his cock still buried inside her. She refused to look at him again, and her gaze stumbled over her body. The shame of her nudity, all laid out in the light, was sharp and swift as it clenched her insides in a blinding chokehold.

Her arms trembled wildly, her hair sticking to the sweat on her face. The evidence of her arousal smeared her inner thighs. But the worst of the view was her oversized breasts bouncing lewdly as he began to thrust anew with hard-hitting strokes.

"Please cover the windows." She knew he couldn't. They were two-stories up, with no attached curtains or blinds.

He put his face in hers, the pink scar on his cheek bunching with his smile. "You realize, what exists in the light doesn't go away in the dark."

Fuck his condescending smirk. Shadows hung like drapes on the three windowless walls surrounding them, hovering just out of reach, but soon they would close in with the setting sun. The approaching darkness in this unknown place both comforted and scared the shit out of her.

His eyes wandered down her body to lock on where they were connected. All that distended flesh was likely wrapped around his cock, folding up and down his length, so fucking grotesque it made her eyes burn.

"Stop looking." It was a tear-choked plea, one he acknowledged with a furrowed brow then rejected as he sat up, gripped her ass, and angled his head, watching himself slide in and out.

She thrashed and jerked, but her efforts didn't distract him from staring at her pussy.

A twitch tugged the lower lid of her eye, jumping manically, angry and relentless. She squeezed her eyes shut and breathed slow and deep. Numbness settled over her arms, and a throb awoke in her chest, like an over-pressurized artery pulsing above the muscle. If only it was a heart attack.

Instead, it was the smothering pain of panic crashing over her. She tried to calm it by focusing on something other than the sight of her body. She studied his heavy-lidded eyes, strong nose, and full mouth, all arranged in perfect symmetry. The angles of his face followed lines of natural geometry. Uniformed cuts of muscle sculpted his pecs and abs.

He was a kidnapper, a rapist, and she ached to be repulsed by him, just to prove she was sane, but she couldn't. And she wasn't. His scarred beauty radiated seduction and danger, a deadly combination.

She'd told him he would see why she'd given up modeling, yet he continued to fuck her as if he hadn't seen every inch of her terrible nudity. His arms braced beside her waist, his biceps flexing as his cock pistoned in and out of her, scrambling her thoughts, overwhelming her.

The dime-sized scar in his shoulder was the last thing she saw as tremors attacked her nervous system, seizing her body and arching her back. Blackness invaded, the clouds faded from the windows, and she fell into nothingness.

A hand slammed into her jaw, shooting a stinging fire through her nose. She blinked, gasping for air, and his scowl bleared into focus.

"Stay with me, goddammit." Silver flames lit his eyes, sparking above her in blurry, iridescent flashes.

He pulled out, ripped off the condom, and pumped his hand along his length, hard and fast. Bending over her, he propped himself up, his arm straight, biceps straining as his fist stroked. His eyes locked with hers, and his mouth opened with a guttural shout as come squirted over her mound, belly, and chest.

She stared at the globs streaking her body, dazed. Why had he come on her and not in her?

He answered her unspoken question when he swirled his fingers through the ejaculate, spreading it over her skin as if rubbing it into her pores, marking his territory.

"Beautiful." His voice was thick with lust. He leaned down and lapped at it, collecting a white puddle on his tongue.

Before she could analyze the come licking, he crawled up her body and captured her mouth. His salty kiss swirled past her lips, aggressive and consuming. She tried to fight it, but she was too weak, too lost to the drugging glide of his lips, the salacious pressure of his teeth, and the undivided focus of his desire.

He'd seen every shameful flaw, and still he kissed her as if he believed she was beautiful? She closed her eyes and could almost taste a man beneath the cruel lash of his tongue. The flavor bore a hint of cleanliness. Earthy. Carnal. Human. It gave her hope that a modicum of kindness might've been buried in there, too. No doubt it was a hope fabricated from desperation.

He broke the kiss, and his tongue darted out, trailing the seam of her mouth. "If turning off the lights is the only way you can get off, you need to replace it with something else." His lips whispered over her cheek. "With trust."

"Are you shitting me?" She twisted in the restraints, kicking and heaving against his heavy body. "You fucking raped me!"

A dark cloud rolled over his face, and his eyes grew unfocused, his voice eerily quiet. "To call that rape insults the brutality inflicted by the worst kind of man." He blinked, and his eyes cleared. He rubbed his forehead, dropped his hand, and his mouth tilted in a crooked grin. "You liked it too much."

Fire spread over her body, lighting up her nerves and burning her throat. "I'm tied down, dammit. I didn't have a choice." She didn't have a choice to like it? Okay, not a whip-smart response. "Untie me." She glared at him through blurry eyes. "Or do you plan on raping me again?"

"Maybe." He winked. "If you beg."

The fuck she would. "Is your name really Van?"

His fingers caressed a path around the outer swell of her breast, over her ribs and hip, and slipped between the raw skin of her lower lips. "My mother named me Van Quiso." He shoved two fingers in her opening and curled them, coaxing her muscles to clench. "You'll refer to me as Master." His timbre was a velvet sheath swaddling an obnoxious order.

He shifted down her body, hovering like a dark mountain of dread, and wedged his massive shoulders between her thighs.

Her heart rammed against her ribs in a violent protest. Oh God, she never wanted anyone down there. Not after Brent. It was her biggest shame, her eternal regret. "Please, don't. You don't understand."

He bared his teeth, grinning, and bit down on her clit. White-hot pain pierced through her pussy in concentrated heat. She cried out as his teeth continued to pierce and yank the sensitive nub, his tongue flicking back and forth as swiftly as his thrusting fingers.

She screamed thick, sobbing shrills of agony. Hot tears rolled down her face, her cries garbled and raw. He released her, kissing the sore flesh. The tenderness only made her cry harder.

She was on display, naked and hurting, weak and defenseless. And her future would only get worse. What would happen to her without her routine, trapped in some unknown location, at the center of a madman's attention?

For two years, she'd hidden herself in the darkness of her self-pity.

She wasn't living. She was barely surviving. The idea of returning to her house was as grim as staying here, with him. Was this the beginning of a new misery, where her days were consumed by a rapist who made her come? The thought trembled through her. That was a whole different kind of sick.

As the edge of pain dimmed, the pinch of something else took hold, a realization as spiteful and psychotic as the monster before her. It hardened her spine and sharpened her focus.

He might've had the upper hand, but he couldn't control the mess in her mind. If he planned to keep her around, he'd damned well better be prepared. She was going to make his life a living hell.

He reached for the buckles around her ankles. "You ready?"

She was ready, for what she had no idea. She'd been beaten, drugged, taken from her house, and raped. She was already fucked in the head, her dignity long gone, and now she was backed into a corner she couldn't escape. She had nothing to lose.

She raised her chin and met his eyes. "Yes."

# FIFTEEN

The shackles around Amber's ankles fell away. She yanked her legs together, knocking her knees, and the sudden movement sent stabbing pain through her hips. But it was anger — the sudden violence of helpless fury — that sharpened every nerve-ending in her body.

Van watched her from beneath hooded eyes and reached for her wrists. "You're an unforgettable fuck, Amber."

She ground her molars, her voice low and harsh. "And you're a fucking rapist."

His eyebrows pinched together. "You're pissed, but you went over the edge and exploded around my dick." He freed one arm and murmured, "You needed that."

The conversation was surreal, as if they weren't discussing an event she would relive and mourn every day for the rest of her life, however short that might be.

The final shackle dropped, and blood tingled through her hands. She scrambled toward the edge of the bed, but he grabbed her ankles, and dragged her back, wrestling her to sit sideways in his lap.

She fought him, slapping and snarling, teeth bared, her muscles screaming with venom. But amidst her struggles slithered the chill of helplessness. If she managed to overpower him, to outsmart him, *to escape*, where would she run? Outside?

Was she seriously trying to convince herself that a naked cuddle with a rapist was less scary than whatever waited beyond the front door?

He took advantage of her hesitation, his nudity slipping around her and his hands controlling her legs until she straddled his lap, sitting chest to chest, his arms locked around her back. Hot skin pressed against hers, slick and hard and entirely too close. She shoved against the twitching muscles on his chest, but his embrace was implacable, a steel cage of limbs.

His lips brushed the sensitive spot beneath her ear, and he breathed deeply, smelling her.

She shivered. She needed clothes, a shower, her routine, and...courage. Her fingernails dug into his back as she scanned the clutter strewn throughout the room. There, her robe, tossed over her duffel bags on the floor in the corner. The rest of the room... Oh my God.

A beer bottle sat on the dresser. Dirty socks piled beside the bed as if he'd just kicked them off and left them there. Two hangers hung on the closet doorknob. The nightstand... Wait. What?

Her aquarium sat against the far wall, filled with the broken fragments of her life. What did he intend to do with it? Would he torture her by destroying them beyond recognition? Would he be so cruel? She sat taller on his lap, her breasts dragging unnervingly against his chest, her voice cracking. "Why is that here?"

The gentle tiptoe of his fingertips along her arms aroused unnerving sensations over her skin. He nuzzled her neck. "It means something to you."

A lump swelled in her throat. It was just a career, but it signified the beginning and end of a normal life. She stared through blurry eyes at the one possession she would've lamented leaving behind.

As heartless and forceful as he was, nothing cruel lingered in his expression now. He studied her with daunting tenderness and an innocent sort of curiosity, and she felt knocked off balance. And naked, which had nothing to do with her lack of clothing. What if he threw the keepsakes away? Or used them against her? "It's just some broken memorabilia."

He held her in place as he massaged the soreness from her wrist. "It was the only sentimental belonging in your house, and you had it displayed." His touch moved over her wrists, gentle and attentive. "You liked to look at it, which tells me someone else destroyed it. Who?"

An angry pulse throbbed behind her eyes. Brent had taken a sledgehammer to everything that mattered to her. Except her career. That was on her. But she wasn't about to tell Van any of that. He didn't know about her ex-husband, and she couldn't afford to expose any more of herself beneath his perceptive eyes. So she decided on stubborn silence.

His hands moved to her calves and ankles, kneading the muscles, coaxing circulation, and easing her stiffness. She didn't trust his tenderness for a second, and her vulnerability escalated with each soothing caress.

He seemed to be distracted with his hands busy on her legs. She could slip off his lap and run.

And run where? The closet? Or she could endure his touch and try to figure him out. "What are you doing?"

"I got carried away. I never checked the cuffs, and they were too tight." His eyes were fixed on his fingers, but she sensed his attention was singularly focused on her. On her shallow breaths, the prickles bumping up her flesh. On what she might say next.

His profile was so painfully striking as he bowed his head, lips parted, face soft with affection. Any woman would've fallen into his bed at the crook of his finger. Hell, she'd offered the night she'd met him, and didn't that just dig under her skin? "You turned me down; then you returned and took me by force. Are you a serial rapist? A stalker? A murderer?" She trembled to put the space of the room between them but forced her eyes to his and whispered, "What are you?"

Something slipped over his expression, a menacing shield that turned his jaw to stone. He gripped her waist and set her on her feet, pushing her away. His elbows dropped to his knees as he watched her from beneath sharp brows, eyes creased in searing slits, voice quiet. "I'm the heir of torment, Amber."

She stepped back, hands shielding her groin and breasts.

He rose and held out his arms, unabashedly nude. "I'm the slippery footprints in your carpet. The creaking floor that steals air from your lungs. The hand that holds the gun." He paced through the room, snagging a pair of jeans from the floor, and met her eyes. "I'm the inescapable curse that caught you when you opened your door."

A shiver rippled through her and settled into her bones. Not a hint of arrogance in his words. Just the steady monotone of unresisting acceptance. As if he'd rehearsed that creepy speech or had at least given it a lot of thought.

She darted for her robe, shrugged it on, and turned to face him with a semblance of courage now that she was covered. "You don't have to be those things." She pushed back her shoulders and gave him a practiced response of her own. "You could be the nemesis of torment."

He pulled on the jeans, regarding her with an unreadable expression. "Is that what Dr. Michaels told you? Some cockamamie horseshit about confronting fear with its adversary, courage?"

How did he know who— Of course. Her call log. Yeah, that was exactly what Dr. Michaels had said. She refused to tell him so, and while seeing him clothed from the waist down should've mollified her somewhat, she couldn't relax. He was too unpredictable. He probably let her put the robe on just so he could tear it off and rape her again.

She glanced around the room, stepping backward and tripping over scattered clothes and shoes. Without thinking, she gathered up shirts, pants, and dirty socks and walked them to the hamper in the closet. "Am I your first?" First stalking? Kidnapping? Rape?

"No." The single word pierced through her back and stabbed her heart. "Your next door neighbor was my first. Her lover was my last. There were seven in between."

Nine slaves. What happened to them if he was still free to keep taking people? Her neighbors were still alive, obviously, but how?

His footsteps creaked the wood floors behind her, thankfully shifting farther away. She needed room to breathe, to focus. Squatting, she tackled the clothes on the floor. The scent of aftershave and the musk of man billowed around her as she stuffed the hamper, hung the belts, and searched for some order in which to place the pile of boots, sneakers, and sandals. But it wasn't enough to soothe her blooming panic. Her neighbors had survived him? They were alive and free right next door to her house? Had he let them go?

"Stop that." His strides neared, pausing right behind her. "Don't ever pick up my shit."

The harshness of his tone jerked her to her feet, and she spun to face him, chin raised. What she really wanted to do was cringe in the corner and hide from the seething brick wall, now wearing a t-shirt, jeans, and an icy glare.

She swallowed hard and found her voice. "My neighbors are your *old friends*? The reason you were on my porch?" Had there been any truth to his comment about watching them fuck on their table? She didn't know them, had never met them. "But they're free?"

"Liv and Joshua got away." His eyelids dipped halfway, shuttering his eyes, but his face softened, almost peaceful-like, as did his voice. "They all got away."

Why was he telling her this? To make sure she understood she was just one in a long line of violated bodies? She felt sick and inconsequential. Put in her place with a smart smack of reality. She was nothing to him but an easy fuck no one would miss.

But the others had escaped? Hope swelled through her insides, bright and full, lifting her nausea. He would grow tired of her neurotic quirks, if he hadn't already. Maybe he'd return her to her house before the mortgage defaulted. Maybe he'd kill her.

"Whatever you're thinking, *don't*. The circumstances with the others were different." He reached out and grabbed her chin, forcing her to look at him. "I ran a sex trafficking operation, Amber. Liv was the deliverer with too much damned power. *She* freed them. Not me."

"Oh my God." Her knees buckled, and she stumbled back into a clump of hanging clothes, clattering the hangers. *Sex trafficking. Slave.* Her lungs squeezed, and her blood drained to her feet. "I can't— Oh God, Van. Please, you can't do this."

"Goddammit," he snarled. "I don't do that shit anymore." He

wrenched her out of the closet by her arms and shoved her toward the stairs. "You're not going anywhere. You're *mine.*"

"What do you mean?" She tried to turn, to see his face, but he kept pushing her. "What do you want?"

His arm snagged her waist, pulling her back to his chest, and he half-carried her down the spiraling staircase. "You said you were ready. We're starting in the bathroom."

Ready for what? Would he rape her in the shower? Drown her in the bathtub? She twisted, her toes skidding over the steps as he descended. "What starts in the —"

A blast of sunlight hit her face. Floor to ceiling, the two-story wall of glass towered over her. Trees of every size and shade of green spread out as far as she could see. Trails wound through clutches of thick trunks. Any random person could've been out there, gawking at her through the windows.

She flinched away from the exposure and curled against his chest. She wasn't dressed properly. Her hair hung in strands around her face. Full-body tremors arrested her lungs and strangled the shriek in her throat. He hooked an arm beneath her knees, another at her back, and carried her through the room of windows.

She screamed then, clutching his shoulders and hiding her ugly tears in his neck. "The windows...the windows. Please..." She sobbed, desperate, miserable, her skin rippling with terror. "You have to close them." She clawed at his back, choking.

His arms dropped her, yanking her hands from their grip on his shoulders as she fell. Her back hit cushions on a couch with a full frontal view of the windows.

She scrambled backwards, fighting for air and losing her robe in her hellfire hurry to get away. He watched her, his brows sharpening into a *V* over narrowed eyes. Fuck him. She kept going, backing up and over the arm of the couch. Her ass crashed into a small table and sent it sprawling to the floor with her. The hard tiles bit into her tailbone, and tears burned her cheeks. *Escape. Hide.* Where?

The great room extended into an open kitchen and more windows. The stairs went to the loft and no escape. A door below the railing opened to...the bathroom?

Gasping, she jumped to her feet, staggered, and righted herself in a clumsy spin of naked limbs and jiggling tits. She was so fucking humiliated. Her chest contracted painfully, and her shoulders ached with tension.

The path to the door stretched out in an eternal walk through windowy hell. Eight running steps. Two sets of four. *Focus on that.* Her knees wobbled as she lurched forward, her body growing heavier with each step. Goddammit, she could do this.

His arm caught her waist and dragged her to the couch, flipping her to her back. She kicked and spit as he landed atop her, pinning her arms above her head and kneeling on her thrashing legs.

"Jesus." His Adam's apple bobbed, and his beautiful face contorted into a blur. "Calm the fuck down."

She roared and bucked beneath his crushing weight. "Let me go!"

"Are you possessed?" He leaned in, nose-to-nose, stealing her oxygen. "Are you going to start spitting Latin and tell me to lick you?"

His amused tone heightened her embarrassment and fueled the panic. The windows closed in, compressing her chest. She grabbed at the cushions and dug deep, for air, for strength, determined to have the last word. In one rage-filled burst of breath, she shouted, "Shove it up your ass, you cunting dick!"

He jerked back, and faster than the hammer of her heart, his fist slammed into her face. Fire burst through her cheek. Then the sun burned out.

# SIXTEEN

A fuckstorm of conflicting emotions pounded in Van's chest. He sat back on the couch and stared at the gorgeous, complicated woman beneath him. All it had taken was a swift punch to the cluster of nerves below her ear, and the panic attack went *poof*. Lights out. But every time he hit her, it cut open a squishy, remorseful spot inside him, one he didn't know existed.

This wasn't discipline training. It wasn't kinksual pain play. He wasn't experiencing any of the violent, fist-swinging rage Liv used to bring out in him. This was Amber, and hurting her when she was scared felt so goddamned unforgivable.

He rubbed a hand through his hair and jerked at the strands. Fuck, he needed to tread more delicately. Just like the others, the abduction and the sex had pissed her off, but the windows? He shifted to take in the peaceful landscape of wilderness, a view that soothed him on his worst days but terrified the fucking sense out of her.

If she were just dealing with the trauma of captivity, he wouldn't have been second-guessing himself. But the agoraphobic and OCD triggers added layers of complexity. Once upon a time, it might've been an interesting experiment to play with—tormenting her with sex and pain then forcing her outside—just to see which would break her first. But the appeal wasn't there. In its place coiled something else. He wanted her whole.

He climbed off the couch and yanked the drapes shut, buttoning up all the windows on the first story. He glanced at the top row of glass and sighed. Nothing he could do about those.

The open-plan cabin included a kitchen, sitting room, bathroom, and loft. The bathroom was the only windowless space. Except the garage... No, he wasn't ready for her to see his little hobby.

He returned to the couch where she lay exquisitely nude and lost in her dreams. The point of her stubborn chin softened in sleep. Her lips parted seductively, sloping into a small, slender nose. Collarbones pressed against delicate skin, and the fullness of her tits rose and fell with even breaths.

Her ribs were too sharply visible, but he'd fix that with a heartier diet. Despite being underweight, her sleek curves would've filled any man's spank bank. And other than her implants, there were no scars, no abnormalities, which made her poor self-image completely unfathomable. Time to reconcile that.

He gathered her in his arms and carried her to the bathroom. With her limp body perched on the counter, he slapped her face. "Wake up, sweetheart."

Her eyes fluttered, and a scowl bent her lips.

God, how he ached for her to smile at him with those captivating eyes all lit up and dimples denting her pretty cheeks. But why?

His chest tightened. He knew why, and it surfaced a childhood pang, the old starving need to see his mother gaze upon him with the same kind of smile, just once. Just a hint that she might've loved him. But all that memory offered was a boy's squashed hope and a dead mother.

He grunted deep in his chest just to hear the masculine sound of his very adult voice. He wasn't that needy boy anymore. He didn't have to depend on his mother or look to Liv for happiness. He could take what he needed from whomever he wanted.

He shook her, and her head rolled on her shoulders.

"Stop fucking hitting me." Her voice growled with grogginess, her hostile look lost through heavy blinks.

He supported her neck with a hand and softly traced her frowning lips. "When was the last time you smiled, Amber? A real smile?" Liv used to smile at him. When she was plotting his death.

Sitting on the counter, she glanced around the bathroom, orienting herself, as the tension in her body awakened beneath his fingers. When her startled gaze locked on the covered windows beyond the door, her shoulders relaxed, but her hands jumped to cover her tits and lap—and the dried come that coated her skin beautifully. Did she really think she could hide from him?

Gripping her wrists, he pinned them to the counter behind her and wedged his denim-clad hips between her thighs.

Strands of blond hair stuck to the tracks of dried tears on her face. Her brown eyes were so light beneath the glare of the vertical sconces they burned a golden hue. Even tinged pink from exhaustion, they radiated a blinding energy. Absolutely stunning.

Her brows pulled together as she regarded him. "My last smile?"

He nodded, and because her lips were so fucking tempting, he leaned in and kissed them. Just a tease of warm, gliding flesh.

She didn't kiss back but didn't pull away either as she spoke against his mouth. "You were on my porch and asked me if I was going to give you herpes."

The race of his heart drummed in his ears. She'd smiled at that? *He* had made her smile?

She cleared her throat and put an inch between them. "I should thank you for wearing a condom, but I'm not feeling very thankful at the moment."

Shifting her wrists to one hand and pressing them against her back, he opened the drawers beneath the vanity. "I'm clean of STDs, checked regularly. I'll show you the bloodwork later." He leaned back and gave her a few moments to scan the contents of the drawers.

One held six shades of brown hair dye and multiple boxes of each. Her eyebrows and lashes were dark, but since her cunt was shaved and her roots didn't show, he wasn't sure which was closest to her natural color. A home STD test kit waited in the other drawer.

Fascinating how her eyes dismissed the test and instead studied the boxes of dye like they held all the mysteries of the world.

He bent his knees so their faces were level. "I'm going to release your arms. You are *not* to cover yourself."

Her jerky nod didn't tear her eyes from the drawer. When he let go, her hands flew to her hair, her fingers dragging and catching on the tangled length. "You want to change the color." Her combing fingers sped up, shaking and restless. "You don't like it blond?"

Jesus. Her question was unexpected, but he should've seen it coming. It was her nature to please. To please him. And fuck no, he didn't like the bleached-out look against her warm skin. He wanted it the same dark brown as Liv's. And his mother's. Which was way too fucked up to admit out loud, even for him. "*You* don't like it."

Her eyes flashed to his, and her mouth formed a beautiful, gasping O. "I don't..." Her brows furrowed. Then her nostrils flared on an inhale, and her gaze hardened. "Why would you assume that?"

"You fuss with your hair like it's the bane of your existence." He shifted forward, sharing her breaths. "What you really want is to be accepted the way you are."

He'd pulled that last part out of his ass, but given the sharp jerk of her shoulders, he hadn't been off the mark.

"Which one is your natural color, Amber?" He tapped on the boxes.

"It'll take at least two boxes." She pointed to the deep brown black.

"That one."

His mother's color.

He pretended his stomach didn't just drop to the floor as he gathered the packages. He didn't let her wear a towel as she bent over the sink. Didn't fluster her with questions as she silently rubbed the dye into her hair. But he couldn't stop his fingers from tracing the bumps along her arched spine and watching her skin prickle beneath his touch.

While the dye set on her hair, she peed on the test stick and let him take her blood and swab her mouth and pussy. When he told her to turn around so he could swab her rectum, she backed into the wall, her eyes round and fearful. "No. Please. That's...that's...just no."

He stepped into her space, using his bulk to crowd her. "Ever had a dick in your ass?"

"No!" Her tone was furious and her eyes blazed, but her chin shifted subtly up then down.

He rested a forearm on the wall beside her head. "Did you know body language betrays a lie? For example, the liar might nod while denying she enjoys getting her ass stretched by a cock."

A swallow bobbed in her throat as she stared up at him with glassy eyes. She licked her lips. "It's been two years. I'm clean...there."

"Let's let the lab decide that. Turn around."

"I'll do it myself." A ragged whisper.

He glowered down at her, giving her an eternity of strained silence to contemplate the consequences if she continued to push him. With black dye smearing her forehead and her hair in a lump of wet mess on her head, she looked deliciously vulnerable. Her chin quivered for a breathless moment; then finally, she released her lungs and faced the wall.

Squatting behind her with the swab in hand, he pried her firm cheeks apart. She was so damned tense, and he refused to fight her. "Tell me about your autographed books."

The muscles in her ass twitched and relaxed. "They're just signatures."

"Personalized to other people. Widen your stance."

After a stubborn moment, her feet shifted apart.

He caressed the crease between her thigh and cheek, thrilling in the responsive quiver. "How did you get them?"

"I bought them on Ebay. I like the stories. And the sentimental signatures. The little notes for other people. Normal people."

Ah. "But you don't know them. They may very well be more fucked up than you and me combined." He slid two fingers between her now slightly less tense cheeks, exposed the sweet little pucker of her anus, and swabbed.

Enough time had lapsed between preparing the test swabs,

reading the instructions, and collecting the cultures. The color should be set. He patted her hip and stood. "Jump in the shower and rinse your hair while I package up the samples."

Still pressed against the wall, she looked over her shoulder at him with a strange expression on her face. Dark shadows bruised her eyes, her posture slumping. No doubt she was exhausted, hungry, and still working through her shock of the last couple hours.

He turned toward the vanity and listened to her footsteps shuffle to the shower.

Thirty minutes later, he stood behind her as she stared into the mirror. He'd used the hairdryer on her hair and let her keep the towel tied around her chest. Rich deep brown fell like a waterfall around her shoulders and curled damned near to her waist over the white terrycloth. The color highlighted the dark lashes fringing her eyes and illuminated the glow of her honey skin tone.

She was even more beautiful than his mother. Mesmerized, he couldn't look away. "What do you think?"

She glanced at his eyes reflected in the mirror, her fists clenched around the top edge of the towel. "What do you — ?"

"No." He gripped the counter's edge beside her hips and pressed his chest against her back, glaring at her. "I asked what *you* thought of it."

A noise squeaked in her throat, and she took a long moment to study her reflection. "It's...me."

His chest pinched. "And *you* outshine any ideal you try to cover yourself with." Her jaw tightened but he didn't miss the catch in her breath. He placed a kiss on her shoulder. "Let's go eat."

"Where's my robe?" Her hands flew between her legs, covering the gap in the towel with a fan of trembling fingers. "Dammit, Van. Eyes up here." She bent forward, trying to further hide her cunt.

He scrubbed a hand over his face. This was such bullshit. Obviously, he wasn't getting through to her. Fine. He would just force her to show him what the problem was. He dug beneath the sink, removed a large handheld mirror and set it on the wide space of counter beside the sink. Then he patted the oval of reflective glass. "Hop up. Legs spread. Knees that way." He pointed at the mirrored wall behind the vanity.

Her head instantly started shaking side to side.

He grabbed her jaw, cupping her cheeks and stilling her. "If you don't hop when I say hop, we're going for a walk." He jerked his head toward the door and the windows beyond. "Out there."

When he released her, she climbed onto the vanity, her limbs shaking and the cords taut in her neck. With her ass on the handheld mirror and her legs spread, her bent knees pressed against the wall mirror. It was an awkward position, but she'd just have to deal with it. He yanked away the towel and tossed it behind him.

Her hands started to move to her pussy, but she caught herself and clutched her knees instead. Good girl.

Leaning against her back, he trailed his fingers around her ribs, beneath her tits, crossed his arms around her waist, and hugged her to him. "How long have you been a shut in?"

"Two years, three months, and five days." She peeked at him from beneath her lashes.

He scraped his stubble against her cheek. "What happened?"

Her finger tapped restlessly on her knee. "I got scared."

"More scared than you are now?"

She nodded, swiftly and passionately.

Damn. He was no psychiatrist. But he knew how to manipulate to get what he wanted. "Does this" —he cupped her pussy— "have something to do with it?"

Her breaths quickened, and her face contorted in pain. Fuck, if she had a meltdown, he'd get nowhere. He moved his hand, placing it over her breastbone, and touched his lips to her ear. "I won't touch your pussy, but I want you to look at it and tell me what you see."

"Why?" Her eyes roamed his face in the mirror, pleading. "What are we doing?"

He was digging too deep, too fast, but he wasn't a patient man. "Let's call it an exorcism. I'm not officially trained, but I'm well-versed in demons."

She watched him, maybe hoping he'd change his mind. Or stalling. But she was a smart girl. She'd make the right choice.

Slowly, her eyes shifted, wandering the room. Then breath by breath, they lowered. Down, down, a little hitch in her chest brought them up before they lowered all the way.

He didn't prompt her, didn't move. He simply took in the splendor of the view between her legs.

Swollen, juicy lips formed a deep crevice of dark flesh, hiding the opening that had felt so fucking tight around his cock. Heat rushed to his groin, hardening him against his jeans and tightening his balls. The hood of her clit was still a beautiful shade of red from his teeth. He wanted to keep it that way.

Her voice shattered his reflective thoughts. "It's grotesque."

What the fuck? He bit down on his tongue to keep his roar from escaping. After a few deep inhales, he asked softly, "Who told you that?"

Her lips pressed together, and her body turned to shivering stone in his arms. After another battle of glares in the mirror, she looked at her hands where they were fisted on her knees. "Lots of people."

"I want names." Blood rushed outward from his core, heated and violent, hardening his muscles around her. "Start with the first fucker who fed you that bullshit."

"What are you going to do?"

"Whatever I want. Give me the name here or outside." He was one second from hauling her naked body through the woods. Thank Christ, his closest neighbor was two-hundred treed acres away. He trusted the waist-high trip wires he'd set up around the perimeter. One touch and the alarm in the cabin would blare. "Choose."

"Brent." Her voice was so soft he would've missed it if he weren't reading her lips.

"Who the fuck is Brent?"

She closed her eyes, opened them, and found his in the mirror. "My ex-husband."

He held his expression blank as his stomach bucked and burned. Not once in his research had he stumbled on an ex-husband. His first instinct was to blame the cocksucker for her disorders then find him and kill him. But he needed the story so he could show her how very wrong it was.

"Eyes on your pussy while you tell me exactly what he said. All of it, from start to finish."

She shifted her ass on the handheld mirror, which gave them both another angle of her beautiful cunt. When her gaze lowered to it, she clenched her teeth. "I've never talked about this."

He dropped his mouth to her shoulder and murmured, "I swear, Amber, I'll burn off my dick if I ever use this to hurt you." He meant it with a startling passion.

She kept her eyes on her pussy, but her gaze shifted inward as she leaned her back against his chest, her shoulders curling forward. "We were at an after-party for the semi-finalists in an international beauty pageant. I might've won the competition, but I let my stupid insecurities destroy my chances, my career, my marriage. My life."

# SEVENTEEN

Memories of that night two years ago built behind Amber's eyes as she stared at the flabby flesh between her legs. She wanted to hide it, to hide *from* it, but she couldn't look away. Exposing her shame and *talking about it* was fitting, right here, right now. When her fractured life couldn't sink any lower. With a man she should be repelling rather than attracting.

"It was the eve of the final competition." Her voice wavered. "All the icons of the pageant industry were there." The Master of Ceremony, former pageant winners, handpicked members of the media, and a host of celebrity models and photographers. "It was a night to impress and network with the who's who among the business."

Van's chest pressed against her back, centering her, his attentive silence an unexpected support. Despite being physically abusive, not once had he degraded her verbally. Wrong or right, it was enough to propel her. "Tawny was there."

"Tawny?"

She tensed. Oh fuck, why had she mentioned her sister? Would he go after her next?

His palm caressed her belly, a vulnerable place to touch her. *He'd punched her there.* So why did the intimacy of his hand feel so good?

He kissed the juncture of her neck and shoulder. "If she means something to you, I won't hurt her. I'm only interested in what happened."

"She means a great deal to me."

"A best friend? Or a sister?" Understanding warmed his voice. He had no reason to fake that. He could've simply forced her to answer.

"My only sibling. She's a mid-level fashion model, dabbled in pageantry, but didn't have the same success. She was always at my side."

Clinging to Amber's circle of friends, looking for the big break in her own career.

He pushed her hair over one shoulder, and his lips brushed the back of her neck, raising hundreds of tiny bumps across her skin.

She cringed, but didn't lean away. "Brent was entertaining a crowded table with his usual charm when he asked me to grab him a beer. That was his thing. Work the crowd while I...I was an introvert." Her stomach turned, and bile simmered through her chest. "When I returned, more people had gathered around him, and he was...fla— flapping his arms in the air. Men and women, dressed in tuxes and evening gowns, were doubled over, howling with laughter and wiping tears from their eyes."

Van's chest hardened behind her as she contemplated the ugly dark folds of skin around her vulva. "I knew it had something to do with me, something awful." It usually did. Her voice strained. "He was a crowd pleaser. Everybody loved him." Which was why she fell so hard for him, so fast, at the naive age of eighteen. Her head bent forward, her entire body aching, as visible tremors coursed through her. "Always the center of attention. Even when it was at my expense."

"Why?" His sharp tone cut through her. "What did he gain from that?"

Her spread legs shook beneath her hands, and her heart twisted painfully. She searched for the right answer, the one Dr. Michaels had helped her come to terms with. "We met in high school and married at eighteen, right about the time I entered the world of pageantry. Things were good. Better than good." A flutter brushed against the ache in her heart and faded just as quick. "Time and the stress of my career changed him."

By age thirty, Brent's physique had softened with extra weight. He never looked less handsome to her, but it bothered him, especially as her body continued to firm and tighten with her pursuit of fitness modeling. "He grew angry and unhappy, and I was the target for his bitterness, a way to redirect his insecurities from himself. That realization didn't come until later. At the time, I felt like a constant disappointment."

Her legs squeezed closed, protectively, but Van caught her thigh and gave her a warning pinch on the tender skin inside her knee.

When his hand returned to her belly, she let her legs fall open and swallowed around the surging emotion. "He nitpicked and scrutinized *everything*, convinced me to...uh...well, to get this awful boob job, bleach my hair, and bake in a tanning bed. I wanted to please him, to absorb his sadness, so I guess I let him slowly transform me. But his insults grew crueler, more public."

It was when Brent stopped looking her in the eye, when he

stopped looking at her at all, that hurt the most. To think she'd kept the light *on* back then, hoping he would *see* her, so driven to please him. She was so goddamned tragic.

Van's thumb shifted upward, along her sternum, and traced circles in the hollow of her throat. "He's fucking weak."

"Says the man who hits women." She braced herself for a strangling squeeze of his fist.

The thumb stilled, and his teeth lowered to her nape, scratching gently, his breath shooting sparks of heat down her spine. "I'm far worse than your sissy bitch of an ex. Don't ever forget that."

Her spine tingled anew, itching to put space between them. At the same time, it'd been years since she felt this at ease with her body. Not that she was relaxed. Far from it. Hell, she was sitting on a mirror with her legs open. *With the lights on.* Her muscles ached and trembled, and her hips burned. But the pain was a startling distraction. Her vision wasn't consumed by black snow. Her heart wasn't flat-lining. The absence of a looming breakdown made her head spin.

He kissed her neck and placed his palms on her inner thighs, widening her legs. "Continue."

Cool air drifted over her labium, bringing with it the chill of memory. "Right." She cleared her throat. "Well, I approached the table, and dozens of eyes flew in my direction, leering, crinkling with laughter. Lowering to my groin." Which had suddenly felt obscenely pronounced in the tight satin of her gown.

Truth was, she'd grown insecure about the way her lips had stretched over the years, enough to stupidly mention it to Brent while he was fucking her the night before. A desperate attempt to seek his approval. His only response had been a series of grunts.

Tears rose up, then and now. She exhaled through it. "Brent was too busy flopping his bent arms like a chicken and squawking hysterically to notice my return. 'Flapping wings,' he said. God, it was...so loud. So fucking mean." When he'd finally made eye contact with her, he leaned over to Tawny. *I feel bad for her. You should see how the skin hangs. It's grotesque.*

Sharp pain seared through her sinuses, stabbing needles behind her eyes. "Then he played the role of concerned husband, asking if anyone could recommend a...a g-good labial plastic surgeon to help me with my...*problem*." She whispered the last word as if that would make it less real.

It had been a defining moment. The accumulation of all his hurtful words, the years of insecurities that came with posing before judges, and her lifelong battle with OCD had mounted inside her, pressurizing, as she stood amidst the laughter, moments from losing her polished demeanor.

Van tilted his head. "You looked up images on the Internet, right? You would've seen how completely normal your cunt is."

She wobbled on the counter, nodding. "Those pictures made me feel worse. Outside of the few deformities posted on medical sites, the Internet is full of porn and beauty and perfection. Normal thirty-year-old women don't post those kinds of images." She tried to close her legs, and his grip on her thighs stopped her.

"Then you recognize the difference between a deformity and an eighteen-year-old porn twat." His hands found her fingers and moved them to her inner thighs, holding them there. "What did you say to Brent after the surgery comment?"

Van's nonjudgmental interest bolstered her, and she sat taller, less shakier. "It was clear he had described my vagina to a room packed with my colleagues, people who could make or break my career. In that single lonely heartbeat, I woke up. I realized he didn't love me. How could he? You don't treat someone you love with such vicious cruelty."

Van shifted against her, and a swallow sounded in his throat. "Love and hate are closely related expressions of the same intensity. Both require passion, and neither follows logic. If he didn't love you, he would've treated you with shrugging detachment."

His response resonated with what she knew of his own volatile behavior. She didn't *know* him, but she imagined he could love someone as fiercely as he hurt them. It would take a strong, willing person to survive his brand of passion.

With his hands caressing her fingers and thighs and his face nuzzling her shoulder, his affection momentarily eclipsed his earlier abuse. But he would hurt her again. She needed to pin that to the forefront of her mind and never confuse possessiveness and control with love. The way she had with Brent.

A glance at her pussy transported her back to the ballroom, and the remembered shock of what happened dragged her tongue over numb words. "The beer I held out dropped to the floor as I repeated out loud, 'Flapping wings.' It was the first time I'd heard that particular insult, and I wish I would've yelled it, owned it, with fucking venom. Brent didn't bother to turn around, simply glanced over his shoulder and told me to fetch him another beer."

Van's fingers wove through hers, digging into her thighs, and his breaths grew sharper, faster. "Amber—"

"Let me finish." She wanted to relive her anger, feel it thrash through her body and feed on its strength. "Tawny leaned back in her chair beside him and asked with drunken liveliness, 'Your lips are so stretched you can fly with them? Really, Amber? You gonna fly across the stage tomorrow and collect the crown with a sweeping vaginal thrust?'"

Van's eyes flashed to hers in the mirror. "I hope you smacked the mouth off that whore."

She flinched. "She was drunk." Tawny had a sick mother just like her and would always be her sister, the girl she raised and loved unconditionally. Even when Tawny stood by Brent during the divorce. And after. The heavy, achy weight of responsibility pressed down on her chest. "You promised not to hurt her."

"I won't." His gaze didn't waver from hers. "Unless you ask me to."

"Never." She unloaded the gravity of her heart in that single impassioned word.

His arms fell away, his body heat gone. She watched his reflection pace the large bathroom, hands in his hair, red splotches creeping from the neck of his t-shirt. Even when irritated, he moved with a swagger in his step. The lift of his arms raised the hem of his shirt, exposing the cut *V* of his abs and the bounce and flex of cotton-stretching muscle. His jeans rode so low on his trim hips a dark line of hair surfaced above his belt.

On the next pass, he slipped a toothpick in his mouth and stopped behind her, his expression turbulent. He gripped her thighs, holding her legs open, and gave her the full potency of his silver eyes and growly voice. "You should've yanked up your dress and showed those fuckers your beautiful pussy."

Oh God, he was fuming. On *her* behalf. It should've scared her, but in that fleeting moment, she trusted he wouldn't turn his anger on her. "I did. I removed my panties and ripped my designer gown from ankles to waist, right up the middle."

His eyes widened, and his mouth hung open, the toothpick protruding from the corner. She liked that. When his lips tilted in a lopsided grin, she loved it, so much so she wanted to smile with him. But she could still feel her fury from that night, her blood simmering at the surface, scorching her skin.

"I gathered the satin fabric behind me, turned in a circle, and let the room have their fill of my flapping wings." Brent's face had turned ashen, but she'd been too heartbroken to care. Somehow, she'd managed to grab her panties from the floor and walk out of there with the confidence of a beauty queen, head high, long strides, one heel before the other, hands relaxed at her sides. The nervous laughter of two hundred people had followed her out the door. "I left Brent that night. I was disqualified. Tried to enter other pageants for the next year. I never stepped on stage again."

"Your disqualification remains a mystery on the Internet. No one talked to the press? No camera phone shots of you in your ripped gown?"

Every nerve in her body bristled on high alert. Of course, he'd researched her. He was a *stalker*. "The event was an invite-only affair for the semi-finalists. Since the pageant hadn't aired yet, the attendees were confidential. No cameras allowed. After, the pageant officials were tenacious about keeping the details hushed." They hadn't wanted to tarnish their reputation with the disgrace of a contestant.

Van's palms slid down her thighs and paused an inch from her outer lips. "No one has seen this since that night?"

She shook her head. "Not even a doctor," she said absently, distracted by the view of her pussy framed with the thumbs and fingers of his huge hands. It looked the same but strangely...protected. What if Van had been there that night, standing beside her with his broad shoulders, alluring scar, and intimidating eyes? Would they have laughed then? Would she have cared what they thought? Such an absurd, disturbing notion, yet imagining it sparked a burst of warmth in her chest.

"When I look at your tiny pink lips," he said softly, "I want to slide my tongue between them and suck the sweetness from your tight hole. I crave your taste, the velvety feel of you in my mouth and around my cock." His eyes found hers in the mirror, a smoldering collision. His pupils dilated into bottomless pools of danger, pulling her in. "Your pussy is exquisite, Amber. A perfect mold of flesh and fantasy, of throbbing blood and healthy life. Nothing compares to the grip of your wet heat. *Nothing*."

He ground his erection against her back, but she didn't think he was trying to be lewd. Nor did she believe he'd force her to have sex on the heels of revealing her humiliating story. He was merely proving his words the one way he knew how, and she wanted to believe them.

When he stepped away and handed her the towel, she knotted it around her and stared at his outstretched hand. *Don't let your guard down.* With a steady breath, she gripped his fingers and followed him out of the bathroom to the kitchen.

The drapes on all the ground-level windows kept her breathing at an even tempo, but the layers of dust on the furniture, the crusty dishes on the counter and in the sink, and black smudges on the tiles ratcheted her pulse to ear-ringing anxiety. She pulled away from his hand and sprinted to the sink, the tremors in her legs numbing her feet.

Where to start? Oh God, she would never get this place clean enough. She ducked her head, searching for the soap, the scrub brushes, the dishwasher... Where were the damned—?

His hand wrapped around her throat and yanked her back. Deep grooves formed in his forehead, his eyes narrowed and steely. "Sit the fuck down." He shoved her by her neck until her ass hit a chair at the table, seating her.

Utensils and canisters cluttered the counters in no logical order. Streaks of grime coated the cabinet doors. God only knew what she'd find if she opened them. Her lungs tightened, her inhales shallowing, coming faster.

His fingers returned to her throat, forcing her chin up. Frustration hardened his eyes, but it didn't channel to the soft rumble of his voice. "There's no way a room full of shallow fuckwads turned you into this. When did it start?"

Nothing was that simple with her. "I have—" She choked around his grip, and he dropped his hand to her lap, squatting before her. She coughed, glaring at him. "I have a genetic connection to agoraphobia, OCD, and substance abuse." *Don't look at the burnt splashes of food on the stove. Don't look at it.* "My mother predisposed me to some nasty traits." And she was seconds away from having a full-on freak-out amidst his nuclear level of disgusting clutter. She leaned into his face, her chest pumping with heavy breaths. "You should probably return me. I'm no good."

His jaw set. "If you lose your shit, I'm tossing you on the porch." He stabbed a finger at the front door.

In that moment, she despised him. Her eyes and chest ached, and she wanted nothing more than to stick it to him by stepping over that porch and running to safety. But there was no safety out there. Her safe place was unreachable, and once the mortgage foreclosed, it would be gone.

He stood. "You're going to sit there and tell me about the anxiety while I fix dinner."

When his back turned, she closed her eyes, shielding herself from the cluster-fuck-chaos of his kitchen, and drew a ragged breath. "Eighty percent of patients with my conditions have first degree relatives who suffer from panic attacks. My mother is a doozy of mental illnesses and was committed to Austin State Hospital when I was twenty-two. Tawny was twelve when I took her in."

The glide of his feet over tiles drifted toward the fridge. "Does your sister have these conditions?"

"She has her own obsessions, but nothing like my mom and me." Strange how she could talk about this with a man who would hit her as readily as kiss her. It took twelve phone calls with Dr. Michaels before she'd opened up. Probably because she wasn't trying to impress Van. He'd brought her crazy into his home, so he could suffer the ugly details or fuck off.

"Where's your dad?" he asked.

"He left when Tawny was a baby. He couldn't handle it." She didn't blame him for leaving her mother, but leaving her and Tawny? That was unforgivable.

She rested her closed eyes on her hands, elbows propped on the table. "I used to manage the anxiety with medication until I became addicted to the pills. With the help of one of my therapists, I learned how to focus it outward. Pageantry and modeling was a distraction." Though not a healthy one.

Dishes and silverware clattered behind her. Then the microwave beeped four times, grounding her.

"After the night in the ballroom, I held myself together for three months. Brent and Tawny had been my only potential support network, and when I lost them, I had no one. Still, I bought that house, applied for competitions, and taught myself leather-crafting to keep busy." To keep herself sane. She crossed and uncrossed her legs beneath the table. "Then the panic attacks started. The first one happened in a clothing boutique where I ran into a group of models who had been there that night. When they saw me, they laughed and whispered. But they made sure I heard what they were saying."

The panic attack had left her crippled and sobbing on the floor for hours. The manager had to drive her home. "I never returned to that store or any other boutique again. One by one, the attacks surfaced in different places. I'd see someone leer at me at the gym, smell something in a store that reminded me of that night, and an attack would drop me to my knees. I couldn't go back to those places, and my world grew smaller and smaller. Eventually, I stopped going anywhere."

The chair beside her screeched across the floor, and the scent of chopped onion, peppers, and cilantro tickled her nose. She opened her eyes to find a platter of folded shells resembling enchiladas.

"Enfrijoladas." He cut into a corner with a fork and held it to her mouth. "Corn tortillas dipped in bean sauce. Open."

"You just made this?" He could cook?

"Last night. For you."

A shiver licked down her spine, a reminder that he'd been stalking her, planning her capture. "I'm not hungry." How many calories were in the shavings of white cheese alone? Two days worth, at least.

"This" — he wiggled the fork— "or the door."

She slammed her teeth together. She was a captor's dream. No steel bars needed here. Just threaten her with an open door, and she would fall at his feet. Well, she wouldn't make it that easy for him. "Four bites."

He smirked and pushed a glass of water across the table so she could reach it. "Three."

Tension vibrated her shoulders. Three was fewer calories, but it wasn't *four*. His smirk meant he knew how much she depended on that number. So much for being difficult. She opened her mouth, too tired to dwell on numbers or the fact that he was creeping her out by feeding her.

He slid the fork between her lips, and a zest of full-bodied seasonings mingled over her tongue. Spicy but not too hot, the taste of Mexico melted in her mouth. He watched her with an expectant expression as she chewed.

His last name was Quiso. His pale gray eyes looked European, but with his dark hair and tanned skin, he could easily have a little Mexican in his woodpile.

After he fed her two more bites, she asked, "Did your mother teach you how to cook?"

He laughed, but there was no humor in the clipped tumble of huffs. "If Isadora couldn't smoke it or inject it, she didn't bake it."

Oh. He'd said she was dead. She gripped the towel covering her lap, curiosity scrabbling at her tongue. "Your father—"

The fork clanked against the plate. He stared at the table, eyes shuttering as his silence tightened around her. She tensed for the impact of his fist. But what he hit her with was far more jarring.

"He was a human trafficker like me." His empty voice coiled the tension in the room. "Brought me into the business when I was twenty-five." He looked up. "When Austin appointed him Chief of Police."

She stopped breathing, her head spinning with the biggest news story to come out of Austin. *Police Chief linked to the kidnapping and rape of two missing persons.*

"Eli Eary," she whispered.

"Good ol' Dad. Quality role model for Austin's youth." Disgust and sarcasm layered his tone, but it also held an edge of sadness.

His father trafficked slaves. His mother was a drug addict. She looked at him, *really looked* into his insidious silver eyes. What must they have seen in his thirty-something years? Had he spent his entire life in a dark light, dragging the sins of his parents behind him? How could he not be anything but fucked up?

*Don't make excuses for him, Amber.*

He dug into the food and spoke while he chewed. "You followed the news story?"

"Some. He kidnapped that girl and held her for years. And the football player from Baylor." Enslaved them in a suburban house doing unimaginable things to them. "They shot him."

"Yep." He leaned back in the chair and leveled her with his luminescent gaze. "Don't remember their names, do you?"

She shook her head, dread creeping into her bones.

He chewed, swallowed. "Liv Reed and Joshua Carter."

*Liv and Joshua got away. They all got away.*

The trembling started in her chest and rippled to her arms and legs. They lived right next door all this time? The reason he was on her porch?

She could guess why he'd returned for them, and it slammed her heart into a laborious frenzy. Even if she could return home and save her mortgage, would she feel safe living beside Liv and Joshua? Van would come back for them. For her.

"You should really get out more." He raised a glass of water to his lips, grinning.

She choked, wanting to argue this unbelievable story. "The news reports said he worked alone." Her voice strangled, rising in pitch. "There wasn't any mention of a son."

He drained the glass, set it down, and leaned in to stroke her jaw. "Because I don't exist."

# EIGHTEEN

As Amber paled and scooted her ass away inch by inch, Van questioned the brilliance of telling her who he was. He put his elbows on the kitchen table and rubbed his aching head. Despite how familiar he'd become with her strained fearful look, she now stared at him through new eyes. He already told her he'd trafficked slaves. Apparently, connecting him to the infamous Eli Eary had sent her over the edge. Literally.

She'd scooted so far, she fell over the side of the chair and crashed to the floor, giving him a glorious view of all her taut little lines and curves beneath the splayed towel. He bit his lip, halting his grin. Her clumsiness in these frazzled moments was such a contrast to the image of her decorously posed on a stage.

With a huff, she jumped to her feet and retied the knot at her chest. "What do you mean, you don't exist?"

*Here we go.* He'd opened the door. Might as well give her a tour of the shit hole. He dug a toothpick from his pocket and slid it between his teeth. "Eli Eary—we called him Mr. E—never mentioned me to anyone in his lawful life."

"Why not? You're his son."

"The bastard son of his first *slave*. Not something you brag about over donuts at the police station." He gnawed on the toothpick. "And in his criminal life, I only existed to the slave buyers—who don't talk because they're dead. And the slaves—who don't talk because they killed the buyers."

She touched her throat, her voice disbelieving. "That's how the others got away?"

Should he worry about her connecting Liv's escape with hope for her own way out? Nah. She couldn't even look at the windows, let alone step outside. And by the time she overcame the agoraphobia, she would be too attached to him to leave. "Yep." Liv had been a very naughty girl, but her ability to outsmart him and Mr. E lifted his chest with pride. "I didn't know Liv had freed the others until I started watching her."

"*Stalking* her." She flashed him a reproving glower. For long moments, she didn't move, but she seemed to be calming herself. It was a fascinating thing to watch. The heave of her torso slowed, and her hands loosened around the knot of the towel. She had no idea how strong she was. "You said you were twenty-five when he brought you into the...business. Does that mean you and your mom had escaped before that?"

Not quite. He smiled as his acidic existence burned him from the inside out. "Mr. E took my mother from a US-Mexican border ghetto when she was sixteen. He broke her, impregnated her, and returned her where he'd found her." She'd been his first, after all. His guinea pig. And a pregnant slave, so far beyond mentally ruined, had no value on the market. So he'd thrown her away like a used condom.

She stepped toward the kitchen table and sat two chairs away. "And you went with her?"

"Yeah." The unwanted spawn. He rolled the toothpick with his tongue and relaxed against the chair back as every organ inside him twisted and turned. He'd only ever shared this with Liv, and he'd been weak from her bullet when the truth spilled out with his blood.

Her slim eyebrows pulled in, her face pinched in thought. "What did her family do when she returned? Wasn't there retaliation? An investigation?"

He laughed and shook his head. "My mother was a run away, and we lived in a *colonia*. The dumping grounds for America's uneducated, discarded waste. No drinking water, no working sewers, no *law*, and certainly no care for someone else's problems." A wave of bitterness tightened his muscles. It was no wonder he took pleasure in human suffering.

She gripped the knuckles of one hand. He waited for the four cracking pops, a mechanism he'd noticed she turned to when she was upset. But they never came. She flattened her palms over her thighs, staring at them, and spoke quietly. "You were cursed at birth to be fucked-up. Just like me." A ragged inhale. "Honestly, I'm surprised you're so..." She closed her eyes.

He leaned toward her, his heart knocking at his ribs with anticipation to hear the rest of that thought. "I'm so...what?"

Her eyes cut to his, and she shrugged. "You're smart."

The compliment curled through him, loosening his shoulders and thickening his tongue. He'd never considered himself smart. He researched anything and everything that interested him, but he certainly wasn't educated in the traditional sense. "Mr. E taught me what I needed to know." How to read expressions, lure the unsuspecting, calculate human reaction, and how to break the strongest will. "But I couldn't tell you what the square root of sixteen is."

She moved her mouth as if tasting her precious number. Then her eyes glimmered. "Liar."

True, but that was the extent of his math skills. Feeling playful, he smirked. "You know what the square root of *us* is?"

She cocked her head and wrinkled her nose. Then her lips curved, dimpling her cheeks. "Fucked-up." The strength of her brilliant smile hit him smack in the chest with a shimmering burst of warmth and connection.

He was so fucking tempted to grab his chest and trap the feeling there, that strange exuberant joy. Whatever his expression held made her lips soften. The seam of her mouth slowly separated, the rosy flesh clinging together then letting go. Something was inching its way into the air, energizing the space between them, and she was two chairs too far away.

Carefully, he slid back from the table. Her shoulders tightened, and her chest expanded on an inhale. He stood and covered the distance between them with lazy deliberate steps, marking her subtle breaths. When he reached her, he lowered to his knees.

Her gaze dipped to his mouth, and her tongue darted out to tap her upper lip. "What's with the toothpicks?"

The question stiffened his back. He'd acquired the habit as a means to intimidate. Nothing conveyed *scary motherfucker* like removing something from his mouth, something he would've appeared to be concentrating on, to focus all of his attention on a frightened little slave.

No way would he remind her what he was and ruin the moment. "It used to be a tree trunk. I'm so badass I chewed it down to a toothpick."

She shook her head, gifting him with another sweeping smile.

His dick swelled. He flexed his thighs but couldn't shake the grip of his arousal. It surged blood down the length of his cock and lowered his voice to a gruff rumble. "Admit it. Ain't nothing sexier than me on your ass, gnawing a toothpick."

She reached up and flicked the protruding end, making it quiver like an arrow. Then she exploded with laughter. "Yeah, you're soooo hot when you have wood in your mouth."

Aw God, the husky rhythm of her laugh could light a fire in a cold dead heart. "I'd rather have *you* in my mouth. Specifically, your perfect, tight cunt."

A flush crept across her cheeks, but her touch lingered, brushing against the toothpick and slipping to the corner of his lips. Her fingernails scraped the stubble on his cheek, and her eyes followed the movement, lashes heavy and dark against her glowing skin.

This tenderness...it was like nothing he'd ever experienced. It made his heart race and his fingers shake. It both alarmed and invigorated him. He didn't want it to end.

He held still, aching for her kiss. Not to take her lips but to give her his, just to experience a moment of surrender, to be at her mercy. Throughout the toxic span of his sexual history, he'd only had one relationship, and Liv had fought him through every damned interaction. He'd never allowed another to initiate a kiss, not even when he was used as a boy or later as a whore. What would it feel like to receive genuine affection?

Her face neared, perhaps an unconscious movement, and her exhales caressed his chin. He knew what this was. Stockholm Syndrome was a foregone conclusion, a symptom of being captured. But that didn't stop him from parting his mouth, hoping for something that couldn't be explained away by a criminal psychologist. The toothpick dangled between his teeth, seconds from falling. She plucked it away and replaced it with her lips.

Every cell in his body zeroed in on the soft glide of her mouth, the gentle suckle of his lower lip, and the taste of spices and honey swirling over his tongue. His entire fucking world flipped inside out, everything he knew about intimacy crumbling away to be replaced by something softer, farther-reaching, and intensely terrifying.

He tried not to fall, told himself it was dangerous, but her kiss grew in confidence, demanding more, stretching so fucking deep she was swallowing him whole. If she reached his soul, he would've given it to her. If the cabin burned down around him, he wouldn't have noticed. He was a goner.

Her jaw stretched wider, and he opened his, letting her explore his mouth with licks and nibbles. Her little bites stroked a feverish heat over his skin, and his brain melted into useless mush. Soon, he couldn't feel his body at all, didn't know where he was, as every sensation concentrated on the warmth of her lips, the dance of her tongue, the beat of her pulse beneath his palm.

Ah, there were his hands, wrapped around her neck, his fingers a restraint made of flesh and bone. He savored the acceleration of blood pumping through her carotid, the delicate sinews yielding to his will, his grip immovable yet soft and cherishing.

His experiment in surrender over, he moved on autopilot, reclining back and taking her with him. As he wrapped her legs around his waist, she tried to break the kiss, but he was in charge now. His mouth was insistent, his tongue holding hers down. His hands found her ass beneath the towel, and his fingers curled into hard, hot muscle.

No doubt she would fight him. Her muscles would go rigid, her jaw would stiffen, and—

Whoa. Her body liquefied against his chest, her arms folding around his shoulders. Her tongue followed his, and a quiet moan vibrated in her throat.

Fuck him, but her submissiveness was her most powerful compulsion, one that would haunt him and possess him until he owned her body, soul, and tangled mind. He ground his hips against the bared apex of her thighs, dragging her closer with his hands on her hips.

They kissed for a delirious eternity, their breaths fusing in a caress of wet licks over heated flesh. He wanted more, his cock wanted in her, and his groan vocalized his need. He flexed his ass and rocked his erection against his zipper, against her cunt, his jeans too damned itchy and tight.

She wriggled in his lap and sucked on his tongue, seemingly as lost as he was. Until she tensed, silencing their smacking sounds.

No telling where her mind just went. His thoughts floated somewhere between *Fuck her now* and *Don't fuck her up*. He let her pull back and grimaced as she shifted on his aching, swollen cock.

Her lips, glistening and swollen, taunted him as she spoke. "What are your plans for Liv and Joshua?"

A sour taste hit the back of his throat. He stalked them because he was sick. Obsessed. Lonely. But more than that, because they had access to a life he wanted. *Sweet, round face. Brown curls. Precious. Innocent. His only living blood.*

He couldn't admit to Amber how much a relationship with his daughter meant to him, how Livana was the only pure thing that had come from his miserable life. Maybe Amber wouldn't say anything out loud, but he didn't want to see the doubt in her eyes, the glaring rebuttal. *You're just like Mr. E. You're not good enough to be a father.*

A fission of pain ripped open behind his eyes. "I wasn't going to take them. Or hurt them." He hated the desperate edge in his voice, the frantic need for her to believe him. He gripped her neck. "I told you I'm out of the slave business."

"Then what am I?"

What *was* she? Broken like him but better, brighter, an unexpected discovery, like the gems in her shattered crowns. "The greater half of fucked-up squared."

She sighed. "I think your math needs some work." She glanced down at the flat expanse of her tummy where it lay bare beneath the separation of the towel.

The cleft of her pussy pressed so seductively against the ridge of his strained jeans. She ran a hand down her torso, and her shoulders bunched. A frown gripped her face, the only warning he had, before she shoved off his lap and stumbled back.

What the fuck just happened? "What's wrong with you?"

Her face twisted, and she hugged herself. "My stomach hurts."

He studied her tightening posture, bent spine, and defensive tuck of her arms. "Maybe you need to take a shit."

She cringed. "You did *not* just say that."

He'd bet his right testicle she'd never so much as farted in front of her ex, let alone discussed her bowel movements with him. He shrugged. "A good dump always makes me feel better."

"You seriously don't have any boundaries."

Boundaries were for the scared and weak. "At least I'm not constipated. Want a laxative?"

"I'm not—" She stomped a bare foot on the floor four times and squeezed her arms around her abdomen. "You're right. I need to go to the restroom."

Because he didn't have an iota of desire to watch her shit, he stood outside the closed bathroom door and gave her some privacy—the *only* privacy he would ever allow her. Hands in his pockets, mind at peace, he marveled at how much warmer the cabin felt with her presence. Someday, she might consider it her home, her safe place, with him. But it would take time to trust her not to hurt herself, to not harm him.

As he waited, that thought began to niggle. Nothing in the bathroom could be used as a weapon, and the door didn't have a lock, but something didn't feel right. She hadn't just asked to use the bathroom. She'd scowled at her body and triggered some thought that had her hugging her belly.

He grabbed the knob and hit the door open with his hip.

She was bent over the toilet, hacking quietly, too softly, as if she'd invented the art of graceful barfing. Even then, he might've blamed his cooking if she hadn't lowered her eyes to the floor and pawed at her hair with anxious hands. If she were truly sick, she would've ignored him, too focused on the pain.

She solidified his suspicion when she opened her mouth. "You trying to poison me?"

Her tone was too inwardly focused, too ashamed. If she thought he'd put something in the food, she would've gone at him with fire in her eyes.

His hands clenched and unclenched. He should've known. She was too fucking thin. "You're a puker."

She wiped her mouth with the back of her hand and said to the floor, "I never asked you to take me." She looked up and shouted, "Or my fucked-up problems!"

Fuck that. She was *his* to care for, to revere and keep safe. He didn't care what her *problems* were. He wouldn't allow her to treat her body this way. "Where is the girl who had enough pride in herself to stand on a stage and invite judgment? I *demand* more from you."

"Let me give you a quick lesson on vanity." She seethed through her teeth. "It's sensitive and shallow. If you overfeed it, you'll make it puke."

That mouth would get her nowhere. If she was going to behave like a brat, he'd treat her like one. He released a frustrated breath, calming himself, and removed her toothbrush from the drawer. "Brush your teeth."

She gave him a nasty little glare then did as she was told. She must've been counting in her head, because she muttered "Four" around the foam of toothpaste each time she moved the bristles to a new tooth.

He pinched the bridge of his nose. She was fucking exhausting, and he hadn't even begun the discipline that was coming for her unacceptable behavior.

When she finished rinsing, he yanked the towel from her body. Before she could protest, he threw her over his shoulder and hauled her out of the bathroom with a firm grip on her ass and thigh. She kicked and punched as he carried her through the sitting room. Her tiny fists hammered his back, propelling him through the kitchen and into the mudroom.

The tall cabinet held everything he needed. Pinning her tiny, bucking body to his shoulder with one arm, he gathered rope, cuffs, condoms, and his favorite whip. Then he reached for the door that led to the woods out back.

A painful wail tore from her lungs, her nails clawing his back. "What...what are you— No, I can't. Can't go out." Her breathing came in choking stops and starts. "What are...you doing?"

He'd spent seven years breaking people. Could the same methods un-break someone? It would certainly make her think twice before puking again. "Punishment, darling." He threw open the door and stepped outside.

She convulsed in his arms, totally missing out on the surreal skyscape, the fading mist of violet clouds, and the full moon ascending above the horizon of timber. As she strangled on her breathless protests, he strode toward the tree line and into the twilight of what might be the longest night of her life.

# NINETEEN

Amber's screams clawed their way into Van's heart as she flailed and sobbed in her wrist bindings. Fucking hell, why did he care? He wasn't an unfeeling man, but his emotions usually resulted in a ruthless, more external reaction, like a black eye on the person who caused them. This unexpected compassion smacked the damned sense out of him. What the hell was he supposed to do with that?

He cinched the last knot around the tree and recalled what he'd read about agoraphobia. Systematic desensitization was the term many articles used, and his takeaway was simple. *Expose her to the phobia. Let her panic, watch her freak out, and don't let her give in to her response, which is avoidance.*

It was supposed to be a gradual process, but easing into things wasn't his style. And while he could've handled Amber's punishment inside the cabin, she needed to learn how to cope with and overcome the fear. He wanted to become the *habitual response* she turned to.

His own purpose hadn't wavered. Helping her would help him. A whole, recovered Amber would prove he was a better man, that he could be a good father. If he succeeded, she would stand by his side and maybe even *hold his hand* when he met his daughter for the first time.

Hanging from a massive horizontal branch by her arms, she kicked her feet through the dirt, contorting her torso and gulping for air as if each breath were her last. A string of hyperventilating shrieks followed. Spasms shook her body, and the demon returned in the form of flinging spit and snapping teeth. "I hate you." More heaving. "Fuck you." Her teeth chomped at the air between sputtered insults.

He'd managed to dodge the majority of her rabid bites, but she'd sunk her canines into his arm twice before he'd securely tied her to the branch. She'd burrowed beneath his skin in more ways than one, and he couldn't help but treasure the imprints she'd left on him.

Her arms wrenched against the restraints, and her eyes rolled back in her head. "Oh God, it hurts. Take me back." A howling wail. "Need inside, inside, inside…"

Her chant ebbed into a mumbo jumbo of hiccuping sobs and indiscernible words. He'd read that panic attacks could last anywhere from minutes to hours. Sooner or later, she'd wear herself out. Or pass out. The latter wouldn't save her. Not anymore.

When her ankles were locked down with rope and tied to the trees on either side with two feet of space between her feet, he checked her limbs for blood flow, making sure the cuffs weren't cutting skin. Then he stood before her in the spotlight of the full moon, made brighter by the beams of floodlights illuminating the yard.

Her body faced the woods, her back exposed to the swath of lawn between the cabin and the tree line. The placement gave him enough visibility and room to maneuver. He'd also hear the house alarm if the perimeter wires were tripped.

Strangled noises coughed in her bucking chest. She was beyond speech now, seemingly lost to the frenzy in her head. Brown ropes of hair clung to her frame in sweaty strands, her eyes bulging as she fought for every rasping breath.

Seeing her dark hair and agonized features flared a deep, long-buried memory. His mother used to wear the same defeated look before the drugged haze of detachment had permanently emptied her expression. He would *not* allow the same thing to happen to Amber.

He paced out eight steps behind her and tested the weight of the whip's handle. Shaking out the fall, he let the six-foot thong ripple over the ground. His target, in all her magnificent nudity, shook wildly before him. Her arms stretched over her head, secured by wrist cuffs and rope, and the muscles in her back bounced beneath the unblemished canvas of her skin. The stunning sight took his breath away.

He delayed a moment to clear his mind and refill his lungs. Then he bent and locked his elbow, moving his arm upward and flowing the whip out behind him. At the twelve o'clock position, he relaxed his arm straight down and released the plaited leather through the air with a *crack*.

The fall landed with pinpoint accuracy, raising a pink bite just above her ass cheek. She flinched, and her violent thrashing slammed to a stop. Shock? It only lasted a heartbeat before she flung herself forward, caught by the rope, and cried out loudly and mournfully.

In the past, those pained howls would've hardened his cock into a burning steel rod. He would've imagined beating the shit out of the weak boy he'd once been and gotten off on it—as vile as that was. But his dick didn't jerk, his body pliant and cool, his mind completely focused on what she needed. Too many fears were coming at her all at once, probably faster, harder, and more intensely than anything she'd experienced. He wanted to shelter her from the onslaught. He wanted to see her eyes shine bright and protect that light. He wanted to free her.

A swallow lodged in his throat, and the handle shook in his hand. Where were these thoughts coming from? And what if he made her worse?

If the whip brought her unfathomable pain, she would avoid the outside more, *unless* she was able to engage with the pain and connect it with pleasure and arousal. It was the response he hoped for. Otherwise, this would end in disaster.

With his feet spaced shoulder-width apart and the grass tickling his toes, he shifted his left foot forward. Hips loose, left hand up and out for balance, he settled into a relaxed stance and waited for the shaking to stop.

For the span of a dozen pummeling heartbeats, his uncertainty shifted. His dominant hand warmed and strengthened as it held the whip *selflessly* for the first time. Until now, it had struck only because it felt good, because it satisfied a craving. He tightened his fingers around the stiff leather grip as Amber's panting cries surrounded him, begging wordlessly for his help.

He let the whip fly. Over and over, the lashes kissed her back, her ass, and her trembling legs. Whether he wanted to deliver a light sting or a muscle-bruising blow, his body knew what to do, his attention centering on her responses. The uncurling of her fingers, the loosening of her knees, the clench of her thighs, every answer contrasted with and complemented his strikes, each stumbling sigh playing different tones of the same melody. The song of unbidden surrender.

As the physical pain overpowered the emotional, her body liquefied. Nerves, muscles, and vocal chords, once stressed to their max, appeared to be softening, dissolving into a gentle sway of limbs and hushed moans.

His arm burned with exertion, his t-shirt soaked with sweat. He lowered the whip, catching his breath, and angled his head. The moon cast a globe of light on the glistening arousal slicking her inner thighs.

Pride lifted the corners of his mouth and expanded his lungs. He was the Master of a glowing red ass and a soaking pussy, of an agoraphobic who hung naked in the woods with a sigh on her lips. Damn straight, he owned that.

He set down the whip and approached her back, pausing close enough to let her feel his body heat without touching. Not one lash had broken the skin. He'd gone easy on her, though she probably wouldn't thank him for it. "What are you feeling, Amber?"

Her head rolled forward, and a shiver rippled her shoulders.

He walked a wide circle around to her front, slowly, confidently, his gait a habit of lethal charisma, as her heavy eyes tracked his movements. A kiss away, he cupped her face and raised her chin. "Tell me."

She licked her lips, her eyelids half-mast. "I...I need..."

She'd better say *him*. He *needed* her to say it.

Holding her jaw with one hand, he dropped the other to a taut nipple, brushing it with a knuckle in teasing strokes. "What do you need?"

She arched her spine, pressing her heavy tit against his palm. Her eyes rose to his, brightening with unspoken thoughts, then drifted over his shoulder and widened. Her next inhale caught in her throat. "Take me inside." She sucked in sharply, her jaw stiffening, her voice rushed. "Need to go back. Oh God. Now."

Panic gripped him, and he twisted his neck, scanning the timber behind, his muscles swelling to attack. But nothing moved amidst the skeletal silhouettes of the sleepy woods.

A throb lit behind his eyes. Shit, her phobia was contagious, and of course, it was still there between them, a gasping fucking presence. What had he expected? A miraculous cure beneath his whip?

He checked his blooming anger and kept his tone calm yet authoritative. "Focus on me, Amber. On my hands." He flicked her nipple and trailed the pads of his fingers around the curves of her breast, lifting the warm, dense weight. "Fucking love your tits. The velvety texture, the little hard buds." He pinched a nipple, made it harder.

Her eyes shifted, and when they found his, they softened. She leaned toward him, her arms trembling in the cuffs.

"Focus on my lips." He took her mouth, and after a few coaxing nips, she melted into him. He kissed her with a deep ache in his chest, a burning need for her total attention. Sucking and licking, he dominated her mouth, fingers plunging into her hair, angling her head to deepen the kiss.

The phobia might've slipped in, but she was still entranced in subspace. All the endorphins and adrenaline that had been released with the pain would be buzzing through her body, floating her in a warm, drifty cosmos that gravitated toward her Master.

As their tongues swirled together, tangling and tasting, his hands edged around her breasts, down her flat belly, and tiptoed over her hipbones. Her skin prickled with goose bumps, her pelvis lifting toward his, enthralling him.

He continued his caress to the creases between her mound and hips, sliding down her inner thighs, and returning to her waist. A vibration thrummed beneath her flesh, heating with circulating blood. He knew how to toy with her, when to ease off, teasing the anticipation by touching everywhere but the one place that would send her into a blissful spiral. He broke the kiss. "Tell me what you need now."

A visible tremor skated over her. She tried to bend her elbows, unable to budge the rope, and dropped her head to his chest. "I...I'm scared."

Quiet, desperate, her admission shivered through him. He needed to hold her, to assure her. If he released the cuffs, would she try to run? Doubtful, but if he was wrong, he'd catch her.

With years of practice in rope work, he freed the French bowline knots in seconds. He caught her wobbly descent, mindful of the welts, and carried her to the thick carpet of grass. When he laid her on her side, she curled in on herself, her face distorted in terror, and her body wrenched into the violent throes of panic.

It happened so damned fast, locking her muscles and pinching her breaths. He watched helplessly, gripping the back of his neck. He could take her inside — *avoidance*. Or he could try something else — *distraction*.

He rolled her to her back and blanketed her body with his, bracing his legs and arms on the outside of hers, caging her in, knowing the coolness of the grass would soothe the lashes. "No one can see you. Look. You're completely covered beneath me." Not that a soul would dare step foot on his land. The *Fuck Off* signs he'd posted had been anything but welcoming.

She grabbed at his ribs with rigid fingers and pulled him closer, rooting her body into the core of his while fighting for breath. Fuck him, but he wanted to be her security, her anchor, her fucking everything. Not as her captor but as her lover.

As she burrowed deeper beneath him, her fingers stumbled against the waistband of his jeans. Maybe it was accidental, but she didn't jerk them away, rather they inched inward along his tightening abs.

A heady rush of exhilaration connected his spinning emotions to his groin. His cock, instantly hard and hungry, strained against the zipper. He ground the aching thing into the dip of her clenched thighs, and she responded in kind, bucking and gasping as her fingernails dug into his stomach.

His heart raced. He wasn't alone in these feelings. She needed him as much as he needed her, physically as much as emotionally.

He ducked his head and captured her mouth, kissing her deeply and thoroughly. She met him, her tongue sliding against his, but her breathing didn't slow its sharp, shallow rhythm.

The grass was cold and damp beneath his forearms where they bracketed her head. He ran his hands through her hair and gathered the thick mass, using it to hold her still while he plunged his tongue between her sweet lips.

The panic hadn't fully tapered, evidenced in the heave of her chest and the jerking of her body against him. She kept her elbows tucked in and her shoulders curled between his as if she truly believed he was shielding her from her biggest fear.

He strengthened the kiss, fucking her mouth with his tongue, stealing her breaths and, hopefully, the noise in her head. The earthy scent of soil and the musk of their mingled sweat bathed his inhalations as he chased her tongue, pinning it and releasing it in a sensual dance.

As her breathing slowed from anxious to aroused, he wedged a hand between their bodies, caressing her belly and lifting his hips to glide lower. When he reached the hood of her clit, he watched with awe as her eyes closed and her chin rose, exposing her neck.

Warmth sifted through him, lifting his broken soul to the surface. Where was the temptation to jump on that vulnerable throat and crush it with a ruthless hand? He wanted to own her, but not if it scarred her. She was his weakness, and with a confidence that punctuated every revelation he'd come to accept since he'd taken her, there wasn't a damned thing he'd do to change it.

Stretching his fingers to slide along her slit, he inhaled her heavy exhale, taking in the minty scent of toothpaste. Each twitch in her body sizzled along his nerve-endings, and his cock throbbed to shove itself inside her hot little cunt.

When his fingers furrowed through her damp flesh, she tensed. He removed his hand and touched her cheek, drawing her eyes to his. As she focused on him, her mouth parted and her expression gentled, but he could see the memory of him raping her straining that sensual, seductive-looking gaze.

Guilt, intense and agonizing, shredded his insides. His stomach hardened, and he dropped his forehead to hers. He'd fucked up when he'd forced himself on her, scaring her in a way he wished he could take back. "I'm sorry."

Whatever she heard in his voice, perhaps the reedy vulnerability in his otherwise controlled tone, brought her hands out from beneath him to grip his jaw and guide his face into the light.

She stared up at him for a long, terrifying moment, her eyes searching, her lips rolling together. Then her fingers moved to his temples, combing through the hair over his ears, tenderly, lovingly, in a way he didn't deserve. Her gaze didn't waver from his as she swallowed. "I will never forget. But maybe someday, I might be able to forgive."

A surge of emotion pulled at his jaw and gathered in his throat. "I don't deserve forgiveness."

She tugged on his ears, drawing his mouth to hers, and gave him her assurance in a kiss. He answered it, furiously and passionately, as a fire swept over his skin. Their mouths slid together for a blissful forever, exploring and learning, giving and taking, and still, it wasn't enough.

With her thighs imprisoned between his legs, her chest safely covered by the width of his torso, she seemed stable. Relaxed even. Her hands and arms had returned to their tucked concealment between their bodies, which put her fingers at the perfect position to bump against the swollen bulge in his jeans.

Given all the kissing and foreplay, she had to know where this was leading. Without releasing her mouth, he slipped a hand over her silky abs, sliding downward to the heat of her cunt. She didn't flinch. In fact, her kisses grew hungrier, breathier. Her nipples hardened, dragging against his chest.

A testing reach just inside the folds of her pussy soaked his finger. He pulled back his hand and brushed the hair from her face with steady fingers while his insides shook with profane need. His cock jumped, so fucking painful in its bent position it slammed his teeth together. His whole body seemed to know she was ready. As badly as he wanted to tug himself out and shove inside her, he couldn't.

He should ask first and heed her answer. Fuck, had he ever done such a thing? And open himself to rejection? Hell no. His jaw stiffened.

But if she didn't say 'No,' if she accepted him into her body through a will of her own, it would invite trust and maybe a deeper connection.

Which could expose him to a different kind of pain, a hurt far worse than Liv's bullet in his shoulder.

He stroked her cheek, her chin, and her waiting lips. "I want to fuck you, Amber. But I won't take you again without permission." And there hovered the most frightening thing he'd ever uttered. What if she never gave him permission?

She stared into his eyes, her mouth squeezed shut as if to trap the noisy breaths flaring her nostrils. Christ, the wait was torturous. Her rejection scared him as much as he had scared her. Then she spoke. "I need you inside of me."

He stilled as her words pinged through him like raindrops striking tin. Steady rain on a rusted tin roof, with his doll safe and unbroken in his lap, his mother sitting beside him, a warm breeze lifting her hair and brushing it against his face. And maybe she patted his leg as if she wasn't bothered by his company. Yeah. Amber's words were as consoling as that, his single happy memory.

He stared back at her, wanting to ask if she was sure and not daring enough to open his mouth. But her expression said it all. Firm eye contact, a soft blush, and parting lips that built into a gentle smile.

With shaky fingers, he fumbled for his buckle, loosening it and tackling the button, the zipper. His breaths caught, impatient and awkward. Holding his body over hers to maintain her veil of security, he tugged a condom from his pocket and rolled it on.

His cock jutted out, hard and ready, nudging the valley of her thighs. The position of her legs, pressed together between his, would limit his thrusts. He didn't care. He wanted to fuck her right there, outside, knowing he would love it, that she would, too.

He pressed the swollen head against her slick pussy, leaned down, and thrust his hips forward, slamming into her tight body. The hot flesh of her sheath rippled around him, squeezing, welcoming, fucking consuming him. His head fell back on his shoulders, a moan sighing from his gaping mouth.

Ah God, nothing was grotesque about her cunt. Its pretty shape, its gripping strength, there was no place he'd rather be.

He stroked in and out, her velvety warmth sucking and releasing him, shooting sparks of electricity over his skin. She flexed her hips upwards to meet his thrusts, pulling a groan from deep inside him.

His hand cupped the fullness of her breast, his palm rolling over the hard bud of her nipple. Too soon, his release rushed forward. He held it off, angling his pelvis to grind against her clit. With a few hard rotations, her breathing changed, growing faster, more shallow.

She didn't cry out as the climax took her, but he felt it throb around his cock, tightening every muscle in her body. Her fingernails scratched at his ribs. Her heels scraped through the grass between his feet.

His overwhelming satisfaction burst into exploding ecstasy. He ejaculated so hard and long stars invaded his vision. He might've thought he died if not for the kisses she peppered over his chest, grounding him.

He couldn't speak, couldn't breathe, couldn't *move*. When he finally found his voice, he stuttered with stupidity. "I can't even...that was..."

"What mutual pleasure feels like?" Her voice was husky. And bratty.

He sank his teeth into her shoulder, not to break skin but hard enough to leave a pretty bruise.

She screeched and writhed beneath him until he let go. "What was that for?" Her gaze was wide and shiny, glaring up at him, but a smile twinkled at the edges.

"For being a brat." He grinned, floating on a cloud of lingering bliss, and rolled off to free her of his weight and remove the condom.

Her choking gasps were the first indication of his fuck up. Her hands flew to her chest, her eyes darting wildly around her.

He rolled back, landing atop her and covering her thrashing body as best as he could. But he knew he'd lost her the instant she grew rigid. A scream roared from her throat, cut off, and she bucked in his arms.

Just like that, she was back to square one.

# TWENTY

Shadows crept from the woods, inch-by-inch, breath by ragged breath, closing in and swallowing Amber's ability to run, to crawl, to scream. The ground spun beneath her, tossing her body and splintering her chest. Her lungs burned, and her bones melted into icy liquid. Too helpless. Too exposed. *Nowhere to hide.*

The earth began to suck her in, twisting oxygen-depriving tendrils around her neck. As she struggled against the chokehold, a heavy presence grabbed her and pulled her into a prison of strength and darkness.

She curled into that shelter. It felt safe, beautiful, and she didn't want to leave it. How could that be? Maybe it stemmed from her belief that every man possessed the ability to cause wonderment—even dangerous, vicious men. As she flailed through her mind, searching for escape, she found Van's wonder, his hand, reaching out through the terrible noise.

It lifted her, yanking her farther away from the horrors of outside and into a quiet cradle of warmth. His arms folded beneath her back and legs, and his chest flexed against her cheek as he carried her, his body propelling forward.

Overhead, the moon shone bright and full. The sight of it was startling, wonderfully overwhelming, and her emotions poured out in a burst of sobs.

He sped up, running now, as fast, as hard as his breaths. Through the door and up the stairs, he held her like glass. Like her aquarium, fragile and transparent, brimming with brokenness.

The world stopped spinning as the mattress caught her limp body, but her mind continued to trip. She tried to organize the mess of her thoughts, floating through them, unsure where to begin. Where had her brain been the last hour? Skipping around in a nutter's wonderland of slippery delusions? She lay there, numb and empty, as if she'd just been ripped from a drunken haze.

The cool conditioned air bit over her skin, intensifying the heat in the lashes on her back and legs. She was grateful he'd brought her inside, but she needed to lay into him for whipping her.

Maybe later. She couldn't find the energy to be pissed. Exhaustion pulled at her muscles and burned her gritty eyes. But something else muted her anger as well. Curiosity? Or shame.

Once the initial shock of his whip had faded, her body had drifted into a strange weightless suspension of time and place, her mind so centered on the next strike, all the threats of outside had evaporated from her senses. The crack of the whip had stung, sure, but the pain had been fleeting, hypnotic. Nothing like the agony of a panic attack. Even more confusing, it had turned her on.

A jolt of remembered pleasure zinged up her inner thighs. All those floaty feelings had orbited around Van. She'd wanted him so badly, she'd fucked him. No, not fucked. She'd welcomed him like a wanton thing, grinding against his erection, begging. And he'd given it to her, a deeply physical and soulful connection, so unlike the cruelty of the rape. In fact, none of her sexual experiences compared. Not even with Brent. Especially not with Brent.

Had Van whipped his other captors? Surely, they hadn't felt the same profound intoxication? Had he fucked them, too? Her neck stiffened, and her chest ached with an irrationally selfish emotion. They had been sex slaves, normal people forced into a horrible situation, where she was...she was just sick.

The mattress jostled with his movements behind her. He kept the light on as he shifted toward her back. When he touched her, it was with cool, wet fingers. Whatever he was rubbing into the welts was tingly, soothing, and there was way too much care in those gentle strokes.

It hurt to swallow, her throat raw from screaming, so she closed her eyes, relaxing into his touch. Her head grew heavy on the pillow, the aftershocks of the last panic attack still trembling through her veins. Too soon, his fingers disappeared. But he replaced them with his body heat as he tugged the covers up and tucked them in.

Two years of shutting off the lights and closing the shades, and she hadn't been able to conquer the fear. Maybe it needed to be whipped out of her. *Inside the house.* No doubt he would do it again. She should just wrap her arms around it and embrace it.

With the same illogical impulse that had propelled her to kiss him in the kitchen, she rolled to face him, first to her belly then to her side. When she met a broad hairless chest, her heart stuttered. Had he removed his pants as well? The wall of muscle an inch from her nose tempted her to follow the dusting of hair below his abs and find out.

His arm slipped around her, and his thumb glided lazily over her nape. He smelled of earth and warmth and virility. His pecs twitched and rippled beneath golden skin, each brawny brick of his torso chiseled in a uniform sculpture of strength. Jesus, the man's body didn't know when to quit.

Apparently, hers didn't either, given the sudden throb of heat between her legs. She clenched her inner muscles and shivered. His unlawful beauty and sneaky moments of tenderness both scared and captivated her, but more than that, he compelled her.

She wedged a hand between his bicep and ribs, snaking it around his back and inching closer, so close there was no question about his state of dress.

The short hairs on his thighs tickled as his strong legs intertwined with hers. His cock, soft and thick, laid against her hip. She shivered again and knew he'd felt it when he released a soft hum.

She pressed her lips to his hard chest and savored the catch in his breath. His skin tasted salty, his raw outdoorsy scent chasing the spice of his cologne. He was quiet, perhaps thoughtful, as he snuggled against her, seemingly content with her affection, neither dismissing it nor demanding more. Laid-back, unassuming Van was irresistible.

She wriggled upward along his body, kissing his sternum, the side of his neck, and lingered on the dime-sized scar on his shoulder. A bullet wound? Had one of the slaves or the buyers shot him? Or were there other fragments of his criminal life she knew nothing about? "How did you get this?"

"Not tonight, sweetheart." The tired rumble of his voice settled over her, and the caress of his thumb moved from her neck, down her spine, pausing mid-way. To avoid the welts?

Leaning back, she peered up into his eyes and found the silvery depths tinged with lazy fatigue. She loved that look on him, but it couldn't be trusted. "My back doesn't hurt."

"It will tomorrow, brat. You need to drink water." He reached behind him and grabbed a plastic cup from the nightstand, knocking random clutter to the floor. He didn't bother picking it up. He simply rolled back and held out the cup with a raised brow.

God, what must the floor look like? Clothing and crap scattered with no order and configuration? "The mess—"

"The mess is mine. Drink."

She gritted her teeth. "Last time you told me to drink—"

"I won't drug you, because I'm not taking you anywhere." He leaned in and kissed her forehead. "You're exactly where I want you."

Her heart thumped, the foolish, gullible thing. She narrowed her eyes. "Why?"

"Because I like you."

She expected a charming grin, but what he gave her was an expression etched with honesty.

"Jesus, you look so beautiful right now." His timbre was rough, throaty.

Her mouth fell open. She was a fucking mess. Mental issues aside, she didn't wear a stitch of makeup, and her hair tangled around her neck and shoulders from rolling in the grass. She wanted to point this out, but he regarded her with such intense focus, it was easier to drop the subject. She glanced at the waiting cup.

How long had it been sitting on the table, amongst watches and hangers and discarded candy wrappers? Was there dust and bacteria in it? She wrinkled her nose. "How fresh is that?"

His eyes hardened into steel blades. "Too damned tired for this, Amber. Don't test me."

Just like that, his command was back, a reminder of his volatile nature. She accepted the cup, draining the lukewarm water, her throat tightening in pain and revulsion with each swallow. He took it from her, tossing it somewhere on the floor. With all the other mounting debris. Where there were no lines, no structure, no routine.

Her scalp tingled with rising anxiety. *Stop thinking about it.* "I'm going to make your life hell."

His head lowered to the pillow, his eyes closed. "My life is already hell. An eternal dark walk of the damned."

A bit dramatic, but no question he was damned, as was she. But there was warmth in his dark walk. Intense warmth with rock hard arms that held her close. She couldn't figure him out and, at the moment, didn't have the strength to try.

"Did you count the swings of the whip?" he murmured against her forehead. "In little groups of four?"

Her head jerked back. Count the—? No, it hadn't occurred to her. Her teeth clamped down on the inside of her cheek, sparking a burn in her eyes. How could she have forgotten to count? She'd been so scared of the woods stretched out before her, gawking at her nudity. Then the sting of the whip came, and her mind had just...blanked. He'd distracted her in a way no one else had been able to do.

"Didn't think so." His face was softly vacant, but a smile lightened his tone. "Twenty-three lashes. Not twenty. Not twenty-four."

Twenty-three marks on her body. An uneven number without balance or special meaning. Her pulse raced. The fucking prick did it on purpose! "Give me another whack of your whip. Just one." She leaned up, patting his whiskered cheek, but he wouldn't open his eyes. "It'll be quick. We can do it right here." She cringed at the frantic pitch in her voice.

"Begging already?" His lips bowed up beneath her fingers, his eyelids smooth and closed. "Go to sleep."

She glared at him, fingers itching to slap his peaceful face. What would he do? Give her another twenty-three lashes? Pin her down and fuck her? Take her outside? The last thought jerked her hand away.

The longer she studied him, the more conflicted she became. The sharp angles of his jaw, the slope of his perfect nose, the fringes of dark lashes, and the jagged edge of the scar that cut so deep into his cheek it must've hit bone. He was stunning, painfully so, but nothing in his features revealed *who* he was.

His lips relaxed, the muscles in his face loosened, and soon his chest settled into an even rise and fall of sleep.

For the next hour, she deliberated over what to do. She was a captive to this man. She should've been plotting her escape with fearful breath. Only she didn't feel scared, and *that* should've scared her the most. Instead, she was enraged, dreaming up ways to stick it up his ass and rotate it because he'd refused her a twenty-fourth mark. So yeah... All kinds of logical reasoning going on.

The bedside clock flipped to 12:04. It had only been twelve hours since she'd sent Zach away. No one would've noticed her disappearance yet. Or ever. No missing woman reports. No investigations. She was a nobody and had no one to blame for that but herself.

Van hadn't moved in his sleep, his heavy arm hanging limply around her. How could he have let his guard down so easily?

Because he knew she didn't have the balls to leave the house.

Well, fuck him. He was possessive and controlling, and she couldn't mistake that for care or concern. Everything he did was calculated, and all she had to combat him with were her wits and courage.

Courage?

Right. With a long inhale, she dug deep, pulling it from somewhere, certainly not from her hammering heart or queasy stomach. Then she shimmied out from beneath his arm. When her hair caught in his fingers, she bit down on her lip, her pulse thundering in her ears.

He didn't stir.

Slowly, breathlessly, she unwound the strands from his grip and slipped to the floor. Peeking over the edge of the mattress, she watched his breathing for a long, agonizing minute. Then she glared at the clutter. *Don't pick it up.*

With the grace of a queen balancing in six-inch heels, she tiptoed around the mess, stopped to remove a casual halter dress from one of her bags on the floor, and gave her aquarium a longing look. *Come on, Amber.*

*You can't take it with you.*

She hugged the dress to her chest and dashed down the stairs on silent toes. In the bathroom, she pulled on the knee-length halter, ran a brush through her hair, and scoured the cabinet. Lotions, soaps, toothbrushes, and tampons filled the drawers, but no makeup.

She gripped the edge of the counter. He'd grabbed all these things from her house but not the one thing she needed to escape. How could she go outside without her cosmetic armor?

A skitter of panic seized her muscles as her reflection glared back in the mirror. Pallid skin, dark shadows beneath dull eyes, and lips twisted with disgust. She couldn't let anyone see her like that.

*Excuses.* She didn't need to look her beauty pageant best. She just needed a goddamned backbone. What kind of captive dolled herself up before making her great escape?

The stalling, crazy kind. God, she really annoyed herself sometimes.

She crept through the stillness of the house, the windows closed up, and the loft looming above like a watchtower. Was he watching her? Not a flicker in the soft lamp light on his nightstand.

Releasing a thready exhale, she moved to the kitchen. No cell phones or phone jacks. No knives or scissors in the drawers or on the butcher block. Not that she could've found a goddamned thing in the junk overflowing from every cobwebbed cranny. People really lived like this? Thankfully, Brent had been tidy, though thinking on it, she'd stayed on his heels, fixing everything he'd touched. And hadn't cleanliness been a point of contention between her father and OCD mother, one of the many reasons he'd left?

She opened the silverware drawer, at least the semblance of one. It also held oily screws, toothpicks, and pencils. She grabbed a fork and held it up.

What was she going to do with that? Hell, what would she do with a knife? Wasn't that something an escapee would carry while running for her life?

*Until she had a meltdown, stumbled over her feet, and stabbed herself.*

She abandoned the weapon idea and considered the cluttered drawer. She could put a really good dent in this while he slept. She'd start with the utensils and realign them in their appropriate sections. First, she'd have to find the sections, remove the crumbs, scrub the bottom, and —

Shit, she was doing it again. She was supposed to be escaping. As she continued to mentally clean and organize the drawer, she backed away from it and took the final steps to the mudroom.

Inside were two solid doors. One leading out back, and the other? A garage and maybe a getaway car?

Gripping her knuckles, she popped through the joints, working herself into a frenzy of indecision. Fuck, she hadn't driven in two years. And wouldn't he hear the garage doors go up?

She approached the back door and stopped a foot away. When her toes curled, she looked down in shock. She wasn't wearing shoes. *Brilliant, Amber.* No makeup, no jewelry, her hair unwashed and uncurled, she wasn't even close to being put together. Then there was the fact she had no clue what she'd do if she actually made it off the porch and encountered another person. Would she ask for help?

If she didn't face plant in a full-on breakdown, she'd spazz out over her appearance and run in the opposite direction, as pointless as that would be. But where would she go? She didn't even know where she was. Could she go home? He'd track her down, of that she was certain.

Assuming he was still asleep, she'd have a head start. She touched the knob, gripping it with a sweaty hand as her nerves flared tremors down her spine.

God, she'd rather be sleeping with him, nuzzled up against his hard body, soaking in his warmth. She could stay...

To what end? She'd heard about the psychological effects of captivity, how capture-bonding could fabricate emotional ties. He'd hit her, whipped her, raped her. *Don't fucking forget how dark he can be.*

But his darkness had showed her the moon for the first time in two years.

The tarnished metal grew slick beneath her palm. Her brain told her heart she needed to leave, but her hand wouldn't turn the knob.

Her chin trembled, and her grief rushed forward in a riptide of shaking limbs and burning tears. Dammit, she was so tired, so emotionally mixed-up. She wasn't strong enough to open that door. Not now, maybe not ever.

Deep down, she knew she'd never make it off that porch, but fuck, her pathetic self couldn't even try.

Her knees gave out, and she slid to the floor, so fucking dramatic in her misery. How had she ended up here? Not in this house, but at this level of utter weakness?

Dr. Michaels had said the *how* wasn't important. It was the *now* that mattered. *Does the* now *stop you from eating, sleeping, smiling, interacting...living?*

Van seemed to encourage all those things. She folded her arms on her bent knees, head on her forearms, and stared at the gray tiles between her feet. Gray like his eyes, the perfect blend of light and dark.

She sat there, displaced and achingly tired, until her tailbone complained and her eyes grew heavy. *What's it gonna be, Amber?* A life under his roof or a life filled with puking, sleeping pills, deliverymen, and loneliness?

She could always leave later, on another day. No, the unmade decision would linger and taunt her and drive her crazy.

For a girl who lost her shit when a sock found its way into the wrong drawer, she wasn't foaming at the mouth right now, in this house of clutter. Maybe there wasn't such a thing as a *wrong* drawer. Maybe *here* wasn't wrong. With different drawers. A different routine. With a man who might be able to love *her* as fiercely as he hurt.

She rubbed her eyes along her arms, wiping away stray tears. Lifting her weary head, her gaze crawled across the floor to the kitchen and froze.

Leaning against the fridge opposite the mudroom, he stood in the dim glow of the stove light. Wearing black athletic pants, legs crossed at the ankles, arms folded across his bare chest, he studied her with a calm, unreadable expression. She swallowed hard and dropped her eyes. Jesus, even his bare feet were intimidating.

Who knew how long he'd been standing there, watching her? She'd been so caught up in her pity party he could've been there the whole time.

He didn't move or speak, his stillness thick enough to strangle the air. What if he made her leave?

That was when she felt it, deep inside, breaking free. Her missing backbone. It straightened her back and invigorated her with a thrilling rush of strength. If he didn't want her, he could...he could go climb a wall of stretched-out vaginas.

She met his eyes. Pale, piercing eyes that told her he knew her next four steps before she did. With her eyes, she said, *Bet you didn't see this one coming.*

She rose—gracefully and steadily, despite the burning in her legs—and walked to him. The proximity forced her to look up to hold his gaze. Arms relaxed at her sides, posture strong and proud, she smiled without force or agenda. She smiled because it felt right. "I've decided to stay."

"Uh huh." The corner of his mouth ticked up. "Too scary out there?"

She glanced over her shoulder, acknowledging the door, and looked back at him. "Well, there's that. And while I could continue to fight through it and maybe someday make it beyond the porch, I've lost interest in escaping." She put the strength of her backbone in her voice so he would hear her earnestness in the most absurd, childish, fucked-up reason ever. "Because I like you, too."

# TWENTY-ONE

Van had perfected the pose of lazy nonchalance years ago, but as he leaned against the fridge, he embraced it for no other reason than fucking exhaustion. Of course, Amber would pit her fear of him against the agoraphobia. But the first night? Good thing he'd wound her hair around his fingers like little trip wires.

No one could say she wasn't tenacious, especially considering her willingness to risk another panic attack so soon after the last one. No sweat off his balls, though. He'd been too curious to stop her. Besides, it moved her a step closer toward acceptance of her new life.

So he'd followed her down the stairs, blending into the shadowed corners of the cabin as she fought her demons in the bathroom and kitchen. When she'd opened the silverware drawer, he'd been ready to stop whatever cleaning fest she might've been envisioning. Honestly, his cabin could use a good scrub, but not at the expense of the OCD thing. He wanted to shake up the disorder, not enable it.

Big brown eyes glared up at him, her expression expectant, and challenge evident in the lift of her chin. Damn, she was willful and tireless. He was a year younger than she was, yet her energy ran circles around him. Apparently, he needed to workout more.

Judging by the fists that now moved to her hips, she was waiting for him to respond to her announcement. Impatient little twit. He'd already picked through her words, not only what she'd said but how she said it.

*I've lost interest in escaping.*

The steady resolve in her voice and her unwavering eye contact had been convincing. But her revelation wouldn't keep her from going outside. He'd make sure of that.

*Because I like you, too.*

Five easy words, but the promise they imparted filled him with fierce belonging. And an uncomfortable amount of sentimentality. He rubbed the back of his neck. He needed sleep. They both did.

"How about you *like me* upstairs...while we sleep." He added that last part to make his intentions clear. Though he could be up for something else with a little coaxing.

She smiled, and the illumination of her eyes flooded the kitchen with light. "Yeah, okay. I'm beat." Her voice hardened on the last syllable, asserting her disapproval of his heavy hand.

*Bring it, baby.* Fuck, he looked forward to her fight. After a good night's rest.

He let her lead up the spiraled stairs because really, how could he refuse an opportunity to be eye-level with her backside? And fuck him gently with a two-by-four, she flexed that ass with the grace of the gods. The sight of her round cheeks straining the fabric of her dress would chase his dreams for an eternity.

Then he remembered he hadn't packed any of her panties. Christ, she was too damned tempting. Halfway through the climb, he shoved the dress up to her waist, found two unmarred spots of supple flesh, and pinched the hell out of them with both hands.

Her shriek echoed through the cabin. "Hands off my ass!" She reached back, wriggling to his delight, her fingers curling around his wrists. "I mean it."

He released her, chuckling. "Darling, my hands and your ass are meant to be together. Don't fuck with destiny."

She sighed, adjusting the dress, but he didn't miss the smile dimpling her face.

"You're insufferable." She shook her head, then flew up the remaining steps, and vanished into the loft, leaving him standing there grinning like a fool. A deliriously happy fool.

The scar on his face bristled with his smile, itching. His lips fell, his fingers rubbing his cheek. She could cut him far deeper than a bullet or a knife.

He clenched his jaw and gripped the railing. He couldn't fathom backing away from whatever this was. There was so much about her, her unpredictability and her routines, her strength and her brokenness, that made him want to go all the way, wherever that might take him.

Tonight, he would sleep with her in his arms. She deserved someone better, but at the very least, he could come to bed freshly showered.

Her footsteps pattered around in the loft. All the dangerous weapons were locked up. He dashed to the bathroom and grabbed a five-minute shower.

When he climbed the stairs again, it was with renewed purpose. At the top, he found her digging through her bags. "What are you looking for?"

"Pajamas." She moved to another bag.

He hadn't packed those, either. "Wasting your time." He shed the towel around his waist and stretched out on the bed, arms folded behind his head, blissfully naked. "We both know you sleep like this."

She didn't look at him, but her arms stopped moving, elbows deep in a bag. "I hate that you know that."

He could see how the stalking stuff might bug her, but... "I won't apologize for that." His obsessive habit had led him to her. "Come to bed."

He anticipated another fight, one where she would refuse to undress and he would win because, well, he always won. But in bewitching Amber-fashion, she shocked him again.

Rising to her feet, she faced him with her hands on the hem at her thighs and tugged it up and over her head. Gorgeously nude in the glow of the lamp, she walked to the hamper, folded the dress, and placed it on the pile of dirty clothes. She stared at it for several heartbeats with her lips pursed and her eyebrows pulled in.

He shifted to his side, lifting on an elbow. Was it the sight of her laundry mixed with his? Or maybe she had some kind of ritual that involved sorting clothes in multiple hampers? Would the absence of her system trigger another breakdown? He refused to go to her. He wanted her to come to him when she was upset. "Amber?"

She looked up, and her fingers flew to her knuckles. *Crack-Crack* —

"Amber." He put force in his voice and grabbed the edge of the blanket, pulling it over his lower half and holding it up in invitation.

Her eyes darted to his face then lowered to his sleepy dick. She continued to stare, cracking her knuckles, as he recited the U.S. Presidents. "Washington, Adams, Jefferson" — *Madison* — "Mac...No, uh, Roe —"

"What are you doing?" She lowered her hands and approached the bed, head cocked.

*Good girl. Keep walking.*

His arm was growing tired of holding up the blanket. "Who was the fourth president?"

"Madison." She blinked. "Why?"

He was bored a couple years ago, in between slaves, and passed the time by memorizing all the presidents, first ladies, and trivial facts about each. Now he used it to distract her from a meltdown, as well as to keep his dick from hardening and scaring her away.

"Takes my mind off things." He glanced down at his flaccid cock and could feel the weight of her eyes there, too.

In the next breath, the lamp clicked off, and her knee landed beside him. Before he could catch his breath, she curled around him, arm hooked at his back and leg nudging between his.

Christ Almighty, what a goddamned fulfilling feeling, her hard feminine muscles and soft curves all up against him. He rolled to his back and savored the warm weight of her tight body pressed against his side. She felt fucking amazing, all relaxed and accepting, holding him as if she appreciated the intimacy as much as he did.

This was his new favorite position, and his dick wasn't even inside her. Hell, he wasn't even hard.

How was it that just twelve hours ago he'd held her at gunpoint, drugged her, and forced himself inside her. How could she have admitted she liked him or have any desire to snuggle against his body? But she had, and she was.

She wasn't normal.

He released a long, conflicted breath. They would never be normal. It just wasn't in their blood. He gripped her thigh, hooking it over his, and coiled his fingers around her hair. Fuck normal.

Her exhale warmed his neck, and the pad of her thumb traced his collarbone. "When was the last time you slept beside someone?"

"More than a year ago." Which didn't exactly conjure sweet memories. On those rare occasions when Liv actually stayed in his bed, he'd never felt so alone. "She was the only one. What about you?"

"Brent was the first and last." Her tits pushed against his ribs as she breathed in. "What was her name?"

"Liv."

Her fingers jerked against his chest, but her lips pressed a soft peck on his shoulder, just beside the bullet wound. He'd tell her about that, about all of it, eventually. The idea of keeping anything from her was ludicrous. And so unlike his relationship with Liv, which had died at the hand of secrets.

Tonight had been the first night he didn't drive to Liv's neighborhood in over six months, and he hadn't even thought about it till now. Thinking of her tended to stir up a turmoil of conflicting emotions. But at the moment, all he felt was a dim ache somewhere behind his heart.

"Do you love her? Is that why you were on my porch?"

There were no quick responses to that. "I'm going to delay the answer to your last question because we're both tired. As for the first, I like to think of it as a seven-year fever." Which had burned into a hotheaded, delusion-inducing illness.

His admission hovered in the darkness, smothering like a miasma he'd accidentally let in.

Her quiet voice scattered the thick air. "My fever lasted fourteen years."

*Fourteen years.* That sleazy asshat didn't deserve fourteen seconds with her. "You know how to treat a fever?"

"Mm. I'm too tired to think of something witty. Go ahead."

"Rest and lots of *fluids*." He lowered his voice. "Obviously, not at the same time."

"Oh my God." Her groan dissolved into a soft lullaby of laughter. As it whispered through him, he realized the reason his days felt so empty was because they hadn't been filled with that sound.

He touched his lips to the top of her head, grinning. What a sentimental asshole.

For the second time that night, he waited for her breaths to tumble into sleep. This time, they did, pulling him along with a smile on his face.

The next morning, he woke wearing that same damned smile. But it didn't last. He was alone in the bed and the loft.

He shot up, his feet tripping over the floor. Only he wasn't tripping on a goddamned thing. Not a shirt or a magazine or a discarded pack of cigarettes in sight.

Fuuuuck. She'd been up for awhile.

The bedside clock read 10:43. He released a relieved breath. It was still early. He raked his hands through his hair. That was early, right? Jesus, what time did she normally wake?

He dug through the hamper, pulled out a pair of jeans, sniffed them, tossed them, and dug again until he found a fresher pair. Laundry was on the agenda at some point in the near future.

Tugging on the jeans, half-walking, half-hopping, he didn't bother with the zipper or button as he sharpened his attention on the stifling quiet downstairs. Would she have left? *Could* she?

A rush of blood heated his neck and face, his fingers curling into his palms. He plucked a toothpick from a holder on the dresser and sprinted down the stairs.

# TWENTY-TWO

Halfway down the stairs, the scent of lemon and bleach reached Van's nose. Damn, damn, damn. He quickened his descent on silent feet. At the bottom, his gaze landed on the shiny kitchen counters, small appliances and canisters sparkling in a neat row, and Amber's ass hanging out of the fridge in her bend to scrub the deepest corner.

He pinched the bridge of his nose and let his frustration wave off his back. As much as he loved the sight of her in those little shorts cleaning his house, he wanted her to do it for *him*, not for her illness.

Shoulders back and chest out, he moved to the kitchen with heavy, wide steps. By the time he reached her, she was organizing condiments in the fridge door.

She spun when his footfalls landed behind her. He held his head down, his hand casually rotating the toothpick in his mouth. When her toes flexed against the tiles, he removed the pick, slowly placing it on the counter, and gave her the full force of his eyes.

She tensed, her pupils widening, her lips pinched in a line. The overhead light reflected a metallic glow around her, her dark hair freshly washed and dried. She drew in a lungful of air and grinned with overly bright eyes. "Morning. Sleep well?"

Apparently, he'd slept too well. He hadn't even heard her shower or run the hairdryer. But did the little vixen really think her pleasantries would distract him from the hand that was adjusting the mustard label in the fridge door behind her?

He stifled the laugh bubbling up inside him. Jesus, from the booty shorts and tit-hugging tank top to the fluttering eyelashes and saucy attitude, the whole package was cute as fuck. *And defiant.*

"Best sleep of my life. You?" He turned away, feigning disinterest in his now spotless kitchen, and reached into the overhead cabinet. His bare feet didn't stick to the tiles like they usually did. She'd been awake for a long-ass time.

"I slept well." She hadn't moved from her position by the fridge. If she was wary of him, she had every right to be.

He removed a box of Froot Loops and opened the package with intentional slowness as his mind sped through the next ten steps. "Have you eaten?"

"Nope." A casual response, yet it vibrated with caginess.

He kept his back to her but could feel the heat of her eyes stroking the muscles he'd worked hard to maintain. "How about some cereal?" Froot Loops was a midnight snack. No way would he feed her that junk. Nutritious meals only. Eggs and bacon, fucking protein and shit.

"Uhm. Sure."

Without turning around, he held the open box over the floor and dumped it upside down. Colorful O's tumbled around his feet. He stepped side-to-side, crunching them into a satisfying dust of sugar.

Her breathing grew loud and rushed behind him. "Oh my God." Then louder. "Why?" She released an ear-splitting shriek. "I just mopped the floor!"

And he would clean it later. He wasn't a damned slob. Sure, he slacked on the laundry and didn't give a fuck which shelves the cups went on. But she wouldn't find moldy food or mouse droppings or hoarding stashes of crap falling out of the closets. He pivoted slowly to check on her.

Pressed into the gap of the open fridge door, arms wrapped around her rib cage, shoulders curled in, and eyes wildly darting over the floor, she definitely struggled to hold it together. He was about to make it worse.

He emptied the last of the box, tossed it on the mess, and strode toward her with an air of calm and focus. His unyielding grip on her elbow shuffled her sideways as he closed the fridge. Then he backed her into the counter and put his face into hers. "You will *not* clean up after me."

Her strong-willed chin appeared, jutting up and out, ready to fight. "I can't live like this. This" —she thrust a trembling finger at the floor— "is *not* okay."

"That's right. So here's how it's going to be." He clutched the counter on either side of her hips, arms straight, with two feet of tension rotating between them. "As long as you are obsessively clean, I'm going to be obsessively *not clean*. For every inch you give, I'll match it. We'll eventually meet in the middle." He lowered his head so she could see his eyes. "Got me?"

She didn't look at him, her gaze locked-and-loaded on the floor as if waiting for the crumbs to sprout hundreds of tiny stingers and attack. He knew what was coming, tipped off by the slow deep inhale and the twitch below her eye, and he let it happen.

Her knees bent fast, her body dropping to the floor. Free from the corral of his arms, she scrambled to the mess, sweeping and scooping, her breaths rushing in her frenzy to shove tiny handfuls into the box.

With an even pulse and loose muscles, he lowered to sit beside the huffing tornado. Cereal crumbled beneath his ass and legs as he leaned his back against the cabinet. She didn't seem to notice him, too consumed with black and white, linear numbers, and clean floors...her tragic need to perfect everything.

He'd had enough. She didn't weigh more than a buck-ten soaking wet, so it didn't take much effort to drag her, chest-down, across his thighs. With his forearms braced on her back and legs, she was effectively pinned.

Furious eyes flashed over her shoulder, and her legs kicked uselessly against the floor. "Let me go," she snarled, her fists still clutching handfuls of cereal.

Without moving the arm on her back, he yanked her shorts to her knees. Beautiful, bare, and blotched with tiny pink bruises, her ass flexed and prickled with goose bumps. The arnica gel he'd rubbed into her muscles the previous night would've reduced a lot of the swelling and stiffness. But he caressed a palm over the silky skin to make sure.

Her glutes didn't flinch, her fight still concentrated in the thrashing of her arms and legs. And what a fight, all muscle and soft skin and seductive curves writhing on his lap, her ass right there for the taking.

He was already hard—it was inevitable. He shifted her hips so that her clit lay directly over the swell of his erection through the open zipper, ensuring that every wriggle would stimulate her. *And him.* Then he waited for the next buck of her ass.

It rose. Fell. She gasped as her clit hit his dick. *Fuck.*

He swung his arm, laying into her round cheek with a solid, stinging smack. She writhed, the movement grinding her bundle of nerves against him, tormenting him. He spanked her again, over and over. Her flesh heated beneath his hand, her breathing catching and releasing, growing louder, and staggering into a chorus of moans, hers and his.

After the fifth whack of his hand, he trailed the tips of his fingers over the glowing burn. "Who am I, Amber?"

Her arms slid across the floor, the cereal evidently forgotten beneath them, as she snarled with a thick voice, "Van Quiso. Filthy spawn of the devil."

He gave her five more fiery strokes of his palm, harder and more concentrated than the first five. Then he pinched the heated sore flesh. "Try again."

She released a hiccuping wail, her attempt to squirm away from his grip fruitless. "Mm-m-master."

"Good girl." He glided a finger between her legs, slipping through her slick heat and thrusting to the knuckle. Tight, pulsating muscles gripped him, sucking him in, speeding his pulse.

Bound by his arm on her back, she could only kick her legs and accept the pleasure he allowed her. In turn, her responsive cries propelled him to a euphoric state of lust.

He added another finger and banged her cunt, twisting his wrist and massaging her G-spot as she groaned and rubbed her clit against the sensitive ridges of his cock.

Christ in heaven, the need to fuck her was a raging thing inside him, tearing him to shreds in its attempt to rip out and shove in her. But he couldn't force her.

He bit down on his lip, tasting blood, and dropped his hands to the floor.

Panting, she lifted her head, looked up into his face with heated eyes, then at his hands, back at his face. Her expression fell, and she slid off his lap. "Why?"

Why did he spank her? Or why did he stop? He grabbed her shorts, halting her attempt to pull them up. "I control this." He gripped his dick with his free hand, squeezing hard to dull the ache, and lowered his voice. "And this." He released his cock and gestured around them, encompassing the cereal, the covered windows, the overhead lights, and her gorgeously flushed body. "I control all of it."

She studied him for a silent moment then slipped her legs out of the shorts in his grip and rose. His muscles stiffened to chase, but she didn't run. She backed up until her ass hit the fridge, nude from the waist down, nipples pressing against her tank top. Her heavy-lidded eyes locked with his, her jaw lowered and closed with a whispering inhale. A wordless *Yes*. An undeniable plea.

Climbing to his feet, he tucked himself into his jeans and pulled up the zipper. Then he stalked toward her, mirroring the tilt of her head, knees and shoulders loose, and his gaze holding her prisoner. A breath away, he paused, soaking in the subtleties of her tipped-up chin, parted lips, and glossy but resolute eyes.

With the next breath, he lunged, hands on her jaw, fingers spread around the back of her head. His elbows dropped, shoulders raised, and he yanked her to him, lifting her on tiptoes, guiding her mouth, taking it. His grip twisted through her hair as he drew in her upper lip and shoved her against the fridge, following her with the weight of his body.

The kiss went fucking wild, their lips mashing in a frantic battle. His tongue plunged her mouth, attacking, thrusting in and out, possessing her movements, owning her. Breath for breath, lick after lick, he ate at her mouth, tasting, devouring.

He dropped his hands to her breasts, squeezing ruthlessly as he rolled his cock against her cunt. His tongue tingled, his skin burned, and his head swam. God, she was a drug, and he was so fucking high.

She gripped his biceps, bit at his lips, and threw her arms over his shoulders, her fingers scratching the fuck out of his back. He shuddered, loving it, but he was in control.

Reaching back, he grabbed her wrists and slammed them above her head. Their bodies ground together, his forearms pressing hers to the fridge, their tongues dancing and clashing. Chest-to-chest, hips fused together, he flexed his ass, dry humping her like a horny teenager.

Jesus, fuck, he didn't care. He wanted her.

He leaned back to study her face and found strong smoldering eyes, sharp breaths, and swollen wet lips. Whatever she saw in his expression made her mouth chase his and her fingers curl around his hands. They kissed endlessly, fueling the fire and pushing his control long past the point of discomfort before pulling back and starting all over again.

When he broke the kiss with a hand on her jaw, they panted as one, mouths open and so close their bottom lips brushed. She peered at him through lowered lashes, and he stared back in awe. What trembled between them wasn't an *if?* Or even a *how hard?* Those were foregone. The question they shared was simple.

*Ready?*

With his body holding her weight against the fridge and her arms restrained by his hand overhead, she lifted her calves, sliding them up his legs. Her feet dug into the back of his thighs, pulling him impossibly closer and trapping his cock between them.

She kissed his lips and leaned back as her gaze caught on the overhead light and froze. Along with her breath.

*The goddamned lights.* How could she not be over that?

His fingers fell from her rigid face. Fuck him, he was in hell.

# TWENTY-THREE

Amber squeezed her eyes shut, stomach tightening with nausea, and tried to pull free of Van's grip. Her hands wouldn't budge, held by one of his above her head. "The lights."

"Jesus, Amber. I've seen every gorgeous inch of you." His breath was so close, heating her cheek and vibrating with frustration. "Open your fucking eyes."

She stared up at his striking face and attempted a confident expression. But his gaze immobilized her much more effectively than she could pin him. His pillowy lips semi-puckered with sulkiness, and his intense eyes creased at the corners. Irritation? Uncertainty, too, given the grooves in his forehead and the twitch in his jaw. It was a raw look for him, one that ripped at the places she was already torn and stitched her back up with stronger seams.

Too many terrifying possibilities bounced between them, tingling over her scalp. She could give him a physical connection in the dark, her method of maneuvering through lovers. It would keep her heart safe and her mind focused on the real dynamic of their relationship. She might've decided to stay, but she was still his captive.

As she dropped her toes from his thighs to the floor, he crowded in, melding their bodies together, his feet on the outside of hers.

He gripped her jaw roughly. "You've been in the dark too damned long. The lights. Stay. *On.* Why does that scare you?"

Her heart cramped in its thundering torment against her ribs. As he glanced down at her most intimate places, he didn't seem disgusted. But her filter questioned it. He would get halfway through fucking her and see a flaw he hadn't noticed, an unsavory part of her body brought to light.

"It's...I don't...God, this is hard." She breathed in deeply. "I feel exposed. I can't...I don't handle rejection well."

His eyes flashed, and his nostrils flared. He released her and backed away, but his gaze stayed with her. "Your piece of shit ex abused that beautifully unique part of you that needs to be accepted."

Said the former sex trafficker. She shook her head, unsure how to respond to that.

He gripped the zipper on his jeans and dragged it down, slowly, torturingly, his eyes heated and locked on hers. Without looking away, he hooked his thumbs in the waistband, shoved them down, and kicked the pants to the side. His cock stood hard and swollen between his legs. A curl of heat twitched through her, and her pussy clenched.

He reclined on his back amidst the destruction of Froot Loops and propped up on his elbows. "Now I'm exposed, too. Waiting for *your* acceptance."

There was something changing inside him. She couldn't name it, but she could see it creeping to the surface in the stiffness of his muscles and the clench of his fists as he lay on the floor. It seemed to be feeding on feelings that gravitated around *her*. Was he aware of it? She wanted him to know she could *see* him, that she wanted to accept him.

"You look uncomfortable." She cringed at the stupidity of her statement.

"Yeah, well, this position doesn't bring out the best in me. I'm not a bottom, babe." His eyes darted away as he blew out a long ripple of air then looked back at her. "And you're not the only one susceptible to rejection."

Who would've rejected *him*? She wouldn't, not anymore, but he was covered in cereal. It stuck all over his skin in multicolored crumbs. Who knew what other nooks and crannies it was finding its way into? Just looking at it made her itchy and sweaty.

The other post-Brent men she'd slept with had been so much easier to deal with. They didn't ask questions, didn't pay attention, and certainly didn't fuck her on a crumb-encrusted floor. They pounced; then they bounced. On her terms. "Can we go upstairs?"

"How about you follow your nose down here and taste the rainbow?"

Her heart pounded anxiously at the thought of rolling around in that, but the pleading expression on his face splintered her anxiety painfully down the middle.

She knelt beside him, shuddering as cereal adhered to her legs. Picking off four pieces, she searched for the box to discard them. It would only take a sec—

"Amber." His demanding tone made her drop the crumbs. His

long, skillful fingers drummed on the tiles in such a seductive way she might've leaned down and sucked one into her mouth if not for her repulsion at the crumby floor.

The spilled cereal beckoned her, her mind grouping the O's in fours. She'd scoop them up in those groups then clear the crumbs away from the grout lines. "You ask for a lot. Lights *and* dirt."

"I'm not asking. We are going to have lit-up, dirty sex because you are *not allowed* to look at the mess."

Her gaze flicked to his. "I...I don't kn—"

"You are going to straddle my cock because you need to come. And you deserve that release because you won't be looking at the mess ever again." His glare was as fierce and unwavering as his tone. "Not once. Understand?"

No one had ever talked to her like that, and it gnawed away a chunk of her anxiety. "Okay."

"I'll be right here the whole time." He lowered his back to the tiles and opened his arms, his eyes potent and knowing. He *saw* her yet didn't utter a single hateful word.

Her heart raced as if being chased, hunted. He could catch it, take it, right now, and she wouldn't stop him.

She straddled one of his thighs, a compromise, and nestled into his waiting arms. His relief was palpable in the sighing embrace he gave her. She breathed it in, wanting him, and suddenly determined to give him something she hadn't given a man in two years.

Wriggling out of his arms and down his leg, she didn't look at the crumbs grinding into her knees because he'd commanded her not to. He'd given her the liberty to ignore it. And though his arms were no longer around her, she felt him holding her as she obeyed his order.

A thrill of pride ran through her, as if she'd never ignored untidiness before. She probably hadn't.

She bent over his hard length and wrapped her fingers around it. Satiny skin over rigid steel heated her palm. He was big, not overly so, but he looked massive in her tiny hand. He felt empowering in her grip.

She ducked her head and took his cock into her mouth. His choked breath spurred her to draw him deeper, her fingers pumping the root in sync with her sucking. Pools of heat collected between her legs, simmering to a needy throb. She started to close her thighs to dull the ache, but he lifted his knee, rolling it against her pussy.

His hands flew to her head, digging into her scalp. His hips bucked and his hard body trembled violently beneath her, reducing his rugged timbre to throaty grunts. Seeing him so painfully aroused, so vulnerable in her mouth, was addictive. And she held the power to relieve him.

This was what control felt like. She licked and nuzzled his glans and slid his length over her lips and cheeks, smearing saliva and pre-come across her face. It was liberating.

The hands on her head clenched, and he yanked her off of him. "Condom."

"I don't..." She glanced around the kitchen, knowing full well there were no condoms. She'd been through every shelf and drawer. "Where?"

His eyes closed, and his face twisted in agony. "Check the pockets of my jeans. Hurry."

Sliding off his leg, she snagged his jeans and found a condom in the front pocket. Did he always keep rubbers on him? Given the relaxed wear of the denim, he'd likely grabbed the jeans from the hamper, stocked with a condom. "Got one."

He fisted his cock, stroking it, root to tip. His knuckles flexed in his exertion, his eyes burning with silver flames.

Sweet mother, that image hit her right between the legs, sending her inner muscles into a hot spasm. She ripped open the package, rolled on the rubber, and straddled him, his cock a long, stiff invitation against her pussy.

He leaned up, and she met him halfway in a sweeping of lips. He grabbed the back of her neck and pulled her to him as he dropped against the floor. Their tongues tangled, and their hands slid everywhere, bumping and caressing in urgent exploration, kindling her arousal from a low burn to a wildfire.

She shoved her fingers through his hair, her hips working into an electrifying grind against him, each flex hitting her clit against the head of his cock, the smooth hardness of his length sliding between her labium. Fuck, what would he feel like without the rubber in the way?

"Aw God, put me in," he groaned against her mouth.

The sound of him begging surged heat through her blood. She reached between them with shaky fingers, positioned his cock, and the hard tip pushed through her opening.

His head fell back, and the cords of his neck strained as she slid down his length. He stretched her deliciously as she worked him in, sinking inch by inch, until he was buried to the root. So deep, so full, her needy flesh rippled around him, shooting sparks of pleasure through her body.

She attacked his mouth as she rolled her hips, ravenous and impatient, sucking on his lips, nipping at him. Her fingers found his hair, stroking and pulling as he fucked her. His large hands on her hips held her in place, his thrusts rocking into her in long, powerful strokes.

He was merciless, his muscles flexing beneath her, his balls slapping her ass with every drive of his cock. His hands moved to her breasts and pinched her nipples so hard the sharp pain sent her over, so fast and explosive, she hadn't felt its approach.

The orgasm slammed into her, and she pushed up, back bowing, riding the wave after wave of ecstasy. Her head fell back, mind empty, her body soaring through the tingling sensations.

He let out an unintelligible curse, thrusting hard and fast. His hands dropped to her waist in a bruising grip as his strokes jerked, lost rhythm, and slammed deep inside her. "Unnngh." His jaw hung open with short, ragged exhales. "Uh...ungh..." He shuddered as he spent his seed, his heavy grunts rumbling into a throaty growl.

The kitchen rotated around them, heaving with the sounds of their heavy breaths. Eternal seconds passed before feeling returned to her fingers and toes.

He looked up at her, his eyes dilated and heavy-lidded. "C'mere."

She lowered her body, her arms winding around his broad shoulders and his heart pounding against her ear on his chest. He hugged her to him, his cock growing soft inside her.

"Ready to eat?"

She released a sated laugh. "Such a man. Sex and food."

"Life's two main ingredients."

After they brushed the crumbs from their bodies and dressed, she sat at the table and watched him scramble eggs and fry bacon. She and food had a hate-hate relationship, so she'd never bothered to learn how to cook. He didn't seem to mind, seeing how he'd told her to sit and rest.

The smell of grease filled her nose and roused her hunger. By the time he brought the plate and two glasses of milk to the table, a rumble had gripped her stomach.

One plate. One fork. He perched before her, his thighs on the outside of hers, lifted a forkful of eggs, and held it to her lips. She accepted willingly, wantonly.

He broke off a piece of bacon. "You didn't look at the mess on the floor while I cooked."

It wasn't a question. He knew she hadn't. She chewed, swallowed, and opened her mouth for the bacon bite. When her lips wrapped around his fingers, he drew them out slowly and stroked a knuckle across her cheek.

"What does the anxiety feel like?" he asked, softly.

She sipped the milk to clear her throat. "When it's bad, I don't have control of my body. It feels like something huge and chaotic is wearing my skin, thrashing around in it, stretching it, and I'm stuck in there with it, helpless."

He fed her another bite, thoughtful, listening. Maybe he didn't understand, but he seemed to be trying.

"Sometimes it's subtle, just there beneath the surface. If I'm distracted, I won't identify it until it's passed. I've tried to study it as it happens, to better understand it. If I lay still and really focus, I can almost grab hold of it. It's as if my brain has its very own body and something is brushing up against it, something that shouldn't be there."

"Do you feel it right now?" He watched her with those perceptive eyes that could reach deeper inside her than any other part of his body.

"I feel..." Panicked? No. Troubled? Not exactly. "Out of alignment."

His eyes glimmered. He liked that answer, and it made her insides flutter.

As he finished off the breakfast, she realized she'd stopped counting the bites when he prompted her to talk. Probably his intention. He didn't seem to do anything without an agenda.

There were still a few bites left, but her stomach hardened, way too bloated. She shook her head at the next forkful. "Tell me something about you. Something that's hard for you to talk about."

The fork paused then lowered to the table. He glanced at the mudroom and back at her, his thumb moving restlessly along the edge of the plate. Then it stilled. "I'll show you."

He stood, and without waiting for her, strode to the mudroom, opened the garage door, and stared into the dark hush, his features empty and distinct.

His expressions would never expose *who* he was, but judging by his sudden remoteness, whatever waited in the garage would.

A cold sweat broke out over her skin, but she rose to follow him, determined to know him. As she walked right through the middle of the smashed cereal without looking at it, her head tilted back, her arms relaxed at her sides, and her strides carried her to him with grace.

He glanced at her with cool, unreadable eyes, and she curled her fingers around his limp hand. Then she followed him through the door.

# TWENTY-FOUR

The fluorescents overhead buzzed in the darkness a half second before the garage flooded with light. Amber blinked rapidly, her lungs tightened, and her hand released Van's fingers with a jerk.

Where she expected chains, whips, torture equipment, and hell, maybe a car was something much more startling.

Dolls and mannequins in every size and state of repair lined workbenches and shelves, hung from walls, and overflowed crates and boxes. Detached arms and legs scattered the floor. Headless bodies slumped in piles with limbs tangled together, the hinged eyes and painted faces frozen in apathy.

The humidity in the two-bay garage stifled her breath, and a chill settled into her bones as she took in the largest collection of mannequins she'd ever seen. There was something very sad about their condition, the way they were tossed aside, neglected...yet *kept* all the same. A graveyard for broken dolls? Or some kind of a sick tribute?

He left her side and strode toward a large table in the center of the garage, its surface cluttered with paints and tiny tools and doll parts.

She didn't follow but instead walked a wide circuit around him on shaky legs, hands at her sides, her attention imprisoned by the horde of soulless faces. What would a man as virile and rugged and *manly* as Van want with dolls?

Her steps took her through a maze of baby dolls, toddler-sized dolls, and nipple-less mannequins, all bald and naked, most damaged beyond repair. Her stomach turned, but she wanted to understand the source of her apprehension. He didn't seem to have any friends or family. Were these...things a distraction from the loneliness when he wasn't abducting people?

The agony of being alone and feeling unwanted was a cruel affliction. It could make one desperate for any kind of connection. Maybe even a connection with the plastic replicas of the real thing. Or with deliverymen in the dark.

Had all those men she'd slept with been some kind of coping mechanism for her loneliness? That might've been part of it. Like a fourth of it. Yeah, and the other three-fourths of the reason was simply payment for her deliveries. It'd been a fair trade. She hadn't been using them, right? Her ribs squeezed, and she shoved that thought away.

She passed a tall display cabinet with a glass door, the only one like it in the room. The two dolls inside... What the hell?

A plastic woman sat nude on a chair. She was similar to Amber's height and held a child-sized doll in a red-checkered dress. The woman's brown marbled eyes stared with a glassy, far-away look. Even more eerie was the red line hand-drawn from one glass eye to the pink painted mouth. A scar drawn exactly like the one on his face. She shuddered, gasping, and covered her mouth with her hand.

The dolls in the cabinet were the only two in the garage with hair, the strands intricately woven together in various shades of brown. Why weren't they damaged like the others? Why were they the only ones safely displayed behind glass? What did they mean to him?

They held answers. Shivering curiosity drew her hand to the knob on the glass door.

"Don't touch those."

His harsh voice made her jump, and she yanked her hand back. Shit. She shook off her nerves and turned to face him. "You collect dolls." *Hollow-eyed, creepy-ass plastic people.*

Perching on a wheeled stool, he rolled toward the table and placed his palms on the surface, staring blankly at the clutter around his hands. "I make them, collect them, and...break them."

An emotionless response, but layers hummed beneath the words. He leaned back, knees spread, hands folded between his strong thighs. He watched her from beneath dark eyebrows, his full lips relaxed and pouty. He was somewhat childlike, surrounded by dolls, sulking and rolling on the stool. Yet he commanded the room with the intensity of his sullen temperament, all that muscle, and...the stretch of his jeans cupping his cock so erotically.

She jerked her gaze up. The man was fucking sexy as hell, doll fetish notwithstanding. She swallowed and continued her exploration around the perimeter, attempting to make sense of it. As she wandered, she peeked back every now and then, finding him tracking her every movement with hooded eyes.

A weight bench sat at one end, surrounded by a mess of mismatched dumbbells. She hoped to learn a lot more about him than the location of his damned workouts. When she reached the farthest corner, she faced him again. "Why do you break them? You don't sell them?"

His huge hands cradled a small headless body, his thumb moving over a two-inch hole punched through the torso. "I'm more interested in quality control." He tossed it behind him.

She flinched as the doll skidded across the cement floor. He broke dolls for fun. Her heart crashed into a roaring panic. Had he harmed a real child at some point? Was this his way of dealing with that? Or maybe he had been the child?

Her spine crawled with millions of icy pinpricks. Her feet stuck to the floor, the span of the garage separating her from the darkness surrounding the man she might've gravely misjudged. "Why do the dolls need quality control?" Fear quivered in her voice despite her best attempts to stifle it.

He rose from the stool and walked toward a box of undamaged bodies with a terrifying calmness. Paralyzed, she watched as he yanked out the plastic mold of a baby—its limbs attached—and dropped it on the floor. Then his bare foot came down, smashing the body with one stomp.

She stopped breathing. Was this some kind of reenactment? Horrified, she wanted to look away, but she couldn't. She had to know.

The torso cracked beneath his foot, and the head popped off. Dizziness swarmed her head, sending her ears ringing in a frenzied pulse.

With hands on his hips and his head tipped down, hard eyes rolled up and locked on her. "That's why."

She wrapped her arms around her waist, her fingers sticky and trembling. Quality control meant he was looking for flaws, right? Was he looking for a doll that could survive a heavy foot? That didn't make any sense. Oh God, she didn't want it to make sense.

Breathing deeply from her diaphragm, she smothered her dread with a strong voice. "I don't understand. Why are you smashing them like that?"

He looked away, his lips in a flat line, seemingly refusing to answer. But he wanted to. She could see it in the rise and fall of his chest and in the shift of his eyes as they studied the collection, searching for the words.

Endless seconds passed, the stillness strangling, before his Adam's apple bobbed and his fingers twitched on his hips. "It was the first and last toy I owned. A goddamned doll." He laughed nervously, his hand lifting to rub the back of his neck. "I don't even know how I got it. Probably from one of those missionaries who would pop in to deliver food and Jesus pamphlets."

A clot of emotion gathered in her throat. Something had happened *to* him. She lowered her hands to her shorts, gripping them. "This was when you lived in the *colonia*?"

He nodded and crouched over the broken doll, glaring at it. "I was a nine-year-old boy. What the fuck was I doing with a doll?"

His tone was angry, at odds with the tender way his finger traced the jagged hole in the doll's torso at his feet. He seemed to be lost in memory, his silence hardening the lump she couldn't swallow. She stepped forward, aching to erase the distance, but the jerk of his shoulders halted her approach.

"He was a huge man. My mother was a whore, sold herself for the needle, and he was just some random john, but he was the first one I remember. He fucked her right there in front of me. She was so fucking high I don't think she was conscious." A tremor shook his body, and he sat back, legs folded against his chest, his arms wrapped around his knees. "And there I was, curled up in the damned corner, hugging that doll, kissing her ratty hair like she was my only friend. Hell, she *was* my only friend."

He put his hands over his face, and his shoulders hunched like a scared little boy. Her heart clenched painfully, and her eyes burned. She wanted to hold that little boy so damned badly.

Straightening the legs of her shorts, she moved with fast, quiet steps. Then she dropped before him and mirrored his pose with her arms around her knees.

His hands lowered and dangled between them. He didn't look up, didn't acknowledge her at all. "When he was done with my mother, he turned to me. I wouldn't let go of that doll. He was so goddamned strong I couldn't stop him from ripping Isadora out of my hands."

"Isadora? Your mother?"

His head cocked, and his eyes narrowed in confusion on the broken doll between their feet. He squeezed his legs tighter against his chest, his body curling inward. He was shutting down.

In a bold gesture, she reached out and placed her hand on his cheek, stroking her fingers through the thick hair above his ear.

He shook his head, eyes on the floor, then leaned into her touch. "I'd named the doll after my mother."

There was no embarrassment or resentment in his tone, just...sadness. He loved his mother, that much was clear, and evidently that love wasn't reciprocated.

A burn seared through her nose. She envied his devotion. She didn't know her mother well enough to love her. There'd been no connection, no relationship. Just illness. She rocked forward to her knees and wrapped her arms around his shoulders.

His legs dropped, and he pulled her against his chest, speaking softly into her hair. "When he stomped on the doll, her body split in half, and the arms and legs tore off. Just like that, she was dead."

She rubbed his rigid back, her own muscles stiff with anguish. The attachment he must've felt for that doll amidst such a neglected, fucked-up upbringing... God, he must've mourned her. The doll. His mother. She glanced over his shoulder and took in the menagerie of brokenness with new eyes.

It was tragic and beautiful and inspiring. She didn't know the depth of his suffering, but the coping, the struggle to self-medicate? She knew all about that. The memory of his doll had stuck with him, and he'd recreated his appreciation for it, clinging to the notion that he could somehow repair what had happened, that he could fix the past with the present.

She didn't think that was possible, but what did she know? Just because she hadn't been successful at taking back her own life didn't mean he couldn't find some kind of peace in creating an indestructible doll.

He adjusted her legs so that she straddled his lap and squeezed her chest to his. His arms were strong and immovable around her, his body a powerhouse of muscle. But she felt the scared boy in the hunch of his shoulders and the restlessness of his fingers gripping at the shirt covering her back. That little boy felt like her insides, fractured and hurting, lonely and scared, but brimming with the desire to love something or someone and to be loved.

His cheek rubbed against hers, but his arms turned to stone and his chest expanded with a long, tense inhale. "After he smashed the doll, he pressed my face into the dirt and fucked me." Her heart crushed instantly at the emptiness in his voice and the impact of his words. He released a slow breath and kissed her brow. "I came to grips with that a long time ago. He was the first but certainly not the last. For the next four years, many of her drug dealers turned to me when she was too stoned to put out. She OD'd when I was thirteen."

Amber held him tightly, her hug expressing what she couldn't with her voice. When he leaned back, his eyes were clear and searching. His gentle expression filled her with heartache, but she also felt a strong surge of something else. "I'm proud of you."

He cupped her face, his thumbs caressing her cheeks as his eyes followed the movement. "Mm. Not much to be proud of, Amber. By age thirteen, I was a whore just like her."

Her jaw stiffened, her words rushed and heated. "You were young. It was all you knew. And you broke free from it. You didn't let it kill you."

"Don't make excuses for it." His eyes sparked. "I don't."

She wanted to argue, but his hard, domineering glare was back. She bit her lip, her mind swimming through everything he'd told her. "So you're trying to make a doll that doesn't break?"

His gaze traveled through the garage, probing the broken body parts. "I've tried. They all break eventually." He laughed. "I'm convinced their hollow bodies are filled with mysterious energy, just waiting to cave in. Like dark matter. Can't fuck with science."

She stroked a finger over his jaw, savoring the connection. "Dark matter holds the universe together."

His lips twitched. "It also threatens to destroy it."

Were they talking about the dolls or him? She pointed at the plastic woman and child sitting in the cabinet. "What about those two? They're not broken."

His eyes closed, opened, and he patted her leg, lifting her to her feet as he stood. "That's enough for one day. I've got shit to do."

More secrets then. She stared at their shiny blank faces, and they stared back, trapping their story behind painted lips. "You'll tell me when you're ready?"

He nodded and led her to the door with light steps as if he'd shed the weight of the world. So why did she feel so heavy? It was admirable what he was doing, making and breaking dolls to redeem his childhood. To redeem his mother.

But she wouldn't dress it up. He was her mirror in a way. They both carried a million cracks beneath the skin. Even under the stark light of the fluorescents, it was hard to see which of them was more broken. But for the first time, she felt like she had to vanquish her mental illness not for herself but for someone else. Because she was broken *with him*, and if she fixed herself, maybe she could make him a little less broken, too.

# TWENTY-FIVE

The first twenty-four hours in Van's cabin had been both terrifying and eye opening. Amber's surroundings and the man she shared them with challenged the routine and order she desperately clung to. Her world had become a state of nonlinear catastrophic exasperation.

As the hours bled into days, the next three weeks were very much the same. Every day was just like the first, the punishments and the tenderness, the panic attacks and the sex. She made his life hell, and he whipped her for it. She adored him, when she didn't hate him.

He followed through on his promise to be as messy as she was clean. When she scrubbed the shower walls, he coated them with motor oil. When she picked up his socks, he decorated the house with tampons, tying the strings in knots so complicated she couldn't undo them.

Three weeks with him made her fear a little less. She still couldn't face the outdoors, yet every day he forced her out. Sometimes, he required a single step on the porch. Most days, he hauled her kicking and screaming to the tree where he whipped her and fucked her into an adrenaline-induced state of elation.

But as the weeks passed, she could still feel that intangible thing in her head, scratching against her brain like it wanted out. Something else lived in there, too, making her anxious. Her dependency on routine and straight lines was shifting. She was becoming too centered on Van.

She was aware of it, knew it was unhealthy, and still she listened for his footsteps and watched his expressions with a pounding heart. Whenever he left the house to jog in the woods or run errands, she awaited his return with an uneasy amount of panic.

Then there were his secrets. How did he get his scars? Why did he keep those dolls in the glass cabinet? Why wouldn't he tell her? She'd developed a new obsession, a dangerous one.

On day twenty-four, she sat alone in the garage at the worktable and tied off the final stitches on a doll. The body was made of leather, strong and durable, and stuffed with wool batting. She'd glued and sewed the plastic limbs and head to the leather torso. Van had painted the face with red puckered lips and twinkling blue eyes. The long straw-colored hair had taken him hours to weave.

She finished it off by dressing it in a blue gown with yellow bows. When she held it up for inspection, a feeling of breathlessness came over her as heat radiated through her chest. *Try to break this one, Van.*

She hopped up, carrying the doll with her, and stopped at the display cabinet. The angle of the light cast her reflection in the glass door. She guiltily tugged up her shirt and revealed her tummy. Having neglected her purging habit in Van's ever-watchful presence, she'd gained weight. At least six pounds, maybe more.

Bile simmered in her throat. She tucked the doll under her arm and pinched her hip, a repulsive hunk of flesh. Saliva burst through her mouth, overwhelming her with the sudden need to spit. She clamped her lips closed, fighting it.

Maybe he wasn't telling her his secrets because he'd lost interest in her. She hadn't made much progress combating the OCD, and she fought him every day when he dragged her outside. That must've been it. He was tired of her.

With her self-berating thoughts banging in her head, she left the garage in search of him. To show him the doll, to hold him, kiss him, talk with him, it didn't matter. She needed his strength and their connection.

When she stepped into the kitchen, she slammed to a halt. He leaned against the counter, sipping a glass of tequila, dressed in a suit. His strong, freshly-shaven jaw and thick, dark hair were just two of the countless traits that made him painfully attractive. He wore a narrow black tie and black button-up shirt beneath a suit that matched the striking color of his pale gray eyes.

The spice of his cologne reached her nose, seductively tempting her arousal. And taunting her insecurities.

Did he want to go on a date? He knew she couldn't. Oh God, she couldn't. She bit down on her cheek. *Stop being so self-absorbed.* Maybe this had nothing to do with her.

She swallowed her dread. "You look...Wow." She wanted to eat him. She laid the doll on the counter and reached up, adjusting his collar and stroking her knuckles over his jaw. Then she slid her palm down his tie. "Why are you dressed up?"

He drained the glass of tequila and set it beside the doll. "I'm going out."

A cold fever flashed through her cheeks. Dressed like that? A date with someone else? Her hands shook, and she gripped them behind her back. "Where?"

His eyes, *God those eyes,* pierced through her like knives. Then he sharpened the cut with his answer. "I'm going to see Liv."

# TWENTY-SIX

Probably an inappropriate time for Van's cock to get hard, but fuck him, Amber's jealousy was as sexy as her tight little body. He leaned against the kitchen counter, shoved a hand in his pocket, and gave his dick a firm pinch, not that it helped.

Her jealousy, however, was bred from her poor self-worth, which was the root of the bulimia, the need for perfection, and the avoidance of outside.

She held her composure admirably, but that didn't mean her insecurities weren't bursting at the seams. Her hands were behind her back, so he leaned in, straining to hear the crack of her knuckles. The popping didn't come, but her cheeks flushed a lovely shade of pink. And was that a growl in her throat?

Somehow, she pulled off a pleasant voice. "Why would you need to see her?"

Because his daughter was growing up without him. Because his infrequent visits to Liv's window over the past three weeks weren't turning up any information. There'd been nothing on her possible connections with the cartel or FBI; nothing to tell if she was using those connections to trap him in the event he attempted to contact their daughter.

His involvement in Mr. E's operation was still unknown to authorities. If he surfaced, it would threaten his freedom and ironically Amber's. Liv would rat him out if she sensed even a hint of danger with regard to their daughter. Prison was *not* an option.

The one thing he wouldn't do was take Livana from her stable life with Mr. E's widow. Despite his history with kidnapping, he would *never* do that to his daughter. Fuck, he just wanted to be a part of her life and needed to make sure Liv understood that.

He turned the glass of tequila on the counter round and round as he collected his thoughts. Telling Amber about his purpose with Liv meant revealing his parenthood and exposing the looming reason he'd taken Amber, why he'd worked so hard to help her conquer the disorders. She would eventually find out his intention to use her as a character reference with Liv. How would she react to that? Would she think he was using her? Was he?

He used her body for his pleasure, and he depended on her strength to be a better man. But most days, it was a damned struggle to reconcile his goal with all the sentimental crud sticking to his heart. He was so wrapped up in Amber, adrift in the most thrilling moments of his life, he'd lost his bearings.

Amber's health and happiness were as important to him as his daughter's was. In fact, his goals with Livana had become secondary to his relationship with Amber. And that scared him to fucking death.

As he stared into the worried brown eyes of the woman he'd come to adore more than any person in the world, he realized she owned him as much as he owned her. He clung to that heady, full-body feeling because it infused his every thought with hope.

It was also turning him into a cherry-scented, floaty-hearted sissy fuck.

Why did he need to see Liv? He twisted his lips into a charming smile, but the effort hurt. "She has something I want."

At an arm's length away, she glanced down at her tits, then her hips, and looked away with a pained expression. No doubt she'd filtered his words into something like *Liv has something you don't have*. She was oblivious to the effect she had on him. How could a woman so fucking beautiful be so damned blind?

Good thing he had some time before he needed to leave. "You'll be punished for that."

Her gaze jerked back, and she crossed her arms. "What the fuck did *I* do?"

"I want *you* to answer that question, and after your punishment, I might" —he drew out a long breath, letting her mind flicker through the possibilities— "allow you to come."

"You're an asshole."

"Noted." He was delaying the eminent conversation regarding Liv, but toying with her was a delicious distraction. He rested his ass against the counter, tilted his head back, and stared at the ceiling with a dramatic amount of interest in the white brush-strokes. She would tell him why he was punishing her eventually.

She tapped her fingernails on the counter, blew out some heavy exhales, and stomped her foot twice. *Not four times.* "Fine. I don't know what you want from Liv, but it makes me feel" — she groaned — "inadequate."

He awarded her honesty with the full commitment of his gaze. "Be specific."

She pinned her lips together, fisted her hands on her hips, and glared at her feet. "Jesus, you're annoying." She peered up at him, then back at her feet, and mumbled, "My boobs—"

"I can't hear you."

She huffed then hardened her voice. "My boobs are fake and plasticky. She's probably beautifully natural."

He hooked a knuckle beneath her chin, lifting her face to capture her eyes. "She's both beautiful and natural" — her jaw stiffened, and he squeezed it— "but she's got jack shit on a beauty queen."

Her chin pressed down on his hand, stubbornly and uselessly. "What else?"

She shifted her weight from foot to foot. "My hips are fat." Her voice wobbled into a seething shout. "And that's *your* fault!"

There it was. He'd been waiting for it. Bulimia was the quietest of the disorders, the one they hadn't discussed since her first day here. But he never left her alone until her food settled, strictly limiting her opportunities to puke.

He crouched at her feet and gripped her thighs beneath the short skirt, lifting the hem to her waist with the slide of his hands. "You're done with your calorie-counting world of size zero."

"There's nothing wrong with size zero. Runway models—"

"If you want to look like a starving creature, you better have drool clinging to your chin and your mouth reaching for my cock." He leaned forward and sank his teeth into the flesh on her thigh.

She jerked in his hold, and he bit down ruthlessly into her flexing quad. If she'd gained any weight at all, it was muscle. She was a fucking machine during their morning workouts.

He kissed the two half-moon indentions he'd given her and pressed his nose against her bare pussy. Christ, he loved that she didn't have panties at his house. As he breathed in her sweet scent, her hips trembled beneath his grip. It had only been two hours since he'd fucked her, yet his cock was as stiff as the night he'd met her.

He lowered the skirt and stood. "Wipe your mind of all your preconceived notions of how you think I see you." He touched her cheek and really looked at her, the glow of her skin, the dark fall of hair around her shoulders, her sultry fuck-me lips, and the rise of her full tits. Defined biceps, slender throat, petite nose, everything about her ensnared him. He could stare at her for hours, losing himself in her beauty. He brushed her hair behind her ear. "How do I see you, Amber?"

Her eyes were bright and glassy, peeking up at him through dense lashes. "You think I'm...pretty."

Not the word he would've chosen for the exquisite view before him, but it pointed her the right direction. "Good girl." He kissed her softly, happily, humming his contentment. "Now you can ask your questions."

She fingered the lapels of his suit jacket, sliding her hands up and down the folds of finely woven wool. "What does Liv have that you want?"

"Mm." He fisted his hands behind his back. *Stop delaying, dickhead.* "It's time to visit that display cabinet."

She arched her eyebrows. "You're ready to tell me?"

Fuck no. "Yeah."

He led her to the garage, loosening the tie and rubbing his tight neck. He'd practiced how he would tell her for weeks, but as they stood before the lifelike reminders of the family he'd longed for, his carefully composed speech disintegrated, and his polluted heart clawed out of his throat.

"In thirty-three years, there have only been four people I've given a shit about, that I'd even consider putting before myself." He opened the glass door, his mouth dry. "The first two didn't love me back."

"Your mother and Liv." She stated it not as a question but as a realization as she stared at the dolls, her elbows tucked to her sides, her fingers trembling on her bottom lip.

He touched the hair on the mannequin, his token of Liv. But as the soft strands slipped through his caress, he didn't feel the usual heaviness in his chest. Instead, his pulse raced with nervousness. He hadn't intended on telling her about the hair, but he longed for her to accept *all* the ugly parts of him.

"I made this with Liv's real hair. Collected it for years from her pillow, her hairbrush, and directly from her scalp." At the time, he didn't know why. A compulsion maybe? A sick one. He removed his hand and shoved it in his pocket.

"Oh, Van, I can't even..." Her voice strained with disbelief, and she cleared her throat. "Why?"

He was damaged, in the most irredeemable way. He brought shaky fingers to his forehead and gave her his back. He hated this feeling, this fucking vulnerability. "This was a mistake."

"Van Quiso." Her clipped tone vibrated with impatience. "You put me on that bathroom counter with my legs spread and made me talk about some scary shit. You owe me." She sucked in a long breath and softened her voice. "I want to understand why you kept her hair. I want to know everything about you."

Her words moved him. And the sudden support of her arms wrapping around his waist and her chest against his back found him and held him.

"I have a memory of my mother under the tin roof of our makeshift shelter. She wasn't crying or stoned. She was just sitting there, *being*." He placed his hands over Amber's on his abs, absorbing her warmth. "She was sitting so close her hair touched my face and shoulder, and I imagined maybe that was what her fingertips would feel like or her kisses." His voice thickened, his chest aching. He coughed into his fist.

She slipped under his arm and cupped his face with fire in her eyes. "My mother couldn't look at me because I reminded her of her illness. She gave birth to me, this child who embodied the worst of her sickness, and nothing I could've done would change that." She caressed his chest. "I guess what I'm saying is...I get it. I wanted you to know I understand."

He coiled his fingers through her hair and put his lips on her forehead. He was his mother's repulsive reminder of her slavery. Of course, he knew that, which was why he needed a relationship with his daughter. To show her she wasn't a thing he resented. To give her a father's love. "The third one doesn't know I exist."

"The third?" Her brow wrinkled beneath his lips. She pulled back and peered around his shoulder at the display cabinet. "The small doll is the third person you...she's..." She swallowed, hard.

"Livana will be eight next month." Another birthday he wouldn't be a part of. His throat burned with painful frustration.

She nodded, a jerky movement, as her gaze shifted over the doll, swimming with thoughts. "Livana. Liv and Van."

*Livana.* The name he'd given to the child that was snatched away the moment she was born. Mr. E hadn't even allowed him to hold her.

He touched the scar on his cheek. "Mr. E gave us matching scars when I got her pregnant."

Her eyes squinted, probably narrowing on the hand-drawn scar on the mannequin.

With his hands on her waist, he turned them to face the cabinet, standing behind her with his arms around her mid-section, holding her tightly in case she ran. "Mr. E and his wife raised Livana." His voice clogged, thick with painful memories. "My father prohibited us from seeing her outside of the videos he sent."

"Videos?"

"His *incentives*. To ensure we didn't fuck up the meetings with his slave buyers."

"My God—"

"I knew where Livana was the whole time and kept it from Liv." Though he'd never been allowed contact, he'd secretly watched his daughter from a distance. "Liv would've gone after her. It was too risky."

His stomach hardened with guilt. He could've helped her get their daughter, but in doing so, he would've lost Liv. In the end, he lost her anyway. He closed his eyes, breathing in the clean scent of Amber's hair, and opened them. That same end had brought him a woman he would never deserve. "When she shot me, I told her everything. I'd planned on telling her anyway. Mr. E killed her mother, and I knew Livana was next."

"Jesus." She pivoted in his arms and ran her palm across his shoulder, over the bullet wound. "She shot you and your father." She chewed on her lip, watching the caress of her hand. "And she escaped. So why did she never mention you to the police?"

"She'd killed seven slave buyers. She thought she killed me. And she hasn't heard from me since the day I wired her six of the seven million we'd earned in trafficking."

She stepped away from him and paced along the wall of doll parts. "A payoff?"

"An apology."

She pinched her bottom lip, wearing a pensive expression. "And she has something you want. Which was why you were on my porch."

"Mr. E's widow has my daughter. But I know Liv has unrestricted access to her."

"You're a stalker." She reached up and traced the gnarled seam of a doll arm. "You're also a fugitive, and your daughter lives with the Police Chief's widow." She dropped her hand and looked at him with confusion etching her beautiful face. "I'm sorry, Van, but I don't understand what you hope to gain by seeking out Liv."

He put his hands in his pockets to hide his shaking fingers. "She could bring me along on her visitations with Livana. She could introduce me as a friend or an uncle, and someday, when Livana's old enough, when she trusts me, I could tell her."

Her lips tilted into a frown, her eyes downcast and glossy as she shook her head. "Why would Liv agree to that? Van, she must be terrified of you. She'd never let you near Livana."

His pulse sped up, his voice hard. "I'll convince her I can be a good father, that I'm not a threat." He moved toward her with determined steps and gripped her head, tilting it back, trapping her gaze. "You're doing so well, going outside every day. You could tell her how much I've helped you and convince her I've changed." Adamant resolve strengthened his posture, and he channeled that strength to his eyes. "Come with me."

# TWENTY-SEVEN

The flash of Amber's eyes and the set of her jaw made Van's stomach drop. Fuck, his words had come out all wrong. They clotted the space between them, shoving them apart.

She yanked her head from his hands. "*That's* why you've been forcing me outside? You thought you could fix me, that I could vouch for you?"

The sadness in her voice ripped him in half, but he refused to let go of her or give up on this. He grabbed her wrists and held them against his chest. "You could tell her I'd be a good father, that I would never hurt my daughter."

A tremble skittered across her chin. Her arms twisted in his hands, her fingers clutching his jacket. Then, in an unexpected move, she lifted on tiptoes and pressed her mouth against his.   ·

The beat of his heart stumbled as she kissed him without resentment or anger or any of the reactions he'd feared. He was numb with shock, dizzy with lust, swirling his tongue over her lips. Fuck him, *those lips*. He needed them on his body, on his cock. He needed to tug it out and shove it inside her, to bury himself in the place she accepted him.

She broke the kiss and spoke quietly. "I don't think you'd hurt your daughter like you've harmed all the other women in your life." He opened his mouth to agree, and she pressed a finger over his lips. "In fact, I think you're done treating women that way."

"I am—"

"Shh." She dropped her hand. "You would be a great father. Fierce and protective and attentive."

God, that felt good to hear. He pressed his lips tight to keep from smiling like an asshole.

Her eyes darted away, and she leaned back. "But I can't be the one to confirm that, Van. I can't..." She shook her head. "I can't leave. I'm not fixed."

There lay the crux of his conflict over the last few weeks. He didn't just want her fixed for his purpose. He pulled her back to him with her forearms pinned against his chest. "That's not why I want you. I just want...I need you to *want* to be by my side."

She sniffed, her eyes closing then cutting back to him. "You said there were four? Four people you cared about?"

Ah, there was his little *count*ress. He might've grinned if his chest didn't hurt so badly. "Number four..." He blew out a breath, lowered his brow to hers, and told her the truth. "When I met her, I wanted to pick apart her mind and play with the pieces. I wanted to become her obsession, her solitary devotion, her fear." She tensed and so did he. "But along the way, *she* picked *me* apart. I'm the one who is obsessed, devoted...scared. Come with me to see Liv?"

She wrenched from his hold and backed up. "I can't."

He prowled after her. "You handle the agoraphobia just fine while hanging from a tree in subspace." She stumbled against the wall, and he closed in, blocking her on either side with his arms. "You don't even know you're outside when I'm fucking you beneath the shelter of my body."

"Right." She straightened her spine, hands clenched at her sides. "So you plan on whipping and fucking me during this meeting with Liv? 'Cause I'm not sure that'll help your fatherly image."

"No. I'm just saying you can do this without the mental distractions. I won't leave your side, Amber, and I would never let anything out there harm you in any way."

She shoved against his chest with a shriek and slipped beneath his arm, shuffling backward. "My enemy isn't out there, Van." She thrust a finger at the garage doors. "It's here." She gripped her head. "Right here. I sit in this house day after day and tell myself I'm strong, that I'm better than this. But once I step outside, something takes over. Something more powerful than me invades my body and I can't fight it. I try." She sobbed. "I fucking try. But it brings me to my fucking knees. Every. Time."

He reached her in two strides and lifted her into his arms. His chest was so fucking tight it felt like his heart was shrinking. He couldn't fail her. He wouldn't. He carried her out of the garage and through the house. "When you're ready" —he climbed the stairs— "you'll be there with me."

With a heavy sigh, she hugged his neck. "So you won't go see her? You won't leave?"

God, she sounded so relieved, and he was about to steal that away.

He set her on her feet beside the railing in the loft. "Liv is singing in a bar tonight. It's neutral ground, a good place for me to feel her out."

"What?" She gripped his hair and pulled his face to hers. "You can't. She'll turn you in, Van. You can't go."

He removed her hands from his head, walked to the nightstand, and grabbed a length of rope. "Do you need to go to the bathroom?"

She gaped at him. "No. Why?"

"On your knees." With the rope taut between his fists, he returned to her with a clear sense of purpose in his strides. He promised her a punishment, and he expected her to remember. She must've read the intention in his eyes because she lowered to the floor.

"Arms up and together."

She obeyed, but of course, she couldn't keep her mouth shut. "You can't punish me for having thoughts, Van. They're just thoughts!"

Insidious thoughts that fed an eating disorder. He wound the rope around her wrists—nineteen times because she'd told him once it was her least favorite *anti-number*—and tied it off at the base of a banister beam on the railing. An anchor hitch knot she wouldn't be able to undo with her bound hands.

The restraints were just preliminary, to prime her for the punishment she would receive when he returned. The rope prevented her from standing and leaping to her death, but she could lie down. Which was a mercy because she would be there awhile.

He left her with a lingering kiss and adjusted his tie on the way to the front door. A sudden thought veered his path toward the kitchen counter, to the doll she'd left there. He picked it up and lifted the gown, pressing his thumbs against the seams in the leather torso.

"Stomp on it." Her voice drifted down from the loft.

He spun and met her gentle eyes peering through the railing overhead. When she gave him an encouraging nod, he set the doll on the floor and slammed his loafer into the soft belly. The limbs bounced but remained attached. He cocked his head, heart thundering. With an unsteady hand, he scooped it up and raised the gown. No holes. Every stitch intact.

The tingling started in his hands and spread out through his entire body in a warm feeling of weightlessness. "You did it," he whispered then raised his voice. "You fucking did it."

When he looked up, her gorgeous, teary smile lifted him on his toes. He wanted to tell her that she had to come with him, that he needed her because he loved her, that she found him and released him with a fixable doll, and maybe, just maybe, she could fix him, too.

But the warmth that nuzzled every tattered shred of his being didn't come from some doll. It was brought to life by her unfathomable understanding. She could have called him a creeper and spit on his collection. Instead, she supported it by devoting thought and effort to make it better, not for herself but *for him*.

He wanted to tell her this, wanted her to know how much her actions moved him. But as she sat back and pulled her bound wrists to her chest, her smile soft, her lashes lowered, she seemed to already know. So he settled on a thickly uttered "Thank you."

"You're welcome."

He placed the doll in a paper bag and tucked it under his arm. With one last glance at Amber, he squared his shoulders and hardened his expression. "I'm whipping your ass when I get home."

She nodded, her eyes gleaming with an inner light. "I know. Just come home."

Fuck, he loved her so much it hurt. If anything happened to him, if he wasn't able to return, would she die of starvation? He shoved a hand through his hair, his fingers clenching. "I promise."

# TWENTY-EIGHT

Van stepped into the thick black foyer of the *Curie Lounge* in downtown Austin. Pockets of dim light flickered above the tables. Every chair in the house was filled, maybe a hundred or more live-music enthusiasts sitting back, enjoying a drink and a sexy voice. They wouldn't be disappointed in the latter.

Humming through the speakers was the sound that had haunted him for years. There were no instruments. Just the terraced rippling of her voice, reverberating seductive notes along a man's cock, reaching deep inside him, the only warning she gave before she ate his soul and spit it out. He shivered.

She stood beneath a spotlight in the corner of the large room, eyes closed and sheathed tits to feet in a black gown as she sang a bluesy melody with a sultry sway of her hips.

Remarkable how he didn't entertain a single obsessive thought for the woman. Amber had truly cured his fever.

Pinching the paper bag between his arm and side, he scanned the lounge for her clunkier half and his gaze collided with Joshua Carter's wide eyes at the far end. The man shot from his chair, all six-foot-two of him, his expression shifting from shock to fury. The burly linebacker glanced at Liv, ten feet away, and back again.

Joshua wasn't a bad looking guy. Age twenty-two or twenty-three with black hair, he had that chiseled jaw women loved and green eyes, which were really narrowed and pissed right now. But even so, Van would've gladly fucked him if he didn't have something better waiting for him at home.

And that something was tied to his banister, waiting for his cock.

Damn, he needed to speed this along.

As Joshua strode toward him, choosing a path that blocked his view of Liv, he let his gaze rest on those furious flames of green sparking in the dim light. A year ago, he'd been Joshua's captor. He hadn't fucked him, but there'd been some non-consensual kissing and dick stroking. A friendly greeting was probably too much to ask.

Because of the money he'd wired Liv, Joshua knew he'd survived the gunshot wound. Beyond that, did his former slave assume he was still trafficking slaves? What were the chances they'd even hear him out?

He slid a toothpick between his lips and closed the distance. This should be fun.

# TWENTY-NINE

As Van approached the charging ex-football player, it reminded him of a game of chicken. Who would yield first? Or the worst possible outcome, neither of them. Amidst a crowded bar of patrons, the confrontation needed to be handled delicately, which wasn't a strength he'd mastered.

At the center of the room, Joshua's hand landed on his shoulder in a hard grip, those tightly pinned lips lowering to his ear. The voice he'd heard groaning orgasmically through his mics for six months was now harsh and clipped. "What do you want?"

Van leaned back, deliberately removed the toothpick, and glared at the hand on his shoulder until it dropped. "What, no hello kiss? Afraid my tongue might make you come again?"

A sharp inhale. "Go back to whatever hole you crawled out of. Right now."

So much anger in those eyes. He didn't remember wrangling that much of a reaction when the man was bound and nude in his attic. "Down, boy. I'm not here to fuck you or your girl. I just need to talk with her."

Joshua glanced over his shoulder at Liv, and Van used the opportunity to catch her eyes.

As her gaze clashed with his, she belted her voice through an eerie cascade of notes, the scar on her cheek a shadowed line beneath the angle of the lighting. She excelled at hiding her emotions beneath a cool facade, her intentions well disguised through cunning and underhandedness. She appeared to be lost in song, but she was probably planning the hundred and one ways he would die when she finished the set.

Whether it was by coincidence or design, she ended the melody with a hum, and stepped out of the spotlight, heading directly for them amidst the rise of applause.

When she reached them, her hip-swishing gait carried her right on by and to an isolated table in the corner. Joshua trailed her like an obedient puppy, and they slid into one side of the booth.

Returning the toothpick to his mouth, Van took the opposite seat and set the doll beside him. Liv knew he'd collected dolls over the years. The night she'd shot him, he let her see replicas made with her hair for the first time. He hadn't seen her reaction. No doubt it was one of horror. He'd never explained what they meant to him. Maybe someday he could trust her enough to tell her.

Folding her hands on the table, she appraised him with God-knew-what swirling in her dark brown eyes. Her hair was shorter now, shoulder-length and fringed around her pale face. She was still beautiful. In an inhuman, callous kind of way.

Once upon a time, he'd been turned on by the perplexity of her masked expressions. Now, he felt strained to his limits. A twinge lit behind his eyes.

She tilted her head. "I see you haven't lost the toothpick."

He rolled it between his lips and grinned. "I see you haven't lost your puppy." He glanced at Joshua's scowl and back at her.

"Where's the hoodie?" The bubbled pink gash on her cheek moved with her lips.

His own scar itched, but not with the same tingling connection he'd once felt. Maybe he'd imagined that bond. Perhaps their shared pain hadn't really been shared at all. He slid a palm down his tie and tapped the heel of his leather loafer beneath the table. Fuck, he was sweating already. He needed to lose the jacket. "People change."

She held herself so impassive, so stock-still, one might question if she were breathing. "Why are you here?"

Typical Liv, skipping past friendliness and shoving straight to the facts. He could only blame himself for her coldness. Beneath that defensive shield lay the warm and caring woman she was, the girl who existed before he'd taken her.

The year that separated them should've tempered her visage, and maybe it had. Most likely, she wore her protective mask now because of *him.* His stomach sank. He was there to change that.

"I've stumbled upon something incredible" —someone with a wealth of spirit and strength, someone he *hadn't* ruined— "that has put all my mistakes in perspective. I've found a reason to try harder. To be a better man." Ah, there it was. A flicker of warmth beneath her frozen face. "I *know* I'll be a good father."

Her thawing expression hardened into ice. "Absolutely not."

Joshua grabbed her folded hands and squeezed. "Hear him out,

Liv." Green eyes locked with his. "You found someone?"

More like she found him. His very soul lay in the palms of her bound hands. He nodded. "I love her."

Liv's lips twitched, barely a tic, but it could've been a smile. "Does she know what you've done? Did you tell her about us, all *nine* of us, and your father?"

He tapped the toothpick with his tongue and reclined against the seat back. "She knows everything."

"I'm happy for you, Van." It was undetectable in her tone, but a glimmer of sincerity touched her eyes. Then it was gone. "If she loves you in return."

"She loves me."

"So where is she? You're hardly a man who would leave his girl unattended. Why isn't she with you?" Her emotionless voice set his molars together. Worse was the diligence in her questioning. She didn't believe the relationship was consensual. She would've been right two months ago.

He held her unwavering gaze. "She's agoraphobic. She can't leave the house."

"Convenient." She inhaled a subtle breath, and her tone hardened. "Cut the crap, Van. No manipulations. No bullshit. Tell me what you want."

He held his hands still on his lap and maintained strong eye contact. If he showed any sign of nervousness, she'd jump on it. "I want to meet Livana. Take me with you on one of your visitations."

Joshua bent forward, his dark brows lowering over narrowed eyes. "You know about the visitations? You've been watching Liv?"

"Of course he has." Liv stared back without a hint of surprise on her face. She was smart. She had to have known or at least suspected. "Stalking and abducting is what he does."

His cheeks burned, and his body tensed. Yeah, he had been stalking. "She's my daughter, too." How could he explain?

"Do you have someone tied up in your house right now?" she asked.

Fuck yes, and he was two seconds from shoving out of there to be with the one person who had faith in him.

She leaned closer and lowered her voice. "How many times a day do you beat her and make her suck your cock?"

He launched toward her, mirroring her pose. "Asks the hypocrite who fucks her slave boy on the kitchen table with a strap-on."

She put a hand on Joshua's suddenly heaving chest and sat back with a satisfied smile. "Only one way you'd know that. Some people *don't* change."

The toothpick snapped between his teeth. He spit it on the floor and faced her again. "Come to my house. You can meet my girlfriend. She'll validate everything I've said."

A waitress appeared at the table, beaming a smile at Liv. "That was an incredible performance, Miss Reed. The manager wants to meet with you before you leave to discuss a regular schedule."

Liv nodded. "Thank you."

"Can I get y'all any drinks?"

"No, we're good. Thanks." Joshua waved her off and folded his forearms on the table. "Why on earth do you think I'd ever allow Liv to step foot in your house?" He continued in a harsh whisper. "You blackmailed her for seven years. Beat her. Raped her. Gave her no choice but to train and sell slaves." His voice pitched in a state of disbelief. "You kept her daughter from her."

"Besides that," Liv cut in, "Van has a *talent* for training people to obey. I'm sure a sweet submissive girlfriend would say just about anything."

He tightened his fists beneath the table and whispered furiously, "That's logical *if* I were trying to con anyone else. But you have both been there. You'd recognize coercion from a mile away." He turned to Joshua. "And you read people better than anyone I know." He flicked a hand at Liv. "If you can see through her fucking masks, you should damn well be able to see through mine and my girlfriend's."

His former slaves stared at him with furrowed brows as if they were considering his words.

"I'm just asking for a chance." His words rushed forth with the pump of his heart. "I've done some horrible things, and I want a chance to protect her from the kind of man I used to be. I grew up without a father's love, and I want to fucking be there to give her that."

Their silence wore on. He scrubbed his hands over his face, and when he looked up, her expression sent a chill down his spine. Not her usual detached frigidness. In its place were soft, sympathetic features that didn't belong there. He didn't want her looking at him like that. She was about to break his heart, and he couldn't bear to hear it.

"No," she said. One soft, excruciating word.

The pain exploded in his chest, and he struggled to breathe through it.

She wasn't done. "You coerced me for seven years, and I let you. But this isn't about me. It's about Livana. I can't let you" —her breath hitched, and her jaw stiffened— "I *won't* allow you to fuck with her."

"Liv, I would never—"

"If you go near her, I won't involve the authorities." Her eyes blazed with rage. "I'll kill you myself, and when I dispose of your body, no one will ever find it."

His heart pounded, and his stomach soured with regret. He'd told her the same thing once.

Her voice dropped to a heartless rasp. "You know why?"

The answer he'd given her a year ago about her own death crawled from his thick throat. "Because no one will care enough to search for it." *Or wouldn't be able to cross the porch to search for it.*

Joshua wrapped his arm around her shoulders. She leaned against his chest, her eyes closing not with satisfaction but with heavy sadness.

He should've stood and walked out of there, but he needed to know his options. "You won't kill me."

Her eyes flew open. "No? How do you think I freed eight slaves and ended your father's operation?"

The real question was how she disposed of the buyers' bodies. "How did you come by your cartel connections? It was Camila, wasn't it?"

He hadn't been able to confirm the connections, let alone link them to the first slave they'd kidnapped together. But her averted gaze validated it.

Fuck.

*Liv had cartel connections through Camila.* If he approached Livana, he was a dead man. His pulse thrashed, and he yanked at his collar. Fuck, fuck, fuck, fuuuuuuck!

He felt sick, his throat tightening. He reached for the paper bag beside him, removed the doll with a shaking hand, and held it out. "My girlfriend and I made this. Will you give it to Livana?"

She cringed. "Ugh, you still have those things?" Her face distorted with disgust as she climbed over Joshua's lap and strode away.

Fucking moronic how he'd thought bringing a doll to the meeting in place of Amber could've proved anything. Didn't matter that it was handcrafted, beautifully detailed, and made with so much goddamned hope. His daughter would never see it. His gut clenched.

Joshua gave him a pitying look. "Van..."

Fuck him. He shoved the doll back into the bag and got the fuck out of there.

The leaded weight of his feet dragged through the parking lot, the humid air pushing down on his shoulders. When he reached the Mustang, he stripped the jacket and tossed it in the back seat. With his hands clenched around the wheel and the doll in his lap, the weight of the night came surging in, burning his eyes, clotting his throat, and filling up every splintered crack inside him with thick, oily crap. Yet he felt so fucking empty.

He opened the glove box and shoved the doll inside. Then he slammed it shut and numbly stared at the closed door.

A knock on the driver's side window kicked the air from his lungs, and he jumped.

Joshua stood beside the car, bent at the waist with his hands on his knees. "Roll down the window."

He rubbed the ache in his chest and turned the window crank, offering the man a bored expression.

"You had a look about you in there," Joshua said, "when you talked about your girlfriend. A peaceful look."

Joshua was a charging protector as much as a touchy-feeler, a reminder he was going to be a preacher before Liv took him. He was hardwired to see the good in people.

And Van wasn't in the mood for it. "Get to the point."

"Get your shit together, man. You've got a month. Meet us at this restaurant. I jotted down the date and time." Joshua shook the napkin. "Liv will feel less threatened if your girl is with you. So don't show up without her."

He didn't like this numbnut dictating his schedule, but he buried his arrogance. "Liv won't agree to this."

"She's scared, Van. But she'll be there. I'll make sure of it." Joshua's mouth tilted in a half-smile.

Well damn. Their relationship dynamic was baffling. Clearly, Joshua was a sexual submissive, but maybe he wore the pants when he didn't have a dildo in his ass.

He reached for the napkin, and Joshua snatched it back, eyes hard and assertive. "And stop stalking my girlfriend."

"I don't need to." Nor did he want to. He grabbed the napkin and rolled up the window on the fucker's gloomy face.

Hope. It was just a tiny twitch in his chest, but it was there.

As he drove back to the cabin in Cedar Creek, that hope dwindled by the mile. He had a month to slay Amber's beast. His ears pounded. The more he thought about it, the more he wanted to slay it literally.

He turned off the exit and drove to the suburban house in Austin he'd visited a few times in the last three weeks. She might've been predisposed to the disorders, but they hadn't taken over her life until her stupid motherfuckering ex brutalized her from the inside out.

He parked in front of the two-story house and shut off the car. Residence of Brent and Tawny Piselli, insurance salesman and aspiring model. Proud owners of two yappy dogs and a sprinkler system. Only thing missing was the white picket fence.

He cracked his neck from side to side and tried to shake the tension from his hands. He wanted to kill both of them, but he'd promised he wouldn't harm her sister.

The picture window glowed with light from the sitting room, flickering with movement inside. Tawny's Audi wasn't in the driveway, and Brent always parked in the garage.

His pulse elevated, driven with a desire for vengeance. He burned for a fight.

*My enemy isn't out there, Van. It's here. Right here.*

Maybe Brent's death wouldn't help her, but it sure as fuck would release the burning misery built up behind his eyes. He wanted to dominate, to hurt. He wanted to fucking see blood. Fuck the consequences.

He flipped open the glove box, reaching inside for the pistol. His hand brushed the paper bag, crinkling it.

*You would be a great father. Fierce and protective and attentive.*

He would be a great inmate. A kidnapper, a rapist, a sex trafficker...a murderer.

His head hurt, and his damned body felt like a thousand pounds, every tense inch of it sinking into his stomach. He tore the bag off the doll and bent the legs to sit it on the passenger seat beside him.

*You're trying to make a doll that doesn't break?*

*I've tried. They all break eventually.*

Except the one Amber built.

The image of her soft smile and bright eyes shining through the railing invigorated him with a warmth that could only be connected to life.

Not death.

He didn't have to be a kidnapper, rapist, sex trafficker, or murderer. Not anymore.

He slapped the door on the glove box, closing away the gun, and started the car. He had a promise to keep and a sexy ass to beat.

# THIRTY

The front door closed with a heart-jolting thunk. *He made it home!* Amber rolled off her back and scrambled on her knees to the railing. Clutching the wood spindles, her fingers ached with the physical and emotional strain of the last few hours.

The steady fall of leather soles on tile swished through her ears, centering her. Liv hadn't turned him over to the police. Huge exhale. Maybe he hadn't gone home with her. Deeper inhale. His beautiful, naked body wasn't in a bed right now, wrapped around the woman who'd given him a seven-year fever. He was home, safe. Hers.

His broad back came into view, and she trembled with anticipation. He'd lost the jacket, the black dress shirt stretching across his shoulders. He must've known she was watching him, but he didn't look up. *Please, look up.*

His casual gait veered through the great room, the tips of his fingers sliding across the sofa back and tapping along the edge of a desk, his powerful legs moving slowly yet systemically. He stopped at the center of the window wall with his back to her and stared at the drapes. His head tilted to the side.

Every muscle in her body turned to ice. "Van?" Her throat convulsed. "Van? How'd it go?" *Oh, God, turn around, turn around. Please stop looking at those drapes.*

He slid his hands into the pockets of his gray suit pants, the fabric hugging his tight, narrow ass. His feet spaced shoulder-width apart, his posture terrifyingly relaxed. "Tell me the worst thoughts you entertained while I was gone."

His vibrating timbre was so low, so commanding, she melted into the floor. "I imagined you hauled off in handcuffs and how I wouldn't be able to come to you."

"What else?" His baritone echoed off the two-story ceiling.

She swallowed. "I thought about..." She swallowed again, aching for him to turn around. "You and her...together."

A twitch rippled across his back. "Say it, Amber."

Her stomach twisted with shame. "I pictured you...making love to her."

"Thank you." His head lowered a millimeter. "Now tell me why *you think* I would do that."

She closed her eyes and tightened her fists around the spindles. "You shared seven years with her. You collected her hair...your matching scars." Her voice quivered, her eyes opening and clinging to the back of his muscular frame. "You have a child together."

"I haven't touched her in over a year, and tonight I felt no desire to." His back rose with his inhale. "I enslaved her for seven years because I was selfish. The hair, the scars, Livana...all examples of my selfishness. That's not love, Amber, which was why I never thought to free her."

He reached up, tore open the drapes, and wrenched them off the wall. Wheezing, she jerked away from the railing, caught by two feet of rope.

Fabric and metal poles tumbled to the floor as he moved from window to window, ripping and tossing. She curled into a ball, chest heaving, her face buried in her bound arms.

Every clatter of metal and rip of sheet rock made her heart jump in terror. Her breathing reached an all-too-familiar velocity, burning her lungs and beading sweat along her scalp.

Eventually, her breaths were all she heard as silence settled through the cabin, thickening, waiting. No footsteps on the stairs. No commanding voice. Was he waiting for her to pull herself together?

Her limbs shook, and her pulse ripped through her veins, but breath by painful breath, she reined it in. He'd opened the windows because he wanted to free her. He waited patiently because he believed in her.

She gathered all her courage to accept that knowledge and crawled back to the railing on wobbly knees.

He stood at the bottom of the stairs, pinching the button on the shirt cuff at his wrist. As he loosened it and moved to the other wrist, he lifted his eyes, locking them on her. Intense eyes. Dangerously beautiful eyes. She didn't need to look at the windows behind him because she held those eyes, because they told her he loved her.

He didn't look away as he climbed the stairs and rolled up his sleeves. He held her gaze as he reached the loft and removed his belt, dropping it on the wood floor before her. He didn't break eye contact until he knelt at her side and ripped the straps of her tank top.

The openness of the windows crawled on her skin. So she sat on her hip, leaning toward him, and let his touch, his eyes, and his spicy scent swallow her senses. The nylon rope bit into her arms, rubbing against her clammy skin, but she welcomed it, gloried in the restraints he'd given her.

Sliding the shirt to her waist, his fingers stroked a trail of fire down her breastbone, over the lacy bra cups, and across her belly. "Lift your gorgeous ass."

His whisper pulled that fire inward, heating her blood and curling tendrils of warmth through her pussy. She raised her hips, lost in the potency of his hands on her body. There was something unequivocal about pleasing a man as controlling and calculating and *adoring* as Van Quiso. No need to think. She simply obeyed, placing all her pleasure, and her pain, in his strong and capable hands.

His full lips parted as he glided the shirt and skirt down her legs, his sharp silvery gaze totally and completely focused on her. No matter what kind of confrontation he'd just come from, he was here now, gifting her with the command of his concentration.

With only the bra and rope left on her body, she met his eyes comfortably and confidently. "Will you tell me about it?"

"After your punishment." He licked the corner of his mouth, perhaps seeking the toothpick that wasn't there. "On your knees."

She obeyed, eyes glued to the swell of his groin as he stood and unbuttoned his shirt. When he shrugged it off and tossed it somewhere near the closet, she yanked against the restraints to go after it.

He chuckled, damn him. Whatever. She'd pick it up later. Right now, she had something better to do, like take in the sight of his magnificent body.

His abs flexed with his reach for the leather belt on the floor and contracted with his stretch as he straightened. Veins ran beneath the skin of his forearms, bulging over muscle, pumping with the movements of his hands folding the belt.

Her fingers tingled to run down his chest and around his back to feel his taut muscles and absorb the smooth texture of his skin. More than that, she wanted to bask in the heat of his belt on her ass.

Dangling the strap at his side, he unzipped his pants and slid his hand inside. "Do you know how fucking hard you make me?" He removed his hand and grabbed a fistful of her hair. "Spread your knees. Arms up and elbows out. Like you're hugging a six-foot cock."

Her mouth watered, and her pussy throbbed with liquid heat. When she assumed the pose, he stepped into the ring made by her bound arms and yanked her by her hair until her cheek pressed against his hip.

The strength of his thigh supported her as he pivoted to face her, his cock hard and pulsing and tenting his slacks an inch from her face.

She slid her cheek against it, reveling in the curved shape and the way it jumped against her touch. Her arms tightened around his thigh, and she ground her clit against his shin, humping his leg and throbbing with need. "Van—"

"Who am I?"

She smiled. "The ruler over lights and porches and window shades and spectacular messes and—" The yank on her hair made her smile harder, and she answered honestly and respectfully. "Master."

He caressed the edge of the belt over her cheek. "Describe your pussy. I want details."

"It's wet, leaking onto my legs. And it hurts. It's clenching like crazy." Her admission intensified the throb. "Van, I need you."

"What does it look like?"

She choked. Dammit, why did he have to go there?

The belt whistled through the air and landed across her ass with a searing sting.

She grunted against his hip. "It's swollen."

"More." He swung again, hitting her other ass cheek.

Her thoughts blurred with shameful images, but she would tell him, and maybe he'd spank her harder. It didn't matter why he belted her as long as he continued to do so. The pain was a need, a distraction, and a connection. "It's stretched, loose, chewed up, and used."

He laid into her, beating her ass just as he'd promised. She didn't count the swings. She never did, too consumed by the fiery sensations blazing through her body, the press of his cock in her face, the exertion of his breath, and the bolster of his leg as she hugged it tighter with every stroke. The pain was binding, an extension of him, an outpouring of his very essence, his darkness and devotion, his damage and strength.

He could whip her against a tree, fuck her beneath the moon, or tie her down on the porch and mar her flesh with the cuts of his teeth. It didn't matter, because wherever he took her, no matter how brutal or dark the destination, there would always be warmth. Because he would be with her.

The belt clattered to the floor. He slipped his leg from her embrace and tackled the knots, unwinding the rope from her arms. The room spun around her, but her world was aligned. Because he was right there, his arms beneath her legs and back, his chest against hers. He lifted her and laid her on the bed.

She melted into the mattress, ass tingling, her pussy spread and soaking and aching to be filled. He stripped his pants, his erection long and thick, as he climbed over the edge of the mattress.

He wedged his shoulders into the gap of her thighs and breathed against her pussy, "I don't see anything here that's stretched, loose, or chewed up. But the last part, well..." He pressed a finger in her opening and stirred it around the edges, shooting pulses of heat through her inner muscles. "It's definitely used. I've made sure of that."

He dragged a slow, torturous lick through her folds, and her hands flew to his hair, her pelvis bucking to meet his mouth.

"Fuck, you taste like heaven. I could eat you all night...*after* you tell me more about this hang-up. That brain-damaged prick you were married to didn't come up with his insult by looking at you. I'm beginning to think he never looked at you at all."

The truth of his words tensed her legs around his shoulders.

He kissed her cunt with an open mouth and a swirling tongue, devouring every inch of her slick flesh. Hot, wet, "No, he picked up on your insecurity and exploited it to get his rocks off." He lapped at her clit. "Tell me the source of your insecurity, and I'll let you come."

His sucking resumed, his lips sliding over her, his tongue thrusting and circling. His skillful mouth smothered her with overwhelming pleasure, and just as the orgasm rose up, he pulled back. Fuck! Then he went at her again, eating and biting and pushing her toward the edge.

She vibrated with need, the urgency to come overwhelming. "He wouldn't go down on me. He...he talked about the girls who ran in my circle, about how tight their cunts must've been and how he wanted to bury his face in that." She blew out a tired breath. "He hadn't gone down on me in years, and I...I thought it was my pubic hair so I shaved. It didn't help, so I decided there was something wrong with me."

He looked up, his lips glistening, his eyes twin flames of silver. "His fucking loss." Then he immersed his face in her folds and blew her fucking mind.

Her legs trembled, and her fingers twisted and yanked his hair. The attack of his teeth and tongue sent her soaring with weightless wings, the release spinning her out of control, her back arching and her toes curling.

When she landed, he caught her, shifting them to their sides, face-to-face. He pulled her thigh over his hip, his cock nudging her opening. "Your pussy belongs to *me*. You're not allowed to insult it. Not in your head or otherwise."

"Okay." She smiled, and it must've looked as loopy and satisfied as she felt.

With a finger gliding around the tip of his shaft and spreading her open, he worked himself in. His hand flew to the back of her head, and he groaned into her hair as he thrust.

The invasion was full and snug, every inch of him warming and stroking her insides. Her muscles contracted around him, all thought, all feeling, centered on where they were joined. He pumped faster, pulling her head back by her hair and taking her mouth. My God, the man could kiss. She could come just from the slide of his tongue.

She opened her eyes and found him watching her with affection and a thrilling amount of lust. He hadn't grown bored with her. He wanted this. He wanted *her*. Not Liv.

As he began to plow into her with intoxicating roughness, she returned to his mouth, biting his lips, her fingers tracing the ridges of flexing muscle along his torso. He slammed into her, grinding against her clit, and pulled out in long strokes, repeatedly, pushing her to the edge, teetering...

He rolled her from her side to her back and deepened the thrusts. His head dropped to the pillow, his softly-shaven cheek rubbing against hers, his breaths sharpening. "Fuck, Amber. So fucking close. You need to come."

She clutched his ass and clamped down around his driving length. Four more grinding rotations, and she let go. "Aaaagggh, God, I'm coming." As strong as the first, the surge lifted and carried her through waves of drugging pleasure.

His hips jerked. "Fuck." He buried his face in her neck, his palm covering the side of her head, his powerful body trembling through jerky thrusts. "Fuck. Me, too. Fuuuuck."

She held him tight as he fell apart above her, his weight a crushing security and his groans quenching her undying need for his appreciation.

As his muscles relaxed and his cock pulsed inside her, a voice whispered at the back of her head. "Van? The condom?"

He barked out a laugh and rolled to his back, taking her with him and slipping out of her, his seed smearing against her thigh. "Little late for that, babe." He reached between them, swiping a finger through the mess on her leg and sliding it into her mouth. The clean salty flavor mingled with his saliva as he kissed her slow and lazily. He leaned back, grinning.

She pinched his ass. "You have a semen fetish."

"I like the way it tastes on our lips, and so do you." He kissed her again. "The test results came back today. You're clean."

She relaxed against him, draped over his body, her cheek on his chest, smiling happily. Not that she'd worried about STDs, but he'd put her on the pill when she arrived — using a no script online pharmacy — and she hadn't had sex without a condom since she'd been married. "No wonder that felt so good."

"Mm." He stroked her hair with one hand and cupped her ass with the other. "I went to Brent and Tawny's house tonight."

*Fucking whiplash.* She jerked back and collided with his unreadable gaze. "Why?"

He forced her face back to his chest with a strong hand and held her in place. "I drove there to kill him. Decided not to."

Her heart raced. She hadn't even considered the possibility. "You're not a murderer."

A heavy sigh expanded his ribs, and his thumb drew restless circles over her jaw where he held her against him. "A year ago, Liv was brutally raped by a slave buyer. I felt responsible because I'd sent her to him fully fucking aware of what kind of monster he was. When I found out, I shot his wife just to torture him. Then I..." He exhaled. "You don't need to hear the details. I killed him."

*Torture.* Van had no doubt brought unholy vengeance on that man. His breathing labored, and his hand loosened on her head. She rose up and searched the hard lines of his face. No remorse or horror painted in those lethal features.

"Protective till the end," she whispered.

"The very end, in fact. I packed up after that to leave the operation for good."

"But Liv shot you before you got out?"

He twined their legs together. "Yeah."

"Your avenging-murder days are over?"

"We'll see."

Right. If someone harmed her, all bets were off. The thought filled her with a selfish kind of comfort. She slid a toe up and down his calf. "You're not going to rehang the drapes, are you?"

He laughed. "Nope."

That was a problem she'd worry about in the morning. "What happened with Liv tonight?"

He combed his fingers through her hair and stared at the ceiling. "You were right. She's too scared to trust me. Can't blame her." He lowered his eyes to hers. "They want to meet you. Joshua specifically. The meeting is set a month from today." The fingers in her hair curled, pulling the strands and speeding her pulse. "In a restaurant."

The spectacle played out in her head. A slobbering panic attack, nothing like the little gasping hiccups she'd been having outside the cabin. More like one of those spit-flinging episodes that bucked her body all over the floor and rolled her eyes into the back of her head. Patrons would gape in horror and spill their drinks. The manager would call for an ambulance. And Van would be humiliated.

A silver light focused on her, funneling her feral thoughts back to the loft, the bed, and the hard body cradling her. His eyes glowed with acceptance, hope, faith. He looked at her with the kind of love that would transcend any answer she gave.

With a trembling smile, she nodded. "I'll try."

# THIRTY-ONE

Amber did try. Hour by hour, day after day, Van watched her tackle her fear till her body gave out. He supported her the best way he knew how, with a commanding presence, a steady hand, and an aching yet prideful heart. But he eased up on pushing and dragging her in his usual way, because dammit, she was hard enough on herself.

Even now, five days away from the meeting with Liv and Joshua, she lay passed-out in the front seat of the Mustang, covered in sweat and dark hair tangled around her. Because she'd demanded he drive her to the edge of the two-hundred acre property.

He paced beside the open passenger door, the gravel driveway crunching beneath his sneakers. Even through muscle spasms and hyperventilation, she'd fought with white knuckles on the dashboard to remain conscious.

The tightening in his gut told him she wouldn't make it inside that restaurant. If she didn't, he would never hold it against her. But how well would *she* accept her failure?

He searched his pockets for a toothpick and came up empty. Fucking hell.

He lowered onto the edge of the seat beside her and stroked the soft, damp skin on her cheek, traced the lashes beneath her closed eyes, and pressed his thumb against her full bottom lip. He yearned to take her back to the house before she woke, but he'd agreed to her plea.

*If I pass out, please don't drive me back till I wake. I need to fight through this.*

The phobia was so deeply worked into her mind it felt more powerful than the two of them combined. But she *had* made progress.

She'd conquered the uncovered windows within one week. Hell, she didn't even mess with her hair anymore when she passed by them.

The bulimia seemed to be subdued because she didn't obsess over her body image anymore. She never tried to cover her body from him, her appetite had grown to a healthy level, and a few times, he'd caught her looking at her reflection, not with disgust, but with approval flickering in her eyes.

The OCD had become a trivial thing. She still counted and popped her knuckles when she was upset, and she would always be an orderly little neat freak. But it didn't control her life. Not like the agoraphobia. Not like *him*.

Her eyes fluttered open, flicking over the surrounding windows, groggily orienting. Her fingers curled in her lap, and her breathing hitched.

He cupped her face to direct her focus on him. When their eyes locked, he was transported back to the first time they met. On her porch, him with his dick in his hand, her all dolled up for a date with the mailbox. Her brown eyes, round as saucers then, had been so terrified.

The very same terror stared back at him now. He tensed, and the surrounding timber stilled, too, waiting for her reaction.

Her breathing tightened, followed by the usual shaking, wheezing, and sweating. Her choking sobs wrenched at the air and weighted his stomach with lead. He crawled into the driver's seat, closed the doors, and sped back to the house, his heart stumbling all over itself. This wasn't working. Nothing was working.

After he fed her lunch, she sat at the kitchen table, staring at the remnants of oyster bisque in the bowl. Her shoulders slumped, her head lowered, and she wouldn't maintain eye contact.

He wore a path on the tiles around her chair, his muscles stiff and his throat tight. Joshua had given him a chance to win Liv's trust. Would this meeting be his only chance? It seemed like an all or nothing kind of opportunity, to prove to Liv he had a girl who wasn't coerced or enslaved.

But her dejected posture made his stomach sink. "Fuck the stupid meeting, Amber. We can attempt another one at a later date. Whenever you're ready."

Her chin hardened. "Where's the man who broke into my house and fucked with all my stuff? Stop being gentle with me. Van. You're the only person who has ever given enough of a shit about me to shove me out the door." She stood, fire sparking in her eyes, and pointed a finger at him. "I need you to shove me across the porch on my face if you have to."

His heart banged against his ribs with furious agreement.

"We're doing this." She squared her shoulders. "*I'm* doing this."

But she was doing it *for him* and only because he would be there. If she failed, her devastation could be self-damaging, and he couldn't allow that to happen.

He pressed his lips together and rubbed his forehead. She was a stunning, naturally-submissive, *housebound*, consensual slave. He should've been out-of-his-mind ecstatic. But if he had one regret in their two-month relationship, it was his stupid, selfish fucking mission to be her obsession. If he hadn't come into her life, maybe she would've lost her house. But more than likely, she would've landed on her feet because she was bullheaded and strong as fuck.

None of that mattered now. He'd fed her, protected her, *controlled* her every damned move, and in doing so, he'd robbed her of her self-reliance and replaced it with an unhealthy dependency. Him.

She blew out a breath and cocked her head, her eyes suddenly bright and mischievous. "I have an idea."

Just like that, she brought a smile to his face. "Does it involve bleach and scrub brushes?"

She tapped her chin. "Hmm. I'm thinking gasoline." Her eyes glimmered. "And fire."

An hour later, he stood beside a well-fueled bonfire roaring twenty-paces from the cabin. The heat from the flames and the aroma of wood smoke had an old-fashioned way of fortifying the spirit and moving the psyche into a place of deep contentment.

He looked up to find her leaning against the doorjamb, just inside the back door. Her arms wrapped around her torso, her expression strained with panic. No doubt she wouldn't be stepping over the threshold. But beneath the fear lay a softness in her eyes, a kind of peaceful resolve.

She'd said the fire could burn away the past, melt the painful memories, and make room for transformation. It was worth the try.

He gave her one more questioning look, arching his eyebrow. *Are you sure?*

At her nod, he lifted the aquarium of tiaras and chucked it into the fire. The flames crackled and sparked, skittering red-hot embers across the ground. Metal and glass wouldn't disintegrate, but it would certainly fuse into an unrecoverable blob.

A glance over his shoulder rewarded him with a view more magnificent than a million fires, her smile as radiant as the iridescent glow of gems melting in her tiaras.

He reached for the garbage bag he'd sneaked outside, her words floating through his head.

*It's just stuff attached to broken memories. Burning it will inspire new ones to grow.*

By *stuff*, she'd meant her crowns, but he had memories, too. He removed the contents, her *OhmyGod* rippling the air as he fed the blaze with dolls. Two plastic bodies, brown hair, and a red-checkered dress vanished behind a black fog of smoke. It wasn't a cremation. It was simply the end of a life that hadn't been a life at all.

Looping his thumbs in his front pockets, he strode toward her with an easy, unhurried gait. Hope lightened his chest. It had been there for a while, but it strengthened as he took in the promise sparkling in her eyes.

# THIRTY-TWO

Five days later, Van waited in the kitchen, chewing the ever-loving fuck out of a toothpick. He tossed it in the waste-bin and yanked at the sleeve of his suit. *Come on, Amber.*

That morning, he'd bought makeup, hairstyling crap, a black dress, and heels. And she'd been holed up in the bathroom with that shit for an hour. They needed to leave immediately to arrive at the restaurant on time.

Deep breath. Fuck, he was wound tight. But he wouldn't rush her.

Still, he hoped she was held up by a curling iron and not a change of heart. How could he not be hopeful about what the night could bring? It could crash through the agoraphobia as well as open a door with Livana.

Or it could end in tearful hyperventilation.

The bathroom door opened with a whoosh that sounded like the air rushing from his lungs. Sweet mother of sin, he'd told her cosmetics would defile the natural perfection of her face, but as she lingered in the doorway, shoulders back, arms at her sides, one long leg bent before the other, he stood tongue-tied and stupefied.

The raw, disheveled knockout he drooled over every waking hour had transformed into an untouchable, world-class beauty queen. It was impossible to keep his cock down while admiring her tight body wrapped in hip-hugging silk. Dark hair curled around her face and chest. Deep crimson painted her lips, and her thick lashes went on forever, highlighting her shining eyes.

Toned legs flaunted delectable flesh from thigh to ankle, her feet arched in the black fuck-me heels he hadn't been able to pass up at the boutique, and her smile... Fuck him.

He wanted to lick along the curves of her tits rising above the low neckline and bite the taut nipples pressing against the silk. The view spoiled him, and there wasn't a man on earth who deserved to look at her. "Let's stay home." Christ, he needed to be inside of her.

The smile gracing those red lips widened. "You look good, too, Van." Her gaze roamed his body, turning the stiffness in his pants into a throbbing monster.

Her nostrils flared as if she were trying to smell him from across the room. "So incredibly handsome. Wish I had panties." She twisted to look at her ass. "When I sit down, I'm going to leave a wet spot."

Fuck it. A quickie against the wall wouldn't make them *too* late. He strode toward her and grabbed her hips, leaning in to take her mouth.

His lips crashed into her halting palm. "No kissing." She pinched his chin. "You'll smudge the makeup."

Then she definitely wouldn't be down with what he had in mind. He adjusted his erection and straightened his tie. "We better go or we won't be going at all."

Her easy playfulness vanished instantly, and she cast a fearful look at the front door.

Even a non-agoraphobe would've approached this meeting with a healthy amount of nervousness. Hell, his stomach would be all kinds of fucked up by the time they arrived. With any luck, she would be too anxious about being outside to muster any additional worries about impressing his former slaves. She had enough to focus on.

"Hey." He cupped her face, turning her eyes to him. "I parked the Mustang right outside the door. Just like we practiced."

She nodded with an expression so fearfully hopeful, it hurt to see it. They'd driven to the end of the property every day for the past week. Yesterday was the first day she hadn't fainted during the two-minute drive.

He gripped her hand and led her calmly to the front door. "Your steps are mine, Amber. I won't leave your side."

If they made it out of the driveway, it would be her first time off the property since he'd abducted her two months ago.

Her breath stuttered as they hit the porch. It was spastic by the time they reached the end of the driveway. He rolled to a stop and softened his voice with patience. "How are we doing?"

She popped her knuckles, her eyes squeezed shut, her chest jumping with shallow breaths. "Just keep...going. Don't stop."

She'd told him once how strangers' eyes felt like loaded guns aimed at her head. She was about to face a firing squad, and she'd bravely demanded that he keep going.

He slid his hand around the back of her neck, beneath her hair, and squeezed. "I love you, you crazy woman."

Her head nodded with a jerk, her smile quivering the corner of her mouth. "You, too," she whispered. "Now drive."

He gripped the wheel and began the painful trek toward downtown Austin.

Thirty minutes later, he parked the car in front of a quaint Italian restaurant, his stomach in knots. The sign read *No Parking*, but he didn't give a fuck. The tension in the car had been rolling off her since they'd left, and the combustion was three, maybe four breaths away.

Releasing their seat belts, he twisted toward her and grabbed her ice-cold face. "Amber? Talk to me."

Her eyes were closed. They had been the duration of the drive. Another wave of tension vibrated off of her. She opened her mouth to speak, and her voice cut off with the wheeze of her lungs.

Goddammit, she wasn't ready for this. But if he drove her home without letting her try, it would steal the decision from her. "Look how far you've come. You can do this, sweetheart."

Blindly, her hand fumbled for the door handle. It shook so badly, she wouldn't be able to pull the latch even if she found it.

"I'm going to get out and open your door for you."

She answered with a heart-breaking sob, but he didn't miss the slight nod of her head. With heart-racing strides, he rounded the car in the three seconds. But he was too late.

When he opened the door, the look on her face lanced a new scar, right through his heart. Her eyes were wide and terrified and locked on the restaurant's glass windows, on the patrons inside. Makeup streaked her cheeks, marking the paths of her tears, her complexion ghostly white. Her fingernails dug so deeply into her palms, when he pried them loose, blood smeared over the broken skin.

"I can't… I can't… I can't…" She choked between wheezing breaths.

His blood heated, and his chest tightened. She'd wanted to do this, wanted to be pushed. Well, not like this. No goddamned way. He'd have to carry her inside, and her humiliation from that alone would only cause her more suffering.

He kissed her gasping mouth, hard and angrily, and slammed the door. He'd brought this pain on her. He'd fucking failed her.

On his sprint back to the driver's side, he glanced through the restaurant window. Liv and Joshua sat in a booth in the back corner, heads bowed over a shared menu. His gait slowed, but only for a second. There'd be another time, another chance. And if not, fuck them. He'd find different way, one that didn't destroy Amber.

He climbed behind the wheel and found her slumped over her lap, her head crooked in an awkward angle. The backs of his eyes burned as he reclined her seat back and positioned her limp body beneath the seatbelt. Then he drove his broken doll home.

# THIRTY-THREE

Hope had a way of leading a guy on, offering tantalizing glimpses of possibilities and enticing him to the edge of belief. But it didn't put out. Van had been on the giving end of such things throughout his criminal history, which made it even more harrowing to watch Amber succumb to hope's cruel disappointment.

A month had passed since the drive to the restaurant, and she'd regressed, immediately and spectacularly.

"Get up." He stood over the bed where she spent the majority of the day, every day.

She rolled to her back, blinking heavy eyelids, and held out her arms. "Make love to me." She dropped her arms and looked away. "Please?"

His body felt cold, his heart weighted down with the ache it had been carrying for too damned long. Maybe her devastation was partly due to her disappointment in herself. But he knew the bigger part was in her inaccurate belief that she'd disappointed him.

He yanked back the sheets and let his weight press down on her nude body. He could never deny her, not even now in her numb state of existence. With a hand on her face, he held her eyes and gave her the words he repeated daily. "I love you, I want you, and I will never ever be disappointed in you."

She kissed him. Her usual response, maybe some kind of coping mechanism.

He matched her licks and nibbles then took over, leading her, controlling this. It was what she wanted and what he needed. He released his belt and opened his jeans, her hands already on his cock, stroking it to readiness.

As he worked himself into her wet heat, her eyes glowed. These were the only moments when he saw that light, the only way he seemed to be able to bring her out of her head. Not the belt nor the whip nor his restraints affected her. Not even when he hauled her outside every night. She'd lost interest in everything but him. And his cock.

It wasn't healthy, and it didn't help her. He was a toxin, polluting her mind and making her worse. If he let this go on, he would destroy her.

He brought her to climax, and as he followed her over the brink of momentary bliss, her words rushed in, punching an agonizing hole through his heart.

*You're the only person who has ever given enough of a shit about me to shove me out the door.*

As he held her limp body in his arms, the vibrancy in her eyes dulled to blankness. She sank into the mattress, her heat pulling away, and a frigid void slipped between them. It was slow and subtle and perhaps unintentional, but her detachment strained and ripped every nerve-ending in his body.

God, he wanted her light back. He would ejaculate inside her over and over if it could fill her with life. But the sex was fleeting. If anything, she was colder and more despondent after they made love.

He wanted to argue that he loved her too much to *shove her out the door.* Truth was he loved her too much not to. Just like her behavior with the deliverymen, she was only getting by without getting better.

And he'd become another Zachary Kaufman.

Her independence was the key to unlocking the windows and returning the light. Without it, there was no life.

That night, he made the most painful decision he'd ever made. He drugged her dinner, packed up her things, and gave her back her self-sufficiency. He returned her to her house and reinstated her life, a better life, without him.

For hours, he lingered in her bed, wrapped around her unconscious body, immobilized by the gravity of his decision and struggling to breathe through the agony of it. Soon, he would have to rise from her side and give her the only thing he had to offer—life itself.

Death seemed easier than this godawful burden of losing her. But she had a hell of a fight ahead of her, and if she could suffer through that, then he could endure the loneliness that awaited him.

He couldn't stop the tears burning his eyes as he pressed his lips against her unresponsive mouth. He was numb to the violent tremors wobbling his steps as he staggered down the hall without turning around. He squeezed his eyes shut as he stumbled into the garage, the excruciating pain in his chest eclipsing the crash of the concrete floor against his knees.

He left the door opener on the shelf and forced his legs into the minivan. The he backed it onto the driveway and climbed out. Shades covered every window on Liv's house, blatantly shutting him out. Not that he was in any state to give a fuck.

He reached inside Amber's garage and pressed the door button on the wall. His chest burned and his throat ached as he stepped back and wrapped his arms around himself to keep from stopping the doors' descent.

When the garage doors sealed shut, the silent finality of it ripped out his insides and beckoned the enclosing darkness with the sound of his sobs.

# THIRTY-FOUR

Amber woke with an ear-ringing headache. She hadn't even opened her eyes and her body already ached with grief, sagging into the mattress like a useless weight. She'd gone to bed hating herself for what she was doing to Van, and just like every other night, sleep hadn't absolved her.

Her hand slapped over the mattress, searching for the warmth of Van's skin, his strength, their connection. Her fingers collided with papers.

She jerked up on her elbows and rubbed her eyes, blinking against the illumination of a nearby lamp. She rubbed and blinked again.

White walls bled into a shadeless window, glowing with sunlight. Her mouth dried as she soaked in the white carpet, white quilt, the duffel bags by the door... Oh God, her bedroom.

Dread iced through her veins, curling frigid fingers around her throat. The house should've been foreclosed, empty, gone. And where the hell were the shades? She sucked in a shaky breath and shouted, "Van? Van, where are you?"

She scrambled off the bed and raised trembling fingers to her lips, straining to hear his footsteps.

The A/C unit hummed outside the window. The shower down the hall dripped. *Plop-plip. Plop-plip.* The water was on? What the fuck for?

Beside the lamp, the bedside clock glowed 6:19 AM. Electricity, too? Her heart stopped then went ballistic, tightening her skin and firing up her muscles.

She sprinted through the house, searching room by room for answers, for him. Not a single shade on the windows. The fridge and cabinets were filled with food. *Food from the cabin.* She opened the garage door and shivered at the dark, cavernous space. No Mustang. No Van.

Returning to the kitchen, she gripped the edge of the sink and looked up. The window and backyard stared back. Her heart froze, and she dropped to the floor, out of sight. Was he out there? Was he coming back?

Unbidden, his words came rushing in, stabbing through her heart.

*I enslaved her for seven years because I was selfish. That's not love, Amber, which was why I never thought to free her.*

"Noooooo." A roar burst from her throat, heaving her chest and burning her eyes. That couldn't be it. This wasn't freedom. It was some kind of a mistake, a misunderstanding. Oh Jesus, she needed to talk to him.

She reached up to the counter with a blind hand, found her phone, and swiped through the contacts. No calls. No new numbers. She tossed it across the floor and stared at it, helplessly. She'd never seen him use a phone or e-mail. He probably didn't even have those things.

*Because I don't exist.*

Her heart rate accelerated. Where was the cabin located? Somewhere outside of Austin. With trees. Lots of trees. Fuck! How could she have never thought to ask?

*Because she never intended to leave.*

She slammed a fist against the cabinet, rattling the doors. The one and only time she'd traveled the route from the cabin while conscious, she'd kept her damned eyes closed.

Her breath caught. Were there papers on the bed? She ran back to the bedroom and crawled over the mattress. The sight of the folded letters turned and twisted her stomach. Her hand flew to her belly, massaging the anguish there, her fingers brushing cotton. She looked down at the cami and panties that covered her body.

Blood drained from her face, her cheeks numb. He'd dressed her and left her. A quiver gripped her chin. She rubbed it roughly away and gathered the papers.

They shook in her hands as she sat on her heels and flipped through them. The first was a receipt for her mortgage. Zero balance, the house was paid off. A pang rippled through her chest.

Next were printouts of all her credit card statements and utility bills. *Zero balances.* The ache in her chest swelled to her throat.

The following letter showed an unfamiliar bank account in her name, the balance printed in bold font. *$100,000.* Enough to live on for years. Burning pinpricks hammered behind her eyes.

She choked, buckling over her knees. Sobs tumbled out, painful and wretched. Oh God, it hurt. He'd left her. Left her without shades on her windows. Left her with a secure and stable and financially-free life.

To free her.

She gritted her teeth, the papers crumpling in her fists. Stupid, stupid, stupid man. Why would she want any of this if she didn't have *him*?

She opened the last letter, a handwritten note scrawled with loose penmanship.

*I will always love you, I will always want you, and I will never ever be disappointed in you. -Van*

It was a good-bye. A fist-through-the-fucking-heart goodbye. The tears surged, hard and ugly and agonizing. She flung herself off the bed and staggered through the room with a helpless, rage-filled cry, her arms sweeping everything in her path. The lamp, the TV, and the duffel bags hit the walls and bounced along the floor, thumping and exploding.

Her vision blurred. Her legs crashed into furniture. Her teeth sawed her lips until blood coated her tongue. Her fingernails shredded and ripped in her attack on everything she could destroy.

At 8:27 AM, she sat on the floor with her back against the dresser. Her lungs burned, her cheeks cracked with drying tears, and her heart jabbed at her ribs with each thump of its sharp splintery edges.

"Well done, you crazy fucking bitch." Her voice scratched her raw throat, but she deserved it. "First prize for world's ugliest temper tantrum. Yay."

She took in the aftermath with little interest. Pillow stuffing covered the floor. Dents peppered the sheet rock. The small TV lay on its side with cracks spider-webbing over the screen.

Where was her anxiety for straight lines? Her impulse to tackle the mess?

She dropped her head back against the dresser and closed her eyes. She couldn't think about that right now. Something else was pressing against her brain.

He lived thirty minutes from that restaurant. If she knew which restaurant it was, she could narrow her search for the cabin. She jumped to her feet and strode toward the wall that faced Liv and Joshua's house, pressing her cheek against it. Maybe Van had given them his address? At the very least, they knew the restaurant.

And so her harrowing journey to their house began. By the end of that first night, she was able to peer out of every window without losing control of her breathing.

By day five, she started keeping her front door open, letting in bugs and sunshine and the gawking of neighbors in passing cars. She sat on the threshold, trembling and gasping, but she didn't pass out.

On day nineteen, her ass hit the bench on the front porch for the first time in two years. She'd stumbled into it, actually, in a breathless fall of exhausted, quivering muscles. She might've clapped her hands if they weren't squeezing the weathered slats in a death grip.

But she did manage a smile, the first smile to touch her lips since the night they'd left for the restaurant. God, he'd looked so handsome in his suit. He'd been so nervous and...turned on by her.

Her heart pinched, and her smile wobbled away. She missed him, deeply and painfully. His absence was a constant wrench of every breath as if her lungs could never quite fill without him.

She uncurled a hand and raised the hem of her old t-shirt, wiping the humidity and sweat from her face. He would've been proud of her. Fuck that. *She* was proud of herself.

"I'm sitting on his bench," she announced to the coverage of bushes, the sunlight soaking into her damp hair. She ran her fingers over the wood, hoping to absorb some part of him that might still be there.

She glanced at the closed-up windows on Liv's house and nodded. She'd get there.

That night, she lay on top of the covers in bed, nude and as content as she could be without him beside her. As she fantasized about his heat sliding over her skin and his tongue controlling her mouth, her hands roamed her body.

Her house might've been a mess, but she'd maintained her daily regimen of cardio and strength training, and that effort flexed sensually in the hard hillocks of her ass and firm flesh on her hips. Her muscles and curves felt beautiful beneath her fingertips. And so did her pussy.

She stroked her fingers down her mound and between her folds as her thoughts filled with silver eyes, a thick cock, and seductive lips. The deep, reverberating voice in her head commanded she fuck herself. So she did, with urgent, wanton thrusts of her fingers. When his voice told her to come, she shouted his name to the ceiling.

There was a good chance she'd never find him, that she'd never be able to show him how far she'd come. But as the next two weeks passed, she protected her new self-esteem, nurturing it with every little progressive step. She refused to even consider puking. She made trips to the mailbox, reconnected with Dr. Michaels, and reinstated her leathercraft business, adding leather dolls to her list of merchandise.

She hadn't worked up to leaving the yard yet, but as the weeks passed, conquering the agoraphobia became more about self-reliance and less about finding Van.

Still, night after night, she sat on the bench and waited for him.

She'd always thought it would take a tragic event to rip down the walls of her phobia: her house catching fire, terminal cancer, *abduction and rape*. Yet, on day seventy-six, something unexpected finally propelled her over the property line and onto Liv's porch.

Love guided her shaky legs beneath the luminance of the moon.

She loved herself enough to raise a sweat-soaked fist and knock on the door. And she loved him enough to smooth her breathing when a gorgeous brunette poked her head through the crack.

A pink scar, just like Van's, twitched on Liv's cheek as she tilted her head. "Yes?"

She curled her fingers in the fabric of her shorts, relaxed them at her sides, and lifted her eyes. "I...I...uh..." Her voice quivered, and the air thinned. "I live next door. I'm—" She wheezed with burning lungs, and Liv's emotionless expression didn't help her nerves. "Sorry. I'm a bit panicky."

A car motored down the street behind her, and she jumped. *Jesus, get a grip.* "I'm...I *was* Van Quiso's..." What was she? Slave? Girlfriend? Lover?

Those dark eyes turned to stone. "What the fuck did he do?" Liv opened the door all the way and stepped toward her.

Her muscles heated, and her own eyes hardened. And she didn't step back. "He loved me enough to shove me out the door." Oh fuck. *Awkward.* She glanced over her shoulder, cringing at the open space of the shadowed street. "Can I come in?"

Ten minutes later, she sat in a brown leather armchair with a mug of coffee in her trembling hands. Liv and Joshua perched on the couch across from her, Joshua's arm wrapped around Liv's shoulders. No doubt they assumed the worst about Van, and her need to rectify that spilled the words from her mouth.

They listened without comment or expression as she told them her story. The agoraphobia and OCD, the reason Van was on her porch, the abduction and rape, the dolls and the restaurant, his forceful attempts to overpower her disorders, his longing to have a relationship with his daughter, and his final unselfish act. The how and why he shoved her out the door. On the surface, the events were horrific and unsavory, but she spoke of them with a passion that made her eyes burn, her chest swell, and her lips curve upward. "I love him."

"I see that." Liv reclined against the couch back, her denim-clad legs crossed at the knee and hands folded in her lap. "Stockholm Syndrome is an intense—"

"I have an addictive personality, Miss Reed." She set down the mug and faced the woman head on. "If you want to psychoanalyze me, please consider all of my *syndromes*. As well as your own capture-bonding relationship." She flicked her eyes at a grinning Joshua.

A smile bent Liv's otherwise unreadable expression. "Touché."

Her shoulders relaxed. "He healed me in a way none of my therapists had been able to do. He freed me."

Liv hummed, and the soft, reverberating note sent an exquisite chill through the air. "And you want me to allow him contact with Livana?"

She nodded. "I also want you to help me find him. The restaurant you named only limits my search to...oh, the greater Austin area."

"*He'll* find *you*. He's nothing if not dedicated to his stalk—" Liv smiled. "Pursuits."

She left Liv's house with a yearning to believe her. Hell, he wouldn't have to look far.

For the next two months, she waited right on that bench. She'd trimmed the bushes so he wouldn't miss her if he drove by. So she wouldn't miss him.

Often, she lay on the wood slats and fell asleep under the canopy of stars. During the day, she expanded her business and paid her bills. She kept a routine, but it was *flexible*. One time, she even took a cab to the grocery store. A panic attack cut her shopping trip short, but she'd managed to get herself home without assistance.

She didn't subscribe hope, but she refused to let herself slip by without a constant goal to work toward. Sitting on that bench, night after night, was a full-on confrontation with her fears. For an agoraphobe, that kind of courage was hard to come by. She collected her courage from every tiny advancement she made in her recovery, saving it up and making herself stronger.

If he never came back for her, she *knew* she was brave enough to continue alone.

# THIRTY-FIVE

Not a second went by when Van didn't question the choice he made that night. Every window, every speck of dust, even the bedside lamp was a painful reminder of what he'd given up. The most agonizing choices were the right ones, but acknowledging it didn't make it any less agonizing.

Six months had passed since he'd kissed her drug-slackened lips in a torturous goodbye. He didn't just miss her lips, but goddammit, he missed them so fucking much.

He missed the sound of her knuckles cracking, her little gasps of panic, and her constant bratty comebacks. He missed working out with her in the mornings and making love to her in the afternoon. He missed feeding her and whipping her and studying all the quirky nuances that made her blush and scowl and throw her head back with laughter. And he missed her in his bed, the firm curves of her body all tucked up against him.

The silence of the cabin was excruciating without her. Even the simple act of breathing was met with a hollow echo that left everything cold and empty.

Like most nights, he drove aimlessly up and down the streets of Austin, heading anywhere except back to the lonely cabin. The leather doll she'd made was a permanent passenger on the seat beside him, a reminder to not show up at her house and demand she come back. He held no doubts in her ability to recover. The doll beside him was a symbol of her strength. And he'd made her weaker. As long as he didn't interfere, she would find her tenacity again.

He turned onto a dark, narrow street. Austin didn't have ghettos, and certainly nothing as decrepit as his childhood shacks, but there were pockets that bristled with crime and broken families.

Up ahead, a small silhouette moved on the side of the road, bobbing and darting beneath the canopy of an abandoned gas station. He slowed the Mustang, motoring closer, the street empty and unlit. He turned into the lot, and the headlights flashed over the tiny features of a five- or six-year-old girl sitting against the concrete wall, legs curled against her chest.

Where was her mother? There was no one around, and she was way too young to be out alone at eleven o'clock at night. Hell, he'd spotted a prostitute just two blocks back.

He stopped the car and opened the door to the sound of her soft sniffles. Approaching her cautiously, he asked, "Are you lost?"

She hugged her legs and shook her head.

With a hand on his hip, the other rubbing the back of his neck, he looked around. Apartment buildings, dark commercial properties, and empty parking lots lined the street. "Where's your mom?"

She pointed at the apartment tower down the road and sniveled.

"What's your name?"

"Leslie," she mumbled.

He crouched at her side. "Leslie, how about you head home? It's not safe out here."

Tears burst from her throat as she shuffled away from him.

Fuck. He crossed his arms around his knees to keep from going to her. Last thing he needed was someone accusing him of being a pedophile. "Go home, Leslie."

She shook her head in hard, jerky movements, the whites of her eyes glassy and wet in the headlights.

His skin tightened, and nausea hit his stomach. He knew that look, one bred of abuse and neglect. He forced himself back to the car and sat there for endless minutes, staring straight ahead, his eyes watering. What could he do?

He slammed his hand against the steering wheel. He'd gone through such a long period of feeling nothing, refusing to allow his miserable past to morph into a selfish need to run back to Amber. But his heart was growing frailer by the minute. He fucking needed her.

But he couldn't just leave this little girl. If she were Livana, he'd remove her from her toxic home.

*Kidnapping.*

Okay, not an option. He snagged the doll and returned to the girl, dropping on one knee before her. "Whatever it is, Leslie, it's not your fault." What else had he wanted to hear at her age? "It's okay to be scared. Your mother loves you."

Jesus, he sounded like an asshole. But when he handed her the doll, she hugged it to her chest. Then she sighed.

It was a tiny thing, that sigh of happiness, but from it breathed a rush of wind that liberated him. He could return to Amber, not as a stalker and rapist but as an honest man. She could love him back or reject him because she deserved to make that choice. The choice he'd wanted so desperately as a child.

He climbed into the car and made an anonymous phone call. Then he moved the Mustang down the street and kept an eye on her. Fifteen minutes later, red and blue lights flashed around the corner. The police wouldn't always be there for her, but maybe they would help her tonight.

He didn't look in the rear-view mirror as he pulled away. Amber was forward, Livana was forward, and that was where he needed to be.

As he made the twenty-minute drive to her porch, his anxiety rose to a level Amber would've been all too familiar with. What if she'd taken another lover? Another deliveryman? What if Livana had moved elsewhere? Christ, he should've kept an eye on them.

With a churning stomach, he passed the side street he usually parked on. A few seconds later, he pulled into Amber's driveway and turned off the car.

Something moved on the porch. A stray cat? No, a person-sized shadow, sitting right there. He strained his eyes through the dark, waiting for them to adjust. Dark hair, wide eyes...Amber? Face frozen in...Panic? Confusion? Shock?

He fumbled for the door handle, catching it on the second pass. His legs shook as he rounded the front bumper, his eyes glued on the woman rising from the bench.

Sliding the hood off his head, he quickened his gait, his heart slamming into his throat. *She's on the porch. Outside. And she's not flipping her shit?*

Fuck him, she did it. A smile stretched across his face. Of course, she fucking did.

She leapt off the porch and ran toward him, her legs flexing in tiny black shorts, her gorgeous tits stretching her t-shirt.

He held out his arms to catch her, his pulse racing in anticipation to hold her body, to kiss her lips —

Her hand landed across his face in a stinging slap. "Six months, Van Quiso." She smacked him again, her eyes blazing. "One hundred and eighty-three fucking days!"

Her tiny fists went crazy, raining down on his torso in pummeling strikes. She got in some bruising punches, but dammit, he couldn't stop grinning. God, he missed her feistiness.

When she lowered her arms and gazed up at him, her beautiful makeup-free face softened beneath the glow of the streetlight. "You came."

Christ, he wanted to kiss her. "You waited."

She raised a finger, pointing at the bench. "Right there. One hundred and sixty-four nights."

His heart squeezed. With pain. With pleasure. "What did you do the other nineteen nights?"

Her lips slid into a foxy grin. "I made little Van voodoo dolls and stabbed them with toothpicks." Her smile fell. "Are you seeing anyone?"

The worry pulling at her expression made him sick to his stomach. He cupped her face and guided her mouth to his, just close enough to kiss. "There's only been you, Amber." He brushed their lips. "If we're not counting my hand."

He captured her mouth, or maybe she took his, but their tongues met with equal hunger, lips mashing through drugging licks. When he tilted his head and demanded deeper entry, she surrendered, melting against him with her fingers in his hair.

His kiss grew punishing, urgent and rough, his hands more so. He found her tits, pinching them hard enough to make her yelp. He sucked on her upper lip, his cock throbbing against his zipper, as he caressed her firm cheeks beneath the shorts. Jesus, he'd missed her ass, and he was going to fuck her right there on the driveway if they didn't move inside.

When he pulled back, she slipped out of his arms. Walking backwards, hips swaying, she gave him a playful smile. "So you haven't had sex in six months?"

He stalked after her. "No, baby. What about you?"

She shook her head — *thank Christ* — then took off toward the front door, vanishing inside the house. He trailed her, his blood pumping from his heart to his dick, his jeans a painful constriction.

A quick scan through the front room gave him a sense of how much had changed, like the single clock on the wall and the way the pillows were strewn across the couch. There was no clutter, no dirt he could see, but the house didn't have the same severity it once had. Perhaps it was the addition of color. A red throw blanket, an orange rug, and a yellow vase in the corner.

He found her in the kitchen, her eyes glimmering right before she slipped out the back door. What was she up to?

Another thing he'd missed were her endless surprises.

He stepped into the backyard, the woodsy smell of hickory scenting his inhales as he prowled toward her. She waited beneath a tall lattice trellis that adhered to the house.

He reached above her head and yanked on it. "This is new."

Lifting her lids, she peered up at him. "When I put it together, I fantasized about you tying me to it, taking my ass with your belt. Then with your cock."

His nostrils flared with a deep, joyful breath, and he kissed her mouth, passionately, letting her feel what her words did to him. "I regret that it's been six months since I've told you I love you." He brushed his tongue inside her lower lip. "I love you. And I *will* whip and fuck your ass against this trellis when we move it to the cabin."

The release of her breath wisped over his lips. She gripped her shirt and yanked it over her head. "I missed the way you make love to my mouth."

What the hell was she doing? Oh shit, there went her shorts. He gripped himself through the jeans and tried to restrain himself. He should scan their surroundings, check for gawking neighbors, but he couldn't drag his eyes from her, too afraid if he looked away, she'd disappear.

She hooked her thumbs into the sides of her panties. "I missed the warm, wet feel of that first slide of your tongue against mine, the way you tease and pull back. Mmmm. Then you take over with your big, manly confidence and control. I miss that, Van."

Her panties slid to her ankles, and she leaned against the trellis passively, submissively, awaiting his command.

His arousal fed so greedily on her submission, there wasn't a chance in hell he could stop this. A glance at Liv's house validated his position was in eyeshot of her back door. Fuck it.

He released the zipper on his jeans, and his already excited cock jumped as he shoved his pants and briefs to his knees. "Still on the pill?"

She nodded, her smoldering gaze fixed on his cock, making him impossibly harder.

"Arms above your head. Press your wrists against the lattice as if my ropes are keeping them there." He watched with his whole body as she obeyed with quivering breaths and an adoring gaze.

His cock twitched with the need to thrust deep inside her. "Describe your pussy."

Her breath sped up. "It's tight, Master. It hasn't been wrapped around anything but my fingers in six months. It's wet and beautiful and yours."

He stared at her with wonder, like a witness to the fall of prison walls and the freeing of a courageous heart that had been trapped inside. She stole his breath.

He covered her mouth with boiling, ravenous kisses as he fingered her cunt, finding her wet and tight and undeniably beautiful. Using the strength of her core muscles, she lifted her legs and twined them around his waist, her eyes as hungry and desperate as he was. He replaced his fingers with his cock, pressing against her opening, and hissed through his teeth as he entered her in one long thrust.

Heat rushed through his body, concentrating on where they were joined. To feel this connection after so goddamned long, Christ, it was like a welcoming song, a homecoming. It shook the very foundation of his soul. "Fuck, Amber. I missed you."

Clutching the diagonal rungs of the lattice, she whimpered against his chest. He ground his hips and flexed his ass to deepen the penetration.

He ran his hands over her full chest and around her curvy hips, pulling her to him with a fury of slamming drives. She didn't lower her legs or let go of the trellis as he gripped her hair, jerked her head back, and bit her below the ear. Despite the threat of outside, her movements were more confident than they'd ever been, her pelvis circling and rocking as she met him thrust for thrust.

His release swelled to the brink of explosion, and he grunted. "Come for me, Amber. I want to hear you."

She threw her head back and let go, her body shaking and her moans warbling into the night sky. It swept him away, wrenching the orgasm from his body in trembling waves.

As he came down, their lips met in a kiss so simple and tender, so honest and familiar, it left him split open and helplessly, shamelessly, filled with devotion. He pulled her to his chest, and they stood in silence, their arms wrapped around each other.

"Told you he'd find you." Liv's voice chimed through the darkness.

He yanked up his jeans and glared at her over his shoulder. "Do you mind?"

"Not at all." She leaned against the deck railing and watched them pull on their clothes. "Stalkers are hard to get rid of." Not a hint of emotion on her face, but a smile lifted her voice. Yeah, Liv had been a stalker once, too.

Amber's arms coiled around his waist, her cheek resting on his chest. "This one's not so bad."

"So you've said." Liv straightened and walked toward her back door. Then she paused, her eyes locked with his. "When you're done there, swing by. You still owe me a meeting."

He tightened his arms around Amber's back and closed his eyes as a weightless rush drifted over him. When he looked up, Liv was gone. But her offer lingered. He pressed his lips against the top of Amber's head. "You've been busy."

She shrugged. "She has something you want."

His pulse raced. "You think she'll—?"

"Go find out."

Ten minutes later, his racing heart neared detonation as he stood outside a spare bedroom in Liv's house. He squeezed Amber's hand and strained his eyes to make out the shadowed shapes within the room.

"She's just staying the night," Liv whispered. "If you wake her, I'll kill you."

He was already moving through the dark room, his mouth dry and adrenaline surging through his blood. Amber lingered in the doorway, her supportive smile holding him upright.

Stunned and hypnotized, he reached the bed and soaked in the shaded blur of Livana's dark eyelashes and dainty features. Her tiny fingers curled around the pillow, her slender frame cocooned in bedding. Christ, she was even more precious in person.

Reaching down, he ran trembling fingers over a wisp of her hair. The soft texture seeped through his touch, vividly bright and so damned real.

He could stand there all night, and he did for a long time, breathless and overcome. A cleared throat in the hallway jerked him into awareness, and slowly, reluctantly, he stepped away.

Liv waited outside the bedroom with Amber and Joshua, rigid in her statue-like posture as she watched him approach. When he reached her, her eyes flickered, right before he yanked her into an embrace.

Her arms hung at her sides, her body stiff and unyielding. Beside her, Joshua leaned against the wall, his gaze soft and thoughtful and fixed on Liv.

Van lowered his forehead to her shoulder. "I'm sorry. For keeping her from you. For taking you from your mother. It's too late for apologies. Fuck, I know this, but I'll do whatever I can to make it up to you."

Tense seconds passed, then her arms rose and folded around his back. She squeezed tighter, her voice thick. "This is a good start."

He raised his head and shared a look with Amber over Liv's shoulder, one that promised new memories. Joyful memories. She pressed a knuckle to her mouth and gave him a tearful smile.

He released Liv and moved to her side, where he belonged, surrounded by the radiance of her presence. As he stared into the brown eyes of the woman who embodied impossible dreams, he felt the future in every cell of his body. It felt crazy and beautiful and decisively unbreakable.

# THIRTY-SIX

*Three years later...*

Amber was outrunning him, fucking running circles around him. But really, how could he complain? Watching her ass flex in those painted-on athletic pants took his mind off his burning muscles and overworked lungs.

As the sun disappeared behind the skyline of downtown Austin, the city's towers glinted with the lingering rays of yellow and gold. Too bad the humidity didn't vanish with it. He wiped his forehead with the sweatband on his wrist and quickened his pace to catch up with that gorgeous ass.

Maybe fifty paces ahead of him, she pivoted, running backwards and grinning at him like a goon. "What's the hold up, old man?"

Old man? He was still a year younger than she was, even if she hadn't broken a sweat. Fucking show-off.

Pedestrians and fellow runners scurried out of their way. A dozen teen-aged boys paused their soccer game to watch her run by. He gave the fuckers a threatening glare, and they snapped from their gawking and returned to their scrimmage.

He and Amber could've easily jogged in the woods at the cabin, but the social surroundings were good for her. And there was another reason he'd chosen this park.

In an hour, he would be meeting with one of his former slaves, Camila, on the south side of the pond. He'd learned she was attempting to bring down a new slave ring in Austin and was in over her head. Even with her cartel connections, it had been too ambitious and risky as hell. She needed help, and fuck him, but being a husband and a father fueled him with a crazy amount of protective drive, which included a bloodthirsty need to wipe the city of sex trafficking.

Amber was skittish about his involvement, but she would come around. He wouldn't give her a choice.

Up ahead, an old lady and her Boston Terrier stepped into Amber's backward running path. If Amber didn't turn back around soon, she was going to collide with them.

"Amber." He panted for air. "Watch yourself."

As she spun around, he glimpsed the tightening of her fist and the flinch of her shoulders. No one around her would notice the traces of her anxiety, the way she cracked her knuckles too often, the tiny hiccups in her breathing, and the trickle of sweat between her breasts. They would only see the confident woman she was with a knockout body and face so ethereal it compelled longing glances.

Every day she left the house was a workout for her. The agoraphobia would always be there, but she made it her bitch with an inspiring amount of courage.

He caught up with her on the bend around the pond and ran at her side. Christ, he loved seeing her at his side. Good thing, too, since they worked together every day out of the garage at the cabin. Her leathercraft business had trickled into the doll market, and they were inundated with orders.

When they reached the next bend, his pocket vibrated. He checked the caller ID and grabbed her elbow, veering them off the track.

Slowing to a stop and hunching over with a hand on his knee, he lifted the phone to his ear. "Hey, sweetheart."

A melodic voice tinkled through the phone. "Daddy?"

Damn, he would never get tired of hearing her call him that. And it was the only greeting she gave before charging into the reason for her call. "You can't just go around threat—"

"I'm doing great." He smiled, feeling the easiness of it inside and out. "How are you?"

"I'm fine." She sniffed then rushed on in her high-pitched voice. "But Katie told Jena, and Jena told—"

"Livana." He used his warning tone, winking at Amber. "Slow down."

Amber bent at the waist in a stretch that put her chest on her thighs and her ass in the air. He leaned with her, mesmerized, as blood rushed to his dick. He dropped the phone.

She gave him an upside down grin, her ponytail swishing over the ground.

He returned the phone to his ear and pulled his shirt over the front of his pants.

" — can't do that," Livana said. "Are you there?"

"Yeah, honey. I dropped the phone. Start over."

"Did you threaten Danny Taylor?"

Oh, that. "I didn't threaten him. I simply enlightened him."

Amber straightened, shaking her head and licking the corner of her curved mouth, the vixen.

"Mom already said I could go to the dance." Livana's voice pierced through the phone, cool and sure and just like Liv's.

By *mom*, she meant Mr. E's widow, Carolyn Eary, her legal guardian who raised her from birth and still provided the roof over her head.

What had started out as Liv introducing him as a family friend was now a unique, and often delicate, arrangement. He'd spent a lot of time with Carolyn in those first few months, feeling her out. When he finally revealed his identity, she was understandably skeptical of his intentions. But he'd proved himself as he'd done with Liv, and a year after he'd met Livana, Carolyn told her whom her biological parents were.

Livana knew nothing of their criminal history, but she did know how to play all three of them to get what she wanted. Carolyn was a fucking pushover. He was a drill sergeant. But Liv was the wild card.

"What did Liv say?"

"She said to ask you."

"I didn't hear you ask."

Even irritated, her sigh was the sweetest damned sound. "Daddy, can I please go to the dance?"

"You're too young."

"I'm twelve!"

He dug a toothpick from his pocket and slid it into his mouth. He was done jogging for the night. Amber was in the midst of another erotic stretch and his focus was shit. "You can go, and I will chaperone."

A long pause. "Ugh. Fine."

Well, that was easy. Maybe she didn't realize he would be at her side the entire evening. "Love you."

"Love you, too."

He pocketed the phone and scanned the park for a spot that would offer the most privacy. When an outcrop of rocks up ahead caught his eye, he gripped Amber's hand and led her to them.

Behind the cover of a huge boulder, he pressed her against the flat surface and kissed her deeply and thoroughly. "Go to the dance with me, Mrs. Quiso."

She answered by returning his kiss and flicking her tongue wildly and aggressively. They'd been married for two years, but every day felt like a honeymoon. He ran his hands up her spandex-clad thighs, cupped the hard muscles of her ass, and caressed the soft curves with his fingers.

Yeah, sex in a public park wasn't the best idea for a guy who wanted to remain under the radar. But as she flexed her hips, tangled her tongue with his, and aroused every nerve-ending in his body, his only thought was *Yes*.

She reached for her shirt and pulled it over her head, her tits tumbling over the cage of her sports bra. Jesus. Whether in shackles and hanging naked from a tree or seconds away from losing her panties in a park, her ability to shock and awe him was infinite.

Curling her arms around his shoulders, she rose up on tiptoes to meet his gaze with bright eyes. "Still want to put a baby inside me? Fifty-percent chance you'll get another girl."

"I'll take anything you give me." He ground the aching ridge of his erection against the *V* of her thighs. "Right now, you're going to give me something wet and tight. Turn around. Arms above your head."

# DISCLAIM

# PAM GODWIN

Book 3

# PROLOGUE

With a swing of the hammer, Matias pounded a steel tent stake into the arm pinned beneath his boot. A normal man would've flinched at the godawful howls of pain. The man he used to be would've puked out his guts at the feel of tendons snapping beneath the crude impalement. But focused fury was his internal companion, a ruthless beast risen from the ruins of his former self.

Hazel eyes, identical to his own, stared up at him in pleading agony.

He swung again, burying the spike into flesh. Shredded screams fused with the damp air of the shed as metal pierced muscle and tissue, finding purchase in the dirt floor.

Four stakes secured Jhon's arms and legs. The hooked heads protruded from bleeding holes, neutralizing any attempt to thrash free.

Matias removed the final stake from his pocket. The one that would end his brother's life.

Luring Jhon to the abandoned farm was easy. Beyond the open doorway, thick foliage cloaked the mountainside, rippling toward a tributary of the Amazon River below. The blue haze of humidity filtered the sunlight and blanketed the atmosphere in a wet sheen.

The remote site in the Colombian jungle indulged his brother's greed to expand cocaine production. The absence of witnesses made it an ideal place for Matias' revenge.

With shallow breaths, Jhon blinked slowly, fighting to maintain consciousness. "Don't do this."

The same words Matias uttered the night he was ripped from his home. *From Camila.*

He was a world away from the Texan citrus grove where he spent the first eighteen years of his life. A world away from the girl he'd tried — and failed — to protect.

He pressed the stake against the hollow of Jhon's throat, his voice an avalanche of gravel. "Why *her*?"

"She was —" Jhon wheezed past gritted teeth. "Something you cared about."

"She was family!" And so much more.

Speared to the ground, legs twitching against the spikes, Jhon hardened bruised eyes. "*I* am your family."

Only by blood, which stank of corroded iron and betrayal as it seeped into the soil.

Matias pushed on the stake, digging between corded sinews and breaking skin. "Where is she?"

Camila hadn't contacted him in six weeks. The moment his phone stopped ringing, he knew.

A malicious grin cracked Jhon's pallid face. "Sold."

*Slavery.* That much he'd figured out, but it didn't stop the torment from exploding anew and ravaging his veins with fire. "Where? Who has her?"

"She's dead, little brother." Jhon swallowed against the steel point, raising his chin to drive the stake deeper, taunting. "You're chasing a ghost."

A ghost with an invisible trail, likely smuggled to the farthest corner of the world, to be used, broken, and disposed.

The truth resounded in the empty chasm of his chest, a painful splintering quickly snuffed out by the nothingness that consumed him.

He was wasting his time with Jhon. His brother was too cunning, too loyal to the organization, utterly single-minded, and willing to die to protect the only secret Matias wanted.

*So be it.*

He reared back the hammer and struck the stake, slamming ten inches of steel through Jhon's throat. The gurgling cough ended too soon. Just like all the others, his brother's glassy-eyed silence didn't soothe Matias' hunger for retribution.

Jhon's death was neither the first nor the last. In the months that followed, Matias sank deeper into the unforgiving armor of brutality. He belonged with the cartel, among the corrupted and the heartless, and used every resource available to search for her.

Obliterating men as despicable as himself provided an outlet for the rage he was unable to quiet. He understood the need to gut betrayers and decapitate adversaries, to torture for information, build stronger compounds, and effect armies. He became one of them, embracing their predatory existence and embodying a reputation that made the worst of his kind fear his name.

But it didn't bring her back.

It didn't bring back the citrus scent of her golden skin when she'd dozed with him in the grove. The way her shiny black hair whipped against her back as he chased her through knee-high grass. Or the spark in her brown eyes right before she launched a lime at his head. Slowly, his memories of her decayed.

Twelve months after her disappearance, she'd become a mirage in his wasteland, distorted at the edges and flickering out of reach.

He lay on his bed in the newly renovated Colombian compound, hands clasped behind his neck, eyes closed, trying to forget, if only for a few minutes. The faceless blonde between his legs helped with that, bobbing her head and working his cock to distraction.

His lower body clenched, balls aching and tightening as he strained for release. "Faster. Suck harder."

She quickened her movements, the suction of her mouth hot and wet and —

A distinctive ring tone sounded from across the room. *What the fuck?*

"Did you hear that?" He jack-knifed into a sitting position and shoved her off his lap.

She dragged the back of a hand across her swollen lips.

The ringing echoed again, chiming a tune he hadn't heard in a year, waking a phone only one person had the number to.

He vaulted off the bed. "Get out."

With a racing pulse, he sprinted toward the dresser. Following the muffled bleeps, he dug through piles of weapons, papers, and clothes that scattered the surface. There! He grabbed it.

*Unknown number.*

His hand shook as he tapped the screen and accepted the call.

Dead air.

No, no, no. He missed it. Hitting the call back button, he rubbed a hand down his face. *Come on, come on.*

The screen flashed. *Call failed.*

Vicious rage tore through his body, inflaming his muscles. He spun and found the blonde taking her sweet-ass time dragging on clothes, her gaze on his softening cock.

He grabbed a chambered .45 from the dresser, flicked off the safety, and aimed it at her head, his voice cold and lethal. "Get the fuck out."

Eyes wide, she snatched her shirt from the floor and shut the door behind her.

He set down the gun and returned to the phone, deafening in its silence and still plugged in since the day he left it on the dresser. *Call me back, goddammit.*

It was illogical to hope. Camila was gone. Anyone could've accidentally dialed him. But wasn't hope the reason he'd kept the number all this time?

He stared at the blank screen, willing it to come back to life.

A moment later, it lit up. *Unknown Number.* The cascading ring tone penetrated his chest, stabbing interior scars with excruciating precision.

Tempering his breaths, he answered. "Who is this?"

Silence. Then a soft exhale. "It's me."

He stopped breathing, every cell in his body screaming in denial. His countless enemies were insidious in their efforts to destroy him. How hard would it be to procure this number and impersonate her husky voice?

He lifted his arm, zeroing in on the white pockmark on the inside of his wrist. "How old was I when I got my first scar?"

"So paranoid." A sigh ruffled through the ear piece. "Guess that means you still work for them."

His jaw set, his tone clipped with suspicion. "How old?"

"I was…uh, six. So you were eight?"

He gripped the edge of the dresser, his rib cage tightening. But any one of their friends or neighbors could've been tortured for that information.

Relaxing his grip, he sharpened his voice. "Tell me how it happened."

"I hate your asshole games."

Exactly how Camila would've responded, and the lack of warmth in the voice was perfectly her. But he couldn't trust it. "Tell me."

She growled in frustration. "You slipped in a stream and punctured your arm on a rock."

That was the story they told their families, an innocent lie to protect a mangy dog. Only Camila knew the truth.

His hope crashed, burning in his stomach. "Wrong answer."

"Seriously? We swore to take that secret to our graves." She cleared her throat. "Rambo wasn't a bad dog. He just didn't appreciate you taking his bone. You deserved that bite."

*Camila.* All the air evacuated his lungs as his mind spun and wrenched apart his painfully constructed acceptance of her death. Convincing himself she was gone had been a grueling effort in self-destruction, reinforced with irreparable distractions. The business, drugs, women, blood… So much fucking blood.

He couldn't feel his legs beneath the grip of shock, his mouth dry and acidic. "You're not dead."

"Nope," she said, casually. Too detached, even for her. "Did you look for me?"

Every damn day. "Are you safe?" He snagged a pair of jeans, his hands sweating as he shoved them on. "Where are you?"

"I'm safe, but listen, I just escaped a fucked up situation and need to lie low for a while."

Escaped? Impossible. No one *escaped* a highly-organized human trafficking ring. Especially not a seventeen-year-old girl. *Eighteen now.* She'd been in captivity for a fucking year. Did they beat her? Rape her? Take her virginity?

His insides boiled with murderous wrath and overwhelming guilt. They were supposed to be each other's firsts. She was only sixteen when the cartel came for him, and though he hadn't seen her since that night, he'd waited for her, holding on to an impossible dream through their secret phone calls. Until she vanished.

"You haven't asked what happened to me." Her tone hardened. "You already know, don't you? How?"

He couldn't tell her, not until he was certain she couldn't run from his answer. "I need to know where you are and how you escaped."

"Who do you work for?" she asked.

"You know I can't tell you, *mi vida.*"

"Don't call me that." A muffled rustle of fabric followed, conjuring an image of her pressing the phone to her chest. "Dammit, I want to trust you, but you have to give me something. Anything. What happened to the boy whose thoughts completed mine? What did they do to you?"

That boy was dead. How quickly they'd returned to their exhaustingly endless argument, one he refused to feed. "Tell me where you are."

"Will you help me?"

"Always."

As she rattled off directions to an isolated reservoir in Texas, he scrambled for a pen and scribbled down the details. *Two hours outside of Austin.*

It would take him a day to travel there from the bowels of goddamned Colombia. "I'm on my way. Just…stay put."

"Oh, I'm not there." Her breaths quickened, as if she were walking at a swift pace. "That's where I left a body. I need you to get rid of it since, you know, you're still in the *business.*"

His skin chilled with the ramp of his pulse. "What body?"

"The sick fuck who bought me."

The phone's power cord snapped from the outlet as he charged toward the shirt on the floor. "You killed him?"

"Doesn't matter. But I'm using his phone and need to toss it like yesterday."

*Fuck! She's going to get herself killed.* And now his number would show up on phone records for rival gangs, FBI, fucking anyone to track.

He paced the room as a year's worth of ruthless crimes caught up with him. "Who else have you called?"

A pause, filled by the rush of her breaths. "Just you."

Relief loosened his gait. "I have to kill this number." He gave her the number to his main phone and made her repeat it several times. "Only use burner phones, and *mi vida*? Don't try to contact your parents."

"Why the hell not?"

They were dead. Buried beneath the scorched landscape of the citrus grove.

He evened his voice. "You'll endanger them."

She made a despairing noise, a small thing, but it was a hint of emotion nonetheless. She was closed-off by nature, reserving her softness for the few who earned her loyalty. He'd been on the receiving end of that once, had forgotten what it felt like.

The reminder was a molten shock to his system, intensified by a combustible storm as he imagined what she'd endured in the clutches of her kidnappers.

Who had touched her? How deep were her wounds?

His hand clenched and loosened on the phone. "How many motherfuckers do I need to kill?"

"I'll handle it. Just deal with the body. I need to go—"

"Give me a way to contact you." So he could locate her. And reclaim her.

"I'll be in touch."

"Don't you fucking hang—"

She disconnected the call.

# ONE

*Ten years later…*

"Lower. That's it. A little lower…" Camila rocked her hips beneath the scratch of whiskers. "Right there, *churro.*"

*Churro, my ass.* This underweight stick of a man reeked of sweat, stale smoke, and neglect. Or maybe it was the mattress.

Not that she expected a pleasant experience. The man between her legs worked for someone vile. Someone who didn't deserve to live. Shame she didn't know who that someone was. But she was here to find out.

Bony hands curled around her waist, his wet mouth slithering across the waxed mound of her pussy. *Here we go.*

A purr vibrated her throat, her pleasure as fake as her role tonight. But damn if she didn't sound convincing. With her legs spread, back pressed against the mattress, and a hundred-and-fifteen pounds of athletic nudity on display, she could rob a man of all common sense.

As soon as she could seduce him into position, she'd take more than just his wits.

He shifted lower, curled his tongue inside her, and *Whoa! What the –* A charged warmth of bliss shot across her skin and bowed her spine.

"*Mierda*, yes!" She turned her neck, hiding the shock on her face.

Holy hell, he knew how to give head. She melted against the suction of his lips, clinging to the tingling rush of sensations. As far as surprises went, she could roll with this one. She might even come.

With wicked flicks of his tongue, he peered up at her, his pupils bloated in the dim light of a floor lamp. "Condom?"

He wouldn't get that far, but he'd picked her up at the local bar under the assumption she wanted to fuck.

"Got it covered, baby." She grabbed his brown hair and held his mouth against her pussy. "I'm almost there."

An orgasm wasn't in the plan, but fuck it. He did things with his tongue no warm-blooded woman could refuse. Tenacious and sinful, he licked in and out and all around, reviving the ever-present ache inside her.

His unappealing looks didn't matter. Whenever she climaxed, it was always the same face behind her eyelids. Jet black hair. Dimpled smile. Sun-soaked complexion. Strong jaw. *Strong everywhere.* With eyes like ripe limes, golden in the center and ringed in deep green.

At least, that was her silly, childhood memory of Matias. The past twelve years — doing whatever unspeakable shit he did — likely marred his beauty. Time had certainly hardened his voice. Wrapped it in ice.

But she could hear his timbre in her head, sharp and incisive. *Come for me, mi vida. Come now.*

Heat bloomed low in her pelvis, gathering into a rhythmic pulse and tumbling her over the edge. She detonated on the stroking tongue, grinding and panting with abandon. *Damn.*

He raised his head and snaked a hand over her abdomen, his gaze hungry and full of intent. He could look at her however he wanted as long as his fingers continued their prowl upward.

Inching along her ribs, he teased each bone in his path toward her tit. His position was just…about…

*Perfect.*

She captured his arm, shifted it diagonally across her chest, and held it tightly against her. Tight enough to widen his eyes.

Strengthening her grip, she lifted her knees above his head and pinned his neck between his own shoulder and her inner thigh.

"The fuck?" He writhed and twisted, trying to jerk free.

His other hand swung toward her face, but she knocked it away and clamped her legs around his thrashing neck. Jesus, he was strong for a skinny fucker.

She yanked harder on his arm and adjusted her hips, maneuvering him into a restrained position.

*Finally.* Adrenaline surged through her veins, and her breaths came in short bursts.

Realization glistened in the stark white of his eyes, and he snarled like a rabid animal.

*That's right, baby. I know who you are. You're so fucked.*

He bucked his chest against the mattress, his teeth snapping too damn close to her stomach.

"I have kids." His sunken cheeks blanched, his voice a choked rasp. "I'm a father."

Good for him. She had a father once. And a mother and sister. Her heart twisted, the loss as raw as the day she discovered their deaths. They would never know what happened to her. Would never know she made it out of that attic of shackles and horrors. She'd escaped a fate worse than death.

The same fate this piece of shit inflicted on others.

"You should've thought about your kids…" She hooked her foot beneath her other knee and squeezed her legs. "Before you stole someone else's."

The compression of her thighs and the pulling grip on his arm crushed his bicep against his throat, strangling his ability to speak. And breathe.

Her muscles strained to defend the position as he kicked and rolled his hips. Keeping his arm pressed beneath his chin, she swatted away his attempts to punch her with his free hand. Over and over, he flung his fist toward her face, fighting for blood, for air, wild in his desperation.

*No bueno.*

If done effectively, the chokehold would cut off the blood flow in the arteries on both sides of the neck. It should've been over within seconds. Why was this motherfucker still squirming?

She tightened her legs and cocked her head, studying the waning twitches in his body. Unconsciousness would come soon. She settled in and tried to steady her heartbeat.

Months of stalking Austin's worst criminals had led her to Larry McGregor. Mailman by day and slave trader by night, he spent his downtime hooking up with sleazy women at the local bar. Bet he regretted that vice right about now.

Her thighs tensed, burning to snap his neck. But she needed him alive.

Surveillance confirmed he held a teenage girl in an abandoned barn twenty minutes outside of Austin. Knowing her team was extracting the girl at that very moment should've made it easier to breathe. But there were more Larrys, more enslaved girls, the trafficking network in Austin vast and well-funded.

The only way to stop it was to cut off the head. First, she needed to know how to find that head.

Larry's body fell limp between her legs. She waited a beat, pushing at his gaping jaw before slipping from beneath him and checking his pulse. *Slow and even.* Unlike her own.

From her purse on the floor, she unwrapped a maxi pad and removed the plastic cable ties she'd hidden in the cotton. How long before he woke?

Fuck, she was out of her realm here. She wanted to end him, but if she didn't secure the information she needed, another would take his place, and another, and another. This would be her first attempt at torture. Did she have the balls to do it?

She quickly zipped his wrists to his ankles and stuffed the maxi pad in his mouth, her fingers twitching through the movements. Matias would have a body to dispose of soon enough.

*Matias.* Every call she made to him brought a new line of questioning. His *and* hers. Neither would budge in their secrecy.

A sudden chill crept over her. Just thinking about him made her feel vulnerable and...naked. She slid on her dress and heels.

She hadn't seen him since he was eighteen, not since the day those hard-looking men led him out of the citrus grove. Over the years, he told her he was *obligated* to stay with them. Were they cartel? He refused to confirm her assumption, but he didn't deny it either. What was she supposed to do? Trust him? No way in hell.

He was a thirty-year-old...what? Grave-digger? Hitman? Underling for a drug lord? Whatever his line of work, he always got rid of dead bodies for her. The first was the man who intended to buy her. Followed by six more buyers and their bodyguards for her six fellow slaves. Her last call was four years ago. To collect Van Quiso's body.

She retrieved her phone from her purse and pulled up her contact list. A shudder raced through her as she stared at the last number dialed.

*Van Quiso.*

The man who kidnapped her when she was seventeen.

The man who imprisoned her for a year and trained her to be the perfect slave.

As it turned out, he hadn't died from that gunshot wound in his shoulder.

No matter how hard she tried, she couldn't parse her feelings about that. They ran too deep, too entangled and confusing, much like everything else in her life. So she detached from it, held herself at a distance, and focused on the goal. She had a slave trader to torture and kidnapped girls to save.

She tapped his name on the screen. As the call connected, her heartbeat roared past her ears.

Van answered with silence.

"It's done and ready for pick up." She steeled her breath.

"On my way." He disconnected.

She slumped on the edge of the mattress, her shoulders loosening.

Ironically, asking her kidnapper to help her take down other kidnappers wasn't the worst call she had to make. That special pang of dread was reserved for her impending conversation with Matias.

God, she missed him. Almost as much as she feared him.

# DISCLAIM

A soon-to-be dead man lay hogtied beside her, eyes closed and mouth stretched around the balled up maxi pad. She could dispose of the body herself. At the risk of getting caught and sentenced for murder.

If she involved Matias, he would shield her from the law. At the risk of him finally locating her.

Then what? Whatever connection they'd shared as children was a distant memory. She knew nothing about the man he'd become.

If his overbearing, razor-sharp tone over the phone was any indication, he hadn't lost his protective ownership over her.

But she hadn't spoken to him in four years. What if he'd forgotten about her? What if he was married?

Her heart punched painfully, and she reached up to rub her chest.

There had been a time when he'd gallantly stood between her and anything that threatened to harm her. If he knew she was taking dangerous risks, would he try to stop her? She was so close to finishing this. So fucking close.

And maybe she was protective of him, too. Maybe she still cared for him against her better judgment. If that were true, she couldn't take him where she was going.

She needed to forget about him.

Except she couldn't. In the back of her fucked up mind, she looked forward to her next kill just so she'd have a reason to hear his voice again.

# TWO

Camila paced beside the floor-to-ceiling windows in Van's living room, her impatience burning a short fuse. She dragged a hand through her hair, fingers snagging in the shoulder-length, black strands. She needed a fucking haircut.

She needed a lot of things.

Sighing, she turned to Van. "Why won't he fucking talk?"

After a week of interrogation, Larry McGregor was a goddamn mute. Strapped naked on a table in Van's garage, he'd endured sleep deprivation, starvation, solitary confinement, and her endless threats of permanent disfigurement.

All he had to do was tell her who he worked for and where he was supposed to deliver the girl he'd kidnapped. Two simple answers and his suffering would end.

Van reclined on the couch and rolled a toothpick between his lips. "You need to up your game."

"Oh, please enlighten me." She narrowed her eyes, her voice edged with bitter resentment.

She'd spent an eternal year in Van's shackles, learning obedience one welt at a time. At least this house didn't have an attic. She didn't need any more reminders of him whipping her body and picking apart her mind. He probably would have taken her virginity, too, but the man who had intended to buy her wanted that sick pleasure.

Van never managed to break her, though. What made him think he could give advice on breaking Larry McGregor?

Tossing his chewed toothpick on the coffee table, he removed a new one from his pocket. "Threaten his kids."

As a father, Van knew all too well how effective that was. But she couldn't do it. Even if it were a hollow threat, she refused to stoop to that level.

"No innocents."

She'd been an innocent kid once, one of the reasons Van had captured her. Back then, he was a vicious son of a bitch. Still was. But the past four years had diluted some of his poisonous nature. Or maybe his wife had something to do with that.

Unfortunately, his wife had put a full stop on Camila's plan to chop off Larry's fingers.

"Amber?" she shouted toward the second-story loft, where the strange woman had vanished moments earlier.

Amber approached the railing upstairs, her brown hair cascading in curls around her model-perfect face.

How Van had been able to coerce a beauty pageant queen into marrying him was anyone's guess. He'd kidnapped her, for fuck's sake. Yanked her right out of her house and imprisoned her in this remote cabin, not to be sold, but to be used as his own personal sex slave.

The kicker was, he'd stopped his kidnapping and slave trading after that. Amber forgave him, and they fell in love or some shit. Their relationship smelled like an epic mindfuck, but on the surface, it seemed to be working for them.

Amber fingered her curls as if ensuring each one lay exactly right. Then she brushed the front of her sundress, erasing imaginary wrinkles.

Yeah, the woman had issues, and loving Van wasn't the weirdest of them. She struggled with severe OCD and agoraphobia. When Van snatched her, she hadn't been out of her house in two years.

Lowering a hand to the railing, Amber stepped down the spiral staircase, one toned leg crossing in front of the other like she was walking the runway in a fashion show. "Did you need me?"

Camila met her at the bottom step. "I'll cover the garage floor with plastic. I promise I'll keep the mess...not messy."

"No. That's—" Amber clutched her knuckles, popping each one systematically. "The blood will splatter. I'll never get it off the concrete and—"

"Amber." Van appeared at her side, gripping her fingers and stilling her favorite coping mechanism. "Crack your knuckles again, and I'll tie you to the tree outside."

"Right," Amber said on a stiff inhale. "I'm good. We're good."

She stared at her husband for a long moment, each second stretching into something intimate and unspoken as her expression heated. Jesus, did she want him to tie her up? This was Van Quiso of all people, prince of sadism and non-consensual kink.

The four-inch scar that bisected his cheek was the first thing any terrified girl would notice. Followed by his obscenely oversized muscles, tousled brown hair, and the saw-blade angles of his face. There was no denying he was insanely attractive. *Insane* being the quintessential word here.

Amber pulled her attention away from him, shifting it across the room, eyes squinting. Hard.

Camila followed her gaze to the coffee table, returned to Amber, then back to the table. Van's chewed toothpick lay alone on the dust-free surface. Knowing him, he probably left it there to fuck with her OCD.

"You guys," Camila said, shaking her head, "are seriously whacked."

Hands fisting on her hips, Amber straightened her spine. "Says the woman who wants to cut off body parts in my garage."

*Touché.* Bringing Larry here had been a matter of convenience. The closest neighbor was miles away, and Van kept the property locked down like a fortress. As for his willingness to help her? Well, maybe that was his way of atoning for being a former human-trafficking asshole. Whatever helped him sleep at night.

"Fine. No blood." Camila crossed the room and took in the heavily treed landscape beyond the wall of windows. "I need to increase the Krokodil injections."

Created by mixing codeine with paint thinner, gasoline, and a few other nasty ingredients, the drug was more addictive than heroin. She didn't cook it long enough to remove the toxic impurities, hoping that would speed up the side effects, such as gangrene and pneumonia. Eventually, blood vessels would burst, and the flesh around the injection point—where she deliberately missed the vein—would rot and fall off the bone in chunks.

"How do you avoid a lethal dose?" Van leaned against the windowed wall, gnawing on a toothpick.

"No idea." She wasn't a druggie, had never even smoked tobacco. "I'm going to check on him."

Passing through the kitchen, she took in the polished appliances and spotless countertops. Exactly what one would expect in a house occupied by someone with OCD.

There was nothing lavish about the cabin. The fixtures, the furniture…it was all simple. Practical. Made her wonder what Van did with his wealth or if he'd even kept any money from his trafficking days.

She opened the door to the garage and found Liv and Tate bent over Larry's nude body.

It was surreal seeing them here, willingly standing in the home Van shared with his wife. His *domain*.

# DISCLAIM

Liv Reed was the first person he'd captured, his first slave, and the one he'd hurt the most. After he broke the rules and raped her, he got her pregnant and couldn't sell her. Buyers wanted virgins. That had earned Van and Liv matching scars on their cheeks, courtesy of Mr. E.

Mr. E, now dead, had run the operation, raised their daughter, and controlled Van and Liv by threatening the little girl's life.

It was impossible to look at Liv without feeling a torrential mix of nostalgia, pity, and gratitude. While Mr. E had forced Van and Liv to capture and train slaves — nine in total — Liv covertly and brilliantly killed the buyers each time she delivered a slave. She did that for *years*.

Tate looked up from the table, his dark blond brows pulling together as he scanned Camila from head to toe. He'd been the sixth one Van and Liv enslaved.

Imagining a strong-willed, masculine guy like Tate Vades being forced to suck Van's cock... Camila knew it had irreparably damaged him. But he hid his demons beneath a disarming smile.

"Doing okay?" He met her gaze, a thousand more questions swirling in his crystal blue eyes.

"*Muy bien.*" She really wanted to know how *he* was holding up, but if she asked, he'd give her a similar bullshit answer. "You don't have to be here, you know."

When she told her team a few months ago that she'd asked Van for help with this phase of her plan, Tate had blown a gasket. But if Liv could trust Van — enough to let him be part of their daughter's life — they could rely on him for this.

"Van doesn't scare me." Tate crossed his arms, the sleeves of his t-shirt straining across his biceps. "I'm not going anywhere, Camila."

He hadn't left her side since the day she rescued him. They lived together, worked together, his shadow always hovering like a protective brother. Except the way he watched her was more like a boyfriend. One who refused to have sex with her.

Maybe he kept her in the friend zone because of what they'd been through. Or maybe it was because of what she'd become.

"This is going to be unpleasant." She approached the table where Larry lay motionless, his arms and legs bubbling with sores. She gave Tate a stern look, silently reminding him she was going to break another law. Murder another man. Throw away another body. "You can go before —"

"Stop." He gripped her jaw and brought his mouth to her ear, his voice low. "I owe you my life, so just...shut the fuck up about it."

"Fine." She turned her head, breaking his hold.

As the first slave to be freed, she spent years helping Liv extricate Tate and the others. That included dismantling Mr. E's operation, killing the buyers, and using her connection with Matias to dispose of the bodies.

503

The freed slaves could've gone back to their lives if they'd had families or something to return to. They didn't, instead joining Camila in her effort to take down a new trafficking ring — the one Larry worked for.

"He's still not talking?" She prodded at the gangrenous, pus-filled flesh on Larry's forearm.

"No." Liv frowned, the scar on her cheek wrinkling. "I have to leave in a couple hours."

"You have Livana this weekend?"

"Yes." The tightness around Liv's mouth relaxed, replaced with the warm glow of maternal love.

Van and Liv shared joint custody with Livana's adoptive mother. It was a strange arrangement, one they fervently protected. Which meant they kept their involvement in Camila's illegal activities to a minimum. Had it been Van's weekend with Livana, he wouldn't have permitted Camila and her team of ex-slave vigilantes anywhere near his house.

Larry flicked open his eyes and thrashed his head, his rotten flesh tearing beneath the cinch straps.

To think, addicts purposefully shot themselves up with this shit. Cheap ingredients, easy to make, and a *killer* high? Yeah, no thanks.

She touched the abscess on his arm, and a layer of skin the width of her hand slid free and splatted on Amber's pristine garage floor. Her stomach revolted.

"Shit." Tate rubbed the back of his neck. "Amber's going to have a full-on seizure when she sees that."

Not if they cleaned —

Holy fuck, was that a bone shining through the hole in Larry's arm? Bile simmered in the back of her throat.

"What are you doing to me?" Larry groaned, his eyes clearing.

Good, he was lucid. She turned to grab a syringe, but Liv was already there, holding it out for her.

"This," Camila said, positioning the needle an inch from Larry's flaccid dick, "is Krokodil. It's been eating you from the inside out. Given the dead flesh on your arms and legs, I bet your guts don't feel very good right now."

"You fucking bitch." He shifted his hips, unable to distance himself from the syringe. "Get away from me. I need a fucking doctor."

"Sure." She sweetened her tone. "Just tell me who you work for."

He dropped his head back and fell still. Gaze-locked-on-the-ceiling still. Something seemed to settle over him, the tension in his body draining away. Resignation? The motherfucker better not be giving up.

"Whatever you do to me," he said, eerily calm, "*his* retaliation will be tenfold. You have no idea who you're fucking with, you stupid cunt."

Tenfold? Maybe so. Whomever he worked for would probably go

after his family.

"I'm going to put maggots on this." She traced a finger around the rotted cavern in his arm. "Move along the whole zombie thing you've got going on."

Tate grimaced, looking as nauseated as she felt. Liv somehow managed a bored expression.

"Do it." Larry closed his eyes. "I don't fucking care."

Okay, forget the maggots. She jabbed the needle into the root of his dick.

His back flew off the table, the rest of him restrained by straps as he screamed and flailed.

Holding onto the syringe, she hovered her thumb over the plunger and waited for him to calm down. "When and where is the girl supposed to be dropped? Give me that, and I won't rot off your junk."

He shook against a full-body spasm, his eyes bulging as he stared at the needle stuck in his delicate flesh. "Ten at night." He spat out a month, a day, and GPS coordinates.

Oh, thank fuck. It was only two days away, but she was ready, having tracked and hunted this operation for four years. Her veins sizzled with the need to finish this.

As Tate left the garage to shout the coordinates to Van, she removed the syringe.

Larry cried out in relief then glared at her with bloodshot eyes. "He's going to kill you. You'll beg for it before he's done."

She tried not to let that threat worm its way inside her, but it penetrated her resolve and formed ice in the marrow of her bones.

Shaking off the dread, she turned and found Liv drifting along the wall where dozens of dolls and mannequins hung from hooks. Van's garage was a workshop. His little shop of glassy-eyed horrors.

She took a step toward Liv then thought better of it. "Hey, Liv? You okay?"

Liv stiffened, her hand lifting to smooth down her straight, black hair. "I used to hate these things. Part of me always will, you know?"

When Van collected slaves, he also collected freaky plastic people. Now he made dolls out of leather and gave them to homeless kids.

Still fucking creepy.

Liv relaxed her posture and strode back to the table, her graceful legs encased in black denim. Her moods were difficult to follow, switching on and off like the masks she used to wear.

"Did he tell you why he has a fascination with dolls?" Liv asked, tone silky soft.

Camila shook her head. She and Van didn't have a let's-share-stories kind of relationship.

Sadness etched Liv's slender face. "Maybe he'll tell you some day. It puts all of this" — she gestured at the wall of leather bodies — "into perspective."

Curiosity itched beneath her skin, but Van's doll fetish would have to wait. Liv held out another syringe, this one with a thicker needle, the tube filled with Pentobarbital stolen from a vet clinic.

As Camila reached for it, Liv pulled it back, her voice low. "Let me do this for you."

Liv had killed slave buyers with blades, bullets, and even her bare hands. She certainly had the stomach for it. But Camila had helped with some of them. She could do this.

"Thank you." She held out her hand. "This is nothing compared to what I have to do next."

"What are you planning, Camila?" Liv released the syringe, her expression a cold mask.

A shiver rippled through her. *That* had been the tone Liv used when she held a whip, posed to strike. When Camila's world had been confined to four windowless walls in a soundproof attic.

Deep breath. She was here because she didn't want other girls to end up in chains, where they would learn how to beg for an orgasm, how to stroke a man's cock, and how to relax into the bone-rattling bite of a whip.

She forced her attention on Larry, his eyes closed and breathing even. Passed out. Maybe already on his way to death.

Aiming the syringe over his heart, she slammed it down and drove hard and fast. When his eyes flashed open, she depressed the plunger and held a finger over the pulse in his throat until his eyes closed and his heart stopped.

She stood there for a moment, waiting to feel something. Like what? Killer's remorse? Was that a thing? All she felt was purpose. It strengthened her backbone and energized her pulse.

"Got to make a call." She headed toward the door.

Liv caught her arm and swung her back around. "What's your next move, Camila?"

That was the tricky part. Liv, Tate, none of her team would like it.

"I'll fill you in." She pulled her arm from Liv's grip. "But I have to deal with the body before it stinks up Amber's garage."

Liv studied her face, probing too closely, too deeply. "You're carrying a torch, girl. The damn flames are burning in your eyes. Someday soon, it's going to devour you." Liv's expression softened. "You can't save them all."

"I know." But she could save a lot of them.

In the kitchen, she grabbed a new burner phone from her bag on the counter and headed toward the front door.

Van blocked her path, arms crossed over his chest. "Who do you call to deal with dead bodies?"

"An old connection." She trusted Van more than she ever thought possible, but she didn't trust him with this.

"What the fuck kind of connection? Liv said you did side jobs for some cartel. Are you bringing that shit to my front door?"

She might've mentioned something along those lines at some point. She didn't do anything for any cartel, but it was highly probable that her connection did. "I'll move the body off the property. They won't come anywhere near here."

His jaw stiffened. "The same thugs that were supposed to dispose of *my* body."

"Hey, man." She held up her hands and met his frigid gray eyes. "I'm not the one who shot you."

His gaze turned inward. He scratched his shoulder — the old wound hidden beneath his shirt — and the corner of his mouth twitched. "Good thing Liv missed my heart."

Was that a good thing? Maybe so. If Liv had aimed true, Van wouldn't have lived to help them in the most valuable way possible. Financially.

"The thing I can't figure out, though..." He narrowed his eyes. "How did you know I didn't die? Liv says this guy, whoever you're about to call, doesn't have a way to contact you. If he didn't tell you I wasn't there..." He tipped his head to the side. "Were you watching the house?"

"No, I..." *Jesus fuck, this is an awkward conversation.* "I went there to clean up the blood. Except you didn't leave any behind, and your car was gone."

He nodded absently, seemingly absorbed in thought, so she slipped around him and opened the front door.

"Camila."

Her breath caught. Christ, would she always flinch at the bark of Van's voice?

Standing behind her, he squeezed her shoulder and removed his touch. "I'm sorry."

For which part? Snatching her from her front yard? Tying her up? Spitting in her face? Shoving his cock in her mouth?

"For everything." His footsteps retreated, leaving her shaken and off-balance.

Dammit, not the best frame of mind for the call she had to make.

It had been four years since she'd spoken to Matias. Did his promise to always help her still hold true? What if his number was disconnected?

Only one way to find out.

Her heart hammered as she stepped into the chilly darkness and dialed.

# THREE

The vibration of the phone shattered the chilly stillness in the SUV. Matias glanced at the screen, and a smirk pulled at his lips.

There had been a time when a call from an unknown number had sent his heart rate into a frenzy. But that was years ago, before he'd invested in spies, surveillance, and drone technology.

Parked on a barren road in the outskirts of rural Austin, he stretched out in the driver's seat and met Nico's gaze in the rear-view mirror.

"You gonna answer that, *careverga*?" Nico dropped his head against the backseat and closed his eyes as if he didn't give a fuck either way.

The pompous ass had apathy down to an art. Nico could yawn through mass beheadings and play games on his phone during gunfights, but everything he did was calculated. His brutal intellect and mafia-style code of respect made him the most feared cartel capo in Colombia.

Matias knew the man behind the reputation, though. He trusted Nico, not only with his life, but with Camila's.

"She made me wait four fucking years." He held the vibrating phone in one hand and a wide screen tablet in the other. "I want to watch her sweat."

Live video streamed on the tablet, transmitted from a drone that circled four-hundred feet above Van Quiso's cabin. The quadcopter's modified cameras, with high-powered lenses and night vision, provided a bird's eye view of her position on the front porch while remaining outside of her range of hearing.

His phone cycled through another burst of vibrations and fell quiet.

"Well done." Nico's voice, while monotone to an irritating degree, held a tinge of amusement. "If she doesn't call back, you'll be an unbearable *hijueputa*."

"She'll call back." Matias tapped on the image of her head, initiating the drone's active track feature.

The small, self-flying aircraft adapted to its surroundings, using sonar detection to avoid anything in its path as it followed her movements through the yard. The aerial footage flickered between nebulous and grainy, but when he magnified the picture, he could make out the pixelated curve of a hand as it raked through her hair.

Was she thinking about him? Wondering if he was dead or alive? Probably cursing him for not answering the phone. What would she do if she knew he was parked less than a mile away, watching her?

She paced a circuit across the front lawn, activating perimeter lights that illuminated her slender frame. She stopped, kicked at something in the grass, and raised a hand to her ear.

His phone buzzed again. *Unknown number.*

He found Nico's reflection in the mirror and arched a brow.

"Don't look so smug, *ese*." Nico loosened the knot on his tie. "She'll run the other way as soon as she learns what you've done."

Camila didn't run from anything. Not even when they were kids. No, she would look him dead in the eye. Then she would kill him.

He placed the phone on the dash, set the call on speaker, and answered the way she expected. "Who is this?"

"Hey. It's been awhile, huh?" Her voice was strong, confident, but in the video, she doubled over, a hand braced on her knee.

His insides constricted in sympathy, stirring up years of anguish. Did she resent the time and distance between them as much as he did? Not likely. If she did, she would've fucking called.

He seethed with the urgency to go to her, drag her into the night, and chain her to his bed.

Just like Van Quiso. Only worse. He would never let her escape.

She would seethe and snarl and fight every step of the way, and he would absorb her hatred because, in the end, it'd all be worth it.

His skin warmed despite the cool air blowing from the A/C. Adjusting the vents toward his face, he wrapped his voice in silken tones. "It's been four years, *mi vida*. Where are you?"

"You first." Her blurry image resumed pacing. "Where do you live, and who do you work for?"

He caught Nico's glare in the mirror, those notorious eyes sharp with warning. *Don't you dare.*

"Ask me something meaningful." He flicked his attention back to

510

the screen. "What do you really want to know?"

"Hmmm." The drone lost her image as she stepped beneath a large oak tree. A moment later, she appeared on the other side, headed toward the sedan parked in the gravel driveway. "Are you...okay?"

His breath hung in his throat. It was an unexpected question, but one he could answer honestly. "I will be when you come to me." *Willingly.*

"How would that work? Would we meet at Starbucks, smile over the rims of our *tintos,* and take turns asking questions that go unanswered? Or would we skip the bullshit and jump right into fucking and fighting?"

"*No quiero café.* I want your smiles, your fighting, and your fucking." His cock jerked. "I want *you.*"

"If you wanted me, you would've found me. Unless you stayed away because..." She hummed, a husky, feminine sound. "You want me too much."

"You think I'm protecting you from myself?"

If only he were that selfless. His hands were bound. Not in the way he intended to bind hers, because dammit, she didn't have an excuse for avoiding him.

Outrage hardened his voice. "Why haven't you contacted me?"

"You tell me," she said, acid dripping from every syllable. "I don't know what you do, what you're involved in. I know your voice, but that's where it ends. You're a stranger. Would I even recognize you if I passed you on the street? For all I know, you're an undercover cop with a wife and kids in the suburbs."

He didn't blame her for being paranoid. Her hellfire mission to take down a very specific kind of criminal had led her to commit felonies that were punishable by death. But did she honestly believe he would betray her?

"You don't trust me." He squeezed the steering wheel.

"I trust you enough to ask for help."

"I see. And here I thought you called because you missed me." Except he knew she'd brought an unconscious man to Van's cabin. "You have something for me to get rid of?"

"Yep."

"But you won't be there when I collect it?"

Silence.

"How is that trusting me?" He watched the screen, mesmerized.

"I trust you with this." She sat on the hood of the car and lowered her head. "To stand by your word and not leave my package where someone could stumble across it."

The Austin PD never closed the missing person case on Camila Dias. The last thing he wanted was them to find her now and charge her with capital murder.

"Will the package be there this time?" he asked.

"Yeah. The last one" — she glanced up at Van's house — "was a slippery sucker."

Not that slippery. When he'd arrived to collect Van's body, the bastard was driving away from the house, bleeding from a shoulder wound and clinging to the steering wheel like it was the only thing keeping him alive.

The situation had presented two options. Shoot her kidnapper in the head as he drove by or follow him.

Following Van had been the best decision he ever made. A few weeks later, Van had led him to Liv Reed, who unknowingly took him right to Camila's front door.

That was four years ago. Four years of monitoring her impressive operation. He had the patience of a goddamn saint, but his intentions were far from benevolent.

He wanted her with a vehemence, but the timing was crucial. The agonizing wait was so very close to being over he could feel the adrenaline coursing through his system.

"Where am I picking up the package?" He knew she wouldn't send him to Van's property.

As she gave him an unfamiliar address, he mapped it on the tablet. Enclosed by farmland and dirt roads, the drop was only ten minutes away. Of course, she assumed he was out of town. Otherwise, she would've dumped the body before she called him.

This was the point in the conversation where she expected him to ask her shit like, *What are you involved in? Who did you kill this time? What have you been doing the past four years?*

He needed more from her. Something deeper, vulnerable. "Are you afraid?"

"No."

"Ah, but you answered too quickly. Have you forgotten I know when you're lying?"

Silence stretched, followed by her sigh. "Maybe I am."

"Afraid?"

"Maybe. Sometimes..." She jerked her head up.

Something moved at the edge of the screen. A man came into view, approaching her with a human-size bundle rolled up in a sheet. Terrible goddamn timing.

The camera angle shifted as she slid off the car and walked toward the house. "I need to go."

"We're not finished." He tensed, unable to dampen the vitriol in his voice. "Do *not* disconnect."

"Slow your roll, sparkle. I'll call you right back." She hung up.

# DISCLAIM

He slammed a fist into the dash, cracking an air vent and shooting a jolt of pain up his arm.

"Feel better?" Nico asked dryly.

"Fuck off." He glanced at the rear-view mirror and met Nico's eyes. "Did you get the address?"

Matias could make the call to have the body picked up, but the order carried more urgency when it came directly from the boss.

"*Sí, pendejo.*" Nico opened the back door and stepped out, his black suit made darker against the backdrop of the surrounding woods. Turning, he leaned back in and nodded at the tablet. "You need to put a leash on that. Fuck her ass into submission."

Hard to argue when fantasies of destroying every hole in her body had kept him in a hyper state of arousal for over a decade.

Nico shut the door and paced away from the SUV, his profile stark against the glow of the phone at his ear.

Neither of them had time for this side trip to Austin. Not with the heroin shipment arriving in Orlando tomorrow and the operatives they were currently moving across the Chihuahuan Desert. Smuggling drugs and terrorists into the States was a lucrative business, but risky as hell, especially with federal agents sniffing around the compound in El Paso.

Nico sure as fuck didn't want their resources allocated to an unprofitable cause like Camila Dias. But the man owed his power, his wealth, and every phlegmatic beat of his heart to Matias. Nico might bitch and argue, but he wasn't going to tell Matias *no*.

The drone changed course, following her as she helped load the body in the trunk of the sedan. That done, she turned toward the man at her side.

The video was too muddy to make out details, but the way he crowded her, standing too fucking close, gave him away.

Tate Vades towered over her by a foot, his shoulders twice the width of hers, and one of his arms was sleeved in black ink. His blond-brown hair, blue eyes, and muscled physique made him an ideal sex toy for a slave buyer with an appetite for strong men on their knees.

Tate's buyer, however, didn't live long enough to drive away with his new slave. Matias had collected the body himself, as well as the 5.7×28mm casings that had been left behind. Rounds that could've only come from Camila's FN Five-seven pistol.

Fuck him, but he couldn't get enough of her murderous spirit.

Apparently, neither could Tate. For the past six years, he'd become a permanent fixture in her life. Given their close relationship, it was no surprise when she reached up and placed a hand on his jaw.

*Step away, Tate.* Matias zoomed in on the sliver of space between their unmoving postures. His molars crashed together. *Step the fuck back,* hijo.

Tate raised an arm above his head, holding something away from her. She gripped his neck, her other hand swiping at whatever he kept out of reach. The car keys? Were they arguing over who would deliver the body?

The guy was eager. Eager to protect her and fight for her cause. But if he wanted his dick to remain attached to his body, he'd get eager to remove her hand from his fucking neck.

Their arm-waving dispute ended when Tate broke free and climbed into the driver's seat of the sedan. *Good boy.*

She watched him drive away with the body, a hand on her hip and the other holding her phone.

Matias flexed his fingers, cursing every second she delayed. *Hit redial, Camila.*

A heartbeat later, she did.

He accepted the call on speaker. "Are you afraid of me?"

"Which answer will change the subject?"

"I'll take that as a *yes.*"

She walked to the yard, prompting the camera to pan to the side. Stopping beneath the perimeter lights, she lay on her back in the grass. Her hair fanned out around her in shiny, black tendrils, like tributaries of the Amazon River at night.

The sound of her breaths marked the space between them. So close he could see her and hear her, yet still too far away. She was stalling, turning his nerves into a breeding ground for desperation, anger, and desire.

"All right. I'll give you this," she said. "I'm afraid the reality of you won't live up to the memory."

His heart stuttered painfully. Her confession was so fragile, bleak, and...inaccurate. But he'd thought the same about her once, before he started watching her. The tough girl from his childhood had grown into every bit the fierce, beautiful woman he'd imagined she would be.

"I miss...us," she whispered. "But I'm afraid, if we met again, I'd find that the concept of *us* is just a jagged mote of a memory. I don't think I could handle that. I want that part of my life to remain real. Untarnished."

She had no idea how much of her childhood was a lie. But the thing between him and her?

"What we had...*have*..." He closed his eyes, fighting the impulse to snap at her for doubting them. "It doesn't get more real than that."

"People change. How can you be so sure?"

Over the years, his need for her hadn't faded. It had become a living, starving thing inside him, ruling his fucking world. There was something else, though. Something beyond his desire to take, overpower, and claim.

It felt like a dark, festering mass knotting around his organs, strangling him with nothingness. Did it have a name? He rubbed his forehead, searching for a way to identify the persistent, agonizing…what?

He opened his eyes. *Loss.* That empty feeling, the hollow pit in his soul, was her absence. He mourned her. Deeply and endlessly.

"Remember the shack on the north side of the grove?" He traced the edge of the screen, lost in the fuzzy outline of her lying in the grass.

"*Mierda.*" She laughed. "I was convinced a cannibal lived there."

"Not just any cannibal. A big, hairy one that buried bones —"

"*Children's* bones."

" —under the floorboards." He grinned.

"I didn't make that shit up." She sounded defensive, but a smile teased through her voice. "Or maybe I did, but I swear I heard their cries from my bedroom window."

"That was Lucia riding her boyfriend in the backseat of his car."

"Oh, God."

A heavy hush settled between them. He wasn't sure if she was thinking about her sister or the night she finally entered the shack.

"You were so determined to get me to go in there." She let out a ragged exhale. "I was horrified by the idea."

"Do you remember what I told you?"

"The fear will haunt me," she said quietly, "until I step inside and show it my teeth."

"You took that quite literally."

He hadn't known the true meaning of *painfully hard* until he'd watched her strut her sexy ass inside that dark shack, holding the flashlight like a weapon and baring her teeth.

The moment she'd realized there was no cannibal, no rotting bones, and that she'd well and truly conquered her fear, she aimed the beam of light on her stunning smile and said, "Wanna know who I love? That guy."

She'd turned the flashlight on his face, and he'd felt her blinding declaration like a magnetic pulse. It had electrified every inch of his body, lighting up his chest and settling at the base of his cock.

They were virgins then, her sixteen, him eighteen. In the months leading up to that night, they'd fumbled and groped without clothes on, learning how to make each other come with fingers and mouths. But the look she'd given him in that shack, her eyes aglow in the shadows of her defeated fears, he knew she'd been ready. For all of it.

He'd pinned her against the crusty wallpaper in the shack's only bedroom and fingered her until she screamed her declaration over and over. Until his conscience had forced him to step back.

Glancing over his shoulder, he spotted Nico behind the SUV, puffing on a cigarette.

He turned back to the phone. "I should've fucked you that night."

"I should've let you."

His chest clenched. They hadn't wanted their first time to be in a smelly shack. So innocent. Foolish. He thought they'd have more time, more opportunities, a lifetime of them.

Instead, he gave his virginity to a prostitute in a smelly alcove beside a dumpster.

"I wish I'd known," she said, voice clipped, "that was our last time together."

Neither of them had known what the next day would bring. She still didn't know it was the Restrepo cartel that had led him away with a gun pressed against his ribs. Or why.

"When did you lose your virginity?" All these years, and he hadn't been able to uncover her sex life. Or come to terms with it.

"I could ask you the same thing, but let's not do this to ourselves, okay? The answers hurt too much."

The misery in her voice gave him comfort. Thinking about her with someone else ate at him like a sickness. With her knock-out body, lethal confidence, and fuck-me eyes, she could have her pick of drooling dicks.

In one of her nine phone calls to him since her escape, she swore Van did not take her virginity. Outside of that, however, she remained tight-lipped. She didn't discuss sex with her roommates, didn't bring lovers home, didn't publicly date.

If she fucked, it was in secret and beyond the reach of his cameras.

She sat up and looked at the cabin. "Before I go..." She climbed to her feet, her voice quiet, serious. "I told you what I was afraid of, but you didn't tell me. What haunts *you*?"

"You." He gripped the back of his neck, eyes fastened on the screen. "Your fear of *us*. When are you going to step inside and show it your teeth?"

"Will I need a flashlight? Or a gun?"

"Neither." He sharpened his tone. "Tell me when."

"Someday, maybe."

"Not good enough." He drummed his fingers on the console.

"Someday, later."

"No—"

She ended the call.

*Fuck.*

Someday was the right answer. She just didn't know how soon. Everything was finally falling into place, giving him the opening he'd waited years for.

He wouldn't be leaving Austin without her.

# FOUR

Camila slipped into the cabin and kicked off her flip-flops. *What the fuck was* that?

Her hands shook, her skin fevered, and a deep ache pulsed between her thighs. Not just because she wanted him. Because she'd heard the desire thick in his breath.

As she headed toward the kitchen, muffled voices drifted from the direction of the garage. Christ, she needed to pull herself together before she went in there.

Curling her fingers into her palms didn't stop the trembling. Damn Matias Guerra to hell! Was it not enough that he'd abandoned her and taken her heart with him? Evidently, the prick wasn't finished tormenting her.

She could've handled the questions he used to throw at her, had been prepared to redirect and volley them back. But his *are you afraid* tactic? It was dirty and below the belt.

Only he knew how to dig through her tough exterior, grab hold of her fears, and force her to examine them. She shouldn't have called him back, but like a scab itching to be picked, her obsession with the past overruled her need to heal.

His gravelly timbre had rolled time in reverse, his words transporting her to the safety of the citrus grove. It was as if she'd been talking to *him*, the boy who showed her how to make a slingshot fork from an orange tree, how to swallow while kissing to avoid unwanted saliva, how to do so many unforgettable things, like fall in love, the *conchudo!*

She paused in the kitchen, brushed the dust off her jeans, and attempted to straighten out her thoughts. Eighteen-year-old Matias never kept secrets from her. But the man he'd become was a mysterious, unreachable black hole.

Maybe she was just as closed off as he was, but he at least knew what she was involved in. Since the day she'd escaped, she'd told him she was killing slave buyers while he told her *absolutely nothing.*

Was he still involved with the armed thugs who'd taken him away twelve years ago? Or had he moved on to something worse? Something so awful he wouldn't, *couldn't,* share anything personal with her?

"Why didn't you come back for me?" she whispered, gripping the edge of the counter.

Why did his secrecy feel like a betrayal? Like he'd chosen his sacred thug life over her?

If he loved her, he would've returned for her, taken her with him, and prevented everything that followed. The attic, the bone-deep bruises, the chains of isolation, and the darkness that still pervaded her thoughts, following her everywhere. No, not following. *Smothering.*

That was the rub, wasn't it? She'd trusted him to protect her, to always be there, and he'd deserted her, left her to her fate.

She massaged her temples. Why was she wallowing in this quagmire of imaginary angst? It felt a whole lot like self-pity, a bullshit mentality she refused to subscribe to. She'd never been a victim, didn't need protection or rescuing, and sure as hell didn't need a dick to get herself off.

What she needed was a mind-numbing drink.

A quick sweep through Van's cabinets uncovered an impressive collection of tequila. *Praise Jesus.* Popping off the cap, she drank straight from the bottle. Ah, God, it was the good stuff. Smooth and crisp, the agave slid down her throat like peppery, sweet water.

A few sips turned into a few more. She drank until her tongue tingled and her nerves dulled. She drank until the front door opened.

It snicked shut, and footsteps echoed through the cabin. Tate emerged around the corner, eyed the bottle, and winged up an eyebrow.

"Trouble in Crazy Town?" He nodded at the garage door, where the murmur of their former captors filtered through.

"Nope." She capped the bottle and put it away.

"Your phone call?" His forearms flexed at his sides. "The body—"

"Will be taken care of." She shifted her weight from one foot to the other. Or maybe she bounced.

The alcohol buzzed through her veins at a nice, even keel. Not enough to make her stupid, but it was doing its job. Tate's judgmental scowl had zero effect on her giveafuckometer.

The front door opened again, and a moment later, familiar green eyes came into view. Black hair outlined a golden complexion, boyishly handsome features, and straight white teeth. No one smiled quite like Slave Number Nine.

"Hey, you." Joshua Carter didn't waste time closing the distance and wrapping her in a hug.

"Hey." She laughed, arms clinging to the packed muscles beneath his Baylor University t-shirt.

The warmth in her cheeks wasn't from the booze. There was something about Josh, a rare kind of inner light that enabled him to focus on the good in every person and situation. Hell, he'd married Liv — *after* the woman had kidnapped him, beat him, and pegged him with a strap-on. Underneath his rock-hard, linebacker physique was an endearingly squishy and very forgiving soul.

Or perhaps he was just as fucked up as the rest of them.

He released her and scanned the cabin's open layout, his face growing taut. "Where's Liv?"

Camila tried not to let his preoccupation with his wife affect her, but there it was, pinching her chest. She didn't want Josh, but she envied what he had — someone to look for and be concerned about. Someone to love.

Maybe she'd misjudged her tequila intake. It had turned her into a sensitive little girl.

"Liv's in the garage." She stepped out of his way. "Thanks for driving Tate back."

As a high school football coach, Josh had a legit career to protect. But he'd offered to meet at the drop location so that Larry's car and the incriminating DNA inside it could be disposed with the body.

He and Liv were the only ones in their little circle of freedom fighters who weren't considered missing or dead. They had a relationship with his parents and Liv's daughter. A family to spend holidays with. In that regard, they had more to lose than the rest of the group.

"Wish I could help more." With a pat on her head, he disappeared into the garage.

Tate crossed the kitchen and leaned into her space, his arm braced on the wall behind her.

Her eyes fluttered closed as the scent of his skin permeated the inches between them. His masculine proximity charged her nerve endings and heated her blood. He smelled balmy like a summer afternoon in the grove. Like a breeze ripened with the aroma of lemons and loam. Like the Texan sunshine when it emblazoned his hazel eyes —

She looked up, her gaze colliding with Tate's icy blue glare.

"What's going on with you?" He bent his knees, putting them nose to nose.

A dull throb swelled between her legs, engaging her inner

muscles. "I need to get laid."

She needed so much more than the fleeting relief of an orgasm, but she'd settle for a kiss from a man who cared enough to give her one.

His gaze fell, heavy with regret. He didn't have to read her mind to know what she really wanted. Hands bound, ass spanked, hard, brutal fucking—they'd discussed her desires in detail until it'd become a laughable tirade. But that only made the stricken look on his face harder to stomach. He knew how goddamn lonely and hungry she was, and still, he rejected her.

She knew he was attracted to her, but he shut down whenever she approached the subject. Maybe her tastes were too dark for him, too much like what he'd endured. Or maybe they weren't dark enough.

"We only have two days." She ducked around him and headed toward the garage. "We need to talk about what happens next." A plan that was guaranteed to receive a concerted *fuck no* from him and the others.

After gathering everyone in the living room, she explained how she intended to use Larry McGregor's information to infiltrate the human trafficking network in Austin.

Anticipating the most resistance from Tate, she paced the edge of the room, eyes trained on his bowed head as she outlined the initial steps. He didn't move from the chair by the windows, his gaze glued to the floor.

Van didn't show the same restraint.

"You've lost your fucking mind." His entire body bunched and flexed as he balled his hands into fists. He probably would've leapt from the couch if Amber wasn't sitting on his lap. "You want me to sell you? As a *slave*?"

Liv and Josh sat side by side on the love seat. Their rigid postures, narrowed eyes, deeply furrowed brows—they looked like Bonnie and Clyde's disapproving cousins.

Camila pursed her lips. They didn't have to like it. They didn't even need to be here.

"We don't know who these people are." Van dragged a hand across the scar on his cheek, his tone harsh. "And you want me to just show up and hand you over? First off, they're expecting Larry McGregor."

"They're expecting a girl, tied-up and blindfolded." Camila lifted her chin, even as her insides rioted at the idea. "Larry could've sent anyone to deliver her."

"Okay, fine, but you're like...what?" Van sneered. "Thirty-years old? One look at you, and they'll laugh their fucking asses off. Right before they cut out your throat."

"*Despégala pues!*" Her face caught fire. "I'm twenty-eight, dickhead."

"He doesn't mean it," Tate said softly. He didn't raise his head, but his eyes drifted upward and locked on Van. "She could pass as eighteen, and you know it. Look at her. They'd pay double the asking price to get their hands on her."

A heavy feeling sank in her stomach. She wasn't surprised Tate defended her, but she'd expected a godawful fight from him. No way was he okay with her plan.

"They trade in untouched, *underage* pussy." Van folded his arms around Amber, taking her with him as he leaned forward, his glower carved from stone. "Have you forgotten how I know that, Tate?"

"Not one person in this room has forgotten who you are, *Van*." Tate bolted from the chair and faced the wall of windows.

Arms across his chest, spine stiff, Tate stared out into the darkness. Or maybe he was glaring at his reflection. She knew he hated the way he looked, but he hated Van more for capturing him because he was attractive.

Van closed his eyes, his expression unreadable. Amber curled tighter against his chest and whispered in his ear. Across the room, Josh reached for Liv's hand and pulled it into his lap.

They had all been Van's slaves once. And there were more at home—Ricky, Tomas, Luke, Martin, and Kate—all nursing their own invisible wounds under Camila's roof. She didn't spend as much time with Van as she did with the others, but the dynamic between him and his former captives was improving, slowly adapting into something a little less hostile.

Van had been the one to initiate a truce. The money Mr. E had collected—the payments from buyers who didn't live long enough to indulge in their purchases—totaled in the millions. Van could've hoarded that money after Liv killed Mr. E, and maybe he did keep some of it. But he'd given an ungodly amount to the nine people he'd abducted and tortured.

Camila's share funded her vigilantism. Did that mean she owed him her forgiveness? She wasn't sure she'd ever reach that level of acceptance, and she wasn't the only one.

Every person in the room fought inner battles, their fears birthed in the same attic, their perspectives cut by the same whip. Tragedy had shackled them together, but when the locks fell away, they remained unified in their soul-deep appreciation for freedom. They understood one another in a way no one outside their group could.

That intimate camaraderie was palpable now in the stillness that enveloped them. The silence didn't isolate her. It connected her to them, her fellow survivors, her fighters, her closest friends.

"Camila wasn't underage," Tate said, glancing over his shoulder at Van. "She was seventeen when you took her. When you *chose* her."

*Not helping.* Camila pinched the bridge of her nose. "Tate —"

"I didn't choose her." Van addressed Tate, but his eyes drilled into hers.

"What do you mean?" A chill hit her core.

"I was given your identity, location, and the buyer's contact number for the delivery when I finished your training."

She looked at Liv for validation.

"You were our first transaction." Liv absently traced Josh's fingers where they tangled with hers. "The only one Mr. E set up for us. Van and I handpicked all the others."

Her hand slid up Josh's thigh, fingernails scraping across denim, teasing the curve of his groin. She might've picked Josh because he met the buyer's requirements, but in the end, she'd chosen him for herself.

"I'm sure your plan is one-hundred-percent vetted." Liv stood and folded her hands behind her.

The capped sleeves of her corset-style shirt accentuated her delicate shoulders. The tiny waistline flared over the curves of her hips, drawing the eye along the tight fit of black denim on her legs. She wore casual clothes like lingerie, as if every cinch of fabric and peek of skin was deliberately designed to tantalize and distract. If she hid a knife behind her back, it would go unnoticed. Until it was too late.

"You're fully prepared to walk into a nightmare. *Your* worst nightmare." Liv prowled toward Camila, her lilt hypnotic, seductive. "You've envisioned the vilest scenarios even as you know your imagination hasn't scratched the surface."

True, she'd mentally prepared herself, but it didn't stop her heart from racing. "Yes. Of course."

"They'll restrain you." Liv circled her, trailing fingers along her arms. "Humiliate you. Whip you."

"I survived it all before." She stood taller.

"They'll rape you." Pausing inches from her face, Liv glared with enough potency to summon goose bumps. "You haven't survived that."

Liv's fathomless brown eyes brimmed with tortured experience. Torture she'd both inflicted and received.

"I was trained how to submit." Camila rolled back her shoulders. "I know how to keep my head down and attached to my body. I'll survive."

As if she'd have a choice. She wasn't naïve. She could be raped, mutilated, *then* killed. But she wouldn't let fear put the brakes on this plan. At that very moment, there were girls, trapped and alone, suffering the exact things Liv outlined.

"Maybe so." Liv stroked a finger along Camila's hairline, her gaze following the movement. "But I can't let you return to that life."

"I can't let other girls — other people's *daughters* — endure that life without doing something about it. I'm not asking for your permission."

Liv closed her eyes. When she opened them, her resigned expression said she wouldn't fight this. Nor would she support it.

"Your daughter is waiting for you." Camila stepped back. "Go home. Keep her safe."

Closing the gap, Liv framed Camila's face with her hands and touched their foreheads together. With a brush of lips, she delivered a kiss, closed-mouthed but no less penetrating. "You *will* come back."

With that, she left. Josh lifted Camila in a rib-breaking hug then followed Liv out, leaving Camila alone with Van, Amber, and Tate.

"Liv's right," Van said after a long period of silence. "You survived *me*, but I'm not *them*."

"So you won't help me?" Her stomach knotted.

She'd chased this trafficking operation for four years, and this was the first time she'd petitioned Van for help — beyond his financial support and the use of his home. She needed him now to deliver her into hell, because he was the only one who could.

"I know you're not them." She approached him, hands at her sides.

He leaned back on the couch, his eyes flinty and cold as he stroked Amber's hair.

"I also know," Camila said through a dry throat, "you have the grit to drag me in there by my hair, force me to my knees, and leave me there without a backward glance."

Tate turned from the window, devastation rumpling his handsome face.

She would've rather asked him to play the part of the asshole slave trader. He might've been able to pull it off. Right up until it came time to leave her.

"Let's say I can fill that role." Van dug through his pockets and paused when Amber held up a toothpick. He bit it out of her hand, rolled it to the corner of his mouth, and looked at Camila. "You're not a virgin."

Her mouth fell open. "What? How would — ?"

"I was trained to spot these things, and you…" He waved an arm, gesturing up and down her body. "You're like a walking advertisement for fluid exchange. Hungry flesh and — "

"Van, take it down a notch." Amber smacked away his waving hand and turned to Camila. "What he means is you radiate sex. It's beautiful, really, how comfortable you are with your body and sexual appetites. You wouldn't be that way if you hadn't experienced pleasure with another — on your terms."

Okaaaay. That was weird and intrusive and… Good God, was she that transparent? She locked down her muscles, trying to shut off any and all sexual oozing. But now she was hyper-aware, and the heat of Tate's gaze roaming over her tight tank top wasn't helping.

"Whether your experiences were good or bad," Amber said, "you long for more. I can tell because your hunger, it…it sensualizes the way you carry yourself and how you interact with people. Like him."

She followed Amber's gaze to Tate.

Confusion stormed across his face as he stared at her. Had he assumed she was a virgin? She'd confessed her desires to him, but she never told him about the long line of nameless men, the years of meaningless sex, all her failed attempts to find something or someone that would touch the places inside her she couldn't feel anymore.

Camila refocused on Van. "So you have virgin radar. Congratulations. But it's been a long time since I've had sex." She'd given up on one-night stands over four years ago.

"Your hymen doesn't grow back, girl." Van smirked around the toothpick. "They'll check."

"You didn't."

"I didn't have to."

Right. All he'd had to do was beat her into submission. But none of that mattered. The purpose of this tangent was to make a point, one Van had walked right into.

"When they check me" — she hid her disgust beneath a lazy shrug — "they won't be able to sell me off."

"They'll kill you." Van grinned, the fucker.

"They'll keep her." Tate rubbed the back of his head. "That's her plan."

"Bingo." She sat on the arm of the love seat. "They won't kill me, because I have a working vagina, and I'm not ugly."

"You're gorgeous," Amber said with a small smile.

"Thanks. So they'll take me to the head asshole. I'll cry and beg for my life. Of course, that'll just turn him on. He'll try to fuck me and…" She looked at Van, his gaze bright with curiosity. "I'm not the same girl I was in that attic."

"I know."

Was that pride in his voice?

She'd spent the past ten years in dojos, learning how to use her body like a weapon. "I may not be able to defend myself against a gang bang, but I know how to unman a dick when it's between my legs."

"Larry McGregor?" Van raised a brow.

"Triangle choke. Killing him would've been easier than knocking him out."

"Jesus, Camila." Tate's chest rose and fell. "What if you're outnumbered?"

"That's where the tracking device comes in. I know a guy. A dentist." She opened her mouth and tapped the molar that would cost her fifty grand to drill tomorrow. "I've had him on standby to do a special kind of dental restoration."

"A GPS chip in a dental filling?" Van rolled the toothpick between his lips. "Smart. But the battery life—"

"It'll last two weeks, sending a signal every thirty minutes. It only uses the battery when I'm moving."

Oh, the creative and illegal things one could buy on the web's black markets.

Van sawed his jaw side to side. Was he loosening it up to snap at her? Or was he thinking through her plan?

He blew out a breath and looked her firmly in the eye. "I'll do it."

Amber gripped his hand as relief fluttered through Camila's veins.

"Tate." She met his frigid eyes. "You'll track my position through the chip?"

He blinked, nodded. "Two weeks…You'll most likely be in the belly of the operation before the battery dies."

She hoped. "If I'm successful, if I kill him, I'll contact you, and you won't need to do anything." She rubbed her slick palms on her jeans. "If you don't hear from me, you'll have the location of the operation and—"

"We'll save you." The conviction in his voice vibrated through her.

"No." She matched his tone.

She picked at her cuticles, forcing her shoulders to relax.

"You and the others…" *The freedom fighters.* She smiled at that, because she knew she could count on her team. "You'll finish where I failed."

# FIVE

Two days later, Camila sat on Tate's bed, transfixed by the contours of muscle playing across his back as he dug through a mountain of dirty clothes. His sex appeal aggravated the nervous energy twitching through her, but she couldn't look away. There was something she wanted, something Tate could give her.

"I need to talk to you."

"I'm listening." He shook out a wrinkled shirt, sniffed it, and tossed it back in the pile.

Van would arrive in three hours—three hours until she surrendered her freedom. Maybe only for a couple of weeks. Maybe forever.

The gravity of *forever* had plunged her into hours of introspection, creeping paralysis through her limbs and gnawing at her resolve. She wasn't putting herself in chains simply for the cause of justice. There was a darker motive. A selfish desire to overpower the fears that haunted her. Her enslavement had wrought a deep dissatisfaction with her own life, and though her body had healed from the trauma, her bleeding soul demanded she do this.

With a roll of her tongue, she sought out the new filling in her molar. Indiscernible to the eye, the composite material felt foreign and obtrusive in her mouth. The GPS chip, however, instilled a sense of confidence in her plan. Seeing her movements on the software program and knowing Tate would be tracking her made her feel a little less alone.

She thought about giving Matias' contact information to Tate. If Tate didn't hear from her, he could pass along her last known position to the one person who might increase her chance of survival.

But she didn't want to go into this with that seed of hope. Didn't want to find herself tied to a bed in a pool of her own failure, waiting for someone who might not come for her. Matias had already abandoned her once. For that to happen a second time? The destitution that would follow might very well kill her. He was the only person from her past she had left.

Therein lay the root of her loneliness. Van had given her a taste of how depraved men could be. Matias had shown her how to turn innocent love into a lifetime of bitterness. The only sex she'd experienced had been quick, unsatisfying fucks.

She'd known Tate for six years, and now, in her final hours of freedom, she wanted to know him on a deeper level.

"I've never made love." She held her breath.

He paused with his hand in the pile of clothes and glowered over his shoulder, his eyebrows drawn together. "Wait...so you *are* a virgin?"

"No. I'm—" She straightened her spine. "I've never had sex with someone I know."

Strangers, all of them. No connection. No emotion. Just sex. She blamed herself for that. She didn't let people in, didn't trust anyone outside of those she lived with.

His lips pressed together in a grimace as he turned away.

Was he judging her? Self-righteous anger burned beneath her skin.

Digging at the bottom of the dirty clothes pile, he smelled another shirt and reared back with a pinched face.

"This one should work." He tossed it at her.

It landed on her lap, and a waft of mold and sweat hit her nose. Jesus, did he have a month's worth of wet towels in that pile? For a guy who was fussy about hygiene, he had some strange abhorrence to doing laundry.

He joined her on the bed, lifted a lock of her hair, and sniffed it. "You stink, but not enough."

"What?" She slammed her teeth together and immediately slackened her jaw, remembering the expensive electronics in her molar. "I haven't showered in three days."

She'd spent hours working in the garden and running outside, letting herself get sweaty and dehydrated. A glance at the mirror earlier confirmed she looked appropriately filthy and starved, like a girl who'd been locked in Larry McGregor's barn for a week.

"I'll smell straight-up offensive after I put on this shirt." She set it aside and met his eyes. "You're evading my question."

"You didn't ask a question."

No, she hadn't. She didn't want to demand it. "It's different, right? Better when you have sex with someone who cares about you?"

He leaned forward, elbows braced on his spread knees, and stared at her out of the corner of his eye.

As secretive as she'd been about her one-night stands, he was even more surreptitious, sneaking out at night and stumbling home in the early hours of dawn, refusing to tell her where he went. Maybe he was searching for something, too.

"You care about me." She looked for a flicker of affirmation, any indication of softening in his stony expression, and found none. Her stomach sank. "At least, I thought you did. I mean, I'm grateful you're not fighting me on this plan, but why aren't you?"

"Let's not do this, Camila." His gaze ping-ponged between her and the floor.

"Which part?"

"All of it." He rose, stepped away, then hesitated, changing direction mid-stride to stand over her, hands on his hips. "I won't ruin our friendship by muddling it with sex. Nor will I let you walk into"—he waved an arm, seemingly wrestling for words—"into a place resembling Satan's fiery asshole thinking you don't have my support. I'm here for you, and I'll be here when you return."

But what if she never came back? What if she died, forgotten and alone, having never experienced the kind of love that connected two people in the most intimate way?

He crouched before her and gripped the backs of her calves, his hands warm and welcoming on her skin. "Is there a chance in hell I could talk you out of this suicide mission?"

"No." Definitely not.

"So what's the point in trying? It's not like you need my approval."

His push back would've shown she mattered. Maybe she wasn't the center of his universe, but it would've been nice to feel…what? Commanded? Forced? Reined in by someone who loved her enough to care about her wellbeing? Maybe she just wanted to be fucked so hard she felt it emotionally, spiritually, instead of just physically.

A lump knotted in her throat, and she swallowed it down. She was letting her emotions run rampant, twisting her into a jumble of contradiction. Had he opposed her mission, it would've pissed her off.

She'd been chained up, beat up, kicked down, and held in the dregs of her weakest point. But she never stopped fighting, never gave up. She'd mustered what little courage remained and chose to live, to learn, to hate and kill, to do whatever it took to not just overcome, but to evolve.

He knew all that, and the intense gleam in his eyes said he was confident she'd do it again.

"I would've showered," she said with a soft smile, "if you wanted to tie me up and fuck me."

"If things were different, if *I* was different, I would've put you in the shower and never let you leave."

Warmth spread through her limbs. "You sure you're not gay?"

"Yeah." He laughed. "I'm sure." He cupped her face, his nostrils flaring with a deep breath. "I hope you find what you're looking for."

She imagined the moral corruption she would find — men who perceived women as nothing more than livestock to sell, fuck, and piss on — and the hairs on her neck lifted.

Tate pulled away and shot a longing look at the doorway.

"I'm not very good with goodbyes." He scratched his neck, avoiding her gaze. "So…"

"Go on." She shoved his shoulder, blinking through the achy burn in her eyes. "Get out of here."

He didn't look back as he escaped. The sound of his footfalls quickened down the hall and faded in the distance. When the front door slammed, the bang ricocheted through her chest, releasing a stream of silent tears.

She let them fall, promising herself they'd be her last until she saw him again. Then she dried her face and changed into his pungent black shirt.

For the next three hours, she made her farewell rounds through the sprawling, ranch-style Austin house. She shared a bedroom with Kate — one of the last slaves under Van's reign — while the five guys took over the other four rooms. The attic was finished, but no one would sleep there.

They were millionaires, thanks to Van. They could buy seven estates, retire in luxury, and live anywhere. But they clung together in a modest suburban neighborhood not far from Liv and Josh, in a house they'd made their home.

Heaviness pressed against her breastbone as she recapped the plan with her roommates. No one cried. No one tried to talk her out of it. Their need for retribution darkened their eyes and strengthened her backbone.

When Van arrived, she followed him to his car, leaving her friends standing bravely stoic on the front porch.

Barefoot, wearing only a mid-thigh shirt and panties, and accompanied by Van's menacing silhouette, she looked like a woman begging for someone to call the cops. Thank God, the street was empty and shrouded in darkness, but the evening heat weighed heavy, making the atmosphere feel stagnant and dead.

A hint of smoke tinged the air. She glanced around, tracking the scent until she spotted the red flare of a cigarette bobbing in an alcove beside the garage. Tate only smoked when he was irate, but she knew it was him, a brooding sentinel in the cover of night, always watching.

She gave him a chin lift, the motion jerking with the anxious rhythm of her heart.

Van stopped beside his '65 Mustang GT and opened the trunk. The hood of his sleeveless sweatshirt cast his face in shadows as he removed a coil of rope and a black scarf.

When he turned toward her, the moonlight caught the opening of his hoodie, revealing an expression cut straight from her nightmares. His eyes, like steel blades, flayed her skin in an icy chill and bled her pores with sweat.

"Are you numb with terror yet?" He cocked his head.

"Getting there." She tightened her muscles, fighting against the violent tremors gripping her body.

"Good." He grabbed her hair with unnecessary force and shoved her toward the shallow, coffin-like interior of the trunk. "You should be petrified."

# SIX

Camila wasn't claustrophobic, but after a forty-five-minute ride in the trunk of Van's Mustang, the tiny space had morphed into a malignant presence. It pressed in from every direction, growing heavier, tighter, restricting her movements. *No room. Too cramped. Can't breathe.* She needed air. She needed *out!*

*But I put myself here.* Inhale. *I'm in control.* Exhale.

Except she wasn't. Blindfolded and pinned on her side, she'd already given up her freedom. And this was the easy part. If she couldn't endure a trunk, she wouldn't survive the rest.

*I'm a slave again.* She focused on breathing—in, out, repeat, repeat, repeat—while centering her mind on submitting and surviving.

Her eyelashes dragged against the scarf, and her wrists burned in the scratchy bindings at her back. Van had tied the rope so tight it cut off blood flow, turning her hands into unfeeling stumps.

But it was necessary. As necessary as the melodramatic show she would put on for her captors. She needed to appear crippled with fright, her mind so horribly wounded they would only see a quivering, harmless girl. They would carry their traumatized little Trojan Horse past their security, and there, ensconced in the heart of the operation, she would strike.

The tires spun off the pavement and continued on bumpy ground, spitting gravel against the chassis. Larry McGregor's GPS coordinates put the rendezvous at the edge of a cotton field. This must've been it, the final stretch of the drive. Her lungs seized with renewed panic.

Too soon, the car slowed, stopped, and the engine shut off. The sudden silence mired into her bones, shoving her deep into buried memories of the night she met Van. His hand over her mouth, the stabbing pain through her head, the blackout, the wooden box…

The trunk creaked open, and a blast of arid air filled her lungs, bringing with it a resinous perfume. A hint of camphor. The approach of cotton harvest.

She licked parched lips, tasting the dusty drought of summer as she eased up on an elbow, hands numb and restrained behind her. The blindfold stole her vision, and given the hour of night, there would be no light seeping in. But amid the chirrup of nocturnal creatures, she heard him, his rustling movements closing in. She braced for a ruthless hand to yank her out.

"If you get yourself killed," Van whispered, shockingly close, his breath at her ear, "I'm going to hunt you in hell and blister your fucking ass. Hear me?"

"Noted." She swallowed.

He pulled her from the trunk by her leg. Her back banged against the bumper, her hands and eyes useless as she tumbled downward and crashed against the solid dirt.

Pain jolted through her thighs, and pebbles dug into her knees. She dropped to her hip, but his hand caught her under the arm, wrenching her up and dragging her backward.

She stumbled, pivoting in an attempt to blindly walk forward. Without slowing his gait, he swung her around and shoved her in the right direction. Then his fingers found her arm again, jerking her against his side.

"They're watching." He kept his voice so low it was barely audible beneath his breath. "Two Range Rovers. Fifty paces ahead. They're exiting now."

The slam of a car door sounded in the distance, followed by several more in rapid succession. Footsteps approached. Many. But how many?

Her chest heaved. She tripped over a rut in the dirt, and her bare feet scraped against sharp rocks. She let out a whimper for effect, but also because she wanted to scream at him to take her back. She couldn't do this.

Blood roared in her head, her breath catching, stacking, choking, her mind spinning. *I can do this. I can do this.*

Van didn't let up, playing the part with his bruising grip and ground-covering strides. This was why she'd asked him. Tate would've carted her out of there at the first sign of her distress.

She staggered alongside him, dragging her feet and stopping, only to get hitched forward again. She wheezed and mewled in pathetic intermittent noises. She couldn't have faked a full-body tremble, but it was there, attacking her with a force that chattered her teeth.

Oh God, what if she couldn't do this? Why the fuck did she put herself here?

His thumb dug into her bicep. Then it tapped one, two…five times.

*Five men.*

Why so many? Mr. E's operation ran for years with only two captors. Her blood pressure skyrocketed.

She wasn't counting the steps, but it felt like a lot less than fifty when Van suddenly halted. He didn't give her time to slow, using her momentum to thrust her to her knees.

Free from his grip, she lurched sideways, scooting awkwardly without her hands in a pretense to escape.

Van caught her neck with his sneaker and slammed her face against the brittle soil, holding her cheek to the earth with the weight of his foot.

"Whoa. Lower the guns," he said, and the press of his shoe vanished. "Don't worry about her face. It isn't her best feature."

*Fucking cocksucker.*

She shrank into a fetal position, cowering in the curl of her shoulders, and feigned a series of breathy sobs. What she really wanted to do was tug down the blindfold and take inventory of the men and their weapons.

"Which one of you Zorros is in charge?" Van asked.

*Zorros.* He was telling her they wore masks. *Clever.* She might see their faces eventually, but Van would walk away without their identities.

*It'll be okay. I have the GPS chip.*

"Call me *Jefe*," a man said from twenty-some-feet away, his voice soft and raspy. "She's a virgin?"

He carried an accent, a tincture of south of the border, where *Jefe* meant *Boss*. But there were a lot of Hispanics in Texas. He could've been her neighbor, her gynecologist, or the guy who bagged her groceries.

"She says she's a virgin, but I didn't check." Van's sneakers scuffed in place. "I didn't want to go prodding around and break something."

Vile amusement slithered through his voice, but no one laughed.

Dumbasses. A girl could be a virgin without an intact hymen. Lots of things could stretch or tear it. Horseback riding, water skiing, doing the splits, vibrators…

"Where's the money, Jefe?" Van asked, all humor gone.

Gravel crunched beneath advancing footsteps. Something heavy landed beside her head, followed by the sound of a zipper.

"Pass along our gratitude to *Señor* McGregor," Jefe said, maintaining his twenty-foot distance. "We look forward to more business from him."

*Sorry,* ese. *Larry McGregor's doing business with the Chief of Hell.*

Van lowered, his breaths near, and she curled tighter into a ball as if his proximity had conditioned her to do so.

"It's not all here." Van huffed. "This wasn't the agreed price."

What the fuck was he doing? He had no idea what was negotiated.

The man who had approached with the money treaded away, only to return a moment later. A second bag dropped on the ground.

"My mistake," Jefe said. "Now take it and go."

*Well played, Van.* Had he not questioned the payment, they would've known he was a fraud. Her eyes drifted closed behind the blindfold, but her relief was short-lived.

The bags lifted, and Van's presence retreated. She clung to the sound of his diminishing footfalls, aching for him to turn around.

*Don't go.*

What if there were too many guards and the operation was bigger than she'd estimated? What if this was all for nothing? Her surveillance had uncovered dozens of low-life scumbags like Larry McGregor. Men living normal lives—when they weren't stealing young girls and selling them to...*who?*

She'd imagined an operation like Mr. E's. Small and efficient with a network of Larrys on one end and buyers on the other. But five men had been sent to collect her. Five! How many were waiting at her destination? They could be gangsters, snuff filmographers, drug lords, chainsaw massacrers...

Van's Mustang growled to life, and the tires skidded. *Leaving.*

She was alone. Outnumbered. She didn't know what they looked like, what they were armed with, or who they worked for. And now they owned her. They could do whatever the hell they wanted to her.

Sweat pooled beneath her braless breasts as the rumble of Van's car faded into silence. There was no turning back. It was done.

"He's headed your way," Jefe said.

Dread churned in her gut. Who was he talking to? Someone on the phone?

"No, let him pass," Jefe said. "Just make sure he gets on the interstate. We'll wait."

Van was smart. He would know if someone followed him, and he sure as fuck wouldn't try to come back for her.

Her stomach clenched. With her hands bound behind her and miserably numb, she couldn't remove the blindfold. Only slightly less bothersome were the strands of hair stuck in her mouth. She tried to spit them out as she tracked the creaking of leather, the fall of heavy boots.

She'd expected a gang of uneducated hoodlums to fall upon her with grabby hands and verbal threats. But they remained silent. Disciplined. Like an army of professionals. Somehow, this was worse.

She dragged herself to her feet, teetering on shaky legs. "C-can someone…r-r-remove my blindfold?"

Well, that sounded effectively timid.

The air shifted in front of her face. She stopped breathing. Someone was there, close enough to touch a fingertip to her forehead.

She recoiled, but the hand stayed with her, trailing over the blindfold, down her cheek, and freeing the hair stuck to her lips. Her pulse raced, and the muscles in her neck strained against the pressure to hold still. She burned to slam her head forward and break his fucking nose.

*Give him a weak little girl. Let him believe you're not a threat.*

"Please don't t-touch me." She bunched her shoulders to her ears and tucked her chin to her chest.

Brushing the strands from her cheek, his finger followed the line of her jaw, pressed beneath her chin, and forced her face skyward.

She didn't have to pretend to be scared. The reminder that this man bought and sold humans was enough to get her throat working, her fear bobbing in her exposed neck.

The finger on her face disappeared, and metal clicked behind her. She jerked. Too late.

A slim ring of steel snapped around her forearm. More clicks, and the manacle cinched tighter. *A handcuff.*

He slid it down her arm, securing it above the rope on her wrists. Where was the second cuff?

Her answer came when he gripped her arm and the metal on his wrist clanked against hers. Her pulse thrashed in her ears.

What kind of man was she handcuffed to? Was he young or old? Covered in scars? Did he fuck his victims after he killed them?

"Let me go." She raised her voice several octaves and pulled against the restraints. "I won't tell anyone. I haven't even seen your faces."

She shook her body, hoping her freak-out was believable. Inside, she was frozen with terror, but showing her emotions didn't come natural for her.

"I wouldn't fight him, *puta.*" Jefe's accent issued from farther away. "He bites."

An image flashed through her mind of an oversized man with a boar's face and dribbling tusks. *And I'm handcuffed to him.*

"Get away." She blindly kicked his legs, snarling as she clawed at the hand on her arm. "I want to go home. Please don't do this."

In a flash, he shifted in front of her and wrapped an arm around her thighs. Her feet lost contact with the ground, and she was lifted up, up, and over his shoulder. She landed upside down, her face against the cotton on his back, and her wrists locked to one of his behind her.

No amount of bucking and kicking would dislodge the hand on her ass or the other one attached to her wrist. But she struggled anyway, which only worked her panties into her butt crack and hitched the t-shirt halfway up her back.

Blood rushed to her head, and hard-packed muscle flexed beneath her. Jesus fucking Christ, maybe he *was* an oversized boar-man.

He carried her a short distance, tossed her onto a long bench seat, and pulled her to sit upright. Leather stuck to her thighs, and rubber mats met her feet.

The boar sat beside her, his shackled arm tucked between her tailbone and the seat back.

"Let's go," Jefe said through the open door on the other side. Then he slid in next to her, his body pinning her against the boar.

Doors slammed shut, and the Range Rover shot forward, bumping along uneven ground.

With the t-shirt rucked around her waist, the cool air from the vent pebbled goose bumps across her thighs. She squeezed her knees together, hating how she couldn't use her arms—to pull down the shirt, to work the blood back into her hands, to stab her fingers in their eyes.

She'd chosen modest navy-blue panties because they resembled swimsuit bottoms. *I've worn less at the beach.* But it didn't make her feel any less exposed.

"Where are you taking me?" She tightened her arms against her sides as pins and needles penetrated the numbness in her fingers.

There were at least three men in the car. The driver and the two on either side of her. Yet no one spoke. As unnerving as it was, it made sense. If she escaped or was sold, their anonymity would protect them.

"I can't feel my hands." She squirmed between them and amped up the spasmodic sound of her whimpering. "What do you want from me?"

Jefe gripped her neck and angled her face in his direction. "Shut up."

She considered throwing a spastic fit until the bite of cold steel touched her cheek. A knife? She made a noise in the back of her throat and squeezed her eyes shut, letting her body go limp in the collar of his hand.

The dull edge slid across her cheekbone, gliding upward and slipping beneath the blindfold. With a flick of his wrist, he cut through the scarf and pulled it away.

Her heart pounded as she squinted through the darkness and found Jefe's black eyes watching her from the narrow opening of a black ski mask.

There was nothing noteworthy about those eyes. Were they even black? Hard to tell in the shadows of the car's interior.

He tightened his grip on her throat, stopping her from turning her head. The mask covered his hair, face, and throat. A glance downward revealed an average-sized physique in a nondescript t-shirt. He could've been anyone.

Beyond the heavily tinted windows, murky fields blurred beneath a starless sky. Which direction were they headed?

His gaze flicked over her shoulder and locked on the other man. Then he shoved her head between her knees.

What the fuck? Bent in half, she got a good view of her filthy feet. They looked so tiny and sad between the men's rugged boots.

She turned her neck to get a glimpse of the boar, but the fall of her hair blocked her line of sight. Fuck.

Jefe touched the blade to her skin again, this time on her wrist. The rope?

"P-please." She sniffled then heaved a couple of shuddering breaths for good measure. "I can't feel my hands."

"Can you be a good girl?" Jefe trailed a finger down her spine.

"Y-yes. Please untie me."

With his hand holding her head down, he cut the rope. The instant it fell away, she snapped her free arm forward and shook out her hand. Ah, fuck, it was so numb. But as the sharp biting sensations rushed in with the blood, it really fucking hurt. The shaking didn't help, and her fingers refused to bend or move.

Her other hand, still attached to the boar, was pulled onto his lap. Jefe released her head, and she straightened, quickly shoving down the hem of the shirt and scanning her surroundings.

Instead of a mask, the driver wore a baseball cap that sat low on his brow. Brown hair? Caucasian? She couldn't tell.

A three-lane highway stretched out ahead, surrounded by black smudges of farmland. No road signs in sight. If they weren't heading back to the city, where the fuck were they going?

The boar's strong fingers massaged her shackled hand, and the cuff on his wrist scraped against hers. The tingling receded, and warmth rushed in. She stifled a sigh and glanced at the hand she was shackled to.

A tattoo peeked out from the cuff of his sleeve. It was too dark to make out the design, but the ink looked faded and old.

Keeping her head lowered, she took in the casual recline of his posture. His legs spread wide, invading her space. He wasn't oversized or boar-ish. Nor was he average.

His muscled thigh felt like stone beneath her wrist. The coarse material of his fatigues cupped an impressive groin, and the waistband rode low on his narrow hips. His shirt had inched up his navel, revealing a dark dusting of hair and deep indentions of abs.

The bastard was honed like a damn blade. Hopefully, his brain wasn't as sharp.

She lifted her eyes, following the bulge of a bicep, the stretch of cotton over ridges of pecs, and…a ski mask. *Mierda.*

Despite the absence of light, the eyes staring back weren't black. Pale hints of color streaked into inky rings. Gold? Blue? Green?

He watched her without blinking, his intensity edged with thick lashes. Something flickered in the depths. An emotion. She was sure of it. Did he want to fuck her? Kill her? No, it was more complex than that. Whatever it was made her heart pump and her mind scream, *Look away.*

But she couldn't. Jefe might've been in charge of this team, but *this* man… He was up to something, and it lodged a boulder in her stomach.

The SUV stopped moving, breaking her trance. Beyond the windshield, the paved road ended at a field, and in the distance sat a small plane. The second Range Rover pulled up beside them and shut off the engine.

*Guess I'll be leaving Austin.*

Didn't matter. The GPS chip worked globally.

When the driver climbed out, the overhead lights remained off. Probably disconnected.

"Stay here." Jefe joined the driver outside, leaving her alone with the man who disturbed her the most.

"Do you talk?" She turned, intending to give him an impatient glare, then slammed her eyes shut.

*You're scared and weak, remember?*

She curled her shoulders forward, balled her hand on his lap, and stuttered, "What are…you going to do…to me?"

"Good question."

That voice… The blood drained from her face. *No, no, no.*

"What did you say?" She met hazel eyes and knew she was seeing things. *It's too dark.*

"What have you gotten yourself into, *mi vida?*"

The vibration of his voice was a strong hand massaging between her legs, so familiar and arousing she couldn't breathe.

She gripped the arm attached to hers and lifted it, using both hands to yank back the sleeve and expose the underside of his wrist.

Swirls of ink blackened his skin, but her focus narrowed on the pockmarked scar of a dog bite. No, this man was probably riddled with knife wounds. Did she even have the right arm?

"How did you get this scar?" She searched his gaze, and it told her nothing. And everything.

Dropping his hand, she went for the ski mask. As she yanked it up his neck, he didn't stop her. Instead, he gripped her hips and pulled her onto his lap to straddle him.

Her heart galloped frantically in her one-handed effort to bare his face. Shoving and tugging the material higher, she uncovered a chiseled jaw, a dusky shadow of stubble, a wide mouth with full lips...

Her throat closed up, and she jerked her hand away. "You're not him."

"I'm not?" His fingers dug into her waist.

With the mask gathered across his nose, she could almost convince herself he didn't look like an older, more distinguished version of Matias.

"He wouldn't be here." A sharp pain twisted in her chest. "He would never support sexual slavery."

A sinister grin curved his lips. *Not* a Matias smile. Except there, hiding in the corners...

She lifted her hand to trace the dimples. The same dimples she'd stared at every day for sixteen years. The same dimples that had flashed whenever he put a spider in her hair or peed on her mother's roses and always when he came in the stroke of her hand. They were the same dimples that had bored into her memories for the past twelve years.

Her heart slammed against her ribs as she yanked off the mask.

Thick strands of black hair fell across a smooth tawny forehead. Dark brows pulled into a *V* over eyes that would glow citrine in the sunlight. If she pressed her mouth against those firm lips, which memory would he taste like? The first bite of a juicy orange? The full-bodied smoke of a bonfire? A refreshing dip in the spring-fed stream?

He was so sculptured and masculine, all grown up, filled out, and sexier than she could've ever imagined.

And he'd come to save her. Whether she needed that or not, he'd actually come for her. Somehow...someway, he'd discovered she would be here and wanted to help her.

She cupped his face, the scratch of whiskers so strange against her palm. "It's really you, *mi vida*."

*My life.*

She raised her other hand to frame his face, but her arm caught. Shackled. Her vision clouded. *No.* Oh God, no, he wasn't her life or her goddamn savior. He enslaved women. Quivering anger spiked through her body. He was...

*My captor.*

# SEVEN

The falter of Camila's breaths, the heave of her full tits, everything about her intoxicated Matias' senses. She was here, *right fucking here*, filling his hands with her tight, trembling flesh.

His reaction to her had been instantaneous, darting a possessive jolt down his spine and thickening his cock. But evidently, she needed more time to adjust. After all, he wasn't here to save her, not in the way she was probably guessing.

Her initial shock at hearing his voice had softened into wonderment, loosening her shoulders and parting her heart-shaped lips. In that moment, she'd seemed lost, completely knocked off her stubborn axle.

Now she glared at him with liquid hatred in her eyes.

Christ, she looked so goddamn fuckable when she was riled. On his lap. Chained to him.

He tightened his fingers around her hips to stop himself from violating every inch of her body. The same discipline he'd exercised the last time he had her alone. *Twelve fucking years ago.* Not that he had anything in common with that dumbass eighteen-year-old boy.

He'd shed his innocence in exchange for power, every last ounce of chivalry traded for brutal dominance. If he hadn't, he would've been gutted and eaten alive.

And the woman who had smuggled her way into his ruthless world, pretending she was there against her will? She now had the audacity to look deceived.

"Did you expect me to be here?" She shoved at him, stealing peeks at the men outside as her legs kicked to escape the intimacy of their position. "This is...it's just too coincidental. How did you know?"

"Don't waste your breath asking questions I'm not going to answer." He held her against him, chest to chest, with her thighs straddling his hips and her cunt pressing on his erection. Exactly where she belonged.

"Tell me you're not with them." Her expression paled in a rictus of angelic horror, her muscles edged with frozen tension as if wrestling to maintain her cover. She had no idea what he and the other men knew about her.

"You should be more concerned about who *you* are with." He held up their handcuffed wrists and gave her a taunting smile.

The bright flash of her teeth drew his attention right before she swung her free hand across his cheek. She reared back to slap him again, but he caught her arm and wrenched it behind her.

"You still hit like a girl." He worked his jaw against the sting.

"*Me lo chupa.*" She curled her lip and lowered her voice to a harsh whisper. "You bought an enslaved woman. You bought *me,* Matias! You know what happened to me when I disappeared, what kind of hell I escaped, and still, you do this?" She yanked her arm in the handcuff. "How could you?"

He could ask her the same question. How could she team up with Van Quiso? How could she let that cock-sucking pervert tie her up, toss her in the dirt, and sell her to a cartel? Damn her for being so fucking reckless with her life.

As she glared at him, her seductive eyes seemed to fight an internal war, demanding answers while begging him to tell her this was all a big misunderstanding.

He wouldn't tell her shit. Showing her over the coming months, one agonizing day at a time, was the only way they would come out of this whole and together.

What was taking the guys so long? Matias glanced through the windshield and spotted a rangy silhouette crawling under the turboprop. Must've been Chispa, their explosives guy. If there was a bomb on-board, he'd find it.

Camila slammed her head forward and bit his shoulder through the shirt.

He jerked her back by the hair, holding her face inches away as he scowled. Jesus, fuck, he wanted to rip into her.

She jutted out her chin, holding his gaze with a voracious amount of attitude while whispering under her breath, "Who do you work for?"

Right about now, she was probably more concerned about what the other men knew about her and her dangerous ruse. There was so much she didn't understand about her situation, and she wasn't ready to learn the depths of his role in it. Keeping her in the dark was the only way this would work.

And the things he would do to her in the dark... He imagined trussing her up on a suspension beam, burying his teeth in her perfect rack, and pounding his cock into the clench of her sinful body. *Dios mío,* she had a knockout figure, with curves to hold on to and toned strength to withstand his cruelest, most sinister appetites.

He ached to unleash the violence inside him, to spread her open and let her feel what the last twelve years had done to him.

Instead, he pinned her hands behind her back and crashed his mouth against hers.

She held her breath, lips pinched, but he pried them apart with his tongue and buried it in the wet heat of her mouth.

Growling against her lips, he thrilled in her struggle, in the way she sank into the kiss while twisting her arms to get away. She could fight her desire, but she couldn't disclaim their unbreakable bond, one that had taken root so long ago in the haven of their citrus grove.

A moan vibrated in her throat as she stretched her mouth and drew his lip between hers, sucking and licking, gnashing and biting.

Electricity surged through his groin and tightened his balls as he devoured the furious lashes of her tongue. She tasted like home, warm and sugary, nourishing and *his.*

The soft familiarity of her lips fueled his arousal while the rigid resistance in her body heated his muscles with aggression. Fucking hell, he got off on her torment, on the stiffness of her spine and the frantic rise and fall of her tits. It only made the slide of her hungry lips taste sweeter, more rewarding.

He ruthlessly ate at her mouth, and she gave it right back, her tongue seeking and whipping with all the mistrust, anger, and years lost between them. Her frenzied inhales quickened his own, their breaths crashing together as her fingernails scratched at his hands.

It had been twelve years since he kissed a woman, and she'd been only a girl then with gangly limbs and tiny breasts. Kissing her now blew away the memories. There was no more shyness, no restraint or inexperience...

Resentment barbed inside him, puncturing holes in his unraveling control. How many men had she kissed? Sucked? Fucked? His vision blurred in smears of red. He needed vindication and intended to take it from her pleading screams, from the give of her body beneath his thrusts. Pain and pleasure. Twisted justice.

*Not yet.*

He tore his mouth away and shoved her off his lap, gasping with the fury of his breaths.

Her gaze flew to the window. Confirming no one was watching? She looked back at him, lips swollen and eyes smoldering. "Fuck you."

"Careful, Camila. You don't—"

She launched at him, teeth bared and fists swinging.

He subdued her easily, wrapping her shackled arm around her torso with her back pressed against his chest.

"Let me go, you fucking traitor."

He covered her mouth with his palm, fingers gripping her jaw shut, as he angled her face toward the window. "You promised Nico you'd be a good girl."

She froze, attention glued to the back of Nico's shirt, and choked an indiscernible sound against his fingers.

He released her mouth.

"*Jefe* is...Nico..." Her free hand touched the glass, and her voice dropped to a whisper. "Nico *Restrepo*? As in capo of the Restrepo cartel?"

Of course, she knew the name, but not because her parents had been Colombian. Anyone who watched the news knew about the ongoing conflict between the notorious kingpin and law enforcement officials in the U.S. and Colombia.

What she didn't know was that the Restrepo cartel had played an instrumental part in her captivity eleven years ago. He needed to guard that secret until she was mentally and emotionally prepared to hear why he was still embedded in the crime family that had banished her to chains.

"Oh my God." She dropped her head in her hand, her expression veiled by the tangled mess of her black hair. "This isn't just some local slave ring."

Not even close. She was headed bowels-deep into Colombia's most powerful criminal organization.

"You work for the fucking *Restrepos*?" She twisted on his lap and searched his eyes. "All this time?"

He flattened his lips into a line, knowing she couldn't handle the truth.

"What's your position exactly? VP of Shipping and Receiving?" She jerked on the handcuff. "Director of Human Slavery?"

Her jaw set in the defiant way that had always made him hard. He dug his fingers into her skin and tried to ignore the roll of her hips over his agonizing erection.

"Oh, right." She tipped her chin up, wearing a corrosive smile. "Even now, those questions are off limits. But you knew I'd be here? You planned this?"

He rapped on the window, anxious to get her across the border and show her what he thought of her questions. He hadn't expected her to confess the reason she was here, but whatever scheming she was still doing in that gorgeous head of hers was pointless. Her fate was sealed.

Nico broke away from his conversation with the pilot, and she instantly hunched her shoulders forward, head down, quivering like the mousy little girl she wasn't. Nico opened Matias' door, concealed by his ski mask and casual clothing, all safety precautions to protect his identity — not from Camila, but from anyone who might've been watching.

"*Listo?*" Matias tightened his grip on her stiffening body.

"Ready for what?" Her voice cracked.

"Something came up." Nico glanced over his shoulder at the plane and returned to Matias. "We're modifying the route."

Wasn't uncommon. Transfers and layovers changed with the intel. Sudden DEA activity, rival gangs mobilizing, anything could've compromised their scheduled stopover.

"Chispa's done with his sweep." Nico stepped back. "She's next."

Matias didn't give her time to fight, hauling her out of the SUV and tossing her over his shoulder. She felt willowy in his arms, but not delicate, not like the tiny girl he used to hoist one-handed into orange trees.

Stifling the twinge of remembrance, he crossed the field, lifted her into the eight-seat Cessna's rear door, and set her on her feet. Inside, he pushed her head down, both of them ducking as he guided her past three rows of chairs and shoved her into the front seat.

She didn't glance at the stripped-down interior, the exposed cockpit, or the absence of anything that could be used as a weapon. Her glare was all for him.

"Where are we going?" She tucked her shackled arm against her waist. "This hunk of metal won't make it to Colombia."

No, but their connecting flight would.

Removing a key from his pocket, he knelt before her and trapped her shins with his thighs. Then he unlatched the cuff from his wrist and locked her to the chair's frame.

The tread of soft shoes sounded on the stairs behind him, followed by the scratch of a familiar voice. "*Dejamos en cinco minutos.*"

Turning, Matias met the cloudy eyes of their most trusted doctor, Picar. The old man's hunched spine and stocky frame allowed him to pass through the cabin without too much bending. But his decrepit appearance was deceiving. Picar earned his name by the way he wielded a scalpel. *Chop.*

Matias shifted out of the way as Picar slipped by and settled into the seat across the aisle from Camila. A black bag sat on his lap, his gnarled hands rooting through it.

"Whose shirt is this?" Matias gripped the neckline hanging off her shoulder, gathering the foul-smelling material in his fist. "If you give me a name, I won't torture him before I kill him."

She averted her eyes to the window.

Van Quiso and Tate Vades were around the same size, but he bet it belonged to Tate. He didn't put it past that bastard to send her off bathed in his own stink.

He ripped the shirt from neck to thighs, baring round, perky tits and dusky nipples. His pulse kicked up, rushing a torrent of heat to his cock.

Her free arm shot up and hugged her breasts. "What are you—?"

"You wouldn't believe the places I find bugs." He battled her gaze, never looking away.

"Bugs?" Lines formed on her forehead.

"Listening devices, GPS chips, countermeasures… They hide in the tightest crevices." Matias clasped her inner thighs and spread them apart, relishing the quiver across her skin.

"You think someone shoved a mic up inside me?" She injected a squeak in her voice and blinked rapidly.

She might've been angling for the scared little girl look, but there wasn't a hint of worry in her eyes. That meant he wouldn't find a bug between her legs. Probably not a hymen either, but he'd wait until they were alone to check that.

"Some chips are implanted in the skin." He trailed his fingers over her panties, along her ribs, and paused at the undersides of her breasts. "Lower your arm."

She heaved out a breath and gripped the armrest, her other hand twisting in its locked position against the chair.

Wedging his hips between her legs, he took his time reacquainting himself with the velvety texture of her golden skin. She'd bloomed into flawless proportion, the firm weight of her tits perfect handfuls and peaked with taut nipples begging to be clamped.

There were no incision marks, no bugs, but it was the twitch in her eye that confirmed he was searching the wrong place. A twitch she'd tried to hide as a kid whenever he'd flirted with the older girls who worked in the grove.

She wasn't scared. She was pissed.

Curious how she hadn't applied the martial arts training she'd learned over the years. He'd given her plenty of opportunities to lock him in a leg choke. Maybe she was waiting to attack him when they were alone, when he wouldn't have back up. Or perhaps Nico was her only target.

Matias moved up her chest, hands roaming over the exquisite lines of her collarbones, along her neck, and paused at her pouty lips. "Open."

Her jaw lowered, but he didn't miss the half-second of hesitation or the flicker in her chocolate gaze. An anxious crack in her facade. After all this time, he could still read her.

He gripped her wrist and held it to the armrest. His other hand flattened her back against the seat.

"Picar." He nodded at the doctor. "*Dale pues.*"

She whipped her head around and glared at the syringe in Picar's hand. "What is that? What are you doing?"

"Something to help you sleep."

"No, I don't need that." Eyes wild, she bucked in the seat, going nowhere. "Don't you fucking drug me!"

Picar leaned over and pierced the needle into her pinned arm, his hands steady despite her thrashing and spitting. When the syringe emptied, he gathered his things and hobbled toward the rear of the cabin.

Her lungs pumped for air, her expression furious, but her body began to weaken, slumping beneath the weight of the sedative.

"*Se arrepiente de esta. Enorme* missst…take." Her head rolled, and she snapped it upright. "I hate you."

"No, you don't. You hate that you fear me." He brought his mouth to her ear. "Step inside and show me your teeth."

"Youuu *chucha* mmmwotherfruck…errr." She blinked heavily, her tongue lolling in her mouth. "Ima gonna…*picar* yerrr bwalllz off…n'kwill…" Her chin hit her chest. "You…dead."

He buckled in her limp body, brushed the hair from her face, and sat back on his heels.

She'd vacillated between weak and pissed, scared and brave, as if trying maintain her ruse with Nico but falling off-kilter with Matias. He knew she was still uncertain about his role in this.

He sensed the little girl inside of her warring with the grown woman. The girl longed for him to be the boy she remembered while the woman knew the truth. But her reality was probably confusing the two, leaving her unbalanced, guarded, and consumed with hatred.

He'd anticipated all of this, and though her hatred felt like a thousand knives twisting in his heart, it was a necessary part of the plan.

If she thought she hated him now, God help her. She had no idea what was coming.

# EIGHT

Distorted sounds stirred at the edges of oblivion. A throb penetrated the darkness and hammered through Camila's skull.

*Matias fucking drugged me!*

She lay on her side, the surface beneath her hard and smooth. No longer on the airplane?

Shoes scuffed nearby, voices jumbled in and out of her awareness, and…

Was that a whimper? Another woman?

Her pulse echoed in her head as she wrestled through the fog of sedation. Her eyelids weighed a hundred pounds, refusing to open. She tried to move her aching arms, but they wouldn't budge in the cuffs behind her. Focusing on her legs, she gave each a lethargic twitch. No restraints there.

She could still defend herself. Maybe after she mustered the strength to open her eyelids.

Where was she? Was Matias with her? The dull murmur of voices continued, but she couldn't hear him.

She managed a few sluggish blinks, wincing against shards of light. The waxy scent of wood polish infiltrated her nose, and with it came traces of cigarette smoke and sweat.

Pushing down the impulse to struggle, she forced herself to remain still, listen, and take inventory. Movement rustled in front of and behind her, but without footsteps or clear voices, she couldn't pinpoint the number of people, who they were, or how close they stood.

The whimper had come from the floor behind her. Other captives? The smoke meant there were probably men present, but the scent wasn't overwhelming. Maybe one smoker?

Her bare thighs chilled in the air-conditioned room, and the bottom edges of her panties were parked uncomfortably high on her ass. At least, her shirt felt dry and clean against her skin. Wait… Matias had ruined her shirt.

Long sleeves covered her arms. If Matias had switched her top, what else had he done while she was unconscious? Her fingers curled, rattling the shackles.

Another whimper sounded behind her, lifting the hairs on her arms. Definitely a second woman. Maybe more. She couldn't think about what that meant. Not right now.

Holding her eyes open, she waited for the bright wash of pain to recede. With her cheek pressed to the ground, she took in the wood flooring that stretched out in front of her. A couple yards away, two sets of black boots and a pair of shiny loafers stood still, toes pointed in her direction.

The voices fell quiet.

A shiver swept down her back. Was Matias among them? Christ, why couldn't she lift her head?

Elegantly carved baseboards encircled the perimeter of the room, broken up by wide doorways bracketed with white pillars. Couches, chairs, and low tables sat off to one side in an array of straight, modern lines and monochromatic fabrics.

Bands of sunlight striped the floor and warmed the backs of her legs. She'd been unconscious the entire night? Long enough to be transported to Colombia, if that was where they'd taken her.

Panic rose, quickening her breaths. *The GPS chip!*

With focused concentration, she moved her sandpaper tongue against the molar and prodded around the edges of the filling. It still felt weirdly numb but…intact. Hope bottled up in her chest. He hadn't found it.

Maybe she wasn't compromised after all. If Matias believed she'd been captured and stripped of her volition, her plan was still viable. Except there was a nasty, decaying hole in that theory.

She'd asked Matias to dispose of Larry McGregor. Although she'd never given a name during their phone conversation, it was safe to assume Matias identified the body as the man who was supposed to deliver her. *Fuck.*

So he knew she was playing him. Did he tell Nico or was he playing his own game?

With a heave of determination, she rolled to her back, groaning as her listless body landed on her shackled arms.

Turning her head, she came face to face with a dark-haired woman on her knees. Mouth gagged with a black bandanna and tears streaking from her wide eyes, she couldn't have been older than thirty.

*She's my age.* Definitely not the prime age for sexual slavery. Maybe these fuckers weren't picky about who they chose to destroy.

Camila's breath emerged on a guttural growl. Her blood boiled, saturating her muscles with heat as she tensed to fight, to defend.

*Too soon.* She needed to get her bearings, gather her wits, and reevaluate her plan.

The woman wore nothing, her beautiful bone structure, swarthy skin, and full-figured curves on display for whoever was in the room. And she wasn't alone. Another Latina woman knelt beside her, and behind them lay a blonde curled on her side with her eyes squeezed shut. All three were naked, gagged, bound, and reeked with enough sweat and fear to sour Camila's stomach.

These women were human beings. They had names, birthdays, and favorite songs. Somewhere out there someone was missing their daughter, sister, friend. Hell, these women were old enough to have children.

And now, they would only have pain.

Camila shook with the force of her fury as memories broke open in her mind. The coarse bricks against her back as she hung from chains. The violet wand burning between her legs. The ring gag. Van's engorged cock. His come in her throat.

The musty stink of the attic adhered to her nostrils and coated her taste buds. She tried to hack it from her system, coughing and wheezing past the dryness in her mouth.

She touched the modified molar with her tongue. At least now, the people in her life knew her location. They would save these women if she failed.

Behind the women, the room spilled into a roofless inner courtyard. Lifting her head, she leaned up on her elbow to see more.

There were no doorways to block the view. The entire wall was missing. Spanish tiles wrapped around an Olympic-sized infinity pool that merged into the most breathtaking landscape she'd ever seen.

A dense jungle of broad-leafed tropical trees and heavy undergrowth stretched to the horizon, cascading upwards over sloping hillsides that rippled into mountain ranges that must've been hundreds of miles away.

She'd never been to the basin of South America, had never even ventured outside of Texas, but she was certain she was staring at the Amazon rainforest.

Dizziness sailed through her, threatening to rob what little strength she'd summoned. Running would be a wasted effort. The compound was likely swarming with armed guards. She wouldn't even make it out the door. If she did, she wouldn't survive a night in the jungle.

Didn't matter. She hadn't come here to escape on the first day.

Pushing up to a sitting position, lightheaded and nauseated, she turned away from the unfathomable view and the terrified women and focused on the enemy.

A man in a black suit stood a few feet away, his eyes inky and unreadable, with a promise of callousness in his resting scowl. In his mid-thirties maybe, he kept his beard and mustache trimmed as short as the black curls on his skull. He might've been attractive if it weren't for the menacing glare that deepened under the mantle of his thick brows.

"Welcome to Colombia." He didn't grin, didn't change his expression in any way, but his accented voice confirmed he was Nico Restrepo.

Matias stood a couple of feet behind Nico. Her heartbeat quivered with both relief and disappointment. He would either help her efforts or try to stop her.

He wore black fatigues and a white t-shirt, with hands behind his back and his stance wide and confident. He didn't look at her, but his nostrils flared. He must've been aware she was peering at him through her lashes.

And she was wearing his long-sleeved shirt.

Why wasn't she nude and gagged like the other women? Was he protecting her in some way? If that was the case, why was she on the floor, bound with the others, as if awaiting sentencing?

Whatever was going on, she didn't want to give them a reason to muzzle her, so she kept her mouth shut as she sat taller and waited for Matias to meet her eyes.

When he did, he rubbed a palm over his thigh, his golden gaze unbending and infuriating. What was he thinking? Was he trying to give her a warning? A silent command? What? The longer she stared at him, the more something didn't feel right, but goddamn, she could stare at him for hours.

Whiskers shadowed his strong jawline. Muscle roped around his forearms and flexed beneath the faded ink of his tattoos. His broad chest, narrow waist, and powerful thighs drew her focus to the considerable package between his legs. If the kiss they'd shared earlier was any indication, she bet he fucked as hard as he looked.

Heat flooded low in her belly, and her nipples hardened. Why did he have to be so distractingly attractive? She pressed her lips together.

His face tightened, and he looked away.

*Shit.* She shifted her attention to the third man who stood beside him, and her breath strangled.

The corners of his pale mouth tipped into a smile that had been sewed together with heavy black thread. It was like something out of a Tim Burton film. His nest of wild black hair, ghostly complexion, and purple bruises beneath his eyes only made his needlework smirk more disturbing.

Were the stitches self-administered or some kind of punishment? Jesus, how did he eat? She shuddered. No wonder he looked deathly anorexic.

"You already met Matias." Nico lifted his phone and nodded his chin at the Goth guy. "This is Frizz. Don't let his youth fool you. He has a supernatural talent with sharp objects."

Her lips tingled as she imagined him attacking with a lightning fast needle. And what did Nico mean by *already met Matias*? Did he not know they grew up together? If Matias was hiding things from him, maybe she could use that to her advantage.

"I have an impatient buyer in the pipeline." Nico swiped the screen of his phone, wearing a scowl that bordered on boredom. "He's bald, fat, and looking for love." He rolled his lips. "Well, maybe not love. Let's call it *commitment.*"

Who the hell was he talking to? Matias stared at the floor. Frizz's threaded grin was aimed at no one in particular. The three women behind her sniveled and shook in their chains.

Camila returned her attention to Nico, her pulse beating a frantic tattoo.

"I need to sell one of you." Nico cocked his head, his gaze flat, dead, as it rested on Camila. "I really don't care who, so you tell me. Which one?"

Her mind spun, trying to make sense of his question. He wanted her to choose a girl to sell. A tremor bowled through her, rocking her body. No fucking way.

Nico snapped his fingers, and Frizz stepped forward.

Dread swelled in her gut as Frizz's emaciated frame ambled through the room. He twirled a finger through his crazy hair and — with the stitches just loose enough to pucker his lips — he whistled something eerily cheerful.

"You're not getting it, *niñita*." Matias lifted his head and met her eyes. "If Nico tells you to do something and you ignore him, he simply cannot let that slide."

*The brown-nosing* hijo de puta! How could he not see this as anything but horrifically fucked up?

She twisted around, her heart lodged in her stomach as she followed Frizz's movements. *What's he going to do? Oh God, what is he whistling?*

When he crouched next to the blonde behind her, his creepy tune cut off. With a sick stomach, she suddenly recognized the melody as the *Kill Bill* whistle.

Frizz wrenched the blonde off the floor by her hair and hauled her over his knee, face up. In the next breath, he held a curved surgeon's needle above her frozen nude body. Black string threaded through the needle's eyehole and ended at a knot that pulled tight against her lower eyelid, which he held pinched between his fingers and pulled away from her eye.

The woman screamed against her gag, her eyes bulging and her lashes batting against the taut thread.

Camila's stomach turned, and saliva flooded her mouth. How the hell had he pierced and threaded her skin that fast?

"Stop!" She swung back toward Nico, hands jerking against the cuffs as she grappled for a way to stall them. "If you...you disfigure her, you can't sell her."

Nico lowered into an armchair against the back wall and lit a cigarette, scratching his trim beard.

"Lucky for us..." Matias approached her, his lean, arrogant stride twisting the hatred inside her. "Mr. Bald-fat-and-committed isn't a picky guy. He only requested tight holes. We can close up the slits he won't be fucking."

All three women burst into pleading, wailing sobs. She wanted to join them, to give in to the hopelessness burning up the back of her throat. But she couldn't. She refused to surrender.

"We'd love to keep all of you." Matias circled behind her.

She shifted to her knees, following him with her eyes.

"But we can't run a business without profits, can we?" Matias ruffled the hair on the women he passed and returned to stand before Camila. "Times are hard, and to stay competitive, we have to sell the merchandise. It's basic economics. Supply and demand. I don't make the rules."

Every word he said fractured something inside her. The demon in front of her wore a Matias-shaped mask, but beneath it lay the soulless reflection of pure evil.

She searched his eyes for a phantom echo of the boy she once knew and found no remorse. Not a hint of goodness in the fiendish smirk he so easily donned on his too-attractive face. It left her feeling more cold and alone than her darkest nights in Van's attic.

This wasn't him. Matias was gone.

Unbidden, a trail of fire crawled up her throat, and her eyes blurred with tears.

"Deciding someone's fate can be taxing." He gripped her chin, squeezing painfully. "All those messy emotions get in the way. It sucks. But it's time to woman up and choose."

Her skin crawled where he touched her, and she jerked her head away.

Frizz held the blonde over his bent knee, his hand poised to finish the stitch over her eye. Fuck him to hell and back.

"*Ir a la mierda.*" Camila angrily rubbed her cheek on her shoulder, trying to erase the fallen tears.

"You need to shut down that hormonal shit." Matias rocked on his heels, seemingly at home in his despicable skin. "Like your *papá* used to say" — he laughed in a deep voice — "I'll give you something to choke on."

Her *papá* never said that, but it didn't stop the smoke from billowing through her chest and strangling her airway. She seethed with the vicious need to wash the floors with his blood.

Nico rose from the chair and strolled over to Frizz. He drew a long drag on the cigarette and, without a whisper of emotion on his face, stubbed it out on the blonde's stomach.

The piercing sound of her howls slammed Camila's heart against her ribs, and the aroma of singed flesh pervaded her inhales.

Frizz launched into his haunting whistle and turned his gaze to the needle in his hand.

"No, wait!" Camila scrambled toward Frizz on her knees, her arms useless weights behind her.

Matias yanked Camila back by her hair. "Choose."

*Fuck fuck fuck.* Her gut instinct was to volunteer herself, but if she did, she wouldn't be able to stop them the next time, and all the times after that. But how could she condemn another to a life of rape and brutality? She couldn't.

She raised her chin and spat the words. "I choose me."

"Too easy." Matias released her with a shove. "You disappoint me. I thought you were made of stronger stuff."

"Why are you doing this?" Glaring at him, she fisted her hands behind her, mentally squeezing his scrotum between her fingers and ripping his balls from his body.

Blood-curdling screams jerked her head toward the blonde.

Frizz had made two loops over her eyes and swooped in for a third.

Oh fuck, oh God, they wanted a decision, but this wasn't a choice at all.

"Her." Camila nodded at the blonde, her voice cracking as she blinked through the onslaught of tears. "Just...please remove the stitches."

Frizz stood and hauled the blonde to her feet. She keened loudly, her head swinging side to side as if trying to shake the threads from her eye. With a grip on her bound arms, Frizz dragged her out of the room and around the corner, trailed by the hiccupping sounds of her sobs.

An agonizing chill settled over Camila. So fucking cold. Her body was a vibrating cage, a prison of ice and violent tremors. The kind of shivering anguish that locked up muscles, sought out bones, and made her want to die. She couldn't feel the sunlight on her back or the wood beneath her knees. Was this what death felt like?

But she wasn't dead. She needed to fight for the blonde woman. For the women at her back. And for all the others bought and sold by these monsters.

"This is your life now." Matias crouched before her and lowered his voice. "*I* am your life. *Tu vida.*" He hummed to himself, a smile pulling at his wretched lips. "When I spread your thighs, you will let me in, because I own these legs and everything above, below, and in between them. You fight me, and I'll take it out on someone else." With a raised brow, his gaze shifted to the women behind her and flicked back. "Now I know you're a smart girl. Nod if you understand."

Her throat constricted. He wanted her to be his slave, to wear *his* fucking chains. Well, wasn't that perfect? She certainly despised him enough to endure that role with an appropriate amount of misery.

*It's just a means to an end.*

Her slave training kicked in, and she lowered her eyes, bowing her head on a nod.

She would outwit him, fool him into thinking she was intimidated by his threats and weakened by her restraints. Then she would confide in him, figure out his angle, and convince him to turn on his boss.

If he refused, she would kill him.

# NINE

Matias knew the instant Camila came to terms with her position as his slave. Her entire demeanor changed, her gaze falling to the floor, shoulders loosening, and spine straightening.

He didn't believe for one second that this was surrender. The betrayed look in her eyes wouldn't be going away for a while, and neither would the damn ache in his chest.

So while she would undoubtedly wear the role Van Quiso had taught her with mechanical perfection, she wouldn't embrace it emotionally.

To obtain what he wanted, what they both needed, it was his responsibility to show her what it truly meant to yield to her Master.

"On your feet." He stepped back and clasped his hands at his back.

She rose gracefully, head down and arms drawn behind her in the cuffs.

Tendrils of black hair fell in front of her shoulders and hid her face, but he was sure her eye was twitching. Good thing he couldn't read her mind. He'd rather not know all the ways she imagined killing him. She wouldn't succeed.

"Follow me." He gave Nico a nod on his way out of the living room without looking back to confirm she obeyed.

Crossing the white marbled floors of the circular foyer, he veered toward the glass causeway that would take him to the east wing.

"Are you going to rape me now?" She appeared at his side, voice devoid of emotion as she matched his strides on silent feet. "Or can I take a shower first?"

He swung around and clamped a hand on her forehead, snapping her face upwards as he stabbed two fingers in her mouth. Pressing down on her tongue while pinning her head back, he trapped her startled gaze with the hard warning in his.

After a few noisy breaths, her jaw relaxed beneath his hand.

*Good girl.* He released her and turned back toward the hall.

Truth was, he loved her verbal banter. It was one of the many reasons he hadn't gagged her…yet.

He held his arms behind him, mirroring hers, and led her out of the causeway, past one of the three kitchens, and through an open terrace sitting area.

The warm breeze filled his lungs with the scent of rich soil, vegetation, and sunlight. The aroma of *vida*. One of his favorite features here was the ability to fold back the walls in every bedroom and living space and create this indoor-outdoor atmosphere.

"I thought mosquitoes were a plague in the jungle." She squinted against the rays that filtered through the overhead trellis. "Or maybe that's the idea. Are itchy, swollen bites one of your many methods of torture?"

"The balconies are above the tree tops, too high for insects. Turn right here." He let her lead one step ahead and into the expansive library so that he could savor the exploratory shifts in her gaze as she took in the estate for the first time. "There are mosquito repelling flowers planted at ground level, and we spray when needed."

"You say *we* as if your ass is out there exterminating bugs." She pursed her lips. "Or is that how you started in this business? Did you leave Texas to become a liveried servant for slave traders?"

"I was never a servant." He clenched his jaw at her blatant attempt to offend him. "But we employ a full staff. The servants live" — he pointed at a building nestled beneath a canopy of foliage — "there."

"Is that where I'll be staying?" Her eyes lowered to his dick and quickly snapped away. "Or do you keep all the slaves in a basement dungeon?"

"No dungeons." The holding cells were in the west wing. "*Tu vida es* with me."

"How does your boss feel about that?" Her gaze swept across his face and returned to the landscape. "Does he always let you keep random slaves for your sick enjoyment?"

"We both know you're not a random slave."

She pulled in a breath. "By *both*, do you mean you and me? Or you and Nico?"

"Hmm." A smile tickled his mouth. He'd let her stew on that for a while.

"What about the slaves in the living room?" she asked. "And all the ones that came before them? Do you rape them, too?"

He grabbed her arm, stopping her forward motion. "I'll allow your questions as long as the conversation interests me."

She limbered up her shoulders and curled her lip.

"Matters concerning Nico and our business are off limits." He tightened his grip. "Before you open your mouth, be damn sure it's a response befitting your station."

She rolled her jaw as if warring with her words, her eyes huge and feral. Then she looked away.

"Yes, Sir." She lowered her head.

Wicked satisfaction zipped down his spine and coiled low in his groin, throbbing urgency along his hardening shaft. He needed to bury himself inside her and fuck her vigorously and thoroughly until they were both spent. Christ, he'd fantasized about it since the moment he started beating off in their grove.

The end goal was to earn her loyalty and gain her consent, an undertaking that would require weeks, months, maybe longer. In the meantime, he was under no delusions that he had the strength or the honor to wait around while she worked shit out in her head.

He was going to use her body in every way he imagined. She could cry, spit, and writhe in her restraints. Hell, she would definitely be doing all of that, and he would devour every explosive second of it while her pussy clamped around his cock.

Keeping his distance from her for the past four years had nurtured vicious cravings inside him, warping his tastes into an almighty need for painful, destructive sex. He was going to fuck her until they were both annihilated. Until their broken pieces scattered in an unholy tangled mess. And when they put themselves back together, there would no longer be hers and his. Only *them*.

He didn't have to look inside her to know what she wanted. She'd come here, *willingly*, as a slave. She could tell herself it was a mission to stop slavery, but he knew she was searching for something to sate that which she didn't yet understand, yearning to face a fear that haunted her since her abduction.

She put herself in a position to be raped and tortured because, deep down, this was her way of stepping inside and showing her teeth.

Dammit, he wanted to belt her for being so fucking reckless. But at the same time, she'd finally given him the opportunity to help her. To be there for her when he'd failed so spectacularly in the past.

It was a reminder of why he'd waited. As much as he wanted her, the end result had always been about her and what she needed.

Releasing her arm, he swiped a hand down his face and stared at the tent in his pants.

# DISCLAIM

*She needs food and a shower, you impatient bastard.*

When he looked up, she tore her gaze away, face flushed. Probably a reaction she hadn't meant to make so obvious, but there it was. He affected her.

He reclaimed her arm and hurried her across a long balcony that served as an end cap for multiple bedroom suites and corridors that led to more bedrooms. Beyond the glass railing lay a deep valley of majestic Kapok trees.

"Who stays in those rooms?" She stared at the closed doors over her shoulder as she passed.

"There are dozens of guards and hired whores who live on site."

"Whores." Her voice tried for deadpan, but it cracked at the edges. "Is this where you've been living the last twelve years?"

"More or less." He tipped his head to the side and watched her eyes track a cloud shadow as it glided across the treescape. "This is our home base. The cartel's citadel." The sanctuary he always came back to.

How many times had he imagined bringing her here just to see her stand in awe of the place he called home?

Her blank expression offered zero fucks, but she wasn't fooling him.

Situated in the southern-most point of Colombia, the fortress was nothing short of spectacular. Bulletproof glass encased the exterior, presenting unobstructed, cinematic views of the self-contained enclosure of tropical rainforest. The kind of views National Geographic enthusiasts would jack off to from any angle in every room.

But security had been the central ethos that had led the construction of every square foot. Panic rooms, iris recognition scanners, tactical cameras, motion detectors, and fortified polycarbonate and ballistic steel building materials made the property virtually impenetrable.

On top of that, very few knew of its existence. Anyone idiotic enough to approach the perimeter wouldn't live long enough to beg for forgiveness.

She would be protected from outside threats, namely his enemies and anyone she might've pissed off in her war against slave traders. But it had taken an exorbitant amount of planning to relocate her here without adversely impacting his objective.

He wanted her completely—heart and soul. While that in itself might've seemed preposterous, his approach to winning her was even more outrageous. But he didn't have a choice. He was competing against a ghost.

His fists clenched. Her heart belonged to a boy who no longer existed. Well, fuck that motherfucker. That was the guy who didn't protect her a decade ago, who let her get kidnapped. That fucking guy failed her. *I failed her.*

He wouldn't fail her again.

"There's a lot of white." She stepped into another living room and nodded her chin at the flooring, walls, and furniture. "White, white, white. Not the best color scheme for blood stains." Her face tightened.

"Bleach is rather effective, but you already know that." Considering he'd disposed of fourteen bodies for her over the past ten years — slave buyers and their body guards. He'd dealt with the bodies, but she'd cleaned up the blood. "This way."

He reached the heavy wooden doors that barred entry to his personal space but didn't unlock them, his focus on the approaching heel-toe click of stilettos in the hall behind him.

"Welcome home, gorgeous," a familiar voice purred.

"Yessica." He turned to greet her, taking note of the way Camila stiffened beside him. "This is Camila." He twisted Camila around to face the other woman. "Camila. Yessica."

Despite the bottle blonde hair, Yessica's heritage oozed from every dip and curve on her body. Like most Colombian women, she had more of *it* on her legs and ass, a cola-shaped figure accentuated by a flat stomach and full hips.

"Aren't you a pretty little thing?" Yessica sashayed toward them, long legs stretching her red floor-length dress and heels tapping against the marble.

Camila looked up at him, eyebrow arched, giving him a delectable view of the twitch in her eye.

Maybe she was jealous, but despite the borrowed t-shirt, handcuffs, and knotted hair, Camila's natural beauty transcended that of every woman he'd ever seen, no matter how extravagantly primped, nipped, or tucked.

Not that Yessica had ever gone under the knife. Her tits were smallish, and she knew how to work them. But that didn't make her any less shallow. Her life's ambition was to be pampered by a wealthy man, and while there was revolution and poverty in Colombia, she refused to leave her homeland under the equatorial sun. So here she was.

"Are you keeping this one?" Eyes on Camila, Yessica trailed a blood-red fingernail along the neckline of his shirt.

"Have you checked your room?" He removed her hand from his throat. "I brought you some gifts from the States."

"Mmmm. I'm headed there now." She smoothed her palm over his shoulder and lifted up on her toes to press her lips against his ear. "Will I see you at dinner?"

"You will."

"Excellent." She turned to Camila. "Nice to meet you."

With a devious grin on her face, Yessica disappeared down the hall, exaggerating the movement of her hips and shoulders.

The ass shaking was usually for his benefit, but this one was undoubtedly meant to unnerve Camila. When it came to her competition, Yessica was one of those kill-em-with-kindness while stabbing-them-in-the-back kind of women.

"How long have you been tapping that?" Camila didn't even try to hide the bitterness in her voice.

"I have an idea." He turned toward the computerized pad on the wall, leveling his eye with the screen. "Let's share our sexual histories while I fuck you in the shower."

The retinal scanner blinked, and the double doors to his suite clicked open.

"God, you're a pig." She sneered. "No, scratch that. You're a disgusting boar."

In a flash, he cuffed a hand around her throat and slammed her back against the wall. "You forget yourself, Camila."

She closed her eyes, but that stubborn chin of hers jutted above his knuckles. "Forgive me, Sir."

The pulse point in her throat thudded steadily against his palm, but the moment he leaned in and touched his lips to her brow, he felt her heartbeat quicken.

Tenderness scared her more than cruelty. What a complicated, remarkable creature. It was no wonder she'd held his attention all these years.

Stepping back, he assessed her gaunt complexion, cracked lips, and sharper-than-normal cheekbones. She hadn't eaten or hydrated since last night, and her arms and shoulders must've been killing her from being restrained for so long. Yet she hadn't uttered a single complaint. She was a fucking trooper, and it only made him want her more.

He ushered her into his private suite, a domain that only three other people could access.

The doors locked behind him as he steered her toward the huge balcony where a dining table waited with an assortment of *arepas* and fruit.

"Sit." He pulled out a chair.

She lowered into the seat and eyed the food. "Impressive service. A benefit of working for a drug lord?"

Something like that.

He removed a key from his pocket, unlocked her cuffs, and set them aside. As she rubbed at her wrists, a pinch of guilt sneaked up on him. He shook it off.

"Put any notions of running out of your head. The only way in and out of here is by helicopter." He flicked a wrist at the roof. "Unless you have some latent survival skills." He gestured at the endless green beyond the railing. "You can try your luck out there."

Anyone else would've freaked the fuck out at the impossibility of escape, but not her. She poured a glass of water from the pitcher, leaned back in the chair, and drank deeply.

Because she didn't intend to escape, not without getting what she came for.

She'd already guessed that he'd expected her to arrive with Van Quiso. But she didn't know the half of it.

He had a myriad of bombs to drop on her, and each detonation needed to be thought out and timed perfectly. Like the one he was about to deliver.

As she piled her plate with *arepas* and dug in, she was probably mentally walking through a plan that relied on one key component if she failed. And she *would* fail.

Dipping into his pocket, he pulled out a tiny silver box and set it beside her plate.

She froze mid-chew and stared up at him, eyes hard and suspicious.

"Open it." He sat in the chair across from her, elbow on the table, chin on his fist. "Go ahead."

Swallowing a mouthful of ham and cheese, she lifted the lid and choked. "You fucking bastard."

Her hand shook, and the box tumbled from her fingers, spilling the smashed GPS chip and pieces of her filling on the table.

# TEN

"This is…" *Fuck, fuck, fuck.* Camila pressed her tongue against the filling in her tooth, struggling to speak amid the turbulence whipping inside her. "Why?"

"You know why." Matias leaned across the small table, hands folded on the white linen and eyes twinkling with smug victory.

Her lungs constricted, making it a bitch to breathe. She was so damn angry she didn't even know what she was asking him.

The doctor on the plane… What was his name? *Picar.* Was he a dentist? Or had someone else drilled into her teeth while she'd been unconscious all night?

"I'm not asking why you removed it." She mirrored his leaning position, bringing her face within a fist's swing of his. "Why did you fix it?" Her tongue swiped over the molar as she glared at the broken microchip beside her plate. "Why fill the tooth and let me think you hadn't found the chip?"

"There were exposed nerves that needed to be sealed before you woke." He shrugged. "I didn't want you to suffer."

*Is he serious right now?*

He smiled, flashing those deep dimples, and it was like staring at a terrible distortion of a precious memory. "The dentist was a trusted associate, exceptional at his trade, and was generous enough to meet us at our layover."

"Where was that?"

"The chip was disabled before you left the States."

Of course. Tate was probably losing his shit over the dead signal. He would track her last known position—likely some shady airport near the border—and assume the worst.

She blew out a breath. The GPS chip had been a safeguard, simply a backup plan if she didn't succeed.

But she could die here. In the cartel's citadel. Tate would never find her, would never stop the depraved transactions that happened within these walls.

She was on her own. A one-woman army against a powerful crime syndicate. And it all hinged on the man sitting across from her.

Matias knew she'd preemptively planted herself here, so there was no point in pretending. Since he hadn't asked her why she did it, he either knew that, too, or he didn't care. How much should she reveal? Maybe she should just lay it all out there and demand he put an end to the slave trading.

Right. When she'd woken in the living room, he was all *This is business* and *Go human slavery!* Had he been putting on a show for his boss, or had twelve years of crime well and truly carved out his heart? She needed to find out what his agenda was, where his loyalties lay, and how easily he could be turned.

"If I hadn't been there last night, would you have come?" She poured another glass of water and drank half of it. "Or would you have bought the girl who was supposed to be there?"

"I knew you'd be there."

"How?"

"I know everything." He grinned.

She seethed. "Does Nico know about our history?"

"I keep nothing from him." He watched her steadily from across the table.

*He could be lying.*

But why would he?

"What about the others?" She set the glass aside. "Do you share your personal life with Frizz, Picar, and whoever else lives here?"

"Some of them, yes. Others haven't earned my confidence." His fingers laced together, thumbs brushing lazily one over the other.

Faded ink sleeved both forearms, and at first glance, the matching designs appeared to be stars scattered among leaves. She lingered over the art, her gaze tracing the shaded lines of... *Not stars.* They were five-pointed blossoms on the branches of fruiting lemon trees. The same delicate blossoms he used to pick for her and put in her hair.

Memories uncoiled, tugging at emotions she'd tried so hard to keep contained. Her stomach hardened as beloved images blotted her vision. She'd spent her entire childhood with him, elbows-deep in lemon trees. His arms had once bore the scratches of mischief and labor. Now, they were permanently branded with those treasured moments, *their* moments, to remind her of everything she'd lost.

"Remember Venomous Lemonous?" His gaze lowered, resting on his tattoos.

"*Si*." She'd hated the old, cantankerous lemon farmer.

She couldn't remember his real name, but he'd worked in the grove most of her life. She and Matias used to sneak under his lemon trees to have…outercourse. Hands down each other's pants, bodies grinding, breaths heaving, tongues entangled. Just when they'd reach the heat of the moment, old Venomous Lemonous would slither out of the foliage, hollering and swinging his damn stick.

"He used to tell me"—Matias deepened his voice and scrunched up his face—"keep your root in your pants, boy, or it will do to her what spring does with the lemon trees."

The memory echoed hollowly in her chest. If Matias had knocked her up, would he have come back for her? Would Van have captured her? Would she be here now, grieving her past?

"Venomous Lemonous must've put the fear of God in you." She released a heavy sigh. "Since you did…you know, keep it in your pants."

Figuratively speaking. He'd never fucked her, but she'd been intimately familiar with every hard inch of him.

"I'm not that boy anymore." He slid his tongue across his bottom lip.

"And not just because you don't keep it in your pants." Roiling heat simmered in her belly.

Hell knew how many women he'd been with, consensual or otherwise. This was the guy that, less than an hour ago, made her choose which girl he would sell into slavery. Who stood by while a woman was burned, stitched in the eyelid, and hauled away. He was felonious, toxic, heartless.

But there was something else about him, something both troubling and captivating.

He reclined in the chair, legs spread wide and hands dangling loosely on the armrests. Dust covered his fatigues, ridges of muscle strained his t-shirt, and what looked like dried blood flecked the skin on his thick neck. No, that wasn't what was unsettling her.

Was it his expression? The way he regarded her, all moody and contemplative? Maybe it was the darkness that shadowed his face. The jet black hair that was clipped close on the sides and choppy on top, the stubble on his jaw and throat, the fringe of thick, smudgy lashes, and the heavy ridge of eyebrows that made his golden eyes glow with an intensity she felt beneath her rib cage. God, how he stared at her…

That was it.

Liv had told her once that a legitimate Master could command a woman using the power of his eyes.

What Camila saw in his gridlocked glare was an indisputable leader. A dominant male. When he fought, he won. When he wanted something, he took it. And right now, he wanted her attention, her nearness, her obedience.

Something inside her clicked into place, her entire body vibrating with the pull of an unbreakable string that drew her to him. She couldn't look away, couldn't breathe or speak.

She rose from the chair and closed the distance, her insides thrashing.

Wrought iron screeched against tile as he scooted back and tapped his inner thigh. A single tap and she was there, standing in the V of his legs, waiting for his next command with equal amounts of wonder and trepidation. *What's happening to me?*

"Remove the shirt."

Ahhh, that voice. He'd always known how to sweeten it to coax her and how to sharpen it in challenge. In three words, he achieved both.

She lifted the shirt over her head and let it fall to the floor.

He didn't move, didn't blink, but his taut inhale sounded like a whip cracking beside her ear. "Now the panties."

Her breath hitched. No underwear meant no more physical boundaries. She squeezed her eyes shut, breaking the spell.

A breeze from the ceiling fan brushed across her bare breasts, hardening her nipples. He'd seen it all before, most recently on the plane, but now that he'd declared his intent to claim her, exposing her pussy would feel more vulnerable, more significant.

She stole a glance at the ruined microchip on the table. She was just one girl, raised on a poor Texas farm. Completely out of her league.

But how many Restrepo enemies had made it this far? Did the FBI, DEA, or Colombian Police even know how to find this place? *No es probable.* Yet she stood within the walls of the cartel's lair, unrestrained and still breathing.

Steeling her spine, she resolved to see this through. For her survival. For the innocent lives they bought and sold.

She hooked her thumbs under the elastic at her hips, shoved the panties to the floor, and kicked them. The urge to curl inward and cover herself made her fingers tremble, but she fought it, adjusting her stance into one that had been beaten into muscle memory. Legs wide, hands behind her neck, back straight, tits out, eyes on him.

The heat of his gaze seared her pussy, and his fingers twitched against the armrests. She wished she hadn't waxed off all her pubic hair. She felt so damn bare and unprotected.

"I miss your soft curls here." He stroked the back of a knuckle across her mound. "No more waxing."

She shivered. She couldn't help it. It was the thick intonation of his voice, a subtle trace of Colombia. When she was sixteen, she'd clung to the gravely rumble of his timbre. And now, fuck, he still had the ability to make her wet with his voice alone.

He leaned forward, his lips a kiss away from her chest, warm breath on her nipples. She stifled a gasp as fingertips grazed her hipbones and roamed over her ribs, his hands shaking.

*Shaking?* She reared her head back. "Are you nervous?"

His expression hardened. He stood abruptly, snatched her wrist from behind her neck, and pulled her after him. Inside, through a sitting room, and down an enclosed hallway, they went.

"Do you know why I'm here?" She quickened her strides to keep her arm attached to her shoulder.

"Because I want you here."

"No, I mean do you know why I showed up with the man in the Mustang?"

"Van Quiso?" He slammed to a halt, causing her to crash into his chest as he whirled on her. "The *hueputa* who tortured you for a year?"

Cords pulled taut in his neck. Muscles and veins strained against the skin on his forearms, and the fingers around her hand cinched so tightly it felt like he was seconds from snapping bones.

She'd obviously hit an overprotective nerve, which was hypocritical as fuck seeing how she'd spent the last however many hours in his restraints.

"Don't hurt him." There was no love lost between her and Van, but she'd been making progress with the man.

"Give me a reason not to," he spat and turned away, yanking her into a massive bedroom.

"He's not worth your time, he loves his wife, and he doesn't give a shit about me. That's three." She glimpsed white walls, white bedding, and white woodwork before she was shoved into an all-white bathroom the size of her bedroom at home.

Oval glass tiles glittered like diamonds around the vanity on the wall to the left. Sunlight warmed her right side, spilling in through the floor-to-ceiling pane of glass that ran the length of the room. In the distance, a pair of blue and yellow macaws soared above the trees and perched in the leafy canopy. She stood there for a moment, contemplating the surrealistic beauty that enveloped her nightmare.

She was in Colombia, her parents' birthplace, with the boy she'd loved and lost—the man who'd become her enemy. The scenery shouldn't have been this awe-inspiring.

The white travertine floors cooled her bare feet as she stepped forward and followed him to the shower at the far end. But as she passed the separate toilet room, her bladder pinched.

He glanced at her face and waved a hand at the toilet. "Go."

A year without privacy in Van's attic made it easy to sit down and pee under Matias' watchful gaze.

"You haven't answered my question." She tore off a wad of toilet paper.

"Do I know why you tortured Larry McGregor for information? Why you killed him and pretended to be his delivery?" He twisted the shower faucet on and spun back toward her with fire in his eyes. "I know everything about you, *mi vida*."

How? A chill raced down her back. That meant Nico probably knew her plans, as well. Unless Matias was bluffing. Maybe he didn't know *everything*.

She wiped, flushed, and walked toward him, fingers twitching at her sides. "Who took my virginity?"

His gaze flew to her pussy, and his hand shot out and clutched the towel rack on the wall beside him. A second later, the brackets ripped from the woodwork, and metal hurtled through the room and crashed near the doorway.

She jumped, pulse hammering in her throat.

"Get in the shower." He thrust a finger at the walk-in enclosure.

The tiled space was large enough to wash a harem of women. She tried not to dwell on that as she stepped beneath the warm spray of multiple shower heads.

He tackled the laces on his boots, toed them off, then moved to his socks, shirt, fatigues, and…sweet God in heaven, he wasn't wearing underwear.

Maybe the steam was distorting her vision, but his cock looked so much longer, thicker, *harder* than she remembered. Where his body used to be tall, slender, and a little awkward, it was now broad, vascular, and stacked with brawn and power. Every inch of him was pure, raw testosterone.

Her knees loosened, and her skin flushed. Was it possible to sweat in water?

"Why did you tell me the GPS tracker was removed?" She gave him her back and grabbed the shampoo. "You could've let me go on thinking I had help coming."

His footsteps squeaked on the wet floor, closing in. She held her breath.

"The sooner you accept your future with me," he said, his mouth at her ear, "the easier this will be for you. Turn around."

She inwardly growled, shaking with the impulse to tell him what he could do with his orders. But she needed to pick her battles.

If she turned around, though, her brain would get all scrambled under the force of his eyes. And his cock, good God, it would be standing proud and right there between them.

*Just don't look at it.*

With a tight throat, she pivoted to face him.

# ELEVEN

Warm water rained down from the array of shower heads, heating Camila's skin. Or was it anxiety making her hot and itchy? Keeping her focus above Matias' waist as she angled her face out of the spray, her gaze landed on another tattoo.

At first glance, it looked like black veins forking over his shoulder. She felt him watching her as he turned to the side, allowing her to see the full image.

The outline of a tree trunk etched across his upper back and spread into leafless branches. The piece was twice the size of her hand and crawled over his shoulder. An orange tree. She'd recognize the rounded, symmetrical shape anywhere.

A closer inspection revealed two images in one, an optical illusion of limbs curving into the figure of a woman with hourglass hips and flowing black hair. Branches formed her slender neck, the bends of her arms behind her, the dip of her waist, all of which stemmed from the *V* at the apex of her thighs. It was eerily beautiful, unique, and really fucking sexy.

But an orange tree? A woman with long, black hair? Surely, it wasn't…

"Me?" She looked up and froze in the prison of his eyes.

He gave a terse nod, lifted the shampoo from her hand, and stepped behind her.

She stared at her toes in the swirl of water. He'd tattooed an image of her on his body.

That should've ignited her with outrage and confusion and sparked all kinds of questions. But dammit, her nerves were frayed, her body too tired to care. Way too tired to stop him from washing her hair, making her sigh with his distracting fingers, and massaging her scalp as the scent of citrus and lavender wafted around her.

After all these years, she still knew the feel of his strong hands, the muscles that thickened his palms, and the surety of his grip. She'd known how his mouth tasted after a long day in the sun, the way he'd moaned when she kissed that spot beneath his ear, and the intensity of his eye contact as he'd chased his orgasm.

"Tell me his name." He shifted around to her front, his hands lathered in soap.

"Who?"

"The one who took your virginity." His voice was soft, at odds with the teeth-breaking set of his jaw.

"Um…" She blinked through the deluge of water. "Oscar."

"Oscar?" He scowled, nostrils flaring. "That's not a name. It's processed meat."

"It *is* a name." She was pretty sure Oscar had been a manwhore, so maybe *processed meat* was more fitting.

"Did he make it good for you?" His tone was incisive, guttural.

"Two pumps and done."

His entire demeanor darkened. She knew what he was thinking. *It should've been him.*

He lathered her body, his hands sluicing soapy water from her neck to her toes and everywhere between. Fingers curved around her breasts, stroking, molding. She twitched away and raised her head, her gaze entangling with the luminous gold of his eyes.

Her breathing shortened, and his touch slid lower, down her sides, around her waist, stopping to palm her ass and squeeze her flesh.

"Matias, don't." She gripped his wrists, tried to push him away.

It only made him clench harder, putting enough pressure against the muscles on her backside that pain twinged through her nerve endings. Weightless energy charged through her — an intense kind of energy that buzzed like an angry vibrator in her pussy.

Straightening her upper body, she flexed her thighs, trying to block out the sensations he stroked between them.

He seemed to be pondering dour thoughts because his caresses grew rougher and less controlled, making her cringe.

"When you escaped Van Quiso and called me…" He crouched before her, eyes on her cunt as he traced the seam with a warm, wet finger. "You were a virgin then."

"Yeah." A shiver trickled down her spine.

She was grateful to have left the attic with that one part of herself intact. At the same time, it became a burden she'd carried for months after.

The label of innocence didn't quite fit after what she'd been through with Van. It'd felt like she was holding on to her virginity *because* of the abuse she'd endured.

When Oscar propositioned her in a coffee shop six months after her captivity, she'd been more than ready to prove she wasn't a fearful victim.

"You should've fucking told me how to find you." Without warning, Matias shoved a finger inside her and used it like a hook to yank her closer.

She gasped. Trying to buck free, she smacked at his arm and kneed his chest, but couldn't dislodge his finger. "I didn't know you anymore."

He'd been led from his home by armed men, and in the few phone conversations they'd had before her abduction, he'd acted so damn secretive and shady. He'd told her nothing, refused her questions, and hadn't come back for her when she still lived in the grove.

"I didn't trust you." She twisted her hips away from his hand, going nowhere. "As it turns out, I have killer instincts."

"You were wrong." He launched to his full height and squeezed her neck as he added another finger inside her, thrusting them mercilessly and wrenching a whimper from her. "And you're wrong now. I will never forgive you for hanging up on me. For making me wait a fucking year before you called again. Making me wait while you spread your legs for other men."

There was so much pain in his voice, in the taut line of his shoulders, the glaze in his citrine eyes, the vicious drive of his fingers making her pussy ache.

"You're hurting me." She clawed at the hand around her neck.

"You hurt *me!*" He tightened his grip, holding her back against the wall. "You were mine, goddammit!"

"Yours?" Her temper inflamed, flushing her system with adrenaline. "When I called that day, were *you* mine? Were you a twenty-year-old virgin holding out for his childhood sweetheart?"

"I did wait for you!" Flexing his hand at her throat, his other withdrew from between her legs to stab through the wet strands of her hair. He yanked at the roots as he tipped back her head. "I waited until I could come back for you. Waited a fucking year. Then you disappeared, and I thought…" The anger drained from his voice, and his forehead dropped to her temple, his breath hot on her face. "I thought you were dead."

Her throat closed up, her eyes burned, and she felt an overwhelming urge to wrap her arms around him.

*He's a slave trader, living in luxury that's paid for in innocent lives.*

"I was gutted." He trailed fingers over her shoulder and around her breast, the hand on her throat loosening. "Consumed with rage. A nineteen-year-old kid with so much hatred eating me up. I fought and drank and killed." He pinched her nipple, squeezing painfully. "Then I fucked a whore in an alley."

Her chest caved in beneath a barrage of jealousy. And rage. So much fucking rage it seethed from her pores. He should've returned for her. Should've talked to her, confided in her, *trusted* her. Then he never would've had to stick his dick in a whore. Fuck him.

"The next day…" He brushed his lips across her cheek. "I got the shoulder tattoo."

A branding of guilt. He deserved it.

Except she understood that odious feeling. She'd starved herself for weeks after she gave her first time to Oscar. She hadn't belonged to Matias, but all of her firsts had been meant for him.

He released her throat, and when he lifted his head, his haunted eyes filled her horizon. Her brain couldn't reconcile the look on his face with the cold-hearted man auctioning off women in the living room.

Going into this, she'd known rape was on the table. She had an IUD to prevent pregnancy, but STDs were one of the many known risks. One risk she hadn't calculated was having sex with Matias. Whether it would be willing or forced, it was a threat to her heart, one that could destroy her.

He gripped her wrists and pinned them against the wall above her head. She anticipated what was coming and couldn't stifle the feelings exploding inside her. Her legs shook, and the inner muscles contracted and heated. For years, she'd imagined him between her thighs, his body a pillar to hold on to, and his groans a comforting embrace.

The lean muscles of his chest flexed, and his full mouth parted as his wet body slid against hers. He pressed his hard length against her pussy, seeking entry, his gaze feral.

He shifted her wrists to one hand and grabbed the base of his cock. Stroking himself, pressing his body impossibly close to hers, he licked the seam of her lips then kissed her like he'd waited his entire life for this very moment. His hard, frantic nips and urgent flicks of his tongue left her gasping, biting, reciprocating.

Hunger coiled between her legs, and her clit throbbed beneath the massaging glide of his length. She wished her arousal was a trained response, but Jesus have mercy, she wanted him. Wanted him in her.

She rocked her hips, needing more friction as she chased his tongue and devoured his lips.

"I've waited so long for this," he breathed between kisses, his eyes molten gold.

Without looking away, he speared his fingers inside her, spread her open, and slid his cock along her folds. Fucking her without penetration.

*Just like old times.*

She tried to disassociate what was happening now from her cherished memories, but the pieces of her that would always want him were breaking open and messing with her mind. As he nudged the broad head of his erection at her opening, her pleasure centers fired in excitement, and her heart pounded frantically, even as her brain screamed *no.*

He stilled, his breath cutting off as his smoldering gaze drilled into her.

Holy fuck, this was it. She couldn't breathe.

The hand on her wrists clamped to the point of pain, and his head whipped around to look over his shoulder.

"I need you in the west wing." Nico's accent echoed through the bathroom.

Heat rushed to her cheeks as she peered around Matias' stiff shoulders. What the hell was Nico doing here? In Matias' bathroom? Without fucking knocking?

"Sorry about the timing, *parce.*" Nico stood a few feet away, hands in his pockets, his scowl prominent amid his dark trimmed beard. "This can't wait." With a sharp glare in her direction, he strolled out of the room.

"Fuck!" Matias released her and shoved his hands through wet hair. "Fucking fuck!"

She sagged against the wall, her body buzzing and head spinning. Just a sliver of another second and he would've been inside her. Their first time together. Connected in the way she'd always imagined. So fucking close.

She should've felt relieved. Should've been over-fucking-joyed by the interruption. Instead, her heart felt like it was shrinking.

Matias smacked the faucet, turning off the water. Then he stood there, swiping his palms down his face, his body a vibrating coil of tension.

How was he okay with Nico coming into his bathroom and ordering him around? It was either a really close relationship or an authoritarian one.

Maybe she should dry off, try to wipe away the last few minutes. As she moved to step out, he beat her there.

Wrapping a towel around his waist, he held one out for her. "Let's go."

Go? She assumed this was a business call. Would he take her with him? Hope bubbled up. She needed to get a lay of the land. *And cool off her damn libido.*

In the bedroom, he dragged on black suit pants, tucking his

erection to the side as he zipped up. *No underwear.*

She bit her lip. What was she supposed to wear? She dried off and looked around.

A wall of windows led to another balcony. A king-sized bed sat in the corner of the room, draped in white fabrics. Couches and chairs formed a horseshoe in front of a fireplace. And a large column stood in the center of the room, rising up to the apex of the vaulted ceiling. Everything painted in white.

"Kneel beside the post." His voice crept over her shoulder, shockingly close.

She turned to face him. He wore a black button-up tucked into the narrow waist of his pants.

In his hand dangled a length of chain. Her stomach collapsed, and she spun back to the post. There, screwed into the wood near the floor, was a metal ring.

"If I told you I wanted to leave," she said, mouth dry, "that I wanted to go home, would you let me?"

"Never." He walked past her, locked the chain to the metal ring, and held on to the leather collar at the other end. "You want to be owned."

"Said no slave ever." She stood her ground. "But I won't try to escape. You don't need to chain me."

He widened his stance, hands clasped at his back with the short chain hanging behind him. But it was the cutting look in his eyes that made her shake from head to toe. It conjured dark enclosed places, ear-piercing screams, and bruising thrusts against the back of her throat.

Her heartbeat went ballistic, banging in her ears. He wasn't Van, but he wasn't Matias, either. The man standing before her made a living off of human pain, and his interest in her was personal.

She lowered her head, her feet moved, and the sour taste of dread flooded her mouth.

Lifting the towel from her grip, he folded it on the floor in front of his shiny shoes. Then he straightened and touched his lips to her forehead.

She cringed, eyes glued to the square of terrycloth, knowing what he wanted and inwardly fighting it.

*You won't win this battle. Focus on the end goal.*

Methodically, one muscle at a time, she knelt for him. Back straight, weight evenly balanced between her hips, palms facing outward on her thighs, eyes on his belt. Then she adjusted, spreading her legs shoulder width apart to allow full view of her pussy, her skin prickling with self-loathing.

"Your orgasms belong to me." He glanced at the ceiling and the camera tucked in the corner. "I'll know if you touch yourself."

She gritted her teeth. *As if!*

"Any man can chain you to a post." He buckled the leather collar around her neck, securing it with a four-digit padlock.

The leather sat snugly against her skin, the gravity of it choking her air.

"Any man can rip off your clothes." He tested the chain between her neck and the wooden column. "Fuck your throat, call you a whore, and you might even like it. That's rough, gritty sex. But it isn't dominance."

Her heart stuttered. He'd described her experience with Van so accurately.

He glided a finger across the line of her jaw, tilting her face upward. "Dominance is when I kiss your brow and you obediently lower to the floor. Willingly. No hesitation." His eyes flashed. "It's when you kneel for me, give me the power to break you inside and out, and trust that I won't. You will surrender your vulnerability without shame, because that's what I want, and what I want, you crave."

"You're delusional." She struggled to swallow. "I'm not—"

"You're not there yet. So in the meantime, I'll settle for rough, gritty sex."

With that, he left her trembling on her knees.

# TWELVE

Instinct guided Camila through the next few hours. Naked and shivering with raw nerves, she'd attempted dozens of combinations on the lock she couldn't see at her throat. She'd tried to unscrew the metal ring on the post until her fingers turned red. Then she'd walked the radius, measuring the span of the chain.

With arms out, she could stretch about six feet in every direction, but the bed sat twice that far. The bathroom, couches, and built-in wall cabinets were even farther. The doors to the hall and balcony closed off the exit points. Another door, also shut, must've led to a closet. There was nothing within reach except the towel and an expanse of gleaming white marble floors.

Not that she intended to break out of this fortress, but dammit, she needed to snoop through drawers and closets to find out what Matias was hiding, anything that might explain why he was so obscure.

She glanced up at the camera in the ceiling. Was he watching her now, waiting for another reason to hurt her?

There was also a building pressure in her bladder. Probably shouldn't have drunk so much water, but *come on!* Van would've at least given her a bucket to piss in.

Restless and wary, she paced circles around the pole like a tetherball, switching directions, and pacing again. She replayed her conversations with Matias, searching every interaction for hidden meanings in his words, clues that would indicate there wasn't a monster behind those mercurial eyes.

But she recalled nothing helpful. Everything he'd said and done implied he was one-hundred-percent invested in the cartel. *And owning her.*

When she'd asked him where she'd be staying, he'd said her life was with him, diminishing any hope of disentangling her past from the present. This was no longer just a battle against slave traders. She would be fighting to protect the heart of the girl he'd abandoned in the citrus grove.

She gripped the chain and yanked. *Fuck!* How long would he keep her locked up?

God, she'd thought she was so fucking clever. Thought she could just smuggle her way into a slave ring and single-handedly take out the asshole in charge.

She didn't know shit.

How arrogant of her to assume she'd end up in the boss's bed. While she didn't want to be anywhere near Nico Restrepo, the alternative called into question some seriously conflicted desires.

She glared at Matias' bed across the room. *Forgive him. Bite off his dick. Fuck his brains out. End his life.*

No, killing him wasn't an option. To put an end to the cartel's slave trading, she needed to get to Nico. To do that, she'd have to win over Matias by any means necessary.

*I'll settle for rough, gritty sex.*

She could still feel his voice vibrating through her, and she shuddered anew. Worse, he knew he affected her. He wasn't a stranger she could inveigle and trick. He could see past her act, undress her mind, and fuck her thoughts.

She tapped her fingers against her thighs and pulled in a deep breath.

When they were kids, she'd anticipated what he wanted and followed his every whim without reservation. Hell, she'd followed him around like a lost puppy. But he was also two years older.

No, that wasn't why. There had always been a captivating shift in the air around him. A dominant man stretching the skin of his prepubescent body. A Master lying in wait.

She leaned against the post and slid to the floor, tucking her knees to her chest. With a shaky hand, she traced the stiff band of leather around her neck. The texture and weight felt like Van's restraints, but the similarities ended there.

Being bound by Van had made her feel defenseless, trapped, uncared for like an insignificant nothing. But this… She pressed her palm against the leather, squeezing it around her throat. Matias' collar felt like armor, *his* armor, protecting her from the world. Why? Because they shared history? Or were his parting words messing with her?

*Kneel for me…give me the power to break you…trust that I won't.*

Funny thing, trust. It was so hard to give, yet easy to rip away. He'd earned her trust through sixteen years of friendship. Then he'd lost it. Not the day he left, but in the phone call that came a month after. It'd been the coldness in his tone and the furtive way he'd steered the conversation away from commitment and love. He'd chosen his future, and it hadn't included her.

She lowered her hand to the round metal tag that hung on the collar, tracing the engraving for the hundredth time. What she wouldn't give to know what it said. Was it his name and phone number like a damn dog tag? A quote from a handbook on how to destroy human lives? Or was it something personal, like his tattoos? Not likely. Dozens of his slaves had probably worn this very collar.

She sucked in a breath, hating that the pang in her chest was jealousy of other women rather than remorse for the abuse that might've occurred. Yet the idea of being owned by him, being the only one he'd ever kept, made her crave things—filthy, kinky things she'd fantasized about during sex.

It didn't matter how skilled her lovers had been, none had taken her to the depths she hungered for. No matter how much she begged, no one spanked her long enough, choked her hard enough, or left her unable to think afterward, lost to sensations. She ached to be fucked violently and loved tenderly, and for the life of her, she didn't understand why.

She wasn't one of those women who needed a man, but she longed to be the kind of woman a man couldn't live without. And while Matias' intentions hovered somewhere between terrifying and soulless, the way he looked at her made her feel treasured. Protected.

His spoken promises should've horrified her. Instead, they poked at the twisted parts of her soul that wanted things she was too afraid to ask for.

What the hell was wrong with her? This wasn't Stockholm Syndrome—she'd loved him before he was her captor. Insanity, maybe? Brain damage? Or just good, old-fashioned stupidity.

As the balcony glowed orange in the blaze of the sinking sun, interior lamps flickered on around the room. Growing more distressed about his return, she resumed pacing, which seemed to ease her irritated bladder. She considered peeing on the floor and thought better of it. Van would've pressed her face in the mess. Who knew what Matias would do?

An hour after sunset, footsteps sounded in the hall. As if compelled by the confident pace of the strides, she knelt at attention on the towel, facing the door. With shins placed against the floor, thighs vertical, and body held upright, she positioned her arms in strappado—behind her back with elbows, forearms, and wrists pressed together with imaginary restraints.

It was sick the way her pussy clenched in anticipation. She'd fantasized being taken by him—forcibly, passionately—since forever, but the circumstances were all wrong. *He* was all wrong. Her insides knotted.

Still, she kept her attention on the door, anxiously awaiting his expression upon finding her posed in presentation.

The knob turned, and the door swung open, revealing the golden flames of his eyes, motionless in a sea of crimson.

Blood spattered his face and throat and caked the ink on his forearms where he'd rolled up his sleeves. His black shirt and pants glistened with wetness, and his hands clenched at his sides as he stared at nothing.

"What happened?" Her heartbeats fell hard, her posture crumbling. "Are you hurt?"

He didn't look at her, didn't acknowledge her in any way as he stepped into the bedroom. No noticeable limping. Not a hint of physical pain or visible wounds beneath the smears of blood.

Stopping at a built-in cabinet, he opened the doors to a wet bar and poured a glass of *aguardiente,* neat, the way Colombians preferred their soft vodka.

She wanted to ask him whose blood he was covered in, hoping with every shuddering breath that the gore didn't belong to one of the captured women. "Matias?"

His entire body stiffened, the glass hovering midway to his mouth. Maybe this wasn't the best time to call attention to herself.

He swallowed back the *guaro* in one gulp, poured another, and carried it into the closet. When he disappeared beyond the doorway, she couldn't see inside, but the retreat of his footfalls hinted at the extensive depth of the room.

She pressed her lips together and sat back on her heels. Did he get in a fight? Torture someone? Stand too close to a ritualistic slaughter?

Her stomach rolled. Maybe this was just a normal day of work for him. Except the crystallized glaze in his eyes suggested that whatever happened had rattled him.

A moment later, he exited the closet, carrying a fraternity paddle, a cane, handcuffs, and a ball gag. His stony gaze landed on her.

"What're you doing?" Her pulse went crazy as she scrambled to her feet and shuffled backward until the chain snapped her to a halt. "I behaved while you were gone. I fucking knelt for you!"

Jesus, he hadn't even changed his clothes, standing there like a blood-soaked nightmare. And his eyes... Something wasn't quite right in the shadows behind those unmoving flames.

He dropped his bundle on one of the armchairs and dragged the chair toward her, its legs squealing across marble.

Parking it just out of her reach, he stood so very still and silent, intent on watching her while her insides fell apart and her bladder screamed to spill all over the floor.

"I have to pee, Matias." Her voice wavered. "And you need a shower. I'll help you clean up."

He continued to stare, studying her in a detached way. No, not studying. He seemed to have retreated inward, mentally shut down. His hand blindly swept over the chair and picked up the ball gag.

*Shit shit shit!*

"Matias? Remember when I got this?" With trembling fingers, she parted the hair on her scalp.

His gaze flicked to the jagged scar above her hairline and returned to her mouth without a trace of emotion.

She was seven when she fell out of the orange tree, busting her head open and bleeding all over the place. "Do you remember what you told me?"

"An ounce of bravery is more valuable than a gallon of blood." His voice was ice grinding against rock. "Andres taught me that. Then he died a coward's death."

What did that mean? His uncle had perished in the fire that had taken her family. A conversation for another time.

"The day I got this scar," she said hoarsely, "you promised me you would never let me fall again."

If she reached out an arm, she could touch his sticky shirt. But she didn't dare.

He stood taller, his chin level with her forehead as he lifted the ball gag. "Open your mouth."

"Don't do this." She shook her head, eyes blurring. "Don't hurt me."

"If you fight me, what will I do?" His tone held no pitch or fluctuation.

*Take it out on someone else.*

She tensed with the compulsion to kick out a leg, knock him off balance, and lock him in a chokehold. Then what? She was chained to a fucking pole.

Her attention flew to the cane and paddle. Deep down, she believed he wouldn't kill her. Probably wouldn't make her bleed either, no matter how badly this would hurt.

She stretched open her mouth.

His lips curved, but there was no pleasure in his smile. No dimples. No emotion whatsoever as he pressed the rubber ball between her teeth and secured the strap behind her head. Thank God, his hands were free of blood, washed clean up to the wrists. Or he'd worn gloves.

"Face down." He stabbed a finger toward the floor. "Legs spread wide and pray to hell."

A punishment position, one that allowed full access to the tender areas of her body. She lost control of her breathing, her tongue pushing against the gag as her skin broke out in a cold sweat.

She must've hesitated too long, because he grabbed her hair and forced her to the floor on her stomach. With his knee digging against her back, he wrenched her arms behind her, forcing her hands in a reverse prayer position and securing them in the cuffs. Then he grabbed the long wooden paddle.

Tremors assaulted her arms and legs, and her throat sealed up. Didn't matter how high her pain tolerance, this was going to hurt like a motherfucker. She might've fantasized about Matias spanking her, choking her, and fucking her to near-death, but the truth was, she didn't *enjoy* pain. Unless…maybe…it was inflicted with love.

*There's no love here.*

Her reflexes begged her to fight him off, but experience had taught her that tensing muscles beneath a strike resulted in days of painful bruising. So when he removed his knee from her back and replaced it with the heat of his hand, she let her body go limp and focused on breathing deeply.

Before she drew her second breath, a whistling scream cracked the air, and the paddle made contact in a fiery explosion of broken skin.

# THIRTEEN

Camila howled against the gag, her teeth sinking into rubber as Matias swung again and again. He'd skipped the goddamn warm up and slammed her straight into a body-twitching, skin-burning overload of agony.

Kneeling at her side with his weight braced on the hand at her back, he struck her ass and the backs of her thighs with deep, swift, penetrating thuds. Had she been standing, the first hit would've knocked her over. As it was, it felt like he was beating her into the floor.

*Stop! Dios mio, es demasiado. It's too much.* Her screams garbled against the gag as every hit vibrated through her like a muscle-thumping bass note, chattering her teeth and blazing fire down her legs. *Please make it end.* She wanted to curl into a ball, close her eyes, and dream all of this away. And never wake up.

The fucking wooden paddle didn't let up, its rigid width covering such a huge impact area she felt it everywhere. Each heavy, hard-hitting blow stopped her heart and lingered long after the next thud. Her vision blurred, her lungs wheezed, and her bladder felt like it was going to burst.

*No más, por favor. No more!*

She attempted to slow down her breathing, but she couldn't tune out the anguish. So she tried to experience it as an observer, focusing on where each burning sensation originated, where it ended, what shape it was, and how deep it sank into muscle and bone. The exercise pushed her through the worst of it, but eventually, dizziness set in, endorphins flooded her bloodstream, and darkness invaded the edges of her consciousness.

Just when she thought she would pass out, he tossed the paddle in the chair. "If you need to pee, do it now."

He didn't move to unchain her. Piss on the floor then? Maybe he got off on that brand of humiliation, but she was in too much pain to give a fuck. Except, when she tried to release her bladder, it wouldn't relax. She concentrated harder. Nothing. Was it shock? Stage fright?

She bit down on the rubber ball and glared at him through her tears.

Caked in blood, expression vacant, eyes cold, he was death and hell and the devil that ruled it all.

Hooking a finger through the ring on the collar, he dragged her to her knees. For an ignorant moment, she thought he was finished.

Without meeting her eyes, he arranged her lethargic, aching body against the post. On her knees, back against the column, and shins bracketing the base, she felt a tug at her wrists. Heavy deadness pulled on her eyelids. She blinked, tried to keep hold of awareness, but she had no fight left.

The smack of a hand across her cheek snapped her awake, and her attention fell on his bloody shirt. *Oh God, this is still happening.*

Her breaths came in asthmatic bursts. She tried to pull her arms forward, but they remained where they were, hugging the post at her back and locked with metal rings.

Saliva pooled around the ball in her mouth and trickled down her chin as her entire body shook beneath a rush of adrenaline and whatever morphine-like chemicals her brain had released. She wished she was drugged or drunk. Or dead.

He picked up the cane, and she swung her head left and right. She couldn't do this. No more pain. *Please, Matias!*

Like the paddle, he didn't ease in. The cane flew through the air and landed on the front of her thigh.

"Noooo" ripped from her throat in a keening, indistinguishable wail.

The cutting stripe seared a trail of heat across her skin, followed by another and another.

Her chin dropped to her chest with the weight of her head, and she watched with horror as each new welt bloomed on her thighs. The cane never slowed. Ladder-like cuts formed, some of them torn and bleeding on the surface. It was if he were trying to mark every inch of skin between her groin and knees.

She'd rarely cried after those first few days in Van's attic, and she hadn't intended to now. Except this was Matias, her childhood best friend, beating her body to a pulp.

Tears coursed down her cheeks, and a heavy, helpless feeling settled in her chest. But amid the heartache throbbed something sharper, darker. Something so very wrong.

Her gaze lifted to the zipper of his pants, where the long, hard outline of his erection strained against the fabric. She looked up at his eyes and found a smoldering flicker had chased his coldness away.

His breathing lost rhythm, and his hand shook as he lowered the cane. He was turned on by this, by her responses, her body? Whatever it was, his arousal fed hers, awakening the nerve-endings in her pussy and soaking her with heat as images of him coming on her abused body flashed through her mind.

Her stomach cramped with disgust and shame. Why was she so fucked up in her head?

If he were any other man, she would've vomited against the gag. The only reactions Van had stirred in her were raw fear and rage. But Matias was deep beneath her skin, his gaze touching her everywhere, heating her from the inside out.

He dropped the cane, and it clattered across the floor.

She sagged in relief, wobbling on her knees as every welt on her body pulsed with the beat of her heart. When she caught her breath, she dragged her gaze to his.

"You're a fucking feast for the eyes, Camila." He stared down at her, no smile, but his dimples flashed.

While life seemed to be returning to his face, she could feel the last trickle of energy draining from her limbs. He caressed her cheek, and she didn't have the strength to pull away. Until his other hand opened his zipper.

Eyes wide, she made a groaning noise against the rubber ball.

His blood-soaked pants slipped down his thighs as he freed his cock. He fisted the length, gliding his hand up and down. A vein bulged along the shaft, the crown swollen and wet with precum. He tilted his head back, and his jaw looked so fucking strong, so powerful shadowed in stubble and clenching harder and harder with each vigorous stroke.

"No teeth, Camila." He pinned her with an intractable glare and released the buckle on the gag.

The instant it fell from her mouth, he thrust past her lips and hit the back of her throat.

She gagged, convulsing and drooling, but he didn't pause or slow.

"Oh fuck." Tremors skated across his thighs as he dragged his length over her tongue. "So fucking good." He circled his hips and gripped the post with one hand while holding on to her head with the other. "Goddamn, I missed your mouth."

Tears blinded her eyes. She choked and sucked air, her hands twisting in the cuffs. She had nowhere to go, couldn't move, couldn't breathe. She sure as hell didn't roll her tongue or do anything to increase his pleasure. She was just a hole pinned to post, a face to brutally fuck.

And he did, every slam of his hips adding another fissure in her memories until the rot seeped out. Van's musky scent. The coarseness of his hair against her nose. The ruthless hammer of his dick in her mouth.

"Stay with me, *mi vida*." Matias gripped her jaw with both hands and forced her eyes to his. "I know what he did to you, and that's not what this is."

Yes, it was! Only so much worse. Van had beaten and tormented her to terrify her into obedience. He'd made her powerless in her pain and humiliated by her pleasure. With Matias, her depraved desires came from a completely different place, the part of her that had never stopped loving him.

He stared at her like he could feel her anguish, as if he longed to take it away. His expression softened, his eyes watchful. *Thoughtful.* So unlike the man who just caned her. Jesus, what the hell was happening?

At least with Van, she'd known he was the enemy every harrowing hour she spent in his attic. But this man? He was the criminal who petrified her and the lover she longed to lay beneath while he did all manner of dirty things to her. It threw her off balance and made her want to lash back with burning revulsion.

Without looking away, he widened his stance, his breaths quickening and fingers tightening against her cheeks. He was close. *Please hurry.*

His body became a piston, flexing and jerking as he found his release. The next thrust sent a shock wave down his thighs. He pulled out then sank deeply, his hands shaking as he shouted to the ceiling. "Fuuuuuck!"

Salty come shot down her throat, and his cock slid free from her lips. She vibrated with a full-body shiver, her lips tingling with his taste and her pussy aching to be touched, filled, pounded.

It had been twelve years since she'd taken him in her mouth. She struggled to make sense of the man staring down at her while her mind clung to the boy who used to guide her lips to him, slowly ease his girth in and out, and encourage her with softly whispered words. The boy who never orgasmed without seeing to her pleasure first.

Now he simply stared down at her as her ass throbbed and her thighs lit with pain, with no relief in sight.

He kicked off his shoes and made fast work of stripping his bloody clothes. Fully nude and partially erect, he removed her cuffs, unlocked the chain from the collar, and lifted her off the floor.

Cradled against the damp skin on his chest, she let her head loll against his shoulder. Every shift against him made the welts on her thighs throb with heat. She couldn't bring herself to do anything but droop in his arms.

He carried her into the bathroom and set her on the toilet. Her bladder released immediately, and a wave of vertigo sent her canting sideways.

His hands caught her shoulders, his broad body crouching in front of her. "You need to eat."

"I need anslers…answers. Shit, I'm slurring." She couldn't make her mind work, every part of her over-stimulated. *Lost to sensations.*

"It's the intensity of the pain." Something slipped behind his eyes, there and gone before she could identify it. He scratched at the blood on his neck. "The adrenaline burns off quickly, but the endorphins linger, creating a *crash.*"

Rage powered through her spent muscles. "How many torture sessions did it take for you to learn that?"

He stared her down as if trying to frighten her. She wanted to smack that look right off his fucking face, but she couldn't summon the strength. So she stared right back, despite the tremble in her chin.

Rather than giving her time to wipe and flush, he scooped her off the toilet and stood her on her feet in the shower.

Soap in hand, he scrubbed them both with clinical efficiency, his expression tight with concentration.

She leaned against his chest, hating that she needed his support to stand, but the floor was tilting. The room darkened. Too dark. She couldn't see. She didn't care.

A towel wrapped around her, then his arms, and she floated.

She must've passed out, because her eyes blinked open to a fully-dressed Matias. He wore a charcoal suit and a gold button-up that he'd left open at the neck. His dry hair spiked in chaotic strands that fell over his brow.

Lying face up on the bed, she was dressed, too…partly. A stiff, silver corset strangled her torso, and lacy black panties rode high on her ass. She looked around the room. Where were the rest of her clothes?

"I need you to get through the next few hours." His hands slid over her thighs, working a glob of ointment into the cuts.

Dread simmered in her empty stomach. "What's the next few hours?"

"Dinner." He capped the tube of ointment and grabbed her hand, guiding her to the full-length mirror propped in the corner.

"Dinner with who? Where? What am I supposed to wear?" She met his eyes in the mirror.

Standing behind her, he combed fingers through her hair, arranging the length to fall in waves around her shoulders. She'd always considered her hair black, but even semi-damp, it wasn't as dark as his.

Same for her complexion. By no means was she pale, but she looked straight-up white next to him.

His frame dwarfed her, twice as wide and a head taller, and now she knew what it felt like to be on the receiving end of that strength. As if his size wasn't intimidating enough, the way he raked his sharp focus over her reflection made her want to retreat to the floor in a fetal position.

He'd shown up in her life out of nowhere, beaten her without purpose, fucked her mouth, then tended to her. He was either pathologically insane or there was something else here at play. Was he putting on an act for someone? For Nico? Or for whoever was on the other side of that camera lens? What was their hold over Matias, and how could she use that to her advantage?

She glanced down at the rows of cuts reddening her thighs. He'd hurt her ruthlessly, callously, but she'd endured the same in Van's attic. It was the slew of unanswered questions that scared her the most, and her mind raced to dissect the last twenty-four hours. But she narrowed her focus to the topic that mattered.

"I put myself here because I want to help people. Women, just like me. I thought..." Her voice wobbled, and as much as she tried, she couldn't drag her eyes to his in the mirror. "I thought you cared about me."

His chest rose and fell heavily behind her, but he said nothing.

"Stop trafficking humans. That's all I want." Her chin trembled. "Please."

"No." One word, crisp and final.

Her heart sank, but she would keep trying, keep pushing for as long as it took.

The metal tag glinted on the collar, catching her attention. She leaned forward, squinting to unscramble the reversed reflection of text.

*Don't fuck with my property.*

Meaningless. Impersonal. Recyclable. Was that how he viewed whatever this was with her?

"Let's go." He gripped her hand and pulled her toward the exit.

"Wait." She tugged at the corset's bust line, where it rested just above her nipples. "Not like this.

The burnish of his eyes darkened ominously. "Exactly like this."

# FOURTEEN

Matias had done some godawful shit over the years. Theft, torture, slow agonizing fucking deaths as he brought unfathomable hell upon too many to count. But he'd never deliberately harmed Camila, not the way he had tonight.

With heavy footsteps and a strangling ache in his chest, he led her out of his suite.

Beating the ever-loving shit out of her had not only killed something inside him, it moved him in the opposite direction of his goal. But those marks on her body were necessary.

Forcing himself in her mouth, though? That had been for him.

The sight of her nude body, kneeling, collared, and trembling when he'd opened the door... Fuck! She'd stripped away her fears for him. It was the most seductive thing she could've done.

And he'd repaid her by fucking her throat raw.

Clawing branches of guilt stabbed in his gut. Not only was he a selfish fucking prick, he was pushing her too fast, too soon. All that talk about dominance and her willingness to submit had been ill-timed. While he'd passionately meant every word, he needed to earn her consent first.

Her bare feet padded along the marble as he guided her out of the east wing and through the foyer. Arms clutching her body and shoulders hunched, she seemed to be trying to hold herself together. No doubt she was exhausted, wracked with pain, and fuming fucking mad.

He would've preferred to leave her in the room, but that wasn't how things worked around here. If a cartel member stole a new assault rifle, he showed it off to his buddies. If a lieutenant or drug lord acquired a new slave, he brought her to dinner. The last thing Matias wanted was to raise suspicion, not after what had happened in the west wing tonight.

In the States, the *war on drugs* put crackheads in jail for little baggies and taught grade-schoolers how to sing jingles about the evils of marijuana. But south of the border? The war was real, and narcotics were just a drop in a cartel's bucket.

Matias covered the gamut of criminal commerce, from trafficking weapons and humans to smuggling immigrants and terrorists — all of which made his wallet fat and his dick hard, proving that he was, without question, a very bad man.

The fucked up part? He didn't give a rat's ass, and that made sweeping Camila off her feet one helluva challenge. Figuratively sweeping, of course. He could force her to her knees anytime he wanted. What he couldn't force her to do was offer her soul in supplication.

He wanted her to love every piece of him, even the most depraved and unworthy pieces. *Especially those.* In return, he would protect her soul, cherish it, and put it at peace again.

He rested a hand on the rise of her ass and slipped a finger beneath the tight cinch of the corset. As much as he enjoyed her on her knees, he preferred this — the rigidity of her backbone — as her gorgeous legs stretched to match his strides.

She wielded the kind of inner strength that would intimidate an average man. He fucking loved that about her. So much so he'd spent the last four years shifting the world beneath her feet to ensure that when she finally offered him her soul, she would do so with her integrity and backbone fully intact.

"Will you talk about what happened?" She peeked at him through her lashes as they rounded a bend in the hall. "About what upset you before you…" She pressed her lips together. "Before you came back to the room?"

The hallway was empty, and they hadn't passed another person since exiting his suite. But the walls had ears.

"No." He studied her huge disappointed eyes and reconsidered. "Maybe later."

The grooves in her forehead smoothed away, and she nodded.

Dozens of residents had witnessed his gory walk from the west wing. That kind of thing was commonplace since they frequently brought captives to the compound to be tortured. A rival gang member here. A government official there. Seemed there was always someone begging for a bloody send-off to hell.

Tonight's dismemberment, however, had been one of their own.

His hand clenched against Camila's ass, and she gasped.

He'd known Gerardo since the beginning and never would've suspected their trusted accountant of leaking information to another cartel.

Valuable information, such as numbers of bank accounts, names of intermediaries, drug transactions, and payoffs to law enforcement officials. The extent of the damage was still unknown.

He hadn't felt this kind of betrayal since... His chest tightened. The day he'd learned Jhon had set up Camila's abduction. The sick son of a bitch. Matias shook with the need to kill his brother all over again.

The drone of voices and laughter filtered in from the veranda at the end of the hall. It would be a full room tonight since most of the operators were in town—forty or so lieutenants and hitmen.

Dinner was held every night on the veranda, and while business wasn't always conducted at this hour, members needed a damn good excuse to miss it.

It'd been over a decade since he'd walked in there with the slightest twitch of unease, but as the dining area came into view, his insides lit with nervous energy. He glanced down at one of the reasons.

Silken black hair, soulful eyes, and a body that wickedly sinuated the lines of her corset. Camila was the only woman he'd ever loved, and he knew—somewhere beneath her campaign to save the free world—she could love him. *Him,* not the ghost of the boy he'd been.

But he needed her to hang on to her hatred for just a little while longer.

Gripping her arm, he pushed her back against the wall of the empty corridor. She stiffened then launched into a muscle-tensing, kicking, shoving struggle. He wrenched her hands behind her and pressed his weight against her chest.

Anyone who passed by would simply see him enjoying his new slave before dinner.

He touched his mouth to her ear and kept his voice at a whisper. "I won't tell you to trust me. You're not there yet. But I want you to listen."

Her jaw tensed against his. Then she relaxed in his hold.

"Nico knows our history, as do the small few in the inner circle."

"Who's in the inner—?"

"Everyone at my table." He leaned back and watched her eyes dilate as she absorbed the information. Stifling the overwhelming urge to kiss her, he returned his lips to her ear. "The rest of that room is on a *need to know*, and they need to know you're just the slave of the month. A fresh hole to fuck. You mean nothing to me."

He released her and stepped back.

"I fucking despise you." Vicious honesty snarled through her voice and hardened her eyes.

He inwardly winced and smoothed his tone to hide the hurt. "Perfect."

Setting off toward the veranda, he didn't look back.

The cartel had never had a turncoat among their upper ranks, and that was the other reason his stomach was knotted all to hell. No matter how many body parts he'd severed from Gerardo, the only thing the snake confessed was that he hadn't been working alone.

There was another mole on the property, and it could be anyone. A maid, an armed guard, a hired whore, or one of the members sitting out there on the veranda. His opponents were many, but this was a rival cartel, gunning to take them out and steal their business.

Where Nico was the face and the name of the organization, Matias was the spine. Their enemies didn't know this, but a spy among their ranks would know where to hit and how deep to cut. If they realized what Camila meant to him, they would start with her.

Hence the barbaric markings on her legs, the slutty attire, and the hatred in her eyes. They would see an abused slave, a piece of property, and *not* a cherished pet he would trade all the secrets in the world to keep safe.

A hush fell over the dining room as he stepped onto the veranda. Eyes lifted, beer bottles froze at mouths, forks settled against plates, and heads lowered. *Respect.* After twelve violent years, he'd fucking earned it.

He gave a general nod to the congregation of men, and they resumed drinking and conversing.

Ten round tables of six filled the spacious, roofed balcony. Of the sixty seats, only a few were empty. Two or three girls knelt on the floor around each grouping, but some members had wives and mistresses who sat in chairs beside them. There were also a few non-members like Yessica, the resident madam, who'd secured a seat at a table.

As he passed Yessica's chair, she reached out and brushed a hand against his cock, her lips puckering in an air-kiss.

He couldn't hear Camila's footfalls behind him, but the sharp exhalation at his back sounded as if she were choking on smoke and ash.

Without acknowledging his slave, he weaved through the dining room, stopping every few feet to shake a coke-stained hand, pat a tattooed shoulder, and answer questions about his recent visit to the States. Frivolous questions about the weather, the watered-down alcohol, and American pussy.

Other than the wandering eyes and looks of appreciation, they seemed to dismiss Camila as his slave and nothing more. She wasn't restrained like the others on the floor, but no one would question how he kept her in check. His brutal reputation glowed in angry red welts all over her legs and ass.

She remained silent, head down, and spine straight. Her mind, however, was likely spinning off its rails, absorbing every detail of his criminal wonderland. Her thirst for information matched his own, but where he'd unearthed almost everything he needed to know about her, she was still fumbling through the dark.

If she looked hard enough around her, she'd find her answers.

# FIFTEEN

Matias took his time making his rounds on the veranda. Amid the holstered guns and scarred faces, the usual laid-back energy circulated through the room, making it easy to hold a smile as he examined expressions for deception, studied postures for restlessness, and refused the drinks offered to him.

Camila followed, sticking close to him, but not too close. He suspected she wasn't seeking protection from the heated stares, but instead trying to evaluate every word spoken and glance exchanged between him and the other members.

He hadn't bound her hands because he didn't want to add more discomfort to her beaten body, but she held her arms behind her anyway. Perhaps it was her slave training. Or maybe she was trying to keep herself from drawing the .45 from his shoulder holster and blowing his brains all over the linen tablecloths.

When he reached the head table, he lowered into his chair and pointed at the floor beside him. She knelt without hesitation, and possessive warmth settled in his chest.

Beside him, Nico frowned at the screen of his phone, eyebrows furrowing and releasing. The man might've seemed disinterested in his surroundings, but he was always watching, constantly on high-alert.

Picar, Chispa, and Frizz were already seated at the table, which left one empty chair. Matias could smell Gerardo's death and deceit wafting from it.

"Someone get rid of that." He waved a hand at the vacant seat.

A man in a black suit emerged out of nowhere and carried the chair away.

Nico glanced up from his phone and rubbed a hand over his dark beard. "Taking this personal, *ese*?"

"Don't pretend you're not." Frowning, he snatched the bottle of *aguardiente* from the center tray and poured a glass.

By now, every member in the room had been briefed on Gerardo's betrayal. However, no one outside of the inner circle knew about the mole that still lurked among them.

Matias tossed a casual glance across the veranda. Men of all ages and style of dress sipped from a range of beer to hard liquor. Their preferences for jeans or suits were as diverse as their motivations. The elders tended to be content in their positions, just buying time while protecting their families — their legacies. The younger members took more risks, always searching for greener pastures, hungry for more money and more power. Like Gerardo.

With a shrug, Nico cast his eyes on Camila. "Any success on the other matter?"

Matias looked down at the swollen cuts on her thighs and felt a deep ache to pull her onto his lap. "Success is relative."

Once he owned Camila's heart, he would spend every day of the rest of his life continually seducing her consent for his brand of fucking.

She didn't seem to be following the conversation, too frozen with horror as she stared at the man and woman on her other side.

Frizz poked a straw through the gap in the threads on his mouth, sucking from a glass filled with a thick, brown puree — probably whatever was on the menu blended into a soup. His other hand stroked the head of the Latina brunette. Tears ran down her face, her eyes dead as she cried silently on her knees beside his chair.

She was one of the slaves brought in with Camila this morning. Nico must've gifted her to Frizz, because she wore Frizz's tragic trademark.

Red *X*'s stitched across the woman's lips, with excess thread dangling from one corner of her mouth like a drool of blood. A needle was tied to the end and swung like a pendulum with each violent shudder of her nude body.

Camila pressed her hands to her stomach. Her shoulders quaked, and she jerked her head toward Matias with accusation and tears in her eyes.

Yes, he'd told her if she fought him, he'd take it out on someone else. That didn't mean he'd protect the slaves from harm.

He bent down and put his mouth beside her ear. "*I* didn't do that."

She gave him a vicious glare then redirected it to Frizz.

Sure, his corpse-like appearance and fetish with sewn mouths was gruesome, but she wouldn't be so quick to judge if she knew his story.

Frizz ticked his head to the side and wiggled three fingers at her in greeting.

She choked and shot her gaze to the floor.

Dinner was delivered in courses by servers in black suits, beginning with grilled lamb *chunchullo,* followed by *sancocho,* large pieces of plantain, sliced avocado, and white rice. The rich spicy scent of the tropical stew blended with cigar smoke and the hum of laughter. Easy conversation added a low-key backdrop. Nothing seemed out of place, which made it difficult to keep his guard up.

As Nico discussed the finer details of yesterday's heroin shipment to Orlando, Matias spooned hunks of salty meat from the soup and fed Camila.

She sat on her heels, knees bent in perfect form, and opened her mouth for each bite without contest. But she couldn't hide the pain etching her face.

There was that pinch of guilt again, twisting behind his ribs.

He glanced across the table and met Picar's cloudy eyes. The old doctor didn't speak very good English, but he excelled at deciphering expressions. Gerardo's double-dealings had begun only two days ago, and it had been Picar who'd noticed Gerardo seemed shady.

Leaning to the side, Picar removed something from his bag on the floor and slid it across the table. Matias recognized the color and shape of the pill, and for a moment, he considered the possibility that it could be poison made to look like Vicodin. But Picar was a devoted husband and father. He had nothing to gain and everything to lose if he fucked over one of his own. Besides, if he'd wanted to harm Camila, he would've done it when he injected the sedative on the plane.

Matias pocketed the pill.

Between spoonfuls of *sancocho,* Chispa and Nico debated strategies on how to deal with the federal agents that hovered around the compound in El Paso. In the distance, thunder rumbled, drawing Matias' attention to the huge archways and columns that encircled the veranda.

Nightfall blackened the horizon, hushing the chirrup of cicadas, but the sound of drizzling rainfall helped to ease his nerves.

He pushed his chair back and patted his lap, watching Camila out of the corner of his eye.

She grimaced, and her mouthwatering cleavage heaved above the bodice of the corset. She could hate him all she wanted. His lap would be a fuckton more comfortable against her sore muscles than the wood floor.

With a deep breath, she rose, her legs trembling with the effort. As she stepped in front of him, she kept her head lowered and arms hanging loosely at her sides.

He turned her to face the table, and sweet mother, her round flawless backside flexed inches away. He wanted to shred the panties, bend her over the table, and sink his teeth in. Followed by his cock.

Heat surged along his shaft as he imagined how tight that little hole would feel clenched around his thrusts. He could do it, fuck her ass right here, and not a goddamn person in this room would raise a brow.

The way into her heart was without a doubt a path of tribulation. But where he put his mouth and cock wasn't the key factor in obtaining his goal. It was the ability to connect with her on a fundamental level.

Curling his fingers over the black lace on her hips, he drew her toward him and settled her on his thigh.

She sat rigidly, hissing from the pain, elbows locked against her sides, and legs shaking. With an arm around her waist, he pulled her back against his chest and scooted the chair forward, sliding her lower half beneath the edge of the table top.

Stiff as a board, she refused to relax against his reclined body. Her breaths sharpened, expanding her rib cage and testing the seams of the corset.

She really wasn't going to appreciate his hands on her, but anyone outside of his table would expect a public display of groping to be the only reason he moved her to his lap.

Over the years, he'd brought slaves to dinner, not for his pleasure, but for the sole purpose of tormenting them. After Camila's disappearance, he'd taken a special interest in slavery. He so badly wanted to sit her down and explain his involvement. Hell, he wanted to explain everything. But she wasn't ready.

Beneath the concealment of the table, he cupped her pussy over the panties. His other hand rested lightly against her throat as he made a shushing noise at her ear.

She drew several more breaths. Then her muscles began to loosen against his legs and chest. An eternal moment later, she let her head fall back on his shoulder. He released her neck.

Her soft hair brushed against his throat, and the heat of her body seeped through the threads of his suit. Christ, he'd waited so fucking long for this, to feel the beat of her heart against his, protected in his home, and held in his arms.

With great reluctance, he removed his hand from between her legs, trailing fingers gingerly around the welts on her thigh. His chest squeezed with regret, and hers inflated with a held breath. Shifting his hand toward his pocket, he slipped the pill between two fingers.

"Open your mouth," he whispered at her ear. "For the pain."

Her instant obedience was a testament to how much she was hurting.

He placed the pill on her tongue and traced the plump flesh of her bottom lip. Then he offered her a glass of water, which she drank greedily.

He didn't have to glance up at the room to know he was being watched. Yessica, for one, would spend the entire evening trying to gauge his interest in Camila. Others would simply be looking for weaknesses. They might work for the same team, but they would kill one another if it meant moving up in the ranks. And Matias held a covetous position.

Giving a slave a pill, however, wasn't uncommon. Ecstasy, roofies, any number of trance-like drugs made unwilling partners more malleable.

He returned her water glass to the table and slid his hand beneath the front of her panties. Her abdomen quivered, and her thighs clenched together like a vise.

"Open," he whispered firmly.

She parted her legs, and he caressed the delicate flesh, slowly, teasingly.

"So I've been thinking…" Chispa stroked the thin mustache on his lip. "We need to work on our PR."

"*Se necesita un cerebro para pensar*," Picar muttered.

"Isn't it past your bedtime, old man?" Chispa grinned.

Picar held up a fist with his pinkie and index finger extended like bull horns. The gesture was as old as Colombia, meaning *Your wife's a cheating whore.*

Matias chuckled. Since Chispa wasn't married, he could interpret it however he wanted.

"You need to loosen up, Picar." Chispa folded his twiggy arms behind his head. "Sometimes you gotta let your ball sac hang like two cacay nuts in a wet baggie to know you're alive."

Given Picar's stony glare, his next gesture would involve making a fist shape out of his strongest hand and slamming it into Chispa's face.

"You two need to get a room." Matias roamed his fingers lazily across Camila's soft folds.

She relaxed against him, breaths even and silent and eyes lowered. He guessed most of that was an act. The painkiller wouldn't have kicked in yet, and he knew she wouldn't miss an opportunity to be as invisible as possible while studying every person on the veranda.

He turned his attention to Chispa. "What did you have in mind for PR?"

Soliciting low-rank falcons was an aggravation, but they were the eyes and ears of the streets and the best access to information on the activities of the police, military, and rival gangs. They also propagated fear. Scaring the *picadas* out of the general public kept people in line and out of the way.

Matias slid his finger through moisture. Warm, wet *arousal*. His cock hardened, suddenly and painfully. His breathing sped up as he stroked deeper, circling the entrance of her pussy without penetrating.

Her thigh kicked up and bumped the underside of the table, rattling dishes.

No one at the table spared her a passing glance, but Matias vibrated with excitement. He knew her mind was fighting this, fighting him, but her body still loved his touch.

"We need a motto." Chispa tapped a fist on the table.

"How about *Give us your shit or we'll kill you*," Nico said with a gleam of amusement in his eyes.

Her breath hitched.

"Or…" Matias stroked his other hand down her arm, smiling. *"There are some things that can't be smuggled. For everything else, there's the Restrepos."*

"Not bad, not bad." Chispa nodded thoughtfully.

Picar swiped a gnarled finger across his eyebrow, his expression dead serious. *"Armas got?"*

"Got guns?" Chispa howled with laughter.

The entire inner circle joined in, hooting and slapping the table.

When they finally settled down, Chispa snorted. "I've got one. *The Quicker Fucker Upper.*"

The laughter began again.

Matias enjoyed nights like this. A departure from the stress of business to drink and shoot the shit. Camila appeared to be focused solely on what his hand was doing, but he knew she was listening, picking apart every word and judging the whole lot of them.

Someday she would sit here among them as his equal and join in the camaraderie. Hopefully, someday soon.

For now, he was content with just holding her while reacquainting himself with her body. As much as he wanted to sink his fingers inside her, he'd rather show her how much pleasure he could give her in private, when he could focus on only her and not on the countless others who might be scrutinizing his motivations.

Frizz reclined in his chair and whistled a song. The table fell quiet, listening as he continued the tune.

"Is that…?" Chispa made a disgusted face. "'Dead Babies' by Alice Cooper? You want *Dead Babies* to be our motto?"

A smirk pulled at strings on Frizz's pale lips.

"Frizz…" Matias rubbed his free hand across his scowl. "Why'd you have to go there?"

Frizz shrugged.

"Moving on…" Chispa shook with an exaggerated shudder. "We also need a logo."

"I'm bored with this conversation." Nico scowled into his beer.

"Dude. All the other cartels have one." Chispa leaned forward, his dark eyes animated. "We can hand out monogrammed switchblades and put up a Facebook Fan page."

"Facebook," Matias said dryly. "What're you going to post? Pictures of dismembered corpses, status updates on our assault weapons sales, and incriminating selfies?"

"Yes, exactly!" Chispa pointed a finger at him, laughing. "Think about how many *likes* we'd get with that shit? Everyone knows mutilated bodies get more shares than adorable duckling pictures."

Because dumbass kids loved to brag about their cartel affiliations and celebrate murderous gangs like sports teams, going so far as to take time out of their midday gunfights to post photos of themselves posing with guns.

"I think we're freaking them out." Chispa lifted his chin at Camila and the Latina on the floor.

He was probably only referencing Camila, but included both women to avoid suspicion. Everyone in the inner circle knew what she meant to Matias and what his plans were for her.

"Nah." Matias tugged on a lock of her hair. "They know we're just fucking around."

She grew limper, more relaxed on his lap, probably fighting sleep. He moved his hand to her waist and simply held her. Her body had endured an intense amount of strain over the past twenty-four hours, and he needed to put her to bed.

After the last course was served, the veranda thinned out, leaving half-empty tables cluttered with full ashtrays and discarded beer bottles. It was time to go.

"Is there room on this lap for me?" Yessica's voice clawed like nails over his shoulder.

Camila roused against him, lifting her head and blinking heavy eyelids as she stared at Yessica.

"Calling it a night." Matias shifted Camila off his lap, holding on to her hips as she wobbled.

"So early?" Yessica propped a hand on her cocked hip. "Send that one off to her room"—she waved a hand at Camila—"and come have a dip in the pool with me."

"We're not dressed for swimming." He tossed back the last of his *aguardiente* and stood.

"Since when do you and I need clothes?" She tilted her head and pushed out her mouth to emulate a puffy-lipped pout.

Her duck face detracted from her pretty features.

Camila stood motionless beside him with her hands fisted at her sides and a twitch in her eye. She was upset, but it had nothing to do with

Yessica. Her attention was glued to Frizz's slave, her body leaning subtly toward the woman on the floor as if she wanted to swoop in and protect.

"Goodnight, Yessica." He curled his fingers around Camila's upper arm and dragged her away from the table.

"I'll walk with you." Nico joined his side.

They strolled in silence toward the west wing. Camila dragged her feet, seemingly losing strength with every step thanks to the painkiller.

Matias' hands flexed with the overwhelming urge to carry her. But preferential treatment wouldn't have gone unnoticed in the busy halls as residents geared up for the usual late night parties in the various sections of the estate.

When he reached the wooden doors to his rooms and found the corridor empty, he lifted her listless body into his arms. She rolled against his chest, and a night's worth of tension uncoiled inside him.

Nico stepped in front of the retinal scanner and opened the door for him. Then Nico trailed him through the expansive living space and into the bedroom.

By the time he laid her on the bed, she was out. Breaths deep and even. Eyelids relaxed. Lashes fanning over her cheeks. Gorgeous as sin.

He rolled her to her stomach and sat on the edge of the mattress to tackle the ties of the corset.

Nico stood at the foot of the bed, watching intently, his natural scowl darkening the edges of his mouth.

"Well?" Matias unraveled the knot at her tailbone and worked his way up her spine, slowly loosening the cinch.

"We still don't know if Gerardo revealed —"

Matias made a slashing gesture with his fingers across his neck and aimed a pointed glare at Camila. He was almost positive she was asleep, but the *almost* was too big a risk. He wasn't ready for her to know this secret, and the gritty details of this conversation could wait until morning.

"We'll just keep doing what we're doing." He reached the last tie on her back and wiggled the corset loose around her ribs. "If the mole knows, he or she will expose it soon enough."

"Camila's going to find out, regardless." Nico clasped his hands behind his back. "I still don't understand how you intend on keeping this from her while she's living here, *parce*."

There were so many things she didn't know, like the fact that he'd had a brother by blood or why her parents died. She didn't know the reason he'd been ripped away from her or what his role was in the cartel.

Soon, she would learn that the reason she was here was not to stop human trafficking, but to uncover the truth.

"Trust me." Matias stood and removed his suit jacket, his hands confident and mind clear.

"I trust you unequivocally with our lives." Nico's eyes flashed, his voice sharp. "That doesn't mean I have to like this asinine plan."

"As you've said for the millionth time."

"Just making sure we understand one another." Nico glanced at Camila's sleeping form, and his scowl bent into a half-scowl. "*Que duermas bien.*"

"*Buenas noches.*"

As the tread of Nico's shoes retreated and the doors to the suite shut behind him, Matias removed the rest of his clothes and locked his gun in the closet. Then he turned his attention to the woman in his bed.

Fifteen minutes later, she lay naked beneath the sheets with fresh ointment on her thighs. She'd slept through it all and continued to sleep as he removed the collar and set it in the drawer beside the bed. Then he tucked in behind her, his chest against her back, and slowly explored every exquisite bend, dip, and slender bone of her body.

Despite the ache in his cock, he was happier than he'd been since the last time he held her like this.

He closed his eyes in memory, and the grass tickled his back. The sun warmed his face. Her skin pressed against his, legs entangled, with the aroma of citrus and earth in the air.

Back then he had to worry about Venomous Lemonous chasing them apart with a stick.

He opened his eyes and brushed his lips against the delicate shell of her ear.

Now he faced a different opponent, one less tangible but far angrier. Her heart might've been locked up like a fortress, but it wasn't impenetrable.

He shut off the light and curled his body tightly around hers.

Twelve years, he'd imagined waking to the smell of sex and contentment and *her* tangled in the sheets around him. Tomorrow morning, that dream would become a reality. And after that?

He had a lot of fucking work to do.

# SIXTEEN

Camila woke to the caress of fingers on her hip and rapid breaths falling against her nape. She blinked in the darkness and held herself immobile on her side, arms hugging the pillow beneath her head, her own breath parked in her throat.

Fingertips trailed along her waist, traced the grooves of her ribs, and lingered on the underside of her breast. Her breath escaped, but she kept it slow and stable, feigning sleep. The same instinct that had *never* saved her in Van's attic.

Did she actually think she'd make it through the night without Matias fucking her? She'd hoped. Like *press my goddamn hands together and pray to whoever's listening* hoped. After he'd beaten her, fucked her face, and fed her on the floor beside a woman with stitched lips, her libido had shriveled up and died.

But she knew better than to hope. He'd already stripped her naked—the corset, panties, and collar gone. Not even the sheet covered her.

Every hair on her body stood up, screaming at her to bite, choke, kick, and run the fuck away. Could she get past the eye scanner? Slip around the guards? Hijack the helicopter? No chance in hell she'd survive the Amazon rainforest.

She was stuck here. *I put myself here.*

Her plan had been ten kinds of fucked in the head.

Masculine heat saturated her back, his legs intertwined with hers, the hard muscles in his thighs and calves flexing with his rapid breaths. And his hand shook, fucking vibrated as he cupped and kneaded her breast.

How long had he been awake? Touching her and working himself into this panting, trembling state?

Maybe his hands shook with all the women he fucked, but at gut level, she didn't believe it.

He wasn't taking. Taking would've been fingers digging, pinching, claiming. No, shaking meant restraint.

If the circumstances had been different, she would've been shaking with breathy enthusiasm. He was the one she'd always fantasized about during sex, but now that she was in his bed, her stomach knotted.

Moving only her eyes, she sought out the clock on the bedside table. *3:13 AM.*

As if the passing of minutes, days, years even mattered. Time might as well have been frozen. Like her lungs. And her life.

He lowered his hand to her hipbone, fingers curling against the juncture of her groin and thigh, reaching, stretching toward her pussy.

Her pulse sprinted, and her mouth went dry. She kept her thighs pinched together and squeezed her eyes shut. *I don't want this. God, please, I don't want to be forced.*

The welts on her skin stung each time she tensed. What if he decided to be really cruel and dig his fingers against them? She'd probably pass out.

With his hand on her hip, he ground against her in tight, slow rolling motions. The hair below his abs rubbed against her ass, and every hard naked inch of him twitched—his chest, his legs, his swollen erection. Goose bumps shivered down her spine.

She feared him as all monsters were meant to be feared in the dark. Only he wasn't under the bed. He was in it, his breath on her neck, skin against skin, and he was hungry.

If she looked over her shoulder, she'd find a monster with eyes of golden green, wearing a face she once caressed and kissed and loved. With hair she'd stroked with intimate affection, the strands in every shade of the deepest black—the color of his soul.

"I know you're awake," he said in a rumbling voice and lowered his lips to her neck, whiskers scratching and teeth scraping.

"I don't want this." Her throat closed up, strangling her voice. "Please, Matias."

He bit her earlobe then suckled the sting. "I'll change your mind."

*Not happening.* Her mind hurdled along a course that ended with a punch to the esophagus, his skull slamming against the marble floor repeatedly, and castration. She couldn't escape, but maybe a chokehold would help him understand how fucking wrong it was to take an unwilling woman.

With a deep breath, she twisted toward him and swung to hook her arms around his neck.

He didn't move, but something caught her hands, holding them to the pillow. The fuck? She tried to yank free to no avail, and her pulse detonated.

The mattress bounced as he leaned toward the side table. The lamp clicked on, and a dim glow illuminated the bed.

Lying on her back, she angled her neck and spotted two skinny ropes between her hands and the headboard. Her blood turned cold.

She knew restraints intimately, had fought them and lost too many times. No amount of jerking and yanking would help her, and the ties on her wrists were the kind that constricted under pressure, the braided nylon so thin it blended with the white sheets. No wonder she hadn't noticed it when she woke.

"Don't test the knots." He crawled over her, easily restraining her kicking legs as he settled his hips between her thighs. Then he braced his elbows on either side of her head, studying her with a predator's vigilance. "They'll only cinch tighter and cut off the blood to your hands."

But her legs weren't tied. She relaxed her arms above her head, her hands curling into fists. "Why am I restrained? I'm not—"

"I want you this way."

"I have chlamydia and...and syphilis and—"

"You're clean." He rocked against her, gliding the rigid length of his cock along her mound, breaths slipping, and lids falling half-mast. "We both are."

She turned her head away. "You don't know—"

"Picar drew our blood and took swab tests on the plane." He gripped her face and forced her gaze back to his. "I've never had sex without a condom."

Neither had she, and she sure as fuck didn't want to start now.

Except she had always wanted this, with him, without anything between them.

*Not like this.*

"Christ, Camila, I've waited—" His fingers slid into her hair and dug against her scalp, eyes searching and voice hoarse. "I've waited an eternity for this."

Molten gold bled into emerald rings around his irises, the bones of his face sharp across his cheeks, square around his jaw, and exquisitely Matias. Women everywhere probably fell at his feet—with or without his command. How many had sampled his warm skin and tasted his firm lips?

Her heart twisted. Why did she care? She didn't, but it still hurt like hell lying beneath him and staring into eyes that had once meant the world to her. And it was only going to get worse. He was going to fuck her and make this ugly goddamn mess of feelings a thousand times uglier and more painful.

A hot ember sat in her throat. She pinched her lips together, refusing to give voice to her weakness. There was no sane reason for her to feel anything but pure fucking rancor.

Yeah, *that*. The anger, the murderous hatred… She grabbed hold of it and let it consume her. Snapping her teeth together, she crunched her abdominals and kicked a leg up and over his shoulder. With a twist of her hips, she landed a knee hard against his jaw, using his shock to drive him to the mattress and into a cry-angle choke.

But without her arms, she couldn't stop him from trapping her leg and rotating it. With her kneecap against his torso and the pressure of his upper body against his grip, her leg snapped straight, hyper-extending the knee joint.

She cried out against the unbearable agony, and the cuts on her legs protested against the strain. She slapped her hands on the bed, thrashing her arms against the rope.

When he released her, the pain ebbed. Until he tossed her onto her back and crushed her with two-hundred-plus pounds of ravenous need.

"Fighting me like that?" He buried his face in her neck. "A *huge* turn on." His hands frantically stroked every inch of her he could reach. "You're killing me."

She shook with volcanic rage. "Then die already!"

A muscle bounced in his jaw, and his eyes flickered with…hurt?

Fuck his feelings. She dug her heels into the mattress and tried to buck off his heavy-ass body.

He let her struggle for the span of a few heartbeats, while he rubbed and caressed and kissed her skin, the fucking bastard. Then without warning, he wrapped a hand around her throat and pressed hard against her windpipe, instantly subduing her.

"If you kick your legs again…" He stared at her like a nocturnal predator, a creature at home in the shadows of hell. "I'll restrain them to the bed, spread eagle."

Flashes of white blotted out his scowl. She couldn't breathe beneath his hand, couldn't speak, but she opened her mouth in a plea for air.

He let go, and she gulped, lungs heaving. She yanked against the rope, unable to pull her hands to her aching throat.

As she caught her breath, he returned his attention to her body, fingers roaming, his mouth feeding on her skin, licking and biting.

"You've always been beautiful." He kissed his way toward her pussy. "Your confidence. Your spirit. Your body." He nibbled on her hipbone. "Look at you. Fuck, Camila. You can't possibly be real."

She deflated beneath him, and tears gathered in her eyes. She couldn't fight against his words. Why was she even fighting at all? She'd known this would happen before she left Texas.

*Because it's Matias.*

The same Matias who chained her to a post and caned her. And he could do it again if she continued to push his patience.

She blinked, and the tears knocked free, trickling down her temples.

His shoulders lowered between her legs, his hands spreading her thighs wide and baring her cunt for his gaze. But he didn't look down, instead holding her gaze for a long, uncomfortable moment. Then his focus drifted to the tracks of her tears.

His expression clouded with an emotion she'd never seen there, not once in the countless times he'd witnessed her cry as a child. Was it guilt? Pity?

Whatever it was softened his features and wrinkled his brow, giving him a brooding, contemplative visage. It only added to his exotic beauty, the stubble on his face dark and dangerous against a complexion that glowed like bronze in the sun. His allure was so intoxicating it was painful to look at him.

"Don't pity me, Matias." She rolled her shoulders against the mattress, stretched her fingers to grip the bottom edge of the wooden headboard, and forced her gaze to his. "It's the wrong feeling for what's happening here."

The muscles in his face tightened, all softness gone. "Pity is not what I'm feeling right now."

He dipped his head between her legs and inhaled deeply. His fingers clamped tighter around the backs of her thighs as he smelled her, dragged his nose through her folds, then buried his mouth.

She arched her back, stunned by the assault of sensations. It took several seconds for her lower body to rouse, but when it did, her pussy throbbed hard and greedily, soaking her with a rush of arousal.

He moaned against her cunt, his tongue strong and firm as it lapped and swirled and dipped inside.

Shame coiled in her belly, and a whimper escaped her lips. This wasn't supposed to feel good. It was wrong, sick, fucked up in the worst way possible.

His eyes stayed on her, his kiss aggressive, frantic, and so damn sexual. Then his fingers joined in, stabbing, curling, and stealing her air. His muscled shoulders contracted with his frenzied movements, pressing against the backs of her legs as he bit and sucked her delicate flesh.

Each lick was a rasping whisper, liquefying everything in its path as it penetrated deep, coaxing and seducing the dark cravings inside her.

She didn't want this. She didn't. Yet her entire body hummed with pleasure. It had never been this good. Ever. Not when he was younger, not with anyone, and she despised him most of all for that.

His groaning kiss might've felt like heaven, but his demon tongue was an enticement to hell. This was worse than him fucking her dry. He was turning her body against her, using their familiar intimacy to make her wet and twist her up.

Arms above her head, legs spread, and nipples erect in the lazy breeze from the ceiling fan, her traitorous body melted beneath the sensual slide of his mouth. She focused on the fan blades, watching them go round and round — *whoosh, whoosh, whoosh* — in rhythm with her heart and the throb against his tongue.

Eventually, his lashes lowered, concealing the predatory glow in his eyes. She found relief in that, until his fingers strummed against her thigh, tightening and loosening, as if he were trying to hide the shaking. He used to do that when they were teenagers, quaking and twitching his hands when he was overly excited and trying not to come.

Her chest constricted. He was a rancid poison, injecting himself into her system. Circulating through her blood. Breaking her down and rotting her from the inside out.

But the poison thinned as she climbed. He floated her up and halfway down again. The smell of his rotten intent still lingered, but underneath, she tasted ecstasy. Because he'd brought her to the cliff, and though she fought against the fall, his tongue was too talented, knew her body too well, and he pushed her over.

She moaned as blissful shocks burst across her nerve endings, spreading outward, trembling her legs, and wiping her mind. She spun through a vortex of unimaginable pleasure where she didn't need air or legs or wings, because he was there, catching her, holding her, and carrying her through the haze. He was with her, protecting. *Mine.*

Her arms twisted in the ropes as she clung to the lingering sensations, quivering and gasping to catch her breath.

When she finally came down, the weight of what just happened pressed against her chest.

He'd made her come, and it left her feeling more alive than she'd ever felt in her life.

And raw. So fucking raw it hurt in places she couldn't identify or reach.

Why hadn't he just raped her without all the foreplay and eye contact? He could've fucked her, gotten off on whatever sick shit he was into, then left her the fuck alone to lick her wounds. She could survive physical pain. But this…this godawful ache inside her? She didn't even know where to start.

"How long has it been?" He kissed the hood of her clit and leaned up on his elbows.

"How long for what?" she snapped.

"Since someone ate your pussy."

"A week ago." She considered leaving it at that, but since he wanted to stick his fucking nose in her business… "Larry McGregor had skills."

"What?" he bellowed and shot up off the bed, his face contorted and fiery red. He swung an arm out and sent the lamp crashing to the floor, spinning the glowing light through the room. "You fucked that worthless son of a bitch?"

"No." Heart thundering, she slammed her legs together and scooted toward the headboard. "I let him go down on me so I could—"

*Shit.* She'd said too much.

"So you could put him in a chokehold," he said, voice cold and deadly calm. "Same thing you just tried on me."

Technically, it was a different chokehold, but she wasn't about to point that out.

He stood with his back to her, the brawn of his ass hard and flexed like a gladiator preparing for battle. She'd seen his nude body so many times, but that was *before.* This body was so much bigger, his thighs cut and dusted with dark hair, his waist narrow and widening into defined shoulders, and his spine straight and confident.

He was power and danger and persuasion, and she was a quivering blob tied to his bed.

Scrubbing a hand over his head, he dragged it down his face, his profile angled downward as he glared at the glowing exposed bulb on the broken lamp. The heave of his back slowed, and he seemed to be reigning in his temper.

He sat on the edge of the bed, his cock still hard and jutting upward as he shifted his gaze to her. "When was the last time you had sex?"

She hesitated. Did the truth really matter? Would it reveal a weakness or some hidden psychological condition he could use against her? She didn't think so. "Four years ago."

"Four—" He choked, his head tilting and expression perplexed.

No, not perplexed. *Possessive.*

Maybe she should've lied.

He crawled toward her with a feral glint in his eyes. She tucked her legs close to her body, but he caught her ankles and dragged her down the mattress on her back.

"Four years ago," he said quietly and wedged his hips between her thighs.

The last time she'd felt his weight on her, he'd been on the thin side of sexy, but now he was stacked with compact muscle, his shoulders beautifully sculptured, and his torso a rippling slab of intimidation. It was like being pinned by a fallen tree. With eight-pack abs.

With a hand in her hair, his other reached down to cup her pussy. His mouth parted with the acceleration of his breaths as he sank two fingers in, teasing and tormenting.

"What about you?" Her voice shivered as she tried to block out the warmth and pressure of his hand.

"I'll tell you." He brushed his lips against hers. "But not right now."

Anger sparked in her veins. Typical evasive Matias, telling her exactly nothing.

He sucked on her bottom lip, his fingers curling lazily inside her. "We always talked about our first time together, how perfect it would be."

She didn't want that memory here. It was too sweet, too fragile. "Don't do this."

"This isn't going to be perfect. It's going to be ugly and conflicted, because you can't get out of that damn head of yours, and I'm too fucking worked up to draw this out. But when I'm inside you, it will always be honest."

Honest? She buried her fingernails into her palms. "Fuck you."

"In a second." He slid his fingers out of her and gripped his cock, seating himself at her opening. Then he held her head in his hands and rested his forehead against hers. "I need you with me, *mi vida*. Forget about all the bullshit and just focus on us."

"There is no—"

He kissed her, forcibly, hungrily, his mouth rough and wet and persistent. She tasted herself on his lips, a despicable reminder that she'd orgasmed on his forked tongue.

His hips rocked, just enough to press his tip inside, and stopped. His legs shook, and his fingers curled against her scalp as if he were struggling with the need to slam all the way in.

"It's just you and me in this bed." He licked her lips and kissed the corners of her mouth. "No history. No future. Nothing but *right now* and *us*."

The intensity of his eyes seemed to say so much more than his words. His pupils pulsed, dark and bottomless but not empty. There was something there, way down deep. Something huge and profound. She peered in, all the way inside his soul, and she felt it instantly. They both did, their breaths hitching as one.

In that frozen space of time, she saw not the monster that sold women into slavery, but the boy who had kissed all her scrapes and scratches, taught her how to face her fears, and promised her he would never let her fall. The bond she had with that boy was still alive, right here in this bed. It was more mature now, scarier, stronger, but it held her just as tightly, demanding she give herself in return, and she wanted that. Desperately.

She nodded her consent, a reflex that immediately warped into regret, then panic, but it was too late.

He thrust, his head falling to her shoulder. "Ahhh, God. So tight." He worked his hips, inching through her wetness and pushing, pushing, to fill her fully. "Fuck, let me in."

Desire thickened his voice and shivered through her. She squeezed her fingers against the headboard and tried to relax her inner muscles, but he was huge, his girth stretching and invading until, finally, he was buried balls deep and panting.

"Oh fuck, Camila. Fuck." His chest vibrating with a deep groan. "Hold on."

Then he fucked her, and she did hold on—to the headboard. Her emotions, however, were slipping through her fingers. She tried to separate, tried not to feel anything as he pounded inside her, his hands everywhere, caressing her chest, her hips, her legs. But it was the potency of his eyes, his gaze never leaving hers, that held her there, commanding her to stay.

He pressed her knees to her shoulders, deepening the angle as he hammered in and out, faster, harder, his passion unlike anything she'd ever experienced. Pleasure fired through her nerve endings, and she tried to pretend she felt nothing, tried to block it all out.

But she felt everything—every slide of his cock and curl of heat, the spasmodic quivers across her skin, and the needy grip of her pussy. Her body wanted this, and she hated it. Hated herself.

He kissed her urgently between heaving breaths, his grunts and groans unrestrained and his body a contracting tireless machine.

With his tongue in her mouth and his bruising grip on her legs, he slammed against the back of her cunt, ignoring the flinch of her body. He took her harshly, fervently, as if he were fucking her with every torment, dedication, and dream in his soul.

This was what was missing in all her one-night stands. This driving vehemence to give and take, the devastating risk to own or disclaim, to just toss it all out there, consequences be damned. She had no defense against this. No amount of shutting down or tensing up could overpower the force of his gaze or the urgency in which he consumed her.

Each drugging stroke tore at the surface of her shields, burrowing into her secret places and unleashing dark things—filthy desires of being taken, used, dominated, and...loved. Exactly like this.

The rope prevented her from moving her hands. His strength stopped her from lowering her legs. The steadiness in his gaze forced her to look at him, and in his eyes, she saw herself in a way that terrified her.

She was a powerless woman beneath a powerful man. She couldn't dictate positions and speeds or the degree of pain and pleasure. She wasn't having sex to wheedle information, control the results, or search for meaning in her life.

Yet there was power in just *being*, in letting it all go as he made the rules, led the movements, and determined the purpose. It felt...*right*. Amid the ugly, conflicted honesty of what was really happening, it was perfect.

She didn't just feel him between her legs. She felt him everywhere, ripping her apart and putting her back together in a way that served him. But somehow, it served her, too.

He kissed her, and she lost herself in the thirsty strokes of his tongue, the heat of his breaths, and the promise of his hunger. She kissed the boy who haunted her and the man who filled her with dread. And somewhere between the shadows of her past and her future, she surrendered.

Whether he saw it on her face or felt it in her kiss, he knew, his eyes sparkling with flickering fire. His hands cupped her head, his fingers shaking and hips ramming as he groaned through labored breaths.

"Swear to God, Camila. I'm trying not to come." He slammed his mouth against hers and devoured her lips with frenzied bites and licks. "I'm not stopping until you're trembling around my cock." He ground against her clit and hardened his voice. "Come with me."

His command triggered a swell of electric heat between her legs. He captured her moan in his mouth, kissing her deeply, assertively, and undoing her completely.

She broke the kiss with a hoarse gasp as the orgasm rolled over her in pounding waves. He rode her through it and followed her off the edge with something akin to awe widening his eyes and slacking his mouth. Without releasing her from his gaze, he came with a rumbling groan that faded into breathlessness as he slowly dragged his cock in and out, drawing out his pleasure.

Remnant vibrations twitched and jerked between them, their breaths jagged, bodies damp with sweat, and his cock still inside her. Once her pulse returned to normal and her lungs caught up, he loosened the knots on her arms and kissed each wrist with heartbreaking affection.

His tenderness made her want impossible things. Happy endings didn't exist in a cartel compound that housed slaves with sewn lips. She was here for them, not him, and he knew it. So why the devotion in his expression? Why bother giving her pleasure at all? Maybe he genuinely loved her. Or maybe he wanted to destroy her. Both options terrified the hell out of her.

She tensed to push him away, his weight suddenly too hot and heavy, but her liquid bones refused to move.

"Camila." He studied her face for a moment then sighed, and pulled out of her.

He left the bed, but didn't go far, disappearing into the bathroom and returning with a washcloth.

Numb and suspicious, she lay still while he gently cleaned between her legs. Then he tossed the towel on the floor, rolled her on her side, and curled around her possessively with his chest against her back.

*Caring for her. Cuddling with her.* Her chest tingled with warmth, longing for more.

It was too much. Too wrong. She wriggled and shoved. "Why are you doing this?"

He refused her the distance she needed, holding her against him with an arm hooked around her ribs and a leg wedged between her thighs.

"I've been deprived of your touch for twelve years." He found her hand in the bedding, twined their fingers together, and kissed her shoulder. "Now that you're finally here, I'll deny myself nothing."

"If I fight and tell you *no*, will you fuck me anyway? Would you have raped me tonight?"

"Yes."

It wasn't his answer that shot a violent tremor through her body. It was the way he delivered it—swift, cold, and with unwavering conviction.

"Shh. I know you're scared." He tucked her hands against her chest and massaged the blood back into her fingers.

"Because you're a raping, slave-trading monster."

"Yes, but once you fall in love with a monster, you no longer fear them."

# SEVENTEEN

Sunlight warmed Camila's legs through the bedsheets. She lifted her gaze toward the glass wall and squinted at the brilliant blue backdrop. Maybe Tate or one of the others was looking up at that very moment, beneath the very same sky, thinking of ways to find her. The likelihood that she'd never see them again made her heart sink, but determination charged through it, energizing her blood.

Except she couldn't move. She could barely breathe in the solid arms that restrained her more effectively than chain or rope.

"When are we leaving this bed?" She pushed against Matias' shoulder, fingers grazing the tattooed branches.

"Someday, never," he said in a sleepy voice, pulling her impossibly closer, chest to chest.

He'd woken earlier and fucked her in the spooning position. She hadn't told him *no*, hadn't said a word when he'd roused her from sleep, rocked slowly into her from behind, and refused to come until she did. And she did come, with the same snarl of emotions as the first time.

But that was a couple of hours ago. Now he seemed content to do nothing but hold her. It felt almost…safe. *Almost.*

The dull pain pulsing deep beneath the welts on her thighs and butt helped her remember what he was capable of.

"Don't you have henchmen to recruit and women to sell?" She lifted her gaze to his.

"You're supposed to be a slave, not a slave driver." His voice was stern, but the glimmer in his eyes betrayed his amusement.

She guessed her own expression wobbled somewhere between *go to hell* and *oh well*. Truth was, she preferred this…this mellow, amicable

Matias. He reminded her of the boy she used to laze around and laugh with. If she kept him in a jovial mood, maybe he'd open up enough to talk to her. Civil conversation would be major progress after yesterday.

As her bladder twitched with pressure, an odd thought struck. "I haven't seen you use the bathroom since I've been here."

"I went while you were sleeping. Even brushed my teeth." He touched his lips to her forehead. "Are you concerned about my bathroom habits?"

"No, it's just…" With her arm resting along his ribs, she traced a finger across the bottom edge of his pectoral, which felt a whole lot like steel. "I guess…I don't know. It'd be nice to see you do something human."

"Look closer then." He lifted her chin with a knuckle and gave her a good look at the hazel swirls of life in his eyes. "I feel pain and hope and fear, just like you." He moved his hand from her face to hold up his wrist with the pockmarked scar. "To this day, I'm afraid of big black dogs. I take melatonin because I have trouble sleeping. I get indigestion when I eat too many *empanadas.*"

Her heart thudded and twisted.

"And I dreamt about this, Camila." He touched her cheek oh-so delicately with the pads of his fingers. "I dreamt about waking up with you for as long as I can remember."

That was… *Wow.* He was sharing, and she liked it. Liked it so much it made her uneasy and fluttery, her lips teetering on the verge of a weird smile.

With a ragged inhale, she lowered her gaze to the dense stubble on his jaw. "Remember when we sneaked into the faculty room at school and photocopied our faces?"

"That's not the only thing we photocopied."

"That was all you." She jabbed a finger at his chest, fighting a grin. "*You* yanked your pants down and sat your butt cheeks on the glass top. My poor innocent eyes."

"You looked?" He leaned back, eyebrows arched.

"Well, um…yeah." It'd been her sixth grade year, so they'd been twelve and fourteen. She'd seen him nude as a child, but that day had been the first time she'd ogled him in all his postpubescent glory. "I don't really remember."

"You're lying." He bit her neck playfully. "You definitely remember."

A full-blown smile stretched her cheeks as she recalled her shock. He'd looked like a man to her then. All that pubic hair—black like the hair on his head. And balls that hung low beneath a cock she'd fantasized about every night for the next three years. To think, he'd waited until she was fifteen before he let her touch him beneath his boxers.

She shrugged. "Too bad we didn't save the evidence. When the Xerox machine spit out that grainy picture of your ass...Oh God, do you remember? I've never laughed so hard in my life."

"Yeah, you peed your pants." His shoulders shook with laughter.

"Down my legs and all over my flip-flops. I had to wear your gym shorts home." She groaned. "I was so embarrassed you saw that."

"Why?" His brow furrowed. "Did I say something—?"

"No, you were cool about it. You were always..." *So tender and protective and perfect in every way.* "You had my back."

She sighed, holding on to the memory and her smile.

"This is what I missed more than anything else." He trailed a finger across the curve of her lips. "You're so goddamn beautiful, Camila, but when you smile, you light up the whole fucking world."

Her lips fell beneath his finger, her chest tightening with the weight of the huge, indescribable thing between them. She couldn't pretend this bond didn't exist. It'd been there her entire life. Even through twelve years of separation, she never stopped sensing it, thinking about it, and now, it sang with his words and vibrated with his touch.

But it was also murky and distorted with ugly truths. He'd purchased her, beaten her against a post, and refused to talk about his job. He was a slave trader, yet he'd helped her dispose of the bodies of slave buyers. Because he cared about her? He was an infuriating contradiction. As much as she wanted to luxuriate in their reconnection, doing so would be a death sentence for the women he preyed on next.

She needed to be smart about it. Nurture the bond. Manipulate it. Keep her fucking heart focused on the reason she was here. Except she wasn't a manipulative person. She was better than that, and at one time, he'd been a better person, too.

She lifted her hand and clutched his. Their fingers entwined, grasping and shooting tingles up her arm.

With a sudden shift that made her gasp, he yanked her up the bed and put them at eye level on their sides, fingers laced between them and his arm locked around her back.

"I know you felt it." He searched her face, lips parted. "Last night when I was inside you, and now. You feel *us.*"

Her chest ached. She tried not to feel anything at all, gulping down her breaths to stay quiet.

"Just stop for a second." He rested his forehead against hers. "Give yourself this, Camila. Let it happen."

"I can't." She leaned her head away. "It's like dangling a prize in a trap."

She desperately wanted to reach for it, to hold him, knowing if she did he'd break her, painfully and irreparably.

"What's the prize?" He watched her intently.

"Happiness without fear. Love without cruelty." She closed her eyes, voice raw with honesty. "You without slavery."

He let go of her fingers and smothered her against him in an embrace that buried her face in his neck. She wished she could see his expression, but his deep, steady breaths told her enough.

"You like my answer." She matched the pace of his breaths as if she wasn't trembling inside.

"Mm."

"What is *Mm*? I don't understand you. You seem to want this, *us*, but you also want your disgusting profession. You can't have both, Matias. Don't you get it? As long as you're enslaving women, I will never stop fighting."

"You're wrong."

"Then explain it."

"Not yet." He pressed his lips to the top of her head.

"Why not?"

"You need to see it for yourself."

*Fucking impossible.* "I need to pee." She squirmed against him.

He kissed along her hairline, his thumb stroking against her spine. With her nose against his throat, the warm scent of his skin overwhelmed her senses.

She told herself he smelled like rusted chains and broken dreams. "I really need to—"

"Go." He lifted the weight of his arm with a sigh and rolled to his back. "Return to the bed, and I'll tell you what happened in the west wing yesterday."

Images surfaced of him covered in blood, a cane in his fist, and death in his eyes. The cuts on her legs twinged in memory, and she shivered so hard she bit the inside of her cheek.

She slipped from the bed and scanned the floor. Every inch of marble was spotless—his bloody clothes, the broken lamp, corset, and panties nowhere in sight.

Without anything to wear, she made her way toward the bathroom. As she walked along the glass wall that led to the balcony, she spotted another balcony jutting from a separate entrance in the curve of the building. After hiking through the compound, she had a sense of its enormity, but seeing all that exterior glass covering multiple floors and balconies, it reminded her of an extravagant hotel with a steel beam infrastructure.

A table sat on the other balcony, the same one that connected to his living room where she'd scarfed down sandwiches yesterday. Now it was covered with domed plates and pitchers of juice. Her stomach grumbled.

If someone had brought breakfast into the suite and cleaned the bedroom, they had access to come and go. Were the servants around here armed? Maybe it was someone who could be overpowered and get her past the eye scanner.

She paused at the bathroom doorway and turned toward Matias.

He lay in a tangle of sheets around his waist, the white bedding aglow against his tawny skin and black hair. With his arms folded behind his head, he looked peaceful, almost harmless. But the way he studied her, his expression covetous and his eyes roaming her from head to toe, she knew there wasn't a harmless fiber beneath all that muscle.

"How many people have access to your suite?" She held her hands at her sides, fighting the urge to cover herself. "You and…?"

"Three others. Nico, Anacardo—"

"Anacardo?"

How did they take themselves seriously with these nicknames? *Picar, Chispa,* and *Anacardo* translated to Chop, Spark, and Cashew. Apparently, the use of sobriquets was a thing among narco-killers?

"He manages my domestic stuff—food, laundry, cleaning." His gaze rose to her face. "You're the third person."

"Me?" A flush of excitement tingled through her, quickly followed by suspicion.

No way would he make it that easy to escape. It wasn't like he handed over keys to the helicopter. Or a training manual on how to fly it.

"I can get past the scanner things?" She shifted her attention to the hall beyond the doorway. If she found a computer or phone, she could contact Tate.

"Your eyes were scanned before you woke yesterday. You have access to certain areas of the property, including my suite."

"Can I go outside?"

"Of course." With his legs spread wide and hands laced behind his head, he didn't seem to have a care in the world. "I thought you had to pee."

She slipped into the bathroom and used the toilet, buzzing with the new information. While she brushed her teeth—with his toothbrush because *fuck him*—she entertained scenarios of freeing all the slaves in the compound and leading them through the rainforest like a Rambo woman. She needed a badass rifle and a bandanna headband for maximum effect. Oh, and some survival skills, because she didn't know shit about trekking through two million square miles of jungle.

The dangers that lurked amid those majestic palms were so beyond anything she'd prepared for. Not to mention, her escape would provoke a manhunt. If Matias was willing to let her go outside, the odds of getting out were probably not in her favor.

But her goal had never been to save herself or existing slaves. She'd come here to stop them from taking more women. If she couldn't persuade the cartel to end that business, she would have to kill them.

Nausea curled in the pit of her stomach.

She rinsed out her mouth and stared at the wide brown eyes in the mirror. The anguish in those eyes was everything. Matias could be the most atrocious man on the planet, but there was no use lying to herself. She didn't have the emotional strength to end his life. Not now. Not ever. As inconvenient as that was, it loosened some of the knots inside her.

When she returned to the bed, he'd shifted into a half-sitting position, his back leaning against a stack of pillows and a tube of ointment in his hand.

As she crawled toward him on the mattress, he tracked her movements and patted his thigh. His ever-present desire to be all up in her personal space might've been a coercive tactic, but there was more to it. Maybe that was the key. She just needed to find a way to peel back the layers, starting with his obvious attraction to her.

Reaching for his waist, she dragged the sheet off with a quiver of fear darting down her spine. She pushed through it, lifting a leg over his nude lower body and straddling his partial erection.

His hands gripped her ass before she sat down, holding her upright on her knees.

Confused, she looked down at his swelling dick.

"Hold still." He squeezed a dollop of ointment into his palms and rubbed the icy balm over the backs of her thighs.

Instant relief shivered into her skin, and she swayed, dropping her hands on his chest.

"This is new." She twitched her fingers, indicating the sprinkle of dark hair on his sternum.

"So is this." He met her eyes as his caress glided over her ass, making wide circles to encompass the curves of her hips.

"Not the scrawny girl you remember?"

"You were never scrawny." The corner of his mouth lifted, and his gaze wandered over her body. "I spent the majority of my teen years hiding a chubby from you."

"You did?"

"You have no idea." He added more ointment to his hands and massaged the fronts of her thighs. "Last night..." His chest rose, fell. "The empty chair at our table belonged to a close friend."

The sudden somberness in his tone stiffened her muscles. She held still, focused on the movements of his hands, willing him to continue talking.

After a nerve-racking pause, he told her about Gerardo's betrayal, the information leaked to a rival cartel, the dismemberment, the blood, and the spy who still lived among them. His voice became rougher, angrier, with every word, leaving her cold long after he fell silent.

With the nudge of his hands, he lowered her to sit back on his thighs, his semi-flaccid cock resting in the *V* of her legs.

"There are other secrets." His jaw shifted. "Valuable secrets that Gerardo may or may not have released."

"Like what?" She liked this, him sharing, her listening, even if the subject matter fucked with her blood pressure.

"The kind no one talks about." He looked her firmly in the eye. "In time, you'll see things as they really are, and when you do, I want you to come to me and no one else."

Warning bells sounded in her head, raising the hairs on her nape.

Maybe he was working against the cartel? Except he seemed to be genuinely hurt by Gerardo's betrayal. What the hell was he hiding? And who was he hiding it from?

*They need to know you're just the slave of the month. A fresh hole to fuck. You mean nothing to me.*

She'd assumed he was just being a dick last night, but now… "Is your paranoia because of the spy or are there others here you don't trust?"

"Trust is earned, and we have a process that vets members and residents. Backgrounds, ranks, and positions are factors in granting access to certain information, but a lot of it is based purely on gut."

"Is that your job? To vet cartel members?"

"One of them." His blank expression lacked all the clues she was attempting to draw from him.

"And your gut steered you wrong with Gerardo."

He nodded, and somehow that tiny admission to making a mistake made him seem more human, more Matias.

His attention lowered to the raised bumps on her thighs. "Now I'm erring on the side of caution, even if it means risking more of your hatred." He gingerly trailed a finger over the worst cut. "I can repair the pain I cause you, but I can't bring you back to life."

"Someone wants to kill me?" A chill coursed, wild and panicky, through her limbs.

"To get to me, they might try."

Did that mean last night, with the cane…? She stared down at the welts.

*I know what he did to you, and that's not what this is.*

Her throat thickened. "You beat me and scared me so I would look like an abused slave instead of your…your…whatever I am?"

"Yes. But don't misunderstand me." His expression morphed into cast iron and sexual heat. "I get off on bringing you pleasure while you're trembling with fear."

"What am I to you?" She glanced at the rope near the headboard and returned to him. "Am I a slave or something else?"

He cocked his head, his hands absently stroking her legs. "You're my life, *mi vida.*"

She swallowed. "Do you beat other slaves like that?"

"You're not asking the right questions."

Jesus, fuck. What questions? Like who did he beat? How? When? Where?

She looked up. "Why do you do it? Why do you capture and torture women? Is it a kinky fetish? Or is this really just a business to you?"

"Right question." His eyes hardened. "Wrong answer."

"*Qué mierda!* Yesterday, you said this is business, supply and demand, and you don't make the rules."

"It is a business and so much more than that."

"Then tell me!"

"The answer is right in front of you." He dumped her onto the mattress and stood, his voice rising to a shout. "All you have to do is fucking look!"

"I am looking, but you're a goddamn black hole." She leapt off the bed, snatched the sheet, and wrapped it around her.

He growled and stormed toward the closet.

She chased after him. "How about you give me a straight answer instead of this mind-fuck game you're playing?"

"Game?" He whirled on her and put his face in hers. "This is *real.* You and me. No games. No mindfuck. If you put aside all the other shit, you'd know with absolute certainty that every breath I take, that my fucking purpose in all of this is for you."

His choked words, stiff neck, and pained, over-bright eyes stopped her heart. He stared at her as if he were desperate for her to not only hear him, but to see what he wasn't saying.

Why wouldn't he just tell her? Was someone listening?

Her eyes widened, and she jerked her head toward the camera on the ceiling. "Who's watching us?"

"I'm the only person who has access to that feed."

"What about listening—"

"There are no listening devices in my suite."

Well, shit. She pulled the sheet tighter around her chest and met his gaze. "Fine. I'll keep looking and figure out what you're not telling me."

"Where are you going to look?" His breathing started to return to normal, the tension in his face dissolving.

"All the answers are here, right?" She touched a finger to the outer corner of his eye.

"*Muy bien,* my beautiful girl."

He bent closer and brushed his mouth against hers. Another brush and another, until his tongue swept past her lips. The gentle kiss deepened, turning breathy and earnest.

His hands sank into her hair, and his erection jabbed at her stomach. But she didn't pull away, her tongue licking his with all the hope he'd planted in her. He'd opened up, and while she was more confused now than before, he'd given her enough to believe that there was something more than a monster behind those golden eyes.

He broke the kiss and cupped her neck. "We need to get dressed and eat. Then I'll give you a tour of the property."

Her pulse kicked up with excitement as he led her into the closet, activating a sensor light in the ceiling.

Rows of clothes on hangers and cubbies lined the walls on the left and right. Straight ahead was another door, this one with an eye scanner.

"What's behind that door?" She nodded at it.

"Skeletons." He grabbed a pair of jeans and pulled them on.

Her mind conjured a torture chamber with dead slaves hanging from chains on the walls. She shuddered, cursing her overactive imagination. "Do I have access to your skeletons?"

"Not until you're ready." He waved a hand at the racks of clothes on the left wall. "That's your side."

Kicking at the sheet that draped her body, she investigated the extensive wardrobe. Cocktails dresses, casual wear, and lingerie filled the space, all with tags and in her size.

She mentally ran through the last twenty-four hours. She'd spent most of that time in this suite.

"When was all this brought in?" She narrowed her eyes at him.

"Does it matter?" He slipped a blue t-shirt over his head.

"Yeah, it really does. Was it here before I arrived?"

"What does your gut tell you?" He touched a fingerprint scanner on a small safe in the wall, unlocking it and removing the Glock he carried in his waistband.

"My gut tells me..." She studied his face, watching for a reaction. "You expected me to show up as a slave with Van."

He seated the gun in the back of his jeans and stared at her, eyes and mouth giving nothing away.

"I can't figure out how, though." She snatched jean shorts from a cubby and held them up with a questioning brow.

"You can wear what you want during the day, but I choose your attire for dinner."

*Fair enough.* "The thing with Larry…that was all kind of up in the air." She dropped the sheet and slipped on the first bra and panties she found—white lacy things—then the shorts. "I followed him for months, knew he was involved in the trade, but I didn't know exactly how I was going to infiltrate until I tortured him."

He leaned against a shelf, legs crossed at the ankles, arms folded over his chest, regarding her with an unreadable expression.

"You must've been watching me for a while." Her stomach clenched with that realization. "But you couldn't have known my plan until I called you that night to pick up Larry's body. And even then, I don't know how you knew." She put on a brown tank top while keeping her focus on him, examining every twitch in his body. "That would've given you two days to stock the closet with clothes in my size, which is really creepy, by the way."

*And immensely satisfying.* How many men had that kind of attention to detail?

Stalkers did. And serial killers. Oh, and psychopaths.

She rubbed the back of her neck. "So am I warm on any of that?"

"You're hot." A panty-soaking smile filled his face. "Really fucking hot."

"You're not going to make this easy on me, are you?"

"The best rewards are the hardest to earn." He straightened and held out his hand. "Let's eat."

Thirty minutes later, she swallowed down the last bite of egg soup and leaned back in the chair on the balcony. It was the best *changua* she'd ever tasted, filling every crevice in her stomach with rich, milky warmth.

A temperate breeze stirred the humidity to a comfortable level, and the landscape pulsed with the sway of large fronds and the bellow of frogs. But the high-pitched, repeating shrills in the distance sounded like something was dying.

"What's that noise?" She reached for her coffee mug.

"Tinamous." He wiped his mouth with a linen napkin. "Mountain hens. They lay freaky alien-looking eggs with an unusual iridescent shimmer that changes color at different angles."

"So basically they lay eggs that scream, *Hey, look over here! Eat me!*"

The corner of his mouth curled up.

"Are they safe to eat?" She wasn't still considering going Rambo, but a backup plan wouldn't hurt.

"The birds or the eggs?"

"Both?"

"Yes." He studied her for an unnerving moment. "Finding food would be the least of your worries out there."

"Same could be said for in here." She pushed away the soup bowl and met his eyes. "You never carry a phone, yet you always answered when I called."

"I don't need one anymore." His timbre deepened. "You're here now."

He'd only carried a phone for her? She folded her arms across her chest, refusing to be sucked in by the sentiment in that.

"Every device on this property is locked down." He touched his fingers together like a steeple. "To make a call or access the Internet, two-factor authentication is required—a pin number and fingerprint scan."

Fuck, there went that idea. She pushed her shoulders back. "I want to call my friends and let them know I'm alive."

"Not yet."

Her pulse jumped. "Does the *yet* mean there might be a *yes*?"

"Yes."

"*Gracias.*" Now for the hard question. "Can I get a private meeting with Nico?"

"No." His tone was final, his direct eye contact impenetrable.

"Because you're afraid to ask him or because you don't want me to talk to him?"

"Neither."

*Interesting.* He'd said the inner circle knew about her history with him and that he kept nothing from them. Maybe he just didn't want to be left out of the meeting. Damn men and their egos. She couldn't think of another way to go about this, though. It wasn't like she could snuggle up to Nico's chair at dinner and demand a meeting from the kingpin. Not without drawing the attention of forty scary-as-fuck hitmen.

"Okay." She sipped her *tinto*, savoring the syrupy cinnamon-coffee concoction. "I want an audience with you and Nico. In private. No one needs to know about it."

He leaned forward, chewing a bite of bacon, studying her. "Why?"

"To present arguments against human trafficking. Offer alternatives. A different perspective."

"You think you can win him to your way of thinking?" His eyes squinted, lit with an inner glow.

"I want the opportunity to try."

Determination and heart—that was what she was made of. If she could interest Nico in the cause, it might distract him from the effect.

If not, she'd paint the glass walls with his blood.

"All right." Matias leaned back in the chair with a pensive look softening his features. "I'll think about it."

"Today?"

"Later."

Later didn't come when he gave her a tour of the property and made her kneel in a corset beside his chair at dinner on the veranda. There was no later when he fucked her against the post, in the bed, and any damn place he pleased.

The wait for later plodded into days. Days twisted into unbearable impatience. But time was inconsequential, so she bade it by being a timid little slave when they were outside of the suite, watching and analyzing. When they were alone, she shared her past with him and didn't push when he refused to discuss the present and future.

Later ended up being two weeks later, but the wait paid off.

He took her to meet with Nico.

# EIGHTEEN

Matias strode along the path on the east side of the property, his boots crunching gravel and an anxious hum in his veins. The gray sky chased away some of the afternoon heat, but the humidity hung on, pasting his thin Henley to his skin.

He released the buttons at his neck and glanced at the woman walking beside him.

A sheen of perspiration glistened on Camila's adorable nose, her eyes sharp and focused on the path ahead. Her long strides exuded self-possession, though her rigid posture suggested she was beating herself with a thousand over-analyzing thoughts.

He hated the distance between them whenever they stepped outside of his suite. It was necessary, but she took it to the next damn level, refusing to look at him or acknowledge him unless he commanded it.

With an irritated huff, she pulled on the thick leather collar around her throat. While it was there as a statement for others, every time he put it on her, it made his dick hard. Even so, he always removed it when they were alone. Someday, she would choose to wear one, a permanent one — for her and him only, fuck everyone else.

"Camila."

The command in his tone lifted those huge soulful eyes. He remembered the way they'd smoldered this morning, dazed with desire, glassy with uncertainty, her thighs trembling and hips rocking as he licked her cunt and fingered her to orgasm.

"I assume you have a speech prepared for this meeting." He clasped his hands behind his back, head forward, and watched her at the edge of his vision.

Her eyebrows pulled together as she gazed back at the estate, zeroing in on windows near Nico's rooms. "Isn't Nico's office that way?"

She scanned the perimeter of trees, pausing on each of the three armed guards who trailed out of earshot. There were five more chaperons she couldn't see. If she knew they were following, she didn't let on.

Matias' suite offered the most privacy, but he wanted this meeting to take place in his personal, most cherished location on the property. He'd never led her this deep into the jungle. She had no idea this little piece of heaven existed.

He'd debated whether or not it was too early to show it to her, that maybe he was revealing his hand too soon. It was her rejection he feared the most. If she didn't give him the reaction he longed for...

He'd man the fuck up and keep working on her.

"We're meeting him off-site." He steered her to the left at a fork in the trail, leading her deeper into the shadowed jungle.

The gravel thinned to dirt, softening their steps, and the thick canopy of smooth oval leaves created a cool shade. He'd taken her all over the property since she'd arrived, never leaving her side when they stepped out of his private rooms. She'd sulked about that for the first few days, as if she'd expected him to give her security access to the entire estate and just let her roam free.

As long as there was still a threat living among them, she wouldn't be leaving his sight.

He stepped closer to her, resting a hand on the curve of her lower back. "Did you prepare a rhetoric of bullet points and pretentious language for Nico?"

The neckline of her t-shirt had slipped off her shoulder, exposing her bra strap. He wanted to set his teeth in the delicate dip between the collar and her ear and bite down just to hear her breath catch.

"I couldn't pull off pretentious if I tried." Her jaw clenched, released. "Never received my high school diploma, remember?"

Several times over the last two weeks, she'd spoken late into the night about her captivity with Van Quiso. Though Matias had learned the details years ago, she didn't know that. It killed him to hear the specifics of her abuse all over again, especially whispered in her soft voice, but he'd held her tightly in bed, absorbing every word, every shiver and teary-eyed glance she shared with him.

She'd also told him things he hadn't known, like how she completed the remainder of her high school curriculum on-line and lamented the fact that she couldn't receive a diploma since she was still considered missing.

While her tenacity never ceased to impress him, it twisted a hellacious knot in his stomach. No matter what she said in this meeting,

Nico was going to challenge her.

To what end would she go to succeed in her mission?

"You're going to wing it, then?" His chest thickened with all the things he wanted to tell her.

"I'm going to stand before him as a slave, not a politician."

"That's your strategy? Persuade him with your heart?"

"I know it sounds illogical. I mean, he's the Restrepo kingpin, for fuck's sake." She rolled her lips between her teeth. "But he's also a person, and people aren't rooted in logic. We're creatures of emotion, bristling with selfish wants, preconceptions, and brutality. But inside every man is possibility." She lifted a stiff shoulder. "I'll just talk to him in terms of what he wants."

While everything she said was smart and fascinating and maybe even partly correct, it sat in his gut like a red hot coal.

He slammed to a stop. "You didn't take that approach with me."

"Because you already had what you wanted." She spun toward him, with a finger hooked under the collar and resentment in her eyes.

He grabbed her throat. "*This*" — he squeezed the leather against her neck — "is fucking window dressing, and you know it. I want the real thing, Camila. I want your submissive soul, sighing and replete, in my hands."

Her face paled as she gasped and clawed at his fingers around her throat. "I can't…I won't survive that."

Goddammit, how could her brilliant mind get this so fucking wrong?

"Not only will you live, you'll be more alive than you've ever been." He withdrew his grip and strode up the path without waiting for her.

When he reached the stone wall of their destination, she caught up with him, arms crossed over her chest, gaze lowered, demeanor subdued. Scaring her hadn't been his intention. Or maybe it had been. Either way, he wanted the light to return to her eyes.

He paused at a heavy wooden door, watching her closely. His hands felt sweaty, his throat parched and scratchy.

"What is this place?" Her gaze skittered along the eight-foot-high rock wall, tracing the length left to right where it faded into the jungle in both directions.

"Go ahead." He gestured at the retinal scanner that was bolted into the stone. "This is the only entrance. The wall keeps out most of the critters, but we still have problems with monkeys and large birds."

His pulse hammered as she leveled her eye with the security panel. He rubbed his palms on his jeans as she pushed open the door. Then he followed her in, clinging to her every movement as she gazed upon the landscape that had taken him a decade to recreate.

Her hands flew to her chest, her gait faltering mid-stride beside the first row of orange trees. Her head swung right, toward the acre that housed kumquat, tangerine, grapefruit, and lime trees.

"Holy shit." Her mouth fell open, and her steps sped up, still unsteady but her excitement palpable.

She walked beneath the limbs, her hand reaching upward. He remained at her side, devouring the bright glow of her eyes, the tremble in her chin, and tentative way she brushed her fingers over the leaves as if she couldn't believe they were real.

She halted suddenly, her attention directed straight ahead on the lemon grove. Her breath cut off. Then she gulped raggedly, again and again, her hand lifting to cover her mouth as the other reached out, blindly searching for his.

He caught her fingers, lacing them with his own, and inhaled the deepest, fullest breath he'd ever taken.

Four hundred flowering trees spread across the secluded five-acre grove, infusing every particle in the air with tranquil memories. There was only one scent as sweet as the fragrance of citrus blossoms, only one sight as beautiful, and she was finally here.

Her wide, unblinking eyes took in the delicate buds, the vibrant colors of the fruit, and the fertilized soil, and he knew she appreciated the labor and passion in a way that had connected them since they were small children. She appreciated his tribute to her.

"How did you —? You did all this…" She stepped toward the nearest lemon tree and gripped tighter to his hand, pulling him with her as she studied the healthy branches. "They're… God, they must be ten years old?"

"Yes." His voice broke, and he cleared it. "Yeah, I've been at it a while. But I've had help. Hired one of the best citrus farmers in Florida about eight years ago."

"Nico let you do this? I mean…wow. There must be four or five acres here."

"Five acres. Four hundred trees. And Nico…" A smile pulled at his mouth. "He questions everything I do."

Most of his arguments with the other man had been over the necessity of the eight-foot wall.

She didn't let go of his hand as she entered the lane between two rows of lemon trees, scattering the bees that hovered around the blooms. Twisted branches arced over the path and tangled together, forming a living trellis of deep green foliage and dangling fruit.

When she tilted her head upward, a tear glistened on her cheek. She swatted it away with a soft smile on her lips.

"It's just like home. The planting pattern. The archway. Every detail." She stopped walking and turned toward him, her gaze on the inked leaves on his forearm, her fingers squeezing tighter around his. "You did this because you missed it?"

He lifted her chin with his free hand and held her gaze. "I missed *you*."

She pulled her head back, and her focus slipped away, seeking the trees, the ground, their entwined hands. When she returned to his eyes, hers were wet with regret. But there was hope there, too.

"A five-acre grove recreating our childhood. Because you missed me." She touched his jaw, the line of his throat, her gaze following the movement. "I understand you were taken by the Restrepos, and I assume you didn't rise to the top-level in the span of a year. So you must've started as a lackey? Is that why you didn't come back for me?"

"Camila—"

"I was there, Matias. Right there in that grove waiting for you for a year before…" She swallowed. "Before it was too late."

"I couldn't." He released her hand and crushed her against him, holding her face to his chest as his insides rioted with invidious memories. "The men who found me—"

"*Found* you?"

Fuck. He should've chosen a different word. "The people who came for me that day made threats."

"What kind of threats?"

She tried to lift her head, but he held her in place so she wouldn't see the vulnerability in his expression. He was having a hell of a time evening his voice.

"They threatened everyone I cared about." He pressed a kiss to her head. "Specifically you."

She stiffened against him. "Why? What did they want?"

He couldn't explain that part without unraveling every fucking thing he'd tried so hard to protect her from. "Camila, there are things I can't tell—"

Her fist slammed against his abs, not with any kind of force, but hard enough to break free of his hold. She spun away, her face emblazoned with rage.

"You knew about my family." She balled her hands at her sides. "The day I called you, when I escaped, you told me not to contact them." Her eyes narrowed. "Why didn't you tell me they were dead?"

"Lower your voice." He folded his hands behind his back and widened his stance.

She glanced around, but the rows of trees blocked her view of the wall. "Is someone here?"

"No one has access to the grove besides Nico, the caretaker, you, and me."

"Is Nico meeting us here?" She pulled on her ear nervously, her attention darting through the branches, as if she were torn between pursuing this conversation and focusing on her end goal.

"He's waiting for us in the gazebo." He turned and pointed down the path through the lemon trees. "Just through there."

"We probably shouldn't keep him waiting then." She moved to walk past him but paused, her gaze lingering on his face.

She'd spent the past two weeks watching everything and everyone around her. There were slaves on the property, in her periphery, kneeling beside her at dinner, all of them gagged in her presence to prevent communication. But just as he'd hoped, the bulk of her searching had been focused on him, on what he knew and what he was hiding.

He needed her to not only see the truth for herself, but to see *him,* the man she was meant to love.

"Your uncle died in that fire, with my family." With trembling fingers, she brushed the tattoo on his forearm.

It wasn't a question, so he remained still and quiet beneath her rare touch.

"I'm sorry." She dropped her hand, letting it hang at her side. "I've been so angry, so suspicious about what happened to them, I've lost sight of the fact that you lost him, too."

He didn't have a regretful bone in his body with regard to that old man. But as far as she knew, his parents had died when he was an infant and the uncle who had raised him on the grove was the only family he'd had. None of that was true.

With an arm raised in the direction of the gazebo, he waited for her to move then followed behind.

Her jean-clad legs carried her out of the lemon grove, the subtle sway of her ass unintentionally seductive in her determination. Despite the confident way she carried herself, he suspected each step twisted her up with nerves. He wished he could carry her out of there and save them both a lot of potential pain.

They turned the corner, and the gazebo came into view. Seated at the table, Nico glanced up from his phone, his brows heavy over dark eyes and mouth turned downward in his usual relaxed expression.

She looked back at Matias, her brown eyes hesitant. Then she blinked, and her focus cleared, her features hardening.

He molded his face into something that resembled self-assurance. He was ninety-nine percent certain he knew how this would end. But it was that one-percent that sank his stomach with dread.

# NINETEEN

A swarm of bees took flight in Camila's stomach as she stepped into the gazebo and met Nico's demoralizing glare. He rarely looked into her eyes, as in not once since she arrived in Colombia. But sometimes she sensed him watching. Like it was his job to watch her without her noticing.

His elusive observance was so much better than this in-her-face staring.

"Matias' little happy place suits you." Nico's gaze subtly skimmed over her body and returned to her eyes, his Colombian inflection falling flat. "You're much more enticing than the fruit."

Okay, that drained her blood straight to her feet. It was a joke, right? Nico might've kept tabs on her, but he'd never given her so much as a glimmer of interest.

His apathy was frightening, and he exuded it as if deliberately playing it to his advantage. Even now, his arms hung limply at his sides, his posture relaxed behind the wrought iron table, almost bored, as his gaze wandered away.

"She likes the grove." Matias stepped around her and pulled out an empty chair, gesturing for her to sit.

She loved the grove. Loved it so much, in fact, she didn't want Nico anywhere near it.

Sitting as directed, she entertained a silly thought about plucking one of the ripe fruits and traipsing the endless maze of paths through the trees. It was how she'd spent her childhood, letting the twisty arms of the branches guide her, never without a juicy snack in her hand.

"I should hope so, *ese*." Nico focused on an errant crease in his black suit pants, smoothing it with a thumb. "You spent an embarrassing amount of time and money growing shit that can't be injected, smoked, snorted, or smuggled."

"That sounds dangerously close to complaining." Matias lowered into the chair beside her, putting her between him and Nico. Folding his hands on the table, he leaned in, eyes on Nico. "You done?"

"I haven't decided." Nico shrugged.

Both men grinned, sharing a cryptic moment of silence. As their smiles faded, they continued to stare at one another. Communicating? Whatever it was hinted at a strange kind of simultaneous trust between them. Their postures remained at ease, their eyes bright. Until Nico shifted to her.

"So you wanted to meet with me to discuss the cartel's affairs?" His tone dripped with censure, expression hardening in a blink, erasing all traces of humanity.

Just like that, he looked every bit the kingpin. Her insides churned.

He didn't belong here in this magical place, where the trees fluttered with vitality, trilling with birds, and saturating the air with the quiet, aphrodisiac sweetness of orange blossoms. Matias had created a miniature version of her beloved sanctuary, knitting her memories into the soil and coaxing them to life. The resurrected ambiance filled her with a sense of innocence, an unexpected warmth of heart that made her want to turn to him with openness and affection.

And hope.

He could tell her a million times he wanted her, needed her, that her disappearance had gutted him, whatever. It was just words. But this…this nostalgic place was infinitely more moving. It was a proclamation that couldn't be cheated or faked.

The maturity of the trees alone proved that a decade had been dedicated to growing it, to nurturing something much too wistful for a cartel compound. Sure, he hired out the labor, but his touch was in the tiniest details, such as the planting patterns, the types of fruiting trees, the yellow twine her *papá* had used to support the saplings, and the unusual way the secondary limbs were pruned—exactly how Venomous Lemonous had taught them.

No one else could've replicated her memories with such painstaking and sentimental precision. She knew without a doubt Matias had been here since the plants germinated and participated in every step of their life cycle.

Because he'd missed her.

It left her feeling groundless, dizzy, and utterly seduced by the idea of *him and her*, by the beauty and promise it bestowed. She could envision living here, being whatever Matias willed her to be, if it meant spending time in this place, recreating stolen moments with him, and cultivating dreams.

Because she'd missed him, too. So fucking much it made her chest hurt.

Maybe that was why he'd chosen this location for the meeting. To bewitch her so thoroughly she'd forget the reason she was here.

Tightening her muscles, she angled her body to face Nico and gave him strong eye contact.

"You might see me as just a slave, but I'm not controlled by fear." She crossed her legs at the knees, the position pulling the jeans tight across her ass as she rested her hands on the table. "I've killed people, and I'm intimately familiar with human trafficking." She paused. "Can I call you Nico?"

"Please do." His eyes flickered, and it might've been curiosity.

"I'm not an accountant, Nico, but I find it hard to believe the slave trade yields as much profit as, say, your drug smuggling ventures. First off, the slaves I've seen on the property are my age. Some are even older. I doubt any of them are virgins."

He exchanged a look with Matias, and she would've given anything to know what was going on beneath their blank expressions.

"Not that I'm suggesting you capture young girls." Her foot twitched restlessly. She stilled it. "I'm just questioning why you capture and sell people at all."

"Tell us your theories," Matias said. Elbow on the table, he rested his jaw on loosely curled fingers, the liquid gold of his eyes sharp around the edges.

Twisting her thoughts to that of a criminal, she voiced a cut and dry hypothesis about how they sought to gain market share and remain competitive against rival gangs and drug lords. She talked out of her ass while trying to keep her opinions on a cohesive level, brainstorming ideas they could relate to, and maintaining an eager, unbiased tone, like she was a fucking marketing consultant for the cartel.

It was ludicrous, listening to herself suggest how they could broaden their drugs and weapons smuggling to other countries, like Australia. But in her desperate mind, smuggling those things were a lesser evil than selling innocent lives.

Neither of them interrupted her long-winded pitch. Matias nodded at some of her points and lifted his eyebrows at others. She avoided those hazel eyes, though, as well as the symmetrical beauty of his flawless face. She tried not to glance at him at all for fear he'd derail her, command her with a look, and make her want things that didn't belong in this conversation.

Focusing on Nico wasn't any easier. He was dangerously handsome, or at least, he would've been if he didn't look so scowly and disinterested all the time. Didn't matter where he was or what he was doing, he gave the impression that he wanted to be somewhere else, like he was too goddamn important for the world around him.

Other than the night Van delivered her to them, Nico always wore a suit. The crisp black fabrics and collared shirts that opened at the neck projected an urbane, cultured persona that was only mildly intimidating if taken at face value. It was what he hid beneath the casual arrogance that had her carefully choosing her words.

Was she talking to a psychopath? An empty soul? A man who didn't rationalize his own behavior? If he was a man at all, then somewhere in there was a heart.

Steeling her backbone, she changed gears without segue and launched into her experience as Van's captive.

"He locked me in a coffin-like box for the first twenty-four hours, wearing only rope around my hands and feet and a ring gag in my mouth."

Her cheeks twinged in memory at the godawful stretching, and sweat beaded between her breasts. With a waver in her voice, she told them how Van fucked that ring gag over and over in the days that followed, how he beat her, spit on her, and stripped her of every ounce of hope and courage, all while refusing to speak to her beyond the bark of his commands. *Kneel, open, suck, cry…*

"I was there a week before Liv stepped in." Camila folded her trembling hands on her lap. "She introduced herself as a deliverer and said I was to be trained as a slave and sold as a piece of property."

She rushed on, giving voice to the worst of her time there. The whips, the rules, the stifling loneliness, each harrowing memory blooming heat behind her eyelids. "You can't comprehend the depths of human depravity until you experience it on your knees, in the dark, your body broken and throbbing, your mind pulling away in an attempt to protect, to endure. But no matter where your thoughts go, there is nothing or no one to cling to. It makes you question the very reason for life, like what the fuck are we even doing here and why are we the cruelest to our own kind?"

Matias stood, fingers sliding into his pockets, and stepped out of the gazebo. He strode away with a wide gait and strong posture — shoulders back and chest out, but she hadn't missed the stark pain in his eyes.

Her pulse quickened. She'd already given him the full unpolished recitation of her year with Van and Liv, hoping to soften his insistence for slavery. Maybe she was finally getting through to him.

Except he wasn't the one she needed to convince.

Nico stroked a finger over the shadowed edge of his thin beard as he watched Matias walk the path to the far side of the grove, fringed by rows of lemon trees.

Matias sat on a stone bench out of hearing range, elbows braced on knees and profile angled so that he could still see her.

For the span of several heartbeats, Nico didn't move or speak, his vacant eyes on Matias as if gazing down a long dark road. Then he blinked, straightened in the chair, and turned his attention to her.

"You know what I see when I look at you?" His tongue slid over straight white teeth. "With your tight body and your anti-slavery campaign? I see a hardcore submissive in deep denial. A well-trained cliché, trying to top from the bottom, all the while telling yourself you want no part of it. Stubbornness and fear have driven you to fight against your nature, but you're only one hard, violent fuck away from surrender. Am I right, Camila Dias?"

Her stomach bottomed out. "No, you're — "

"Those dark desires you try so desperately to hide beneath your quivering victim act? I see the hungry, dirty slut." His accent thickened into a rolling drawl. "Hell, every man here sees it. And wants it."

Ice filled her veins. This motherfucker was either blowing smoke up her ass or he paid attention a hell of a lot more than he let on.

"I'm *not* a slut." She jutted her chin, hands fisting on her lap, and eyes burning with angry tears.

"You're a slut in the most desirable way possible. How many men have you fucked, *chiquita*? How many dicks have left your pussy clenching for something harder, crueler, and more powerful? All those sloppy, monotonous hookups with strangers, while searching for the one who will pound you into submission, searching for anyone who will fuck your convictions into broken meaningless pieces. A search that took you all the way to Colombia, shackled as a slave in a slave trader's bed."

Fuck him to hell! She shook with unholy rage, her gaze skipping across the grove to Matias. He tipped his head in her direction, elbows propped on his knees, but he was too far away to make eye contact. Too far away to hear this fucked-up conversation or to stop Nico. Not that he would. A twinge of hurt stabbed through her.

"You don't know me," she said to Nico while keeping her gaze trained on Matias.

"No, I don't. But Matias does, and he tells me everything."

Her hackles went up. Matias told him all of this? Why would a cartel boss even entertain a conversation about her?

This discussion had taken a turn into Insanityville. She should've brought a pillow so she could bury her face in it and scream. Everything about this felt off. Yet she couldn't stop Nico's comments from sinking in, itching beneath her skin, and sparking a pang in her chest.

She sucked in a serrated breath. Matias should've been sitting beside her, not on the other side of the grove like a goddamn coward. It was as if Nico had waited until he had her alone to unleash his crazy. But why wait? He was the fucking capo. He made the rules, could do whatever he wanted, and didn't have to explain himself to anyone. None of this made sense.

Throwing Matias a frigid stare, she returned to Nico. "Would you have said all of this in front of him? I thought you two were friends."

"I prefer your genuine reactions, not the ones influenced by him as he breathes down your neck." His tight grimace strained the tension in the air. "I want to talk to Camila Dias, not the woman who's Matias' slave."

"No one influences my...anything." Her voice came out small, weak. She strengthened it with a deep inhale. "No one owns me."

"No one owns your soul. *Yet*. But a voluntary captive lives deep inside you, craving to be claimed, used, and fucked in every way imaginable."

"That's slavery, Nico." She seethed with indignation. "A violation of basic human rights. It was a monstrosity two-hundred years ago in the south, and it still is, here, now, no matter how sexy you try to paint it. But clearly, you and Matias and your damn profit margins—"

"Now you've ruined it." His scathing stare made her wilt. He didn't even need to raise his voice.

"Ruined what?" Her throat closed up.

"Your proposal."

"Were you actually considering it?"

He continued to glare, but now that she looked closer, there was something missing in it. The hard lines of his jaw, dark furrow of his brow, flat line of his lips—it was all there to appropriately communicate his displeasure. Deep behind his inky eyes, though, she didn't see the heat or the passion she'd expect in an outraged man.

Maybe she was just imagining it. "Tell me what you want, what to say. If you'll reconsider, I'll take back whatever I said and—"

"See, you were doing so good there. You were respectful of our business and made suggestions for improvement. You initiated trust by sharing your weakest moments with Van Quiso. Then you blew it with your self-righteous, preachy judgment. If I wanted a homily on moral values, I'd visit my mother."

Shit. Fuck. Okay, she could recover from this. "What do you want?"

He leaned in, and the potency of his cologne chased away the perfume of orange blossoms. "I want you."

# TWENTY

"You want *me*?" Camila widened her eyes, her insides shriveling from throat to gut.

"You," Nico mouthed, his face a breath away. "In my bed, riding my dick, and wearing my collar." He flicked the lock at her throat.

A vise gripped her chest, squeezing her air. She couldn't breathe, couldn't think past the words burning through her heart.

"In return, we'll pull out of the slave trade." He sniffed. "We'll stop capturing women in your hometown. We'll stop enslaving humans altogether."

Her muscles were so locked up she couldn't move, but her head shifted, seeking out Matias on the other side of the lemon grove. His attention was on her, his ass still seated on that bench.

"Eyes on me." Nico's bark jerked her focus back.

His straight nose, even breaths, and dark gaze betrayed nothing. His features were so empty, in fact, she decided he was probably a very good liar. That sucked considering every answer she needed was concealed behind those eyes.

She lowered her head, trying to reason through his offer. "I become your willing slave and you end the slavery of all others. That's what you're proposing?"

"Yes."

"If you wanted me, you could just take me, with or without a deal."

"That's not how this works."

Because of Matias? Or something else? The proposal was irrational. He knew Matias had claimed her. Why would he destroy their friendship or risk Matias' loyalty? Her mind whirled to decrypt the undercurrents. There was more to this. Something he wasn't saying.

"I want Matias in this conversation." She met his eyes.

"No." He bent closer, hands dangling between his spread knees and lips inches away. "This is between you and me."

"Does he know you're making this offer?"

His head turned, and she followed his line of sight across the grove. Matias stared back at her for an endless moment and looked away.

Her heart sank. *He knew.* He knew, and he was letting this play out.

Because he chose his job over her.

"Decide, Camila." Nico's rhythmic accent grated across her skin. "The offer's about to expire."

She wanted to kill him. Strip his golden skin right off his face and smother him with it. But she couldn't.

After two weeks of residence in the cartel's headquarters, she'd watched and learned and come to a glaring realization that attempting to murder the capo would result in an epic failure for two reasons. One, he was never without guards. Even now, she knew Matias was armed and would protect his boss with his life. Two, Nico would be replaced, likely with Matias or someone else in the inner circle. Someone who would continue the slave trade.

Nico's offer was her best choice. Not that she could trust him to follow through on his end of the deal, but it would put her in his bed and potentially in his heart. It would give her an advantage, the ability to persuade him, an *in,* that she didn't have with Matias.

But there was one very muscular, dark, and deadly problem.

Fire trickled behind her eyes and burned through her sinuses. "What about Matias?"

"Disclaim him. Choose your crusade over the man who has caused you so much torment. Is the decision really that hard?"

The lump that was lodged in her throat burned hotter. "He'll kill you."

"Do you honestly believe he cares more about you than he does about me?" He arched a brow.

Logic and reasoning said *no.* Matias sat his fucking ass on the other side of the grove knowing what Nico would offer.

She'd put herself here with the very real possibility of death. *To end slavery.* Now she had what she'd come for—the cartel capo, the top fucking guy, telling her she could stop their human trafficking with her surrender. How could she *not* do this?

Something didn't feel right. Deep in her gut was a discomfiting suspicion that she was being set up. And crowding that suspicion was her stupid sentimentality. Did she care more about saving slaves than she did about Matias? Than the boy she grew up with? Than the man who rebuilt her citrus grove?

Could she willingly have sex with another man?

"Time's up." Nico tilted his head, his fingers playing with the short black hair on his jaw. "I need an answer."

"No." The strength of her voice rose from a place of besotted resolve, but it was resolve nonetheless.

With her heart in her throat, she pushed away from the table, strode out of the gazebo, and took the path through the lemon grove, heading toward Matias. There would be a shitload of introspection in her near future, like was that decision ever really hers to make? But she knew with certainty, no matter what happened, she would never regret choosing Matias.

He lifted his head at the sound of her steady footfalls, and when he stood, the relief etching his expression sent her heart racing. And her feet.

Hands behind his back and stance wide, he stared at her without moving, forcing her to take every last step toward him, sealing her future with him. Her choice solidified as she ran, and when she reached him beneath the canopy of leaves, she looped her arms around his neck.

He stood still for a moment, his rigidness choking her heartbeats.

Slowly, confidently, his arms wrapped around her back, smothering her against him. His chest felt hard, burning up through the thin material of his Henley. A vein bulged in his brow, the sinews in his neck strung tight. She stroked his throat, making his breath catch.

"*Gracias,*" he said in a raspy rumble and touched their foreheads together.

Her entire body trembled as she slid her fingers along his softly shaved jawline and stabbed them through his hair. "I'm scared, Matias." *Scared of him. Scared Nico will take her away from him.*

"I know, *mi vida.* I know." He kissed her with a glide of lips and warm gasps. "Thank you for facing your fears with me."

He kissed her again, this time with force and urgency, his tongue sliding against hers and his fingers digging along her spine. Then the kiss was no longer a kiss. It was his lips whispering into her heart and his breaths caressing her soul. He was hers in his citrus grove, and she was his in any manner he wanted.

It was a dream, one that would take a lot of work and even more answers. But for now, she savored it, tasting and licking his mouth. He was hunger and passion, his tongue tangling with hers with a ferocity that curled her toes.

He swung her around, and hard wood met her back. She lifted her gaze to a ceiling of leaves and ripe yellow lemons. Laughter burst from her chest, shaking her against the tree trunk and breaking the kiss.

His hand swept through her hair as he studied her intently, smiling. "What?"

"Kissing me in a lemon grove, Matias?" She shook her head, grinning wider. "I guess if it worked the first time..."

"And the time after that." He kissed her. "And the next time." Another kiss. "Every time, Camila. You've never denied me in our grove."

"No. I suppose I haven't."

The crunch of shoes on gravel sounded behind him, and he sighed, resting his lips against her brow.

"Guess she likes you better than me." Nico stepped off the path, stopping a couple feet away, hands in his pockets and a strange look on his face.

She untangled herself from Matias and shifted away from them.

"You knew what he was going to offer me," she said to Matias.

"Yes." He held his hands behind his back.

"What if I had agreed?" She kept her tone quiet, more curious than accusatory.

His eyes slid to Nico, and they shared one of those unspoken looks she couldn't begin to decipher.

These assholes had planned this, all of it, to test her. More specifically, *Matias* had set it up. Why would Nico go along with it? What did he gain from it? Something about their relationship niggled, and she couldn't put her finger on it.

She backed up a couple steps so she could study them side by side.

Nico was a hard one to decode with his shroud of suits and disinterest. He was a couple inches shorter, maybe ten pounds smaller than Matias, and around the same age. Nico's complexion was a shade fairer, his scowl a hundred times darker, and he was intimidating in the mysterious way he was always inconspicuously watching, always present. *Like a guard.*

Contrarily, Matias was jeans and guns and hot-blooded temper, but he didn't carry the vigilance of a sentinel — which she assumed was one of his jobs. In fact, he had a slew of guards that followed him everywhere.

"Why do you need armed chaperons?" She narrowed her eyes at Matias.

"I know things."

"What things?" She ground her teeth.

"Important things that require security."

"You give me answers that tell me nothing." She rubbed her head. "What is your job in the cartel?"

Nico cleared his throat, drawing her gaze. He looked away, and she swore a smile touched the corner of his mouth. That was weird. And why was his shoe scuffing the ground?

*Because Nico's not who he says he is.*

"All this time, I thought he was your boss." She pointed at Nico with her eyes on Matias. "But he's not."

"Not exactly." Matias scratched the back of his neck. "We're close."

"Close like besties? Or brothers?" She watched them carefully, looking for reactions. "Lovers?"

"No," they said in unison then laughed uncomfortably.

She turned her attention to Nico, who was just standing here instead of hurrying off to run the cartel. Hell, the man spent the majority of his time up Matias' ass. And Matias walked around like he owned the joint, building citrus groves and silencing rooms just by stepping through the door. Then there was his extravagant suite that only a few people had access to. She'd never entered Nico's personal space, but from the outside, it looked like Matias' wing was the prime real estate with the best views.

Nico appeared to hold authority over everyone who lived here, barking orders and sending people scuttling. But when he was alone with Matias, the dynamic between them flipped.

Like now. The three of them stood there, as if waiting for instruction, for someone to say *Let's go*. Naturally, she looked to Matias.

But so did Nico.

Light bulbs went off in her head, and her mouth dried as she aligned the pieces. "Who owns this property?"

"Hector Restrepo built it." Matias leaned a shoulder against the tree trunk, his timbre as steady as his eyes.

She'd heard stories about the old capo in the news and whispers in the halls during her stay here. Apparently, he was a brutal bastard. *Was.* Hector was dead.

"You're not Hector's son, are you?" She directed the question at Nico, but holy hell, she was certain she knew the answer.

He glanced at Matias.

"See, he's looking at you!" She turned to Matias, heart hammering. "Because you're the one making decisions around here." She fisted her hands on her hips. "Who are you?"

"You already know." Matias stared at her, his unblinking gaze knocking the air from her lungs.

*He's the boss.*

*Matias is the goddamn kingpin.*

What better way to protect the capo than to make everyone think someone else was the capo? How had she missed this?

"If you're not the second in command..." She glared at Matias then looked at Nico. "You are."

"Told you she'd find out." Nico scrubbed a hand over his head and scanned the surrounding trees.

"I need to hear you say it." She swayed as her stomach bucked in denial. "Say it, goddammit."

"I'm Matias Restrepo." The name rolled off Matias' lips with mellifluous possession.

Her face numbed with icy prickles. "You're Matias *Guerra.*"

Matias Guerra, the boy she'd spent her childhood with. Camila Guerra, the name she'd doodled on all of her school folders.

Her mind swam, and her pulse spiked. Christ, she'd grown up with a Restrepo family member? And he'd inherited this estate? This business?

"I'm Nico Bianchi." Nico held out a hand. "Matias' adviser, personal guard, and decoy."

*Decoy* echoed through her head. She stared at his offered hand, refusing to touch it, her muscles too stiff and heavy.

Her chest heaved as she peered up at Matias through her lashes. "You're the capo."

"Yes." Matias' tongue darted out, wetting his bottom lip. "This is my cartel."

# TWENTY-ONE

A massive weight evaporated from Matias' shoulders, replaced by a warmth of sunlight that broke through a rip in the clouds. He licked his lips and swore he tasted joy, tasted *her*, the beauty of his *vida*.

Camila paced in front of him, working herself into a sexy mess. Her nipples pebbled beneath her damp shirt, and denim molded deliciously to her tight ass. He wanted nothing more than to strip her bare and fuck her under the blooming branches, just like he'd been meant to do twelve years ago.

But not with Nico here and not while her huge brown eyes were searching for answers.

She'd turned down Nico's offer, surrendered the easier path, and abandoned herself. *For me.*

Just the thought of what that meant left him breathless.

"All these years…" She wandered a short distance away and returned, her eyes cloudy, distant. "You were the boss since the beginning."

Not exactly, but close enough.

Withholding who he was had haunted him since the day he left her, but numerous safeguards needed to be implemented first, with Nico's proposal being the last measure. Eventually, she would understand the prudence in his secrecy.

"This is madness." She raked her hands through her hair and closed her eyes. "I have so many questions I don't even know where to start." Her head snapped up, and she scanned the grove with a startled whisper. "Who else knows?"

Nico raised a brow in an expression that somehow made his frown look pleasantly surprised. He'd had his doubts about her ability to keep secrets, but Matias had always known that when Camila Dias gave her loyalty it was fiercely deep-rooted.

"The upper-ranking lieutenants and hitmen know who their real boss is." Nico watched her, his hands hanging loosely at his sides. "As well as some of the staff and hired whores on-site. But the cartel's thousands of underlings and countless opponents scattered across North and South American? They have no idea."

She cut her eyes to Matias, every muscle in her body radiating anger. "Why didn't you tell me?"

"I don't think she's ready for this conversation." Nico pulled a pack of cigarettes from his pocket.

She clenched her hands. "How about you let me be the judge—"

"Camila." Matias infused his tone with steel. "I couldn't tell you anything about the cartel over the phone. As for why I didn't tell you the past two weeks…" He pointed a look at Nico.

She followed his gaze and chewed her lip. Then her lip started to curl. "You wanted me to think he was the boss so he could offer me that deal?"

Matias nodded, waiting for the explosion.

Spinning toward Nico, she leaned forward and stabbed a finger in his direction. "Your proposal was complete bullshit."

Nico approached her, slowly, dispassionately, and put his face in hers. "Respect me."

His quiet command held a lethal edge that made her breath catch.

As long as Nico didn't put his hands on her, Matias wouldn't interfere with how Nico managed his relationship with her going forward. She needed to adhere to the boundaries Nico had already set and treat him like a superior in front of others. The spy might've known who the true capo was, but no one outside the inner circle knew who Camila was. Once Matias caught the son of a bitch, she and Nico could battle it out all they wanted.

"You said you wanted me to ride your dick and wear your collar." She swatted at a fly near her ear, her complexion red-hot and sexy as hell. "You called me a slut."

"I gave him a script." Matias braced for a Camila-sized fist in his direction. Even he knew his approach had been slightly depraved.

"You what?" Her voice shook, but she didn't swing.

"Give me a little credit here." Nico lit a cigarette and exhaled a puff of smoke. "I improvised some of that. Very well, I might add."

"Let me get this straight." She paced again, which was really distracting because her ass looked damn good flexing in those jeans. "You told Nico to say those things, to *humiliate* me, all to force me into making a choice? You could've just skipped the damn meeting and talked to me like a normal person."

"Then I would've missed your delightful conversation," Nico said dryly, a gleam of mischief in his eyes.

She shot him a glare and returned to Matias. "If I would've chosen him and his offer, you would've what?" Her voice grew louder, her steps falling harder, faster. "You would've told me it was all a game, beat me with a paddle, and sent me to bed without dinner?" She stopped in front of him, her entire body frozen as she seethed. "It's really fucked up that you engineered this just to know what I would choose. Because guess what? I might've chosen you, but I will *not* stop fighting for those women."

There was her backbone, and goddamn, it made him hard as hell.

"She really gets wrapped around the axle." Nico cocked his head, watching her.

"To the point of paralysis." Matias flattened his lips to hide a grin.

"I don't...argh!" She flung her arms up. "I'm trying to make a point."

"She's still going, spinning round and round." Nico took a drag on the cigarette. "She's probably going to rip out her hair."

Matias couldn't stop his chuckle from escaping. Nico laughed, too, and it was crazy to see him drop his facade so quickly in front her. The man had spent the last decade perfecting the cold, psychopathic mask he wore every day. It had become so much a part of him he struggled to shed the act. He must've truly liked her.

She stared at them as their amusement faded, hands on her hips and tension flaring in her shoulders and neck. "Laugh it up, but the joke's on you. I passed your little test, and in the end, I *will* win the game."

He drew in a deep breath. They were just teasing her, but he needed to cut her a break. She wasn't emotionally or mentally in the same place he was. She'd chosen him, but she still saw him as the enemy, the man who beat her, raped her mouth, and sold slaves.

There were several crucial things he was keeping from her. He could spill it all right now, prove that she was fighting the wrong opponent, and she would fall to her knees, overwhelmed with wondrous glee. Okay, maybe he wouldn't get *that* reaction, but she would certainly look at him through a different lens.

That scenario terrified him.

He didn't want her to fall in love with his agendas or crusades. He needed her to love him the same way she'd loved him twelve years ago — truly, madly, deeply, without argument or thought, with a passion that stemmed from an instinctual, unquestionable place inside her.

He needed her to love him the same way he loved her.

"This isn't a game." He stepped toward her until a sliver of space separated them and lifted her chin with a knuckle. "I didn't stage the meeting with Nico because I wanted to know what choice you would make. I did it so that *you* would know."

She studied his face, her pupils dilating with a thousand seeking thoughts. She could think whatever she wanted as long as she was looking at him, *seeing* him.

Gripping his wrist, she pulled his hand away from her chin, but she didn't let go. Her fingers slid over his, absently caressing his knuckles as she stared at him.

"For the record" — Nico flicked ash from his cigarette, eyes narrowed on her — "I meant everything I said in the gazebo, except the part about being in my bed. If I touched you, Matias would rip me from limb to limb."

"True, but I wouldn't enjoy it." Matias smirked.

"*Me importa un culo.*" Nico glanced behind him. "I'm gonna head back to the house. Guards will be stationed outside of the wall."

Then he strolled away, puffing on his cigarette. When he vanished from view, Camila ambled in the opposite direction, fingers tucked in the back pockets of her jeans and her steps soft and aimless. Matias trailed behind her, keeping a few feet between them to give her space.

She stopped at a small patch of grass between two lemon trees, kicked off her sandals, and lay down on her back, just as she'd always done as a child, with her gaze on the overhang of leafy limbs.

"Why do you need a decoy?" She glanced at him and looked back at the tree cover.

He sat beside her and removed his boots and socks, his chest tightening with all the things he needed to tell her.

"I'll start at the beginning." He lay on the lawn, his shoulder brushing hers, the ground soft and cool against his back.

"I'd really appreciate that." She reached for his hand and laced their fingers in the swath of grass between them.

"My mother was Hector Restrepo's mistress."

She kept her gaze skyward, her brows pulling together. "When did you find out?"

"The day the cartel came for me." He closed his eyes against the memory — the fear and confusion, the unholy shock of it all. "She fled to the States when she became pregnant with me. Didn't want me to be raised among criminals. But Hector knew I was his. And he knew how to find her."

"I assume her name wasn't really Maria and she didn't die in a car accident?"

"It was Natalia." He opened his eyes and pulled Camila's hand to rest on his chest, where he hurt the most. "Hector captured her, held her somewhere in Texas until I was born, then had her killed."

Her breath hitched, and she rolled toward him, aligning her body along the length of his, with her cheek on his shoulder. "I'm so sorry."

He wrapped an arm around her back, the other bent beneath his head, and grounded himself in her. She was the honeyed scent of orange blossoms, the light that shone through the trees, the very air he breathed. Hell knew he didn't fucking deserve her.

"To this day," he said, "I don't know if Hector thought I was unworthy to be a capo's son, if he felt guilty for killing my mother, or if he was trying to protect me, but for whatever reason, he kept my existence a secret and gave me to Andres to raise."

"Andres was your mother's brother, right? Or was that a lie, too?"

"He wasn't my uncle or any blood relation. He was just a guy, trafficking drugs for Hector." He paused, letting that settle in with the heave of her breaths.

It took him several years to accept that the man who'd reared him had been nothing more than a lackey doing a job. While Andres had effectively filled the role of disciplinarian, Matias had been deprived of a mother and all the nurturing softness and affection that came with that. But he'd had Camila.

"Did my parents know?" she breathed against his neck.

"Yes, they knew all of it." With his arm around her back, he held her tighter. "Camila..."

She lifted her head at the grimness in his tone.

"Your parents worked for Hector. With Andres' help, they used the citrus grove as a cover for their narcotics trade."

"No." A vehement whisper. "That's not possible. I would've noticed something." She rose up on her elbow, eyes wide and glistening. "We both would've known. No way that was happening under our noses without us stumbling on—" She gasped. "Did you know?"

"I didn't learn any of this until after I left. They used the shack in the woods to store shipments."

"The cannibal shack?" Her hand flew to her mouth. "But it was abandoned."

"Not always."

"That's right." She dropped her arm. "It used to be all locked up. Windows covered. Creepy as hell."

He nodded. As a kid, he hadn't given much thought to it beyond the stories they made up about a reclusive cannibal. "Andres and your father built that metal barn on the south side of the grove when we were older, remember?"

"The one packed with boxes of fertilizer and plant food and..."

"Some of it was legit. Most of it wasn't. When they outgrew the shack, they used that barn."

"*Mierda.*" A dark cloud shifted over her expression, stiffening her jaw. "My parents were simple people. They never would've wanted any part of that."

He placed a hand on the side of her face, stroking his thumb across her sharp cheekbone, fully aware of how hard this was for her. "Hector smuggled them out of the poorest region in Colombia and set them up with a productive business in the States. He handed them a dream."

"In exchange for a lifetime of servitude." A frown appeared on her forehead.

"Yes."

Trailing his fingers around the shell of her ear, he followed the graceful lines of her jaw to her neck and lower, beneath the edge of the leather collar. Her breath quickened, and her hand landed softly on his chest.

"The fire wasn't an accident, was it?" Her fingers twitched against him, and her lip trembled. "They're gone because of their involvement in your cartel? My sister, too?"

"Yeah. I hate this for you. Wish I could protect you from it." He caught the metal ring at her throat and used it to gently pull her face to his.

She let him, but the arm against his chest was stiff, ready to fight. "Did they witness something or do something related to drug trafficking?"

His stomach hardened. Her parents had definitely done something, and it had nothing to do with drugs.

He evaded the question by answering one she hadn't asked. "The night of the fire, I wasn't the capo yet, but Hector was already dead. Died a year earlier from lung cancer."

She searched his eyes, her expression suspicious, and she had every right to be.

"Jhon was running the cartel when your family died." His pulse swished in his ears.

"Jhon?"

"My older brother. Jhon's mother was Hector's wife. Murdered when Jhon was young by a rival cartel."

"You have a brother." She caressed his face, fingers tentative.

"*Had* a brother." He relaxed beneath her touch. "The night Hector died, he handed down the empire to Jhon. The next day, Jhon came for me."

"How did he find out about you?"

"Hector spoke about me on his death bed, delirious and apparently regretful." His throat tightened. "The only two people in the room were Jhon and Nico."

Nico was the only reason Matias knew any of these details.

Her gaze turned inward, no doubt trying to connect the dots. "What happened to Jhon?"

As much as he disliked the topic of conversation, it loosened the knots he'd carried for years. He'd dreamt of this, the ability to talk and share with her again. She'd always been a good listener, the only person he could open up to about anything. This was how it was supposed to be.

"Jhon was a cold-hearted bastard, Camila." He pulled in a thick breath. "He took me from my home, from *you*, when Hector died. He was so fucking narcissistic he wasn't content to just own the cartel. He had to own everything and everyone around him, especially his only brother. So he came for me and controlled me by threatening your life." He shoved a hand in his hair. "Christ, I was just a sheltered, eighteen-year-old kid. I know it's no excuse, but he had a goddamn hold over me, one that kept me fearful and quiet about who I was."

"He didn't want anyone to know you were Hector's son?"

"No. The secret stayed buried the year under Jhon's reign. He treated me worse than a lackey, made me do things..."

He shuddered in memory of the torture, his and others. The metallic taste of blood in his mouth, the endless beatings, the helplessness and anger. So much fucking anger. He'd lost the soul of the boy he'd been and replaced it with a bloodthirsty savage.

"When I talked to you on the phone after you left...Jesus, Matias." She touched his cheek and slid her fingers to his jaw, lingering on his bottom lip. "You were protecting me? From him?"

"Yes." He met her eyes. "Until I didn't."

Her face paled. "Jhon arranged my abduction?"

Jhon hadn't been the only one, but he couldn't bring himself to break her heart. Not here in their grove.

"I'm sorry, Camila." He pulled her against him and wrapped his arms around her back. "So fucking sorry."

"It wasn't your fault." Her breath trembled across his neck.

"It *was* my fault. I pissed him off. My relationship with Nico..." Fuck, he'd been so careless, so fucking naïve. "Nico's father was Hector's best friend. When his father died, Hector took Nico in and protected him like a son. Jhon resented him, viciously, and the feeling was mutual."

"You were close to Nico back then?"

"He was the only friend I had, and other than Jhon, he was the only person who knew I was a Restrepo. We bonded instantly in our mutual hatred for Jhon. Nico covertly fed me information, secrets about the cartel and what Jhon was doing, all in an effort to take him out. In return, I saved Nico's life."

"Jhon tried to kill him?"

"Repeatedly. I watched Nico's back, stopped multiple hits on him.

Instead of killing me, Jhon turned his outrage on you."

She lifted her head, eyes welling with tears. "You killed him, didn't you?"

"Six weeks after you disappeared."

A bird chirped somewhere in the foliage overhead, the grass soft and supportive beneath their entwined bodies. The warm air stirred with their breaths as he lay in silence, pondering the hell that had brought them to this point.

"With Jhon dead, why didn't you come home?" Pain and confusion choked her voice.

"You were already gone." He kissed her softly.

She nodded, and a tear fell down her cheek. "When I called you after I escaped, you could've told me all of this. We could've been together."

"In that year you went missing, I did horrible things in my search for you. Slaughtered countless people. Used every brutal weapon in the cartel at my disposal. Somewhere along the way, I gave up. Gave up on you and myself and surrendered to this life. I became worse than the man who captured you."

She went rigid against him, and he knew she was thinking about the slave trade, a conversation he didn't want to have right now.

"My hunt resulted in more enemies than the cartel had ever faced." He coiled a lock of her hair around his finger. "I couldn't rationalize bringing you into it."

"So you kept me in the dark, made me fear and distrust you, which kept me away."

"Yeah." His chest panged with regret, but hindsight changed nothing. It'd been the right thing to do.

"If you have so many enemies, why in the hell would Nico agree to be your decoy?"

"He owes me his life." He huffed a laugh. "The past decade hasn't been a total hardship for him. I shoulder all the stress and decisions while he struts around with more power and wealth than he would've ever had as a lieutenant. He's been more than compensated for the risk."

She rolled to her back and gazed up at sweeping arms of the trees. "Thank you for telling me. For protecting me from it all these years. I get it. I don't like it, but I understand why you couldn't tell me until now, when you could trust me with the information and protect me from those who want your secrets."

He gripped her hand and held tight as a light breeze rippled over them, rustling the leaves and brushing his skin. Somewhere in the distance, a macaw squawked.

He was so close to winning her heart and yet so far. She seemed to be trying to look past the monster she thought he was, but she still hadn't accepted the real reason she'd come here. Submission and bondage were such dirty, shameful concepts to her. She fought against the healthy, consensual aspects of it by focusing on only the ugly illegal kind of slavery.

She pulled her hand away and touched the collar at her throat. Her nostrils flared, her muscles tensed, and he knew she was preparing an argument.

She sat up and pivoted toward him with a stubborn set in her jaw. "You make the rules around here, which means you have the power to end the suffering of all those slaves. I know" — she hardened her husky voice — "I *know* that with the snap of that one command you would make me happy. So fucking happy, Matias, that I would give you my heart and soul and whatever else you desired."

His stomach twisted and soured. "I don't want your fucking negotiated affections, Camila."

He lurched up and gripped her hips. She yelped as he dumped her on her back and fell on top of her.

With her chest rising and falling against his, she gave him her best glare. "Then what do you want? What can I do?"

He had been inside her pussy every day she'd been here, and other than his massive fuck up when he took her against the post, he'd only bound her with lightweight string. Most of the time, he hadn't restrained her at all. He hadn't spanked her, whipped her, or done anything to cause her physical pain since that first day.

He wanted her willing and begging for bondage. While she hadn't once fought him during sex, her participation had been dubious, as if her body was submitting while her mind screamed *hell no*.

All of this was expected. He knew it would take a lot of time and patience, but it didn't make it any easier.

"I've already told you." He shackled her wrists with his hands and pinned her arms against the grass above her head. "Stop focusing on what you think you know and look at me, at *us*. What are you really after? What do *you* need?"

"The prize." Her eyes flashed. "You without slavery."

"Slave has more than one meaning. Open your mind."

"You're talking about what Nico said to me?" She yanked her arms against the grip of his hands. "My supposed search to be owned and dominated?" At his nod, her gaze widened. "Are those women…? Holy shit, are they here willingly?"

"No." His heart pounded with frustration. "They definitely don't want to be here."

Flickering shadows spread over her face. "I don't understand."

"Try."

She regarded him for a long moment then blinked. "You want me to trust you."

"It's a very good place to start."

She breathed in, out, and again. Then muscle by muscle, she slackened beneath him. Her arms went limp in the grip of his hands. Her legs widened, knees falling open to accommodate his hips.

His nerve endings stirred everywhere their bodies touched — hands, chests, thighs, and…fuck, her cunt burned hot against his cock. Excitement surged through him, coiling like a fist around his shaft. He couldn't stop himself from grinding, his breaths shortening and control unraveling.

Eyes damp and overly bright, she started to tremble, her voice reedy. "One hard, violent fuck away from surrender?"

The words he'd given Nico sounded so fucking erotic whispered from her quivering lips. Surrender didn't come without fear, and she was there — the perspiration on her brow, the ashen coloring in her cheeks, the irregular pace of her breaths. He was going to fuck her and make it hurt, make her scream. But he knew that somewhere deep inside her, she was going to enjoy it, and that probably scared her the most.

"Remove your clothes." He shifted to his knees and tackled his belt.

She hesitated, her gaze locked on the strap of leather he folded in his fist.

"Camila."

She looked up at his cutting tone, and he gave the command again, not with his voice, but with the full force of his eyes.

Her inhale fluttered, fingers curling in the grass. Then, with a nod, she obeyed.

# TWENTY-TWO

Matias tightened his hand around the leather belt, unable to stifle the shaking in his fingers as Camila stood and reached for the hem of her shirt. He could no longer hear the drone of bees, feel the sunlight, or smell the citrus in the air, yet the atmosphere had never been more alive than it was now.

Balancing her weight on the heels and balls of her bare feet, she pulled the shirt over her head. Her slave training was evident in the way she held herself—legs straight, knees unlocked, gaze trained on him. But despite the darkness of her past seeping in, her brown eyes shone through it.

Fuck him, but he loved her inner strength, loved how her chest lifted and arched, her shoulders squared, and how her attention homed in on him as if the movement of her hands was merely reflex. He felt her submission at a molecular level, every cell in his body gravitating toward her, his muscles hungrily aware and throbbing to take what was his. But he remained where he was, three feet away, and devoured her every move.

Keeping her face and chest angled toward him with her chin drawn in, she slowly and gracefully removed her bra, jeans, and panties. Then she straightened, the alignment of her head and neck vertical, arms hanging at her sides without stiffness, and let him stare.

He stood frozen in the wake of her beauty, absorbing her nudity, her willingness, in the place he'd meticulously rebuilt, amid the trees he'd planted and cared for, every seed, yard of dirt, and precious memory put here for her.

Long black hair fell over the slender lines of her shoulders, framing round, perfectly-shaped tits. The curl of her fingers against her thighs drew his gaze to the feminine curves of hips, the flat expanse of stomach, and the shadow of hair that had grown back between her legs.

A growl escaped his throat, and he grabbed himself through the jeans, running a palm against his aching cock. She was built for him, every dip, arch, muscle, and bone, all his to worship and protect.

He prowled toward her, soaking in her quickening breaths and the way her gaze tracked him as he circled her. When he stopped behind her, her toes flexed in the grass. He took his time examining her sinful ass and strong, sinuous backbone before dropping the belt and sweeping his hands down her arms.

The marks had faded to yellowish bruises, and he hadn't needed to cut her again. The first time had been a strong enough statement, and she exuded the timid slave act like a pro.

"Matias…" She shuddered, and it wasn't an act. "I'm afraid."

"Afraid of me? Or this?" He hooked an arm around her and squeezed a nipple, hard enough to make her whimper. "Are you scared to want this?"

"Yes." Her voice wavered. "All of it."

He put his nose in her hair and slid his fingers around the sides of her breasts, the dips in her waist, and lower to cup and stroke her pussy. A rush of warmth chased his pulse, his erection bent painfully in his jeans. His fingers quaked and stiffened in his desperation for her.

"What did I tell you about fear?" He pressed his dick against her ass and lightly caressed her damp folds.

"It will haunt—" She cried out as he pinched her clit, but she kept her hands at her sides and didn't pull away. "It will haunt me until I step inside and show it my teeth."

"I'll be right here with you. Always."

The thudding of his heart beat in sync with the pulsing in his cock. She had no idea the power she held over him, didn't know how dry his mouth had gone or that his insides heated to a fevered level of dizziness. Nothing or no one had ever affected him the way she did. She was it for him, his past and future, his weakness and strength, his meaning for everything.

Brushing her hair to the side, he tiptoed fingers up and down her abs, inching close to her pussy without touching, and back up, lingering beneath her tits before dipping down again. With his mouth at her ear, he nipped her skin above the collar, flicked his tongue, and inhaled her warm scent until her head dropped back on his shoulder, breaths catching.

Her face rolled toward him, and she rubbed their cheeks together, her parted lips searching. He captured her mouth in a collision of gasps and hungry tongues that was neither soft nor gentle. He chased and hunted and fed, his fingers sinking between her legs, thrusting hard, and coaxing a moan from deep within her.

Her lower body clamped around him, her neck angling her closer as she tried to deepen the kiss. Her urgency spurred him on, making him hotter, greedier, more frantic.

"Matias, please." She arched into him, her ass grinding against his painful cock.

He tore his mouth away, his heart tripping at a dangerous level.

"Bend forward." He kissed her shoulder and stepped back, keeping his tone silken, yet inflexible. "Hands on your ankles. Spine straight."

She followed his command to perfection, and he swallowed a groan. Yanking off his shirt, he used it to wipe the perspiration from his brow. Then he tossed it and knelt behind her.

He tried to start slow, his hands exploring her ass and legs, but the more he touched the more he needed. Her skin was so tight, so fucking smooth he wanted to lick and bite every inch of her. So he did, gliding his tongue and teeth across the backs of her thighs as he teased her soaking cunt with his fingers.

The hitch in her breath amped his pulse, but he kept his movements slow, sensual, savoring her goosebumps and the flex of her muscles as she anticipated the path of his lips. She was so fucking responsive he couldn't wait any longer. He buried his mouth between her legs.

"So damn wet, *mi vida*. Such a hungry slut."

With her head hanging upside down, she snarled through clenched teeth. "I'm not —"

"A slut, my gorgeous girl, is brave enough to pursue her own definitions of pain and pleasure. She's willing to explore and search for what she enjoys rather than shun her desires like a dirty secret." He bit the delicate skin between her legs, wrenching a yelp from her. "You welcome sex with open legs, because you understand the benefits, the ecstasy it brings."

"Okay, when you put it that way," she said in a throaty voice.

"*My* slut." He licked her from ass to pussy, his tongue probing in both holes with abandon.

She panted and shook, her tits swaying and head lifting to accommodate her breaths, but she held her bent position with flawless grace. A reminder that she'd endured a year of hell to master that composure. Anger simmered through his blood, but he pushed it down, refusing to let it ruin the moment.

When her moans grew shorter, faster, he knew she was peaking. He stabbed his fingers inside her, and in two hard drives, she came with a choked-off scream, her inner muscles spasming against his hand. Fucking beautiful.

He eased out of her and helped her straighten to her full height, pulling her chest to his as she wobbled.

Lifting her chin, he submerged his gaze in hers and saw unspeakable desire in the watery depths. Love was there, too — the love they'd always shared — but it seemed stronger now, pummeled and tested and resuscitated back to life. And in the strength of that love, he saw the tiniest glimmer of trust, the kind of trust that only a submissive could offer.

As far as she knew, he hadn't done anything to earn her trust, yet she was handing it over, instinctively, bravely, and the only explanation was because she loved him.

He took her mouth, and the instant their lips touched, the fusion was frantic and visceral, hitting him right in the stomach. He felt her in his skin, every gasp, bite, and voracious lick connecting to an emotion that had endured the torment of time.

Her beautiful tongue flicked, twirling in greedy euphoric circles and following his lead as he demanded everything and took even more. She dragged her short nails down his back, bursting his nerve endings into a thousand frenzied pieces.

He pressed his lips to the corner of her mouth then kissed a path to her ear, whispering, "Do you want to come harder next time?"

Eyes beckoning, she nodded, shook her head, then let out a husky laugh. "Will I live?"

"For the first time in your life." He reached up and tested the strength of the thickest branch. "Hold onto this."

Lifting her heels from the soil and stretching her arms, she curled her fingers around the limb.

He snagged her bra from the ground, checked it for wires and found none. "Stand flat on your feet."

When she lowered, she was still able to hang on. He used the strip of black lace to tie her hands to the branch.

"Comfortable?" He kissed her mouth softly.

With a glance at the belt in the grass, her expression tightened, but she gave him a jerky nod.

"How did you get into this...this kinky stuff?" Her voice cracked, and she cleared it. "You've done this a lot?"

"I'll answer your questions, but first, tell me why you abstained for four years."

Her eyes darted away, and she bit her lip. "I slept with a lot of men after I escaped, trying to prove to myself that I was the one in control of my sexuality." She looked back at him. "I was also looking for...I don't know. A connection? But after a while, I decided I had better luck with my vibrator."

Exactly what he'd thought. He clenched and relaxed his hands.

"I did the same thing, fucking my way through countless women." At her wince, he cupped her face and pressed so close he felt her heartbeat pound against his chest. "I was searching for something, too. Anything that might resemble what I had with you. I never found it."

"I hate—" She bit back a strangled noise, and a twitch flickered her eyelashes. "I hate that all those women know you in that way."

He wholeheartedly sympathized with the pain in her eyes. "No one knows me the way you do."

The corner of her mouth bounced. "Smooth talker." She slackened against him, almost as if trying to snuggle with her arms restrained over her head. "None of those women know what your fourteen-year-old ass looks like on a copy machine."

"Or my ass at any age on a copy machine." He chuckled into another long, delicious kiss.

She hummed against his mouth as her tongue traced the seam of his lips.

He brushed his hands through her hair. "What I discovered in my fumbling attempts at happiness is that bondage and pain have the potential to make sex more intense and intimate. People fuck all the time without conversation, commitment, or any emotional connection. But when I tie up a woman and beat the living hell out of her, there's a crucial responsibility that comes with that, one that involves clear communication and acceptance—hers and mine. Those very things enhance sexual pleasure." He paused. "Because it requires trust."

"But the slaves you—"

"I've never fucked a slave."

"Oh." Her brows drew together then released with the flash in her eyes. "But you hurt me without communication or acceptance."

"Tell me why I did it."

"You wanted me scared." She swallowed. "To protect me from your enemies."

"Yeah." His throat thickened. "I'll hurt you again, Camila, and I'll be the one to soothe it. Only me." Lowering his hand, he trailed his fingers over the bruises on her ass. "I'm going to give you a different kind of pain. The kind that comes with acceptance." He felt the heat of her lips brush his. "When trust surpasses that pain, the result can feel incredibly profound."

"Okay." Fear threaded through her voice.

"Imagine what it will be like for us. We already share a connection no other two people have. Our memories, our regrets, and this." He kissed her hard and deep, with the entirety of his soul. "*Us.*"

"You think this is what we've both been searching for?" She subtly rubbed her pussy against the zipper of his jeans.

"Yes." He was certain of it. "Listen carefully. If I hit you too hard or overstep your limits without explanation, you need to trust that I'm doing it for you."

"No safe words?"

"No." He laughed and shoved a hand through his hair. "I'm not running a high-end glitter club here. I'm a fucking cartel capo who hangs people in chains to kill them, not to tickle them with a flogger. Dangerous and crazy is the way I operate, Camila."

"Basically the opposite of safe, sane, and consensual." Her eyes narrowed.

He refused to abide by anyone's rules, but… "I want your consent."

"Jesus. Everything you said was so fucking wrong." She stared at him, absently digging her toe through the grass. "But I don't feel a pressing need to kick you in the nuts."

"You normally feel that need?"

"Maybe." Her mouth flattened, but a smile touched her eyes.

"When I restrain you, it's just you and me." He glided his hands up her arms and squeezed the elastic strap around her wrists overhead. "No safe words. No rules. Have we reached that level of trust yet?"

"I'm trying." She licked her lips. "I want to."

That was closer than she was two weeks ago. His pulse kicked up.

Sliding his hands back down her arms, he rubbed her tits, pinched her nipples, and moved to her ass, her thighs, her pussy. He touched her everywhere, keeping his gaze on her parted mouth and the peek of her tongue as she wet her lips.

The rhythm of her breaths led the pace of his strokes. As she panted faster, harder, he added pressure and speed to his caress. Soon, she was trembling, gasping, ready.

As he adjusted his cock to relieve the agonizing pressure, he grabbed the belt from the ground and folded it in half. She tracked him with half-lidded eyes, her expression aglow more with curiosity than fear. He didn't need to tell her how to breathe and relax into the strikes. She'd been mercilessly beaten against her will more times than he cared to think about.

With a steady inhale, he let the strap swing, landing the initial hits on her thighs and ass. He didn't go easy on her, but he knew he wouldn't. He'd pounded his fists against men to the point of bloodshed and death, and while he didn't hit her with anywhere near that kind of strength, he wasn't a gentle man. Nor was she weak.

Her head fell back on her shoulders as she gasped and whimpered. He worked over her body, striking without pause and watching for swelling and broken skin. But more than that, he studied her eyes, thrilling in the dilation of her pupils beneath her glazed expression of lust.

Good God, she had a high-tolerance for pain. As hard as he was hitting her, she didn't scream or shift her feet. Not even when he reached his groove, his arm swinging with speed and agility, muscles loose, and attention focused.

He walked a circuit around her, slamming the leather against her legs and ass, listening to the tempo of her breaths, and devouring the red blooms across her skin. His heart pounded like it had the first time he'd kissed her fifteen years ago. It was finally alive and beating, no longer lost. It had come back, here, to her in their lemon grove.

Inflicting pain wasn't what made him hard. It was one-hundred-percent about the power in trust. She was giving him this, letting him hurt her while trusting that he wouldn't destroy her.

He returned to her front and struck her tits, alternating between them. She keened, her eyes wide and staring upward as tremors rippled up her legs. He knew she'd hit that altered state of consciousness, where time distorted and pain ebbed. She looked like she was floating, peaceful, high as a fucking kite.

Hands slick with sweat, he moved the strap lower, thwacking lightly over her stomach. When he reached her pussy, he landed a vicious blow against her clit.

"No!" She snapped to awareness, screaming and writhing, knees buckling. "I can't...not there—"

He hit her again and again, pummeling the sensitive nerves, testing her.

"You...sona...fuck...ye...pleee..." Tears skated down her cheeks as she gulped for air, glaring at him and bellowing between sobs.

She'd reached her breaking point, and broken was a place he never wanted to take her.

He tossed the belt.

"Fuck you, Matias." Her voice didn't hold a trace of heat as she slumped. Then she gave him a shaky smile. "That wasn't too bad."

Goddamn, he loved this woman. He released the button and zipper on his jeans, shoving them down as he closed the distance.

With shaking hands, he gripped her hair and claimed her mouth, his tongue probing, caressing, and taking. She tasted like citrus and desire, her lips soft and yielding and *his*. She kissed him with the same urgency, her breaths warm and erratic as she hooked a leg around the back of his.

His balls tightened, and his cock throbbed to the point of pain. He gripped himself, aching to fuck her, brutally, possessively, and if he waited much longer, he was going to come before the first fucking thrust.

With his jeans hanging beneath his ass and a fist around his shaft, he lined himself up and rammed hard, missing completely in his pressing need to be inside her.

"Need help?" She laughed and bit his jaw. "I can—"

He smacked her hard on the ass, and she choked on another laugh. Christ, she made him crazy. He kissed her again, and this time, with a bruising grip on her hip, he slammed inside of her, buried to the hilt.

"Fuuck!" Pleasure shot through his cock, and his forehead dropped to her shoulder.

"Oh, God." She groaned and wrapped her other leg around him, giving him all of her weight and the full use of her body.

Adjusting his stance, hands on her waist, he fucked her with every inch of his soul. She tightened her fingers around the branch and threw her head back, crying out with each unapologetic drive of his hips.

"Look at me." He couldn't get close enough, deep enough, couldn't taste enough of her, or wrench enough cries from her seductive lips.

She gave him her eyes, and he held her there, sliding her up and down his length and jacking himself off in her tight sheath. She felt so fucking good he couldn't stop shaking, couldn't catch his breath.

Without breaking eye contact, they moved together as one, the rock and kick of her hips matching the force of his. They were wild and electric, a violent landslide of grunts, slippery skin, and thundering hearts.

His lungs caught fire, and his pulse hammered as fast as his thrusts, everything inside him simmering, building, pressurizing. The whole damn world felt like it was going to explode, and he didn't care. He couldn't stop. He was so fucking lost in her he didn't want to find his way back.

They were both panting so hard they couldn't keep their mouths connected, but he tried, chasing her lips, licking and sucking and swallowing her breaths as he fucked her.

Her tits bounced with the slam of his hips. Her exhales came in short bursts. Then she was coming, screaming, her eyes wide and fixed on him as if blindsided by the sensations. She shuddered and twitched through it, and when she finally settled against him, he pulled back, slipping his cock free and teasing the tip around her opening. She groaned.

"Again?" He bit her nipple, her collarbone, her lips, then sank back inside her. "Yeah, you can do that again."

"I think…maybe… Yes, please." She smirked, eyes half-mast.

Reaching down to where his jeans had fallen around his knees, he removed the switchblade from the pocket and cut her hands free.

Her fingers flew to his hair, and her mouth attacked his, wet and hot, eating at his lips and licking his tongue.

He flung the blade near his boots, kicked off the jeans, and rolled her to the ground beneath him. With the solid support against her back, he let himself go, fucking her ruthlessly, powerfully.

Holding his gaze, she moved her body in a sensual dance with his. Her hands glided across his back, their chests heaving together, and legs entwined. Shock waves descended down his spine, gathering at the base of his cock. He tangled his fingers in her hair, his hips caught in a desperate tempo. He wanted to last longer, but knew he couldn't.

There would always be later, and tomorrow, and forever.

"I'm going to come, baby." Spasms gathered behind his balls. "You're coming with me."

Her eyes flared with concentration. "Kiss me."

And he did, vigorously, passionately, while fighting the agonizing impulse to release. She flexed and strained beneath him and released a strangled shout against his lips. He stared into her eyes, captivated by her orgasmic bliss, and followed her over.

He came violently, pounding her into the ground, his body convulsing with a series of contractions that pumped deep inside him, ejaculating, filling her up, and the pleasure… Fuck, the pleasure was unimaginable as he groaned and thrust and stretched it out as long as he could.

As their breathing evened out and their bodies went limp, a fog of numbness tingled through him. But he kept his hips moving in slow, satisfied strokes, his gaze centered on his favorite brown eyes.

"That was pretty good." She pursed her lips.

He continued to lazily thrust, didn't want to stop, didn't want to leave the drenched clasp of her pussy. "As sloppy as your cunt feels, I think it was better than pretty good."

Her expression softened, and she ran her hands across his jaw and into his hair. "It was perfect, Matias."

Rolling them to their sides, he kissed her tenderly, achingly, with every ounce of love he felt for her. Her arms twined around his neck, and his cock softened inside her, but she didn't seem to want him to pull out, so he held her closer, kissing her as the sky darkened with the approach of dusk.

They lay there for an eternity, nude, in a bed of grass, surrounded by lemon trees, and he knew. He'd finally succeeded in his pursuit for happiness. Then again, he'd always known that this was how it should be.

She watched him as he watched her, seemingly just as content, but something lurked in the back of her eyes.

He spread a lock of her hair in the grass, snaking it around like a black river. "What are you thinking about?"

"Your spy problem."

He didn't expect that, and his heart lurched excitedly. "What about it?"

"Well, you haven't caught this person."

He arched a brow. "Are you questioning my competence?"

"Yep."

"All right." His chest filled with pride. "I'm listening."

She leaned up on an elbow, and the twin peaks of her pink nipples drew his attention.

"Up here, Matias."

He flicked his eyes to hers and found a glint of amusement there.

"You've been monitoring every outgoing transaction and message?" She cocked her head. "Even phone calls?"

"Everything. Nothing is getting leaked or discussed. We're on virtual shutdown. We've flown in all of our technical geniuses and highest-ranking members to the property and haven't let anyone leave. We have every able and trusted person hunting for this person."

She nodded, her expression contemplative. "Have you considered the possibility that Gerardo might've been lying?"

"The man was in a world of pain when he confessed." His heart skipped. "He lasted through hours of slicing and severing and—"

"He was loyal to this other group then. Loyal enough to endure that kind of torture." She glanced away, scrunched up her nose in concentration, and looked back at him. "What if he was trying to distract you from something? What if he wanted you to congregate your cartel?"

Dread sank his stomach, and his blood pressure skyrocketed. "Fuck. No, that's... Shit, we've focused all our efforts here, searching internally. And we're all together, pulled all of our resources to one place."

"The enemy is out there, doing hell knows what, while your attention is centered on yourselves." She sat up and stared over the trees. "If someone were to...I don't know, drop a bomb on this place, every important member would be blown to bloody pieces. Would the cartel die with them?"

Yes, it absolutely would.

# TWENTY-THREE

A week later, Camila stretched on a lounge chair on the balcony outside of Matias' private living room, listening intently to the drone of voices around her. Not really hearing the words as much as evaluating inflections, pitch, and volume of one voice in particular.

Twilight blushed the sky and cast a radiant glow across Matias' stern expression. Sitting at the wrought iron table cluttered with bottles of beer and *aguardiente,* he strategized and argued with the men in the inner circle.

His timbre was calm and even, but the Texan drawl he tried so hard to hide slipped through, barely there, pulling on some of his consonants. Was he worried? Scared?

He hadn't let her out of his sight in over a week. Whenever he left his suite, he took her with him, to his meetings, to walk the perimeter of the property, to dinner on the veranda. Given the current topic of conversation, she doubted he would be leaving her side any time soon.

Other than the potential danger that threatened his life — as well as hers — she didn't *want* to care if the cartel perished or survived. She needed to focus on the horrors Matias kept imprisoned in the west wing. She'd counted at least fourteen slaves since she'd arrived, and who knew how many others weren't being paraded through the halls like dogs on leashes.

A slaughtered cartel meant less slave traders in the world. She tried to feel enthusiastic about that, but instead, it sank a heavy feeling in her stomach. Did she actually like these guys?

Other than her first day here, the inner circle hadn't treated her like a slave, never even raised a brow when she voiced her opinions or asked questions in the privacy of Matias' suite. Of course, Matias had told her multiple times that his four closest men knew who she was and why she was here.

But she couldn't ignore their depravity. The evidence was etched into the horrified faces of the slaves they kept.

Except every time she looked at Matias, she didn't see a man who wanted to profit from women's suffering. She saw a man who adored her so deeply he would sacrifice everything for her.

It didn't make sense that he loved her while doing the one thing that hurt her the most. But rather than fight him, she watched him, tried to understand his motivations and trust that there was something he wasn't telling her, something important.

*If I hit you too hard or overstep your limits without explanation, you need to trust that I'm doing it for you.*

Was there another message beneath his words? Something below the threshold of her understanding? Because dammit, his involvement in human trafficking did overstep her limits, and how the fuck could he possibly be doing that for *her?*

She wanted to trust him, which was huge and terrifying and really goddamn hard on her heart. It shattered every night at dinner, every time she saw a sewn mouth, a shackled hand, or a fearful set of eyes. She was reaching her limits on trust.

"What about the north wall?" Matias leaned back in the chair, his hand resting on his thigh. "Have we added more cameras?"

Chispa jumped in with a technical report, and Matias asked more security questions, his thumb moving restlessly, sliding over the pads of the fingers on the same hand, back and forth, again and again.

There was so much power in those fingers. They could be cruel, fucking brutal in his passion, but they could also be tender, gentle on her skin in his affection. Whether he was whipping her, caressing her, or fingering her into mindless bliss, those fingers inspired strength and dominance, left her craving more, wanting more of him, needing him to be the man she trusted him to be.

He flicked his eyes to her, to his lap, and back to her face. Her heart raced, her entire body pulling toward him as her feet slid to the floor. She stood, straightened her shorts, and crossed the balcony.

Nico, Chispa, and Picar continued the conversation, but all eyes were on her as she lowered onto Matias' lap. Frizz's watchful gaze was the hardest to meet, but she forced herself to hold his stare and not let him intimidate her. Of all the men in the inner circle, his eyes were softest, a strangely-innocent shade of blue. She couldn't help but morbidly wonder about the mystery he kept trapped behind those threaded lips.

A shiver raced through her, and she tried not to wriggle on the hard bulge pressing against the zipper of Matias' jeans.

For the next hour, she sat sideways on his lap, resting against his chest with her head on his shoulder. She indulged in the vibration of his voice as he rumbled on about security, debating the idea of leaving the property and going into hiding.

If they fled the compound, she wouldn't use it as an opportunity to escape. Maybe she was determined to the point of self-destruction, but she needed to see Matias' slave trade through to the end.

But it wasn't just that. The mere thought of being separated from him twisted her insides into panicky knots. That fear alone trumped the accumulation of every fear she'd ever felt. He was the only person who had ever made her lungs stretch, heart sing, and mind dance. No way in hell was she giving him up.

He slid his knuckles up and down her inner thighs as he talked to his men. One might've assumed it was mindless fidgeting, but the swollen proof of his awareness jerked persistently against her hip.

She sighed. If there was one thing she'd learned in her three weeks here, it was that she loved his cock. She loved the thick girth, the veins that ran along the underside, and the little freckle just beneath the crown. Her pussy clenched as she replayed the way he'd woken her this morning—his dick in her mouth, his musky scent in her nose, and his salty come in her throat.

She'd never considered herself a slut, but after he'd framed the term with admiration, she'd spent the better part of the past week learning how to be more honest with herself about who she was and what she wanted. While his beautiful cock consumed her thoughts, she'd become more receptive to him as a whole, and the biggest piece of that was his dominance.

Sitting on his lap like this filled her with belonging. The strength and power in his body coupled with the tenderness of his touch and the warm scent of his masculinity felt like home and permanence, instilling in her a sense of security. All that searching with other men had been such a wasted effort. No wonder losing Matias had hurt her so much. *He* was where she should've always been.

Nico rolled up the sleeve of his shirt. "All I'm saying is we need to be—" A phone chirped on the table, and he grabbed it, glanced at the screen. A second later, he straightened, his eyes lifting and landing on Matias.

Matias stiffened against her, prompting the same reaction in her muscles.

"They found more." Nico's usual scowl vanished amid the starkness of his unblinking eyes.

"Found what?" She sat up and turned to look at Matias.

His hand went to her face, cupping her jaw, but his focus

remained on Nico. "Where?"

"Three hours north by helicopter. *Permítame un momento.*" Nico stood, lifting the phone to his ear as he strode to the far end of the railing.

She touched the hand on her cheek. "Matias? What's going on?"

His lips formed a pale line, his hazel eyes sharp as he stared at Nico's back and lowered their hands. She searched the other faces at the table—Frizz, Chispa, Picar—and found the same expressions, all of them watching Nico, rigid in their chairs as if bracing to leap up.

"Does this have to do with Gerardo's betrayal?" Her breaths quickened. "Did you find spies?"

Matias gave her a stiff shake of his head, and Nico ended the call.

With a strong, urgent gait, Nico returned to the table, eyes on his capo. "We can make it there without a refuel. Burd will drive us the rest of the way."

"And you trust Burd?" Matias shifted to the edge of the chair.

"We've used him a dozen times. He's a good falcon. But I recommend waiting a while. Maybe next week—"

Matias slammed a fist on the table, stopping her heart and knocking over several beer bottles. "We're not fucking waiting." He launched from the chair, taking her with him and catching her around the waist to support her stumbling steps. "Set up the appointment for tonight. Get the helicopter ready. We're leaving immediately."

"Tell me what's going on." She folded her arms across her chest, shivering against the tension in the air.

"What about the plan we discussed?" Nico scowled.

"Get everything lined up." Matias grabbed her hand and turned toward the door.

"Hey, boss." Chispa stood, rubbing the back of his neck as he lifted a chin in her direction. "Maybe you should sit this one out. We can do this—"

"No fucking way." Matias pulled her into the interior living space. Her scalp tingled. "Hold up!"

"Are you bringing her with us?" Chispa chased after him. "What if something happens while—"

"She's going."

"Matias!" She slammed to a stop, only to be yanked forward again by his strong grip. "Are we in danger?"

"No. We're in a hurry. Pick up your fucking feet."

# TWENTY-FOUR

Matias pressed his back into the plush leather of the helicopter chair. The seven-passenger light twin was built for luxury and comfort, but he was far from comfortable.

Squeezed into the cabin with the entire inner circle and battling for leg room, he felt like rubber bands were wrapped around his chest. Guns at his lower back, shoulder, and ankle dug into his skin. His hands slicked with sweat, and the woman sitting next to him glared daggers at the side of his face.

The past hour had been a whirlwind of weapons collecting, safety planning, and route mapping. Camila had followed him around his suite, huffing and demanding answers, but he'd been too focused and rushed for a sit down with her.

Now that they were in the air and heading out of the Amazon basin, he had three hours to tell her where they were going and what he'd been doing for the past ten years.

A jittery ache kicked through his stomach, and it had nothing to do with the flight. The twin engines purred quietly, and the smooth rotor system propelled the aircraft fast and seamlessly through the atmosphere. With a sticker price of eight-million dollars, he'd more than paid for a shudder-less ride.

"I thought it would be louder in here." Camila leaned over his lap in their rear-facing seats and peered out the window into the dark sky.

"There's a capsule between us and the airframe, and the dual-pane glass helps."

Two rows of three seats filled the cabin, configured to face each other. The cockpit was behind him and Camila. Nico sat on her other side, talking quietly with Chispa and Picar as they bent over the tablet he held between them, studying a digital map.

Frizz sat directly across from Matias, head resting back on the seat, eyes closed, and complexion paler than usual. Matias wished the guy wouldn't participate in these jobs, knowing how they affected him. But like Camila, Frizz was haunted by his own experiences and motivated to retaliate.

"I'm trying to be patient." She sat back and drummed her fingers on Matias' thigh. "Like really trying here."

He hadn't envisioned telling her like this. Of course, showing her had always been the plan, but he would've rather sat her down in private, when she was ready, and explained it all.

His stomach hardened. Fuck, what if she wasn't ready?

He'd removed her collar last night after dinner, and she didn't need it now, not where they were going. She wore jeans, a long-sleeved shirt, and tennis shoes, just as he'd instructed. Everyone in the cabin donned the same look—casual, a little rugged, with footwear that wouldn't slow them down if they needed to run.

Maybe it would be better if she went in blind. With an actual blindfold, because she would never be able to unsee what they were about to walk into.

"Why aren't you telling me where we're going?" She pressed her nails into the denim on his inner thigh. "And why don't I have weapons like the rest of you?"

His breath hitched as hope warred with suspicion. Did she want to shoot him or… "Would you fight alongside us?"

"Yes." She lifted her chin. "I mean, as long as we're not headed to some meeting place to pick up more slaves."

Chispa coughed into his fist, and she whipped her head toward him. Matias clenched his teeth.

"Sorry, it's…" Chispa gave her a sheepish look. "It's the stale air in here. Makes my throat tickle."

*Motherfucker.* Matias schooled his expression, and she looked back at him, shaking her head with wide eyes.

"Tell me that's not what we're doing. You wouldn't…" She searched his face, voice reedy. "You're taking me on a slave run?"

A swallow caught in his throat. It was the moment of truth, a moment of courage, the testing point of her instinct, her trust, and her love.

He held himself still and confident as his stomach flipped inside out. "What does your gut tell you?"

She glanced around the cabin at the guys, and none of them made eye contact with her.

"Look at *me*, Camila." When her teary eyes returned to his, he said,

"What do you see?"

Her hands balled against her thighs as she stared at him, long and hard. "I see a man...the man I—"

"Sir!" the pilot shouted from the cockpit behind him. "We're being tracked."

"Who?" Matias twisted in the seat and scanned the glowing panel of gauges. "Something on the radar?" He didn't have a clue what he was looking at.

"I have it." Chispa bent over a tablet on his lap, gaze focused on the screen. "There's a jet above us. Probably Colombian military."

"Or American." Nico rubbed a hand over his scowl. "We can lose them. It's the helicopters and puddle-jumpers below and around us we need to worry about."

As predicted, it didn't take long for the first helicopter to buzz by, swooping and circling. Matias' pilot outmaneuvered and outran it, allowing a few minutes' reprieve before the next one showed up.

Despite his strung-out nerves and heart palpitations, Matias kept his breathing tempered and mind clear, watching Chispa as the man stared unblinking at the radar on his screen. They'd been through this countless times.

*But never with Camila in tow.*

Her hand clung to his leg, her complexion bloodless beneath a sheen of perspiration.

"Who are they?" Her voice was strangled.

"Deep breath. Good girl. Now another one." He laced their fingers together on his lap. "We're flying over rival territory, so it could be another cartel. Or the military. They're always looking for us, waiting for us to come out of hiding."

"What the hell, Matias?" Her knee bounced wildly against him.

"This is Colombia, baby." He clamped a hand on her leg, stilling her. "The conflict between armed groups like us and FARC and governmental forces has been ongoing for the last fifty years."

"What happens if we don't lose them?"

"They'll track us until we land and try to take us into custody." *Or kill us if it's another cartel.*

"You weren't kidding when you said you had a lot of enemies." She offered him a strained smile.

"No." His mind went through the worst-case scenarios, all of them ending with them getting shot out of the air and her body burning in an inferno of metal and debris. "But I bought this helicopter for its speed. We always lose them."

Two hours and several reroutes later, they slipped beneath the radar and landed out of sight in a sweeping field of darkness.

A collective sigh breathed through the cabin as Nico opened the rear clamshell door. The guys filed out, leaving Matias alone with Camila. He unlatched his safety belt and crouched before her to remove hers.

As he rose to lead her out, she grabbed his hand. "Wait."

He lifted a questioning brow and lowered to a crouch before her. "Camila—"

"Let me just say this." She slid a hand over her collarless throat, her expression deep and serious. "There's always a basis for justifying an action and an outcome for that action. A motive and a result. You told me, in not so many words, that I might not like the result, but to trust the reason you're doing it."

His heart slammed against his ribs as he nodded.

Nudging him backward, she slid off the seat and knelt before him in perfect form—spine erect, shins flat against the flooring, arms behind her, and head held proud. His pulse went crazy.

"I'm giving you the power to break me inside and out, and I trust that you won't." She stared into his eyes and pulled in a jagged breath. "I'm scared, Matias, fucking terrified of where you're about to take me, but I'm relinquishing that to you, surrendering my vulnerability without shame, because that's what you want, and what you want, I crave."

Tingling weightlessness filled his chest as he pulled her against him and crushed his mouth to hers. He kissed her frantically, devotedly, for as long as he could, but not long enough. When he pulled back, she gazed at him with unfettered trust.

"When I look at you, I see the man in the boy I loved." She brushed a finger over the dimple in his cheek.

"I fucking love you." He kissed her again, smiling like a lovesick asshole.

"Wanna know who I love?" She returned his smile and pointed at his chest. "That guy."

"*Gracias, mi vida.*"

"Now where's my gun?" She held out her hand and arched a sexy brow.

He laughed and gave her the 9mm from his boot. "I trust *you* to not shoot me in the ass."

# TWENTY-FIVE

Camila held tight to Matias' hand as a leathery-faced man named Burd drove them along a dirt road in a black sedan. Ice-cold dread swelled in her stomach, and she couldn't swallow past the clot in her throat. She still didn't know where they were going, but that was the point of her trust, right?

However naïve or insane, she did trust him. The thing was, she'd squandered so much time focusing on the slaves at the estate that she'd only seen Matias as a monster. But when she looked at him, really looked hard into his eyes, she saw a monster that would never hurt her without reason.

Alone in the backseat with him, she rested her head on his shoulder and tried to absorb some of his calm strength. Nico sat in front with Burd behind the wheel. Chispa had stayed with the helicopter pilot to wait for a refueling truck.

Headlights bobbed in the rear window. Burd had brought two armed soldiers in ski masks—lower ranked cartel members according to Matias—who followed behind in a separate sedan with Frizz and Picar.

Outside the window, tiny villages twinkled by. Despite the ramshackle sheds and the bleakness of poverty, the communities seemed tranquil beneath the full moon, scattered across the mountains and surrounded by cultivated fields.

During one of her late night conversations with Matias, he'd told her about these poor rural populations. These indigenous people bred their chickens and labored in their fields of corn and coffee. Their children attended the nearest schools, sometimes hours away, and played with dolls and footballs like any other place in the world.

But it was a hard life. Land was expensive, and the whir of bullets and helicopters were a constant invasion. While the people were resigned to it, the buzz of rotors always sent them running for cover, often forcing them to abandon their farms and move elsewhere until the violence ended.

She'd thought about this when Matias' helicopter had landed in the field of an impoverished village. How many families were cowering in their homes, waiting for Matias to leave? How many other gangs were prowling this area right now?

"This is it." Nico's heavy accent rose above the hum of the engine.

The headlights behind her went dark as Burd pulled into a long gravel driveway. A porch light glowed at the end of the drive, illuminating the front door of a rickety house. Several cars parked out front. Overpriced luxury cars that didn't belong in this poor village.

Prickles raced down her spine. "What is this place?"

Nico pulled on a ski mask and twisted in the front seat to toss another mask to Matias.

Her mind flashed with images of the night Van delivered her to them. "I hate those fucking masks."

Matias eked out a sad smile then slipped the ski mask over her head, covering her nose, mouth, and neck. "You'll stay with Nico."

"Why?" Her throat sealed up. "Where are you going?"

"Just until I get through the door." He adjusted the itchy fabric on her face until only her eyes peered out.

He exchanged a look with Nico, and while they both exuded calmness, there was an undercurrent in their confidence. Not fear or worry. Something akin to grief.

What was this place? Why were they here? Her mouth dried, and she grabbed the 9mm on the seat beside her, having no idea why she needed it or who she would be aiming it at.

Halfway up the drive, Burd turned the sedan around and parked, with the headlights shining in the opposite direction of the house. The second car was nowhere in sight.

Burd shut off the headlights but kept the engine running. "I wait here in car." He crammed the words together with a thick Colombian accent.

"Where's the other car?" She anchored her gaze on Matias.

"They'll come in on foot." He touched his lips to the material over her mouth in a whisper of breath.

Every cell in her body sighed then snapped tight as Matias pulled away and stepped out of the sedan. The interior lights remained off, and the door hung open, letting in the rhythmic chirp of insects.

In the next breath, his silhouette melted into the darkness. She felt like she was going to be sick.

The crunch of his boots on gravel faded in the direction of the house. He had about a hundred feet to walk before he would appear beneath the glow of the porch light. If the other guys were sneaking onto the property, this must've been some kind of ambush. Who the hell was in that house?

Nico exited the sedan and stopped by her door, his whisper muffled by the mask. "Keep quiet."

With the 9mm in hand, she climbed out into the balmy night air. She didn't hear people nearby or vehicles in the distance, much less see any signs of civilization other than the house. But she felt something, a prickly unrest crawling through the black landscape.

Was someone out there? Watching them? Maybe it was the skeletal shapes of the surrounding trees or the fact that she couldn't see Matias, didn't like her hearing hindered by the mask, and didn't want to be alone with Nico. Whatever it was, this remote place gave her the fucking creeps.

She leaned toward Nico, closer than she was comfortable, to speak low at his ear. "Why isn't Matias wearing a mask?"

"Someone has to show their face at the door," he whispered, eyes darting to the house and back to her. "I'm too recognizable." He removed a huge handgun from his waistband and flicked off the safety. "This is how we always do it. He'll be fine."

*Always do it.* She searched the eye opening of his mask and found his gaze more alive than ever and tinged with deep emotion. Whatever was about to happen, he seemed uncharacteristically affected by it. That only made her stomach cramp harder.

With a crook of his finger, he beckoned her to follow him up the driveway.

She switched off the safety on the 9mm and gripped it with both hands. Her finger trembled beside the trigger guard, and her breath huffed heat against the mask, wetting the material. Stepping softly through the grass to match Nico's steps, she trailed behind him toward the house.

The only assumption she had to go on was they were breaking up a slave ring. If that was the case, wouldn't they want to make sure she didn't accidentally shoot an innocent? Maybe there weren't any slaves in that house.

Rather than leading her to the porch, he ushered her along the side of it. As Matias climbed the short flight of steps to the front door, Nico kept her in the concealment of the shadows ten feet away. She ducked behind an overgrown bush beside the railing just as Matias knocked.

A mewling noise sounded from the darkness on the far side of the porch. Then it mewed again in a harrowing appeal for mercy — the weak cries of a dying animal.

Her breath came in gasps, and the hair on her nape rose. Nico gripped the juncture of her neck and shoulder with warning pressure.

Matias turned toward the cries, and the muscles across his back visibly stiffened. What did he see? A cat? Dog? She tried to block the mewling out of her head by focusing on Nico's grip.

Matias shifted back to the door as it opened. Nico dropped his hand.

She angled her neck, peering through the branches to see whoever stood just inside the house, but Matias' broad shoulders obstructed her view.

A handgun was tucked in the back of his jeans. Another one sat in a noticeable shoulder holster. His hard-packed body flexed beneath his t-shirt, but in the next heartbeat, his entire demeanor changed.

His hips loosened and his stance relaxed in a picture of suave arrogance. He crossed a foot over the other and propped it on the toe of the boot. With a forearm braced on the door frame, he lifted the other to slide his thumb over his bottom lip.

Wearing a sexy as fuck smile, he rumbled the Colombian greeting. *"Qué más pues, señorita?"*

"My, my, aren't you a handsome one?" a woman purred in Spanish.

Tension shot through Camila's shoulders and neck. Was he here for this woman? To capture her? Seduce her? Maybe this was a brothel of slaves.

*Trust his reasons and keep him alive.*

"I have an appointment." He continued in the native language.

"I might be more your flavor, no? Spend some time with me and find out, *viga.*"

Her Spanish was so thick Camila struggled to translate it. *Viga?* She thought it meant *superior muscles.*

"I have particular tastes, yeah?" Matias moved his hand toward the vicinity of the woman's chest as his eyes swept past her.

Scoping the place?

His fingers stroked something on the woman, something Camila couldn't see but had no fucking trouble imagining. She felt her damn eye twitching and couldn't stop it.

Nico gripped her wrist. Without looking at him, she nodded and forced herself to relax. Matias had said he needed to get through the door. Evidently, that required fondling another woman's tits.

He continued the flirtatious conversation in Spanish, telling her how sexy she was, how *bacano* her tits felt, and that her lips were more deadly than his .40 cal. He wooed and winked and charmed the panties right off her skank ass. Hopefully, not literally. Camila still couldn't see her beyond the door.

Camila kept her finger off the trigger and her breaths steady, but Nico didn't let go of her arm.

"I have an appointment." Matias rolled the syllables in Spanish.

An appointment for what? A prostitute? The idea of him fucking other women was ridiculous. Saving them, though? That made so much more sense. But who was he saving them from? Whoever had arrived in those luxury cars? An icy chill rushed through her core and chased the heat from her limbs. She glanced at Nico, but his attention was locked on Matias.

"You're no fun," the woman said. "This way."

Matias followed her in and closed the door behind him.

"Fuck," Camila whispered, shoving Nico's hand away. "Are there slaves in there? Is this a whore house?"

He launched to his feet, dragging her with him, and pivoted toward the side of the house.

A second later, a solid dark shape darted around the corner from the backyard. Ski mask. Slender build. Large knife in hand.

*Frizz.* She recognized the metal buckles crisscrossing his black shirt.

"Back door?" Nico asked the other man in a hushed voice.

Frizz shook his head, blue eyes glowing in the dim light from the porch. Jesus, he looked different with his stitched lips hidden and his crazy hair tucked away. He looked…normal. Young. Really fucking young, like late-teens. He was just a baby.

Had he been rescued from slavery himself? If so, why would he torment the slaves at the estate?

He held up two fingers and pointed across the yard at the shadowed tree line. Identifying the location of the men Burd had brought?

Holding down three fingers and a thumb, he pointed his knife at the house.

Nico nodded and turned toward her, whispering, "Three men and a woman inside. Shoot anyone you don't know. Try not to kill the female."

What the fuck? The gun rattled in her hands. "Why would I kill anyone when I don't know who they are?"

Those people could be undercover DEA or FBI or just a family trying to survive amid the violence. They could be the good guys.

What if that wasn't it at all? Maybe Matias' cartel captured women who ran slave rings and sold them as punishment. Her heart pounded. Could she hope for such a possibility?

Nico lifted a hand to touch the mask on her face and stopped before making contact. "You're about to find out."

Frizz slipped around them and crept onto the porch, his steps silent and movements graceful. Nico followed, and she stayed on their heels.

They froze at the sound of a wane cry coming from the dark corner of the stoop. Definitely a dying animal.

Frizz moved first, slinking toward it. Thank fuck, the boards didn't creak, but she braced for it, tensing for any noise that might give them away.

She stepped where Frizz stepped and stopped beside him, her eyes straining in the absence of light as she tried to make out the floating shape.

A lamb. She sucked in a breath through the mask.

A newborn lamb, hanging upside-down by its back legs. Its front legs scissored weakly, reaching for the floor but not quite touching. Its mewls were so frail and brittle it must've been hanging there for a long time.

Manic energy surged through her blood, begging her to help it. But Frizz beat her there, knife out and cutting it down before she took the first step.

When he lowered it to the floor, she whispered inanely, "Why?"

"Dinner." Nico turned back toward the door.

*Dinner? Fine, then fucking eat it. Don't torture it first.* What the fuck was wrong with people?

She moved to follow Nico, but her gaze was glued over her shoulder.

Frizz squatted beside the poor thing, petting it and making shushing sounds. It didn't even try to move or run away. Probably too weak. Or maybe it didn't know any better than to trust a guy who sewed up women. Maybe this was an alternative reality, and *she* didn't know which end was up. Whatever was going on, watching him soothe that lamb made her chest so tight she couldn't breathe.

She joined Nico at the door, and he held up a closed fist, signaling her to stop. His other hand gripped the knob, but he didn't turn it, didn't move.

Her pulse spiked. They'd already used up thirty seconds with the lamb. What if Matias needed back up for…whatever the fuck he was doing?

Another count of too many seconds stretched by before a scream penetrated the door from within. Nico swung it open, and she followed him through, gun pointed toward the floor and her pulse pounding in her stomach.

A woman lay unconscious on the floor, bleeding from her temple, but it was the heavy thumps and whimpers coming from the back of the house that slowed Camila's gait.

Frizz swept around her and knelt beside the woman as Nico took off down the long hall that led toward multiple closed doors, his pistol trained and ready. He slipped into the first room and shut the door. Grunts immediately sounded through the wall, followed by something crashing.

With wobbly steps, she moved in that direction, but a hand gripped her ankle, causing her to stumble. She whirled and met Frizz's wide gaze where he knelt on the threadbare carpet. He shook his head frantically and pointed at the floor beside her feet.

He wanted her to stay? But Matias was back there. What if one of those grunts was his? She didn't even know who was in those rooms. Slaves? Being forced at that very moment? Oh God, she hoped she wasn't right.

Her hands shook around the stock of the gun, palms soaked in sweat as she inched toward the hallway.

A different door opened up ahead, and a fat naked Caucasian man stepped out, his penis fully erect beneath his jiggling belly. Her heart stopped.

He looked at her and narrowed his eyes on the gun she pointed at him. "Who are you?

The mask protected her identity, and Nico had told her to shoot anyone she didn't know. But on what grounds? Because the man's dick was hard? Maybe he'd been jerking off. Completely naked? No fucking way.

She steadied the iron sights on his chest. "Who are you?"

# TWENTY-SIX

Camila kept the 9mm leveled on the naked man's torso, her chest heaving, knees wobbling. She wet her lips, and her tongue brushed against the mask as she slid a finger over the trigger.

A pained male voice bellowed from the back room, followed by a succession of crashing sounds. The naked man widened his eyes, glanced over his shoulder, and darted that way, toward the last door where the screaming came from.

Her pulse thundered in her ears as she pointed the gun at his back. Fuck, she'd never forgive herself if she killed an innocent man, but he if touched that door knob, she wouldn't hesitate to squeeze the trigger.

"Stop or I'll shoot!" She ran after him.

The next few seconds flashed in the span of two anguished breaths. She passed the fat man's room in the first breath, glimpsed a baby doll on the floor, a bare mattress, and the lopsided pigtails and tear-soaked eyes of a girl no older than nine huddled nude in the corner.

*No no no no!* Her second breath came with an explosion of fire as she aimed her horror-stricken fury on the fat man, trained the gun a few inches higher, and sprayed his brain matter across the wall.

Her next breath died in her throat as she screamed in horror. But nothing passed her lips. Not a sound. Not a breath. Every living thing inside her was sobbing in the room with that little girl. This wasn't shock. She stood frozen in a place she wasn't sure she could come back from.

The remaining two doors opened at the same time. Her arms moved on reflex, the gun swinging left to right as she waited for another naked dead man to step out.

Nico emerged first, eyes scowling through the ski mask and red dots peppering his gray shirt.

"Camila." Matias stepped out of the last room, wearing a mask of blood. He raised red-smeared hands and took a limping step toward her. "Lower the gun."

What was in those other rooms? She wanted to ask, but her voice had left her. Maybe she already knew the answer. Her brain felt fuzzy, and she shook. Fuck, she shook from head to toe.

Nico stood nearest to her. Close enough to reach out and grip the barrel trembling in her hands. She let him take it.

Matias glanced down at the fat man and lifted his eyes to her, wearing a blood-speckled smirk. "You're so badass."

She stared at the body blankly, didn't feel a twinge of regret.

Favoring his left leg, Matias slowly erased the distance with his arms stretched open. She walked into his embrace and dropped her forehead on his blood-soaked chest.

He pulled the mask off Camila's head and held her against him as footsteps sounded behind her. Tiny cries trickled from the three rooms, and his arms tightened. *More little girls.* She fought back the rising, burning need to sob and glanced over her shoulder.

The men who had arrived with Burd strode through the front room. Nico and Frizz stepped aside, their tight expressions no longer hidden by masks.

The soldiers pulled off their own ski masks, revealing feminine faces and long hair. Not men? The rest of their womanhood remained hidden beneath fatigues and loose shirts.

Matias shifted Camila out of the way as the women split off into separate rooms. A moment later, Picar shuffled in, carrying a medical bag.

A tidal wave of questions and confusion slammed into her. Two women and a doctor. Presumably, there were three young girls in those rooms, and two more dead pedophiles. All of this had been planned out and executed with one goal. Matias had come here to save those girls.

She struggled to stand upright against the pounding, overwhelming barrage of emotions. Working her throat, she couldn't separate the numbness from her voice. "Can I...do something?"

What could she do? Comfort the girls? Play nurse? Clean up the bodies? Fuck, she wasn't emotionally fit for any of that. She needed to sit down.

Matias turned her toward the front of the house. "You need air."

She needed to know he was okay. With a surge of determined concentration, she shifted back to him and crouched to examine his leg. Her fingers slipped over blood in the ripped part of his jeans on his thigh. "How bad?"

"I'm fine." He pulled her up and nudged her toward the door.

# DISCLAIM

As she crossed the front room, she glimpsed worn wood paneling on the walls, ratty furniture, dishes piled on a counter in a kitchen that was more like an extension of the front room with a stove, sink, and fridge shoved against a wall.

A little pink backpack and a fuzzy stuffed rabbit sat the corner. Her fingernails pierced into her palms.

The woman lay on the floor, eyes blinking rapidly, face streaked with tears, and lips sewn shut. *Just like the slaves at the estate.*

Camila froze as the last three weeks started to click into place.

"Who is this woman?" She stopped a few feet from Frizz.

His lips rolled behind his own stitches as he looked to Nico, who stood in the front doorway, smoking a cigarette.

"That woman," Nico said through a puff of smoke, "is the girls' mother. Ages nine, eleven, and twelve. The same girls she offered to sell to our slave ring."

His eyes shifted to the hallway. Then he turned away.

The same girls she'd pimped out to those dead men.

Camila's vision turned red with murderous rage. "Why is she still alive?"

Blood surged to her arms and legs, her hands fisted, and her pulse screamed through her veins. She flung herself toward the woman, claws out, teeth bared, desperate to scratch eye balls, rip out hair, and ram something sharp and lethal down that vile gullet.

Matias caught her around the waist before she reached the despicable waste of life.

"Shh." He turned her to face him.

"The slaves at the compound..." she choked. "They're not innocent?" A wave of chills swept through her, followed by a rush of heat as her mind assembled the pieces. "You torture slave traders. Then you sell them."

"Oh, I kill them, too, like the one in the back room." He stared into her eyes, his face splattered with blood and the hazel depths of his gaze stark with sadness. "But every woman and man we capture and sell deserves a fate worse than death. Some traffic humans. Others are like her, sell or whore out their own children."

Her stomach swooped and flipped. The ages of his slaves, his complete lack of sympathy for them, his reason for doing it...

*The answer is right in front of you. All you have to do is fucking look.*

He'd wanted her to see a man who loved her so much he would never become a slave trader. A man who loved her to the ends of hell and back as he tracked down the worst kind of monsters and stopped them from harming others.

She swayed with dizziness, her eyes burning with the onset of tears. "I need to sit down."

He moved her outside to the porch, and she instantly glanced at the dark corner, searching for the lamb. It was too shadowy, too quiet, so she stepped in that direction.

"Frizz wouldn't have left it there." Matias' timbre caressed the rawness of her nerves.

"Oh." She frowned. "Do you think...?"

"He ended its suffering?" He nodded. "And moved it somewhere you wouldn't see it."

She stared out into the gloom of their surroundings, probing for the little lamb's body. Her stomach squeezed painfully. It was silly to care about a dead animal considering what she'd just witnessed. She must've been stretched thin on heartache.

"Sit with me." He held out his hand.

She joined him on the steps, where they sat side by side and gazed at the vastness of the black sky. A moment later, Nico brought out a couple of towels and returned inside.

Welcoming the distraction, she focused on cleaning Matias' face, wiping the sculptured edges around his strong jaw, stern brow, and the strands of his thick black hair. His gaze never left hers as she used the corners of the cloth to clear away the splatter around his eyes, perfect nose, the creases in his ears, and his dimples when he smiled gently.

Then she used the clean towel to dab at the knife wound in his thigh.

"Picar needs to look at this," she said with an achy voice, her mind spinning in a million different directions.

"He's busy." Matias grimaced when she pressed too hard. "Frizz can stitch it."

"Frizz!" she shouted over her shoulder. When he appeared on the porch, she lifted the towel. "Need you to sew up a stab wound."

His eyes glimmered, and he rushed back into the house. When he returned moments later, he carried an armful of bandages and supplies that he'd probably swiped from Picar's bag.

He cut Matias' jeans away from the injury and set to work, cleaning and preparing the wound.

She lifted Matias' hand and used one of the bandages to clear away the blood. "How long have you been doing this?"

"Ten years." His fingers curled around hers.

"A year after I was captured."

"Yeah. It took some time to organize."

"Jesus, Matias." Her heart panged. "You could've told me this during any one of our phone calls. I would've joined your efforts and helped you." *We could've been together all these years.*

He shook his head. "I was in a bad place those first few years. I killed more slave traders than I captured. So fucking reckless and dangerous and *angry*." He lifted his chin at Frizz. "This guy kept my head on straight."

Frizz paused during a stitch and stared at the ground.

"You've been doing this with Matias since the beginning?" she asked Frizz, studying his youthful face. "How old are you?"

Frizz closed his eyes, opened them, and reached for the knife beside his knee. Then he lifted the blade to his mouth and cut each stitch, one by one, pulling away the threads as he went.

Matias squeezed her hand, and she squeezed back, her insides twisting in knots.

"I was eight when Matias found me." Frizz's voice cracked, soft and chalky with disuse.

Her heart clenched.

He glanced toward the house, but his gaze turned distant. "He pulled me out of a place just like this. My old man..." He cleared his throat, his inflection gentle and distinctly American. "My father used to sell me to men like those in there. The men wanted to hear me cry and beg. When I wouldn't do it, my father hurt me very badly."

An ache pressed against the backs of her eyes and seared through her chest. She wanted to reach for him, hold his hand. Matias looked as if he wanted to do the same, but didn't move, so she followed his lead.

"I like to sew my mouth." Frizz licked his bottom lip. "So I won't forget."

"So you won't forget...?" The lump in her throat burned painfully.

"I'll never give them what they want." He stared at his unmoving hands, fingers clenched around the needle. "They'll never hear me beg, never force...themselves in my mouth again."

She tried to keep the tears at bay, tried not to look at him with pity. All she could think about was an eight-year-old boy, abused and molested, living with a cartel and following the capo around while he slaughtered predators.

Maybe it was the best form of therapy. Hadn't she done the same thing?

"What happened to your father?" She had a damn good guess.

"Matias castrated him." Frizz smiled. "And cut out his tongue. He removed other organs, too. *Then* he killed the bastard."

Her stomach curdled. "Is there anything left of the man in the room you were in?" she asked Matias, nodding at the house.

"Pieces." Matias looked over at her and shrugged. "I have a really sharp knife."

"Good." She lay her head on his shoulder. "Did the little girl...did she watch that?"

"I sent her to the closet the second I charged in." He tensed, relaxed. "Those girls will be removed without witnessing the gore."

She traced the ink on his forearm, following the branches with a finger. "Okay."

Frizz sewed up Matias' leg wound in silence. Then he restitched his lips without a mirror, his fingers expertly moving the needle through the existing holes. She watched through a new set of eyes and no longer saw a scary freak. As he poked the needle through his flesh, she thought of it as a lip piercing, a rebellious expression of self. A *fuck you* to dear old dad.

When he finished, he gathered the supplies and strolled into the house, whistling a cheery, unfamiliar tune.

She sat alone with Matias for an endless moment. The heavy hush between them bled into the darkness, dampened by the buzz of winged insects.

"When we get back, I'm calling my friends, Matias." She slid her hand over his thigh. "They need to know I'm okay."

"Anything you want." He turned his face toward her and put his lips on hers. Slightly open. A tiny gliding movement. Then he kissed her nose.

"Why didn't you tell me about the slaves three weeks ago?"

"I wanted you to love me despite this." He pulled away, bracing elbows on his knees, and stared straight ahead.

"I would've loved you no matter what. It was inevitable."

"Through all your one-night stands, what would you have done if one of those men told you he saved child slaves? Would he have become more to you than just a hookup?"

She rubbed her forehead and stared at him sidelong. "That's such a crazy *what if*. I don't know." But she did know. She would've clung to that connection.

"Your heart beats for the end of slavery. If you found that same passion in someone else, *anyone* else, your heart would've cemented you to him." He met her eyes. "I didn't want to be just anyone. I wanted to be *your* one, passions and pursuits aside. I wanted you to choose me for *us*." He looked back at the landscape. "So I let you see whatever you wanted to see at the estate and waited until you saw *me*."

She swallowed thickly. "The amount of fear and doubt and fucking dread I've gone through over the past few weeks…"

"Vulnerability has to happen for love to be real."

Profound and really smart, but also… "This is crazy." She scrubbed her hands over her hair. "You could've just told me your slaves were horrible people, and bam, you would've had me just like that."

"Too easy. You're not getting it." He shifted to face her and gripped her chin. "I refuse to settle for anything less than what we had as kids. You loved me when you were sixteen for no other reason than because your gut told you we were meant to be together. But age and experience fucks with our instincts. Our minds get in the way and try to reason and rationalize every goddamn emotion." He released her chin. "I stripped those rationalizations away and forced you to focus on what you really felt, not what your mind told you to feel. And you believed. You believed in us without seeing...this." He gestured at the house.

"Faith," she whispered.

"Faith in *us*." He focused on her mouth and leaned in, kissing her in that tender way that always made her melt.

"Seems like you went through a lot of trouble for such a blurry concept," she said against his lips, her vision smudging with tears. "Who does that?"

"People have been killing each other because of faith for hundreds of years." He smoothed a hand across her cheek.

"Because of religion, Matias, which is based on control and fear."

"But it starts with faith. Some believe strongly enough they die for it." He leaned in and touched his forehead to hers. "You took that step tonight. You believed in us so passionately you walked into that house and risked your life."

"You're insane." She wrapped her arms around his wide shoulders and sighed. "I love it. Everything you said was wild and inconceivable and could be argued until the end of the burning sun, and that's why it makes sense." She kissed him, softly, deeply. "Every reason, justification, and argument leads us to the same result. We're together because that's where we belong."

He pulled her into his arms, and they settled into a cradle of silence. Voices and footsteps trickled from the house. The constant noise of whirring life echoed around them, and a thickening mantle of sorrow and relief smothered the air.

"How are you doing with this?" He nodded at the door.

"I experienced that whole thing way, way down deep." An unreachable shiver jolted inside her. "All those feelings are still there, lodged somewhere between my heart and stomach. When they decide to resurface, it's really going to hurt like hell." She rubbed her face. "Those girls, Matias...God, I can't...I just can't think about it."

"Don't." He kissed her cheek, brushing his nose against hers affectionately. "It gets easier, I promise. And I'll be right at your side every step of the way."

Golden fire, kindled in a Texan citrus grove and forged in a decade of hell, burned in his eyes.

She drew him close and touched her lips to his scruffy jaw. "What happens to them now?"

"The women will take them to a foster home, one of the many I vetted and trust. I fund every step of their recoveries. I also put the fear of God in those foster families to ensure they provide the best environments for the children I send to them."

"There's my crime boss." She stared up at the sky and smiled to herself. "You're a good man, Matias."

"Then I haven't scared you enough." He lowered his mouth to her shoulder, pressing a kiss there while never taking his eyes off her. "I'll have another chance to do that before we head home."

"What do you mean?"

"The Córdoba cartel is waiting at the helicopter to ambush us."

Her face went cold. "What?"

# TWENTY-SEVEN

"What do you mean? Why are we just sitting here?"

Matias felt the worked-up rasp of Camila's voice like a hungry tongue on his cock. "We have time."

"Time for what?" She sprung nimbly to her feet and stepped off the porch.

Dark jeans stretched over her sexy curves, paired with a plain black t-shirt that molded to her perfect rack. Illuminated by the glow of the porch light, shiny black hair framed her gorgeous face and hung in windblown waves around her shoulders. There wasn't a square inch of imperfection anywhere on her.

The savage need to claim her in front of God and everyone stirred in his blood. *Wrong fucking place and time.*

She stood in front of his perch on the steps, putting them at eye level. "This better not be one of those I-ask-you-don't-say-shit conversations."

He combated her glare, but goddamn, she made him hard as a rock. "We're catching a different ride home." His annoyance with the deal Nico made coiled tension into his shoulders. "I lost my favorite helicopter."

"Wait. Hold up." Brown eyes full of spark, she anchored her hands on her hips in the feisty pose he'd loved since they were kids. "You said there's another cartel waiting to ambush you?"

"Yes. Los Córdoba."

"How do you know this?"

"I set it up."

"You *what*?"

He smirked, enjoying the angry flush in her cheeks.

She cast her gaze heavenward. "*Santa Madre de Dios*, give me the strength to *not* strangle this man."

The crunch of tires on gravel sounded in the distance and grew louder up the driveway just as Nico stepped out of the house.

"We're on our way," Nico said into the phone at his ear. Ending the call, he strode down the steps past Matias.

As the black sedan pulled up behind Camila, she pointed at Matias. "Keep talking."

"In the car." He moved off the porch, toward the driveway, and opened the rear door for her.

Burd relinquished the driver's seat and headed into the house. As a lower-ranked member, he'd been vetted for the vigilante portion of this trip, but not for the next part.

"Are the others coming with us?" Camila stared after Burd as she slid into the backseat.

"Frizz and Picar will stay with the girls for a couple days." Matias latched her seatbelt, trailed a finger across her bottom lip, and shut the door.

He met Nico's eyes over the roof of the sedan. Matias preferred to be the fake bodyguard and chauffeur—the guy no one paid attention to or targeted. But as Nico climbed into the backseat beside Camila, Matias reconsidered the whole decoy thing.

It was purely an emotional reaction after a godawful night. He didn't want anyone else protecting her or sitting by her. He sure as hell didn't want people thinking she belonged to Nico.

Fuck, that sounded ridiculous, even in his head.

Wiping a hand down his face, he lowered into the driver seat, cranked up the A/C, and drove away from the house. He only had about ten minutes to prepare her before they reached their rendezvous point.

"Last week, you gave me an idea." He adjusted the rear-view mirror and found her steady brown eyes. "I decided that we didn't have a mole, but we needed one."

"I'm not following." She shook her head.

Nico powered on his tablet, and the glow from the screen brightened her face.

"We know Gerardo leaked information to a cartel." He eased onto a dirt road, watching the side mirrors for other vehicles. "We just didn't know who he worked with or if he exposed our two biggest secrets."

"I assume one is your identity. The other..." She frowned in concentration. "The location of your headquarters?"

"Yes. For the past week, I kept all our lieutenants congregated at the estate and inconspicuously beefed up security, all while giving whoever was watching our business activities the impression that we were still focused on finding a spy." He hit the gas on a straight empty road surrounded by fields. "We kept our ears to the ground, listening for whispers about an attack against the estate, and uncovered nothing. Not a peep. The location of our headquarters remains a secret, but…" He propped an elbow on the console. "The information Gerardo leaked put our smuggling routes at risk."

"They're going to attack your supply lines?"

"The most profitable ones. Our rivals want that business more than anything." He clenched his jaw. "I've let them think we're too distracted to notice what they're planning. And I gave them a different distraction—another Gerardo."

"You gave them a mole? Inside your cartel?" She leaned forward, watching him in the mirror with wide eyes.

"A fake one." *Mierda,* he loved her interest in his business. "Chispa sent out feelers, making contact with our enemies under the guise that there was unrest within our ranks and he wanted out. He dangled valuable secrets, trying to lure the group that turned Gerardo."

"I bet your enemies crawled all over themselves trying to recruit him."

"Of course. But only one cartel could confirm their involvement with Gerardo." Matias drummed his fingers on the steering wheel.

"Los Córdoba?"

He nodded. "They know things only Gerardo knew."

"That's the group you set up to ambush you?" Her voice pitched with disbelief. "Why the hell would you do that?"

"*Oiga,*" Nico said. "He's getting to the good part."

"Chispa made a deal with Los Córdoba." Matias veered onto another dirt road. The lights of the nearest town glimmered on the horizon, but he made another turn, driving away from it and into the darkness of barren landscape. "In exchange for their protection, Chispa gave them the names of our liaisons and security details on the narcotics business we run through our El Paso compound. He gave them everything they need to steal that operation from us."

"What?" She gasped. "You forfeited your entire El Paso division?"

"To convince them to trust Chispa." Matias shrugged. "The Feds are days from taking it anyway. Los Córdoba doesn't know that. Besides, someone suggested we start looking at new smuggling routes like Australia."

She flopped against the seat back and groaned. "Me and my fucking mouth."

"Love fucking your mouth, *mi vida.*" He held her gaze in the mirror.

Nico cleared his throat. "Turn right at the fork up ahead."

"I'm still waiting to hear about this ambush." She raised her brows.

"Mm." Matias squinted at the road, watching for the turn off. "Chispa contacted Los Córdoba when we left him at the helicopter. Told them where he was and that Nico Restrepo would be returning soon. Perfect set up for them to trap us. I'd be really surprised if the Córdoba capo isn't there just to watch Nico get killed."

Her gaze darted to Nico, her mouth hanging open. "Okay, we're obviously not returning to the helicopter." She looked back at the mirror. "When you don't show, they'll know Chispa set them up." She narrowed her eyes with suspicion. "You did something, didn't you? Did you assemble your own surprise attack on *them*?"

"Love the way your mind works." He grinned.

"I have a contact on the Colombian police force," Nico said.

"Not an ally." Matias spotted the fork and turned off. "Just a guy Nico makes deals with."

"Oh my fuck." Camila touched her throat, her gaze flickering between him and Nico. "You sent the police to ambush them? What about Chispa? Won't they take him into custody?"

Nico powered down the tablet. "I negotiated the release of Chispa and Don — the pilot — in exchange for the location of this ambush."

"But the police are keeping my fucking helicopter." Matias gritted his teeth.

"I should be getting a call anytime from my police contact," Nico said. "Hopefully, they'll have Álvarez" — a glance at Camila — "he's the capo, in custody and put this headache behind us. Los Córdoba won't survive without him."

"Jesus." She slumped in the seat. "What if Álvarez isn't there?"

"Then he got a very strong message from us." Matias spied a helicopter-sized blob in the field up ahead.

"Don't fuck with the Restrepo cartel?" she breathed.

"Exactly." Nico removed his seatbelt and leaned forward to speak low in Matias' ear. "You're out of time, *parce*. You need to tell her."

"Tell me what?" She unlatched her belt, her gaze skittering over the field and landing on the helicopter.

The moment Matias parked beside the twin-engine, Nico swung open his door and stepped out.

"Camila." Matias shut off the motor. "This is the helicopter I keep in Bogota. I had one of my guys fly it here along with someone —"

"Oh my God." She stared out the passenger window, breaths quickening as her hands fumbled with the door latch. "Is that...?"

He followed her gaze to the man hopping out of the aircraft.

Muscled physique, dark blond hair, arm sleeved in ink. Yep. "Tate Vades."

She flung her door open and ran. Had they been on a busy street, she probably would've leapt over cars in her urgency to reach the bastard. Matias rubbed the bridge of his nose and followed her.

With her arms wrapped around Tate's shoulders, she lifted on tiptoes and pressed her cheek against his neck. "What're you doing here?"

Matias flexed his fingers and forced his feet to remain planted a couple yards behind her.

Tate met his eyes, expression tight. "You didn't tell her?"

Expecting the piercing anger in the question, Matias lifted a shoulder. "I ran out of time."

She stepped back, staring at Tate then glaring at Matias. "Why is he here?"

"You had three weeks!" Tate threw his arms up.

"I've been wooing her." Matias straightened, clasping his hands behind his back.

It'd been critical that she didn't know about Tate's role until she'd given herself to Matias fully and completely. That hadn't happened until she knelt for him and told him she loved him on the other helicopter only a couple hours earlier.

"*Wooing?* Is that what you call it?" Camila held his gaze as she stabbed a finger toward Tate. "Explain this."

The pilot started up the helicopter with a squealing whine of the engines. The tail rotor and blades turned, spinning faster and ruffling her long hair.

"Hash it out in the air," Nico shouted as he strode by with his nose buried in his phone. "We need to go."

Matias and Nico quickly changed into the clean clothes the pilot had been instructed to bring, and twenty minutes later, the helicopter reached coasting altitude.

The cabin was comparable in size to the other one and refurbished to enable passengers to talk without headsets. But it was older and made for wear, reminding Matias of the interior of a commercial airliner. That was fine since it was primarily used by his lieutenants and hitmen.

Nico and Tate sat with their backs to the cockpit, facing the bench seat Matias shared with Camila.

"They got Álvarez and most of his top men." Nico held up a text message on his phone, grinning. "Chispa and Don are going to lay low for a few days before we send for them."

*Los Córdoba is finished.* Now Camila could safely wander the estate as his equal.

Matias closed his eyes in relief and reached over to clasp her hand. When her soft fingers closed around his, he knew that everything would be okay. They were headed home, and while she was probably ready to chew him a new asshole over Tate, she was here, holding his hand, her thumb stroking his. Because she loved him. Best fucking feeling in the world.

"Are we worried about being tracked again?" she asked.

"Not till we get closer to home." He took in the beauty of her profile—long lashes, high cheekbones, supple lips—and drew a deep breath. "I met Tate four years ago."

She glanced at Tate, who nodded.

Her eyes closed. "I assume that wasn't coincidental." She cast a sideways glare at Matias. "How did you find us?"

For the next few minutes, he explained how he'd arrived to collect Van Quiso's body the day Liv Reed shot him, and how Van, bleeding and barely alive, led him to Liv, who unknowingly took him right to Camila.

She tipped her head as she listened, and when he fell quiet, she didn't blow up or rush him with questions. She simply waited.

"I watched you for a couple of months. Determined your patterns, your goals, who you were closest to." He lifted his chin at Tate.

Her former roommate sat directly across from her, his knees brushing against hers.

"Matias approached me at a bar." Tate bent forward and gathered her hands in his. "He told me your history with him, how you guys grew up together, that he was the one you called to deal with the bodies, and that he loved you. So I knew you trusted him to some degree." His leg bounced. "He told me he was the boss of the Restrepo cartel and that he was the kind of guy who took what he wanted. But he couldn't take you because you'd been captured before. He couldn't just rip you away from your life because he'd never win you that way." He smirked. "He pitched this crazy fucking plan to me, Camila."

"What plan?" She pulled her hands gently from his.

Next to Tate, Nico put in ear buds and reclined in the seat, closing his eyes. He'd heard this story so many times, had been there through it all. Matias didn't blame him for shutting them out.

Tate gave Matias a questioning look, and Matias gestured for him to continue. It would be better for her to hear this part from him.

"There was a slave ring in Austin. Just a couple of local guys. Not affiliated with anyone. Those are the guys you initially started tracking."

"Oh, God." She ran a hand through her hair. "I can totally guess where you're going with this."

Matias put a hand on her thigh, and she didn't push it away. She didn't touch it, either.

Tate gave her a small smile. "Matias told me that night he intended to kill off that slave ring and replace it with his own people. He would continue to operate it, except the slaves would be fake. Actresses. All of it staged to draw you in. And he needed my help."

Her face turned white.

Matias tried to hold his breath, but he couldn't. He needed to make something very clear. "I know you would've taken down that operation within weeks. You're so damn tenacious and brave those motherfuckers didn't stand a chance. But I was selfish. I wanted you fighting at my side, in Colombia, against some of the worst slavery on the planet. I needed you."

She rubbed her forehead and closed her eyes, her expression giving nothing away. Then she looked at Tate. "So you went along with this?"

"Not immediately. I left the bar with my goddamn head spinning." Tate pulled her arms down and forced her to look at him. "A month later, he flew me to Colombia and took me on one of his raids. It was a fucking barn..." He swiped a hand over his mouth, his blue eyes darkening with memories.

A shiver raced through Matias as he recalled that night. He'd never been enslaved, but the depravity he'd witnessed over the years had deeply connected him to her cause. All the effort she invested — the spying, planning, and risking her life — meant as much to him as it did to her. She was *his*, and he was wonderstruck by her ambition. She hadn't let her own captivity ruin her life. She was too strong a woman to hide in fear. Instead, she used her knowledge and experience to save as many lives as she could.

She would've eventually expanded her campaign beyond Texas, and it was his responsibility to be there, protecting her when she did. There were so many predators in the world, breeding the kind of horrors she fought against. Like the barn.

"There were children," Tate whispered, "naked and shackled, being auctioned off." His shoulders shook, and he met Matias' eyes. "Matias saved every one of them and left an unholy massacre in his wake."

"You fell in love with him that night." The stubborn set of her chin eased as she studied Tate's face.

"Uh." Tate laughed and raked a hand through his blond hair. "As much as a straight guy can appreciate another man, I guess. I was willing to do whatever he asked of me."

At some point over the past four years, Matias developed a soul-deep respect for the guy. Deep enough that he would kill anyone who tried to harm Tate.

"Your heart beats for the end of slavery." She echoed Matias' words to Tate. "You found that same passion in Matias."

It was exactly the thing Matias needed to hear her say. She understood him in a way no one else could.

"For sure." Tate wiped his palms on his thighs, avoiding Matias' stare. "By the way, he was dead set on capturing Van and Liv and selling them into slavery."

"What?" She froze.

Matias still wanted to punish them, but… "Tate filled me in on how they were coerced into human trafficking, so I made an exception and spared them."

"Thank you." She played with the ends of her hair. "I'm still reeling over the fact that you and Tate know each other." She eyed Tate suspiciously. "Four years ago, you left for a week to go on a soul-searching road trip across the States."

"He was with me in Colombia," Matias said. "After the raid at the barn, he stayed at the estate for a few days."

"Why did you involve Tate at all?" she asked.

"He was the closest I could get to you." Matias' stomach sank just as the helicopter dipped and recovered altitude. "He watched over you, protected you, and called me every day, letting me know every detail of your life, including the things you confided in him."

"What things?" she growled, shooting a glare at Tate.

"This is why I wanted you to have this conversation before I arrived." Tate frowned at Matias as he leaned back and folded his arms across his chest.

Matias caught her chin and touched her mouth with his, quick and chaste. Then he released her, but kept his face close. "You told him your sexual cravings. Your desire to be held down, controlled, fucked hard—"

"Okay, stop." She leaned back. "I know what I told him." She turned her glare on Tate. "Not cool, man."

Without Tate's intel, it would've taken Matias a long damn time to figure out she was a sexual submissive. He knew she leaned that way as a sixteen-year-old girl, but she'd also been young and innocent. After her abduction, he'd been shocked as hell to learn that her submissive cravings had only deepened.

"He told me things, Camila." Tate cocked his head. "*His* sexual preferences. You were both in my fucking ear. Him wanting to dominate you. You wanting to be dominated. I knew, without a doubt in my mind, you were perfect for each other. So I helped him out."

"With his plan," she said. "And that was…?"

"To get you to come to me willingly." Matias paused as the helicopter shuddered through turbulence. "I knew, eventually, you would try to infiltrate my fake slave ring disguised as a slave—"

"Oh, no." Her face turned ashen. "OhGodOhGod, I tortured and killed Larry McGregor."

"He was a legit scumbag," Matias said. "At first, you were

tracking a real slave ring. I took those guys out, trickled you a few leads, planted people in your path, but after four years, you weren't biting." He smiled. "You were really cautious, and I'm fucking proud of you for that. But I was growing impatient. So I hand-selected Larry McGregor, a bona fide kidnapper. He'd never murdered anyone. Still, it was a risk I didn't like. Tate ensured me you would go back to his house and immediately choke him out." His nostrils flared. "Except you decided to—"

"I had to get him in that chokehold." She straightened and lifted her chin.

"Wait." Tate widened his eyes. "Tell me you didn't fuck—"

"I didn't." She sniffed. "What about the girl in Larry's barn?"

"An actress," Matias said. "I placed her in Larry's path."

She stared out the window as the helicopter vibrated and swooped with sideways movements and occasional rapid changes in altitude. He already missed his smooth-gliding Bell 429.

"I was making a difference in Austin," she said quietly. "So why do I feel like such a dumb, predictable pawn?"

He didn't want her to think he'd used her passion against slavery to trick her. Nor did he intend to belittle her extraordinary accomplishments.

His stomach hardened as he formulated his words. "You took down Van Quiso's operation, did you not?"

"With help."

"How many of your freedom fighters volunteered to infiltrate a slave ring as a slave? Look at me." When she did, he rested his forehead against hers. "The only predictable thing about you is your prowess. Frankly, I'm blown away by your badass-ness, Camila Dias. As a capo, I can't *not* recruit you. As the man who loves you, I can't *not* be at your side while you put yourself in danger."

She drew in a ragged breath. "You manipulated me."

"And you manipulated me, sneaking your sexy ass into my cartel with the intention of removing my head from my body."

"Well, yeah." She laughed nervously. "I...uh, decided that was a terrible plan."

"Thank fuck for that."

The helicopter wobbled, and she leaned away, tilting her head as she stared at Tate. "How did you get to Colombia so quickly?"

"I've been in Bogota since you left," Tate said. "Waiting for this guy to fly me to you."

"Oh." Her eyebrows drew together. "Do Liv and Van and the others know?"

"Yeah." Tate picked at a hole in his jeans. "I filled them in after Van dropped you off."

"Bet you had a good laugh when I had that chip put in my tooth." Her jaw hardened. "That damn thing cost me a lot of money."

Tate grimaced. "Sorry about that."

She blew out a breath. "This is a lot to take in."

"You wouldn't have come to me any other way." Matias gripped her hand. "I couldn't capture you, couldn't chain you to my bed and force you to love me. It would've created a huge ugly thing between us. So I devised a plan that would bring you to Colombia, one that wouldn't put you in a situation where you'd be consumed with trying to escape."

"Wow," she whispered, staring at their entwined hands. "Fucking brilliant, really. I never once tried to escape. My interest was solely on you and your slaves."

*Exactly.*

Tate angled his body toward the window and closed his eyes as a smile played on his lips.

"You looked past my criminal activities." Matias traced her fingers where they curled around his. "The weapons, drugs, torture, my position in the cartel—all of it. You wouldn't have accepted any of that had I knocked on your door and explained it to you."

"You're right." Her grip tightened, and the vertical lines between her eyebrows deepened. "I probably would've stopped calling you if you'd told me you were a capo. But that doesn't mean I'm not angry about your secrecy."

"I'll make it up to—"

The soft weight of her hand covered his mouth.

"You're going to make it up to me by stepping out of my way when I take over your anti-slavery operation." She raised her brows in challenge.

He pulled her hand down and held on to it. "How about a compromise? I'll stand by your side while we run this thing together. It'll be one of my priorities, but I can't leave the cartel. I have too many enemies. If I walked away from this life, I would lose the protection and resources it gives me. It would be a life on the run, and I wouldn't be able to keep you safe the way I need to. Believe me, *mi vida*, I will chain you to my bed before I sacrifice your safety."

For the first time since she stepped onto the helicopter, her eyes shone bright.

"I never asked you to leave this life, but sometimes…" She leaned up and peppered his mouth with quick electric kisses. "Sometimes I might ask you to chain me to your bed."

# TWENTY-EIGHT

The next morning, Camila stood in Matias' closet—*their* closet—and stared at the door that hid skeletons. It'd been a low priority on her list of things to puzzle out, and he'd said she would have access when she was ready. She wasn't sure she'd ever be ready.

She continued to stare at the mysterious door as she dressed for the day. A simple white sundress. Flip-flops. No bra or panties, since he had a habit of ripping them in his haste to remove them. And no collar because she didn't find it in its usual resting place beside the bed.

He always removed it at night—a thoughtful thing to do since the stiff leather was uncomfortable to sleep in. But she felt naked without it. Disconnected from him.

He wasn't around to ask about it. A few hours earlier, he'd left her utterly exhausted and satisfied after waking her with his mouth on her pussy. As she'd drifted back to sleep, he'd kissed her and told her to find him when she was ready for the day.

She smiled as she strode out of the suite and wandered the halls, searching for him. She passed dozens of guards and other cartel members, and no one gave her a questioning look as to why she was collarless and strolling alone. Had he made some kind of announcement?

Twenty minutes later, she found him on the terrace by the pool, deep in conversation with Nico and Tate.

*Tate.*

Seeing him here really fucked with her reality. In a good way. Her worlds had collided, but instead of everything crumbling down around her in a fiery crash, it all just kind of…gelled.

Even so, she'd had a long talk with him and Matias on the flight home about how all their planning behind her back was the same as lying, and lying was the opposite of trust, and if they pulled that shit again, she wouldn't be as forgiving.

On the far side of the terrace, Matias sat with his back to her. As she emerged from the interior living room, he turned immediately, like he had some kind of internal radar tuned in to her location.

His white t-shirt pulled across his muscled shoulders and put his gorgeous ink on display, giving him a rough and dangerous look that made her heart shiver. He was powerful and infuriatingly domineering, but he was also so deeply sentimental she felt like a cold-hearted bitch in comparison.

He gave her a wink that liquefied her insides. Then he turned back to his conversation.

A quick scan of the terrace revealed two paths to reach him. One would take her around the left side of the lounge chairs. It was a few extra steps out of the way, but far more appealing than the other choice.

If she took the direct path alongside the pool, she would pass Yessica and the bevy of giggling women in string bikinis. Since she hadn't left Matias' side over the past three weeks, his presence had served as a buffer between her and these women. A conversation with them was overdue.

She looked at the safer path longingly.

*Don't wimp out, Camila. Show them your teeth.*

Squaring her shoulders and straightening her spine, she chose the path of most resistance.

The giggling stopped as she approached the lounge chairs, and four pairs of mascara-caked eyes locked on her.

"I heard Matias removed your collar." Yessica fingered an olive out of her martini — *at ten in the morning?* — and popped it in her mouth.

So Matias had made an announcement, but it could've been anything. *The slave is off her leash. The slave was never a slave. The slave is my life, and I'm going to marry her and have lots of babies...*

She sighed. How to reply?

Touching a hand to her naked throat, she went with honesty. "I miss it already."

Matias sat some thirty feet away, his upper body twisted in the chair and hands gripping the armrests as if moving to stand. She gave him a sharp shake of her head, and he relaxed, but didn't turn away.

A warm wind rustled across the terrace, rippling the water in the pool and producing a backdrop of whooshing noises. She doubted he could hear her from where he sat.

"Don't get too comfortable." One of Yessica's friends, a pretty blonde, adjusted the strap of her red bikini top. "He's not a one-woman kind of man."

"Oh really?" Camila kept her tone light and playful as her stomach boiled with acid. "How's that?"

"Well, we've all fucked him." The blonde gestured at the other three women. "He visits lots of beds. Never sticks around." She shrugged. "He's the boss. Too important to be tied down."

Camila tried to ignore the twitch in her eye and the pang in her chest as her smile strained her face. She focused on the fact that this woman had casually mentioned Matias' role as the boss in front of his supposed slave. Now she really wanted to know the specifics of his announcement.

"But he seems to prefer Yessica." Another blonde plucked an olive from her bloody mary and tossed it in Yessica's modest cleavage.

They all laughed as Camila tried her damnedest to keep her fists from bloodying their noses.

"He makes his rounds, but he always comes back to me." Yessica stretched in the lounge chair, her tiny swimsuit revealing far more of her Latina curves than it covered. "I'll just hang out here until he comes in me…I mean, comes to me again."

"Huh." Camila gave her a thoughtful look. "When was the last time he came *in* you?"

"It's been…Oh, you know." Her eyes darted away, and she grinned, but it was taut at the corners. "He holds out for a while then he comes to me all pissed off and sexy. Sweet Jesus, that man gives good angry sex."

Camila's stomach threatened to hurl. She felt Matias gaze hot on her face, but she refused to look at him. It was crucial that she establish her position here without his dominating interference.

"And good gifts, too." Yessica's eyes sparkled. "He always gives me dresses and pearls and makeup—"

"Does he give you the belt?" Camila asked sweetly.

She really didn't want to hear this answer, but she needed to understand if Yessica had been just an orgasm to him or if she was one of the women he'd shared a more intimate relationship with. The kind that involved pain and acceptance and trust.

"A belt?" Yessica pursed her lips. "You mean, does he beat me?"

"Yes. Did he whip your ass with a belt?"

She snorted then exaggerated a full-body shudder. "No, sweetheart."

"Interesting."

"Why is that *interesting*?" She narrowed her eyes.

Her friends found interest in their fingernails, drinks, and the grout in the tile flooring.

"Any woman can get dresses and pearls and makeup, but only the special ones get his belt." Camila leaned over Yessica's chair. "I'll say this one time, and this goes for all of you." She waved a hand, indicating the collective whole of prostitutes. "Do not touch him, invade his personal space, or proposition him. Do not do anything that disrespects me. If I get a whiff of it—and trust me, ladies, I'll know—I'll have your asses removed from this estate. I have no problem with the services you provide around here, but going forward, Matias is no longer a client. Are we clear?"

Paralyzed silence.

Camila sighed. "I asked a question."

"Yes." Yessica ground her teeth. "We're clear."

"Cool." She gave them a cordial smile. "*Chau pues!*"

She turned and headed toward him, her steps lighter, easier. As she closed the distance, however, jealousy tried to work its way into her resolve. She pushed it back with the reminder that she'd fucked countless men, causing Matias the same amount of pain.

When she reached his table, she moved toward the empty chair, but he gripped her arm and pulled her onto his lap.

"Do I want to know what that was about?" He brushed his lips against her ear and nibbled.

Tate angled toward Nico, distracted by whatever was displayed on Nico's phone.

"No more gifts for Yessica." She twisted to look at Matias.

"I don't shop for her." His eyes glimmered. "I receive all kinds of shit when I travel to the States. Presents from my business partners. I give her the girly stuff to divide among the whores."

Relief settled through her. "Well, maybe just give that stuff to a homeless person or something."

"I can do that." He nuzzled her neck. "What else?"

"They won't be propositioning you anymore. Hope your ego can handle that."

"I'll live." He nipped the skin beneath her ear.

She shivered with pleasure. "What did you announce this morning?"

"I briefed my lieutenants on your status and had them run the update down their chains of command. Everyone who stays here now knows you're my equal."

"Your equal?" Her heart slammed against her rib cage.

"My life," he said matter-of-factly.

A wave of heat gathered between her legs. As significant as his statement was, it also carried an undertone of need. Every interaction he shared with her was sexual in its delivery. He knew how to arouse her with his growly timbre, a look in his eyes, a caress of his breath against her skin. He didn't even have to touch her to satisfy her. It was his demanding hunger — that of a confident, dominant man — that she responded to, lifting her face to the rumble of his voice, offering herself to his desires.

She held her mouth against his, touching, not touching. Teasing. "I have two requests."

"I'm listening," he breathed against her lips.

"I want..." She touched her throat. "I want my collar back. Or better yet, I want something permanent and comfortable and *ours.*"

His body went hard a millisecond before he gripped her neck and captured her mouth with his. The kiss was potently seductive, possessive, and consuming, stealing her air and awakening every cell in her body.

Too soon, he pulled back, breathing heavily. "The other request?"

"I want to see the closet."

# TWENTY-NINE

Matias led Camila into the closet of their private suite and angled her in front of the retinal scanner. His breaths quickened as the lock disengaged. What waited behind that door, the pieces he'd been holding back from her, were the knots of guilt he'd carried for years.

"I'm nervous about this." He stepped behind her and wrapped his arms around her chest, kissing her shoulder and savoring the feminine scent of her, bathed in the clean bite of citrus and lavender. "I'm not one of the good guys. I've done things for which there might be no forgiveness."

"I disagree. You've eliminated bad guys far worse than yourself for over a decade." She touched his inked forearm and turned her neck to press her lips against his bicep.

"Hold on to that thought for the next few minutes." He let go and nudged her through the doorway.

She looked up at the ceiling as motion lights flicked on then turned in a circle, scanning the shelves of the small second closet. "Boxes? Plain, non-threatening cardboard. Definitely not what I expected."

He went to the top shelf on the right and pulled down his two favorite boxes.

"We'll start with these." He passed her one and carried the other into the bedroom.

They placed the closed boxes on the bed, and he stepped back, hands in the pockets of his jeans.

"Open them." His pulse accelerated, and a damp mist formed on his brow.

She flashed him a concerned look and opened the first box. Gasping, she removed picture frames filled with her and him, her and her sister, Lucia, and even photos of the old stray dog, Rambo. The citrus grove was the backdrop in most of the images.

"How did you get these?" Her hands trembled as she flipped through bundles of loose pictures.

He'd grabbed what he could that awful night, leaving behind the photos that included her parents. "There's more."

Eyes glistening, she darted to the second box and pulled out a slingshot fork from an orange tree, her favorite raggedy doll as a child, and his denim jacket—the one she'd stolen from him when she was fourteen and refused to return.

His heart hammered in his chest. There were a dozen more boxes of memorabilia in the closet. He'd gone through them so many times over the past eleven years he knew the contents by rote. He used to think he'd found comfort in them on his loneliest nights, but looking back now, he realized those memories had only made him lonelier.

"Matias…" She wiped the back of her hand across her cheek, erasing a fallen tear. "I thought all this stuff—" A sob rose up, but she choked it back. "I thought it was lost in the fire."

His eyes felt gritty and hot, but he didn't look away.

She pulled the jacket to her nose and inhaled deeply. "It still smells like you." Her gaze turned inward, and little lines formed on her brow. "Did you go back there after I disappeared? Did you see my parents before they died?"

Yes, yes, and fuck those motherfuckers to hell.

With a heavy breath, he sat on the bed and patted the spot beside him.

She set the jacket down and joined him, her shiny eyes searching his face. "You're scaring me."

Perhaps he would always scare her, but she wasn't a runner. She would fight him, maybe even kill him someday, but she would never leave him. He found a strange sort of comfort in that.

"Six weeks after your disappearance, I killed my brother, Jhon."

She gripped his hand and kept her teary gaze on his.

"A few weeks after that," he said with a tight throat, "your sister disappeared."

"Lucia?" Her voice whipped through the room.

"I had some guys watching the grove. I was in full-time-guns-out search mode, pulling every resource I had, trying to find you, hoping you'd show up there. When Lucia didn't return home from work one night…" He insides clenched with guilt. He should've been watching her sister, protecting her. "I knew."

"What did you know?" A lethal chill spiked her tone. "Where is she?"

"She's gone. I'm sorry, Camila." Pain stabbed through him. "She was abducted. Killed."

Her hands flew to her mouth, her eyes wide and wet.

"I prayed to hell I was wrong." He pulled her against his chest and stroked her hair. "Weeks went by, and your parents never reported her missing."

"She would've been…nineteen." She gripped his t-shirt. "She was an adult—"

"She was a missing person, Camila. *Missing*, and no one was fucking looking for her."

"No." A keening noise sounded in her throat. "I can't hear this…"

"You have to hear it." God knew, he needed to put this to rest. They both did. "Jhon was dead. Nico was the new face of the cartel. But Andres and your parents knew who I was, knew I was a Restrepo and the real capo. So I paid them a visit."

Her tears soaked his shirt, her cries silent beneath the rush of her breaths.

He held her tighter, running a hand through her hair as his chest squeezed painfully. "Your parents denied any involvement in her disappearance. Said she ran away, she was trouble, and more bullshit on top of bullshit. Goddammit, I was so fucking pissed. And desperate. I had their houses bugged and their phones tapped. A few days later, I got my answer."

Her breaths cut off, her shoulders hitched around her ears. Her entire body froze as if waiting to hear what he knew she'd already figured out.

"When Hector and Jhon died, they left behind an army of loyal men in my cartel. Men loyal to *them,* not to me and certainly not to Nico. This insurgency tried to overtake the cartel, and it took me months to root them all out."

Her chest began to heave again, and her fingers dug into his arm. Having lived at the estate for a few weeks, she knew enough about cartel politics and understood how easily an uprising could occur in the wake of a fallen leader.

"These men who wanted to take over…" She gazed up at him, eyes tinged pink. "They went after you by going back to the place you grew up? To threaten your loved ones?"

"Yes. Except the only one I loved was already gone." His insides tightened. "Camila, your parents…"

"They negotiated, didn't they?" Tears skipped down her cheeks.

"They didn't want to lose the grove or their lives, so they gave up Lucia in exchange for protection."

"Why?" She reared back, teeth gnashing, and voice angry. "If my

704

parents knew you were the capo, they would've come to you. And who the hell did they need protection from?"

"They needed protection *from me.*"

She sucked in a sharp breath. "I don't understand."

He angled toward her, shifting as close as possible with his thigh pressed against hers and his hands cupping her neck. "I was hunting through my ranks, torturing and killing those who were involved in *your* abduction. That's how I learned that Andres and your parents…" He paused, closed his eyes briefly, then looked at her. "They gave *you* up to Jhon to save their own lives." When her face crumbled, he rushed on. "When I killed Jhon, they knew I would come for them."

The brokenhearted look on her face and hitching sound of her cries sent a sharp bolt of agony through him. He pulled her onto his lap and held her for an endless moment as her shock morphed into full-body trembling. He rocked her and shushed her, his own eyes burning with so much goddamn remorse he couldn't catch his breath.

Eventually, she settled into soft sniffles, and he moved the boxes to the floor to lay with her on the bed. Side by side, faces inches apart, she stared into his eyes as hers became clearer, more lucid.

"How did you kill them?" She balled her hand in the bedding between their chests, but sympathy flooded her expression.

He pulled in a dry breath. She knew her mother had been the only mother he'd known. While her parents had never really accepted him, never thought he was good enough for her, it still killed something inside him when he pulled the trigger.

His rage, though… That had made it easier. It was such a deadly emotion, rising up from a dark place and taking over without logic or attention to consequence. His anger had been pure passion — raw, vindictive, and his only friend that night.

"Bullets. One shot each. Quick. Andres included." His voice was scratchy, hoarse. "Then I gathered your personal things. Set the fire. Covered my tracks."

"Where's Lucia?" Her voice was so small and hesitant he knew she didn't want the answer.

"She wasn't in that fire, but she's still gone, *mi vida.*" He'd give anything to return her sister to her.

She lifted up on an elbow. "Where is her body? Do you have that proof?"

"No, but I have an investigation that proves her death. Every trail I followed, every name of every person involved is in one of those boxes in the closet."

"Show me." She jumped off the bed and straightened her white dress over her legs as she headed to the closet with way too much hope in her steps.

He couldn't bring back Lucia, but he could help Camila through the healing process as she grieved her sister all over again.

Two hours later, he sat with her on the bed amid papers, maps, printed photos of locations and slave traders — the entire portfolio of his two-year investigation. An investigation that ended with Lucia inside a transport that crashed in Peru. No one survived in the cargo full of trafficked slaves.

Camila stared at a newspaper clipping, her eyes glazed as if not really seeing it. "She's gone."

Her cheeks were sunken in, face pallid, and the paper trembled in her hand. She needed to eat, rest, take a fucking step back from this, and let her heart breathe.

He gathered the papers and started boxing everything up. "Tate asked about Lucia years ago then again this morning. He doesn't believe me and wants to retrace my steps, see if he can find something I missed."

"Really? Why?"

"I think he's just being a competitive asshole. Honestly, I don't understand his motivation, but he can take a stab at it if he wants. There's nothing to find that I don't already know."

She smiled sadly. "Guess he has a lot of free time now that he doesn't have to babysit me."

"He never looked at it that way." He softened his expression. "If I hadn't threatened his life four years ago, I'm pretty sure he would've gone after you for himself."

"I always wondered what his deal was." She shook her head. "I'm still trying to process the last four years." She watched him put the box with the others on the floor, her eyes narrowing as he sat beside her on the bed. "What else are you keeping from me?"

"You have all my secrets now." He rubbed a hand up and down her arm, reflecting on her comment about the last four years. "But there's one question I never answered."

"I don't..." She blinked, and blinked again, lips parting. "What question? My brain is crap right now."

"That last phone call you made to me four years ago..."

"To collect Van's body?"

He nodded. "It changed my entire world, Camila. Following Van, finding you, approaching Tate, my plan to win you. During those four years, you were all I thought about. In my head, you were already mine, and I was yours. After that phone call, I remained one-hundred-percent faithful to you."

"You didn't..." She bit her lip as the corners of her mouth tipped up. "You didn't have sex for four years?"

Neither had she. It'd been an unknown connection between them, both of them abstaining as if fate had already intervened, pulling them together.

"I didn't touch or look at another woman," he said. "Whatever Yessica told you—"

She gripped the back of his neck and kissed him, putting every ounce of her grief and love into the vibrating hum of her lips. When she touched her tongue to his, his brain ignited, and heat spread from his chest, loosening the coil of remorse in his gut.

He broke contact and pressed his forehead against hers, his breaths erratic as he caressed the line of her jaw, kissed the soft skin there. Never had he felt so loved, so wanted. And deep beneath their connection was something more, something darker, sexual and potent, and he knew. It wasn't just his desire he sensed. It was hers.

"I'll be right back." He carried the boxes to the closet, making several trips, and returned to her with a smaller box, wrapped in black velvet.

Sitting cross-legged at the center of the bed, she reached for it, her eyes swollen from crying and nose pink. Her fingers trembled with the latch as she stared at him with a glint of excitement peering through the shadows on her face.

"Go ahead." He sat beside her, his breaths cut short. He'd waited for this moment for so long.

She lifted the lid, lips separating with a ragged exhale as she touched the platinum, double-link chain inside. "It's beautiful. When did you get it?"

"Years ago." He kissed her mouth. "I've *never* collared another woman. The leather collar was intended to be a statement to others and sturdy enough to be used when I restrain you." He ran a thumb along her wet bottom lip. "And I *will* restrain you."

She leaned into his touch, her eyes shutting for a moment then opening to stare at the collar in her hand. He removed it from the box and held it up so that she could read the inscription on the round platinum tag hanging from the O-ring.

*Su vida.*

"His life," she whispered and blinded him with a teary smile.

Then she lowered her head in offering. With shaky fingers, he fastened the lobster clasp at her nape and felt his whole world click into place.

"*Gracias. Te amo.*" She wrapped her arms around his shoulders and pulled him to lie beside her, resting her cheek on his chest.

"I love you, too. *Más que nada.*"

She squeezed him tight, and her grip on him alone told him she was happy to be with him, that she trusted him. Didn't matter how they arrived at this point, they were here, folded together, him holding her close to his side, and her closing fingers over the tag at her throat.

His heart sang beneath her cheek, his body vibrating with each breath they drew in sync. He internalized every twitch across her skin, the brush of her eyelashes against his shirt, the scent of her hair in his nose.

He tipped her face up and put his mouth on hers. She melted into him, snuggling in, and they stayed that way, wrapped up in each other for the rest of the day. When he had lunch brought in, they moved to the balcony where they ate *arepas* and curled up together on a wide lounge chair.

As the sun sank behind the vivid green landscape, they shared stories, painful stories, of their time away from one another. The men they'd killed, the nights they'd spent alone, and the searching, always searching for *this*. At some point they fell asleep, entwined together beneath the warm blanket of the black sky.

He woke with her sitting on his lap, leaning over him with her thighs straddling his hips, and a look of intent sparking in her eyes. The timer on the bedroom lights had clicked on, illuminating her white dress in an ethereal glow.

Pulses of heat charged sharp and low in his pelvis. He never would've imagined she'd want him so soon after the news he'd shared with her today. But this was Camila, his fighter, his backbone, a woman of carnal flesh—a yearning, determined, courageous woman. And she loved him.

She bent forward and propped an elbow on his chest, balancing her chin on her knuckles. "What if I asked you to just lie there and let me ride you for a while? Think you could handle that?"

Her husky voice curled around his cock, instantly turning him into iron.

"Yeah, I can—" Hunger strangled his words and shot through his veins, hot and restless.

Straightening, she pulled the dress over her head and dropped it. Her tits lifted with her inhale, peaked with hard rosy nipples, and her body gloriously nude except for the silver choker at her throat.

"I've never seen anything more beautiful." He breathed her in and smelled the sweetness of her arousal.

His pulse hammered, and his blood simmered, begging him to take her, to bury himself inside her. His hands flew to the button on his jeans, fumbling in his urgency.

She helped him, her fingers moving over the zipper, her breaths growing louder as they tackled his clothes, stripping off his shirt and pants. When she straddled him again, her hand closed around the swollen heat of his erection.

A groan pushed past his lips, his hips rocking, thrusting his cock into the vise of her fingers as he stared with wonder into her eyes. She stretched over his chest, fusing her mouth to his, and he was lost. Floating, reaching between her legs, stroking her wet pussy. He battled her tongue, moaning with garbled demands that she keep stroking him, kissing him.

"Ride me, Camila." He bit her lips and smacked her ass. "Sit on my cock and fuck me."

And she did, sinking down and shuddering around him. He grunted as she eased up and down, slowly, tenderly, hips circling and hands planted on either side of his head. He stroked her tits, leaned up to suck on her nipples, his balls tightening with blissful pressure.

His eyes never left hers as she moved over him, her cunt clamping down and stealing his thoughts, his breaths, and every tormented ache inside him. In that exquisite moment, there was only her and him, the tight warm clench of her body, and the glorious sight of her riding his dick.

He reached for her hands and held them against his chest, held onto her gaze. "You want to be owned."

"By you? Forever. Promise me."

His heart swelled. *"Sí prometo."*

When she came, she took him with her in a detonation of electricity that left him with no doubt who owned him, body and soul.

# THIRTY

*Four months later…*

The reek of cigarette smoke and the clinking sounds of china swirled around Camila, mingling with the gentle breeze that drifted across the veranda. Her insides vibrated with the murmuring voices of forty men—dangerous men—but none as powerful as the one stroking her thigh.

Matias Restrepo owned every person in the room, but she was the only one who owned his heart.

She reclined in the chair between him and Nico, her belly full after an exorbitant five-course dinner, and pulled a long draw from her beer. She looked forward to these gatherings now that she didn't have to spend them on her knees. In fact, no one knelt on the floor anymore.

At her request, Matias had banished all of the imprisoned slave traders to the west wing. There, Frizz could sew up their orifices and Matias could sell them off at will. She supported whatever punishments were inflicted as long as she didn't have to look at it while she was eating.

That wasn't the only change that had happened since Matias had announced her as his equal.

As it turned out, Yessica hadn't been able to keep her hands to herself. Two weeks after the conversation by the pool, she propositioned Matias in the hall with her hand on his cock. He told Camila about it after he transferred Yessica—along with every resident prostitute he'd ever fucked—to his compound in Mexico. Sadly, that left only a couple women at the estate.

Camila was working on rectifying that. She'd recruited her old roommates in Texas to join her here. Now that she'd taken over Matias' anti-slavery operation, she needed more people she could trust. Her friends were hesitant, but considering the offer.

Tate sat across the table from her, listening to Chispa enthusiastically explain how to make a woman squirt. With a chuckle, Tate slid his eyes to her and winked. She shook her head, smiling.

He'd visited her a couple times in the last few months, but this time, he was just stopping by on his way to Peru, where he intended to follow up on Matias' investigation into Lucia's death. Her heart punched full-speed toward hope, but Matias tried to keep that reined in. He didn't want Tate's confirmation to bring her more grief.

She glanced at the man who protected her soul as much as her body. His muscled arm lay across her lap, his thumb stroking the denim on her inner thigh. In his reclined position, his brawny chest stretched the cotton of his black t-shirt. A foot rested on the knee of his opposite leg, drawing her gaze to the delicious way his jeans cupped the bulge of his cock.

When she looked up, his eyes were on her, invading, pressing deep inside her, into places only he could reach. Places that feared him as much as loved him. But she no longer had to carry those vulnerabilities alone. He wanted all of her, cherished every one of her weaknesses and strengths. And whenever she offered herself to him, put herself fully into his hands, he silenced her doubts and insecurities.

The expression he wore now looked as if he wanted to invade her in a different way. His gaze heated with golden flames, his arms and torso flexing, seemingly restless. Wide shoulders, trim waist, hard abs—it was all there, one layer of clothes away from stealing her breath.

Without warning, he stood and threw back the last gulp of his *aguardiente*. "*Buenas noches*, guys."

Then his hand was around hers, dragging her away from the veranda. She jogged to keep up, her pulse sprinting with excitement. Damn his dangerously flirty *fuck me* eyes, but she couldn't get back to their suite fast enough.

He didn't release her until they reached the bedroom. She made a beeline to the bed, stripping her clothes as frenzied need stretched inside her, heating under her skin and throbbing between her legs.

She dropped her blouse, jeans, and removed her undergarments, her back burning from the heat of his gaze. But he hadn't followed her?

She turned. The sexy bastard leaned against the wall by the door, arms crossed over his nude chest and a bare foot hooked around his ankle. He'd removed his shirt and boots, but the jeans remained, the zipper partially lowered to reveal the dark patch of hair around the root of his erection—which was bent downward and tucked beneath the denim.

Her pussy contracted, and her nipples hardened. "Are you going to—?"

"Stand with your chest against the post. Hands above your head."

It was never a request with him. He commanded, and she obeyed. In the bedroom, with that aggressive look firing in his eyes, she wouldn't have it any other way.

She lingered for a moment, unable to avert her gaze. Inky black hair lay in haphazard spikes and fell across his brow. His expression was dark and severe, but his dimples were there, reminding her of the boy who'd stolen her heart.

The muscles in his torso were flawlessly defined, layered in ridges that were honed in combat. Whether he was training for a raid or running into a gunfight, he was built for this life. His job still scared the bejesus out of her, but she was confident in his ability to stay alive.

She resisted the urge to cross the room and put her hands all over him, because seriously, no man should look that good. With a sigh, she faced the post and reached her arms toward the ceiling.

His footsteps approached, and her breaths picked up. His masculine scent attacked her senses as he stopped behind her, crowding into her space in the possessive, overbearing way she loved.

"I'm going to hurt you," he breathed in the space beside her ear.

She shivered.

"Then I'm going to replace the hurt with something else." His chest slid against her back, his hand closing over the chain around her neck.

"With your cock?"

"Yes." A smile teased through his rumbling voice. "With my cock."

"I accept."

"I'm not asking." His hand lowered to her pussy, cupping and squeezing. "This is mine."

"Oh, you arrogant ass. You want me willing—"

He slammed a palm against her backside, shooting fire across her skin. Her breath left her so quickly and thoroughly she was still struggling to catch it when he disappeared in the closet and returned again.

With leather cuffs and a string of chain, he locked her wrists to the eye bolt in the post above her head. Stepping back, he simply stared at her. Patient. Watchful. He just…stared. After a long, unnerving moment, he grabbed the cane from the floor.

Then he hurt her. Holy fuck, he hurt every inch of her ass and thighs.

She screamed and writhed and cursed him to hell, tucking her hips against the post and trying to keep her lower muscles loose beneath his strikes. She begged him to stop, but those tattooed forearms persisted, welting her skin with hard, erratic blows. Beneath the searing pain, however, something else bloomed, something stronger, deeper.

*Trust.*

She believed he wouldn't take her too far, wouldn't give her more than she could handle. It was trust that had connected them as children, and it linked them now, more intimately than she'd ever bonded with another person. Her entire body followed his movements, shivering with the rapid gusts of his breaths and giving beneath the drive of his strikes.

It was trust that aroused her pleasure, igniting heat between her legs and damping her inner thighs. He was hurting her to remind her that she trusted him with her whole heart.

He dropped the cane and pressed his chest against her back, soothing her with shushing noises. She melted against him, rolling her head back on his broad shoulder and savoring the heat of his body.

His lips glided along her jaw with caressing licks, his fingers sliding between her legs, stroking and working her into a panting, hungry animal. She ground her sore ass against the opening of his jeans, sending bites of pleasure and pain through her body.

He ran his palms over the backs of her thighs, rubbing the hurt there, tracing the creases between her legs and butt. He groaned as he dragged an invasive stroke up the crack of her ass. Then he released her shackles.

Carrying her to the bed, he chained her hands to the headboard and removed his jeans.

He didn't make her wait when he settled between her thighs and notched his cock against her pussy. The instant he claimed her mouth with his, he thrust.

Pleasure lifted her off the bed as he hit deep with long, stroking stabs, shoving a moan from her throat. With his elbows braced on either side of her head and his biceps the size of her thighs, he moved his cock inside her, never looking away.

"Love you," he mouthed.

"Love you." She pulled her arms against the chains, aching to touch him.

Eyes burning bright with the ferocity of his love, he reached a hand over her head and laced his fingers with hers.

He'd finally captured her, enchained her, and she never wanted to escape.

# The DELIVER series continues:

# OTHER BOOKS

**LOVE TRIANGLE ROMANCE**
TANGLED LIES TRILOGY
One is a Promise
Two is a Lie
Three is a War

**DARK COWBOY ROMANCE**
TRAILS OF SIN
Knotted #1
Buckled #2
Booted #3

**DARK PARANORMAL ROMANCE**
TRILOGY OF EVE
Heart of Eve (novella)
Dead of Eve #1
Blood of Eve #2
Dawn of Eve #3

**DARK HISTORICAL PIRATE**
King of Libertines (novella)
Sea of Ruin

**STUDENT-TEACHER ROMANCE**
Dark Notes

**ROCK-STAR DARK ROMANCE**
Beneath the Burn

**ROMANTIC SUSPENSE**
Dirty Ties

**EROTIC ROMANCE**
Incentive

## ABOUT

New York Times and USA Today Bestselling author, Pam Godwin, lives in the Midwest with her husband, their two children, and a foulmouthed parrot. When she ran away, she traveled fourteen countries across five continents, attended three universities, and married the vocalist of her favorite rock band.

Java, tobacco, and dark romance novels are her favorite indulgences, and might be considered more unhealthy than her aversion to sleeping, eating meat, and dolls with blinking eyes.

EMAIL: pamgodwinauthor@gmail.com

Made in the USA
Monee, IL
08 November 2023

46052693R00420